FROM THERE TO ETERNITY

——— FROM ———

There to Eternity

ALAN COLLEY

SERENDIPITY

First published in 2004 by
Serendipity
Suite 530
37 Store Street
Bloomsbury
London

British Library Cataloguing-in-Publication data
A catalogue record for this book is available from the British Library

ISBN 1-84394-093-0

Printed and bound by Alden Group, Oxford

To Judy

Often seasick but never daunted

*My constant companion throughout our travels
and for most of my life*

ACKNOWLEDGEMENTS

Valerie Elliston, for reading the original long-hand manuscript and encouraging me as it progressed.

Carole Allington, for converting my long hand onto disk with flashes of inspired guesswork.

Graham Godfrey, for constructive criticism that I resented but needed, and after reflection took on board. An inspiring tutor on the period in which the book is set.

Ken and Rita Sharpe, authors of the booklet *Christ's Colchester Killers*.

Prologue

IN THE BEGINNING

Whatever the conjunction of stars and planets, or of celestial beings of a spiritual rather than material nature that eighth day of Martius, it was beyond the wit of soothsayer or astrologer to predict the consequences to follow; to see that the collision of the only two boats on that storm tossed sea would result in the bonding of a man and a boy in a relationship that would send ripples spreading throughout the known, and as yet unknown world, until the end of time.

The slave trader from Gaul and the supply vessel from Carthage, were brought together by a storm of unexpected severity, even for the first month of the year.

The captain had demurred at the order for his ship to sail with a convalescing centurion and the news of the recent victory of the 12th Legion, but Lucius Maximus was eager to impress Emperor Tiberius and the Senate, and had overruled him.

He now lay unconscious, hit by a flailing spar following the loss of their sail, and had he been in command a lookout would have been kept at the bow. But in the struggle to survive the overwhelming seas, half the crew had become incapacitated in one way or another, and the only option had been to head due east on bare poles, running before the wind and the huge following waves that threatened constantly to turn them over should they broach-to. Equally fearful had been the risk of being driven onto a lee shore, where they would be wrecked, but that risk was now diminishing, the wind easing as the coast appeared on the horizon. Now those men who weren't lying helpless in their vomit and excrement could be rallied to man the oars and bring the vessel around to run up the coast, although now lacking any steadying sail it rolled horrifyingly, disrupting the rhythm of the rowers so that they could not get up much way as they moved north.

This alone saved them as they rammed unimpeded into the foundering hull, the drowned slaves still shackled to their stations, where they had been as their boat had been overturned by waves, the like of which will be not be seen twice in any decade. So instead of staving in its stem, their vessel mounted the other like a rutting whale, cracking open its hull and sending the coffin and its occupants to the sea floor.

Fear of sinking was in every man's mind as they scrambled to their feet from where they had been thrown and gradually something resembling order was restored, the oars were manned and the boat resumed its course.

Marc had seen the inevitability of the collision as he was tossed by the crest of successive waves high enough to see across the intervening water separating him from the converging vessels, and in interrupted cameos saw the drama unfold with each wave. That he wasn't drowned, shackled with the other slaves, was only attributable to his age and his usefulness at serving the crew, so he had been thrown clear as their ship capsized. Now his youthfulness refused to accept the inevitability of drowning, and repeatedly he clawed his way to the surface for another lungful of air, waving his arms frantically in the brief intervals before he was submerged.

The man at the steer-board saw the movement but disregarded it, his glazed eyes searching the coastline for the beacon that meant Ostia and survival.

Again that human flotsam in the water raised a despairing arm, and this time he was seen by the centurion, who moved quickly to the steer-man.

"Pick him up!" he ordered, pointing well off their heading to where he had seen the feeble gesture, but his command was ignored.

He shook the man by his shoulder.

"Did you not hear me? I said pick him up!"

"What and risk sinking like those?" he snarled, pointing at some bodies floating nearby. "We've trouble enough as it is!"

"Do as I command or I'll throw you in and take over the steering!" growled Brutus, the livid scar disfiguring his forehead contributing greatly to the menace of his words.

Turning up into the wind spray flew the length of the boat, but Brutus was oblivious to everything except his purpose as he leaned over the rail with boat-hook readied in his hand. He saw the frightened face upturned towards him, and realising he was rescuing a boy, felt a surge of confidence he would be able to manage alone, as he was not going to get any assistance. He knew he had to get it right as there would be no coming around for a second chance with such a demoralised crew. But the pitching of the boat was outside his control and as they rose on a nasty, steep wave, the boy was so close he saw his eyes wide in astonished horror as the boat fell off the crest, crashing down on him and forcing him deeply under.

Despairing, Brutus ran the length of the boat, pushing anybody and anything that impeded him aside, only to see Marc break the surface some way astern and beyond his reach. As he knew he had failed, the centurion was anguished beyond any consolation and a feeling of defeat overwhelmed him, as irresistible as were the waters that had overwhelmed the slave trader.

The boy, however, was a plaything of the gods, and the spar still dragging astern, which had been essential earlier as a drogue to slow and hold their hull steady, now seized him in its embrace, securely hooked where the towing line was fastened. As the centurion hauled in the line and heaved the half-drowned boy onto the deck, he knew their future course was to be determined by the vagaries of the Gods that had thrown them together.

4

THE STORM CLOUDS GATHER

The four youths waited silently, sitting high up on the bluff looking down the valley to the far coastal plain towards Caesarea, from where their anxiously awaited victims would appear and their lives would be forfeited.

All had been said over the past weeks leading up to the Passover celebration, to friends, family, tutors, lovers, rabbis and the 'The Sons of Light', the Essenes amongst whom they had been welcomed as searchers after the truth. The farewells had been more poignant as they were sworn not to tell anyone of their resolution and speculation was rife concerning their intentions amongst their aristocratic families. Whether they were undertaking a dangerous enterprise, perhaps aligning themselves to a band of zealots, or undertaking a venture involving a long journey, or even entering one of the monastic communities that flourished in the desert as proselytes, was pure conjecture, and no amount of pleading could establish what they were about to do.

Their parents weren't to know that news of the recent beheading of the Baptist had crystallised the youths' resolve to avenge the wrongs that were perpetrated on their persecuted race, and as they waited neither of the four could remember who had first suggested they pledge themselves to assassinate both King Herod and Pilate, although Jesus Barabbas had suggested the site for this ambush of the rulers as they made their customary journey to Jerusalem for the Passover.

Whether it was chance or fate that they had heard details of Pilate's movements first, the outcome was that they were now poised for one of the most audacious ambushes ever undertaken, to assassinate Pilate within the cohort escorting the Procurator and his wife from Caesarea to Fort Antonia.

The only road had been upgraded by the Romans, but still followed the old Phoenician trade route, and where it climbed from the coastal plain took a tortuous route, winding its way through the hills to the plateaux of the Judaean wilderness, and it was this ascent that was the chosen site of ambush because of a remarkable natural phenomenon. A spring gushed out of the hillside and ran down the cutting that had been hewn out of the rock by the Phoenicians, wide enough not only for the road but to fringe it with a row of evergreen oaks on each side, which over the centuries had flourished, meeting to form a shaded avenue extending to nearly a mile. There was no other place along the entire route where concealment and surprise were possible and Barabbas had chosen well. Their preparations had been assisted by the sicarii, the dagger-bearers, a group of nationalists to whom political assassination was an art, and from whom they had learnt how to use the dagger to achieve their objective silently.

But fate plays cruel tricks and when they first spotted the column of soldiers and wagons approaching they were unaware of the altercation between Pilate and his wife that had resulted in Claudia Procula refusing to accompany her husband. In the carriage instead were eight Egyptian dancers from the most prestigious dancing academy in Alexandria, and in close attendance were two albino eunuchs, their constant guards. The whole group was a present from the Procurator to Herod, and aware that each dancer was a virgin Pilate knew how acceptable they would be to the king, and he hoped thereby to ingratiate himself into the affections of Salome, Herod's step daughter, herself an accomplished dancer who had excited him into attempting an indiscretion, although she had rebuffed every advance he had made.

Claudia Procula was fully aware of her husband's sexual proclivity, and prepared to tolerate it mostly as he was no longer welcome in her bed. But since she had learnt of the beheading of John the Baptist as a result of the intrigue between Herodius and Salome, she had developed a deep hatred of the Herodian dynasty and was resolved to avoid contact with them at any price.

Upon viewing the approaching column each of the four assassins incised his right wrist, and exchanging hand shakes and embracing, covenanted on their conjoined blood to see their self appointed task carried out or to die in the attempt, and then took to the trees.

The approaching column slowly moved beneath them, the dozen mounted officers leading the first detachment of foot soldiers and then the convoy of horse drawn vehicles.

Barrabas was surprised at the two turbanned eunuchs flanking the matching black horses, but Pilate's carriage was unmistakable with its polished wood and shining brass and richly adorned canopy, and he had no time to consider the implications as it moved directly underneath. A brief signal was all that was required to initiate the ambush, and as their thrown knives pierced the backs of the unsuspecting escorts, the youths swarmed down to take control of the carriage.

Barabbas cut the driver's throat and seized the reins as his comrades burst in upon its occupants. The screams that rent the air over the muffled sound of the plodding horses and sent the birds wheeling, also galvanized the soldiers at both ends of the column, and even as the confounded youths abandoned the carriage and fled, their fate was sealed, the sheer rock faces precluding any escape as the troops converged on the ambush from all directions.

The conspirators, bunched together defensively, presented their puny daggers against the swords of the encircling troops, as the enraged prefect shrieked out his command, "Take them alive, whatever you do don't kill them!"

Slowly the soldiers closed in on the youths, the Roman shields denying them any target while irresistibly they were forced backwards until they found themselves pinned to the carriage where their plan had gone so disastrously wrong. They were disarmed and seized, permitting Pilate and his officers to see the outcome of the ambush.

"What do you want done with these scum?" asked a company commander, as their captors attempted to force them to grovel, nearly breaking their arms, so enraged were they at the audacious attack and how close it might have come to achieving the unthinkable.

Ominously Pilate said nothing and appeared not to have heard, but his brain was taking in every detail and the implications of the outcome in different circumstances was stoking up a fury that could not be assuaged. Finally he turned and said, "Find out their families and who is behind this ambush!" and turning he stumbled out of the shade of the trees and sat himself on his horse to take stock.

Then to the tribune who was waiting in attendance he issued a command, "Fell every tree and make a funeral pyre for these two Egyptians and the driver such as the Pharaohs never witnessed in a thousand years. Bring the girls over here and see what they want done to their attackers?"

"But your excellency, it would take weeks to cut down the trees even if we had come equipped for such an undertaking!"

"Then we will proceed to Jerusalem, but I want this valley cleared by our return!"

The officer interrogating the youths now approached with a puzzled and anxious expression.

"They can't be made to say anything," he blurted out. "I've never known such stubbornness, and even separated and tortured they remain mute!"

"Right, choose one of them for Herod to question, his methods are more subtle than any soldiers, the others we will take to Jerusalem by wagon," and seeing the disbelief in the eyes of his officers, he gave a malicious smile as he finished his sentence, "nailed to the underside!"

This time there was even greater disbelief in their faces as Pilate told them precisely what he had in mind.

The traumatized dancers understood little of what was said, but when they saw the youths being fastened naked to the underside of the wagon, one of them broke from the group and tried to pull the soldiers away.

"They no hurt us," she pleaded, "they only boys. Give beating and let go."

Pilate, reflecting on what the outcome would have been had he been in the carriage with his wife, was deaf to their entreaties and ordered the girls be removed.

Within the hour the column had resumed its progress. Three of the youths were fastened naked to the wagons by ropes, no nails being available to comply with the Procurator's order, but suspended so that they would drag along the road every foot of the way. After the first had been fastened face up, Pilate had the inspiration of tying the remainder facing down.

"Let them see the ground for which they are prepared to murder and to die!" he said, gloating with satisfaction as the preparations were carried out.

Barabbas, secured to the hindmost of the four wagons, was forced to endure the suffering of his comrades as they left a bloodied trail across the wilderness. He felt every hurt as they were dragged over stony protrusions or through rough scree slopes and heard their rasping breath and involuntary cries. Gradually their breathing became impossible to discern, their cries ceased to be audible, and no more blood issued with each fresh mutilation as the road erased every trace of their humanity.

Barabbas died a thousand deaths on that interminable journey and only hung on to his sanity by fanning his hatred to white heat.

"Nothing must ever erase this hatred of Rome that I will carry to the grave with me," he vowed, "and when I cross beyond the veil to join my friends I will indict Pilate for their murder and mutilation before Israel's God, the supreme judge."

When they entered Jerusalem the three youths were dead, indistinguishable to their loved ones, as those secured face down had lost every feature, mutilated beyond recognition.

"Cut them loose," ordered Pilate, and the ropes were severed leaving their bodies to lie where they fell. "Drive on to Fort Antonia, and let these unruly people learn that Rome will not tolerate insurrection."

Barabbas was dragged through the streets and thrown in the dungeon.

The dancers had been crying inconsolably and were resolved to show their sorrow by dancing a dirge such as only the mysterious art of the Egyptians was capable of, a lament that would convey their spirits to the underworld at peace.

Quickly the word spread, the devastated families came and sorrowfully gathered their brave and unfortunate sons, and crowds gathered baying for Roman blood, the zealots recruiting support for an uprising at every corner of every street.

The sisters, Mary and Martha, and their brother Lazarus came but were unable to identify their cousin Jeremiah, although they knew with awful certainty he was one of the two because of his association with Joshua, the son of Jairus, one of the rulers of the Temple, and the only recognisable body amongst the three.

Joab was the third, son of Danial and nephew of Simon of Cyrene.

The wailing and lamentation sounded long into the night, and clothes were rent in many a noble's household. Mary and Martha occupied themselves with preparing herbs and spices and unguents for anointing their corpses, and quietly discussed the significance of them all having the letter J as the initial of their forenames.

"The same as that of our Lord!" commented Mary prophetically, giving a shudder and looking searchingly at her sister.

Even as Pilate had been dragging Jesus Barrabas in through one gate of the city, Jesus of Nazareth was entering through another riding a donkey, and his followers and the crowd were placing palm fronds on the ground and calling,

"Hosanna to the son of David! Welcome the prince of peace!"

Jerusalem

CHAPTER ONE

"By the thunder of Mars," ranted Tibullus, his disdainful patrician features now suffused with anger, "is a slave to deny me discharging my commission!"

"No, your honour, and far be it from me to presume to obstruct you. Centurion Brutus still sleeps and it would add greatly to his indisposition if you were to rudely awaken him with your order that his rest day is revoked." Marc regarded the tribune anxiously, who was fidgeting indecisively, turning the scroll in his left hand while his other hovered restlessly on the hilt of his sword as though he wished to draw it and expunge this further humiliation in blood. "Please be patient and wait but five minutes in the mess while I summon my master to attend you."

Choking back any reply Tibullus turned, kicked open the door and stamped his way along the passage, wondering how a slave could know anything of the Prefect's command and muttering to himself angrily, "Indisposition, be dammed! I suppose he'd be indisposed if zealots were storming the fort."

But his mind was dwelling on today's earlier humiliations. The first had been Pilate demanding he bring him a bowl of water, so that he could publicly wash his hands of the whole sordid business, and then when he had had the audacity to dry his hands on the tribune's cloak because nobody had thought to provide a towel.

Was no one aware he was cousin to the emperor, or were they showing their contempt for Tiberius, and if so they would rue this day later. Now he was no better than a messenger simply because Pilate wouldn't trust a lowly courier. Not that the commission was really that important, he was making a mountain out of a molehill! Why was this execution so much more important than any of the others?

But the altercation in the passage way had penetrated into Brutus' room, enough to alert him to trouble and cause him to roll onto his stomach and pull the pillow over his head. Two weeks he had worked from sun-up to dusk, as the tens of thousands had streamed in for the Passover, contending with the gradually escalating excitement at the approaching festival, and the unrest fomented by zealots stirring up a revolt against the Romans. Today however, he was stood down, and to him the next twenty-four hours were as sacrosanct as the Sabbath was to the most pious of Jews, and so he tried to block out the urgent whisperings of his slave, as he dissuaded the irate tribune from bursting in on him, but was unable to ignore the tantrums that followed.

For Marc the necessity of waking Brutus was something he would willingly have deferred, but he knew the patience of the tribune was already tried to its limits, so gently but persistently he shook him by the shoulder.

The centurion's head was muzzy and there lurked a deep-seated ache behind his unopened eyes. In his mouth a stale taste reminded him how steadily they had been drinking the Cretan wine throughout the night. He pushed the hand away, denying the right of anyone to intrude upon his oblivion, but the shaking became more insistent and was accompanied by softly spoken words:

"Please wake up master. It's most urgent."

Brutus opened one eye and saw the concerned features of his personal slave. He raised his hand, now not to reject the intrusion, but to fondly ruffle the blonde curls surmounting the anxious, broad Celtic face.

"Forgive me for waking you, honourable father, but Tribune Tibullus brings a message of the greatest urgency from the Prefect of Judaea."

Brutus could not restrain a smile at his slave's formal address, which he had insisted on using from the day he had plucked him from the sinking slave ship outside Ostea port three years earlier.

"All right, Marc, you do well to rouse me," he murmured doubtfully, "ask the tribune to give me a few minutes to gather my wits together before such a portentous meeting."

Brutus tentatively raised himself from his couch. A bowl of spring water was placed on the small table and momentarily he glimpsed his reflection in the still water. Close cropped, graying hair surmounted his lean face, slightly too long to be handsome in the classical Greek image and too deeply etched by laughter at the corners of eyes and mouth. These lifted in a rueful smile as he ran a finger down the livid white scar from hairline to bridge of nose, and gave thanks to fortune that he had not lost an eye. He had been aware of the Negro's raised scimitar even as he had plunged his sword into his body, but unable to withdraw it in time to parry the blow he had twisted away, and only the agony of that eviscerating stab had saved his sight and probably his life. His brown eyes twinkled momentarily at the vivid memory and then clouded as he cupped his hands to slake his parched throat before plunging his head into the bowl.

"Already it's warm in this accursed country!" he said, grasping a rough linen towel to rub his dripping hair, his thoughts moving on rapidly to the significance of a message from the Prefect, and deep misgivings that it meant trouble.

Ten minutes later, it was an alert and wary centurion who exchanged courtesies with the tribune. Tibullus was brusque to inform him that he had been assigned command of the cohort for today's crucifixion.

"Three trouble-makers are to be executed. Two are of little significance, merely brigands and zealots. The third, however, is a Galilean miracle worker named Jesus, and among his followers are some that would gladly foment rioting. Great crowds follow him wherever he goes and he's always coming into conflict with the priests in the Temple."

"That's hardly cause to crucify him," protested Brutus.

"Pilate thinks likewise. He had him scourged and then wanted to free him. However the Sanhedrin accuse him of blasphemy. They say he proclaims himself to be the Jewish Messiah, the Son of God, and King of the Jews, and thereby he challenges the authority of Herod, and even of Emperor Tiberius!"

"Josias is duty officer today, he should have been given this command?" exclaimed Brutus angrily.

"Centurion Josias has a high fever. The Prefect has washed his hands of responsibility for this man's death, which rests with the Sanhedrin. However, he is concerned at the possibility of public disorder, especially as there is a great deal of unrest following that abortive attempt on Pilate's life, and he wants you carry out the executions decisively and speedily. He doesn't want anything to interfere with his celebration of the Passover this evening as a guest of King Herod."

With that the Tribune saluted and withdrew.

It was a thoughtful and troubled man he left behind, as Brutus was aware how anxious Pilate was concerning the feast that King Herod was throwing that night which had been the dominant topic within the mess these past days. The dancers he had brought were still distressed by his brutality to the boys who had ambushed them on the road, and the rude treatment they had received when they pleaded to be excused performing.

In his room Brutus was surprised to find everything laid out and immaculate. His tunic, body-armour, cloak and sword were readied and Marc was standing by anxiously.

"By Jupiter. You've known all about this for some time, haven't you?" Brutus growled.

"We knew Josias couldn't do it, so it was certain you would be given command."

"Oh was it indeed," roared Brutus, "and since when has the prattle of servants dictated the running of the Imperial Roman army?" He looked quizzically at Marc, "Tell me, what does everyone say about this Jesus?"

"That he's a great teacher and a great miracle worker. Centurion Andreas' servant was at death's door until he entreated Jesus to heal him, and he did!"

"That might have been just coincidence, people can get better however desperately ill they may appear! Who hasn't seen so-called miracles? Why shortly before I found you trying to swim ..." and his voice trailed off, as he remembered by how fine a thread had the boy clung on to life. No other slave had been saved from that ship. "Yes, when I was a legionary in Carthage I saw a man throw a thick rope into the air and then climb up and disappear. We were amazed at such magic. The next day there he sat in the same place ready to do it all over again. Another time in Egypt, a man threw a stick at our feet where it turned into a venomous snake. Did we scatter from it! And did we feel foolish when he picked it up and it was only a stick? Magic, miracles, ba!"

Marc grinned. He was used to the centurion's dismissive manner, especially when he felt he might be out of his depth. Brutus was a man of action, not of words. Listening to soldiers' stories around their campfires, he had been stirred by legendary tales of heroic deeds, in many of which his master had played a significant part.

Suddenly with anger Brutus exclaimed, "These cursed, bigoted fanatics should be left to butcher each other. But no, the priests play cat and mouse with Pilate and we legionaries end up doing their dirty work!"

As Marc watched him stride away to dine, he wondered anxiously how today would end.

After breakfast Brutus put on his full uniform, but as it was not yet time he decided to review the arrangements. Accompanied by the company sergeant he strode over to the guardroom where the prisoners were being held, and as they drew near they heard the excited voices and entered the gloomy building to silently witness what was happening.

In the middle of the room stood a tall man, naked except for a bloodied loincloth. He was facing away from the door, towards the one embrasure through which filtered the only daylight to alleviate the gloom. The weals and cuts on his back bore livid and angry testimony to the scourging he had received, yet still he stood erect, long blood-congealed strands of hair falling abjectly from an entwined nest of thorns pressed onto his brow.

Surrounding him, a few slovenly guards were challenging him to show what kind of a king he was to wear such a crown. A jailer lashed out, striking the man across the cheek, a metal ring on his finger causing further bleeding from a fresh laceration.

"Who struck you then, prophet?" piped the assailant in an exaggeratedly shrill and hysterical voice. "And where will the next blow fall?"

The recipient's complete disregard of the blow amazed Brutus. He knew had he received it, he could not but have flinched, whatever his resolve.

Then calmly, as though in some way he alone was aware of their presence, Jesus turned and faced them. His features were striking and characteristically Semitic, prominent, high cheekbones, a strong, rounded brow and hawkish nose, accentuating the depths from where his eyes regarded Brutus. Alert and perceptive they instantly recognized his significance.

"Is the hour to hand?" asked Jesus, only a slight catch to his breath indicating his inner tension.

Brutus was unable to reply, such was the impact of the scrutiny of his questioner. He lost all sense of reality and was hardly aware of the question, only that he glimpsed some mystery in the face of this new man. Then, like an echo from some great depth, the question he had to answer reverberated in his head. He recoiled at the enormity of that which he had been ordered to do, to crucify this man, and desperately he searched for a way out.

Did he have to execute him? Was he powerless to do anything other than drive the nails that would impale him and hang him humiliated, one more Roman sacrifice!

"You must do that which you must," said Jesus holding the centurion's eyes steadily, radiating such compassion that he knew his innermost thoughts had been discerned, and that neither could escape their destiny.

"Within the hour," he heard himself saying, and turning, stumbled out of the room. Only then was he able to regain some vestige of control, and he said urgently to his companion,

"See that the guard in charge is demoted, and cancel any rest days for the others. What we witnessed in there is very disturbing and the conduct of those men drags all of us down. I want an example made of them. I have urgent matters to attend to, so assemble the escort in thirty minutes, and dispose the cohort along the route to Golgotha."

Departing swiftly, Brutus made his way into the narrow alleys that abound just within the western wall of the city. There he sought out Labun, a skilled wood carver, and after ten minutes earnest discussion retraced his path to his quarters.

Summoning Marc, he asked him to prepare his ceremonial cloak and insignia. These he had last worn on the legion's triumphal parade before the emperor in Rome two years earlier, and catching Marc's inquiring look at this request, he said:

"Nothing else would befit the death of this king, and I need you to carry my spear!"

All these arrangements were unprecedented for a common enough execution, but as commanding officer were at Brutus' discretion. He had won the distinction of flying a pennant bearing the imperial Roman eagle on his spear, by virtue of being spear throwing champion the three previous years.

Accordingly it was a resplendent centurion who led his company to the guard-room, where leaning against the wall were three lengths of newly adzed timber.

The prisoners were brought out by their subdued gaolers, and a pathetic procession now formed, four soldiers around each of the prisoners, led by the centurion and his slave. A heavy bulk of timber was hoisted onto the shoulders of each victim and Marc flinched to see this inflicted on the raw striped back of one of them. Although he slightly bowed under the weight, no expression of pain showed on his face. He had a far away look, as though his mind was detached from his suffering body and had moved a long way on, beyond the pain and humiliation.

But Marc was suffering. Although he had witnessed many executions from afar, never had he been asked to participate so intimately, and he looked despairingly at Brutus, only to be dismayed at the rigidly stern face of his master.

It would have surprised him, had he known the inner turmoil that the centurion was enduring. He had previously felt little aversion to such executions, having reconciled the arbitrary justice to the need to impose law and order. But today so great were the surges of emotion following one after the other, that it was only the iron discipline of a quarter century of soldiering that held him to his purpose. That and the final words of the Galilean, "You must do that which you must!"

Slowly the procession moved off but with few people watching, as most of the Jews were involved in their Passover preparations. None of the victims was steady on his feet, the two zealots as a result of the wine they had drunk and Jesus from the scourging he had received. Brutus wondered how any man could still be walking, let alone shouldering the heavy timber to which he was to be nailed, after so severe a lashing.

They came to a steep incline, where the deep guttering from an intersecting alley created a high step. Here Jesus stumbled and fell to lie dazed on the unyielding cobbles, and before anyone could react a girl tore herself from the restraining hands of her father and darted through the escort to kneel at his side. The soldier making to seize her found his wrist held in the crushing grip of the centurion looming over him, his angrily blazing eyes, taut facial muscles and rigidly held body reflecting his inner tension.

The girl anxiously searched the face of the unfortunate man as she cupped her fingers under his chin and turned him away from the filth of the gutter towards her. His eyes were closed as she removed her neckerchief with her free hand, moistened it at her mouth, and stroked the worst of the grime off his brow and cheeks. She saw his eyelids flutter and then found she was drawn into the depths of compassion that radiated from him, as he quietly lay just looking thankfully at her. No words were needed to convey his appreciation of her brave, loving gesture, and she felt a searing pain within her breast.

Brutus heard his sudden exhalation and realised he had been holding his breath, throughout. Simultaneously he saw the cringing soldier he was clasping and released his painfully bruised wrist.

Turning he saw the man who had vainly tried to restrain his daughter. He was well built and about his own age, so seizing his spear from Marc, he placed the flat of the blade on the man's left shoulder and said, "Carry the cross of the Galilean."

The man moved to the side of his kneeling daughter and said a few words into her ear as he knelt down and lifted the heavy timber. Jesus tried to regain his feet, and found his hands grasped in those of the maid as she helped him up, until he was standing over her. Still not a word passed between them, but before releasing her hands the man placed them to his lips. This was too heart rending for the girl, and bringing her hands up she covered her face as her body convulsed to her sobs. Jesus had his wrists loosely tied and resumed the inexorable journey to the cross.

Brutus looked for Marc to carry his spear, and felt no surprise that he had left him and was standing with his arms embracing the distraught girl as each sought some consolation from the other.

Placing the spear on his shoulder he resumed walking, the storm of emotions ceased and he knew the desolation of being completely alone. His feet still moved, but leadenly in a world without sound. He heard neither the jeers from the bystanders, the scrape of metal studded sandals, the clink of sword against armour. He was a somnambulist, walking through a nightmare where horror succeeded horror, intensifying as though under the control of every malign influence.

Emotionally he had passed into a void, in which he was detached from reality, but to an observer he appeared normal as he performed all his duties. He supervised every aspect of the execution. The nailing of the zealots was carried out first, their convulsions at each hammer blow as wrists and heels were pierced being ignored, as were their cries at the elevation of the crosses, as their weight fell on those nails.

Jesus lay impaled, stoical in his acceptance of his suffering, until Labun arrived with a carved board, which read 'King of the Jews.'

A watching Sadducee would have seized it and broken it on the head of the unfortunate Labun, had not Brutus intervened.

"Nail it here!" he said, pointing to the cross just above the thorn crowned head, and ordered the protesting priest be escorted away, ignoring his threats of the dire consequences that would surely follow. He then commanded the waiting soldiers to haul the cross upright.

Jesus spoke quietly to those hanging on each side of him and then closed his eyes, as though to exclude all that was external and distracting, and to focus on the inner self and the eternal, from where he sought the strength to endure his agony.

Then came the long hours of just waiting and watching, as slowly the life force of each victim receded.

Nothing that Brutus saw or heard seemed to disturb his imperturbability, but everything was being scratched with the point of a stylus on the waxed board of his mind, until it was as scarred as the back of the Galilean.

He watched the sky darkening and the hastily brought torches being set up to garishly illuminate the impending climax. The flashes of lightning and the rolling thunder were counterpoint to every word spoken from the cross. He observed the small group of distraught women nearby, and wondered at the absence of any men.

"Has this prophet no followers?" he asked himself.

Then, as though in answer to his query, a man joined the group and embraced the grieving women.

The air around grew heavy with cumulative energy, as though it were the source of all the lightning that surrounded them. The Galilean lifted his head momentarily and looking towards the heavens cried out,

"It is finished!" and died.

The profound silence following the cry from the cross was desecrated by the ingratiating pleading of a priest.

"This man has said he will come back to life and lead his followers into his kingdom. Can we be quite certain that there is no risk he might only appear dead and still be alive? You must ensure he really is dead as he seems."

The centurion turned from him contemptuously and cursed the Gods. He wondered at the death of this new man he had encountered for the first time this day, and if his role in the execution had been inevitable, as was now his final action.

Responding to some deep compulsion, he drew his sword and with both hands on the hilt lifted it up to eye level, before driving it with shattering impact at the rock on which he stood. He then picked up his spear and moved to stand under the lifeless figure looming over him. He raised the point until it rested against his side, just below the rib cage, and then with one convulsive movement thrust it upwards to pierce the quiescent heart. Only a trickle of blood ran from the wound to stain the pennant.

A palpable silence hung all around.

Withdrawing his spear, Brutus looked at the blood stained effigy of the eagle and tearing the pennant from the staff let both fall before turning to face the onlookers.

"Truly this was the Son of God!" he called out, and then darkness enveloped him.

The darkness that overwhelmed Brutus was absolute as he lay comatose at the foot of the cross. Marc and the young girl, Miriam, had stood inconsolable and distraught witnesses to the crucifixion, but as the centurion lay inert they ran to his aid, only to be repulsed by a phalanx of legionaries, who were improvising a litter from spears and cloaks and would allow no one near.

Marc was convinced his father lay dead, struck down in retribution by the God he had affronted. Miriam felt any words of reassurance futile and meaningless, the whole tableau was so desolate.

Dejectedly they followed the pathetic procession to the barracks and watched the centurion disappear into the sick room. Although it was mid afternoon it was dark as night, and Marc stood disconsolate, as though lost and unable to move, so seizing his arm Miriam urged him to come to her home. It never entered her mind that by this action she was defiling the Passover as she led the distraught boy to their elegant house which was close by the south gate of the city, where her parents were anxiously watching out for her.

No explanations were needed. Her father's involvement in the tragic events of the day and his silent witness of the dramatic climax had had a profoundly disturbing effect on him. He knew in some indefinable way that today some pivotal change to the direction of all their lives had occurred. Although he was deeply troubled, his relief at the safe return of Miriam allowed him to welcome the young stranger to whom their beloved daughter had so obviously been drawn.

The celebration of the Passover was more restrained than usual that night, and for Marc it was a revelation of the relationship of these strange people to their God, unlike anything he had previously known, as they sang their ancient songs and read from the Hebrew scriptures. He knew nothing of the meaning, but he was deeply moved by the reverence in which they held their tradition.

Frequently glancing at Miriam he saw her eyes twinkling with amusement under her long dark lashes, and then she would explain something in Greek or Aramaic, or when these failed she used sign language equally effectively.

The head of the house was named Simon and his wife was Naomi. Their business had brought them from Cyrene in Africa to Jerusalem, at the intersection of all the main trading routes.

Looking pensively at Marc he said, "Where is your country, you are too fair to be from these parts?"

"From Britain sir, across the sea from northern Gaul. My family is at an oppidum near the coast, but I haven't heard anything of them over the past three years since I was captured when my brothers and my father were slain in Gaul."

Recounting this event had brought tears to Marc's eyes, and Miriam and Naomi exchanged concerned glances. He quickly regained his composure and continued.

"Our family had strong tribal links with Castillon in Gaul which was besieged by a legion under Quintilius Varsus. We raised two ships and my father and we three oldest sons, with two score of other men, sailed across to help them. By the time we arrived the battle was over and the town sacked, but gales stopped us sailing home. The Romans were merciless, slaughtering all but the few that they took for slaves."

Miriam was sobbing uncontrollably by this time. Her upbringing had been sheltered, and her parents had tried to protect her from encountering the violence that surrounded them as Rome suppressed any insurrection. Generally they had succeeded, but as from today they all knew that childhood world had come to an end.

"These Romans are so obsessed with violence and killing they slaughter anyone in their path," snorted Simon holding a kerchief to his nose, "they're all the same, brutal and vicious, and anyone associated with them ends up brutalized or their victim!"

"Not my master, sir," interceded Marc, "he's like a father to me, kind and caring, but he's incredibly brave and quite fearless," he stopped for a moment his voice trailing off and a wistful far away look stole across his face, "if he's still alive? I wonder if I'll be able to see him when I get back?"

"Won't he be glad to see you, you will have so much to tell him?" said Naomi, perplexed.

Marc was silent, seeking the words that he couldn't find.

"He is the centurion, mama!" said Miriam.

The colour drained from her father's face as he realised the enormity conveyed by those few words.

"Not the centurion in charge of the crucifixion?"

Miriam gave a barely perceptible nod, and Naomi gasped in horror, closing her eyes and covering her face with her hands.

"How terrible for him and for you," said Simon hearing that cry ring out again resonant with despair, "but you can be confident he was only unconscious not dead."

Naomi moved to the side of Marc and placed her arm around his convulsing shoulders. Miriam moved so that she could grasp her mother's free hand. Her father closed his eyes and raised his hands palms upward in silent prayer.

For many minutes nobody moved, nobody spoke.

Then Simon said, "Mysterious are the ways of God. You must not think that your master killed this Jesus as it was at the insistence of our priests and elders that he was crucified. The Prefect wished to release him but because of his excessive brutality to some of our sons a few days ago the whole city has been close to an uprising. It only needed the priests to give it their blessing and there would have been a full riot, so he gave in to them when they demanded this Prophet's execution. There is a deep mystery here. When the centurion ordered me to carry the cross I was outraged. I dared not refuse, but wanted to. When I stood beside Miriam and stared at the tortured face and into those tranquil eyes, I knew he was no criminal, but still I find myself involved in his crucifixion.

"Maybe in time God's purpose will be clearer. We had a prophet called the Baptist who might have explained all, but the same Herod Antipas who mocked this Galilean had the Baptist beheaded. We live in troubled times, so tell your master many of us had a hand in the execution of this prophet."

They were all subdued and quiet after this long speech, but Miriam in her heart was very grateful, and Marc certainly less disturbed.

Back at the barracks there was considerable activity centred on the unresponsive figure of the centurion. Physicians and soothsayers gathered round the bed tried unsuccessfully to elicit some response. Pins had been applied to sensitive areas, even a glowing taper to the soft inner surface of the arm, but all to no avail. The hair of a rat burnt close to his nostrils produced no reaction, other than that of his tormentors. His eyelids had been held open and a light deflected with a large crystal onto the unresponsive pupil. A needle had been inserted deep under his fingernails.

Now they were at a loss what to do further. They knew his pulse was slow and steady, as was his breathing, but all muscle tone was absent. He lay totally inert.

"A cerebral stroke undoubtedly," said one distinguished physician.

"A cataclysmic seizure," said another, and the two of them disputed angrily across the supine patient.

A soothsayer thought a bolt from Jupiter or Mars was more likely, the immediately preceding actions of the centurion outraging any self-respecting deity.

The two physicians stopped their dispute to ask what he meant.

"Why he deliberately shattered his sword after the death of this prophet and announced that he had killed the Son of God."

The physicians looked at each other in amazement, ended their dispute, shrugged knowingly and left, shortly to be followed by the soothsayer. Finally the centurion was completely alone but whatever the outward appearance, inwardly he was in turmoil.

He found he was standing on the summit of a mountain and all around him was the desolation of a vast plain, arid and without any vegetation as far as the eye could see. Numerous, sluggish flowing rivers meandered from the base of the mountain in every direction to disappear at the horizon. Suddenly from many points around the periphery, phalanxes of legions appeared each led by a standard bearer with insignia borne high. The bearers were dressed in the skins of wild animals - lion, tiger, bear, and wolf, leopard and cheetah.

They tramped in straight lines across the plain to the insistent beating of drums, deviating for neither hill, valley nor river, but any river they surged through changed to blood red. Even the sky at the far extreme of vision turned red, like the impending threat of the final sunset.

As the columns of legions converged they merged at the centre, coalescing into a monstrous body, from which extended limbs pulsated to the beat of the drums. A great cry went up and simultaneously every legionary brought his shield over his head, hiding the man underneath and conferring to the whole, a hideous, scaly image of some primeval beast.

Brutus sought to find a name for this fearful apparition. As he watched with fascination a long, spear tipped tail reared into the air and flicked menacingly to and fro.

A shadow fell across the plain and looking up he beheld a huge imperial eagle swooping on extended wings. Grasped in its talons was a naked girl and as it passed over the monster its tail impaled the girl and the eagle released its hold.

"It's a scorpion!" shouted Brutus, as he watched it dismember and devour its victim.

The eagle returned with a child clutched in its talons, which the creature dealt with likewise.

The third time the eagle returned it brought a young man. At the moment the scorpion struck Brutus recognized the features of his slave and he screamed,

"Not Marc! Oh God, not Marc!" but could do nothing to save him.

Again the eagle returned this time bearing a lamb, but even as the monster struck, a flaming sword flashed across the sky severing its tail. Beside him on the mountain-top stood a dazzling figure of human form, his face bright as the sun and legs like pillars of fire. His vesture was a cloud and there was a rainbow about his head.

The scorpion reconstituted another tail and struck again, this time at the heavenly figure, but again it was severed with one blow. This was repeated, again and again until the scorpion started to collapse, letting out a hideous shriek, its body disintegrating and its dismembered limbs convulsing in an uncoordinated, macabre manner until finally they lay still.

Brutus dared to look up at the face of the victorious figure and he beheld those same searching eyes he had seen in the face of the Galilean.

He sat up in bed and realised he was drenched in perspiration and his heart was pounding furiously. The tension ebbed away.

"Truly he is the Son of God!" he exclaimed and then he fell into a peaceful sleep.

CHAPTER TWO

Anxiously seeking reassurance that things were as Simon had said and that his master was still alive, Marc made his way to the sick room immediately on his return to the barracks, to see the centurion sleeping peacefully. He had been greatly comforted by the kindness shown to him by Miriam's family and as it was his first encounter with Jews at a personal level, if they qualified for that description having their main home a thousand miles away in Cyrene, he wondered if they were truly representative of their race.

Simon had explained that for any Jew Jerusalem would always be home, no matter where they travelled. His two sons, Alexander and Rufus, were in charge of the business in Cyrene, otherwise they would have joined with the family for their Passover celebration.

Relieved at the sight of his master he was suddenly overwhelmed with tiredness, and hurrying to the slave quarters collapsed thankfully onto his straw filled pallet and briefly let his mind dwell on sweet recollections of the past day, before sleep overcame him.

He was awakened, by the insistent shaking of his friend Scio.

"Marc, wake up," he was calling, "centurion Brutus is at breakfast and he's asking for you!"

"But I saw him in the sick room last night, and thought he would be there a long time," mumbled Marc, quickly pulling on his tunic.

"Not he," said Scio, "and it's funny to see the physicians trying to shepherd him back there. I think they're upset that he has recovered as they had lots of investigations planned today."

"Well I wouldn't like to see any of them try now," grinned Marc as the two boys hurried across to the dining room, arriving just in time to see two irate physicians stalking out.

Inside the large mess, a dozen or so centurions were laughing uproariously. They had just witnessed the shorter, and more pompous of the physicians attempting to direct Brutus to the sickroom by pulling at his sleeve. Turning to face the insistent man, the centurion had seized him by his tunic and lifted until their eyes were at a level, his feet a full six inches off the floor.

"Sir," said Brutus "if you pester me or put a hand on me again, I promise you will need a lot longer in that sick room than me!"

Whether he intended to say any more nobody knew, as there was a rending noise from the man's tunic, and Brutus was left holding the rapidly detaching lapels as the physician equally rapidly regained the floor. Spluttering and protesting, the two doctors had little option but to beat an undignified retreat.

At the sight of his master, so great was Marc's relief that he ran to the centurion, and raised his clasped hands together above his head in joyful salute before kneeling at his feet.

"Greetings master," he cried with elation, "the Gods have indeed answered my prayers."

"Thank you, Marc, I was as concerned for you as you have been for me. I am summoned to attend the Legate shortly so will you lay out my ceremonial cloak and tunic?"

"What about your sword?" asked Marc, remembering how dramatically it had been shattered the previous day.

"I won't be needing it again," replied the centurion decisively, evoking surprised murmurs from some of the officers.

Returning to the centurion's quarter Marc did as he had been bid. He saw the empty scabbard and beside it the hilt of the sword, with the remnant of the shattered blade, and wondered how it had got there and what significance to place on those words of his master. It was unknown for a centurion to be without his sword when in uniform, except in their quarters and the communal mess.

The Legate's office was the opposite side of the large parade square, and was the most imposing of the complex. It was fronted by a colonnaded terrace, raised some ten feet above the parade ground and approached by a wide sweeping stair which Brutus ascended to make his way to the broad oak door, guarded on each side by a sentry.

"Brutus to see Legate Venestus," he said.

The sentry saluted and knocked on the door, which was quickly opened by the sergeant. Seeing the centurion, he too saluted and excusing himself, he withdrew into the room, only to reappear quickly and usher Brutus inside.

"Glad to see you're well, sir, and you've come at a most opportune moment!" he said.

"Thank you, sergeant, I too rejoice to be back," replied the centurion, his eyes glancing around the room, containing a great many more people than he had expected.

"A chair for the centurion," called the Legate, clapping his hands, and Brutus quickly found himself seated with a few other officers to the left side of the Legate's imposing desk. Facing him was an agitated conclave of priests and Pharisees, many of whom seemed to be talking simultaneously at the Legate.

"Silence!" he commanded. "I wish to summarize what I understand you to have said. Firstly the body of the crucified Galilean Jesus is lying in a rock tomb given by Joseph of Arimathea, as was approved by Pontius Pilate when you had no better proposals. Secondly, there are widespread rumours that this Galilean claims to be the Son of God, and has declared he will come back to life on the third day following his execution, which is tomorrow. Thirdly, you are afraid his followers will steal his body from the tomb and when it is seen to be empty, claim he has indeed risen from the dead."

Most of the Jews nodded in agreement although one elderly priest dissented protesting, "I urged that he be thrown in the common pit alongside of those zealots that were crucified with him!"

Venestus ignored him and continued, "And lastly, you want us Romans to mount guard over this dead man's tomb until the third day has passed."

"It will certainly save you and us a great deal of trouble if you do, your honour," said the high priest, "such rumours could cause rioting!"

The Legate looked at Brutus quizzically. He had been concerned to hear of the end drama of the crucifixion and shared everyone's amazement at the centurion's recovery.

"What is your opinion, centurion?" he asked.

All eyes turned on Brutus who was not expecting to be asked for any comment on such matters. Rising to his feet and looking at the Jews, he said scathingly, "I hold no political views, but I can speak for every legionary in the Roman army when I say have nothing to do with this matter. It would dishonour any Roman soldier, to stand bodyguard over this dead Jew. They have their Temple guard, let them guard their own!"

There was an outpouring of protest from the Temple delegation, but Venestus quickly came to his feet, banging the table to bring them to order.

"An excellent proposal, centurion," he beamed, "set your own guards around the tomb for as long as you wish, Rome will have no more to do with this matter."

With that he indicated everyone was to leave other than Brutus, and within five minutes they were sitting on one of the large couches in the adjoining anti-room.

"Well, Brutus, we all greatly feared for you and are glad to welcome you back to the land of the living."

"Thank you sir. I have had a daunting twenty-four hours."

"But you are recovered well and seem your normal self?"

"No, with respect sir, in some ways I will never be normal again. You have never encountered this Galilean have you?"

The Legate shook his head.

"Then you will find it difficult to understand what I am trying to say, but this man Jesus has incredible powers of changing the way you look at the world, and how you feel about yourself. I know nothing of his teaching, although like every-one I know he is reputed to be a great healer. As an instrument of Rome I had to execute him, but now I am driven to find out all I can about him."

"That will not be easy to reconcile with serving in the imperial army!" said Venestus.

"Then I may have to ask you to allow me to leave sir, in two years I will attain veteran age anyway."

"Let's not talk about that, Brutus, it's early days yet and you may feel differently later. I particularly want to discuss the Martial Tournament tomorrow."

This was an annual tournament that followed the Paschal celebration, when the Roman cohorts that had been drafted in from Minoa, Caesarea and Capernaum to augment the local garrison, could relax and enjoy competing against each other prior to dispersing.

"This year the Syrian contingent will certainly win the archery and they also pose a real threat in the javelin. You are by far the best spear thrower from the Roman legions and should be able to match their champion Maas, who has a formidable reputation. Livy and Marcus are throwing for the other cohorts but we need you to throw for us. Do you feel up to it?"

Brutus smiled, and affirmed he would enjoy competing against this Syrian, and after a few more pleasantries and some light refreshment he returned to his quarter.

Marc was awaiting him eagerly. He hadn't yet had any chance to talk to his master, although discussing events was something that Brutus had encouraged from the beginning of their relationship. In this respect he was very unlike his comrades, all of whom kept their servants very much at arm's length and never confided in them. They regarded slaves as an underclass collectively, and individually as a possession, with greater usefulness but less value than a horse. Many centurions had offered Brutus a good price for his pretty slave, but knowing their idiosyncrasies, of brutality, of indifference, of sexuality, he never considered accepting any offer.

As he was assisted out of his armour and into his robe, he said, "Well Marc, tell me what you made of yesterday?"

"Oh master, please forgive me for deserting you when you needed me."

"Never mind that," smiled the centurion, "with such a pretty Jewess needing comforting I would have broken ranks had I been your age. No, tell me what impact this Jesus made on you, and his execution."

Marc frowned pensively, but took a while to collect his thoughts into a cohesive pattern, before he was able to reply.

"I think yesterday was the worst day in my life - worse even than when my father and brothers were killed at Castillon. Risking death in battle is natural to both Celt and Roman, but the death of this Jesus just didn't fit into this at all. Jesus seems only to have been healing the sick and crippled, and advocating peace and forgiveness, so what you had to do yesterday seemed a terrible crime. I wondered how you could carry it through, I would never have been able to, and when you collapsed at the end I realized what a tremendous strain you had been under and feared you were dead. Only when I returned from spending the evening with Miriam's family, and saw you sleeping peacefully did I feel reassured."

"Miriam is the young Jewess, I suppose?"

"Yes sir, she is. Her parents tried to help me and made me see that it wasn't you who killed Jesus. The Roman army was the executioner, but only at the insistence of most of the priests and elders among the Jews. Not all, as one or two strongly objected. Jairus, who is the ruler of the synagogue at Capernaum, did everything he could to stop them. Even though his son was one of those boys Pilate murdered so ruthlessly and he was desperately anxious to reprieve Barabbas, he was not prepared to see Jesus executed to achieve it! Simon, Miriam's father, says two months ago Jairus' daughter was at death's door and only because of Jesus is she alive now, and he also says that a great many were involved in executing this man - if he is just a man?"

"Do you wonder at that? When I cried out, that I had killed the Son of God, I really and truly believed it. So awful did it seem that I no longer wished to live, and when I drew my sword it was in my mind to thrust it into my body. Then I recalled those words that the Galilean spoke to me, when I had my mind full of crazy thoughts of rescuing him. He said, 'You must do that, which you must!' Only then did I realize I was bound to him by destiny. So I plunged the sword onto the rock instead of into myself, and resolved never to use it for Rome again."

Marc had gone quite pale at the thought of how close he had been to losing his second father. An overbearing feeling of thankfulness caused him to grasp the hands of the centurion, which were raised and clasped as though still around his sword. Gently he pulled them down and inclined his face so that his cheek lay on them. The tension ebbed from the centurion, and he withdrew one of his hands and placing it on the boy's head drew him thankfully to him.

"Come my son," he said, "let's go and practise with the spear."

CHAPTER THREE

The location for the games was to the south of the city where a dried up riverbed spread to a broad plain, creating a natural amphitheatre flanked by low hills on two sides. On these gentle slopes were assembled the legionaries, separated into the cohorts from various regions of Palestine, each with their distinctive colour tunic.

A large cedar rostrum dominated the games arena and assembled on it were all the dignitaries, resplendent in their white togas or royal robes. Herod Antipas was seated with the Prefect of Judaea, the former in regal purple, flanked by his colourfully attired wife, Herodias, and his sultry, but strikingly beautiful step daughter, Salome, whose nubile body was emphasised by her sleeveless cream gown.

Each dignitary, whether patrician Roman or royal Herodian, was attended by a retinue of slaves, whose role was to ensure that every creature comfort or whim of their masters or mistresses was provided for.

In contrast to the formality on the rostrum, a great number of hawkers and entertainers were freely mingling among the soldiers and there was a carnival atmosphere now their duties controlling the vast influx of Jews were over, and most of the visitors were returning home.

Led by the chariots the competitors had earlier paraded before Pilate who presided over the games, and were now scattered at various points of the arena, actively engaging in diverse rivalries, which were proceeding to an exciting climax, each cohort having had some success. The archery, wrestling, horse racing and pig chasing and spearing were out of the way, only the javelin contest and the chariot racing remained.

Brutus was convinced balance was the critical factor in javelin throwing, together with that coordination of eye and muscle which only practice can bring to perfection. Accordingly he had sat whittling shavings from the shafts of his javelins, until he felt they were perfect, then a last honing of the blades, and he was as ready as he could be.

A trumpet blast summoned the four javelin competitors to the rostrum where the Prefect received their salute, and signalled for the draw to be made. The steward approached each champion to draw a stick to which was attached a piece of coloured silk, determining both the position from which each would throw and the order of throwing. They then proceeded to their throwing marks, narrow boards positioned twenty paces from the targets, which were set in a line close to and just to one side of the rostrum. The order of throwing was to commence with the furthest from the rostrum.

This was the first time Brutus had encountered the Syrian champion Maas, and they appraised each other keenly. The centurion noted the poise of his opponent who was of average height and whose every movement affirmed a natural athlete.

The eyes he encountered were dark and steady in the smooth olive face, reflecting the supreme confidence of the habitual victor.

There fell an expectant silence as Livy took up position for the first throw.

As a single trumpet blast shattered the silence, he took a short run and launched his spear to impale the yellow silk close to its centre, and the roar of approval from the crowd was loudest from the Minoans as they rejoiced in their champion's success.

Maas's run up to his line was almost leisurely, and his delivery of the javelin so precise, that Brutus knew it would find the centre of the green silk even as it struck home.

The centurion was confident he could match him at this distance, if he isolated himself from distraction and focussed his attention on the scarlet silk. His discipline and self-control held firm, and he felt no surprise when his spear found dead centre.

The calibre of all the contestants made it necessary to increase the throwing distance by a further ten paces. At thirty paces the slightest misjudgment would be magnified, as would the element of chance.

Marcus was the first to suffer as a consequence for as he released his javelin a sudden gust of cross-wind carried his spear just off target and he was eliminated. Brutus knew the same could happen to any of them.

Livy was the next to go. He was throwing at the limit of his control and his second spear went slightly wide.

Now only Maas and Brutus remained and the distance was increased by a further ten paces. Brutus knew this was at the very limits of his throwing, but still he and Maas were finding the bull consistently, to the vocal jubilation of their cohorts.

Herod, shrewdly assessing the merits of each, turned to Pilate and said, "Would a small wager interest you?" a glint of excitement enlivening his normally imperturbable features.

"Most agreeably, Tetrarch," replied Pilate welcoming some diversion, the precision of the javelin throwing having become almost boringly predictable, "but which champion do you favour?"

"Oh, of course the Syrian," laughed Herod, "I could hardly expect you to relinquish your claim on the Roman! Say one thousand denarii?"

"Agreed," said Pilate, his smiling face belying his surprise at such a large wager, "but let's increase it by one hundred at each throw."

Both men settled down to watch the contest with renewed interest.

Not so Salome, who had become increasingly bored, now that the well-muscled bodies of the contestants had lost any novelty and their javelin throwing was so consistently accurate. She turned to Herodias and said, "Mummy, wouldn't it add greatly to the excitement if an element of risk could be injected into the throwing?"

"What sort of risk have you in mind my dear, something is needed to liven it up?" replied Herodius with a lethargic yawn.

"I'll think on it," she said, "I'm sure I'll come up with a better idea than just wagering silly money on it!"

"I'm sure you will, dear!" nodded her mother approvingly.

There arrived a hiatus as the tattered silks needed replacing. Salome talked excitedly to Herod who raised an eyebrow and then turned to engage Pilate. For two minutes the men conferred with considerable animation, then the worried looking Prefect signalled the Chief Marshall to draw near. A disputation arose between the two men, but finally at Pilate's insistence the marshal made his way to the men affixing the new targets. They stopped their work to listen to him and after registering surprise and some discussion, one hurried off and reappeared with two short pieces of wood, that they nailed to the frames of the silk bulls so as to make handles.

There was a heightened expectancy amongst the spectators but for Brutus there was only a feeling of apprehension. The marshal approached the two champions and spoke a few explanatory words to them.

Brutus shook his head in disbelief and challenged the marshal to repeat his instructions. He then turned and strode resolutely to the rostrum and stood rigidly at attention facing the Prefect. It was with difficulty that he checked an angry outburst, but as Pilate looked at him disdainfully he called out clearly in the absolute silence that had fallen on the arena.

"Permission to speak, Sire?"

Pilate inclined his head slightly his face registering irritation and anger.

"Please countermand your order regarding the javelin contest, Sire."

"Request refused!" snapped Pilate looking angrily at the Legate seated nearby, who was obviously puzzled as to the cause of the dispute.

"Then I withdraw and Maas is the champion!" Brutus called out, and turning smartly on his heel moved towards his team, who were thrown into consternation at the clamour he had left behind him.

King Herod and the Legate could only restrain Pilate with difficulty.

"Don't make a scene with the whole army as witness," urged Herod, "there will be anger enough within his cohort and ample opportunity to punish his insolence after the games. Listen to the uproar."

The arena echoed to the angry protests of the legionaries as they reacted vocally to the abrupt and unsatisfactory end to the contest.

As Brutus collected his javelins preparatory to departing a deathly silence fell and glancing around the centurion's eyes were drawn to the targets, where an elderly slave was being positioned so that he could superimpose the green silk he held in his hand, over that on the target. Even at this distance the spasm of the man's facial muscles and the rapid tic of his eye were discernible, and his hand was trembling so that he had difficulty in holding the bull. Marc had gone deathly white as he empathized with his fellow slave and realised he might have had to do likewise.

Maas, positioned to start his run, threw a glance at the centurion, who glimpsed the first suggestion of anxiety in those previously confident eyes. Then each step he took towards the line seemed suspended in time, one following the other rhythmically until the front foot was firmly planted on the board. The arched body with extended arm performed a beautiful sinuous movement to launch the spear towards the target where it impaled the bull frame, drawing a great roar from a thousand throats, not one as yet aware that the slave's thumb had been amputated at the knuckle. As the blood spurted and he collapsed under the horizontal spear the roar of the crowd was stifled, to be replaced with many a gasp as Brutus ran to reach the prostrate man.

Bending he lifted him effortlessly and carried him to the Capernaum team, where he offered him to the stunned Maas who could only shake his head as though in disbelief, so Brutus laid him gently at his feet. Returning to his own team he took up one of his javelins and strode towards the rostrum, as he did so loosening the cord around his waist.

Nobody moved in the silence gripping the arena.

Kneeling before Pilate the centurion broke the shaft of his spear across his knee, and binding the shorter piece across the longer, wordlessly planted the cross into the ground directly in front of the stunned Prefect.

It was only as he turned and moved away that Pilate screamed out,

"Seize that man!" but no one did!

Pilate's eyes were riveted on the cross. He recognised its significance and fear clutched at his heart.

The only smile was that of Salome.

Back in the barracks, the centurion and his slave waited silently for something to happen. Both knew that his challenge to the order of the Prefect, and subsequent refusal to comply, had publicly humiliated Pilate and that retribution was inevitable.

Finally Marc could bear the silence no longer. He was frightened and needed reassurance.

"Thank you, honourable father," he said, "I would have held the target for you had you asked."

"I know you would, you aren't lacking in courage. It wasn't that I doubted you or myself for that matter. I had a very disturbing dream on the night of the execution which I have mentioned to no one."

The centurion paused for a moment, staring into space, before continuing,

"In it the whole imperial army, every last soldier became part of some hideous and menacing scorpion. They coalesced to form the parts of its body, and its function was to kill. The imperial eagle would fly to it with sacrificial victims each of which it impaled and devoured. Everywhere was barren and desolate, and I realized then that it was so because Rome is indifferent to how much blood she sheds in her insatiable conquest of the world."

He stopped for a moment as though recalling his vision before continuing, "One of the victims carried by the eagle was you, and I could only watch helplessly as you were sacrificed to this bloodthirsty monster. Today that same image came into my mind and was the reason I refused to allow you to be drawn into the contest between Maas and myself, no matter what the cost."

Marc knelt at his feet his eyes misting with tears, and taking the centurion's hand, he placed it to his lips before laying his face on Brutus's knee.

"Truly I am the most fortunate of slaves, but I am fearful for what they may do. Pilate was enraged, and would happily have struck you down there and then. That little harlot Salome was smiling all the time, and it was she who goaded Herod to behead the Baptist. Now what might they do to you?"

Brutus smiled, "Not put my head on any plate for certain!" he exclaimed. "As a centurion I may be disciplined for insubordination, but as a Roman citizen I have many rights that even this vengeance seeking Prefect won't dare to trample on." He shrugged his shoulders as though dismissing any relevance of Pilate to himself then continued,

"I haven't told you of the end of my dream yet. After I saw you sacrificed, the eagle was carrying a lamb as the next victim. But suddenly I was no longer alone watching helplessly. Beside me stood a mighty champion of the Gods and from the crest of the mountain he struck down that scorpion with a flaming sword. Time after time his sword struck home, until the monster lay dismembered in its death throes."

He saw Marc's face looking at him with astonishment.

"But then Marc, and this is the most marvellous of all, I saw his face and it was that of the Galilean. I awoke at that point and all my agony of spirit fell away. I can't explain the peaceful feeling that followed, but I still have it. I was near to death but that man brought me back to life."

They were interrupted by the arrival of a messenger from Legate Venestus requesting that both Brutus and his slave attend a military court that would convene in the Prefect's Audience Hall in one hour.

"My compliments to the Legate. I will be there, but is the attendance of my slave necessary?"

"Bring the boy, you are ordered to bring him."

"Is this a Courts Martial?" demanded Brutus.

"I think not," said the messenger, "it's similar, but not that formal," and turning on his heel he left, leaving two puzzled and apprehensive people behind.

CHAPTER FOUR

Pilate's residence was not far from the barracks, but in contrast to the austere fort was a riot of colour, six slaves being designated solely to the watering of the flowers and exotic shrubs, which he had acquired from the extremities of the known world. Indeed it was rumoured that they were the main reason he had taxed the temple so heavily to pay for the aqueduct he had had constructed.

The opulence of the residential and administrative buildings was a great source of pride to the prefect and it was common knowledge that he and King Herod openly competed for pre-eminence.

As they crossed a narrow court between high walled buildings a young girl appeared briefly in a doorway, only to withdraw and as they drew alongside reappear, and make a little gesture of her hand catching Brutus's attention. He turned to his preoccupied companion, and said, "Your young Jewess, Marc?"

Mark looked around and saw the gentle lift of her hand.

"Miriam!" he exclaimed a ruddiness suffusing his frank open features, emphasizing the boyish freckles across the bridge of his nose and his cheeks.

"I think she's anxious to tell you something," laughed Brutus, "stop looking as though you've been caught up to mischief, and talk to the poor girl. We've a few minutes in hand, so catch me up by the Prefecture."

When Marc finally caught up with the centurion, not only was he breathless from running, he was excited and impatient to tell Brutus his news.

"Master, Miriam has told me something startling," he panted out, "all to do with the crucified Galilean and an empty tomb!"

"Slowly now Marc, get your breath back, and tell me exactly what Miriam said, leaving out any endearments of a personal nature."

Marc smiled ruefully.

"From a wealthy Jewess to a slave? Little hope!"

But it was said so vehemently that Brutus knew he was getting too close to his slave's heartfelt longing.

"You won't always be a slave, you know Marc, but tell me Miriam's news."

"She says the Galilean has risen from his tomb, just as he told his followers it would be."

Brutus stopped in his tracks and looked searchingly at Marc.

"Would that it were true. I would be the first to want to believe it. Only the day before yesterday I was with the Legate when the priests requested soldiers to guard the tomb. Venestus told them to post temple guards, just so as to stop his followers from stealing his body. Yesterday was the third day, while we were at the games. I wonder what can have gone wrong?"

"Need anything have gone wrong, Master? Simon of Cyrene knows Joseph of Arimathea who gave the rock tomb and personally saw Jesus laid there and the tomb sealed before the temple guards took up their positions. After they found the stone rolled away from the entrance and the body gone the guards first went to Joseph hoping he knew what had happened. When he was surprised at their news they were even more fearful of punishment and wondered what to say, having no idea how anyone could have got past them!"

"And what advice did he give them? To get as far away from Jerusalem as possible?"

Marc smiled,

"No, quite the opposite. To report the event to the Sanhedrin just as it happened."

"Rather them than me. Those pious priests and scribes won't welcome the news that the body has been taken from under the noses of their own guards."

But even as he dismissed it, he was beginning to question his scepticism. He had declared Jesus to be the Son of God - but which God. Rome worshipped so many and he believed in so few, if any.

Arriving at the entrance to the Proconsul's audience chamber, Marc was left waiting outside as a sentry led the centurion before the assembling court.

The auditorium was an imposing building, colonnaded down both sides with a large central assembly area.

Brutus was ushered in to find Pilate seated on a raised dais at the far end. At a table, forward of the prefect and to his left sat the Legate and Tribune Tibullus, and opposite them two scribes.

Herod Antipas had just arrived with his court officials and a chair was placed for him beside Pilate. After a formal exchange of greetings the two men conferred for some minutes, before an increasingly impatient Pilate called the assembly to order and nodding to the Legate ordered the prosecution to commence.

Venestus arose and demanding that Brutus stand forward, addressed him formally.

"Centurion Brutus, serious charges have been brought against you by various persons. They are - Firstly, you contemptuously refused to represent the Imperial Roman Army as its champion. Secondly, you refused to carry out a direct order of the Prefect of Judaea. Thirdly, you knowingly and deliberately broke your sword and your spear in two separate public gestures of defiance. Finally, that you insulted and assaulted in your dining hall the physician Creticus. How do you plea to these charges?"

Brutus studied the faces of his accusers. Mostly they were stern and unfriendly, but in the eyes of Pilate blazed anger and hate. Herod seemed unmoved, as though indifferent to the outcome, but on scrutiny his hooded eyes were cold and menacing, as are those of the venomous reptiles. He realized how alone and friendless he was before them, and simultaneously he realized he was confronting those same rulers who had caused the Galilean to hang on the cross.

He recalled those momentous words, 'You must do that which you must,' and turned challengingly, to refute the charges and place the fault where it belonged.

Confronting Pilate he began his defence, aware that there was no less a threat to Marc as to himself, should he be found guilty.

"Four days ago I carried out your commands to the letter, and I crucified an innocent man because your hands were bloody with that of the youths you had mutilated. You had so roused the populous against Rome you had to appease the priests, as one word of encouragement from them would have started the riot that

31

was simmering. You wanted to hand over Barabbas to King Herod for questioning and then to crucify him, but you dared not, and you wanted to set the prophet free, but again you dared not, so you capitulated to the demands of the Sanhedrin, and then washed your hands of his blood!"

All eyes were riveted on Pilate who had gone deathly pale. He realised he was losing the initiative and the accused was turning the accusation back on him.

"Today I requested you countermand your order at the contest and you refused. Have you washed your hands of the blood of the slave of Maas?"

"As to my sword and my spear, yes I broke them both. Not in defiance as your charge imputes, but in disgust at the perverted use of them that was forced on me. My profession has been an honourable one until now, and I take pride in the small part I have played in maintaining the rule of Rome throughout much of the Empire. Suddenly, my profession has been dishonoured twice by the command of the prefect of Judaea, because the Jewish priests wanted a miracle worker preaching a message of peace, of love of God and love of neighbour, neutralized. I carried out your command because I am used to obeying orders, and likewise when I had to ensure Jesus was dead, I plunged my spear into his heart. These shameful actions I performed at your command but I resolved never again.

"The contest of champions is worthy of the highest honour, yet even that you sought to debase by your obsession for novelty and bloodshed. I refused your order because it would have been dishonourable to comply with it. That is my defence and I demand my right to appeal to my Emperor if these charges are to be pressed against me."

Everyone was on his feet. Pilate was shaking with suppressed rage. He had been deeply wounded in his vanity, and his authority had been challenged in a manner to which he had no reply.

Even his immediate subordinates, the Legate and the Tribune, regarded him with anxiety, as though they knew his cause was lost and they wanted to dissociate themselves.

Brutus bowed to the assembly. "You know where to find me," he said and turning he walked out of the room.

Pilate and Herod withdrew into one of the private rooms of the residence. Both were used to having their own way in matters within their jurisdiction, and this reversal had left them subdued and resentful.

Herod looked quizzically at Pilate.

"This precious centurion has injured us," he said, "and I for one seek vengeance." He had appraised the weakness of character that made Pilate malleable, but felt it prudent to broach the subject carefully.

Pilate snorted, and looked up eagerly as the king continued, "If he had been captain of my guards he would have had the skin flayed off his back by now. However I realise the immunity enjoyed by a Roman citizen and a centurion, so we have to be more careful, but there must be some way of injuring him."

"If you have a plan it will be music to my ears," said Pilate, feeling the first glimmer of hope in what had been a disastrous day.

"He seems to be inordinately fond of that slave of his," mused Herod, "and my stepdaughter has expressed an interest in adding him to her retinue. Would that be possible?"

"Well he is the centurion's property and short of purchasing him, no!"

"But I have people who are very skilful at arranging matters. It would not be difficult to make him into a thief, and would he then enjoy the protection of the centurion?"

"No. He is not a citizen. If you found him to be a thief you could throw him into your dungeon. There would be nothing the centurion could do to stop you."

"Oh we wouldn't let a pretty boy like him languish in our dungeon," smiled Herod whimsically, "that would be an awful waste."

"You have my full approval whatever your purpose might be," exclaimed Pilate enthusiastically,

"Leave it in my hands, prefect," said the tetrarch of Galilee.

Rising with a restless urgency to put his plan into operation he quickly took his leave of Pilate.

Back at the barracks, Brutus and Marc were discussing the happenings of this day. It seemed unbelievable that four hours earlier the two champions had been competing with their spears. Marc had been amazed when the centurion had marched boldly out of the court, signalling that they were free to return to their quarters, but he hadn't got a word from him all the way back.

"Don't leave," he said when Marc, having assisted him out of his uniform, was wondering whether to go, "I have something urgent that I need to discuss with you. Sit down boy."

He made a gesture towards a stool, which Marc drew up to the couch.

"I am going to give you your freedom," he stated simply, unaware of the devastating impact these eight words would have on Marc.

"But master I am truly happy to be your slave," said Marc with total sincerity, a worried look stealing across his face.

"You can serve me just as well were you my son, why, you often call me father. Don't look so worried, Marc. It is my intention tomorrow to see the adjutant and have him write out a certificate of manumission, which makes you a free man. At the same time I will apply to adopt you as my son."

Marc was on his knees, holding the hand of the centurion so very tightly and incapable of adequately expressing his feelings. His face radiated his joy and his youthful eyes were misting.

"This is like a wonderful dream to me," he said. "When I saw my father slain, I was overcome with desolation. I fought as well as I knew how but the Roman soldiers were too skilful and disarmed me easily. In my early days as a captive, and later sold as a slave, I often wished I had been killed alongside of my brothers."

He stopped, trying to control his voice and check the flow of tears he tried to brush away.

Brutus for the first time became aware of the down that covered his lip and lower jaw and realized he was no longer the boy he had rescued. He swallowed hard, tears might be quite acceptable from his intended son but would seem unmanly from a world-weary centurion, as he saw himself.

"Only after you plucked me from the sea did I stop wishing myself dead. As I grew to know you, I realised how kind the fates had been to me." He glanced mischievously up at the centurion and continued, "I saw behind the tough warrior a kind and sensitive man."

Brutus pushed him away with a laugh, so that he rolled over and lay on his back.

"Well, you saw more than was there," he said dismissively.

"Why I believe if you saw a roaring lion you wouldn't run. No, you would go up to it, ruffle its mane and say, stop looking so threatening and behave like the kind, sensitive lion you really are."

Marc was rolling around laughing uncontrollably and Brutus too was roaring with laughter louder than any lion. As their laughter subsided, one glance at the other set them off again, tears rolling down their cheeks. They viewed each other through distorting moist eyes, and lost sight of the threatening world gathering around them, more dangerous to life or liberty than any lion!

CHAPTER FIVE

Shortly after breakfasting Brutus was with the adjutant.

Firmus was a retired centurion who at the expiry of his service had married a Palestinian woman and remained in Jerusalem. One of his appointments had been that of quartermaster to the 10th Legion in Carthage, when Brutus had been but a company sergeant. He was so steeped in matters military that the local commander had welcomed him, created the post of adjutant for him, and now relied on him completely. Firmus was also shrewd about legal matters and ways to circumvent problems before they got out of hand.

They greeted each other warmly, with that cordiality that exists among comrades who have shared and overcome dangers.

"Well and what can I do for you?"

Firmus' eagerness to help showed in the way his face screwed up in concentration as Brutus explained how events beyond his control had taken over, and finally driven him to challenge Pilate's order, with all the consequences that followed.

He also stated his intentions relating to Marc.

After some deliberation the adjutant said, "There's no question you are in a grave situation. You have made an unforgiving enemy by challenging Pilate at the games, and at the tribunal afterwards. I have heard of all that you said, and knowing you as I do realize you had no choice, but Pilate will do everything he can to harm you."

He stopped for a moment, and then as enlightenment dawned he continued, "Is this the reason you wish to adopt your slave, to protect him by conferring Roman citizenship on him?"

"Well not exactly. I have been intending to do it many months, but yes these past few days have added urgency."

"What's special about this slave of yours? Many of us are fond of our slaves but we don't want to adopt them."

"It's impossible to define. He has so many qualities I would hope to find in a son. Loyalty, courage, modesty and we have some great laughs," and he paused for a moment remembering the hilarity of the previous evening.

"Did you know I plucked him out of the sea near Ostia? He was the only survivor of a sinking slave ship. Our helmsman was so afraid he wouldn't go to his aid until I drew my sword and told him he had two choices. Either he put the helm over to assist the drowning boy or I would throw him over and he could swim to his assistance."

Firmus laughed, his monkey-like face screwing up into a thousand wrinkles as he pictured the scene in his mind.

"And no doubt you meant it," he gasped, wheezing as he tried to quiet his breathing.

"Well he thought so anyway, which is all that counts. I hadn't thought of the possibility of his demurring."

This sent Firmus into another paroxysm of coughing and spluttering, but eventually he regained his more normal composure.

"It sounds to me as though your relationship with your slave was determined by the Gods," he said, "and I'm far too superstitious to frustrate them in any way. I will do all I can to help."

He thought silently for a while, then said,

"Your position is untenable anyway, but if you wish to adopt your slave it becomes more so. I think we have no alternative but to request the Legate to give you a discretionary local discharge on full pension. You will be a free man then, able to return to Rome or travel anywhere throughout the Empire. I will have your papers of discharge signed by the Legate this evening, and also draft a certificate of manumission for your most fortunate young slave. Come back later and I will have everything ready for your signature. Go now, and return all your military equipment to the quartermaster, and bear in mind you and your slave have no quarters in the barracks tonight."

Encouraged, Brutus returned to his room where Marc was eagerly awaiting him, and after explaining what was happening, they spent a busy hour sorting out what the centurion could keep from all that he had accumulated over the years.

Borrowing a small handcart, Marc loaded it and together they pulled the vehicle to the quartermaster's store. When everything had been handed back and signed for, Brutus turned to Marc, "Take these denarii and find us a room for tonight. Don't hurry back but meet me at the adjutant's office an hour before dinner."

Marc departed joyfully. There was a distinct spring to his step, as he strode purposefully towards the city of David on his last appointed task as a slave.

Marc didn't hurry. Although he had no idea what finding a room for the night might entail, he knew where to find help for this task. He stopped frequently at anything that caught his attention, and it was amazing how much seemed different today.

Here a carved door drew his eye, an attractive shop front, a glimpse of a colourful court revealed through a half open door, an old silversmith polishing a bracelet in the window of his tiny workshop. Suddenly he realised he had new eyes, those of a free man.

Had his eyes been more perceptive he would have noticed the dark bearded Induranean, if for no other reason than the crescent shaped scar that disfigured his gaunt cheek.

The man moved in fits and starts as he followed him inconspicuously, his hawk-like eyes quietly appraising his prey.

Coming to a small square Marc disappeared into a narrow doorway at the far side, while the man continued into the adjoining alley, where he crouched in an area of deep shadow and appeared to be drowsing.

The doorway let Marc into an enclosed courtyard with a flight of stone steps leading to a broad terrace, above which loomed many tall houses, joined in one continuous façade. Each was distinct and different from its neighbour as though separated also in time, as indeed they probably were, the city having evolved over many centuries. He went up to a carved cedar door and knocked three times. Miriam appeared, looking a little breathless, having run down the narrow staircase, and her eyes lit up on seeing him and the eager, expectant smile enlivening his youthful face. Very few words were exchanged before he entered, and after a cursory look over the courtyard Miriam closed and bolted the door.

"You've come at a momentous time, Marc. We have one of the followers of Jesus with us and what he's saying is hardly believable!"

They hurried up the staircase and entered a much bigger room than he had expected. Seated on a low couch was the largest man he had seen, so large that, seated as he was, his eye was on a level with the dozen people standing around him. He held his immense head proudly and his voice boomed and echoed around the room as he continued uninterrupted, "Mary was quite breathless and unbelievably excited as she ran up to us. She called out joyously, 'Our Lord is risen,' and fell at my feet saying, 'oh Simon the tomb is open and an angel is there proclaiming the greatest news. It's unbelievable!' While our brethren were getting the precise details of what she had seen, my natural impatience asserted itself and I had to run to the tomb to see for myself.

"Arriving there I saw the stone rolled back and the gaping, dark entrance to the tomb. I entered with trepidation, fearful as much as hopeful, and then in the gloom I saw the discarded sheet and the folded cloth, and only then did I believe. But you must listen to Mary, she heard the first words of our risen Lord."

Marc's eyes had not once deviated from the face of this incredible man. He saw the high forehead projecting to strong brows, like two buttresses of an impregnable fort, and the intensity glowing in the deep-set pale blue eyes, and remarked the broad bewhiskered cheeks and the generous full lips speaking through his golden beard.

Only when Mary moved to stand beside the fisherman did he emerge from the trance that held him, and he recognized the beautiful woman as one of those who had mourned at the foot of the cross. Her unusual milk white skin accentuated the redness of a full, exquisitely sculptured mouth and the soft rose pink glow over her high cheekbones. Her mass of sleek black hair was loosely wound in plaits and gathered like a crown.

As Marc recognized her, so he saw reflected in her eyes her recognition of him, and also a sadness, which softened and momentarily dulled their shine. He knew she was seeing again that desolate scene they had witnessed together. Then she threw him a brilliant smile and he warmed to her, and luxuriated in her soft, lilting, melodious voice as she began to speak.

"My friends, Mary, mother of James, Joanna and I carried spices and ointment to the tomb at dawn. Imagine the anguish of our hearts at the dreadful end to such a wonderful promise. We hadn't slept all night, having agreed we would do this last service as our farewell to our Lord."

She stopped for a moment, as though recollecting the exact sequence of events. Nobody moved or spoke. The very air seemed charged with energy as the drama was being recounted.

"As we approached the tomb we saw two guards standing close to its entrance and the stone was still in place. We wondered if they would help roll it clear when suddenly there was a great trembling of the earth, so that we clung to each other for fear of falling. Then a figure clothed in light was rolling the stone clear. His face shone like lightning and we dared not look into his eyes. As we stood hesitating and afraid he spoke these wonderful words to us: 'Do not be afraid, I know well that you have come to look for Jesus of Nazareth, the man who was crucified. He is not here, he has risen as he told you. Come see the place where the Lord was buried. You must go in haste, and tell his disciples that he has risen from the dead and now he is going on before you into Galilee, where you shall have sight of him. That is my message to you.'"

There was a stunned silence for a minute, as they pondered these wonderful earth-shaking words, and then everybody started to talk simultaneously until Simon raised his hand.

"I'm sorry to introduce some sobering news following the wonders Mary has revealed to us. You heard it mentioned that two Temple guards were at the entrance to the tomb. We have had word from our few friends in the Sanhedrin, that the elders have taken council together and concocted a lie to cover the glory of the truth.

"The guards have received great riches, and been sworn to declare they accepted a refreshing drink from one of us, which was drugged so that they fell into a deep sleep. While asleep, we disciples are said to have stolen the body. I tell you this so that you know there are powerful and unscrupulous forces arraigned against us, and we must constantly be on our guard."

As he said these last words he glanced questioningly at Marc before concluding, "I and all the disciples will be going to Galilee in the morning."

In the ensuing babble of conversation, Miriam took Marc's arm and led him over to Simon and Mary, who were conversing quietly. They glanced up and Miriam, pushing Marc forward, said, "This is the Roman slave of centurion Brutus. I met him at the crucifixion and he comforted me greatly."

"There was precious little comfort there for anyone," said Simon, "but I would to God I had been there instead of skulking in some little hide hole. My courage failed me in the moment of crisis and I will live with it all my life."

"But that's behind you now, Peter," said Mary "and you can be sure you will have many chances to make amends. Now let us welcome Miriam's friend and find out what brings him here."

She held her arms open wide and Marc, as though mesmerized, was drawn into her warm embrace. Her perfume was full of nostalgic memories of being comforted as a small boy. For a brief moment he surrendered himself to the buried past and then he found himself held at arm's length as she scrutinized him with shrewd eyes.

"Come on lad, tell us what brings you here?"

Briefly Marc indicated his mission and how he had hoped Miriam could guide him where to begin. Peter interrupted,

"I know a family nearby that has fallen on hard times and have rooms that might be suitable. Rueben the weaver is now too old to work more than a few hours, and his wife Rebecca has a painful swelling in her belly and an issue of blood, although she is long past child bearing. I'm on my way to them, why not accompany me?"

They were shortly walking through a huddle of small bazaars and narrow streets with open fronted work places, many of which resounded to the thump of heddle beating the weft, or hammer against metal. The walls of the houses ascended on both sides until there was but a glimpse of pale clear sky, and no sunlight penetrated.

"Await here," said Simon, and he and Miriam disappeared into one of the overbearing buildings.

Marc moved to look into a leather worker's shop and stood admiring the skilful way in which the leather thongs were being plaited to make a girdle. Suddenly a voice rang out,

"A thief, a thief. Stop thief!"

He turned to the direction of the voice.

A dark bearded man, in the vertically striped robe of a Samaritan, was pointing his way and calling out loudly as he raced towards him. Marc looked about him urgently but saw only a beggar with a crude crutch hunched over his begging bowl some short distance away. Now the man was close, still calling and gesticulating wildly, and suddenly Marc saw he was accusing him. For a brief moment his impulse was to flee, but he realised simultaneously that was just what his accuser hoped for.

Standing his ground, Marc momentarily caught the eye of the leather worker who had dropped his work and was coming to the door. The next instant he was on the stones under the weight of his powerful adversary, who was pummelling him violently and still shouting loudly his accusation.

A small crowd quickly gathered and chaos reigned as Miriam opened the door and looked out to see what the noise was all about. She saw two of Herod's guards approaching as though by magic, and realizing a serious threat was looming withdrew, closing the door behind her.

Discerning the proximity of the guards the man rose to his feet calling out, "This boy snatched a valuable gold brooch I was taking for repair. He gave me quite a chase but finally I caught him."

One of the guards lifted the dazed boy to his feet, and as he did so a beautifully worked brooch in the shape of a peacock fell to the ground from the folds of his tunic.

"That's it!" said the man, seizing it from the pavement. "Praise the Gods I can return it to my master!"

"That's enough evidence for me," said the guard seizing the purse from Marc's waist, as his companion viciously locked his arm behind him, "let's see what else he has stolen today."

He opened the purse and finding ten denarii exclaimed,

"How fortunate you all are that this honest citizen has apprehended this accomplished thief!"

"But there is an explanation for the denarii, and I have never seen this brooch before. Nor was I chased as I have been standing here for the past ten minutes!" protested Marc.

"I'll vouch for that," stated the leather worker, "he was watching me work a girdle for quite some time."

"You hold your tongue," snarled one of the guards, "he's our captive now and under arrest."

"Quite right officer," said the cripple, who had made a laborious path towards them, "I was going to trip him with this if he had run past me, but this loyal man caught him first."

Just then they were all aware of a huge figure looming over them. Simon caught hold of the tunic of each guard, banging them together so violently that their helmeted heads crashed and he dropped them into a befuddled heap at his feet. Seizing the shaking beggar he planted one enormous boot on his backside, and everyone was amazed as he regained his feet and ran off, leaving his crutch lying in the gutter.

The accuser was scurrying away, recognising that not only was there no profit to be gained from confronting this giant, but he might actually compromise his master if the Romans became involved.

Simon was roaring after the retreating cripple, a huge smile covering his face, "Truly the most momentous of miracles I've yet achieved. I wonder if I should use the same cure more often."

He turned to face Marc and said, "We'll fix up a room for you with Rueben but let's make ourselves scarce for the moment as these two seem to be regaining whatever wits they may have had."

The three of them hurried away, the crowd dispersing noisily.

When they had put some distance behind them they felt able to slow down.

"I can't thank you enough, Simon," said Marc, "this nearly became a disastrous day for me when I had thought it the most wonderful."

He then told them of his imminent freedom and his adoption as Brutus' son.

Miriam's eyes misted, so great was her joy at his change of fortune, and reaching for his hand she clutched it tightly as she was experiencing a delayed reaction and starting to feel faint. Simon, exhibiting inordinate sensitivity for such a big man, detected her unsteadiness and bending gathered her in his arms.

"I have a friend nearby where she can rest," he said, and noticing Marc's agitation continued, "don't worry lad, she will be alright in a few minutes. You aren't familiar with the ways of girls. I'll wager she was thinking of you being thrown into Herod's dungeon, which is tantamount to dying. When you tell your master, I mean father, what passed today, he will realise that you are in great danger as it was no accident that you were accused of being a thief. It was a well laid plan to injure you both, and I delight in being there to frustrate such evil."

Now Miriam was recovering, a little colour was returning to her ashen face and although she was nearly enveloped in Simon's massive beard she smiled weakly up at him and said, "Bless you, Peter!"

"Amen to that!" replied the fisherman.

Marc asked shyly, "Why sometimes are you Simon and then you are called Peter?"

"Well Simon is my name, and everybody has known me so until my Lord Jesus gave me a new name of Peter."

Marc was puzzled still, but Miriam astutely reading his eyes whispered, "Peter comes from petrous meaning a rock."

As Marc raised his eyes from Miriam's face to Peter's he lost his confused look and they all burst out laughing. Peering closely at Miriam, his eyes twinkling with delight Marc said, "Is there a girl's name that comes from pebble?" and they burst out laughing yet again.

They had arrived at a door which Peter was about to enter as Marc realised he should be meeting Brutus, so he made a hasty departure and caught up with him as he was crossing the parade ground. Small groups of legionaries were breaking off from weapon drill and as the man and boy passed, they raised their weapons in respectful salute. His legionaries had always held him in high regard and there had been a lot of debate throughout the barracks following the tournament.

Firmus had the documents ready as promised. When both had been signed he rolled each and placed them in small lacquered cylinders, which he then sealed and stamped.

"Keep these very safe," he said, "the one will ensure that wherever there is a Roman garrison you receive your pension, either in kind or in denarii. The other will guarantee you are a free man and as the adopted son of Brutus a citizen of Rome."

He then requested that Marc wait outside as there were some military matters to discuss and when they were alone he said, "It will be dangerous for you and your son if you stay in Jerusalem. The Legate and Tribune Tibullus had little regard for Pilate before the games and now they have none. Tibullus will shortly be returning to Rome and will undoubtedly inform Tiberius of the shortcomings of his Prefect."

He stopped for a moment, uncertain how to advise, but then continued, "Pilate and Herod have now made common cause to harm you. You can take care of yourself but they will find the boy easier. It will take at least a year to remove Pilate, and as Herod finds favour with Tiberius we may have to put up with him forever. My advice is go somewhere outside their jurisdiction. There is a boat sailing for Crete in ten days. I know the captain well and will happily give you a letter to secure your passage."

He finished with a quizzical lift to his voice. Brutus was silent some minutes.

"Thank you my friend. We are both in your debt and will heed your advice. You can be sure we will let you know of our plans, but I have much to attend to here over the next few days. I will certainly be on my guard and if it is in order, I would like to purchase two Roman infantry swords? We're so vulnerable unarmed and I prefer the legionaries weapon to all others and Marc will quickly learn."

"Follow me, that can be arranged without much difficulty," laughed the adjutant.

The two men crossed the parade ground and approached the dining mess.

"I think we may find the quartermaster here and he might be able to help!"

Marc waited respectfully outside and saw nothing of the moving ceremony that was awaiting the centurion. A lookout was posted and at his sign every centurion arose as one to stand in salute to their comrade. The unexpectedness of it nearly unmanned Brutus and he stood wordlessly looking from one face to another. Some he loved more than others, but all he valued as having been moulded and pressed in the same demanding mint as had stamped him.

At a sign from the adjutant they lifted their right arms, held horizontally across their chests, and let free a loud resounding roar. Then, their faces breaking into smiles, they gathered around their comrade. Every word of his speech at the tribunal had become part of the folklore of the garrison, and there wasn't a man who didn't share most of his sentiments.

Outside Marc had quite a long wait, but he rejoiced for his father's sake at each outburst of cheering or banging of the heavy wooden tables.

It was quite dark when Brutus finally emerged, with his sword hanging in a newly worked and beautifully patterned sheath, secured around his waist by an intricately plaited leather girdle, that Marc knew with certainty he had seen in the making. Wordlessly they moved together across and out of the military establishment, and into a less predictable world.

CHAPTER SIX

Rueben's abode was all that they required. He was more than happy to let them have two adjoining rooms for one denari a week, which, though sparsely furnished, provided greater comfort than either had known in the barracks. It was agreed that Marc would assist Rebecca with shopping in the market and the preparation and cooking of the evening meal. She was grateful for this help, as she had been getting steadily weaker as her illness progressed until it had been all she could do to raise herself from her bed for a few hours.

Brutus was glad of the aid of Rueben in finding a tailor, who speedily produced two handsome tunics and a cloak for Marc so he was able to rid himself of his slave attire. So impressed were they both when Marc first paraded his clothes, that Brutus decided to follow suit, and before many days had passed neither of them appeared conspicuously Roman.

Brutus was anxious that Marc gain proficiency with the sword, so each day they walked to a clearing where for hours they could practise unwatched. His duties had frequently taken him into the surrounding countryside so his knowledge of the terrain generally was good. Now, his military instincts sharpened by the danger threatening from Herod and Pilate, they explored all the tracks off the road, the courses of dried up streams, barely passable gullies and hidden caves, discovering previously unknown places to hide should the need arise. They both enjoyed these excursions into the country, and found they were achieving a physical hardiness far greater than either could remember at any time in the past.

Often when resting and enjoying a snack of dates or figs with cheese and bread, they would lie in the shade of some cypresses and talk of their boyhood.

Marc would reminisce about the forests and sea that surrounded the fortified settlement on the coast where he had lived, and the high white cliffs of the large eastern island dominating the horizon. Of the deer and wild boar that they loved to hunt, and the music of harp and pipe that they loved to listen to when minstrels came amongst them.

Brutus always said the same thing when he detected the nostalgic sadness creeping into Marc's voice.

"I would like us to go there one day, Marc," and Marc would smile sadly and wonder if it would ever be possible.

Their rooms were to the south of Jerusalem, in the older part known as the city of David. A gate in the city wall nearby overlooked the pool of Siloan, at the side of which a rough path plunged precipitously down into the Kidron Valley, before meandering gently down alongside the high east wall, and on towards the far plain of Judaea.

Brutus and Marc were walking briskly along the narrow path that followed the stream down the valley. Ahead of them, in the crystal clear air of early morning, loomed the imposing height of the aqueduct, which Pilate had caused to be built at great cost, both of lives and money, and they passed through one of its gloomy arches, to emerge by a low drystone wall on their right, which was the western boundary of an enclosed garden.

"This is the Garden of Gethsemane," said Marc sombrely, and Brutus looked at him questioningly.

"This is where Jesus was seized by the temple guards the night before ..." his voice tailed off, as he could find no words to adequately describe what he felt.

"It all started here did it?" said Brutus, pulling himself up the slope to peer over the low wall.

As a garden it was a disappointment, no riot of colour as in the gardens around the Forum and the adjacent residence of Pilate. It was more densely wooded than the surrounding slopes, and paths ran between the groves of trees disappearing into deep shade.

Marc had joined him and continued, "Simon the fisherman won't talk about it, but I've heard from Miriam that they came here to pray after the Paschal supper. One of the twelve disciples, named Judas Iscariot, had told the temple authorities at what time they were to be here, and to ensure they seized the right man he would greet him with a kiss."

Brutus was quiet for some minutes. Then he said, "I've found it hard to come to terms with what I did that day. Had I been that Judas I would wish I had never been born."

"He threw himself to his death from one of these cliffs some weeks ago," replied Marc.

Brutus shuddered, wondering if the betrayal had been as inevitably predetermined for Judas, as he had become convinced his role had been for him.

Turning away abruptly he regained the path leading to a low bridge a short way ahead. A larger road from Qumran on the northern end of the Dead Sea crossed this bridge and entered the city just to the north side of the temple.

As they approached some dense low scrub where the paths joined, Brutus raised his hand and they both stood listening intently.

This time Marc heard the rustling of the dry foliage close on his right.

Swords drawn, they stood anticipating an ambush, when a weak moan issued from the bushes. Kneeling to peer into the shade Brutus could make out the form of a man lying within. Another moan indicated that no concealment was intended, but rather misfortune was in evidence.

A few hacks at the undergrowth cleared enough space for Brutus to slide through to the injured man, who bereft of all outer garments, was lying crumpled where he had been thrown.

Brutus called to Marc,

"He's barely alive! I guess he's been lying here quite a while as there's no fresh blood. We will need a cart or four men and a litter to move him. Run up to the Temple gate and get help."

Marc set off quickly and the Roman legionaries guarding the gate let him through, directing him to the nearby guardhouse of the Temple.

A few soldiers, having just breakfasted, were standing about idly before moving to their stations inside the Temple courts.

Marc ran to them and started to explain to the nearest, only to be surprised when he turned his back and withdrew into the guardroom. A second showed no more interest but one surly fellow, helmetless and unshaven, came and looked closely, peering at him from different angles.

"Haven't I seen you before?" he said obviously puzzled.

It was then that Marc saw the insignia on his breastplate was that of sheaths of corn as carried by Herod's soldiers, and with a sinking feeling he knew just what was puzzling the fellow. He had recognized his face but not his clothes, and had he been wearing his slave's tunic he would doubtless have been seized.

Mark remonstrated with them at their indifference to the plight of one of their citizens, and expressed confidence he would get more assistance at the fort from the Romans. As he hurried away he was aware of the soldier conversing with another of the guards, and knew they were both studying him intently.

A few minutes later Marc was experiencing exactly the same indifference from the Roman guards. It was a matter for the civil authorities to aid an injured civilian they insisted.

"Take yourself off to Herod Antipas, young lad and see what help he offers," said a senior legionary, but just then he snapped to attention as an officer emerged to see what was going on.

It was the adjutant and he instantly recognised Marc.

"Do you have a problem?" he demanded.

The legionary started to speak but Firmus silenced him with an impatient wave of his hand, leaving Marc to explain. One minute was all that was needed before he turned to the anxious looking soldier and said, "Get moving, Mutatus, centurion Brutus needs help and enough time has been wasted. Ask Scio to fetch the field injury kit, while you bring a handcart from the quartermaster."

The crestfallen legionary sprang into action, and it seemed in no time at all Marc was leading the two soldiers through the gate and down towards the anxiously awaiting centurion.

He had cut a clearer way through to the fallen man who had lapsed into unconsciousness, and using a cloak they improvised a stretcher and manhandled the body to the cart. As they entered through the gate, Marc glanced around and saw among the small crowd the surly guard, accompanied by another similarly attired. They nodded in agreement and the first guard departed hastily.

Marc had the certain feeling they were no longer in doubt as to his identity and wouldn't want to lose him a second time.

Firmus was waiting at the guardroom and with him was the same pompous physician that had felt himself let down badly by Brutus. He looked reproachfully at the centurion and then proceeded to examine the unconscious man. He elicited certain reflexes, at which he expressed his satisfaction and said, "He will un-doubtedly live if this mule headed man," indicating Brutus, "will desist from shaking him about in his cart. He's been badly beaten but no bones are broken, his breathing is steady and pulse not too weak."

"Can you care for him in the sick bay?" asked Brutus. "We can't safely move him further."

Firmus and the physician looked doubtfully at each other, as he continued,

"I know we don't know who he is, but if you look at his fingers and his nails they are well cared for. These marks on his neck and arm indicate he was wearing some fine jewellery that his assailant tore from him, I think you may find him an important person,"

Firmus made the decision to hold him overnight, and the soldiers pushed the cart towards the sick bay with the physician trotting alongside thinking he might do very well out of this.

Firmus and Brutus exchanged a few words before separating when Marc told of his fears, "I've been recognized by the guards that tried to arrest me before Peter intervened. One of them is watching me now."

"I suppose there has always been the chance of this happening. Don't let him think you're aware. Let's walk casually to the old quarter of the city where there are some really narrow alleys, while I think up a plan to deter him."

They penetrated into the maze of small alleys opening here and there into wider courts or crossed by equally narrow intersecting passages, until Brutus suddenly said, "Turn into the next alley and keep on walking when I peel off to one side or the other. Don't look back."

Marc nodded and they both turned into a narrow passage bordered by high boundary walls on both sides, Brutus moving quickly through an open door into a tiny yard crammed full of stacked amphorae. He flattened himself against the wall and waited. There was hardly any noise as the soldier approached to come abreast of the door opening.

For his build Brutus moved incredibly quickly to slide behind the startled man, lock his right arm around his throat and haul him into the yard. The man's hand closed on the hilt of his sword but simultaneously he felt a prick of something sharp just below his ear, into which was hissed the chilling threat,

"Move your sword hand and you're a dead man!"

The man froze, wondering whether to try and break his assailant's grip on him, but recognising the professional soldier he knew he stood no chance.

"Now release the hilt of your sword and move your hand slowly across your chest."

The man complied.

"This is your only warning. If you are as much as seen again anywhere near my son or I, or we have the slightest suspicion of any interest on your part, you will not see another day. If we come across each other in the street move away as rapidly as possible. I am a centurion and enjoy the protection of Rome. Herod cannot touch me nor protect you and I would enjoy killing you if you gave me cause."

Keeping the dagger against his neck Brutus tightened his arm around the man's throat and watched his eyes bulge as he was asphyxiated. Just before he blacked out Brutus felt some involuntary twitching of the man's legs and a sudden weight increase on his tightened arm, so releasing his grip he stepped lightly over the guard as he sank to the cobbles.

Rejoining Marc he said, "I think I've seen him off for good, but this does emphasise the peril we face if we linger around Jerusalem. Maybe it's time we started our travels! How say you, Marc?"

"Have I time to tell Miriam? She would worry greatly if we just disappeared."

Brutus smiled.

"Many a battle has been lost because of the overlong courting of a lady love, but I think we may just delay our departure for one day."

He was gratified to see the tension ebb from Marc's eyes as he returned a hesitant smile.

46

Marc had not been to Simon of Cyrene's house since the evening of the crucifixion, and he was aware that only the most exceptional circumstance would overcome their objection to a gentile crossing the threshold. It was now dark so he was certain he would find her at home, but still he approached the house with trepidation.

The servant who opened the door recognised him, in spite of his greatly altered clothing, and called Miriam who came running, but the joy she felt was tempered by an ill-concealed anxiety, which showed in the worried look of her eyes.

"Oh I'm so glad to see you Marc," she said, "but I'm afraid I can't ask you in, I really can't, much as I would like to."

The crestfallen look on her young visitor's face made her continue with an explanation she might otherwise not have made.

"We have an important visitor come all the way from Tarsus who is talking with daddy. He's a Pharisee and very strict and wouldn't remain in the house if you were to enter."

"Can we talk here then?" queried Marc, "I don't want to go away without you knowing what has happened."

Miriam brought her hand up to her mouth as she let out an involuntary gasp of dismay.

"I'll go and ask mummy if it will be alright to talk on the terrace at the back," she said and quickly disappeared into the house, to run back breathless and excited.

She seized Marc's hand and led him round the side of the house, to a pretty terrace looking over a tiled court with a circular stone fountain in the centre.

"We've only got twenty minutes before I must change to dine with our guest. So tell me everything that's been happening and I want to know all you've done these past few days."

Marc smiled at her excited chatter and he started by telling of the day's adventure. A servant came out and lit two lamps, as it was getting quite dark. Miriam listened without once interrupting, although her face registered the turmoil of emotions she felt more eloquently than words.

"Where will you go? You must go quickly," she burst out at the end, her memory vividly recalling the image of Marc in the grip of Herod's guards.

Naomi appeared and briefly greeting Marc said, "You must go and dress, dearest. Saul and Papa will soon have finished their business and we will be wanting to eat."

"Oh mummy, can you think of anywhere Marc can go where he will be safe from Herod's men?"

"Why don't you ask Alexander, he should be coming by in a few days and there's bound to be a trading boat he knows of going somewhere or other?"

She waved her hand dismissively as she returned to the house.

"I'll talk with my father about it, if there really is the chance of a sea passage soon," said Marc reassuringly, but wishing Alexander's visit was more imminent.

Miriam let him out through the gate of wrought iron set in the wall of the courtyard, but only after she had scrutinized the length of the street. Seeing nothing to alarm her she bolted it from within, fondly watching the boy disappear.

Late that evening Brutus was looking puzzled. It had become a ritual to play the Roman game, Ludus Latrunculorum. Marc had previously invariably been surrounded and conceded but not tonight, for Brutus had been forced to concede the first two games, and he found it hard to take on board the idea of losing.

His sense of humour asserted itself and he clapped Marc across the shoulder and laughed.

"At this rate of progress I think I'm going to have some hard times ahead! Still I've always got dice to fall back on."

"I think I had all the luck tonight," said Marc modestly.

"With your pretty little Jewess as well, maybe?" rejoined Brutus, but wished he hadn't as Marc reddened and had no reply. Changing the subject he said,

"Do you think waiting on her brother is such a good idea? I hope I may have scared that fellow off this afternoon, but he must be only one of many and they will close their net around us if we give them time."

"You must decide what is best as you have so much more experience of defending yourself, but my instinct is to put as great a distance as possible between us and Pilate, and maybe Alexander could help there."

"Let's sleep on it and see what happens tomorrow, it won't take us long to get ready when or whatever we may decide."

Had either known what a momentous day lay ahead there can be no doubt they would have slept less soundly.

About an hour after sunrise they approached the guardroom to Fort Antonia, where the challenging legionary was quick to recognise the centurion and allow them to pass. Crossing the parade square towards the sick bay they discussed how they might find the victim, and in the doorway nearly bumped into the physician Creticus, who was gleefully rubbing his hands and muttering to himself.

"Remarkable, remarkable recovery," he said, nodding with evident satisfaction towards them. "Go in and see my patient, you will have a surprise!"

He seemed to have forgiven Brutus completely and wanted them to acknowledge how successful his treatment had been.

Entering the room they saw lying on his bed a young man dressed in a borrowed tunic with a toga loosely draped over. He smiled a greeting through half closed eyes and addressed them in Greek as though it were his native language. This put both his visitors at a distinct disadvantage as neither was fluent and needed to reply in Latin.

"Greetings, gentlemen. I am in your debt, even to saving my life if you are centurion Brutus?"

Brutus nodded and the man gingerly raised himself off his bed. It was obvious his body and limbs were protesting at the severe beating he had received.

He raised his hand in salute and astonished Marc as he identified himself.

"Alexander, son of Simon of Cyrene, forever in your debt."

Brutus saluted him unaware of the dumbfounded look on Marc's face.

Alexander, however, was aware how profoundly his greeting had disconcerted his young visitor and regarded him with some alarm until finally Marc exclaimed, "Then you must be brother to Rufus and Miriam!"

This time it was Alexander who showed his amazement.

"You know my brother and sister? How can this be? I left Rufus in Libya three weeks ago and my sister Miriam is here in Jerusalem."

"I passed this Passover supper at your parents' home and am very grateful for their kindness," said Marc, and saw that far from clearing things, Alexander looked even more confused.

"Then you are a Jew?" he finally said with an inflection that showed his doubting.

"No, I am a Celt by birth from Britain, but I was captured and enslaved by the Romans."

Alexander had to sit down on the bed. He was staggered at the course of this conversation and found it hard to believe what he was hearing. Finally he said, "Excuse my impoliteness. It is hard for me to believe that my family, so strict in their observance of our custom, sat down to the Paschal dinner with a Gentile as their guest. You must be a most remarkable young man!"

"No, not I," said Marc, "what was remarkable was the sympathy and compassion of your whole family when my world was collapsing all around me and I was completely wretched."

He was momentarily silent as though recalling how things had been that day.

"Only last night your mother told us you were expected and we would do well to enlist your assistance."

"Gladly will I assist you after all you have done for me," said the young Jew, "tell me how I can help."

Just then Firmus arrived and, after inquiring as to Alexander's well being, sat down and asked them to continue.

Marc looked at Brutus, "Sir, it would be best if you told Alexander the whole story!"

Brutus agreed and proceeded to tell him of the crucifixion.

Alexander was incredulous at Miriam's part in the events and even more so when the centurion mentioned he had ordered his father to carry the cross to the place of execution.

"I take it, sir, that my father bears you no ill feeling for what you forced upon him?" he said.

Brutus was disconcerted by this direct question, but before he could reply Marc interjected, "Your father told me a lot at the Paschal meal and he said that he rejoiced to take the burden from Jesus and carry it for him."

Alexander wondered what sort of man this Jesus must have been that his father could behave so out of character.

"And now you tell me this crucified Jesus has overcome death and has revealed himself to his followers."

"Lots of people say he has been seen by his disciples, but the Temple authorities say his body was removed by these disciples after the guards were drugged," said Brutus. "Marc has spoken to a man and a woman who witnessed him alive after the crucifixion, and I promise you he was dead when taken from the cross."

"Can you explain this?" said Alexander doubtfully.

"Well, he was a miracle worker. He is said to have cured the lame, the blind, lepers, those possessed of demons and even brought the dead back to life," said Marc eagerly.

"Do you believe it? Did you ever actually see it happen?" queried Alexander.

"Among the centurions gathered here for the Passover was Andreaus from Capernaum. You know him, Brutus?" said Firmus, and receiving an acknowledgement continued, "Well his servant Dicacus was dying and nobody expected him to live another day. Andreaus heard this Jesus was not far away so he rode with a few followers, found him and begged him to heal his servant. Jesus said he would come to his house and see him, but Andreaus replied he was a Gentile and he wouldn't expect him a Jew and Rabbi to come into his house, but if he just said the word that would suffice. Jesus told him because of his great faith it would be as he asked. He brought Dicacus with him last month and we all saw him serving Andreaus in the dining hall!"

Alexander, bewildered by all he had heard said to Firmus, "I too have been brought back from the dead, by the compassion of your friends here and the skill of your physicians. This sort of miracle is easier to appreciate."

Firmus smiled.

"I suppose you wish to join your family. I will order one of the supply vehicles to take you to your home, perhaps Brutus and Marc will escort you as you still have much to discuss. I wish you a full and quick recovery."

He left to make the arrangements, but was more than a little intrigued at how fine a web was being spun around them all.

The alarm in the house of Simon of Cyrene when a mule cart with two legionaries stopped by the gate was considerable. But when the servants saw two men, one of whom they recognised as the friend of Miriam, assisting the battered and bandaged son of the family, alarm became panic.

Simon, disturbed by all the noise, excused himself from the austere young man, and looked out onto the pandemonium. Instantly recognizing Alexander he hurried to the slow moving party, calling to a servant to fetch her mistress. Father and son met and embraced with intensity, conveying both concern and joy at their reunion.

Naomi and Miriam appeared in the doorway and as the mother was carefully inspecting her injured son, Miriam was insisting on some explanation from Marc.

"Oh, I would love to stay and tell you, but it's not possible to be brief. I'm sure Alexander will tell you everything. We only came to escort your brother safely and don't wish to intrude on your family reunion," said Marc.

Miriam stamped her foot with vexation and tears welled up in her eyes. Marc thought she had never looked so pretty but found himself lost for any appropriate words. His awkwardness was relieved when Alexander said, "Are those tears for me, little sister?" and held his arms out for her to rush into.

So great was her emotional turmoil that Miriam nearly knocked her brother off his feet, and only the support of Brutus prevented his falling.

"Why sister, if you had been with that gang that attacked me there would have been nothing left for the centurion to rescue," he chided her.

She beat her tight little fists on his chest in retaliation, until she saw a flicker of pain and realized how much she was abusing him.

Brutus had now withdrawn and he and Marc were about to leave, as Simon realized what was happening.

"Please don't go now. Come inside and refresh yourselves. There is so much I wish to hear and from the little Alexander has said I know I shall be forever indebted to you," he pleaded.

Brutus smiled uncertainly.

"Two Roman gentiles, sir? I feel we would be imposing on your generosity."

"Oh Jew, Roman, gentile, are we not all children of the living God? Please, I beseech you, spend a little while with us and then feel free to go on your way."

Miriam had now moved up and taken her father's arm, and although she said nothing her eyes were looking imploringly at the centurion who found his resolve wavering.

"For a short while then, sir. Thank you."

At that moment the young man who had been watching from the doorway approached them. He bowed to all and then addressing Simon said, "Our business is about concluded, sir. I am delighted at the safe return of your son. I hope you won't think it ungracious if I leave you to your rejoicing, I have urgent matters to attend to."

"Thank you, Saul, it would be quite improper of me to press you to stay," said Simon. "Do convey our greetings and felicitations to all in Tarsus, it seems ages since we saw your parents."

The lasting impression the young man made on Brutus was the intensity in his eyes, and he thought, "This is a man that it would be impossible to deflect from any purpose to which he has set his mind."

They entered the house and Marc found himself back in the room where they had eaten the Paschal meal. It was a strange feeling to be in the same place where he had sat a frightened and worried slave. Now he was not only a free man and a Roman citizen, but he was with his father and rejoicing at his good fortune. Miriam was seated beside him and he delighted in watching her as Alexander told of his misadventure and subsequent events. In rapid succession her face registered indignation, alarm, horror, relief, joy, sorrow. Even though she knew that Marc was watching her closely her uninhibited youthfulness made her unable to suppress her reactions.

Alexander had arrived at the bridge at dusk.

"A small donkey cart was on its side blocking the bridge and an old man and a young girl were trying to right it. The donkey had been loosed from the shafts and was munching at the side of the path. I was within minutes of home after riding all the way from Bethany and a little impatient, so I dismounted to assist and suddenly half a dozen ruffians had seized my horse and surrounded me. I walked right into their trap like a naïve boy and was furious with myself. I tried to draw my sword but they bludgeoned me into unconsciousness and took everything I had. Doubtless they tossed me for dead into the dense scrub hoping my body would not be found for days, by which time they would be well clear."

Brutus had the suspicions of Firmus to pass on.

"They were probably a band of zealots. Hundreds of them gathered around here at the Passover as usual, but this year they were getting more support than usual after Pilate's brutal mishandling of that ambush. They have disbanded now, but there are a few disaffected bands lurking around, evading patrols and stealing from travellers."

"How horrible of that girl, to throw in her lot with such villains and lure you into a trap," said Miriam, and she was not amused at the laughter that greeted her observation.

"I don't see anything funny about that," she said, her eyes shooting daggers at Marc, who hastily suppressed his merriment and tried to sound contrite.

"Of course there isn't Miriam and what you say is absolutely right. I'm sure our laughter was with relief, and when you said how horrible the girl was, and only the girl, it just came tumbling out."

Miriam felt slightly mollified, but needed reassurance as she thought she detected a barely suppressed lift to the corners of his mouth.

She looked to Brutus for support but he was staring fixedly at the ceiling.

Her father, when she glanced at him was intently studying his finger nails, his mouth open and a bemused look on his face.

As for Alexander, his amusement was so transparent it was only by reminding herself of his bruised ribs that she could refrain from the resumption of the pummelling she had given him earlier.

"Oh mummy, why are men so exasperating?" she cried with feeling.

Naomi got up and holding Miriam's imploring face to her bosom said, "Because they never stop being children, dear. They just grow larger."

Nobody could restrain himself a moment longer and the room reverberated to the men's guffawing and chuckling, to which quickly was added the giggling of Miriam and Naomi.

The servants bringing in flagons of cold sherbert cordial and honey and almond cakes had never known such unrestrained merriment in the household and withdrew quickly.

"It's as well Saul left when he did, my dear, he is of such a serious disposition he would think we've all taken leave of our senses," Simon said drying his eyes.

"If he is from Tarsus, father, is he a merchant we trade with?"

"No Alexander, not any longer, although the family have important links with many trading families such as ours. They are ship owners but that's not why he is here now, he has a much more serious task. Saul is very active as a Pharisee in the community in Tarsus and represents their elders and priests to the Sanhedrin. His business here is to ascertain the policy of the Temple authorities towards the Christ followers, who are as active in Tarsus as they are here." Simon paused as though wondering whether it was discreet to say more.

"What do you mean by Christ followers daddy?" asked Miriam.

"Well, really, followers of this Jesus we saw crucified, dearest. Now they say he has arisen from the tomb his disciples claim this means he is the Messiah. The Greek word for Messiah is Christos, hence Christ followers."

There was a long silence as everyone placed their own significance on what they had just heard. They were all amazed when Miriam broke the silence, "Then that means I am a Christ follower too!"

Brutus and Marc exchanged bewildered looks. The rest of the family was thrown into such consternation by this simple declaration they all began speaking at once. Suddenly Simon stood up and raised his hand for silence.

"I don't think you should make that declaration, Miriam," he said. "You still attend the Temple and worship there. These Christ followers are forming a cult and growing in numbers, and although they still attend the Temple daily they are challenging many aspects of our traditional worship. They refuse to offer sacrifice as atonement and claim that crucifying this Jesus is the final sacrificial offering. You don't associate yourself with this defiance of the Temple authorities."

"No daddy, I don't do that. But I do believe that Jesus has overcome death and appeared to his followers here in Jerusalem. I believe him to be the Son of God and that it was the Elders of the Temple, the Sanhedrin, that caused him to be put to death."

Simon was greatly agitated by Miriam's forthright declaration. Finally he said, "This is as Saul says. Families will be divided within themselves and the whole fabric of Jewish worship will be torn asunder! He says we must crush this movement before it destroys us."

He stood with his gaze fixed as though he were gazing into a frightening apocryphal future. Naomi was sobbing quietly and Miriam went to comfort her. Marc and Brutus arose as one and passing Alexander, Brutus said, "Forgive our departure. We feel this family crisis would be better resolved without us remaining here. We will contact you later. Please convey our regrets that we are leaving so abruptly. Don't worry we will see ourselves out."

Alexander nodded, his mind full of conflicting emotions.

As they passed into the street Brutus looked questioningly at Marc.

"Do you find it strange the turmoil that follows this miracle worker and advocate of peace and love? Perhaps the world is not ready for such a message?"

Marc was unable to reply. He was too deeply moved by all he had seen and heard and in his heart was longing to be standing alongside Miriam saying, "Me too! I'm a Christ follower!"

Marc was impatient to see Miriam and he slept fitfully. After breakfast for which he had no appetite he said, "Sir, I am so anxious concerning Miriam I will be unable to concentrate on anything until I have spoken to her."

"Then go and find her this morning, we can forego our sword practice today. I too am anxious, as I would like to have talked more with Alexander. We are not wise delaying here overlong, and Simon of Cyrene aroused hopes that we could enlist his help. Perhaps you could request to see the son on this errand and you can be sure of seeing the daughter too."

He smiled at Marc, "Don't look so crestfallen. These are momentous times in all our lives. Times of great change, if we are to shed old values and take on new. I resolved to find out as much as I could about this Galilean, and have not found the changes to my life easy so far. So it is with Miriam and her family!" Putting a reassuring arm around his son he continued, "A brave man, and likewise a brave woman, takes change as it comes, responds to any challenge and keeps fear under check. So it will be with you and your friend Miriam."

Marc made his way to Simon's house with his spirit less weighed down after Brutus' words, and was led by a servant into a small study where father and son were rolling up scrolls from which they had been reading.

Both rose on Marc's entry and received him with greater courtesy than he would have expected from two men receiving a mere boy.

"Please convey to your father our profound regrets for our discourtesy yesterday," said Simon, rubbing the palms of both hands together as though at prayer. "You return our son to us, having undoubtedly saved his life, and instead of our thanks are forced to endure our family troubles which thankfully we have now resolved. Please tell us the purpose of your visit."

"Sir, my visit is prompted by two motives. Firstly my heart was greatly troubled by the distress that was obviously caused by Miriam's declaration. I know it is not my place but I felt that I should have been standing beside her instead of fleeing."

"And so you've come to pledge your support now have you?" said Alexander brusquely.

"Well not exactly," said Marc reddening, "I think the moment for that came and went yesterday. I sought only to tell you I do not feel very proud for my part."

"Well said, young man," exclaimed Simon, indicating a chair. "Your honesty and your courage are to your credit. My son and I find it very difficult to accept the testimony of these followers of Jesus and we know very little of his actual teaching. We only know he miraculously healed very many people and then died on a cross which I carried for much of the way. We have been looking at our Prophets, to see if we could find anything they say that might reconcile this apparent contradiction when you arrived."

"And did you, sir?" said Marc eagerly.

"Well one or two rather inconclusive pointers that's all. But tell us of your other motive."

"My father and I have made enemies of both Pilate and Herod Antipas, and they nearly arrested me and would have thrown me into Herod's dungeons, had it not been for Simon Peter. We are convinced they will harm me in any way they can to revenge themselves. Your wife suggested that, as the visit of Alexander was forthcoming, we wait and ask for his assistance. We didn't find time to mention this yesterday, there seemed greater priorities."

"Well it's not too late now. I am pleased to have the opportunity to help you both. I distrust that usurper Herod - he is truly an evil man! My plan is to rest here until after Pentecost in ten days time, by then I should be completely recovered. My purchases will be assembling at Joppa for shipping to Tyre, so say you were to travel with me from Jerusalem after Pentecost or meet me in Joppa in two weeks, how would that be?"

"Thank you, I think to sail to Tyre with you may suit us well. My father will probably prefer to join you at the port as we are anxious to get away from Jerusalem as soon as we can."

Alexander nodded, "Where will you go in the meantime?"

"I am not sure, but Centurion Brutus was talking of travelling to the Sea of Galilee, to Capernaum. When I tell him of your offer we might like to use these days to make that visit."

"You will still be within Herod's jurisdiction in Capernaum, he is tetrarch of Galilee," rejoined Simon.

"I think we feel there is a greater threat here in Jerusalem, where we can be easily watched. In the country nobody would be able to follow us without our knowing."

"I don't think I would relish following you two outside of the city," said Alexander, "but don't underestimate Herod. There are no limits to which he isn't prepared to go for revenge, and he has a tight network of people gathering information throughout Judaea. As a merchant, I'm sure every tax official reports all my movements, so that the authorities can trace me at will. Probably it was not by chance that I was set upon and robbed, more likely my assailants were tipped off!"

"Thank you, I will pass on your warning. Is it possible to see Miriam for just a few minutes, sir?" Marc looked anxiously at Simon.

"I would not forbid it, Marc, were it possible. But my wife and daughter are both at the Temple and likely to be for some time. They are hoping some learned Rabbi there might be able to reconcile the different way they regard this Prophet Jesus." He stopped pensively for a while before continuing,

"I could do with some help myself as I greatly fear he will shake our old beliefs and traditions to the very foundations, and I don't know whether I welcome the inevitable disturbance." He shrugged as though acknowledging how little he could predict, or influence, what lay ahead.

Marc felt completely downcast. He had never contemplated leaving without exchanging even the common courtesies, let alone the intimacies his heart was longing to reveal.

"Then will you please tell Miriam I stand with her in all she declared yesterday," he said, rising to take his departure, "we will keep you informed of our intentions."

Simon saw him to the door and as he walked to the gate called out,

"May you walk with God," and closed the door behind him.

The Wilderness

CHAPTER ONE

"Good," said Brutus, with evident satisfaction at the thought of finally getting away from Jerusalem, "so we leave this afternoon and make our way eastwards to where the Jordan flows into the Dead Sea! That will give us two weeks to explore the region right up to the Sea of Galilee. Can we be ready in two hours?"

Marc nodded agreement. He knew Brutus liked travelling unencumbered, carrying nothing other than his sword and dagger, a good cloak and food and water for one day only. A few denarii would buy them the produce of any villages they passed through, although if nothing was forthcoming, he was expert at living off the land.

Accordingly they took their leave of Rueben, paying a month's advance on their rooms. Rebecca was tearful and hugged Marc mercilessly while he tried to extricate himself from her embrace. Finally, when he had managed, he said, "Since Peter laid his hands on you it's wonderful to see you getting better all the time, so I won't worry about you and you're not to worry about us. We won't forget those dishes you taught me, and every time I think of a falafel I'll think of you!"

Rebecca smiled ruefully and pretended to box his ears and with a wave they began their journey.

Crossing the city they left by the East Gate, heading down into the Kidron Valley. On the far side of the bridge where they had found Alaxander the road diverged, the northerly route heading to Jericho, while the lesser road skirted south of the Mount of Olives which dominated the small range of hills extending eastward all the way to the Jordan Valley.

They had been walking for an hour when they approached a group of women sitting in the shade of some olive trees. Marc thought he recognised one of them and when she raised her hand and waved a greeting his face broke into a smile and his pace quickened.

"Mary Magdalene! What on earth are you doing out here?" he exclaimed, and he pressed Brutus that they rest with them for a short while.

"I could ask the same of you," said the woman smiling joyfully, "except anyone can see you're starting a long journey."

"We are. My father and I hope to spend the night at Bethany and then continue tomorrow down to the Jordan along the old salt road."

Brutus saluted the three women and then looked at Marc quizzically as he recognized none of them, nor could he easily follow the Aramaic they spoke.

"Forgive me," said Marc, "I have the honour to present my father Brutus, until recently a centurion with the Jerusalem garrison. This is Mary Magdalene, the first person to witness to the risen Jesus."

This revelation brought to the face of the centurion a perplexed look initially, followed by one of dismay.

Mary, aware he was troubled but uncertain of the cause, rose to her feet and resting her hand on his arm led him to the other two women.

"This is Joanna, wife of Chusa," she said, "and this is Mary, blessed mother of Jesus."

Both ladies were raising their hands in the traditional Jewish greeting of shalom and averting their eyes modestly, when they all became aware of the torment the introduction caused the centurion.

His face was contorted by spasms of anguish and he held his body as rigid as hammered iron. Mary could feel the tension in the arm she was holding.

Suddenly perceptive, she released his arm and moved to stand in front of him and took both his hands in hers. Her large, lustrous dark eyes were swimming with tears as she whispered huskily, "We have all stood together before haven't we, at the foot of the cross!"

Brutus hearing these, the last words he had expected or wished to hear, sank to his knees, trying to bury his face in his hands.

As Mary found her hands against his face she felt them moistened with his tears, and her compassion overwhelmed her so that she drew him to her, holding his tortured face to her breast. For many minutes they clung together, a silent tableau of suffering and anguish.

Distressed and bewildered the other women looked to Marc for enlightenment. With a sigh he said, "Do you not recognize us from the foot of the cross? My father regaled in the uniform of the centurion crucifying your son, and me clasping Miriam after I had neglected my duty, which was to carry his spear?"

Their disbelief showing in their faces, the women looked from Marc to the centurion, then at each other, reliving that awful time, before drawing together to seek comfort, shedding silent tears of grief.

Marc wandered aimlessly, unable to intrude, feeling isolated and afraid. He glanced up to the summit of the mountain and his eyes were held by a vibrant, glowing luminescence suspended in the sky. It bathed the distant peak with a soft golden glow, which conferred to the daylight an ethereal mysterious quality such as he had never previously seen or imagined. Unable to restrain himself a minute longer, he moved to each group in turn, shaking them demandingly and just pointing. They stood filled with wonder until the glow lost its intensity and suddenly was no more. With it the hurt and anguish likewise disappeared, as though balm had been applied to an open wound. The healing process had begun.

"I know I can't hope for his forgiveness," Brutus said sadly, "I will never be able to forgive myself, but meeting the mother of the innocent man I executed makes what I did unbearable. At the time I wished I had never been born. I nearly impaled myself with my sword and as I stood with sword raised I was only checked from that course by hearing again the last words your son spoke to me. He said, 'You must do that which you must,' and instead, I shattered the blade on the rock at the foot of that cross."

There was silence as these words were pondered on.

Then Jesus' mother said, "I keep being told of the words of my son and I store them like jewels in my heart. You were there, do you not remember his words from the cross?"

Brutus looked puzzled and shook his head sadly.

Mary continued, "His first words were, 'Father forgive them for they do not know what they are doing.' You were included in that prayer, and what the son asks of the Father cannot be withheld by the mother."

"I cannot understand such forgiveness. I did what I did aware how wrong it was, yet that didn't stop me," said Brutus despondently.

"May I tell you my story?" said Mary Magdalene with an intensity that was not to be denied. "Nearly three years ago I first encountered Jesus. At the time I was going through a rough period. I was disenchanted with my way of life, but nothing I did to try to change things helped at all.

"The thing I most craved was love, and I tried to find it in every imaginable way. I loved men and shared my affection with four part time husbands. I loved riches and jewels, and sought both. I loved excitement, and would recklessly seek it in novel ways. I loved power, and tried to get my own way with everyone I encountered. Finally I loved mystery, and delved into the occult and pagan traditions. I must have seemed crazy to most people in the village of Nain where I lived, about forty miles north of here.

"My lovers would sometimes stay away for weeks after I had made a terrible scene, usually because I had been unable to have my own way. I had one real friend, who was always forgiving of my excesses and to whom I could always turn. She was a widow and her name was Sarah. Her only son Joseph was the joy of her life. She did everything she could for him and they would read part of the scripture together daily as he approached his thirteenth birthday, rehearsing the portion of the law he was to read when he became Bar Mitzvah - a son of the law."

Mary paused for a moment and when she resumed she grew sorrowful.

"Two days before his birthday Joseph developed a malignant fever that progressed so rapidly he died on the eve he was to have celebrated his Bar Mitzvah.

"I was distraught with grief and frightened for his mother, as Sarah was inconsolable. Her friends and relatives, gathered for Joseph's celebration, were now having to attend to his burial. It was too terrible for words."

Pausing briefly, while everyone hung on her words, Mary continued.

"The body of Joseph was being carried to the tomb on a bier by two uncles and his two best friends, and as we passed through the east gate a great crowd of rejoicing people came towards us. They fell silent seeing our distress, and then from the midst of the crowd Jesus stepped forward.

"Never had I seen a man like him. Love emanated as though it were a cloak about him. I saw the concern come into his eyes and the grief that pulled at his heart, as it did at mine.

"He said to Sarah, 'Do not weep.' Everyone stood absolutely still anticipating something startling and momentous, but not as incredible as what followed.

"Jesus moved to the side of the bier placed his hand on it and said, 'Young man I say to you, rise up.' And he did, he really did."

An elation and excitement had now come into her voice and Brutus and Marc exchanged looks of wonder, but so spellbound were they, both by the story and the storyteller, neither was willing to break the spell by speaking a word.

Mary continued, "Joseph sat up and spoke to Jesus, who taking him by the arm, helped him off the bier and took him to his mother. I was blinded with tears and beside myself with joy. I knew that my lifelong search had come to an end. All that I had previously sought faded into insignificance. When I managed to fight back my tears and look around for him he had gone, just walked away, and was nowhere to be found, search though I might."

Marc could no longer remain seated. He had no voluntary control of his action as he went across to Mary, kissed her and sitting beside her laid his head on her lap, while she gently fondled his curls, all the time looking steadily at Brutus and smiling shyly.

For some while no one spoke, they each sat reflecting silently on Mary's testimony. Then Brutus said, "Mary, you are a woman I can truly admire, for I recognize a bravery that would shame any legionary in the Imperial army. I know of no one who follows so faithfully her heart, and I rejoice that your searching has led you to find fulfillment.

"I knew that Jesus was the Son of God even as I pierced his heart, so I cannot do other than believe he has overcome that death I inflicted, just as he conquered the hold of death on Joseph. What I still cannot accept is that he can forgive me, or that you can or his mother either."

"Let me tell you the rest of my story and then you may, no then you will realise, forgiveness is far beyond our understanding," Mary said insistently.

Marc thought himself in paradise, as he lay being fondled by this beautiful woman, and listening to her melodious voice.

"After Joseph had been restored to Sarah the whole town and countryside was rejoicing and declaring a new prophet had come to Israel. A Pharisee in the town, named Simon, thought to give a dinner for Jesus and invited all his important friends, and so that all the townsfolk could see, he had the table laid in his court and the gates left open.

"I was standing watching when Jesus joined the dinner party, and I was incensed at the lack of courtesy shown by Simon, who led him immediately to the table and preened himself as though he were exhibiting some rare and wonderful trophy.

"My heart seethed with anger and I had to turn away, and then I remembered I had a jar of precious ointment at home, which I hurried to fetch. Returning to the Pharisee's house I saw Jesus sitting forlorn, ignored by his host whose expectations he failed to fulfil.

"I followed my heart and walked quietly into the court and stood silently behind my Lord. The tears came to my eyes at his humiliation and I knelt at his feet to apply the ointment I had brought. As I knelt there my tears could not be contained, falling like drops of rain onto his feet, glistening like pearls on the dust. I loosened my hair and wiped away my tears, but they were still falling as I anointed his feet with my ointment.

"I never looked up, not once, so I was unaware whether he even noticed me, but I was aware of the Pharisee as he said to his neighbour, 'What kind of a prophet can he be, who would allow himself to be touched by this sinful woman?'

"I knew he was right and great was my anguish that in my heart driven recklessness I had harmed my Lord."

She was silent and as Marc felt a tear on his cheek he knew she was suffering that moment again. He opened his eyes and saw swimmingly the down covered pink of her cheek with the glistening diamonds of fresh tears. Tenderly he raised one hand and with his index finger gently stroked away the tears.

She smiled bravely at him and with a catch to her breath continued her story.

"As I anguished, Jesus turned to Simon and said these words I will cherish all my life long. 'Simon I have a word for your hearing.'

" 'Tell me, master,' replied Simon. Jesus looked at me and said,

" 'Do you see this woman? I came into your house, and you gave me no water for my feet; she has washed my feet with her tears, and wiped them with her hair. You gave me no kiss of greeting; she has never ceased to kiss my feet since I entered. You poured no oil on my head; she has anointed my feet, and with ointment. And so, I tell you, if great sins have been forgiven her, she has also greatly loved.'

"Turning to me he said, 'You have vanquished your demons, Mary. Your sins are forgiven. Your faith has saved you, go in peace.'"

The silence that followed was palpable only the movement of the leaves could be discerned. Brutus moved to her side and kneeling, took her free hand in his and raised it to his lips.

There was not one eye that was not moist as the centurion said, "Mary, this has been painful for you I know, but for me your words are my salvation. I begin to see there are no limits to forgiveness just as there are no limits to love."

"Not my words, Brutus; they are the words of my Lord Jesus."

She began to sing with a bell like voice of great clarity, but with that suggestion of huskiness that imparted a throb underscoring each note. The other women joined in, and although neither understood one word of the Hebrew it was intensely moving and poignant to the listening men.

When they had finished their Psalm the peace that enveloped them seemed to exclude the whole world outside the shade of the olive trees.

With a sigh Mary Magdalene said, "Since hearing those words I have been following my Lord and his disciples and I would follow him to the ends of the earth, and it is hard to believe that anyone who has known him wouldn't do the same."

As they considered the significance of this, a man's voice was heard hailing them from the mountain slope. Then they saw the disciples, some of them running, coming from the summit. Marc recognised Peter who stood out, but the women became agitated because they could not see Jesus in the party.

"He led them up the mountain, telling us women to wait here! Can anything have happened to him?" asked his mother anxiously.

They weren't in doubt for long as the first of the men to reach them, although panting from his exertion, said dramatically, "The Lord has left us to continue his work. He ascended to heaven as we can bear witness, and after he had disappeared into a cloud two angels clothed in white were standing where he had stood!"

"Andrew, are you telling us we are to see him no more?" said his mother in some alarm.

"Well not exactly. The angels said to us, 'Men of Galilee why do you stand here looking heavenwards? He who has been taken from you into heaven, this same Jesus, will come back in the same fashion.'"

"Then have we long to wait?" asked Mary.

"Nobody knows that," said Simon Peter joining them belatedly.

"We asked Our Lord if he meant to restore Israel to her glory here and now, and he said it was not for us to know the times and season which the Father had fixed by his own authority. He has given us a charge to go to Jerusalem and await the coming of the Holy Spirit. This we need to strengthen us that we can witness to him throughout the whole world. So, blessed Mary, it may be a very long time indeed!"

The three women retired together and drew close in mutual consolation. It was now approaching dusk and night draws in quickly at that season.

Marc approached Peter and told him quickly of their plans.

"So Miriam daughter of Simon will be a little down when we see her. Perhaps the news of this momentous day will dispel her gloom a little. We won't entrust much of the food preparation to her, or we are likely to get a burnt offering. Don't worry lad, we will be kind to her and see her through this crisis. All things are in God's hands. Go in peace, you and your centurion."

They parted, each going their own way but all were aware that this was the most momentous of days.

CHAPTER TWO

Even as the disciples were descending the Mount of Olives in a state of ecstasy, and Marc laying his head on the lap of Mary Magdalene was close to paradise, a meeting was taking place in an anteroom of Herod's palace behind closed and guarded doors.

Five men were hovering around a table on which was pinned a taut hide bearing a crude map of Jerusalem and its environs.

Herod sounded angry and impatient as he berated his listeners.

"Nearly four weeks have passed since I gave you a simple task to perform, four weeks during which you have achieved nothing. Worse, whatever you have attempted has been bungled and now our quarry is very much on his guard.

"Fortunately my intelligence comes from many more reliable sources than you, and I have been kept informed of the movements of this centurion and his boy, not withstanding your efforts. Which of you knows where they are now?"

He shot a piercing look at each in turn.

For what seemed an age no one spoke then the Idumaean with the crescent scar on his cheek said, "They passed through the East Gate some hours ago, and having practised with their swords are probably returning to their rooms before dark."

He looked distinctly nervous and his eyelid above the scar was twitching uncontrollably.

"Thank you, Phallu, for your worthless information," sneered Herod, "has one of you anything more valuable to contribute?"

He waited impatiently with his arms folded and a look of seething contempt. Nobody spoke so finally Herod broke the silence himself.

"I thought not. Now that you are known and likely to be recognized you have no worth to me. You are expendable!"

The menace in his voice as he shot out that last word caused an involuntary gasp from Phua, who still smarted with pain from his fractured coccyx, sustained through contact with the foot of the big fisherman.

Herod continued, "So I will give you one last chance to regain some value to me."

He pointed at the map and traced the road to Bethany.

"This is where you will find them, as it is as far as they can travel on foot before dark." His grin was humourless at their consternation. "My jailers have persuaded Rueben to volunteer information of their intentions! From Bethany they will move east towards the river Jordan, which they will then follow north to the Sea of Galilee and Capernaum. I don't want them to reach Galilee and you have to stop them. If you fail, say farewell to your families. If you succeed, I will reward you well."

"We thank your Majesty for his magnanimity," said Phallu. "We failed you because we underestimated our enemy, an inexcusable fault on our part. We are fortunate to have a king who gives us another chance."

He bowed to Herod obsequiously.

"May I ask just one question?"

Herod nodded.

"It concerns the boy. Must we bring him to you alive?"

"Dead or alive, it's of no consequence to me. My stepdaughter has designs on him, but I care not one way or the other. Just do not fail me this time."

He turned on his heel and stormed out leaving consternation behind him.

Phallu was the accomplished assassin among them and so the natural leader. He quickly took control and summoning the guard ordered four horses readied for them within the hour, so that they could move as soon as they had decided their best course of action.

"If we ride hard we can be in Bethany tonight," said Phallu. "It won't take long to find where they are bedded, and as they are unaware we are following, we will have both superiority of numbers and surprise on our side. And it has the added merit that we will impress King Herod by its swiftness in execution, so are all agreed?"

He looked from one man to the next and all nodded agreement.

Dusk was deepening rapidly towards dark. A blood red sunset, now well past, was leaving very little trace behind the centurion and his son. The countryside they were striding through was rocky and sparsely vegetated, and almost devoid of human habitation.

It was with relief that Brutus recognised a low mound of stones, surmounted by some crudely thatched palm.

"We can shelter here for the night," he said moving off the track. "It's a shepherd's hut and even in midwinter we would be able to survive here. I've never searched for it after dark, so I was a little anxious about missing it altogether. I didn't fancy sleeping rough as there can still be a touch of frost at this time of year!"

"Had we failed to find this shelter because of our encounter with the women, I would happily sleep in the open!" exclaimed Marc, the excitement of those two hours still dominating his thoughts.

"See if you feel the same wonder when we have our frugal supper tonight," rejoined Brutus, "but I do know of a good inn for breakfast in Bethany. Come on, let's settle ourselves in while we can still see."

Inside the hut smelt wholesome and dry. A few bundles of thyme and rosemary hanging from the beams indicated recent usage and there was a large mound of dry bracken to sleep on.

Eating the last of their provisions they were both reflecting on the events of the day and had little inclination to converse.

Brutus suddenly exclaimed, "I must be slipping, I haven't given the slightest attention to our safety! By the Gods I could have stumbled into ambush after ambush, so full has my head been of other things. There are some precautions I must take against anyone surprising us!" He sidled out of the entrance leaving the door ajar.

Marc could see the clear stars glittering in the dark, blue black, moonless heavens, which were occasionally blotted out as Brutus moved across the entrance. After ten minutes he returned and impaled the pointed end of a thick stick into the ground, jamming the other under the cross piece of the door.

"I'll be surprised if anyone can approach the hut without our hearing now, but if they do this stick will hold them long enough for our swords to greet them cordially," and Marc knew from his chuckle that he was pleased with his precautions as they bedded down for the night.

The stick being jerked away to ease the door open awoke Marc from his dreams.

Soft moonlight illuminated the interior of the hut and the centurion was silhouetted as he listened intently at the half opened entrance.

Marc heard the pounding of the horses' hooves and moving beside Brutus, saw the four horsemen receding along the track towards Bethany, and they watched until they disappeared round a prominence well down the valley and the sound of their hooves fell away.

"Two soldiers but not Romans," mused Brutus half to himself, "and one of the others riding in great pain in the saddle. It isn't coincidence that they are riding so urgently towards Bethany, where we hoped to sleep this night. They must be hoping to catch us unprepared." He was silent for a minute, thinking things through and Marc knew to keep quiet.

"When they reach Bethany they will make for the inn, expecting us to be asleep. I can guess how they plan to greet us, with the kiss of dagger or sword. They will be surprised to find we aren't there, and very quickly will find out we haven't passed through. Will they come searching for us or will they await us in ambush?" he suspended any conjecture before continuing,

"To search for us would be hopeless, at night and in this terrain. There are a hundred places we could be, and they would have to split up and dismount. So they will stay hidden in Bethany and await our arrival. Come, Marc, we are going visiting now, as they won't be expecting us before daylight!" His eyes were gleaming with eager anticipation of action and the chance that had given them the initiative.

It took an hour to reach the outskirts of the small town, and the barking of a cur in one of the outlying homesteads made them realize it might be difficult to achieve the surprise they had planned.

"We'll forget about stealth until we reach the square," said the centurion with exasperation, "a dog is less likely to raise the alarm if we don't try to steal in!"

To their ears every step on the sun baked earthen road was as loud as the beat of a drum in the clear, night air. Marc felt his heart pounding and his mouth was dry as they passed house after house, his eyes flitting rapidly to every deep shadow where the clear moonlight couldn't penetrate.

Mercifully only the occasional yapping accompanied their passage and if a face appeared at a window, no challenge was forthcoming. Now there were taller buildings joined in a continuous frontage as they approached the square with heavily beamed openings to courtyards or stables gaping dark with hidden menace.

They moved off the road and stood still as their eyes adjusted to the blackness. Marc was the first to become aware of the scrutiny of two large eyes, which were watching them fixedly. He held his breath, his hand plucking at Brutus's sleeve. At the same moment, with a shrill screech and a flap of pale wings the owl flew out into the moonlight. Both jumped at this unexpected cacophony and, with wry smiles at each other they resumed breathing.

Suddenly they heard the snorting that could only come from a horse stabled not far away. A voice rang out nearly above their heads.

"Phua, what's the noise? Is everything alright?"

"Yes, Phallu. A hunting owl made the horses restless. After I've settled them Sohar can relieve me."

"Alright he'll be ready shortly. Keep your eyes sharp, we mustn't underestimate this cursed centurion again."

They heard a shutter close above them and then only the faint whinny of the occasional horse to give them their bearings.

"We must be at the rear of the inn," whispered Brutus. He had his dagger in his hand as he pointed off to his left side.

"I'm going to reduce the odds against us. Stay here until I return and if anyone comes out while I'm away kill him."

He slid off into the darkness leaving Marc with every nerve and muscle taut, and sword drawn in readiness. Any slight sound worked on his overwrought imagination, but somehow he managed to keep his bodily responses in check and avoid any over-reaction. So when he became aware of the presence of Brutus at his side his amazement was complete.

"Caught you napping did I?" he whispered. "Here, put this on and follow me closely."

As Marc wrapped the stale smelling cloak around him he realized it came from the dead Phua. Silently Brutus led the way towards the stable but now the moonlight made concealment impossible.

Hugging the shadow of the wall Brutus hissed, "You cross to the stable but keep your hair hidden and pretend to be busy with the horses and keep your back to the inn. I'll wait here for your relief to come out. If anyone calls just grunt and keep working."

Marc nodded and made a casual shambling passage across the yard. All the while he awaited a challenge with trepidation, so when he heard the opening of a door behind him it was all he could do to resist turning around. Quickly slipping through the half open stable door, his overwrought senses heard the door of the house close. Feeling more secure he could resist no longer, but peered out to see Brutus gesturing to him from where he stood over the body lying at his feet. He knew he was being summoned for the final confrontation.

Leaving the stable Marc looked up towards the house where he hoped to locate the bedroom. One of the shutters was just opening so Marc quickly turned to one side and picked up a large wooden bucket that was half filled with feed.

Stooping under its weight he staggered across the yard, willing himself not to glance upwards to where he knew their adversary was watching his every movement. To divert attention he dropped the bucket, which fell and spilled half its contents, and with a muttered curse he gave it a kick, moving quickly to the door and opening it to enter the narrow hallway with Brutus as his shadow.

It was dark but a wooden staircase was faintly visible to their right, and ascending noisily, Marc hoped his lack of consideration would deceive its occupants. Nearing the top a door suddenly opened, and taper in hand Phallu stood peering down.

Seeing two men he instantly jerked back with a cry and swung the door to slam it shut as Marc leaped forward with sword outstretched, thrusting it into the gap. The force of the closing door against his sword blade threw him off balance as Brutus leapt past throwing his whole weight against it. So powerful was his charge the door splintered off its hinge and burst open knocking the alarmed Idumaean to the ground and before he regained his feet Marc struck, catching him on his neck and half severing his head. Equally swiftly Brutus impaled the man rising from his bed, and as he fell back he knocked over the table.

The fallen taper caught fire to the spilled bedding and in the flickering light from the flames Marc looked at the macabre scene with horror. He saw the first man he had ever killed and recognised the crescent scar on his cheek. He wondered, as the room started to spin around him, why he didn't feel any elation, why only this profound weariness and nausea? As he slumped to the ground and lay inert across the slain man his last thought was at the irony of it all. One minute his head resting and he had known paradise, the next he was plunging headlong into hell.

Much to his surprise, Marc came to many hours later in a bed, and even more was his amazement when he felt a fragrantly perfumed cloth stroking his forehead.

"Why the lamb's awakening at last," fell on his ears with that delicious huskiness that he recognized instantly.

Opening an eye he discerned with a quiver of delight, the features of Mary Magdalene. Wordlessly, as though to speak might end his dream, he raised his hand and relished the kiss she planted on it. As he traced the line of her jaw and then his hand stole across her cheek she sat unmoving, her dark eyes smiling at him.

"Mary," he sighed, "how have you found us here? And where am I?"

Her eyes gleamed mischievously.

"The how is a long story and must be saved for later. The where I can tell you, the inn at Bethany."

Marc shot up in bed and looked around him. He didn't recognise the room but he could hear the sound of horses and harness coming through the shuttered window. He realised his tunic had been removed and he only had on his smalls, and in a panic grabbed the rough blanket that was no longer covering him and pulled it up to his neck. His embarrassed modesty made Mary chuckle.

"Why, you dear boy. I'll leave you to dress yourself and then, when you're more suitably attired for the eyes of a respectable woman, join me for breakfast downstairs." She stooped, kissing him on the forehead, and closed the door quietly behind her.

Marc moved to the window. He looked out onto the stables and yard and he quite expected to see two bodies lying there. Instead everything looked so orderly he had to rub his eyes. At that moment, to the excited whinnying of horses that know they are home, a cart pulled by two bays came to rest in the yard. Seated in it were Brutus and a stranger who obviously belonged to the establishment, from the familiar manner with which he set about removing the harness.

Marc hurried out and in the passage saw the damaged door to the adjoining room propped against the wall, and the memories of the night flooded back. He ran down the stairs and out into the sunlit yard where he found Mary with Brutus.

"We've scattered the bodies on the hill about a mile from the shepherd's hut and set their horses free. Anyone finding them is going to have great trouble piecing together what might have happened, and when Herod hears, he won't believe that just a man and a boy could have slain four of his men."

"I find it hard to believe myself," said Mary looking wonderingly at Marc, "for I thought him such a gentle sensitive boy."

"So he is, Mary," and putting his arm around Marc Brutus gave him a welcoming embrace, "and he acquitted himself so splendidly last night when courage was called for. But it took its toll didn't it? How are you now, Marc?"

"Complete recovered, thank you sir, and totally confused. Can someone please tell me what is going on and how Mary happens to be here?"

"Over breakfast, Marc. I haven't slept all night and right now we all need something to eat."

They sat a long time over their meal enjoying the freshly baked bread, the soft cream cheese and yogurt, the dates and honey, and like the breakfast itself, the story came out morsel by morsel for each to ingest and digest.

Mary started with her story.

"As we got close to the city at dusk we were forced off the road by four horsemen riding through the gate at full gallop. Peter nearly got ridden down and the rider slashed at him with his whip in passing, after which he was very subdued until we were some way towards our house. Suddenly he stopped in his tracks, looked back to the gate and exclaimed, 'Scar-face. Old scar-face who tried to trap Miriam's young friend.'

"We wondered what was troubling him, until he explained how near you had come to being seized by Herod's soldiers."

As she regarded the boy, her concern showed in her furrowed brow and worried eye.

"I felt certain they were intent on overtaking you both and harming you, and was nearly hysterical with fear." She reached for each of their hands and clutched them fiercely. "When we got to our rooms, there was great alarm among the followers. Rebecca had sent word that Rueben had been seized and interrogated by Herod's jailers over your movements. He was brought home in a bad way and very distraught as he had told them your plans. He had endured everything they did to him in silence, but when he recovered consciousness the jailers said they would do the same to Rebecca unless he told them what they wanted to know."

"The bloody swine. The murdering, evil, ill-born swine!" cried Brutus, rising to his feet and grasping the hilt of his sword in impotent rage.

It took both Mary and Marc some while to calm the enraged centurion before she could continue,

"My heart was heavy with grief. I thought of you being overtaken and slain, but something made me refuse to accept your deaths until I saw your bodies. So an hour before dawn I bribed my way past the guard at the gate and started walking. I hardly noticed the beauty of the dawn, but as it grew lighter I was able to hurry. Imagine my joy when two hours later this wonderful man waved to me from a cart." She turned towards the embarrassed and beaming centurion, joy so evident in her face and eyes there was no need of imagination.

"Imagine the surprise of the inn keeper beside me on the wagon when this woman rushed up to us wildly and covered me with kisses, threatening to haul me from my seat," laughed Brutus.

"Only because I wanted you to jump down and rush to meet me. To pick me up in your bear-like Roman arms and share my unbelievable joy you, you imperial soldier," retorted Mary petulantly.

"Had I known the agony of heart you had so bravely carried all night I would surely have done so," sighed Brutus with surprising tenderness, reaching his hand out to cover those of Mary. Both sat silently for some minutes until Marc could stand it no longer.

"Oh come on you two, you haven't told me the whole story!" he exclaimed impatiently.

Looking reproachfully at Marc, Brutus withdrew his hand and said, "After Mary told me of Rueben's interrogation I would gladly have throttled any of Herod's guards, and was glad to have his dead assassins under the cover of the cart. Mary wouldn't believe they were there and when I went to pull back the cover she couldn't look and turned deathly pale so that I feared she might swoon."

"I did no such thing! I've laid out the dead many times and wasn't I on my way to anoint the body of my Lord?" protested Mary with conviction.

"Ah but none of them had been the victim of Marc and his intrepid sword!" replied Brutus, and they all burst out laughing.

"Anyway I told Mary where she would find you. We carried on into the wilderness with the bodies and the horses and just dumped them all over the place. The vultures were waiting as though they had been forewarned, so they won't find much left after today except the horses running free."

Mary shuddered at her mental picture of the scene.

Brutus continued, "The innkeeper is fearful of Herod's anger if he finds out they were slain here, so every trace of them has been removed. Only one servant knows and he will keep quiet. I have hired the cart and two horses for the coming week so we can carry more provisions and have little need to stop in any town. Mary, can you let Simon of Cyrene know that we will join them in Jerusalem at their harvest celebration?"

"That won't be easy as I will be travelling with you from now on," replied Mary casually.

"You'll what?" cried Marc and Brutus simultaneously.

"Well, look at the trouble you get into on your own. Someone has to ensure you don't carry on like this all over Judaea." Her eyes were twinkling at their discomfiture as she continued, "but seriously the two of you will be recognised at every village you pass through. Your quaint Aramaic will give you away if you buy a loaf of bread, and Herod has his spies looking for you everywhere, but not for a party with a pair of horses, a cart and a woman. In the towns we can split up so that Marc might pretend to be a lone traveller, and we could masquerade as man and wife!"

Did Brutus imagine the amused gleam in her modestly averted eye?

Pursuing these tactics she brushed aside any protests they made or fears they expressed for her safety should she be found with them. Ultimately they ran out of arguments and secretly rejoicing at the thoughts of her companionship on their travels, switched to discussing their plans for the week ahead.

"The one thing we mustn't do is deceive ourselves that Herod's threat is over because of what has happened," emphasized Brutus with a grimace. "It will take a day or two for the scale of the defeat we've inflicted to become clear, but it's not in his nature to take reversals lying down. He won't suspect we know he has interrogated Reuben about our plans, and so he will expect us to stick to our intended route, when our greatest danger would be crossing the Jordan into Galilee, where they will be waiting to greet us." He looked enquiringly at his companions.

"Herod is also ruler of Peraea and the Jordan is the western border of that province. There are many places where it is easily crossed now that the rains are over," said Mary.

Brutus looked thoughtfully at a sketch of the region that was laid out on the table. Then he said, "Alright, let's stay within Judaea and Samaria!" Smiling at Mary he continued, "With Mary as guide there must be many places to visit without ever leaving the Roman province. Can you control a cart and two horses Mary?"

Mary looked surprised and confessed she had never tried.

"I don't doubt my control of a couple of men but a pair of horses will be something new," she laughed, and exchanging glances the man and boy wondered how much of her reference was to themselves.

"Well, if you take the reins we will head towards the City of Salt, here at the north end of the Dead Sea," said Brutus, jabbing his finger at the map. "Let's load up and see how well we can do by nightfall."

They were on their way within the hour, well provisioned and having paid the innkeeper handsomely.

There was quite a steep climb out of the town, so Brutus and Marc walked some way in front of the cart as though they were travelling separately; but close enough to throw an occasional look backwards when Mary would give them a cheerful wave.

On a downhill stretch after breasting a rise, the horses welcomed the release from the weight they were drawing and broke into a canter. Mary was surprised at how firm she could be, as she held them back and kept her distance from the men.

"Why, a light rein works as well with horses as it does with men," she mused to herself, and wondered how the men would relish being privy to her thoughts.

Three hours later there were no hills visible beyond the crest some short way ahead where the men were waiting, and as she came abreast of them the whole panorama of the valley of the Jordan opened into view.

Deep in the valley the winding course of the river glittered within lush green-ness, as it meandered down to the wide expanse of the white flecked Dead Sea. Opposite the eastern face of the valley loomed even higher than where they stood, yellow and brown in its bareness with just the occasional terrace of olive trees, or the fresh greenness of young vines scratched onto its lower slopes. Before them the road zigzagged down precipitously, between hills and around prominences broken by clumps of purple or silver or green, where the wild herbs still found nurture from the winter rains.

With a man at the reins of each horse they began their descent, both horses showing their nervousness in twitch of tail and restlessness of eye, or occasional stamp and pawing of hoof. They passed a few mules with bags of salt and the muleteers called out something, which only Mary could understand and to which she replied cheerfully.

"What did they say?" asked Brutus anxiously.

"They said we must be crazy to bring a cart down here. Only the Roman soldiers sometimes do it, and they need ten men and ropes to hold the cart over the steep part around the bend."

"Thanks," muttered Brutus, "and what did you reply?"

"Why that each of my men was the worth of five legionaries of course. What did you expect?"

Even Brutus had to laugh at her audacity, then he said, "We must heed their advice. Just before the bend we will unload and secure the reins to the rear of the cart, so that we have something to haul back on. Mary, you take the horses' bridles while Marc and I see if we can live up to your expectations."

The next hour was the most exhausting and nerve racking any of them had ever known. The first long stretch of the decline was steep, only just wide enough for the cart and in places covered with loose scree.

"If we look like losing control stick this in front of a wheel," said Brutus, handing Mary a heavy, leather sack he had secured with thongs, then easing two planks out of the sides of the cart he positioned them where they could be readily seized and thrust under each wheel should further braking be needed.

It seemed never ending as they literally inched their way down both men throwing all their weight on the reins to hold the cart. Whenever the loose scree threatened their foothold, Brutus called loudly and Mary stopped the wagon from running away by throwing her sack in the path of a wheel. Then the men exchanged reins for planks, positioning them under the two rear wheels until Brutus could relinquish his to Mary and he could return to the body-torturing rein. So they eased the cart down foot by foot, until they had cleared any bad section.

This alternation of progression at least eased the intolerable burden the constant pull of the rein imposed on every muscle and ligament of Marc's sweat-drenched body, the salt half blinding him throughout. All Marc listened for was that cry when he knew he could change rein for plank, and sometimes it seemed never to come, as his whole body ached beyond endurance so that he heard himself praying for it to end. Fortunately they were in the shade thrown by the looming edge of the ravine into which they descended.

As they worked around a tight right hand bend, Marc threw his weight a little too vigorously, and his feet shot from under him and he was dragged on his side as he tried vainly to regain his feet. The accelerating wagon threatened to career off the track completely out of control, and realizing in an instant their plight Mary responded by throwing her weight on to the bridle of the inside horse, which was forced to swerve off the track onto the steep embankment. As it lost its momentum the wagon threatened to tumble down into the gorge to the left, and finally stopped, canting at such an angle they anxiously waited with bated breath.

Regaining his feet, both men were able to exert their full weight as Mary coaxed the nervous horses back onto the track, sack readied until they achieved a position from where they could resume their descent, and Marc's never-ending agony began again until he was convinced it would continue interminably

When finally the command came to stop he would not believe it was anything other than time to change to the plank, and as the motion of the cart halted he moved automatically to the alternate position, from which he peered through salt moistened eyes at the distorted figure of the centurion throwing his arms around Mary, and calling, "We've done it, Mary, we've really done it," and then Mary's swimmingly lovely face was smiling at him too.

He let go of the plank and heard it clatter to the ground. With his fists he brushed the sweat from his eyes and saw a wondrous vision.

The path here widened and inclined gently down. On their right was a terrace planted with olive trees, while on their left a field with young green shoots sloped gently away to a grove of eucalyptus trees. Two children emerged from a thatched hut some short way ahead, followed by a woman prematurely aged by hard living. They approached and looked in wonder at the cart and its owners, the woman nodding as Mary addressed her at some length.

Hurrying away she quickly moved out of sight around a rock face a few hundred paces away. They all sat too exhausted to talk until the woman reappeared with three men, then Mary said, "We will spend the night in a small grain store nearby, and she will prepare us a meal while these men are helping us fetch our things down. We have only one hour of daylight so we can't lie here a moment longer!"

Brutus smiled his acceptance and admiration at the way she had assumed command. He knew she was aware of their exhaustion and had decided to take the responsibility for that night's arrangements.

It was dark before they were seated together enjoying a simple but substantial meal of lentils and vegetables with unleavened bread. The only light was from an oil lamp, but the dancing flame and the shadows imparted a charmed atmosphere to their humble dwelling.

"Mary, you were magnificent today. Had you not come along I hate to think where we would be now," said Brutus, seated on a bale of straw and leaning back contentedly. "I don't know of any soldiers who would have shown such courage or coped as splendidly."

"Thank you, kind sir," replied Mary with a blush suffusing her normal pale complexion, "but having you two I never felt any fear, only anxiety at the strain to your abused bodies."

"I've never known how much my body could take until today," muttered Marc, "and there were times when every muscle cried out for respite. Now my limbs still feel disjointed, pulled and stretched until they hardly belong to me."

"Then slip your tunic off and come and lie here," said Mary irresistibly, "I have just what you are needing."

She delved into a leather shoulder bag, producing a small earthenware jar with a corked lid. Shyly Marc slid almost naked into the pool of light falling on the bedding beside her and as he felt the caress of her touch on his aching limbs and the heady perfume entered his nostrils, he surrendered completely to the first sensual bliss his virginal body had known.

Brutus was held by her eyes regarding him lovingly, as her fingers probed, searching for the aching knotted cores of hurt. He smiled at her, his mind a turmoil of emotions such as he had never known.

"I never knew any woman could be so undemanding or have so much love to give," he murmured softly, moving to sit just to one side of her as she leaned over the supine boy.

"I think love grows in proportion to how much it is nurtured," breathed Mary hesitatingly. "I doubt I can ever have children of my own, my reckless past has

74

bequeathed me that, but this boy pulls at my heart as strongly as though he were of my own flesh. And with my whole being I feel likewise drawn to his father."

Her words might have seemed immodest and wanton, but to Brutus they were as music.

"Oh Mary, I can't deserve your love," he whispered, drawing her dark glossy hair to one side so that his lips could lie on her smooth neck. He felt her shudder as she lifted her head and he let his kiss glide to the concavity at the angle of her jaw and rested there, inhaling her very essence.

"Love is never deserved, it is a gift freely given. That I learnt from my Lord," she breathed so quietly it was hardly audible, and Brutus saw her joy brimming as tears misted her unblinking eyes. Still her fingers worked skilfully along Marc's muscled back and whether he was aware of the change in all their lives that had crystallized in that short time or not, he breathed a sigh of such unrestrained contentment they both perceived it as his blessing.

CHAPTER THREE

A crowing cockerel awoke them to a glorious sunrise, golden hues radiating over the high lip of the canyon promising a hot day. Anxious to get an early start they quickly breakfasted, then loaded the cart and descended to the river Jordan, heading south to where far off they could see the huddle of houses by the lake shore.

Marc walked ahead of the others to give the appearance of travelling separately.

Brutus carried with him the imprint that had been made by Mary nestling against him throughout the night and he rejoiced with every breath that he drew, feeling an eagerness for whatever adventure this new day might offer. Following the wide river as it flowed beside quiet green fields, or groves of olive or orange trees, towards the town, they noted the fording places where the mud brick buildings accommodated the tax collectors, although they were not challenged to pay while they remained on the Judaean side.

Entering the town, stalls were being set up as produce was arriving from the outlying farms, and the cart blended in with those around them.

A military barracks built at the water's edge proudly flew its standard in the light wind and Brutus recognised the wolf emblem as that of the 20th legion, and confidently he made his way over to some soldiers idly standing around, and after a few words was led to the guardroom.

Marc sat and reflected on the change in his fortune over the past five weeks. He had discerned the attachment of Mary and Brutus and rejoiced to see the change in the centurion who now was always seeking ways to serve her. It was almost comical he was so anxious to please, but precipitate, he ended up getting in the way most times.

"They haven't found any of the dead bodies yet," said Brutus breaking in on his thoughts, "or they would be on a state of alert. They are expecting an important caravan from Arabia, and if we wait here a day or two we will be able to join with it to follow the Jordan and enjoy the protection of three companies of legionaries."

"What makes this caravan so special?" asked a greatly intrigued Mary.

"The luxuries they carry! Fine silks from China, jewels from India, ivory from Africa and this year's harvest of frankincense and myrrh from Sheba, and much more besides!"

Mary conceded this was indeed a valuable caravan, and agreed it had to be protected from marauding Bedouin.

"What about Mary?" asked Marc. "Will she be able to travel with us?"

"We'll only go with it if we can all travel together," promised Brutus.

It was now the hottest hour and the sun was overhead as they climbed aboard the wagon and headed back along the river for a shaded pool they had noted on their journey earlier.

They had bathed and were drying their clothes on the hot stones, when the urgent galloping of some horsemen along the road from the direction of Jericho caught their attention. Brutus moved to the road quickly enough to observe the body tied across the flank of the rear-most horse.

Returning to his companions he said, "They've found one of them at least. I wonder why they have come this way rather than head to Jerusalem, which is much nearer to where I left the bodies?"

They were silent for a short while until Marc made his suggestion.

"Is it likely that searching the area around Bethany they questioned the muleteers that Mary bantered with, who would be sure of mentioning passing us and the cart?"

"Did you really say that each of us was the worth of five legionaries, Mary?" Brutus asked anxiously, and when Mary nodded, "then our cover is blown and they will have linked us with you."

Mary looked quite crestfallen and Brutus put a comforting arm around her.

"Don't worry. The trouble is we don't know how much they do know, which makes it difficult to anticipate their next move."

"Why don't you call on the centurion? Even if he has his suspicions he's not going to arrest you," suggested Marc.

"If we go into hiding that will certainly confirm any suspicions he may have. Were I that commander, I would not act against Romans in Herod's cause. Wait here until I return, or should I fail to do so make your way back to Jerusalem and inform Firmus, who will not stand idly by while Herod and Pilate misuse the legion to further their vengeance. As citizens of Rome we are entitled to protection from Herod."

Holding Mary tightly to him for a minute he then departed, resolved to regain some measure of control.

Apprehensive at the turn of events Mary looked for reassurance, but found Marc too absorbed in his thoughts to be very forthcoming.

He was accordingly surprised when she fell on her knees, her hands raised beseechingly in prayer, silently moving her lips as though whispering her innermost thoughts. Sometimes she would remain motionless as though she was listening, her eyes closed, an expression of rapture on her face.

Marc had never known that prayer could be so deeply absorbing and as he watched he envied her at the same time as he rejoiced for her. Suddenly he clearly saw Miriam kneeling at the head of the fallen Jesus on his way to the cross. Overcome with a longing that was too painful to bear alone, he found himself drawn to kneel beside her.

She gave him one radiant smile, as though welcoming him into a communion and then he too closed his eyes and emptied his mind, allowing whatever was there to tumble out.

So they stayed side by side kneeling on the earth, their souls roaming space and time separate from each other, yet joined by indefinable tenuous bonds.

The cry of a rabbit seized by a falcon jerked them back to reality, and Marc heard the horses nervously pawing the ground.

Mary was alerted, but had a tranquillity about her like a cloak and sat watching Marc as he quieted the horses and threw a bundle of herbage for them to munch. Satisfied they were not immediately threatened, Marc returned to seat himself close to her.

She reached out and took both his hands in hers and holding his eyes spoke with that delicious huskiness which always thrilled him. It was as though she were excited and had so much she wanted to say.

"My Lord taught me to pray, as he taught all who follow him and it is the only way I am able to overcome fear. I was thrilled when you joined me as I hoped you were drawn to the power that lies latent within you."

"I was certainly drawn by something and although I have never been taught to pray I found my mind was free of my body, moving outside of me. I was searching for Miriam to tell her I was standing tall beside her, whatever the distance now separating us."

"Miriam is to be your joy, the heavens have ordained it. Just so is Brutus my joy, and I his. As from yesterday we are pledged to each other in this life and, thanks to the power of the risen Jesus, in the next."

Her tears of joy welled up as she gazed at the boy, glistening on her cheek like little jewels. Marc pulled her gently so that her head rested on his chest and nuzzled his face into her mass of glossy black hair, inhaling the perfume that seemed essentially her.

"Then as Brutus is my father will you be my mother?" he sighed, and the powerful tightening of her arms around his waist was the wordless affirmation for which he longed.

"Please teach me to pray, Mary," he said urgently, and then added, "and Brutus too."

The spell was broken and Mary laughingly disengaged from Marc's embrace, rubbing the tears from her eyes.

"Oh my dear boy, I will teach you all I know, but whether your father wishes to join our kindergarten I'm not so sure."

Marc looked a little hurt as he persisted.

"Doesn't he want to learn, doesn't everyone want to learn how to pray?"

Mary restrained her laughter as she realised Marc was struggling to understand something important.

"I'm not sure of the answer to that, Marc. Deep within himself, and maybe within everyone there lies that wish, but not everyone recognises it and you can't wish it for them until they do. All we can do is show how much it means to us and include them in our prayers. I must prepare our meal as Brutus will not think much of prayer if it leaves him hungry on his return," she said moving to the cart.

It was fully an hour before Brutus joined them looking pensive and disturbed, and they knew to wait, as he would not reveal his thoughts until they were clear and he could see what steps were needed.

After they had eaten he said sombrely, "I don't think this is a good place for us to stay anymore. They have found two of the bodies today and the whole wilderness is swarming with Herod's guards and Roman soldiers in a combined search for the other two. They know they will find them dead as they have rounded up all the horses." He paused for a moment, "Decimianus, that's the centurion, asked me if I could give a lead where his detachment might begin their search. I feigned surprise that he should think I could be of any help, but from his look know he has drawn his own conclusion."

He smiled ruefully at the irony of the little charade he had acted out with the centurion. He should have felt able to request his help as a comrade, but some deep instinct had warned him against revealing their involvement.

"Anyway Decimianus states there is uproar in Jerusalem. Herod is incensed and demanding Pilate explain how two ambassadors and their escorts can be slain with impunity in the province under his jurisdiction."

"Two ambassadors indeed! Two assassins and incompetent ones at that!" protested Marc angrily.

"We know that. But you have to admire the way Herod has seized the initiative, and he has shown the strength of his feeling by dispatching a courier to the Governor in Syria complaining of the incompetence of the Prefect. I suppose it's to our advantage that Herod and Pilate are snarling at each other, but Pilate knows he is vulnerable so he is desperate to arrest the killers to re-establish his authority."

"Do they want to arrest you?" asked Mary, her eyes revealing her fears.

"Decimianus hasn't made up his mind and is still weighing up his options. This region, all the way along the Dead Sea is known to be a staunch zealot area and we have often found caches of weapons in caves before now, and there will be many we haven't found. After that brutal killing of the youths who tried to ambush Pilate hundreds have joined them, as we soldiers became only too aware in the run up to the Passover."

"So they could think it was one of those disaffected bands," breathed Mary looking slightly reassured.

"Not really," countered Brutus, "zealots would have stripped them of everything they had, and certainly the horses would have been seized and sold to the Arabs. Decimianus showed me the latest bulletin from the adjutant. Pilate has ordered that the Roman garrisons at Jerusalem, Capernaum, and Caesarea, together with the guards of Herod from his palaces at Masada, Jerusalem and Jericho, participate in a sweep of the whole province west of the Jordan. Any arms are to be seized and the men bearing weapons imprisoned or executed."

Mary and Marc exchanged anxious glances.

"Does this mean we have to surrender our swords and be unable to defend ourselves?" queried Marc.

"If we remain here it does," declared Brutus, "and I can imagine how long we would last then. We must get as far away from the Jordan as we can and find somewhere to hide until we can join Alexander."

"I have a sister Martha who would hide you for sure," said Mary. "She lives at Bethany with Lazarus, our brother who died less than two months ago, but that doesn't concern us now, I don't know why I said it! It just slipped out and he is so often away he probably won't be there anyway."

Seeing the disbelief on the faces of her companions, she realized they were not going to be satisfied with anything less than a full explanation.

"I'd better tell you how it all happened then," she conceded, and as she began it was as though she was seeing it all afresh.

"I had received word that our brother was very ill, and returned home to help care for him. When we saw him becoming worse we sent word to Jesus that Lazarus was near to death and to come right away, but he sent back a message that this sickness would not end in his death but was meant for God's honour, to bring honour to the Son of God.

"So we nursed him anxiously watching him worsen and sure that our Lord had misjudged the gravity of the situation. When he died we couldn't understand why Jesus had not come, he loved Lazarus as his brother and should have been with us.

"We anointed his body, wrapped linen strips around his limbs and a veil over his face and laid him in his tomb. The stone had been in place four days and we were seated in the house with many mourners, when word arrived that Jesus was on his way to Bethany. My heart was too heavy and my faith too weak for me to respond, but Martha went out to meet him, and after they had talked she came back and said to me, 'The Master is here and bids you come.'

"I went out straight away following Martha to where Jesus awaited us near the tomb. When I saw him, I fell at his feet. 'Lord,' I said, 'if you had been here, my brother would not have died.' and wept bitterly." She paused and looking from one to the other saw the incredulity in their faces.

"'Where have you buried him?' he asked and we led him to the sealed tomb. He wept as he stood in front of the cave then suddenly he said, 'Take away the stone.' Martha protested that after the four days he had lain there the air would be foul but Jesus said to her, 'Why, have I not told you that if you have faith you will see God glorified?'

"So some men lifted away the stone and Jesus stood praying. Then he cried in a loud voice, 'Come out, Lazarus, to my side!'"

Mary was sobbing quietly as she relived that momentous event.

"Then he came out. Walking with difficulty as he still had the linen wrapped around him and his face veiled."

Marc gave a gasp of disbelief; not that he doubted anything Mary said, just simply at the staggering, momentous event itself. It defied belief at the same time, as it had to be true.

"The last words of Jesus were, 'Loose him and let him go free'."

Mary was silent now everything had been said, and started gathering up the remnants of the meal as though she was anxious to start off for Bethany. Brutus took her in his arms and insisted she sat down as they still had matters to discuss. She yielded and sat silently her head resting against his chest.

"What a thing you have just told to us. I expect Marc is as eager now as I am to see Bethany again. I thought I would always associate it with the killing of Herod's assassins but now you have born witness to your brother being brought back to life from the grave ... well," his voice petered out as words failed him.

"But everyone in your house saw what happened and must have shouted the wonder of it throughout Judaea and in Jerusalem, so why didn't the rulers welcome him as their champion? Crown him as king?" demanded Marc. "Why crucify him?"

"He never wanted an earthly kingdom and some of his followers with links to the zealots tried to persuade him down that path, but he always refused. He said he wanted to reveal the love of the Father for all mankind, for Jew and Gentile. But after Pilate's brutality that wasn't the message that people wanted to hear. Martha and I anointed those poor boys' mutilated bodies and we cried all the time at the suffering they had endured! If Pilate thought to show the retribution that Rome was prepared to inflict on those who defied her, and deter anyone who might think to do likewise, he made a grave mistake. Instead everyone was looking to avenge them and just waiting for the priests to give their support."

"Is that how near we came, every legionary was aware of the tension and a riot might have succeeded in the short term with the hundreds of thousands of pilgrims gathered in Jerusalem? What stopped the priests, as there has never been any love lost between Temple and Fort?"

"The Temple might have given it their blessing in the circumstance, but they were even more vexed by the defiance that Jesus was showing so openly than they were by Pilate's brutality. This was their opportunity to shut him up and they might never have another. Now they could appease the populous by exerting pressure on Pilate to release Barabbas, and at the same time force him to execute Jesus, which they had been scheming for all along.

"And Pilate would not be averse to such a crucifixion in the circumstances, a subtle reminder to the zealots that he was prepared to line the route from Jerusalem to Caesarea with crucified nationalists, as an emperor had done before, following the slave uprising of Spartacus, when crucified rebels were hung the length of the Appenine Way!

"So you see the inevitability of it all, it was ordained, as was your part on that awful day!" and Mary looked compassionately at the centurion.

"I've heard them say he descended into hell and then conquered death. I descended into hell with him and would have welcomed death, but through meeting you my life has changed beyond belief. I feel a man reborn, embarking on a great adventure!" declared Brutus.

"Reborn! That's the very word Jesus used often. He said unless a man is born again he couldn't know the Kingdom of Heaven. He's said it in the Temple, and the priests asked scornfully if they needed to re-enter their mother's womb. Jesus replied that this rebirth he is talking about is of the spirit not of the flesh. So there's hope for you yet, you Roman bear!" and she gave him a beaming smile.

"Not if we don't get away from here," said Marc, so they fell to discussing the options open to them and concluded the only course was to fall in with Mary's plan and hide at Martha's house.

Brutus and Marc decided to lie low and make their way back along the path to Bethany that night, while Mary would leave the cart at a nearby inn, and make her way on foot to Bethany the next day and take them to Martha. Then at the feast of Pentecost they would all go to Jerusalem mingling with the pilgrims, and join Alexander there to make their way together to Joppa.

For the few hours remaining until nightfall there was no safer and more congenial place to enjoy each other's company than the clearing by the river Jordan.

CHAPTER FOUR

The moon was high in a star filled sky as they crested the western ridge. Their caution had averted any encounters with patrolling troops during the three-hours since dusk, but ahead of them stretched the Judaean wilderness scarred by deep gullies, only the crests of which glistened silvery, beguilingly hiding dangers that lurked within. The occasional fire gleamed yellow, dancing invitingly across the desolate plane with only a few stunted skeletal trees breaking its emptiness.

"Soldiers," said Brutus pointing, "they will have guards posted at a few hundred paces so we must give them a wide berth if we are not to be picked out in this moonlight."

Progress became very much slower now they had to leave the road and move across rough country, and they had frequently to seek cover and allow foot patrols to pass before they could move forward.

By the time they were approaching the town ahead there was the faintest red tint of dawn and the moon was disappearing at the horizon, its fading glow barely showing the darkened buildings. There had been a few encounters with outlying guards, whose vigilance had it been sharper would have detected them, but now they felt they were nearly safe.

Passing the low dwellings on the outskirts, Brutus first heard a whinny some short way ahead. He signalled to Marc and flattening themselves against the wall they inched their way to peer around the corner. In the centre of a square a fire was burning flickeringly, to one side of which stood a supply wagon and two horses. A few soldiers were moving around it and one was beating out the fire preparatory to moving off.

"Syrians!" breathed Brutus, recognising their long yellow skirts and green tunics, "they have a sixth sense and miss nothing so we must lie low until they've gone."

As he spoke, he felt a prickling sensation at the base of his neck, and turning saw four figures standing motionless filling the space between the buildings, their bows drawn menacingly. Marc saw them at the same time and instinctively his hand moved to the hilt of his sword, only to find it covered by the restraining hand of Brutus.

"Very wise, gentlemen," hissed the nearest man with a heavy accent, "we are under no obligation to capture you alive, dead would bring us as great a reward. Unfasten your sword belts and drop them on the ground."

"We are Romans going about our lawful business," replied Brutus attempting a forlorn bluff, "and are on our way to Fort Antonia with a message for Legate Venestus."

"Well, drop your swords and allow us the honour of escorting you to Jerusalem, Herod is most anxious to see you," replied the archer, and Brutus could discern the menace in his smile.

"Do as they say," said Brutus as his sword noisily clattered to the ground.

The soldiers from the square were now covering them from that side and resistance would have been suicidal.

"Take us to your commander!" demanded Brutus. "This province is under Rome and Herod has no authority here, and I think the Prefect would be interested in Roman ancillaries serving Herod's interests."

The spokesmen for the archers demanded that they move away from the wall and then moving behind disarmed them of their daggers.

"You wish to see our commander, so you shall, for he is most anxious to hand you assassins over to King Herod, and then we can stop the search and return to Capernaum."

"We heard of the assassination of Herod's ambassadors at the city of Salt, but centurion Decimianus has been successful in his efforts and we bring news of the capture of many zealots."

"Save your talk for the commander," said the archer, seizing their wrists and binding them tightly behind their back. Then with a succession of forceful thrusts they were taken to the wagon and literally thrown in, landing with bone shaking violence on the boards. Brutus felt his head collide with something softer than wood covered with a tarpaulin. Sitting up he used his feet to push away the cover and in the half-light saw a face from which stared eyeless sockets. A partially covered cheekbone with a scar identified the body and he shuddered at the mutilation inflicted by the carrion eaters of the wilderness.

The company moved off, and in the lightening dawn Brutus saw they all wore the distinctive leather helmets and yellow and green of Syrian bowmen. He also saw Marc with his eyes closed and his lips moving noiselessly, but even as he watched, Marc opened his eyes and gave him a fearless smile.

"I'm practising praying as Mary taught me. She says it's wonderful in a crisis and this must qualify."

Before Brutus could reply a soldier turned and told them to be quiet. They were moving among tents now and the aromatic smell of spices and meat cooking permeated the air. The wagon halted, the tail-board was let down and its three occupants hauled out onto the ground. Two soldiers moved off with the body to enter a tent, and a few minutes later a man emerged, buttoning up his tunic and helmetless. As he strode over something about his walk and his round, bald head, jogged the memory of Brutus and he called out, "Maas, by Jupiter am I glad to see you!"

The man stopped in his track, and then with a great smile creasing his face bent down to study the dishevelled features of the centurion.

"So it's you!" he exulted. "Now it all comes together, why the bodies of Herod's men are being found all over Judaea." He gave a roar of laughter as though he had stumbled across a great joke. Wiping the tears from his eyes he ordered his amazed bowmen to untie their wrists and helped the beaming Brutus to his feet.

"What a dangerous man you are to cross," he said, "I felt that at the spear contest and now I can see how anxious Herod is to put you away, and why Pilate is fully cooperating."

"I'm sorry to spoil your fun but you must know perfectly well it is zealots you are searching for, those responsible for this outrage, not us!" retorted Brutus.

This nearly made Maas collapse, such were the paroxysms of laughter that shook his whole frame, each more violent than the previous.

He lurched towards his tent, signalling impatiently for them to follow, and seating himself at a folding table took a drink from a goblet.

"Can I offer you some of this sherbet?" he asked. "It is most refreshing and you must need something after your exertions."

Responding to the evident good humour of their captor and feeling their situation was improving by the minute they happily accepted. When the servant reappeared with a salver containing a selection of bread and freshly cooked meats and cheeses, they felt their optimism justified, and Brutus glanced at the servant's hands as he withdrew.

"No, I'm afraid I've had to retire poor Anthus after that distressing loss of his thumb," interjected Maas soberly. "He has been a valued slave to me since I was a youth but now he is with my family in Antioch. I really didn't think there was a risk of his being injured until I saw how much he was shaking, but I wanted to be the champion on merit, not by default. I had very little time to consider options, as the tournament was disintegrating with your withdrawal, but had I successfully struck the bull I would have won the right to be champion. As it was I lacked your courage and didn't dare challenge Pilate, although I despised him and what he was making us do, so in the end I allowed him to dishonour me, while you enhanced your honour but became a fugitive as a consequence!"

"I think it was anger that drove me, more than courage. I had only just regained a vestige of self-respect after crucifying the Galilean at Pilate's order, and there he was ordering me to put my slave at risk!"

"You must have great self control as you never showed anger," said Maas, "but now we do have a problem. As you know the hunt purports to be for zealots, the alleged killers of Herod's men, but the capture of you and your slave are a secondary objective as Herod has accused your slave of the theft of a brooch, and you of a personal insult, so he has offered a reward of one thousand denarii to whoever apprehends you. Now my men will feel entitled to that reward."

Brutus said, "We have a friend in Jerusalem who is sufficiently indebted to us to gladly find such a sum. We plan to sail for Tyre on one of his ships after Pentecost. If you can get a message to Simon of Cyrene in Jerusalem I am sure he will ransom us, and we were making for a safe house when your men were too vigilant."

Maas nodded agreement and calling his servant, dispatched him to fetch a scribe. Then they set to, doing justice to the splendid breakfast.

By the time they joined Mary at her sister's home she was nearly at her wits' end with anxiety. She had hoped to find them awaiting her when she arrived at the inn during the early afternoon. Footsore and frightened she had found the innkeeper singularly unhelpful as to where they might be. When he responded to her fourth suggestion that they might have been eaten by a dragon, exactly as he had to the previous three and said that he had no idea of their whereabouts, she stamped out in vexation to enquire elsewhere.

Finally she concluded that Bethany must have a disproportionate lot of idiots and simpletons as she got always the same response.

Then the idea occurred to her that perhaps they had had misgivings about waiting at the inn and had enquired for and travelled to Martha direct. As she made her way there, she passed the field where the soldiers had their tents, telling herself she was the simpleton, for not thinking the obvious earlier.

Finding Martha unaware that anything was even supposed to be happening, she burst into tears, explained who she had hoped to find there and spent the next hour pacing up and down the court, fearfully watching every movement in the street outside.

Dusk was falling when her heart fluttered at the sight of the approaching wagon, flanked on both sides by a column of soldiers. It stopped fleetingly in passing, and as the two men leapt off it with their bundled belongings, she couldn't restrain her cry of joy as they flew in through the gate.

Seized in a great hug and hustled away from the court into the privacy of the cool interior of the house her spirit re-asserted itself, and she pummelled at the defenceless back of the grinning centurion who was threatening to crush the life out of her. Marc was dancing around excitedly as though he could hardly believe they had made it at last.

Martha appeared and stood stock still as the madness cavorted all around her, finally ending only when Brutus released the protesting Mary and he and Marc stood rather sheepishly.

"Please, Mary, forgive us and introduce us to your sister," pleaded Brutus.

This rather amazed both women, as they were not aware of any facial similarity. However in their disapproval of the exuberant behaviour of the men some similarity of expression had been common to both.

"Martha, this is the centurion Brutus of whom I mistakenly extolled his fine qualities of gentleness and sensitivity, and this his adopted son Marc, whom likewise I have mistakenly described as tender hearted and sympathetic. This is my elder sister Martha."

The men bowed and thanked Martha for offering her house as refuge at this critical time for them.

Brutus continued, now in a serious mood, "Please don't feel obliged to put yourselves at risk on our behalf, we would far rather take our chances than expose you to danger."

Martha smiled at him. She had feigned the look of disapproval simply in support of her sister, but now Mary seemed more in control she relaxed and allowed her natural warmth to prevail.

"My house is your house and you are welcome. As for dangers, when are they far away?" She shrugged dismissively.

Seated together taking refreshment Brutus told of their adventures since they had parted. Mary's face reflected her heart so faithfully that Marc felt a compulsion to seat himself at her side and take her clenched fists into his hands to calm her. By the time that he came to the soldier returning with a promissory letter from Simon of Cyrene for one thousand denarii, the colour had left her cheeks and Marc had his hands clenched in a vice.

Finally she stated in a tone that nobody dared to contradict.

"By the living God, that is the last time I ever leave you two to fend for yourselves. You blunder from one disaster to another, from threat of sinking, to shipwreck, because of no one at the helm. Well, I'm at the helm now and I intend to steer a safer course!"

With that assertion she fell silent, relaxed her grip on Marc's hands and resolutely refused to notice the glances exchanged between her listeners. Had she taken notice she would have seen their undisguised admiration.

So when Mary said at breakfast the following day, that the men would be inviting trouble if they ventured out of the house, nobody demurred. Through the open window they heard the march of soldiers, the creak and rumble of wagon and the clatter of horses, and knew that the search for them was gaining in intensity.

When that clatter stopped outside the house both men looked apprehensively at each other as Mary hurried off to find out the cause. Suddenly there was excited talking in the court, before the door burst open revealing Miriam smiling shyly at them. Marc's heart missed a beat as he leapt to his feet and he nearly stumbled in his eagerness to cross the room as Miriam rushed to meet him. They clasped eager hands and stood wordlessly each staring at the other.

Brutus caught Martha's eye and they moved into the court, where Simon of Cyrene and Mary were rubbing down two well-lathered horses. Simon raised his arm in salute and Brutus strode over and grasped it.

"Shalom," said the older man, "it is a great joy to my eyes to see you and the youngster alive and well."

"Only thanks to you," said Brutus, "and we are forever in your debt."

"But how can I ever repay you for the life of a son? What are a thousand denarii to set against that?"

"It is enough to save two lives, as we would not have survived capture by Herod. But how is Alexander recovering from his beating?"

"So well it was only with difficulty I dissuaded him from accompanying Miriam and myself. But two hours in the saddle might have overtaxed him, and he needs to be fully recovered by Pentecost if he is to continue to Joppa as planned." Simon looked around him, "But where has Miriam disappeared?"

The question was too rhetorical to need any reply from the centurion but just then Marc and Miriam emerged hand in hand to join them.

"Isn't it wonderful to find them alive and well papa?" Miriam exulted, her face radiating her undisguised joy.

"We must make a special sacrifice of thanksgiving at the Temple this Sabbath for all of God's mercy to us," declared Simon.

"Yes, let's papa! Can Marc come with us?"

Simon looked at both men quizzically. He was finding it very difficult to accept that the barriers between Jew and Gentile were collapsing under the teaching of Jesus and his disciples. Until he knew what was going to replace the traditional worship he would adhere to the Torah and the Temple.

"I would love to come, is it permitted?" queried Marc.

"Yes, to the court of the Gentiles, which is the outer court. Sometimes the whole world seems to gather there, and the vendors of lambs and doves for sacrifice, and money changers too. It's very exciting and colourful!" exclaimed Miriam.

"I was very moved when I sat with you at the Passover," said Marc. "I loved the psalms you sang and your readings from the Torah. I felt you have a wonderful history, and there's something special about being a chosen race, even in that small glimpse I could see that."

Simon was deeply affected by this spontaneous and natural testimony from the young man and placing his arm around him, he said, "Then Miriam's friend is welcome to join us at our Feast of Weeks this approaching Sabbath and likewise his father is welcome too. I think the apartness may have gone on long enough."

Mary and Martha had joined them now and Mary was quick to urge Brutus to accept the invitation.

"But we leave Jerusalem with Alexander after the Feast and I wish to be with you until such time as we must leave," protested the centurion.

Simon looked searchingly from Brutus to Mary and realised for the first time that an affectionate relationship existed between them, which he felt he should acknowledge.

"May I extend the invitation to all present?" he said looking directly at the two women.

"Thank you sir, were my brother Lazarus and his friends not celebrating here, I would accept gladly. As it is I am needed," replied Martha, with a hint of regret in her voice, "but there's no reason for you to stay, Mary. Come into the house and refresh yourselves".

Bowls of water and towels were brought for the visitors to wash away the dust clinging to them from their journey, before they entered the house.

It was quite natural that the adults should seat themselves on cushions around a low table and the youths on a couch near the open window, where they might enjoy what little breeze there was and the close proximity of each other.

Somehow the conversation moved inevitably to the followers of Jesus and what was happening to them.

"Events seem to happen at an incredible rate," said Brutus, "we were with them three days ago. Was it only three days, it's unbelievable all that has happened since? They had just witnessed Jesus being taken up into the clouds above Mount Olivet and were told to return to Jerusalem and await the coming of the Holy Spirit. Peter and the other disciples were not at all dispirited, only amazed and overjoyed at what they had witnessed."

"I know what they were feeling, it was much the same with Mary and I when Lazarus was brought back to life after lying four days in the tomb." Martha added softly.

Simon's eyes were drawn to Martha by this simple testimony of something so unbelievable, and his face showed his total bewilderment. Miriam, with that ability of women to have one ear focused in one direction while the other is listening everywhere else, moved over to the table and sat attentively at her father's feet.

"We have heard of that miracle from Mary but would like to hear it again from you," said Brutus.

Martha told it, essentially as they had heard it from Mary, but whatever effect it had had on the men paled into insignificance to the reactions of Simon and Miriam. Both were well versed in the scriptures and steeped in the traditions that regulated the lives of devout Jews. Now they were faced with unchallengeable testimony that the Galilean they had witnessed being nailed to the cross, had authority over death itself. Further they were being forced to consider the fault of the priests and elders who had demanded this man's death. But if he demonstrated such authority over death and was the Son of God as he claimed to be, then he surely must be the Messiah they had been awaiting for centuries.

Simon had brought both hands to cover his face and was rocking backwards and forward, moaning softly to himself as though unaware of those around him.

Miriam, relying more on intuition than intellect had moved on, beyond the awfulness of what had been done to Jesus, to the wonder of what he had done for Lazarus and had thereby covenanted to do for them all.

"Listen to Martha again, papa, to what Jesus replied, when she said concerning her dead brother, that she believed he would rise again only when the last day comes."

She reached up to take his hands and was shocked at his ashen face and sunk eyes.

"Listen papa, please listen. This is the most remarkable revelation the world has ever heard and we are privileged to hear it from the person to whom it was revealed. Please Martha tell us again what Jesus replied."

Martha had her eyes closed and her head inclined to one side as though listening.

"Jesus said to me, 'I am the resurrection and the life, he who believes in me, though he is dead, will live on, and whoever has life and has faith in me, to all eternity cannot die.' Then he asked me, ' Do you believe this?'

" 'Yes Lord,' I replied and then I ran and called Mary. Mary had seen Jesus vanquish death earlier at Nain."

"I've already told Brutus and Marc of that. It was Joseph, the son of my friend Sarah, who died the day before his Bar Mitzvah. When Jesus saw the anguish of we mourners as we carried his body to the tomb he came over to us, and seeing the boy on the bier placed his hand on him and said to him to rise up, and he did."

All the time Mary was looking compassionately at Simon, as though she knew the crisis that he was going through and wanted desperately to help.

Simon said, "So here I sit in the house of Martha and Mary and their brother, to whom Jesus has revealed the greatest wonders the world has ever known. How is it possible to doubt what you tell me? I don't disbelieve anything you say but I am fearful. Can we Jews bear the guilt of the crucifixion of the Son of God, the Messiah we have awaited for nearly two thousand years. Or will our blind rejection destroy us?"

He was silent for a minute remembering his part on the day of the crucifixion. How his initial reluctance at carrying the cross had turned to glad acceptance of the burden.

"Our religious tradition might be likened to a well used and very old wine skin. This new wine it is expected to carry is certain to split it asunder!"

"But if we recognise in Jesus the fulfillment of God's covenant with our people for the redemption of all mankind, can't we rejoice in our role?" queried Miriam. "Can't we begin to accept that even his crucifixion was part of God's plan that was assigned to us?"

"To all of us," added Brutus ruefully, "don't forget my role."

"I fear it will not be easy to reconcile the old with the new and that great conflict will follow. For my part I am too old to welcome conflict but I hope with courage to weather it." He gave a wry smile. "But we haven't got very far with our plans to get you to Joppa have we?"

The problems of getting two fugitives to Jerusalem for the imminent feast day, and then on to Joppa took a few hours of discussion, before Miriam and her father were able to remount and ride home. Everyone watching Simon was reassured that he was well on the way to resolving his personal crisis and that he and Miriam were reconciled.

Maas visited them the night before they were to leave and briefed them on the military situation, now that the fourth body had been found and the full extent of the slaughter was apparent. There had been a meeting of all the involved parties at Fort Antonia the previous day, which the Tribune in command of the Capernaum and Tiberius garrisons had attended and subsequently given a very explicit account of to Maas.

"Legate Venestus was chairman as the Field Commander, and there were Tibullus and other Tribunes and a dozen centurions. Pilate and Herod sat on opposite sides of the table glaring at each other. Tibullus reported that two separate bands of armed rebels had been seized. A dozen men were captured in some caves on the West Bank of the Jordan near Aeon and a similar number north of Masada. They had been interrogated and none of them knew anything of the murder of King Herod's officials.

"Herod then demanded they be handed over to his guards for further questioning, and when told they had been executed he flew into a rage. He accused the Tribune of incompetence and Pilate of lack of control of his commanders."

Maas gave Brutus a beaming smile.

"Then your involvement came out and caused quite a stir. Herod acknowledged that he had offered a reward for the capture of your thieving slave who would be rotting in his dungeon had you not protected him."

"What did Venestus say to that?" asked Brutus incredulously.

"Oh he was scathing. He wanted to know why fifteen hundred troops were sweeping the country for zealots when they had other duties to perform. He also asked if there was any evidence that the boy was guilty of the theft, and how had you protected him. Herod admitted that one of his guards had been nearly choked to death in a side street of Jerusalem, and been warned he would be killed if he followed you again."

Brutus and Marc exchanged conspiratorial smiles, while Maas was laughing so heartily that he had to break off for a few minutes.

"Venestus said the whole exercise was a waste of time and a misuse of soldiers to appease the anger of a piqued ruler, and he thought it should be called off. He had the backing of the tribunes and centurions, but Pilate insisted it continue through the weekend. When the legate said this would deplete their resources for crowd control at Jerusalem, Pilate had replied, 'So be it.'"

"It will certainly make it easier to hide in the city, but I'm not sure about getting there," mused Brutus.

"Leave that to me," proposed Maas. "We have to send a supply wagon daily for provisions and it's usually empty, except for the odd body or two!" His eyes glinting, he asked casually, "Are there any more?" and looked regretful when Brutus shook his head.

"If you are ready at mid-morning the wagon, with the same troops who captured you initially, will stop by. You aren't likely to be challenged and it is in the soldier's interest to deliver you safe and sound. Your weapons will be on the wagon.

"Well centurion, you have enlivened a tedious duty and my men and I are grateful. Farewell and may God be with you."

It was with sadness that Brutus returned his salute and watched him depart.

"A fine man and a good soldier. The Imperial Army depends on ancillaries like Maas to hold these far flung provinces."

"And a good friend to us," added Marc. "Could anyone have foreseen at the spear throwing how glad we would be to entrust ourselves to him later?"

Mary had been impatient to know what they had planned and enjoyed it when Marc impersonated the Syrian in some of his humorous outbursts.

"You really are a good mimic, Marc. If you were a Jew you would be an itinerant story teller, wandering from village to village and passing on traditional stories of our race."

Marc proceeded to mimic one of the market traders selling an old, dried-up nanny goat that was long past being edible.

"Look at this beautiful lady, just waiting to drive your lazy old Billy crazy with desire, and this fine udder just awaiting the touch of a healthy pair of kids to make the milk flow again. Milk of such creamy richness Cleopatra could be weaned off asses' milk for her beauty bath." Each phrase was accompanied by such subtly observed gestures, they were all laughing uproariously, and Mary and Martha bid outrageously against each other for such a fine prize.

Eventually sanity was restored and the final touches added to the plan. Mary would leave early and meet them at the north-eastern gate of the city. She would appraise the troop dispositions and look out for possible trouble spots before escorting them to Simon's house.

That night they enjoyed a celebratory meal together, although when Marc found they had roasted a young kid goat, it was hard to dissuade him from embellishing his earlier talent. But there was sadness as they realised that their roads would diverge, so as to make it unlikely they would ever meet again.

CHAPTER FIVE

The Friday began according to plan. Mary departed after breakfast and a short while later a wagon in the charge of two cheerful Syrians pulled up outside the house. Martha was not easily persuaded to relinquish the bear-hugging embrace she gave each man, and she chose to ignore completely the grinning ribaldry of the Syrians who offered to call back on their return, should she still be missing the men.

As they eventually climbed aboard the driver greeted them cheerfully, "Well if your ribs can take that sort of handling without protest, I can't see why our commander thinks that we were over rough when we first met."

Brutus grinned as they waved farewell to a moist eyed Martha.

"Maybe he thought your other passenger had had enough punishment, and throwing us on top was adding insult to injury," he laughed.

The journey was uneventful, although frequently slowed by the large number of pilgrims heading in the same direction. There was a palpable feeling of excitement in the crowd, which was mostly good-natured, although one or two bands of surly young men moved grudgingly to clear the road when challenged.

A mile from Jerusalem, within sight of the city was a military checkpoint, where a large crowd queued to pass the scrutiny of both Roman legionaries and Herod's guards.

"They are looking for you," called out the driver's escort, "but this will be the last place they will think to look, so stay under the tarpaulin until we give you the all-clear."

From where they lay hidden, only voices heard faintly indicated what was happening. They heard the insistent call that the people clear the road ahead and then the crack of the driver's whip, followed by the greater urgency from the hooves of the horses and an increasing protestation from the wagon. Then they slowed before coming to a halt. A Roman voice challenged them, demanding their destination and cargo.

"Fort Antonia to collect provisions for the Capernaum contingent at Bethany," answered the driver.

A new voice interjected, "Any more bodies today?" and then explained he had been on duty three days before when they had brought in Herod's man with his head all but severed.

It made Marc feel very uneasy. He wondered what their reaction would be if they knew he who had nearly severed it was under the tarpaulin.

"No such luck I'm afraid. It's boring now that every inch of the wilderness has been scoured. I don't think there's the body of a dead hedgehog that hasn't been found," came his riposte, and to considerable laughter the whip cracked as the wagon resumed its passage.

Ten minutes passed before a laughing Syrian pulled back the tarpaulin and the sudden strong sunlight nearly blinded them.

"It must have been sticky under there," he said, "and I thought it could have turned sticky for us at one point."

"What would you have done if they had wanted to search the wagon?" said Marc.

The soldier's eyes twinkled.

"We had discussed that situation with our commander. I had my sword readied and would have slain in anger any stowaways found on our wagon."

Brutus gave an appreciative chuckle.

"Your commander is a man of infinite resource, and I grow in my admiration of him every hour."

Pinned in by the press of the crowd and approaching the gate but a few hundred paces away, the driver called, "You will be best on foot now. The crowd will give cover, as there are too few soldiers to check the gateway properly. Good fortune go with you," and they slid quickly over the tailboard and disappeared into the throng.

They passed easily through the gate, carried on a human tide that like the sea is irresistible, and then moved to a quiet tree-lined avenue wondering how they could find Mary in such a crowd.

Marc was disturbed. He had been since hearing the soldier's banter, and finally he had to say what was on his mind.

"Father, did that Syrian mean what he said about killing us had we been discovered?"

"For certain he did, Marc. He would have done it to prevent us being captured, when our lives would have been forfeit and our deaths would have been slow and painful. So a quick slash of sword would have spared us a lot of suffering and we might have revealed under torture the Syrians' involvement, and they would have been executed every last man. I had my sword ready as I would have given the same order to protect my men."

Brutus put a reassuring arm around his visibly shaken son.

"I wouldn't have taken it lying down," he emphasised. "If I had had to kill the Syrians, it would have been with great sorrow. Just so with them had they needed to kill us! Couldn't you hear the rejoicing in his voice as he wished us farewell?"

Marc nodded reluctantly, then said, "Yes, but I don't think I would make a good commander?"

"I think you will make a very good commander, Marc. The well being of your men would be your first concern, you have good judgement and are acquiring weapon skills. Finally although you know fear, you do not let it overwhelm you and I am pleased with how you have accounted for yourself." He paused to give Marc a chance of saying something, but when the boy remained silent continued.

"One thing I want you always to remember is what a stout friend Maas has been to us. They would have had their reward had they handed us to Herod. In helping us he took a calculated risk, which many in a similar situation would not have done, but always prudently to minimize any danger to his men. I respect him greatly!"

"Yes, father. I still have a lot to learn," said his reassured son.

Just then a figure detached herself from the stream of people moving into the Temple precincts, raising a hand in greeting and hurrying to join them. Mary was breathless and agitated.

"I think there are lots of troublemakers here today," she panted.

"If so they are likely to bring the Temple guards or Roman soldiers from the fort, so if anything occurs we will make ourselves scarce, don't worry," said Brutus and received a relieved smile from Mary.

She led them to an elevated terrace in the Court of Gentiles, and pointing to a group of men dominated by Peter, suggested they work their way towards them.

They arrived as a challenge rang out, "You there, the giant. Aren't you the leader of the followers of that heretic who talked of destroying the Temple and rebuilding it in three days?"

"If you mean this Temple of stone, no, but if you mean Jesus who was talking of his body, the temple of his soul, I am leader of his disciples," Peter replied.

"Where is he then, this Jesus you all follow?"

"You know perfectly well he was crucified."

The man sneered, "But what about the three days, surely they're up now?"

"You are well informed. He said after three days in the tomb he would overcome death and so he has. He is resurrected and many of us have seen him and heard him."

"Why isn't he here then? I don't see him," laughed the man, but there was no humour in the taunt.

"You are one of many who have eyes but cannot see, ears but cannot hear. In the fullness of time all will be revealed, even to you!"

"And what of the priests?" demanded the man angrily. "Will they see too?"

"Only if they repent and wear sackcloth and ashes for they seized him and condemned him to die."

The man went berserk. He tore his clothes and his beard crying,

"You heard him, kill these blasphemers! Stamp out this evil sect. Stone them."

The cry was taken up by an orchestrated sprinkling among the crowd, then quickly amplified by the voices of the more easily swayed. The disciples formed a defensive group around Peter who glared defiance at the men chanting around them.

A tall patrician man wearing the Roman toga quietly moved into the middle of the crowd followed by an elderly servant. He scanned the mob scornfully and the chanting subsided, those most immediate to him backing away leaving a clear area between the two factions and him in the middle.

"Must I witness this defilement of the Temple at this important feast? Is this what Pentecost has become, an opportunity for mob anarchy and the violation of your sacred laws?" He glared at the silenced, hostile crowd.

"Don't listen to this Roman. What does he know of our tradition?" called the ringleader trying to rally his faction.

"I know a lot. I have studied the Torah as a god-fearer for twenty years. True, I am a Roman centurion, but I love your traditions and respect that you are a chosen people, chosen to be a light to the Gentiles. I study the scriptures and as a thanksgiving I built a synagogue at Capernaum. Don't you dare to impute I know nothing of your tradition!"

The crowd was fragmenting as those in it by accident dissociated themselves, and those who had planned violence were subdued and hesitant.

"Come, Dicacus," he said, "let us offer a kid for peace at Pentecost," and they walked quietly away.

"Centurion Andreaus!" breathed Brutus with relief, as they moved further into the vast throbbing court.

"Are we safe in the Temple?" asked Marc who had had enough danger for one day.

"If you stay in the Court of the Gentiles yes, but your life would be at risk if you entered the Inner Temple. But there's Miriam and you can be certain she won't take you into any danger," said Mary, pointing to the forlorn maiden standing at a stall that traded in unblemished lambs and kid goats for offerings.

Simon of Cyrene and Alexander were leading a cream coloured kid towards the Inner Temple in time for the mid-afternoon prayers.

Miriam brightened instantly as she saw them approaching. Until this moment she had feared that something would go wrong on the journey from Bethany, but now her face radiated her joy. Marc's heart missed many a beat. She had never looked prettier but it was more than just her loveliness. Suddenly he realised that they were in love and the path of their love was being smoothed for them. The uncertainties were being banished and for the first time he was confident that their love would find fulfilment.

After a few indecisive minutes of wandering around together, Mary dragged Brutus to the booth of a moneychanger displaying an array of trinkets and jewellery, deliberately separating them from the youngsters.

The two youths wandered hand in hand from booth to stall, until Marc finally blurted out, "Can we get away and just be together!"

Miriam squeezed his hand, "Thank goodness you asked. As this is your first visit to the Temple I wasn't sure how much you wished to see. Come on, papa and Alexander will be at prayers for a whole hour."

Her face radiated such joy that Marc wanted to embrace her. Detecting his desire, but decorum presiding over hers, she pulled him through the crowd into the colonnaded cloister adjacent to the west wall, where it was quiet and cool. Sitting on a stone bench looking out on the throng Miriam turned to Marc.

"Can you imagine sitting here not many weeks ago just before the Passover festival? Jesus came through that gate over there with his followers and stood watching all the transactions of buying and selling animals and changing money. A poor woman was crying because by the time she had changed her pittance into temple money she hadn't enough to buy a pair of doves to offer. Jesus went up to her just as the trader pushed her away to serve someone else with more money. She fell and the trader laughed ridiculing her plight, and many joined in the laughter. But not Jesus, he helped her to her feet, then seized the merchant's table and threw it over so that the caged birds and the money were scattered. He then went from one table to another, throwing them over, and seizing a drover's whip started on the moneychangers as well, so that they ran in panic leaving their coins rolling to the ground."

Miriam stopped, a little short of breath, her eyes glittering with excitement.

"He really did that and you saw it?" exclaimed Marc sharing her excitement.

"Not from here. I was down there in the crowd and didn't see very much, but people were running everywhere in pandemonium. Some were calling out a welcome 'Hosanna for the Son of David,' some were calling out with joy at receiving healing, and others were scrambling to pick up the coins from the floor. The Temple guards tried to restore a little order while court officials were tearing their beards and clothes with vexation.

"Someone challenged Jesus if he was the Messiah, the awaited Son of David, but he told them that they had turned his house from a place of prayer into a den of thieves and left, just walked quietly away as though nothing had happened."

"Didn't the temple guards try to arrest him? If I went and started a disturbance I'm sure I'd be arrested," queried Marc.

"Not if half the crowd thought you the Messiah! The guards would have had a riot on their hands if they had tried."

Marc smiled ruefully.

"They would have to wait for the right moment when his followers had dispersed," he said, glancing around apprehensively as talking of arrest reminded him that he was a fugitive and would be seized if he were recognized.

As though she read his thoughts Miriam's eyes filled with tears, and Marc grasped her tight little fists and brought them to his lips. Then opening them he kissed each finger separately, moving from one to the next as though by extending this caress he could postpone forever the parting that was near. All the time Miriam was convulsed with sobs, far too insistent to be contained. The scene in the bright sunlit court ceased to exist for both of them, as hearts enjoined, they lived only for the moment.

"Miriam, I will never again see the world as it has been before because today I have to know if I can pledge my heart to you!"

"Then pledge it, my love, and ease the ache within mine. If our hearts are pledged I can wait however long we must before the fulfilment of our love."

"Not for long, I would be consumed by the fire that rages within me. One month will seem as a year, and a year as a lifetime. I think you are much braver than I, better able to handle adversity."

As Miriam protested at this Marc moved to stand behind her and burying his face in the fragrance of her hair whispered, "I saw you brave the soldiers and give assistance to Jesus when he fell. I was in your house when you declared yourself a follower of Jesus, and that you believed he had conquered death on the cross. I wouldn't have had the courage to do either."

"Jesus gives courage to people, courage to break down barriers, and some people only feel safe behind barriers. As a Jewess my love for you could never have been fulfilled, and until a few months ago it would have been impossible that we could even meet each other. But Jesus has changed that. Our meeting was only because he accepted to die humiliated and rejected by us. Our love was forged on that same anvil where the hammers tempered his nails."

Miriam was no longer distraught and tearful. A joyful radiance was transforming her, as though in her mind she too saw all coming well in time. She looked invincible at the same time as she looked so vulnerable. Marc knew she believed because her trust was in the Galilean and her own brave heart.

From where they stood they had a good view of much of the court. Marc saw Brutus with Mary approach the tall centurion who had confronted the mob earlier. They saluted each other and gripped arms before proceeding with an animated conversation.

The worshippers from the inner courts were beginning to emerge, so the new lovers, hearts enjoined as well as hands, moved from the cloister to join their companions.

As they approached Andreaus he was talking agitatedly.

"They are never going to accept what you say. For two thousand years they have had a unique covenanted relationship with their God, believing each year they will see the arrival of the long awaited Messiah, who will deliver them from whatever bondage they have to endure. We Romans at present, but before us Greeks, Egyptians, Babylonians. Now you ask them to accept that their Messiah arrived, and that they failed to acknowledge him and crucified him for political expediency. No wonder these followers of Jesus stir up such anger when they harangue the crowds here in the temple as they do. The healing miracles have ceased following the death of their leader, so sadly that wonderful phase has finished. I expect to see the whole movement disintegrate soon, and just hope little violence is provoked in the meantime."

"I recognise that your knowledge of the Judaic traditions is much greater than mine or any Roman in the province. But I do know for sure that I killed Jesus with my spear, yet three days later Mary here, entering his tomb to embalm his body with ointment, saw him alive, in the flesh and spoke to him."

Mary modestly inclined her head in affirmation.

Andreaus, disconcerted and shaking his head, queried, "Couldn't you have seen a ghost? A spectral form of his spirit?"

"No sir, truly it was he. He called me by name and he wasn't tormented at all. He gave me a message for his followers, and they have since eaten with him and communed with him until last week."

Mary fell silent and Andreaus looked bewildered by her words.

"What happened last week?" he finally asked.

"Last week all we followers were led by Jesus to Mount Olivet. He asked us women to wait and led his disciples to the summit. Centurion Brutus and Marc joined us where we waited and then all of us witnessed a remarkable glow emanating from around the summit. Then the disciples came down from the mountain without Jesus, and told us they had witnessed him being lifted up into the clouds."

Andreaus was showing considerable strain. His face had gone pale and his jaw was clenched while his unblinking eyes were fixed on some remote point in space. Dicacus appeared elated, only with difficulty suppressing his evident excitement.

Finally Andreaus exhaled deeply and the tension ebbed from him. He said calmly, "These are wonders of which I never dreamt. We are privileged to live at a unique moment in time. If this is God's will nothing can prevail against it running its course; if it is an illusion it will come to nothing. Please excuse us, we still have affairs to attend to. God speed you and your son in your travels, centurion, this province is a dangerous place for you, and for many others," he added, glancing at Mary as he bowed and departed.

This was the signal for them to make their way from the Temple and disperse, Brutus and Marc to celebrate with the family of Simon of Cyrene, and Mary Magdalene to rejoin the followers of Jesus at their meeting room. Marc had never relinquished the hand of Miriam, an assertion of the bond that united them, which they wished all to know. The uneasy looks Miriam received from her family were answered by a steady beseeching smile of overflowing happiness. She knew they had weathered daunting seas, crossed an invisible but formidable barrier, and hoped now to sail in less troubled water.

CHAPTER SIX

That same evening in the familiar ante-room of Herod's palace a heated meeting was taking place. Only Herod Antipas of those who had previously pored over the map was alive to vent his anger on those unfortunate enough now to attend him.

"So the Prefect of Judaea is indisposed. What is the nature of his indisposition, and did you stress our anger, Eliat, at the incompetence of the Roman forces in this matter?"

"Indeed I did, sire. He is indisposed by virtue of his wife and the messages he has received from Caesarea. She has had recurring nightmares concerning the Galilean who was crucified, and threatens to throw herself off a tower."

"Let her, by heaven. Aren't there enough other women in Judaea who would gladly be bedded by Pilate?" roared Herod.

"Undoubtedly sire, but I venture to suggest it would be a foolhardy man who would voice such an opinion," replied his Chancellor wringing his hands.

"Further sire, he absolutely refutes your criticism of the army. He says, two dozen hanged zealots and the seizure of many caches of weapons is no small reward for their efforts. We have here the centurion from the City of Salt, whom you might wish to see. He spoke to the men you are seeking just before you declared your interest in their arrest."

"Well bring him in by Jupiter!" exclaimed Herod, "until now nobody has seen them at all, except for some salt vendors, and my men who are not able to testify to their whereabouts."

Decimianus entered and knelt before the king.

"Tell us of this renegade centurion you met and what you know of his plans."

"He came to my guardroom sire, after descending to the Jordan from the region around Bethany. I thought he and his slave were travelling on foot, but have since learnt they brought a cart down the steep path used by the salt trains and had a woman companion."

Decimianus paused to get his facts in order and to avoid rousing Herod's anger that he had not apprehended them there and then.

"They were anxious to proceed northwards towards the Sea of Galilee, and I suggested they would be able to join the caravan we were expecting."

"Do you think they could have gone that way?" interrupted Herod.

"No, sire, they would surely have been arrested by my men who have had every strategic road watched since we heard they were fugitives. I had my suspicions when one of the bodies was brought down from the wilderness, the body hadn't been stripped, which is unlike the zealots who strip their victims of everything."

"Why in heaven's name didn't you act on your suspicions?" growled Herod, frustrated by the thought of how easily it might have gone his way.

"Because it is dangerous to arrest a Roman citizen and a veteran centurion on no more than a suspicion. Had we been informed that the renegade was protecting his thieving son it would have been different. But that information only came later ..."

"After you had allowed them to disappear without trace eh?" exclaimed Herod derisively, as the centurion fidgeted nervously.

"We searched for them as soon as we had reason, sire," he replied.

"And where do you think they are now?" demanded Herod.

Decimianus licked his lips and felt fear knotting his innards as he replied hesitantly, "I think they have to be here in Jerusalem!"

Herod's head was thrown back at this unexpected reply, poised like that of a cobra, menacingly lethal should it decide to strike.

"In their predicament it's where I would choose to hide. Nowhere else could I remain undetected for as many days as they have. We have searched every cave and gully, but we have had to pare the garrison to the bone to do it. With all the thousands of pilgrims descending on Jerusalem could there be a better place to hide until the search is called off?" concluded Decimianus, with relief at the excitement that had seized Herod.

"By thunder, some sense at last. Well done, centurion, your reasoning does you credit," he exulted.

"You would recognise this Brutus if you saw him?"

Decimianus nodded.

"Then can you take charge of the search here in Jerusalem?"

"I could if I had my century sire, but they are still scattered over the hills of Judaea and it will take a day to regroup and redeploy. Nor can I order this redeployment unless the search of the countryside is called off by Legate Venestus."

"Recall every legionary within fifty miles of Jerusalem and bring them here tomorrow," ordered Herod. "So Pilate is too indisposed to attend our meeting. Very well, Eliat and you other gentlemen," he nodded at the senior administrator of the Temple and the commander of his guard, "we will attend on Pilate and persuade him his interests and ours converge on this issue, and he must order the recall of all the soldiers and saturate the city to flush them out of hiding. Cancel all leave and any rest days! Double the watch at the gates and those mingling with the crowds, both in the streets and in the courts of the Temple! Seize the Jew Rueben for further questioning and find out who this woman is, their companion, and bring her here. Well go. Go! Don't fail me yet again, or by God, you will account for it with your lives!"

In the stunned silence that followed Herod's tirade, he and his advisors departed, speedily heading towards Fort Antonia and an unsuspecting Prefect.

To an outsider observing at a distance it would have seemed everything worked smoothly as though it was nothing exceptional that was being asked. That the biggest manhunt the province had ever known was about to change direction completely was testimony to the lengths that powerful rulers will go to avenge any loss of face or challenge to their pride. Pilate was grudging in bestowing his authorization, but after subtle pressure combined with flattery had been used he acquiesced and signed the order. A dozen couriers were dispatched to every far-flung company and the great military machine was reined back like a team of exuberant stallions to the will of the man holding the reins.

Maas and his company of Syrian archers were enjoying their pretence at searching, confident they would not be found dilatory in whatever they were ordered to do. So it came as a great surprise when they were withdrawn and ordered to Jerusalem at first light. They conjectured on the cause of this new order and wondered if the fugitives they had seen safely on their way had been arrested. Maas insisted if that were so, they would have been sent back to garrison duties in Capernaum not to Jerusalem.

"No, Pilate has deduced they are hiding in the city and they need us to help flush them out. What are we prepared to do further to help them evade capture?" he asked.

"What can we do? We don't know where they are hiding and we take a grave risk if we are found to be aiding them," said the archer who had driven them to Jerusalem.

"We do have a lead, through the man who paid us the reward. We know the house of Simon of Cyrene, and he must be able to get in touch with centurion Brutus," replied Maas.

"Then we can tell Herod's guards where they are hiding, and share the reward a second time," suggested a swarthy veteran named Sisera.

Maas was on his feet, standing menacingly over Sisera with eyes blazing. Seizing his tunic he hauled him erect until he was glaring into the older man's eyes, and very quietly, but clearly enough for every man to hear he replied, "If you or any soldier in this company thinks of handing them over to Herod, you had better think again. No Syrian who honours his parents could consider such a shameful betrayal, and I personally would gladly rid the world of such vermin."

Releasing Sisera, who slumped back cowed onto his stool, Maas continued, "I'm not asking any of you to take the risks we took before, and it may be that we need do no more than warn them. But for myself, I do not think a centurion I would gladly have at my side in battle should be handed as a plaything to that reptile Herod. Anyone with me in offering help should it be needed, stand forward."

All stood and moved into line, even the subdued Sisera who was bitterly regretting his unguarded tongue.

"Fine," smiled Maas, "let us all pull together and we can come through this unscathed."

In the darkened city, in an upstairs room where they often communed, the disciples and followers of Jesus were seated in a number of groups around low tables. These were laden with dishes prepared for their celebratory feast of first harvest, also known as Pentecost. Rebecca and some of the other women were placing the final platters on the tables before seating themselves at another adjacent to the kitchen.

As Peter commenced the blessing there was a loud knocking at the bolted door. Mary, mother of James and John, left the table and descended to find out who was demanding their attention so urgently. She peered out at the frightened face illuminated by the spluttering oil lamp, and recognizing Deborah she led her to the upper room.

The blessing was finished but nobody had commenced eating, their attention on the cause of the disturbance.

"It's Deborah," said Mary, as the woman's alarmed son arose from the table and moved to join her, but his mother waved him away.

"Be seated, David. This concerns only Rebecca and Rueben," she said. "Herod's guards have forced their way into your house and ransacked your belongings. They have also threatened and seized some of your neighbours, trying to frighten them to tell where you are to be found, but luckily nobody knows other than me."

Rueben moved to comfort his distressed wife, while Peter ushered those directly involved into an adjoining room, and taking Deborah by the hand asked, "When did this all happen,?"

"Only half an hour ago."

"Were you careful that you weren't followed here?"

"Yes very careful. I went in the opposite direction and then concealed myself in an alley for some minutes before doubling back."

"Well done, Deborah, we must be constantly on guard. Do you know why they want to find Reuben and Rebecca?"

"To take them to Herod's palace, to answer some questions concerning a centurion and his slave, they said."

There was a gasp of dismay from Rueben as the memory of his recent arrest and beating was still fresh.

"But we haven't any news of them since they started their travels a week ago. What can we tell them?" he said.

"They are asking who the woman is who has been seen with them," replied Deborah.

Peter looked towards Mary Magdalene who had moved quietly to his side.

"So they have a woman companion. I think it best if we keep her identity a secret even from those here in our community. We are as vulnerable to arrest and torture as anyone, and what we don't know cannot be drawn from us. Mary, take Deborah to your table and let her eat with us. We must pray to the Lord for the safekeeping of centurion Brutus and his son, and for the coming of the Holy Spirit to empower us to handle the trials ahead."

He resumed his seat at the table, but it was a subdued community that broke the bread and passed around the wine that night.

Not so in the house of Simon of Cyrene. Unaware of the threat gathering around them and luxuriating in the richness and warmth of the celebration, there was a shared feeling of contentment. For Marc it revived memories of six weeks earlier at the Passover supper, but to Brutus it was all so new and profound. He found himself envying the Jews their uniqueness and their culture.

"Do you know, every Jew within twenty miles of the city is obliged to attend the Temple for this feast, and most of them will stay in Jerusalem until tomorrow evening. Everyone is on holiday. Every servant, every shopkeeper, even those who have slaves must give them today free from any duties," said Simon as Naomi and Miriam brought dishes in from the kitchen.

Marc laughed at the recollection that he had been a slave when he had last sat here.

"Can you imagine Rome if the same rule applied there?" he said. "Why, they say there are two slaves to every free born citizen!"

"And it's probably true," replied Brutus. "We Romans have become totally dependent on slaves and tribute and taxes from our far-flung empire. It is our awareness of this dependence that necessitates our mighty army and our fleets."

100

"As merchants, my sons and I acknowledge the wonderful benefits to commerce your empire has established throughout the known world. So I propose a toast to the Roman Empire, may it gain in enlightenment," said Simon raising his glass to their guests.

"On the matter of commerce," interjected Alexander following the toast, "our ship is nearly laden to sail and I propose leaving for Joppa the day after tomorrow. Will you be able to sail with us in three days?"

He was looking at Brutus as he said this, but from the corner of his eye, saw the start of his sister and the colour drain from her face. Marc, seated next to her felt concern at her reaction but he need not have been anxious. She turned her face bravely towards him and suppressing the tears that were threatening said, "We must get you to Joppa in good time. Your lives will always be in danger until you leave this province behind you. I was thinking to accompany you on Pegasus. You will be riding Mistral, won't you, Alexander?"

"And leading a train of a dozen mules and six muleteers, Miriam. They're a rough bunch but dependable. However it's no picnic, it's tiring and primitive and we may sleep under the stars. What do you think, father?"

Simon pondered as Miriam held her breath watching him anxiously, knowing that she had to accept whatever he said on the matter.

After a brief period which seemed an eternity, he said, "It's a long time since I've seen Joppa. I think I'll come along and bring a cart. There's a wine merchant I know well and if he has as fine wines now as he used to keep, I'll bring back a full cart. The Garrison is always prepared to pay handsomely for an amphora of quality wine," and he smiled broadly at everyone as though he had made a good joke.

"Oh thank you, papa, so I can come, and return with you after they have sailed." Miriam hugged her beaming father and Marc felt great joy that Simon was facilitating their relationship, when many a parent would have obstructed it in every way possible.

"Thank you, sir," he said. "I treasure your daughter and will respect the trust you have shown me. One year, not too distant I hope, I will return and if Miriam is of the same mind as now ask your blessing on our marriage."

"Well spoken, Marc, love is God's greatest gift! We shall see in time what is his will and if it comes about as you propose you can be sure you will have our blessing." He had risen and moved to place a reassuring arm around Naomi, who smiled hesitantly, but thereby associated herself with her husband.

They fell to less serious talk and enjoyment of the feast, punctuated by appropriate readings from the scripture. Miriam produced an eight stringed harp and plucked it to accompany a psalm that she sang, rejoicing in the goodness of God to Israel.

The night steadily advanced and a feeling of security and well being invested the house, to be broken by an insistent knocking at the door. The knock was not over loud and brutal, as foreshadows the violation of a dwelling by intruders, but demanding enough for Alexander to respond quickly.

He reappeared and addressed Brutus urgently.

"There's a Syrian soldier in the hall who needs to speak to you. His name is Maas and he says it is of the greatest importance."

Brutus, alarmed, moved towards the door but Simon stayed him by clasping his arm.

"I know this man and have dealt honourably with him over the reward for our friends here. There is nothing that he has to say that can't be said in front of us all. Please my son, ask him to be so kind as to join us."

Maas was disconcerted seeing the family assembled, but Simon moved to greet him and said, "Thank you for coming from Bethany, and if your business is of such urgency that seconds are critical, say so?"

Maas shook his head.

"Then allow me to present those of my family you don't know, my wife, our daughter Miriam and our eldest son, Alexander. This is Maas who commands a company of Syrian archers, and obviously has ridden hard at night to warn us."

"He has already proved himself a true friend, and Marc and I owe him more than we can ever repay," said Brutus as they exchanged salutes.

"Then please be seated and tell us what brings you here," said Simon.

Maas declined refreshment and came immediately to his business.

"Herod has persuaded Pilate to recall the soldiers from the wilderness and every man will converge on Jerusalem at first light tomorrow. Fifteen hundred soldiers will be redeployed in and around the city by mid morning, and I think they will make a net through which even you will be unable to swim."

For the first time he relaxed and indicated he would be glad of a drink. Naomi passed him a goblet of sherbet cordial, while all looked to the centurion, knowing he was best capable of assessing the significance of this information.

"Then they either know, or have deduced that we are hiding here in Jerusalem," said Brutus.

"That is our conclusion and the reason I have come to warn you."

Maas smiled broadly as he continued, "My company would rejoice to frustrate Herod and Pilate for a second time, and we have a plan which you may agree. The risks to us are small and the chance of success high."

"Why should you risk your lives a second time for us? Herod would demand a brutal reckoning if he discovered your role," interrupted Brutus.

"Let's say that as comrades in arms we share a common duty to help each other. Orders are orders, but you know there are commanders whose orders you obey unquestioningly, and others you want nothing to do with."

He then proceeded to outline his plan.

"A cart, with the drivers known to you and an escort of four soldiers, will be dispatched shortly before dawn tomorrow, carrying some redundant and damaged equipment which they are to hand over to the quartermaster at Fort Antonia. They will then proceed for the Port of Joppa, to meet a company of archers arrived from Antioch. If you could be in the vicinity of the fort, you will have the opportunity to conceal yourselves in the cart before it passes through the Damascus gate and onto the Joppa road. Every hour increases the risk as the soldiers take up their positions, but initially there will be a lot of confusion and much movement, which could be turned to our advantage."

"Your plan is well thought through," said Brutus, "and it is probably our only chance. But a few hours ago Simon and Alexander had an excellent plan but we can no longer delay our departure until Monday, it has to be early tomorrow. How long is the journey to Joppa?"

"One full day's travel if all goes well," said Maas, "so you need a safe house for tomorrow night in Joppa."

102

"Or a safe boat," said Alexander. "I will give you a letter for the captain of the ship, *Medusa*, which will guarantee your welcome, and we can follow as planned on the Monday. You aren't going to be safe until we sail."

Miriam was looking dazed and disappointed, her hopes of their travelling together having been so brutally dashed.

"Can I still come along, papa?" she asked anxiously, and was cheered a little when Simon indicated that still held.

Brutus turned to Simon and asked him urgently, "Will you get a message to Mary Magdalene, she was to have met us at the Temple tomorrow to travel with us to Joppa now we are man and wife, and together we will be sailing to Tyre."

Miriam jumped to her feet and rushing to his side gave Brutus a great hug, which made the centurion smile broadly. She exclaimed, "Why isn't that wonderful! It's so romantic, and it means Marc has a mother now as well."

"I hadn't thought of that," mused Brutus, "I hope Marc is happy about it?"

"Happy! Why I'll say I am. Mary is a truly wonderful woman and I rejoice at such news," and seizing Miriam's hand he squeezed it delightedly.

"Your happiness will be very brief and tragic, if you don't concentrate on your plan for tomorrow," interjected Alexander, rather testily, as their traditional beliefs were once again being challenged.

At the palace of King Herod there was a great deal of activity and tension was running high as Herod paced the anteroom, his face contorted by rage. Messenger after messenger brought nothing that he wished to hear.

"You find nobody I seek, seize nobody of value to us. Are you just stupid or are you deliberately defying me?" he growled, his paranoia beginning to assert itself.

"How can a common Jew and his wife just disappear without trace? Their neighbours know nothing of their whereabouts, despite my jailers' efforts at persuasion."

"Sire, we know they are followers of this Galilean Jesus who have formed a sect that can often be found in the Temple, but never outside of it, as they meet in great secrecy," said an anxious advisor.

"A seditious sect, festering here in Jerusalem and Pilate does nothing to stamp it out? Is he mad or just incompetent? Were I king as my illustrious father, Herod the Great, I would soon eliminate such vermin from the kingdom."

"Indeed, sire, and we would applaud you for it. You may have the chance as smaller but similar groups of followers can be found in the synagogues of Tiberius and Capernaum, within your jurisdiction," added the advisor obsequiously.

"But can we do nothing more in Jerusalem? It's here that this accursed renegade centurion and his thieving whelp of a slave elude us."

"Tomorrow sire we throw a ring of steel around the city so that nobody can get out. Our best men will mingle with the crowds in the Temple and in the streets. These Jesus followers are easy to pick out as they always gather a hostile crowd around them. It would be easy to arrest some for their own protection, and then we should be able to persuade one or more to lead us to this Rueben and his wife and the woman companion."

"Is there nothing we can do now? It's eight hours before the first pilgrims will be entering the Temple. Five hours of darkness in which our quarry may flee the city and escape," pleaded Herod despairingly.

"No sire. There is no chance of them eluding the Roman patrols that encircle

Jerusalem. They are probably feeling secure and unthreatened as they know nothing of your inspired switch of the hunt from the wilderness to the city."

"Oh, come swiftly, daylight. My vengeance is fanned to white heat by these winds of darkness and of night. Everyone, redouble your efforts. We will retire until dawn," with which Herod stalked angrily out of the room.

The dawn of Pentecost was rose hued and portentous, to those who were awake to see it. Herod only saw it as blood red, and exulted that the end was approaching to the chancre that had been gnawing at his mind ceaselessly. To those at the house of Simon it uplifted their spirits with the feeling that all would come well, and that by sunset their anxieties would be over. To Mary and the followers of Jesus in the upstairs room it promised the long awaited coming of the Holy Spirit.

Even the Syrian soldiers accompanying the cart marvelled at the luminescent red glow of the high wall of the city they were approaching, the awesome aspect of the Temple looming above it. They had passed many groups of soldiers, either breakfasting or breaking camp, and had not once been challenged, although they had been the butt of a few jokers calling to them.

Approaching the east gate they were aware of the scrutiny of the sentry, which was occasioned more by curiosity than concern.

"You're early, lads," he called out as they passed through, "you'll be lucky to find anyone awake up at the Fort!"

"Do you mean we will have to batter the gate down to get in?" rejoined the Syrian.

"No, just call out, 'Ahoy guardroom, how many women have you in there?' and see what happens," and the man chuckled to himself at some private joke.

As they approached the heavy double gate a small door to the side opened. A man peered out half blinded by the sun, and made a quick gesture. Two lithesome but veiled women slid through the door and hastily made their way along the cobbled street. Seeing the cart the guard withdrew, and very shortly swung one of the ponderous gates open for them to pass through.

"If you're looking for the quartermaster you will have an hour to wait," he called out.

"We will drop off some damaged equipment, but have to proceed to Joppa for fresh men and their supplies. We need as many men as we can muster if we are going to flush our quarry out of this rabbit warren," called the Syrian.

"By the time you get back it will all be over. Fat chance you stand of seeing the reward," joked the guard, who was surprised at their unconstrained laughter.

It only took them fifteen minutes at the fort before they were leaving the gates behind and entering the narrow cobbled streets. A large tarpaulin covered two crates, between which there was ample space for concealment. The rear flap was down, and as the cart passed a narrow alley, two men emerged, climbed wordlessly aboard and slid into the space between the crates. The drivers' companion turned and repositioned the tarpaulin as one of those escorting raised and secured the flap. It had taken less than half a minute, and had not been noticed by the few people who were about. Five minutes later and to a considerable amount of banter, they passed through the Damascus gate.

"Why do you need an escort of four bowmen for an almost empty cart?" called out one of the sentries.

"Because we won't be returning empty of course, and what we will be carrying lots of people would like to get their hands on," replied the driver.

"Must be a cartful of women then. Make sure you come through this gate when you return."

"They won't be for the likes of you, that's for sure!" quipped the driver as they moved off to more ribaldry.

When they had moved a mile into the hills the tarpaulin was drawn back. Nearly blinded, the fugitives were relieved to sit up and take some deep breaths of fresh air. The grinning Syrian offered them a skin of water from which they both drank eagerly.

"What a relief," said Brutus, "it's so stuffy under that cover I was wondering how long I would last."

"We will post a man two hundred paces in front of us and the same behind. Now you can walk with us, but you must return immediately to the hiding place if either man hails," said the Syrian.

They walked steadily following the road up into the wilderness, yellow and brown and arid. The sun was high overhead and normally they would have sought some shade and rested for the hottest hours, but not today with the urgency of their task. When eventually, the hills no longer ranged ahead, Brutus was hoping they would soon see the Plain of Sharon and start the descent to the wide, lush coastal strip.

Suddenly a voice cried out behind and they saw the rear guard running towards them. Brutus and Marc were quickly onto the cart and hidden. The soldier caught up with them and talked urgently to the driver who called out a warning.

"There are three horsemen closing on us, less than half a mile behind. They are Romans, so stay hidden and we will see what they want."

The cart continued its progress, but very soon they heard the pounding of hooves on the hard road and a voice hailed them.

"Halt there and stand by your wagon"

As they halted the Syrians grouped defensively around their vehicle.

"Why are you moving away from the action? Don't you know the Prefect has ordered every available man to take part in the search for these fugitives?"

"For three days we have scoured the wilderness, and now many of our men have gone down with fever. We have a company of reinforcements and their equipment landed at Joppa, and our company commander has ordered us to bring them into the search. That's where we are going now, to Joppa."

"Forget that order, I give you a new one. Turn back and proceed to Jerusalem. Join the first unit you see on temporary attachment, and participate in the search."

To Brutus the voice sounded authoritative and assured and he communicated his alarm in a whisper to Marc.

"Can you give me that command in writing," stalled the driver, "I have my orders to follow."

"In writing, you insolent fellow? I'll wager you can't read a word."

"Be that as it may, my orders are to take this wagon to Joppa and to collect the reinforcements. I need more than your word to change that, sir."

The driver sounded very resolved and the challenger seemed momentarily disconcerted. The whip cracked and the wagon started to move, when suddenly he called out.

"Let me see what you are carrying that is so important. I command you to stop."

Before the wagon halted Brutus had lifted a corner of the tarpaulin, so that some light penetrated. He signalled to Marc to ready his sword, whispering,

"Only disarm them if possible."

The horses approached, and leaning from his saddle the man grasped the tarpaulin and jerked it away.

The surprise element was complete. None of the riders had weapons drawn and Brutus seizing the hand holding the covering threw his weight on it, pulling the officer out of the saddle pinning him to the board. Marc leapt feet outstretched to hit a second legionary before his sword was half way from its scabbard and the man lost his seat under the impact so they both fell heavily to the ground. The fight was over in a few seconds, as the Syrians surrounded the only soldier still mounted, who thought better than to draw. Quickly the three men were disarmed and sat angrily by the wagon.

"I'm sorry about this gentlemen," said Brutus, "and rejoice that none of you is injured. I am the centurion you are seeking and for whom Herod has offered a reward."

"And is this the thief that you have teamed up with, to the disgrace of the Legion?" asked the officer contemptuously.

"This is my son Marc. The story that he is a thief is a lie. I publicly humiliated Herod and Pilate at the spear throwing, and they have set their minds to avenging the insult. We had to kill four assassins they sent after us at Bethany, that is why the whole legion is hunting for us."

"I was at the games and saw the spear throwing. So it was you who broke your spear in front of the Prefect. Well, well!" exclaimed the unmolested man.

"Indeed. And now we have to flee for our lives, and these brave Syrians are risking theirs to assist us. But the question is, what can we do with you?" he looked pensively at the three.

"Let us go. We give our word we will not give chase or raise an alarm," said the officer surlily.

"Thank you gentlemen but I must decline."

Brutus left them to confer with the driver, who listened intently to what was proposed. He nodded and gave a delighted grin as Brutus turned and rejoined the captives.

"I'm afraid you must come with us. Your horses will be tethered in the shade down that ravine."

He pointed to a deep narrow cleft, winding away from the road to a muddy waddi far away in the distance.

"You can accompany us for a few hours journey and then we will release you. I don't think you would be wise to mention our meeting to anyone, as Herod would think you had failed miserably and vent his spleen on you. Come, let's be on our way."

Within ten minutes the soldiers' weapons and their horses had been hidden and they were continuing their route. After an hour they were descending, and the Plain of Sharon lay invitingly ahead as far as they could see.

At this point Brutus made the men take off their sandals, which he placed at the base of a lone cedar tree where they would easily find them. The three prisoners now travelled in the wagon until they had descended to the plain, where sheep were grazing a wide slope.

"Gentlemen, you are now free to return to duty. I am truly sorry to have inconvenienced you, but on reflection I think you will see the necessity. My last warning is for your own good. We will be far away before you can come after us if you so choose. I would not spare your lives a second time. Herod will enjoy killing you slowly if he ever suspects how close you came to capturing us."

The whole vista of the plain ahead was vibrant with the brilliant whites, blues, yellows and reds of anemone, narcissus, chrysanthemum and crocus poppy. They glowed in the afternoon sun, and it was with elation that the travellers quickened their pace towards the far blue line at the horizon.

CHAPTER SEVEN

From the high window Simon Peter was looking over an amazingly diverse roof-scape, across the city to the pink glow in the east. The hill of Olivet looming over the towering wall was deeply shadowed purple and black, but clearly silhouetted. The rising sun's beams radiated to highlight the wispy cloud with blood red, orange and gold.

Mary Magdalene had moved to his side and they were silent witnesses to the spectacle of the dawn until Peter murmured, "In some way this reminds me of the heavens on the eve when our Lord left us with his promise. Do you remember it, Mary?

"Indeed I do. We all stood spellbound for some time. That was the time that a Roman centurion captured my heart."

"As it still is. What are his feelings for you?"

"He has declared his love, and wishes for us to be joined together as man and wife. I have joyously agreed and will be joining him to sail from Joppa shortly."

"Then I rejoice for you both," said Peter embracing her fondly. "I am certain the centurion and his son will declare for our Lord, from whom your love draws its strength. We will pray for your happiness this morning and you have my blessing."

"Thank you, Peter. This will be the last time I hear you tell of the things Jesus said and did whilst you were together. Could I ask you to tell us of the first miracle, at the wedding in Cana. I've always loved that story and it will have to serve for Brutus and me, as any wedding feast with kin is denied us." There was so much pathos and regret in Mary's voice, that Peter was moved to embrace her for a second time that morning, to comfort her and to strengthen her resolution.

"Always remember, Mary, that you met your love because Jesus suffered on the cross. Now he is arisen he will be with you both, wherever you go and whatever befalls you."

There was a considerable bustle around them as breakfast was being prepared for all those who now slept there, a great many more than the original disciples. There was a loud knocking at the lower door, and one of the followers went to see who it was to disturb them this early. Everyone was nervously silent watching the door, but when Miriam appeared the tension evaporated.

She approached them, knelt briefly before Peter, then told of the events of the night, and the changes to their plans. Peter insisted they move to a quiet room, where they discussed the new situation, and it was decided that Mary would have to spend the night at Miriam's house to be ready for an early start, and where she would be safe from Herod should she be identified as the companion of the hunted Romans.

"Stay around, daughter," said Peter, as Miriam was about to depart.

"Whilst praying this morning we beheld a glorious sunrise. Since I have had a strange feeling of anticipation, and the very air feels vibrant and fills me with energy. For Mary, as a blessing on her imminent union with centurion Brutus, I will tell the story of how Jesus changed pitchers of water into wine at a marriage in Cana. It was his first miracle, the first of many, all of which I recall so clearly. They will be told again and again in the synagogues, so that all Israel comes to believe he is the Messiah."

The hours following breakfast passed in a moving sequence of prayer, psalms and storytelling. During a lull, as people were mingling and conversing quietly, all became aware of a sighing breeze audible throughout the room. It was as the first breath of God that stirred the waters of the deep on the first day, and everyone's attention was held by it.

Peter stood as though in a trance, listening perhaps to an inner voice. As the breeze increased in intensity, so as to fill the whole of the building with its resonance, Peter made a signal to all the disciples and they gathered into an inner circle to pray. So focussed and intense had the wind now grown that the shutters rattled at the windows, the furnishing of curtains and drapes fluttered and cavorted like the vestments of frenzied dervishes. Even in the street outside, the commotion within seized the attention of every passer by, although not a breeze troubled the stillness of the city.

Holding hands nervously Miriam and Mary saw a flickering ethereal fire high up in the roof space. It seemed to be a manifestation of pure spirit, consuming nothing and disowning everything of matter and the physical world. Gaining in intensity it became impossible to gaze on, and the noise of the wind deafened those within. In the brief moments when they dared to look, they saw it descend and hover above their heads before cleaving into separate tongues of fire that moved and rested on each disciple.

Immediately all sound ceased and silence gripped the community, every eye on the faces of the disciples glowing with ecstasy, their mortal bodies sublimated as the Holy Spirit of God entered them.

Peter broke the silence.

"As promised, our Lord has sent his Spirit to dwell with us, as it will do hence-forth until the day of the Lord dawns. Blessed is the Lord God of Israel who works such wonders for his people."

"Amen," said all the witnesses.

"We must tell all nations of this. Nothing like today has been since the world began and all present shall bear witness to it. Let us go to the Temple!" with which he led the disciples from the room.

In the street they encountered a great throng of people, most of them attracted by the extraordinary commotion emanating from the house. They were pilgrims attending the feast and came from all the countries known to Rome. Anxious to learn what was happening, they accosted the disciples as they emerged, bombard-ing them with questions from all sides and in everyman's tongue. The disciples had each surrendered to the Holy Spirit and allowed it to speak through them. So they were empowered to dispute and debate, and relate with everyone regardless of their language or dialect.

Some asked each other, "Are we drunk that we all hear in our own tongue the pronouncements of these simple country folk?" and all the way to the Temple the crowd streamed, wondering and marvelling at what they heard.

Peter protested when someone suggested it was wine that caused such loquaciousness.

"Why these men are not drunk as you suppose, not at this hour. They are manifesting the pouring out of God's Holy Spirit as foretold by the prophet Joel, when he said, 'In the last times, your young men will see visions and your sons and daughters will become prophets and old men shall dream dreams. Then will wonders be seen in heaven and signs on earth and those who call on the name of the Lord will be saved'."

The press of the crowd approaching the Temple was so great that the two women decided to withdraw and make their way directly to Miriam's home to prepare for their journey, and they were struck by the frequency with which they encountered small units of soldiers, who seemed to be at every road intersection or square. Twice they saw men seized and roughly handled before being released and they were thankful that Brutus and Marc were many hours away from Jerusalem.

"Nor have they been captured, as they would have called off the search once they had seized our men," said Mary.

Miriam gave the arm she was holding a squeeze, so close did she feel to her companion, and rejoiced at their shared interest.

"Our men, that sounds wonderful to my ears," said Miriam, her eyes misting perceptibly so that Mary was drawn to kiss her.

When they reached home only Naomi was resting. She had felt too distraught at the happenings of the past weeks to accompany the men to the Temple, and was glad of the diversion of helping them with the preparations for tomorrow's journey.

Simon and Alexander returned many hours later, both were tired and pensive. It was only after some refreshment and a considerable period of reflection that they could be drawn to talk of their experience.

"It's quite incredible at the Temple today. There's an air of excitement every-where and great crowds of people around each of the disciples, all of whom are expounding in great depth on Jesus being the Messiah, the fulfilment of the covenant God made with Abraham, Isaac and Jacob," said Simon sombrely.

"Their familiarity with the scriptures and the Prophets is uncanny. They are quoting from all the books of the Torah, so that even the priests are confounded. Nobody can defeat them in argument. Where have they found this skill at debate, it was never in evidence before?" asked Alexander, his tone indicating his bewilderment.

"Had you been with the followers this morning, you could not but have known. We were witnesses to something incredible, unworldly," said Miriam. "I can only believe it to be as Peter says, the coming of the Holy Spirit as promised by Jesus."

They then recounted all they had seen that morning and when they had finished there was total silence in the room for some minutes before Alexander said, "That explains why they were pouring water on the foreheads of so many in the Temple court and saying 'I baptize you with water, receive the Holy Spirit.' We saw it hundreds of times and wondered what it signified."

"I think it will be the initiation for anyone who wishes to follow Jesus from now on," said Mary, "that and repentance," placing emphasis on the last word.

"We are certainly living at a momentous time. The implications for the wider world I can only guess, but this new teaching will leave little of our familiar world untouched. It will sweep old values away and I only hope it replaces them with something as enriching and worthy," said Simon doubtfully.

For some time they discussed the merits of the new teaching of Jesus. Mary and Miriam were the main protagonists of the new; Simon and his son, doubting and unconvinced, defended the old. Naomi, adhering to the traditional Jewish woman's role, kept her thoughts to herself and prepared their evening meal.

No one was eating in the Palace of King Herod. All night he had been consumed with impatience awaiting the centurion being thrown bound at his feet. He could not countenance failure. They had to be hiding in the city and would be found.

When food was brought to him he dashed the platter to the ground and glared balefully at anyone who thought to eat,

"We'll banquet soon enough when those Romans are in my dungeon," he insisted and was assured by all the sycophants who surrounded him, that they were quite happy to wait.

As the morning passed gnawing doubts began to assail him and, however determinedly he pushed them away, reasserted themselves more strongly with each passing hour. Nobody dared to approach him as he paced the floor of his audience chamber except for a slave, constantly replenishing his cup with wine.

The tension became unbearable even for Herod, and about mid afternoon he suddenly called, "Chancellor, inform Pontius Pilate that we will attend him at Fort Antonia in one hour. Tell him we are singularly unimpressed with the failure of the search so far, and wish for a complete reappraisal of the measures he has taken."

The chancellor bowed, called a scribe to write the message, and dispatched a messenger with great urgency. He returned shortly, with a verbal answer that Pilate would receive them at the fourth hour of the afternoon.

"Why hasn't every house of the city of David been entered and scoured by now?" ranted Herod. "It's probable they are holed up in some stinking hovel there, but our illustrious Prefect hasn't the stomach to do a thorough search."

"Maybe we can persuade him of the necessity. The measures he has taken so far have failed miserably, your highness," fawned his chancellor.

The chair bearers being assembled, Herod and his advisors set off on the ten-minute walk to the fort. The crowds in the street were pressing closely on the cocooned king and lifting the curtain, he was frightened by their proximity.

"Clear them away!" he shouted at the captain of his guard, a young nobleman named Phinehas, who had no experience of crowd control.

Nervously Phinehas drew his sword and pushing his way to the front of the procession, gestured with his weapon for the crowd to clear out of their way. Those immediately in front moved a little to the side, only to be forced back by the press around them, isolating the captain from the remainder of the party. Panicking, he was about to strike out with his sword when he found his arm seized by a smiling, giant of a man. The sword was plucked from his hand only to immediately disappear into the crowd.

"You won't be needing that!" said Peter. "You can't cut your way through. Who is your illustrious passenger to venture out at such a busy hour? Is it some noble-man, who has left his sacrifice to the last minute?"

Phinehas made no reply. He knew he had been made to look a fool and that nothing he said would change it. The crowd was good-natured and lacking in menace, but had the guard and litter bearers completely hemmed in. From where he stood, head and shoulders above those around him, Peter could not reach the enclosed litter.

"See who's inside, Stephen," he called, "and where he's intent on going?"

Stephen pulled back the curtain to find his eyes met by the fear filled eyes staring from the ashen face of King Herod, who was nearly hysterical with fear. Dropping the curtain Stephen called back, "It's the king of Galilee and he looks most unhappy."

"King Herod is on his way to visit the Prefect of Judaea at the fort," stuttered Phinehas, "and I charge you to see he comes to no harm."

"Then we had better provide him with a proper escort!" said Peter pointedly and over the heads of those before them he called loudly, "make your way to Fort Antonia. Pass the word on, all are to head for Fort Antonia."

Swiftly the word spread and as those more remote passed it on, the pressure eased, and then miraculously the crowd started to move along the street. Soon it was moving at a good walking pace and the guard had regrouped around Herod.

The high walls of the fort loomed up and Peter could see the urgent activity of the soldiers as they became aware of the crowd surging towards them. A double row of bowmen appeared along the battlements and the situation looked menacing.

"Sing!" roared Peter, "Sing the psalm of David!" and he started chanting,

> "The Lord is my shepherd;
> How can I lack anything?
> He gives me a resting-place
> Where there is green pasture:

Everyone took up the chant and Legate Venestus, who had ordered out all available troops, visibly relaxed as the tension ebbed out of the confrontation. By the last verse,

> "All my life thy loving favour pursues me,
> Through the long years the Lord's house
> Shall be my dwelling-place,"

a vocal crowd of many thousand was spread out in front of the walls of the fort.

One of the large doors opened, and the Prefect and Venestus appeared as Herod's procession moved raggedly towards them. Peter could see within the massed squadron of mounted cavalry, and wondered how close they had been to a terrible massacre as the party entered the gate and it closed heavily behind them.

He knelt and praised God for their deliverance and all those without did likewise.

Within, there was no praise to God for Herod's deliverance, only vituperation as the various parties started to apportion blame for the sequence of miscalculations and failings that had so nearly led to complete disaster.

Not that Herod was in a condition to say anything, having been reduced to a state of nervous collapse by the imagined dangers enveloping him throughout. He hadn't dared to draw back the curtain and peer out, knowing his guards were completely ineffectual and that his well being depended on the good will of the crowd. Some one looking at him might have remembered a relative languishing forgotten in his dungeon, or over zealously questioned by his jailers. His lack of scruple had made him vulnerable to a multitude of vengeance seekers, so he had remained hidden throughout.

In Fort Antonia, and in the security of a room Venestus placed at his disposal, his spirit gradually revived and with it his foul temper, fanned by the frustration of the day, flamed out of control. Soon he was demanding of the Legate, of Tribune Tibullus and half a dozen centurions the reason the riot hadn't been put down by force.

"My life was in danger throughout, but not one of you attempted to free me from that mob," he remonstrated. "Where is the Prefect? Is he so unconcerned for my safety that he doesn't think to send an escort of soldiers when the city is rioting?" He paused for a moment, partly to catch his breath, but also to allow his audience to reply.

At that moment Pilate stalked into the chamber attended by three advisors. He greeted Herod civilly, although inwardly he was seething, as he had heard the king's tirade. He signalled to everyone to be seated and then expounded on the purpose of the meeting.

"We are all disappointed with the failure of this search so far. We wish to hear what strategy and what disposition of troops has been used, and what additional measures are intended as we seem to be getting nowhere?"

Legate Venestus was the first to reply.

"Sir, we have deployed fifteen hundred men around and within Jerusalem. Every road is covered, every street and square in the city. The Temple court is infiltrated with soldiers who have served with centurion Brutus and had he ventured out of doors, he would have been arrested long ago. We therefore assume they are holed up in a safe house and have not risked moving outside."

"Have you no idea where they might be hiding?" asked Pilate.

"No sir, none!" emphasised Venestus.

"We had a lead, as they have rooms in the old quarter with an elderly Jewish couple. We posted observers to watch the house, but regrettably King Herod's guards broke into the house, and finding no one there seized and interrogated some of the neighbours. Now of course they know of this and our best lead has been squandered."

Pilate looked questioningly at Herod.

"Is it true your men acted independently and raided the house of this Jew?"

A discomfited Herod nodded affirmation.

"But you are outside your jurisdiction. Mine is the only authority for raids on the houses of citizens in Jerusalem," said Pilate reproachfully.

"We had already interrogated this Jew once before, and you made no objection to our acting independently then!" snarled Herod defensively.

"If you mean that abortive expedition of Phallu, and those others who were killed around Bethany, it ought to have dissuaded you from acting independently altogether!" replied Pilate.

Venestus and Tibullus exchanged concerned glances and the Legate felt obliged to ask the question on both their minds.

"Excuse me, sir. What expedition is this King Herod sent these men on? We thought those that were murdered were the king's ambassadors and escort! Now are we to understand that in some way they were acting on information extracted from centurion Brutus' former landlord?"

There was such innuendo in the Legate's question, neither ruler knew what reply to make. The silence seemed to drag on interminably then was broken by Herod.

"My men were sent to find the centurion and his slave. I had some questions I wanted to put to them before they disappeared."

"Do you mean they were to return with your men to Jerusalem? To be questioned?"

"Of course, I mean they were to attend me! Do you think the king of Galilee is going to ride after an insolent centurion and his thieving slave?" snarled Herod.

"And what if they were disinclined to return with your men?" asked Venestus quietly.

Pilate tried to intervene as he saw he was compromised by what was coming out into the open, but such was the intensity of the altercation, anything he said was treated contemptuously, as an irrelevance.

"Then they were to be brought back," growled Herod. "But why am I allowing you to interrogate me? You overstep yourself sir. You should learn your place!"

"This puts a totally different complexion on everything we have been doing these past ten days!" Venestus said, contemptuously turning his back on Pilate and Herod.

Seeing Firmus seething indignantly just in front of him, he said, "Adjutant, how long will it take to stand down all units and call off the search?"

Firmus beamed, his monkeyish face creasing up like a sun dried prune.

"Under an hour, sir, I can draft the order immediately."

The other officers were crowding around the Legate and his adjutant anxious to hear every nuance of what was said.

Pilate was ranting at everyone, but such was the disregard of him he might as well not have been there. To Herod it was obvious that he was a discredited commander, that their common cause was lost, and that there was no point in remaining one minute longer. Fearful and dispirited, he requested the Legate provide an escort of soldiers to see him safely returned to his palace.

"With the greatest of pleasure, sir. Centurion, will you please assemble such troops as you need to ensure King Herod returns safely to his palace," said Venestus, and such was the look of respect he received from the officer, he knew he had made the right decision and there would be no dissent within the legion.

The approach to Joppa for the Syrians and their Roman passengers was protracted but always full of interest. The coastal plain was wide and fertile with outlying farms scattered in fields of grain or vegetables, or orchards of oranges and lemons interspersed with avocado or vines. There was a euphoric feeling, having shaken free of the repressive tentacles of Temple and fort, that seemed to radiate from Jerusalem across the whole of Judaea.

Here, passers by called out a cheerful greeting or a welcome to participate in some refreshment, and there was a singular absence of things military, even to the extent that important strategic places, such as road crossings or fords across rivers, were unguarded.

"They must have drawn every available legionary into the search," said Brutus, "no wonder those horsemen took a great interest in us, actually moving away

114

from the field of action. Do you think we were a bit hard, removing their footwear and giving them such a long walk back?"

"I think they will consider themselves fortunate. It was a brilliant ploy to deter them from coming after us," laughed Marc.

The suburbs of the city were closing around them now, and low buildings lined the road on both sides with only occasional breaks where field or wood approached close. The sun hanging in a cloudless sky drew them westward, and the heat was more easily endured.

Passing a pleasantly situated inn overlooking a large pond, Brutus suggested to the driver that he wished to stop for refreshment, and would like all to join with them. After nine hours on the road this was greatly welcomed and the innkeeper was very attentive, seating them in shade around the pond, while his wife and daughter baked some freshly netted fish over a fire.

Comfortably lying back on cushions and surveying the preparation of their meal, the centurion was expressing his indebtedness to his Syrian friends. They in turn were dismissing all suggestion that they had acted courageously or placed themselves at risk, when their self-congratulatory talk was silenced by the pounding hooves of a hard-driven horse.

They listened in total silence as the horse approached the inn at a gallop and passed. Just as they relaxed, they heard the rider call and draw back hard on his mount's bridle and then the slow, measured pace of his approach to the inn.

Exchanging glances and with a few hand signals to the escort, the fugitives sidled off into the deep shadow of some nearby outbuildings. They watched the innkeeper followed by the soldier approach the seated Syrians to converse briefly, then, they were all excitedly on their feet embracing one another, as the driver sprinted over to where they were hiding.

"The search is off!" he greeted them ecstatically. "The Legate has stood all troops down and the hunt for you is off."

Brutus and Marc looked at each other in disbelief. They had become so used to being fugitives that they couldn't grasp the reality of this change in their fortunes. They recognised the soldier as one they had earlier held captive, but he held out his arm in salute as he approached them and said, "I'm detailed to the fort at Joppa, to tell them that the manhunt is stood down. Couriers have been dispatched to all garrisons and you are no longer at risk of arrest from any Roman."

Brutus pressed him regarding the circumstance of this change in their fortunes, but the soldier knew nothing.

"I have only seen the signed order of the Legate, but from what you have told us I guess our commanders have challenged Pilate on the validity of the whole exercise."

Brutus and Marc were overcome with joy, as were the Syrians. The innkeeper realised the mood had become celebratory, and brought out a skin of his best wine. When the soldier remounted to continue to Joppa he had a distinctly bemused look on his face. His seat in the saddle seemed less than secure, and it was with regret that he took his leave.

An animated discussion of the best course of action in the altered circumstance followed.

"There is nothing for us to collect from Joppa," laughed the driver, "all our supplies are brought in through Caesarea. We would have had real trouble if we had been seriously challenged as we left Jerusalem. Perhaps after the arduous days searching the wilderness, a rest day would be in order. We'll camp here two nights and explore the locality. It will give our commander a chance to catch up with us and maybe we'll be ordered to return directly to our base at Capernaum," he smiled at Brutus, slightly anxious in case they were thought to be malingering.

"We too will stay here the night and find the ship tomorrow. I was anxious to sleep onboard but there is now no urgency." said Brutus.

"Can't we await Miriam's family tomorrow, and all travel the last bit together?" pleaded Marc, "that was the original plan."

"No Marc, although we no longer need to hide on the ship, there are an amazing number of preparations to make for a sea voyage. We must leave at the crack of dawn."

"What sort of things?" asked Marc, dejectedly. "I didn't think we sailed for two or three days."

"Oh it will take us two days to find our sea legs," said Brutus innocently, "and then there are the ship's biscuits."

"The ship's what?" exclaimed Marc. "Biscuits!"

"Ship's biscuits are always riddled with weevils that have to be got rid of."

Marc was regarding the centurion with both alarm and disbelief.

"What are weevils and what are they doing in biscuits we'll be eating?" he asked anxiously.

"They're little brown bugs, usually hundreds of them in each barrel. What they do is lay eggs in the biscuits. When you've recovered from the seasickness a few days out from port, and you're dying of starvation, all there is to eat are these biscuits."

He paused for a minute looking very solemn, but had to turn his face away, towards the Syrian who was also listening avidly,

"Well then you open up the barrel and find the biscuits are all crawling with these maggots that have hatched from the eggs."

Marc's face had been a picture of spellbound repulsion, but there was something in the tone of the centurion as he barked out the last words, and a sudden gleam reflected in the eye of the Syrian, that made Marc move closer to observe them more critically. What he saw made him push the centurion so violently he rolled over backwards, his guffaws of unconstrained mirth shattering the quietness.

"What about a rat hunt while you're about it?" shouted Marc realising how completely he had swallowed everything, "there will be at least one big, brown, Roman rat to get rid of before he lays eggs in the biscuits," pummelling away at the cowering centurion.

"Syrians, to my aid!" called Brutus plaintively, "have you brought me so far, and risked so much, to see me beaten to death by this boy?"

When he saw how little succour he would get from the laughing Syrians, he threw up his arms in mock surrender, to find Marc's arms thrown around his neck, his assailant nearly collapsing with the laughter that shook his body. They lay there quite some minutes as the laughter quieted.

"Do you realise, Marc," said Brutus ruefully, "how long it is since we last had such a laugh? Staying alive has been a pretty serious business for a while, but let's hope that's behind us now."

"Do you think Herod will leave us alone now?" asked Marc.

"No, Herod will never let up. Nor do I believe Pilate will forgive me defying him. We still need to sail as planned, but for me it's wonderful that my former friends and comrades are no longer hunting us."

CHAPTER EIGHT

Early the next morning, Simon, Alexander and Miriam rode their eager horses accompanying a large, lumbering, covered wagon, pulled by a matching pair of drays. The wagoner was a well-built young man named Tobit. Mary Magdalene, seated beside him, thought of her recent role on the descent to the Jordan, and chuckled at her urge to tell her young companion he had a deputy should he have need.

They carried a few boxes of provisions and skins of water for the long, hot day ahead. The train of mules carrying goods purchased by Alexander had left the city at first light and they thought to catch it up about midday.

The men rode ahead, often leaving the road to wander to one side or the other for diversion, but Miriam stayed close to the wagon for the companionship of her friend. Finding it difficult to converse over the noise of the horses and the rumble of the wagon's wheels, she tied her horse to the rear board and squeezed onto the driver's bench.

Although Tobit had been to their house on many occasions, delivering or collecting in connection with some commercial enterprise, Miriam had never really noticed him. Now in the close proximity of the driver's seat, her youthful nature could not be constrained, and she eagerly chatted concerning everything that caught her eye.

Alexander, giving his horse a chance to gallop, disturbed a flock of partridge which noisily rose into the air, wheeling and cawing until the cart was past before agitatedly settling back on the scrub.

"Oh do you know what they are?" cried out Miriam excitedly.

"Rock partridge," said Tobit, "they will have chicks somewhere, hugging the ground like mottled pebbles until the danger is past."

The mention of pebbles reminded her of the nickname that Marc had thought to give her when Peter had carried her in his arms, and her heart leapt in her breast at the thought of seeing him at the journey's end.

"Do you know all the birds?" she asked innocently.

"Some," replied Tobit mischievously, "especially those that are good to eat. Next month we will be netting quail as they fly north, the same as fed our forefathers when they fled Egypt."

Miriam was just about to remonstrate with him, when he pointed to the high hills to the north.

"Look," he said, "there is the king of them all, the Golden Eagle!"

Both women gasped with the grandeur of the vision, highlighted by the sun's rays reflecting off the spectacular spread of the eagle's wings, as effortlessly it circled slowly, urged heavenward by the alchemy of hot sun on bare rock.

"How wonderful, to soar in the sky by just spreading one's arms out like this!" cried Miriam, extending both arms wide and smiling ecstatically.

Tobit, looking up in some surprise, noticed how her simple blue tunic-dress drawn tightly across her body, emphasized her developing breasts, and averted his eyes modestly.

Alexander rode over. Out of the corner of his eye he had caught the gesturing of his sister and was curious to establish its cause.

"Look at that splendid eagle, Alex, I've never seen one before," breathed Miriam reverently.

Alexander followed it for some minutes, then said, "Remember little sister, it's also the badge of the Roman legions and therefore an emblem of our servitude."

"That's typical of Alexander," said Miriam reproachfully as he rode away, "he has no poetry, he's always so practical. My brother Rufus is the poet. His spirit would have flown up into the sky on the eagle's wing."

Tobit felt himself drawn to this spontaneous girl, who refused to be subdued by her brother's cloddishness.

"Alexander is just like my brother Thomas, always both feet firmly on the earth stopping his imagination from soaring," he said. "We were all amazed when he threw in his job and became a follower of this Jesus, the miracle worker."

Both women started with excitement and Mary cried out, "Why I know him well. He's one of the twelve, and I've seen him very many times as I too am a follower."

"He's my twin," said Tobit, "but you wouldn't know it we're not at all alike in appearance, but we're very close and do a lot together, or did, he isn't around much ever since he joined the Galilean. After the crucifixion he was in a very bad way." Tobit stopped, uncertain how much he could say to these women, but one look at their totally absorbed faces reassured him and he continued,

"He was filled with self loathing and thought he was a coward. He fled, along with the other disciples, when Jesus was seized and couldn't find the courage to go to the hill of execution. He stayed home all day like a frightened, caged animal, fearful and inconsolable."

Hearing a sob Tobit glanced at Miriam, her unchecked tears imparting a lustre to her large, dark eyes. Mary put a comforting arm around her, and watching them he became aware of some deep involvement at which he could only guess.

"You weren't there?" he asked. "Not at the actual crucifixion I mean?"

"Oh yes we were both there, although we never knew each other then," said Mary.

"So you know Jesus was dead when he was taken off the cross?" asked Tobit nervously.

"Yes he was dead for sure. Why do you ask?"

"Well Thomas heard a few days later that Jesus was alive, and had appeared and talked to some of his followers. Thomas said he wouldn't believe it unless he thrust his finger into the holes made by the nails and his hand into his side. For four or five days he was so distraught I could no longer bear to be in the house with him. Finally I bundled him into this wagon and drove him to one of the houses where the followers meet, and left him there. I drove away, angry with myself that I could say or do nothing to help him."

"What happened next?" asked Miriam.

"Thomas won't say what actually happened and just clams up when asked. But he came back to us a changed man and declared his Lord had conquered death."

119

"How wonderful to hear, and even more so as we both know it's true!" cried out Miriam with joy, clapping her hands together excitedly.

The pair of horses pranced and snorted as they caught her excitement, and it took Tobit a few minutes to calm them, while Simon and Alexander hovered anxiously close by.

"Miriam, let's walk a while alongside the horses," said Simon dismounting and placing the reins across his arm. "It's obvious something has disturbed them and we don't want them to bolt as we start our descent."

Miriam climbed down and walked demurely alongside her father, having given Tobit a conspiratorial smile and shrug as she climbed down.

"Pull off the road just there!" called out Tobit, pointing at a bare rocky area just ahead. "A mounted column of soldiers is approaching fast, and we don't want to be descending the narrow path when they need to pass."

"Well spotted, driver, that would be very awkward," called out Alexander as they moved over and waited. They all stood watching the column close on them and Miriam felt her heart pounding so strongly, she was afraid of fainting.

"Oh papa, I'm so afraid for Marc and the centurion. Do you think this means they've been taken?" she cried out overwrought with anxiety.

"I'll find out," said Simon, ordering Tobit to break open a skin of water and a case of dates.

As the leading centurion came abreast, he reined back his well-lathered stallion and brought the column to a halt, looking enquiringly at them.

"Excuse me officer, we have been many hours on the road from Jerusalem and feared from your urgent approach that some danger might lie ahead," Simon said, adding ingratiatingly, "would you and your men care to partake of some refreshment?"

The commander was aware of his troops eagerness to be back in their quarters, after so many days and nights searching the Judaean wilderness. However they would have to stop soon, and there isn't a soldier in the world who happily declines a free meal. With a smile he dismounted, followed by his eager troops, to sit in the shade of the wagon and share out the bread and dates and quench their thirst.

"I can assure you, sir, there is no trouble awaiting you ahead. We ride hard because of our eagerness to be back in our barracks in Joppa, after this futile search we have all been engaged in," said the centurion.

"Futile? I heard you had caught many zealots, so why futile?" queried Simon.

"Well that part of the operation was successful but there was a second objective to the search, which we only heard last night has been abandoned."

"Do you mean more fugitives have fled beyond Judaea?" asked Simon.

"I doubt if they have fled, more likely holed up somewhere. No, it's a mystery, but our high command has lost all interest in pursuing them further. It must be a political decision but it means we are now stood down and glad of it."

"I rejoice for you, commander, and wish you a peaceful return," and raising his hand in salute, Simon took his farewell to rejoin his family. He had to constrain himself until the departure of the cavalry, before he felt free to tell them his eagerly awaited news, its impact on Miriam causing some concern as she nearly swooned, so overwhelming was her relief.

In a mood of euphoria Miriam and Mary resumed their seat chatting excitedly until they calmed enough to ask Tobit to continue his story.

"I don't think there is much more. Oh, just one thing that might interest you. My brother has a long scroll of parchment, on which he is writing all the sayings of Jesus from when he first joined, all the time he has been with him. He keeps it in a large jar and seals it with wax whenever he leaves home. Thomas says without this, the words he spoke to his disciples might become altered or forgotten, and he has sworn us to guard it for him while he is away. He sometimes reads from it in the synagogues, even going as far away as Capernaum, but that can lead to trouble with the Sadducees and Pharisees."

"What a shame they remain so blind and so deaf to his words," said Miriam sadly, "but one day they will have to listen!"

Just then her ears heard her name being called faintly on the breeze. Looking ahead she saw a horse galloping towards them, and clinging to it a youthful apparition trying to wave both arms simultaneously and shout at the same time. The tears of joy blinded her as she peered into the sun. She knew it was Marc, and every second as she brushed the tears away with her hands, he drew nearer.

Finally the wagon stopped. Blindly she moved to the edge of the seat and reaching out her hands, felt them clasped securely in those that she loved so much. Suddenly everything became a blur, and the sky wheeled and rocked as she fell into his eager arms and heard faintly his echoing words, "Miriam my love, I'm here and it's all over!"

The Levant

CHAPTER ONE

At the inn all the elements were in place for a memorable evening. The two Romans reunited with the women they cherished, rejoiced at being able to relax their vigilance for the first time in many days. A kid goat enticingly turned on a spit over a charcoal fire, its sweet fragrance competing with the smell of freshly baking bread permeating the large dining room, which throbbed as Jew, Syrian and Roman celebrated victory over the malign designs of Herod and Pilate.

The Syrian bowmen were captivated by the pretty Jewess of whom previously they had only heard, but when they had been approached individually, and Miriam had knelt and thankfully kissed their calloused hands, there wasn't one of the battle hardened warriors who failed to take her to their heart.

"Why are we so honoured, princess?" asked the driver, urging Miriam to her feet.

Her pink cheeks suffused with a dusky reddening in response to the pounding of her joy filled heart, as she blurted out, "Because I owe everything to your courage and generosity. You are truly heroes and I will never cease to be indebted to you."

The Syrian, perhaps for the first time in his life, found himself disconcerted to be the recipient of such gratitude.

"We were never endangered, princess, and a little risk is as salt to our lives and adds savour to the drudgery of soldiering."

From that moment Miriam was 'princess' to all the bowmen, and they would gladly have taken on Herod and his henchman a hundred times as she had conscripted each man to be her champion.

Darkness descended and the room resounded to the festivity as the disparate gathering enjoyed the only feast they would ever share together. The goat was succulent and sweet and their platters were heaped with lentils and green vegetables. Simon and Alexander were enjoying the uniqueness of the camaraderie, something unknown in their more ordered and regulated lives, and there was a general feeling of well being.

Suddenly the door opened and an exultant Maas burst in, to be overwhelmed by the welcome he received as all pressed around him.

"By Jupiter your timely arrival completes our celebration!" exclaimed Brutus, and a place was rapidly made for the overjoyed Syrian at the table. Maas exchanged a few words with his men putting them at their ease, and then glancing admiringly at Miriam exclaimed, "Just in time for such a royal feast, well I count myself fortunate. My men tell me they are all captives of a certain princess."

As Miriam blushed exquisitely at his teasing Maas continued, "I think the commander should be made captive alongside his men."

Instinctively Miriam raised her goblet to her lips and averted her glowing eyes.

"Now I am truly captive," sighed Maas, and all his company cheered.

Marc, rejoicing to be seated beside his love and relishing every nuance in the exchanges between these different people, placed a protective arm around her and was rewarded by her hesitant, shy smile.

A good-natured altercation developed between Maas and Simon, as the Syrian pressed him to accept back the reward.

"My men and I feel we are no longer entitled to the reward as it was never valid in the first place," insisted Maas.

"That may be so, but had you chosen to hand your prisoners over to Herod no one would have been any the wiser, and our esteemed centurion and Marc would be languishing in a jail at the palace."

A shadow fell across Miriam's face as her vivid imagination pictured the awful consequences.

"And instead of joy in our house there would be grieving at the loss of two dear friends," Simon continued. "No Maas, nothing you can say will persuade my son and me to accept back one denarius of that which we gladly gave."

The arrival of a minstrel with harp put an end to any further discussion. His plucking of the strings varied from delicate to vigorous, and his finely modulated voice transported Marc so as to lose himself completely. He only became aware of those around him, as Miriam and her family joined in the refrain with undisguised enthusiasm. Mary Magdalene was both singing and clapping, and catching her eyes, enigmatic and inviting, he felt drawn to join in. Listening intently the Hebrew words came to him, although he knew nothing of their meaning.

"David, melekh Yisrael, hay, hay ve-kayyan."

As his voice augmented theirs, Mary's eyes lit up in mischievous delight, and when she nudged Brutus invitingly and they saw his consternation, it was as much as either of them could do to suppress an explosion of mirth.

As the applause subsided Mary hurried to translate and looking reproachfully at Brutus asked, "Why weren't you singing with Marc those stirring words 'David king of Israel, lives still?'"

Brutus declined to explain and simply asked, "King David was a great warrior, wasn't he?"

"One of the greatest," replied Mary, "and also a great poet, a fine harp player and a prophet. Many believe the second coming of David will herald the messianic age of Israel's greatness."

"That song we just sang, we learnt as quite small children," interjected Miriam. "It's a lovely song of David as a young shepherd, about Marc's age. He was inspired to challenge the champion of the Philistines as the two armies were confronting each other. Goliath was truly a giant of a man, and nobody other than David dare accept his challenge. As they strode towards their duel, the song tells of how five stones each sang out inviting David to pick them up and bear them in his pouch to the contest. Each stone claimed to be associated with some notable event in the lives of one of our Patriarchs. The refrain we sang was the story of the stones."

Miriam stopped, aware she had been talking too much, but she saw she held the attention of all these warriors, to whom tales of epic battles and heroic deeds were their very lifeblood.

"But what of the contest!" pleaded Brutus. "You can't leave us in suspense."

"Oh I'm no good at battles," demurred Miriam. "Alex, you're good at that sort of thing."

"All right, but it is quite a long story and has to be recounted as I learnt it, by heart."

This evoked evident pleasure and anticipation in his listeners, so Alexander began:

"The army of the Philistines and that of the Israelites had been manouvering for advantage for forty days, and they now faced each other from the mountains on either side of the Valley of the Terebinth.

"The Philistines had a champion, Goliath of Geth. He was ten feet in height and his bronze helmet and breastplate were all that one man could carry. Greaves of bronze were on his legs and a shield of bronze guarded his shoulders. As for his spear, it had a shaft as thick as a weaver's beam, with an iron head that weighed six hundred sicles.

"Such was the man confronting the ranks of Israel crying out, 'Here am I, a Philistine born. You that wear Saul's livery, choose one of yourselves to meet me in single combat. If he is a match for me and can strike me down, we will accept your rule. If I have the mastery and he falls, you shall accept our rule.'

"Terror fell upon King Saul and all the men of Israel and their hearts failed them."

Alexander appraised his listeners, as he refreshed himself, and saw they were following every word.

"David, son of Jesse of Bethlehem, was the youngest of eight brothers, three of whom were warriors in Saul's army. Their father sent David bearing ten cheeses, ten loaves and a bushel of flour to supply those with the army. When he reached Magala the army had raised its war cry and gone out to fight. Israel was marshalled for battle and the Philistines awaited them. So David left all he had brought and ran to the field of battle just as out came Goliath, and David heard him repeat his customary challenge. All the men of Israel were shrinking away in terror, and as David stood in awe he heard two men discussing the great good fortune awaiting the man who could overcome the Philistine.

"'King Saul can keep his great riches, and what chance of gaining the princess's hand against such a giant,' grumbled one soldier to his companion.

"David pressed them further on the rewards when his elder brother Eliat over-heard them. 'Why are you here?' he asked angrily, 'You should be minding the sheep instead of hoping to watch the battle.'

"'What wrong am I doing?' asked David, 'and is there not matter here for questioning?' and he continued asking until he came to the ears of Saul who summoned him to attend. 'There is nothing here,' said David, 'to daunt any man's spirits; I, my lord, will go and do battle with this Philistine.'

"'Why you are only a boy and Goliath is a man trained to arms from his youth,' answered Saul. But David told Saul, 'My lord, I used to feed my father's flock. If lion or bear came and carried off one of my rams, I would go in pursuit, and get the mastery, and snatch the ram from their jaws. Should they threaten me, I would catch them by the throat and strangle them. That was my way of killing them lion or bear, my lord, I would slay them and this uncircumcised Philistine shall have no better lot than theirs.'"

Rumbles of approval came from his listeners and as Alexander slaked his thirst, he realized how greatly affected were these soldiers by the story. Maas was staring fixedly into space as though hypnotized, but all other eyes were on him, breath bated until he resumed.

"'Let me defend the honour of Israel,' said David, 'shall this Philistine defy the army of the living God?'

"'Why then,' said Saul, 'go, and may the Lord be with you.'

"He girded David with his armour, helmet and sword, but so unused was the boy to the constraints of these, he disarmed and took nothing but his staff, his leather sling and the five smooth stones of which we have sung.

"The Philistine with his armour-bearer going before him looked at David with contempt. 'What,' he asked, 'do you take me for, a dog that you come to beat me with a stick?' and he cursed David in the name of his gods. 'Come close, let me give you as carrion to bird and beast.'

"'Not so,' cried David, 'though you come with sword and spear and shield, this day the Lord will give me the mastery and I will strike you down and cut off your head. I will feed the birds and the beasts with the corpses of your warriors. God rules the battle; he will put you at our mercy.'

"By now Goliath was coming on to attack David at close quarters with sword raised, his face contorted in anger and vexation.

"David felt in his purse took one of the stones and shot it from his sling. So dexterous was his whirl and so precise was his aim that the stone struck the giant on his forehead, burying itself deeply so that he fell face downwards to the earth. Running to the Philistine, David drew the vanquished man's own sword from its sheath and with it slew him, cutting off his head. As he raised the head of their champion all the Philistines fled in disarray, and with a cry the Israelites fell to slaughtering them all the way to the very gates of Acheron."

As Alexander finished there was a stunned silence and then he was engulfed in the profuse applause of his entire audience, most never having heard of this feat and excited by the intensity of its telling.

It was now very late. The Syrians took their leave to bed down in their tent. Simon and his family and a reluctant Mary followed the innkeeper to the rooms they had for the night and the Romans and Tobit bedded down on straw palisades on the floor.

"You know, father, I have never had such a splendid night in all my life. Thank you for giving me my freedom and adopting me as your son," murmured Marc drowsily as sleep overcame him.

Brutus lay reflecting on the day and wishing Mary were lying beside him, but he was aware of the necessity of observing the proprieties while with Miriam and her family.

The next morning started early with the dawn departure of the Syrians, but not before Maas had given Brutus a letter to give to his father in Antioch, should their travels take them there. The company of archers was to head to Capernaum direct, as the driver had surmised might happen.

Simon and Alexander were anxious to see how the loading of the vessel was proceeding and to establish the day of sailing, and Brutus wished to accompany them, as the boat was totally unknown to him. Mary was more inclined to seek out the synagogue, in the hopes of meeting up with someone who might have been at the Temple over Pentecost.

None of these activities held much appeal for Marc and Miriam whose only urge was to enjoy every minute of the other's company.

"Papa," said Miriam winningly, "you know mama needs a brooch to replace the one that was lost last month?"

Simon nodded absent-mindedly, as he was fitting a visit to the vintner into his schedule.

"Well, would it help you if Marc and I shopped around in Joppa to find a replacement this morning?"

Again Simon nodded encouragingly.

"What is the most you wish me to spend on it, papa, and can you let me have the money now?"

This did gain Simon's undivided attention.

"Not more than 100 shekels if it is of silver and half that if it is copper or bronze. I'll give you fifty and if you find something more expensive ask the trader to bring it to the boat this evening."

This brought a radiant gleam to Miriam's eye as she interpreted it a tacit agreement to their being free the whole day.

"Oh thank you, papa. We'll guard it safely," she rejoiced, placing the coins in her purse carefully and hurrying to finish her breakfast and explore.

"Not so fast, my girl. Make sure you have a good breakfast before you wander into town," insisted Simon, and concealed his amusement at her pretence of eating, for which she was far too excited.

Not so Marc who was demolishing the bread and goat's cheese as though he were famished, oblivious of the reproving impatience of his sweetheart.

Tobit drove the cart into the centre of Joppa, the principal square lying a quarter mile from the busy port. There was a great bustle on the road as they coincided with market day, and all the produce of the verdant coastal plain seemed to be converging on the square. Carts filled with pomegranates, melons, figs, baskets of fruit and vegetables of varying hues picked from early dawn, were vying with mules and donkeys laden with rolls of cloth, skins of leather, salted fish, wine skins, amphorae of olive oil, cheeses.

Such was the abundance that dozens of stalls over-spilled from the square into the adjoining streets and weaving around them boys were herding a few goats here, sheep and pretty young lambs there.

It was a very exciting and colourful scene, and the spirits of Marc and Miriam were leaping, disproportionate to those of their companions who were more preoccupied. Mingling with the crowd and happy to be propelled at the rate of the slowest, the two young people soon became separated from the rest of their party and as they came to the stalls hovered around each, as though they were resplendent with exquisite items gathered from the furthest corners of the world.

That the brooches, buckles, sandals, pots, candlesticks, lamps, tunics, necklaces, combs, ribbons represented the toil of honest local craftsmen meant little to them, but everything had an aura of magic originating from the fusion of their two hearts beating as one.

When Marc preened himself trying on a tunic with an exquisitely cross-stitched hem, the eager trader was disconcerted by the mirth of the little Jewess. It was a reluctant youth who rejected it with a bemused smile of sympathy and a shrug of his shoulder. They hovered some while outside the window of a silversmith who was hammering a silver dish worthy of gracing the finest banqueting table.

"Isn't that a lovely brooch, Marc?" cried Miriam, excitedly pointing to a circle of silver bordering a Star of David with a raised lamb motive in the middle. It was pinned to a measure of purple cloth and indeed looked fit for royalty.

"Do you think it would be within our price?"

"Let's find out," he said leading the hesitant girl into the gloom of the workshop.

Old Abraham looking up from his planishing, lay down his hammer and moved closer as his eyesight was becoming a problem.

"What interests you in my humble shop?" he asked gently, and stood blinking as he focussed on the young couple.

"It would delight me if I have made something worthy of adorning your pretty companion," he said bowing to Marc.

Colouring slightly, Miriam acknowledged the compliment before asking to see the brooch.

He fetched it joyfully, polishing it with a soft cloth he produced from a large pocket of his overall.

"This silver is of the finest and comes from the point of Britain that first feels the surge of the great ocean. I have worked it myself in the last few weeks between the Passover and Pentecost, to reconcile my inner conflict over a prophet, a great miracle worker who was crucified at Jerusalem."

The audible gasp from both listeners arrested him and he looked at them expectantly.

"You must mean Jesus of Nazareth?" gasped Miriam, and at her words the eyes of the old man gleamed with anticipation.

"I do, and now I rejoice because God has answered my prayers. I know you are going to tell me of him, I've had this feeling since I awoke."

"Marc and I were at the crucifixion on that awful day."

Marc could feel her hand trembling, and squeezing it reassuringly was happy to see her head rise resolutely.

"I have to tell you we both believe Jesus to be the Messiah, the son of God and that we are followers of him," she stated simply, and Marc thrilled at her brave words.

Their impact on the man was devastating. He was jumping from foot to foot and wringing his hands continuously as he nodded his head.

"Oh joy, oh heavens be praised, oh welcome, you angels. Come in and seat yourselves and tell me all," and momentarily he stopped his jumping to raise a section of the wooden bench and usher them into the tiny room adjacent to his shop.

There seated on a low divan they told their story of that fateful day. The silversmith greeted every incident with an exclamation, but when Miriam mentioned Mary having been the first person to speak to the risen Lord he was completely overcome. In the silence that followed, he brushed the tears from his eyes and kneeling at Miriam's feet took her hands in his and brought them to his forehead.

"I can see these hands giving that rejected prophet the only kindness he knew on that awful journey, and I bless you for your brave heart. This Mary, she must be a remarkable woman."

"She certainly is, truly remarkable, and she will be like a mother to me," said Marc triumphantly. This brought forth further explanations all of which agitated Abraham increasingly, especially when he realised Mary was actually at the synagogue in Joppa.

He excused himself and bringing the brooch from the shop said, "I want you to accept this from an old man to whom you have brought joyful news."

Miriam was on her feet protesting that she couldn't accept such a gift, however lovely she thought it.

"But you must, my dear, I realise now I made it only for you. The outer ring represents the wide world from where your friend originates, and parts yet to be discovered. The Star of David you already understand, and the lamb at the centre is the sacrificial lamb foretold by the prophets, the crucified Messiah.

"Please take it, it is small enough reward for your courage. I must make haste to the synagogue, I might still find Mary there," and hurrying he left two puzzled people wondering what they should do.

At the synagogue there was quite a lot of activity for midweek, and Abraham was scrutinizing the women's area for an evident stranger when his attention was drawn to the slight, youngish man at the lectern, so fervently was he addressing the congregation.

"I can say to you with certainty this is the greatest threat to face Judaism since the days of the Pharaohs. The spread of this new heresy outstrips the spread of an outbreak of plague and it is twice as deadly, although it purports to be peace loving and God fearing."

There were murmurs of anger from the many listeners and the speaker regarded them sternly until they were quiet.

"You are right to express your anger but who of you is prepared to take action? How often has God in his righteous anger brought retribution on Israel because we have not stood firm and been led astray by pagan influence? But this latest threat is more insidious and more destructive because it comes from within. For sure the Lord our God will vent his anger on Israel if we remain passive or give credibility to their spurious claims.

"Let us examine the teaching of this Jesus, the better to recognise its threat. Before he was crucified Jesus claimed to be the Messiah, the long awaited born of the line of David. That he was a powerful magician and a healer is beyond dispute, but there are many such throughout Carthage and Egypt and Mesopotamia, and they don't claim to be the Son of God."

There were murmurs of agreement and outrage before Saul was allowed to continue.

"Called to account by the Priests for a scandalous scene in the Temple court, Jesus challenged them to destroy the Temple and said he would rebuild it in three days. Such arrogance he knew could not be tested. To compound this he called the scribes and Pharisees a brood of vipers, hypocrites that swallow the property of widows. He likened them to whitened sepulchres, fair outwardly but full of dead men's bones and all manner of corruption within."

The ensuing outburst of indignation was intense and might have continued for some time had not Saul raised his hand.

"Now we come to the poison that if allowed, will fester like a cancer until it destroys us. The followers of Jesus, by stealth, took his body from the tomb and hid it, and now claim he is resurrected from the dead and has been many weeks with his followers. They attend the Temple regularly, and by their zeal and promise of eternal life have persuaded many hundreds of the more simple minded to join them. Some of them may have come from Jerusalem and be seated amongst you now, biding their time to disseminate their lies among you here in Joppa!"

Again he stopped and observed his audience looking around as though suddenly distrustful of neighbour, while calling out for some action to be taken. Saul knew it would be easy to stir them to violence, but also knew this would be counter productive to his mission at this time.

"There is only one answer and I, Saul of Tarsus, am empowered by the Sanhedrin of the Temple to implement it. We must stamp out this heresy as we are authorized by Mosaic Law, even to the extent of slaying those who cannot be persuaded to recant. If the law tells us to stone the adulteress or the unmarried maid who disgraces her family with a man, how much more justified would we be in meeting out the same to the unrepentant heretic!"

The howl of approval at these words sent a shudder through Abraham and he clutched at the pillar to steady himself. This was not what he wished to hear and yet he was appalled that the call for violence had stirred him even as he had rejected it.

Suddenly a voice rang out from among the women and Abraham saw Mary, standing defiantly, a mass of black hair surmounting her beautiful sculptured white face. He knew he was beholding Mary Magdalene and he felt his heart pounding at her fearless challenge.

"May I ask you, Saul of Tarsus, are you really wishing to see us revert to ancient Mosaic practices? That we revert again to stoning the adulteress, and the deflowered virgin? Why not raise a stake here where I stand, and burn alive any misled daughter of a priestly family who may lie with a man before marriage? That is the prescribed punishment of the patriarchs, so is this what you propose, but further to extend it to all those who testify to the fulfilment of scripture and the prophets by the resurrection of the Messiah as we do bear witness."

There was a stunned silence and then as one body the crowd was on its feet, the men hurrying to suppress this unknown harridan who had dared to challenge them so brazenly, flaunting the centuries old tradition of women's subservience.

The women nearby were no less incensed and were clawing at her to pull her down, spitting and slapping in a frenzy of outraged zeal. As Mary was submerged under the press of bodies Abraham felt his head spinning but fought to retain consciousness. Gasping, he moved to the door and wrenching it open staggered into the street.

A company of Roman soldiers escorting a supply wagon moved slowly towards him. The noise from within the synagogue had reached a crescendo and running to the alerted soldiers, Abraham urged them to intervene to stop the murder.

"If it is within your synagogue what concern is it of ours?" demurred the sergeant, who lacked the courage to tackle a riot with his handful of men.

Abraham was on his knees entreating them for the love of God as Marc and Miriam appeared around the side of the synagogue. The clamour and one look at the supplicant old silversmith alerted Marc to some crisis, and he ran to them just as the company was resuming its progress.

"They are mobbing Mary Magdalene to death in there," gasped out Abraham as blackness engulfed him.

"I Marc, son of centurion Brutus, command you to come to the aid of his wife," he cried out, drawing his sword and moving towards the bedlam.

Miriam kneeling beside the inert body of the Jew looked up and saw the soldiers hesitating.

"By the Gods you hold sacred, is your courage going to fail you now and haunt you all your lives?" she sobbed.

It was the spur they needed. Drawing their swords the half dozen of them followed Marc into the synagogue, towards the surging brawling mass of bodies. Striking out with flat of sword and hilt, they fought their way to the struggling inner core, mostly of women, whom they threw off unceremoniously to both sides until they came to the body of Mary Magdalene, unconscious and contorted lying on the blood streaked tiles.

Marc removed his tunic to cover her nakedness and straightening her battered body lay her on her side, praying to her God and to the Galilean as he had seen her do by the shore of the Sea of Salt.

The crowd, shamefaced and subdued, had now withdrawn, many of them nursing cracked heads and bloodied faces as the Romans had given some savage blows. Abraham coming in on the supportive arm of Miriam took in the whole sorry scene at a glance. Releasing Miriam so that she could go to the aid of her friend he approached the group standing apart clustered around Saul.

"I never thought to witness such a desecration of God's house," he said looking directly at Saul. "Saul of Tarsus you have the power to move people by your words but today you do the devil's work."

Saul averted his eyes, as Abraham was one of the most respected of the elders of the synagogue.

"To provoke violence on a woman who does no more than question you, is a desecration of all this synagogue stands for. Unless we call a service of atonement, cover our heads with ashes and you condemn this barbaric outburst, I will shake the dust of this place from my sandals and never enter it again."

Saul was ashen faced and shaken. He had felt he had the crowd in the palm of his hand, mouldable like clay, enjoying the feeling of power and righteousness. To find it slip away in an instant had dismayed and humiliated him. He nodded to Abraham.

"That which you condemn I accept. It is easier to fan the flames than it is to quench the fire, and this unwise woman poured oil on the conflagration."

"She whom you call an unwise woman, is the very first person in this world to see and talk to the risen Messiah after his crucifixion. It was to meet her that I hurried here from my shop."

At Abraham's declaration Saul's face contorted with paroxysms of pain and he clasped his hands over his ears. Staggering away blindly he collided with a pillar cutting his forehead.

"The prince of darkness is descending on Israel and there are few of us to challenge his tightening grip!" he cried, falling on his knees, tearing his clothes and beseeching heaven.

Abraham turned his back on Saul's histrionics dismissively, to give his support to the prostrate Mary. Marc was still praying over her, his eyes tightly closed and his lips moving silently. Miriam was kneeling wiping her bloodied face, which she was inadvertently washing with her copious tears. Abraham bent close to search for any signs of life and as he did so she opened her eyes to peer through the rapidly developing oedema. Vaguely, mistily she saw Marc in her line of vision and smiled serenely as she whispered, "Why Marc, what a diligent pupil you are. Your prayers recalled me from the edge of the pit as I thought to meet my Lord. Bless you my son," and then they closed contentedly as oblivion conquered all the pain.

The soldiers were standing around indecisively and Abraham pleaded for their further assistance.

"Have you space in your wagon to help move this woman to my humble room? It is close by but too far to carry her."

Their leader agreed and two men on each side linked their arms to improvise a litter, as they were used to doing on the field of battle. Reverently, as though acknowledging her courage, they moved to the wagon and laid her on the boards. A blanket was found to cover her and Marc retrieved his tunic. Sombrely they made slow progress through the streets to Abraham's workshop and laid her on the couch where so recently Marc and Miriam had sat entranced by the gentle silversmith.

Miriam took from her purse the silver brooch and held it out to Abraham.

"The whole world reconciled to the Lamb of God through the Star of David … can it be possible?"

"Only in God's own time, my daughter. And through those who suffer and hold fast to their faith," was his ardent reply.

It took Marc some while to find the *Medusa* and he was relieved to see the centurion among the throng loading the ship. Calling above the hubbub he caught Brutus's attention and by his gestures conveyed the urgency of his mission.

One quick word with Simon, and he was pushing his way past the stevedores his face betraying his anxiety. As he came up to Marc and saw his bloodied tunic and overwrought face Brutus braced himself for some crisis but for the first time in his life was totally overwhelmed as Marc told him all that had happened. He staggered and had to lean for support on his son, seized by uncontrollable rigors and unable to breathe or move. The blood surged to impair his vision as his heart pounded and filled his chest with pain.

Marc anxiously held him by the arm and felt the rigidity of his muscles, iron hard and immovable, as had the soldier on the way to the cross when he had tried to seize Miriam.

With a shudder the paroxysm passed and the centurion started to come to grips with the crisis.

"But Mary is alive?" he demanded.

Marc nodded reassuringly, but nothing could erase the anxiety etched on his features.

"How badly is she hurt?"

"Quite badly I fear. We only just got there in time thanks to Abraham."

"Who is this Abraham?" asked Brutus.

"Let me tell you on the way."

"Only after I've told Simon, he must be able to help us find a good physician, and I want her to have the best there is."

Simon had joined them by now aware of some crisis. Hearing what had happened, the colour drained from his face and he was momentarily overcome. Quickly his practical nature asserting itself, he left to consult the port captain calling out as he departed,

"Make sure Miriam stays with you until we get there. I fear such violence is but a foretaste of what is to come!"

Brutus and Marc hurried off and found quite a gathering on the street outside the silversmiths. Entering they were initially unable to see in the gloom, to where Miriam and an older woman were bathing Mary's abused body and rubbing in ointments, the fragrance of which suffused the room.

"How is she, Miriam?" asked Brutus with a catch to his voice, his distress threatening to overcome him.

Both eyes were closed and her face appeared inflated like a blown up bladder. Scratches and weals covered her cheeks, her limbs and her torso, and everywhere bruises were beginning to discolour her exquisite whiteness.

"Oh my brave dear heart," cried the centurion holding one limp hand to his lips and kneeling before her, tears running unchecked down both cheeks, his frame wracked by his sobs. With a glance at each other the two women left the room, closing the door behind them.

"We cannot share his grief, and it will do Mary no harm if we cease our ministration for five minutes," said Judith, a kindly neighbour upon whom the widower had increasingly come to rely in many ways over the years

Shortly Brutus came from the room and thanked the women for caring for Mary before he approached Abraham saying, "Mary is my wife and I thank you for all you have done for her, but for you I think she would be dead. Now someone must be called to account for this unjustified attack. Who instigated this violence?"

Abraham was silent while the centurion fidgeted restlessly. Finally he said,

"In all honesty I don't know. I heard and saw everything but still I don't know. Saul of Tarsus sowed the seeds when he incited the listeners to be prepared to apply Mosaic Law to Jesus' followers, but he wasn't aware of Mary. Then when she challenged him so fearlessly, all hell broke loose, and I think fear is the underlying cause of all that followed. Fear for our traditions as new teaching supersedes the old. Fear of losing those privileges we have enjoyed for millennia of being a chosen people, the elect of God, and finally the fear of the power of the cross. We can't accept that our obduracy deafened us to the messenger of God and we put the Messiah to death. All these things have to be faced sometime, but until then fear will never be far away, and its inevitable destructive consequences."

Brutus looked cheated and paced the room indecisively, as every instinct called for some physical resolution.

Abraham placed a hand on his arm.

"My friend, and I hope I can call you that. Your son and his sweetheart are the promise of the future. A Celt in love with a high born Jewess. You and Mary Magdalene, a Roman centurion with a Jewish wife, you are all part of a changing world. Listen to the teaching of him who brought you together. Reject vengeance and grow in the spirit, or embrace it and wither. I have never witnessed such bravery as that shown by Mary today, but I think I saw in her that which came from her Lord."

The outer door opened to admit Simon and a tall heavily built man who announced himself to be Lucas, a physician of the Greek school. He was very striking with deep set searching eyes peering from behind a hawkish nose, the whole surmounting a bushy, jet-black full set of whiskers, hiding everything below his alertly questioning eyes and his cheekbones. Only these eyes depicted whether

135

he was smiling or frowning, happy or anxious, confident or worried, pleased or angry. At this juncture he was a mixture of all the latter sentiments and he insisted that he and Judith be left alone to examine the patient.

It was a full half-hour before they emerged, Lucas exuding confidence and Judith a quiet satisfaction. Instinctively addressing Brutus he expressed himself in short, curt sentences.

"Remarkable woman! Incredible beating, can't remember worse! No lasting injury as no bones broken or organs ruptured! Good pulse, brave heart! Soon be better! Plenty of rest! Be liberal with the ointment and keep her cool! Plenty to drink and she can eat what she wants! Not to get up from her bed until I visit tomorrow!"

With that he bowed and departed leaving his stunned yet relieved listeners hardly able to believe he was gone.

"What an incredible man," breathed Miriam, seizing Brutus and hugging him with relief, "where did you find him, papa?"

"Through the port captain. He looks after many sick or injured from the boats and is renowned throughout the ports around the Great Sea."

"Well he has certainly impressed me and gives me confidence she will recover. I cannot thank you enough for your help," declared Brutus.

"The Lord be praised," sang out Abraham dancing from foot to foot and beaming at every one in turn.

"Of course she'll have to stay here until she is better. Judith will watch her through this night and we'll make other arrangements tomorrow. One of my friends will find me a bed and I'll hammer no silver while she's here, but instead I'll find out everything she can tell me about Jesus. The Lord be praised," at which he started another little dance

They decided to base themselves at the inn where they had celebrated the previous night, although now there was no celebration, only tense and urgent debate of their altered situation.

Each stated his position in turn, hoping to reconcile their individual priorities and arrive at a common course of action.

Alexander told them the *Medusa* was nearly loaded and would sail in two days, and he could not delay as there was important business he must attend to.

Brutus and Marc agreed it would be at least a week before they could think of continuing, perhaps longer depending on Mary's recovery. Miriam would have loved to remain in Joppa, but had no choice other than to accompany Simon, who stated his intention to return home the day after next. He was aware of how the faces of the youths fell at this pronouncement, but he was anxious to get back to Naomi, and unsympathetic to his daughter's wish for a greater independence.

He said, rather brusquely, "At least you are not as threatened here as you might be. Herod had an agent based here to levy taxes on the merchants, but no longer as most commerce has moved to Caesarea up the coast. He will still have his spies, they are everywhere, so don't be lulled into a feeling of false security."

"Thank you. Your warning is timely, and after today I will be constantly on guard. It is easy to relax vigilance when one threat recedes not realizing another is looming from an unexpected quarter. Tomorrow I will see the local commander and acquaint him with all that has happened and the reason his troops were hunting us around Jerusalem."

Alexander quickly urged, "You must also meet the port captain as he is the best contact to find an alternative ship when you are ready. His name is Ephraim and for many years he sailed his own coaster, but the Romans thought he was supplying arms to the zealots along the coast and one of their galleys rammed and sank it."

"Was he?" asked Brutus.

"Supplying arms? Who knows?" replied Alexander. "He doesn't admit to it openly."

Brutus smiled at the unspoken inference and wondered if this Ephraim would be a reliable ally.

The following morning everyone made an early visit to the house of Abraham. Judith was busying herself heating a broth over the charcoal fire.

"Go in a couple at a time," she said, "but be brief as this is the first time Mary has awoken all the while I have been with her."

They were all subdued as they came from her room as her swelling made her appear grotesque and frightening. Nor was she able to speak much with bruised jaw and swollen lips, or see much through half closed eyes. She did however press one favour on Miriam, who tearfully agreed to return to the inn and she and Marc quickly retraced their path and delving into Mary's few possession found a small package wrapped in a piece of blue silk and tied with linen strips.

"This is what Mary calls her treasure?" queried Miriam looking at the package wonderingly as they hastened to take it to her. Lucas was with her and they had to wait in the shop with Abraham who had but shortly arrived.

"Judith has managed to get Mary to take a little nourishment," he greeted them happily, "so praise the Lord she is on the mend."

Looking at Miriam he asked reprovingly, "Why aren't you wearing the brooch I gave you? It would look lovely on your shawl."

Miriam produced it from her purse and pinning it in position asked his forgiveness.

"Truly I'm sorry. I do love it and am really grateful. I just was so preoccupied with leaving tomorrow and Mary's plight I have hardly thought about anything else."

"Understandable my dear," smiled the silversmith patting her hand, "but life must go on, you must make the most of the little time you have together."

Looking at Marc conspiratorially he suggested, "You should go to the ruins of the old Phoenician Fort which has a wonderful view across the bay and the coastal plain to the Judaean hills. Take a picnic as there is no-one there to sell you any refreshment."

Miriam blushed exquisitely, but the suggestion sown like a seed quickly grew and she left the package with the old man as they blithely departed.

He smiled happily to himself, as Brutus was too preoccupied to be any companion.

Lucas coming from the sick-room, fell instantly into his brusque way of talking. It was as though time was such an imperative that he had devised this way of giving all the necessary information as quickly as possible, thus avoiding any chance of being delayed by any protracted discussion.

"Couldn't be better! Swelling exuberant, nature's method of healing! No fever! Have confidence doing well! Come again this evening!"

Again he bowed and departed.

Even Brutus had to smile at such an amazing performance.

"Well that beats anything for bedside manner!" he said, just as Judith joined them.

"You should see him with Mary," she said, "he's so gentle and patient and kind. All the time he talks reassuringly, and Mary says his hands feel as light as the brush of a dove's wing."

"Glory be," exulted Abraham. "I'll just take in this package that Miriam left with me," although Judith knew this was a pretext for another glimpse of the woman whom she suspected he worshipped.

When he entered the gloomy room he made his way to her bed and whispered, "Mary, Miriam has given me a package for you."

He was amazed as she tried to raise herself but finding the effort beyond her subsided back on to her bed.

"Please hold it where I can see it."

He held it close and wondered greatly at the suppressed excitation her battered features were able to register.

"Now I know a little of his suffering," she murmured, "please put it under my pillow."

Mystified he did as requested and then saw that Mary was sleeping peacefully. Aware of some aura of wonder surrounding them, he knelt reverently and experienced the joy of prayer such as he had but rarely known; a wordless adoration of his God.

The garrison at Joppa was quartered in a very old building situated on a headland overlooking the harbour, the old town straggling back inland on one side and the vastness of the Great Sea on the other. Nobody could recall when the fort was built but it was constructed of massive hand dressed blocks of sandstone, no two of which were identical, but all so precisely butted together the finest wire could not be inserted between, although no mortar was used in the building.

Brutus was seated facing centurion Felix across a narrow oak table.

"I rejoice my men were to hand and responded with such promptitude to the riot. I have the report of sergeant Nathan and it appears you have a son Marc who led a spirited engagement against the mob inside the synagogue."

Brutus nodded.

"Adopted son. My freed Celtic slave who is everything that any father could wish for."

"Not in the report, but spoken of throughout the barracks is a young Jewess, companion to your son, whose words were more efficacious in propelling my men into battle than any you or I might use."

"Ah but that's for want of a pretty face! Wasn't it Helen of Troy, whose face launched a battle fleet of a thousand ships?" quipped Brutus.

"Not at Joppa while I'm in command," said Felix and both men laughed.

Their discussion of all the recent events leading to their present situation was more serious.

"Oh ensign Paulus is still suffering from blisters to his feet, sustained from a long walk without sandals in the Judaean foothills a few days ago. He's reluctant to reveal exactly how he came to be in such an unusual situation …" The question was left hanging in the air and Brutus just stared fixedly into space.

Felix agreed to provision them for their sea voyage when they were ready to go and thought their best chance of finding the right ship was with the help of Ephraim, the port captain.

"Mind you he's no Roman lover, that one, but he is good at his job and as you will be paying him, well …" Felix shrugged dismissively.

When Brutus left he was quite happy in his mind regarding the local situation. He also knew he could rely on the commander of the garrison to inform him of any developments that might threaten.

CHAPTER TWO

By the sixth day Mary was sitting up in bed much of the time, the swelling nearly gone only the residual evidence of the beating she had received showing in the yellow, blue, black, purple and green patches across face and body. Marc was moping around dejectedly, or had been until Mary had suggested to Brutus he looked flabby, and they would both benefit from an excursion into the country and lots of weapon practice.

Abraham had just received a message from the rabbi of the synagogue. They regretted that Saul of Tarsus had been called to the Sanhedrin at Jerusalem, but he had given his support for a service of atonement to be held the following day.

Enjoying the novelty of mollification, Abraham was pottering in his shop when the door burst open, yet all the daylight trying to intrude was excluded by the bulk of the man filling its frame, standing motionless for a few seconds as his eyes adjusted and then demanded with authority.

"Have you Mary Magdalene?"

Abraham affirmed she was there and the man entered and seemed to fill the whole of the shop. As he squeezed past him to close the shop door, Abraham felt a thrill at such a portentous presence enquiring after his heart's treasure. He was Mary's unquestioning slave and he relished being her temporary custodian.

"Simon Peter, fisherman and apostle of the Lord Jesus," boomed the man and Abraham had a job to contain himself, such a passion of delight seized him at beholding this apparition.

"Is that really you, Peter?" called a faint voice from the inner room.

"Who else, Mary?" called out the giant, striding to and opening the narrow door.

As he slid himself sideways through the aperture and entered the room Abraham followed expectantly. What he witnessed was a tableau of exquisite tenderness, the big man moving as daintily as a girl to kneel at the side of the bed and take the hands of the laughing, sobbing, joyous woman and smother them in his luxuriant beard.

"Oh Mary, how I grieved for you when I heard from Miriam of your injury. Brave heart, why can't you wait until I'm around before you take on the whole world?"

"I will next time, I promise," agreed Mary, "but Miriam has only been gone a few days, how can you have got here so quickly?"

"Wild horses and the closed gates of hell could not have stopped me. I walked here straight away. I wouldn't trust myself on a horse, if I could find one to take me!" he said, laughing heartily at his own joke.

"Oh Peter," cried Mary throwing her arms around his great neck, "it is such a joy to see you. But I must look such a mess?"

Peter brushed her hair from her face and with a finger wiped the tears that were coursing over her cheeks.

"You look marvellous Mary, radiant. All the colours of the rainbow, God's covenant with Noah!"

Mary laughed at his making light of her bruises, and suddenly she became aware of the third person in the room.

"Abraham, this bear is really a man. He is Peter, the first disciple of Jesus and the first amongst the apostles and our community in Jerusalem. This, Peter, is Abraham, an elder of the synagogue, a believer in Jesus, and a dear, wonderful man."

The two men embraced, or rather Abraham was engulfed, in the embrace of Peter and as he extricated himself he said excitedly, "I have just received a message from the rabbi that tomorrow they are holding a service of atonement for the brutal attack on you. Would you address the assembly, Peter, you would make a tremendous impression?"

"I'll certainly accept your invitation, we have been talking to every synagogue within a day's journey of Jerusalem and at the Temple. As for making an impression, you can be sure of that after what they did to our beloved sister Mary. Ashes, penance, fasting, all of these will not make amends for that barbaric act."

Mary was a little agitated by the vigour of Peter's chastisement of the congregation of the synagogue, and heaving herself into a changed position she dislodged the packet that had been under her pillow, which fell to the floor.

As Peter picked it up he was aware of some force that constrained him from passing it back. His fingers tingled in an unbearable ecstasy, his heart seemed to suspend beating yet the blood coursed through his body in a frenzy of excitation of limb and eye and ear. He heard the chanting of angelic choirs and the plucking of the nevel and the kinnor, the ancient harps to which David had sung his psalms. These faded and were followed by a fanfare of a hundred shofars, the ram's horns of the patriarchs, and Peter knew he was glimpsing something of 'the day of the Lord'.

All faded and suddenly he was kneeling holding a packet that had fallen off a bed. How long he had been there he didn't know, it had seemed like hours. "What is it, Mary?" he gasped, reverently holding it for her to take.

"The most precious reminder of our Lord, Peter. Do you remember the day I ran from the tomb and cried to you, 'They have carried the lord away from the tomb, and we cannot tell where they have taken him!'"

"Do I remember! James and I ran to the tomb. I entered first and then James followed and we saw the linen cloths lying there, and the veil, which had been put over Jesus' head wrapped round and round in a place by itself. That's when we realised he had indeed risen from the dead."

"After you left I stayed there weeping and then I ventured into the tomb again and saw two angels standing where the body had lain. 'Woman' they said, 'why are you weeping?' 'Because they have carried away my Lord,' I replied, 'and I cannot tell where they have taken him.'"

Abraham was kneeling on the floor in a state of rapture. Every word he heard was a divine revelation, heavenly music to his humble ears, such as he could hardly believe.

"And how were your eyes opened to the reality of the resurrection?" asked Peter, not because he didn't know but because he loved hearing Mary's testimony from her own lips.

"I turned and saw a man in the entrance to the tomb, who I took to be a gardener. 'Sir', I said, 'if it is you that have carried him off tell me where you have put him, and I will take him away'.

He said to me, 'Mary,' and I knew it was he and I simply said 'Master.'" She paused for a moment recalling exactly what had followed, as she was about to reveal her secret treasure to these two men.

"Promise to guard my secret and to reveal it to no man."

"I promise on all the Saints in heaven," said Peter but Abraham was too over-wrought to say anything except 'amen'.

Mary took a deep breath.

"As I left the tomb to come to you with his words ringing in my ears, I saw the veil that had been around his face lying where it had been placed, and I picked it up," and she held up the packet before their astonished eyes.

"Oh Mary," breathed Peter with his first exhalation for ages, "what a treasure to store in your heart."

Abraham put out a shaking finger as though to touch the packet and then hesitated and withdrew it.

"I am not worthy," he said shaking his head.

"There's not one of us worthy," echoed Peter, "the only one who is worthy is the lamb!"

As Mary started to untie the knotted strips, both men realised that yet a further revelation was forthcoming and they watched with fixed eye and baited breath. Gently she laid it on her lap and slowly drew back each corner of the blue silk square. It was as though she were peeling back the delicate petals of an exquisite orchid, knowing that the succulent heart would be more lustrous for its gradual unveiling.

The creamy white roll lay uncovered, just as she had seen it irresistibly lying in the tomb. Now, so gently the movements of her hands were barely discernible, she turned it so that the free end was on her breast and slowly began to unroll it.

No one knew what to expect and the tension was overwhelming. Abraham felt his heart yearning and breaking simultaneously, and afterwards said he died a thousand deaths, each one sweeter than the one before.

"Please Peter," said Mary when she could reach no further, and with humble reverence he unwound it until its entirety lay revealed along her full length. Initially there was a sense of anti-climax, as only a few brownish stains at the very end testified to the Lord's bloodied brow. Then Peter, responding to the urging of some inner voice, drew closed the shutters of the only window, intensifying the gloom within.

Suddenly each of them was aware of an outline etched on the creamy linen cloth and replicated along its entire length. All the prominent features of the face it had enveloped were clearly distinguishable. The round intelligent frontal bulge of the forehead, the orbital rims with the strong brow ridges, the high cheek bones, scarred on one side where struck by heavily bejewelled hand, the hawkish Semitic nose with dilated nostrils, the beautiful strong, sensitive mouth with lips parted as though still echoing "it is finished … finished … finished."

Overcome each felt the presence of the Lord in the room and would not have been surprised had the lips moved.

The impression that the veil bore was not of earthly pigment, pounded in a mortar and applied. It was an emanation, a glowing luminescence that had its elemental origin on the first second of the first day of creation. Here part had been trapped, as it had leapt the barriers of space and time, of that very spirit that binds in a unity the earth to the sky and beyond, to the sun and the stars, even to the farthest reaches of heaven and the uttermost limits of time and back again.

Three times the image was repeated as the veil had three times encircled the head.

With a sigh of unbearable regret Peter rolled up the cloth.

"The power of the resurrection has seared this veil," he said. "Show it to no one until the spirit of the Holy Ghost commands you to. Guard it well, it is the most glorious treasure the world will ever know."

Bending he picked up Abraham, who overcome had collapsed on the floor. Smiling he found room to lay the small old man beside Mary on the bed, and drew back the curtains. As the light flooded in and he looked at Mary, her battered face radiant with joy and the little man beside her, he knew they had shared one of those pivotal moments in time when things are changed never to be the same again. He knelt in prayer.

The atonement service was on the Sabbath at the fifth hour. Peter was very practised at addressing crowds in the Temple, as he and the other disciples had spoken out boldly ever since Pentecost. He was however surprised by the throng filling the synagogue to overfilling, and there was an overspill on to the adjacent street.

Entering, they were invited to take some ashes from a copper cauldron. Abraham applied them to his own forehead but Peter declined.

He said half humorously, "I might well bang a few heads together if I encounter the usual intransigence, so I will reserve the ashes for on the way out."

The service followed the usual pattern of prayer, songs and readings until the rabbi called upon Abraham to say a few words.

He rose and stood solemnly in front of the vast congregation. He closed his eyes his palms extended in prayer for a minute and then spoke quietly.

"My friends and fellow citizens of Joppa, it was I who requested an atonement service for reasons that most of you will now know all about. Earlier this week in this very court, a visiting woman from Jerusalem was attacked and but for the intervention of soldiers would, I believe, have been killed.

"This was no ordinary woman. What ordinary woman would stand up here and throw a challenging question at a visiting Pharisee? No, this was an extra-ordinary woman, not only in her rare courage but in the unique way God has revealed himself to her. It was to hear her tell of the teaching, death and resurrection of Jesus of Nazareth that I had come, hoping to speak to her here in the synagogue.

"But good can follow from evil, and the attack on Mary was certainly evil, but because of it she is now recovering in my humble house, and I have had many chances of speaking with her and shared some wondrous experiences. The greatest consequence, however, is that her friend, and the first follower of Jesus throughout his ministry, is here from Jerusalem where he is the leader of more than three thousand disciples. I ask you to attend prayerfully and in good faith to Simon Peter."

Simon stood up, and as always there was a ripple of excitement at his stature and his imposing aura of authority.

"Elders of the synagogue, citizens of Joppa and friends, I greet you all in the name of he who has sent me, Jesus of Nazareth, who has revealed himself to be the Messiah, the long awaited Son of God."

He spoke at great length about the years he had been with Jesus in Judaea and of the innumerable healing miracles he had witnessed, of bringing the dead back to life, of quieting the elements and feeding multitudes with next to nothing. This was listened to attentively but without comment.

As he moved on to the progressive conflict as Jesus threw down the gauntlet to the established religious leaders, culminating in the rout of the moneychangers and vendors in the Temple court, there were a few loud mutterings and protests, which he disregarded.

Quoting confidently from the prophets he developed the theme that everything in Jesus' lineage, his works, his humiliation and rejection, and his death and resurrection were foretold. They were there to be read in the scriptures by anyone who wasn't blinded by prejudice, or self-interest or self-importance.

At an outbreak of more sustained and intensive barracking some of the elders indicated they would wish to see Peter stopped, but under the urging of the Holy Spirit he was unstoppable.

"Now let us examine the origins of the attack on Mary Magdalene a few days ago. Saul of Tarsus was advocating stamping on us disciples of Jesus. He accused us of fabricating the myth that Jesus had risen from the dead after we had stolen his body, from under the very noses of the guards surrounding the tomb just to prevent such an occurrence. He likens us to a deadly plague, threatening to destroy Israel and our worship of God. That is why he would like to see us stamped out and stoned if we refuse to be intimidated."

He stopped and regarded scornfully the area of unrest where a small number of protestors were trying to incite a greater response from those around them.

"But the violence against Mary has its origins in a much more primitive and deeper urging than that of Saul. It was caused by one thing only, an emotion that has had its hold on every human since Adam was expelled from the garden, and that is fear, naked fear.

"For us mortals banished from Paradise, fear is a vitally important emotion to be heeded and responded to. So we live in fear of God and of incurring his wrath and in fear of sinning, or if we don't we should! So we live in fear of disease and thereby avoid the contamination that spreads leprosy. Likewise the wild animals, the lion, the bear and the wild boar, we fear and avoid. Some things we fear and can do nothing about, the tempest and the raging seas, warring nations, illness, growing old and infirm, famine. But that fear can be the spur to action, to make the best of the situation, but only if the emotion is controlled.

"Often however fear is uncontrolled and then it grips us in its coils and we become fearful. So full of fear that we lose all control. It is this fear we know if someone challenges us on our beliefs, especially those that have been enshrined in tradition. This someone the other day was Mary Magdalene and because you were in the grip of fear you fell into the sins of anger and violence."

Peter paused to allow his words to sink in. He surveyed the crowd, attentive and crestfallen. He knew the time had come to offer the olive branch.

144

"My friends, I can tell you that Mary knew fear and was tempted not to speak up against Saul. But she also knew Jesus and the importance of speaking the message he had proclaimed of love of God, and love of neighbour.

"Oh I beseech you, cast out fear. Embrace this challenge and welcome the changes that have to follow, O Israel, welcome the teaching of Jesus. Let us be the source of enlightenment to the Gentiles, a light to the whole world, God's world. We can rejoice in being God's elect, his chosen people, if we accept Jesus is the fulfilment of scripture, the Messiah, and we can be at the forefront carrying his message to the far corners of the world. I tell you the empire of Rome will be dwarfed into insignificance by that of the risen Lord, but if for us he remains rejected, a man of sorrow acquainted with grief, no more, Israel will have spurned its destiny.

"I can testify to his resurrection and to the power of the Holy Spirit that works through his apostles. Go to the Temple at Jerusalem and ask them in whose name they lay on hands to cure the sick and cast out devils. They will tell you it is in the name of Jesus, a Jew of Judaea, but the Son of God."

As Peter took time to peruse the crowd he was aware of an undercurrent of excitement. It needed only one and so many would follow. But where was that one, he searched in vain. He closed his eyes and in his vision saw the three of them, in the room at the silversmiths. He saw Mary, battered and brave, and Abraham who was holding out something for him to take. What was it? He couldn't make it out in the gloom. He threw open the shutter and as the light flooded in, he saw what it was that was being offered.

His face elated, Peter said, "I want finally to tell of a vision that has been seen here in Joppa!"

An expectant silence fell and everyone was hanging on each word he uttered.

"It is the vision of Abraham the silversmith and my cherished brother in Christ."

The eruption of amazement from the crowd was electric, voices were raised in wonder and every ear was straining for what was to be revealed. Abraham was kneeling his head bowed to the ground in humble adoration of his Lord whom he was now called to serve. He wasn't anxious or troubled, although he had no idea what Peter was about to say.

"In Abraham's shop for some weeks there has been displayed a brooch of silver worked by his skilled hands. Abraham gave it to my young friend Miriam, who has reached her fourteenth year. He gave it as an act of love after he had heard from her lips something of the wonder of the cross. Miriam had witnessed all the events of that terrible day of the crucifixion, and she braved the legionaries when Jesus fell and lay dazed on the pavement, pinned under the weight of the beam. Miriam knelt beside him, and ministered to him lovingly in the midst of the rough soldiers.

"The brooch has an outer circle of silver, heavy and strong. Within is the Star of David each of its points supporting the outer circle. In the centre is the lamb.

"As she stood grieving over the unconscious battered body of Mary, Miriam offered the brooch to Abraham, and said tracing her finger around its edge, 'Can it be possible for us Jews to reveal the Lamb of God to the whole world?'

"Alleluia, I tell you not only is it possible, it will be. That is our father Abraham's vision, it is your silversmith's vision, it is the prayer to the father called out from the cross. It is my vision and it can be yours."

145

A hushed silence hung over the synagogue for a few seconds.

"Eighty souls!" rejoiced Peter, "that really is a big catch for one cast of the net." As his pronouncement boomed out there was an amused exchange of looks between Mary and Marc.

"You still miss your fishing boats don't you, Peter?" queried Mary.

"Not at all. I might have but when the Lord called Andrew and me to follow him by the shore of Galilee, he said, 'I will make you into fishers of men.' I've fished since many times but prefer hauling in men to fish."

"I'll come to the baptism of this latest catch," Mary said firmly, challenging any dissention from the four men who might feel overly protective of her.

"I too would like to come," said Marc reproachfully, as he had expressed a wish to Mary to be baptized. Mary had pressed Peter but he had resolutely refused, saying the time was not right.

The baptism was to be in a secluded cove by the old fort, where Abraham was to lead the converts into the sea. After, they were to share in the breaking of bread and sharing the cup of wine together, but from this too, the centurion and his son were excluded.

Brutus saw and heard everything that passed but kept his own counsel. He knew Marc had wanted to be baptized, and was impatient with Peter for refusing him. He still felt great anger at the Jews for what had befallen Mary, and for demanding the death of Jesus and the consequent role of executioner that had fallen to him.

"I will call on the harbour-master. Now you feel up to sailing Mary, I'll enquire if there is a boat for Tyre in the next week. Keep an eye on her, Marc. Don't let her persuade you she is fighting fit and ready for another battle."

Marc assured him that however much Mary might be spoiling for a fight he would restrain her.

"Me, spoiling for a fight! You speak for yourselves. Just because neither of you has drawn his sword in anger for over a week don't vent your frustrations on me."

"Well spoken, woman," roared Peter and on that note of banter the centurion departed.

Approaching the port office Brutus expected to find the harbour-master there, as he seemed always to be somewhere around the port, the Sabbath being no exception. Sure enough Ephraim was sitting at an oak table entering some sailing details on a large parchment scroll. He waved to Brutus to be seated and when he had made his entry looked up.

"Good day, centurion, what can I do for you?"

"Good day, captain. Firstly accept my grateful thanks for sending Lucas to attend my wife."

"Ah yes. He is a remarkable physician and renowned throughout the Great Sea. Is your wife recovered?"

"Yes thank you. So much so that we hope soon to sail to Tyre as we originally intended."

"That can be easily arranged, many boats go to Tyre from here," said the harbour-master studying his scroll. "There is a Syrian coaster that will be picking up some cargo and sailing in three days time."

"Excellent. We should be ready by then. Will you negotiate a fare for three of us."

"Certainly, it won't be very expensive. Enjoy looking around Caesarea on the way, it really is a marvel to behold with its three palaces, the Roman prefect's and those of both kings, Herod Antipas and Agrippa."

Brutus was hard put to control his reaction at this suggestion. He was caught off guard but was alert enough to detect the veiled challenge.

"I would rather sail to Tyre without breaking the journey. I've seen Caesarea many times, impressive as it is."

"It's such an important port that most boats call there. Your wife might also prefer the passage in easy stages after her recent injury."

Brutus realised that Ephraim was probing and he knew he would be unwise to take him into his confidence. He decided to stall, remembering Alexander's warning of Herod's spies throughout Judaea.

"Well if it is necessary, so be it. Let us see how quickly my wife's recovery progresses. I will call each day and you can inform me what boats are sailing."

Did he see a glimmer of amused satisfaction in Ephraim's eye? Brutus resolved to be very much on his guard and regretted his dependence on the port captain.

He returned to Abraham's house coincident with Peter taking his farewell. He had declared his intention to return to Jerusalem immediately after the baptism.

His tunic still wet up to his waist, Peter was embracing the little silversmith.

"Truly this has been a great day for the Lord. One hundred and three souls from your community, including the renowned Lucas! Many of his calling resent our healing by the laying on of hands." He smiled broadly, "I think they see us as unfair competition."

Mary and Marc kneeled to receive Peter's blessing, after which he bestowed on Mary a dubiously received embrace, as her bruised ribs protested at such abuse. With a final salutation to Brutus, the big fisherman turned on his heel and planting his staff in front of him strode purposefully on his long walk to Jerusalem. He didn't once look back, already his thoughts were facing the challenges to which he was returning.

As his friends watched him recede they were awed by the aura he carried with him, that of a monumental destiny that he was fulfilling faithfully.

There was great tenderness between Abraham and Mary, now that the time was approaching when she would be leaving his home. Though today he had been baptized a follower of Jesus and felt elation, he also felt a great loss looming. Mary adored her kindly custodian of the past week and the silversmith reciprocated her feelings, only with an intensity that was close to idolatry. During the long, pain-filled nights, unable to sleep, Mary had opened her heart to the old man, telling of her years with Jesus and the unbelievable things that had happened.

Twice daily the centurion called at the port office, varying the hour, as he didn't want the harbour-master to anticipate his visits. Twice he had been offered a passage but on boats calling at Caesarea, and each was declined on the flimsy pretext of Mary not being quite recovered.

On the fourth morning he called really early.

No one was in the office and Brutus glanced at the scroll that lay partially unrolled on the table. *Pegasus* caught his eye so that he perused the list of sailings carefully. It was one of the boats he had been offered and declined. Under the column denoting destination, he received a jolt to see it listed calling at Tyre and Antioch. There was no mention of Caesarea. Quickly he ran his eye up and down the scroll and most of them listed Caesarea among the ports of call, but not *Pegasus* although he had declined it for that reason. He realised he had been misled to prevent their leaving on a boat which would have served their purpose well. Ephraim wanted to keep them there.

Quickly Brutus ran his eye down the list of projected sailings but all were calling at Caesarea.

He heard a footfall approaching the office and moved to be nonchalantly looking out of the window as a man entered. He was a thickset man of middle years, whose face bore testimony to a great number of fistfights. Looking suspiciously at Brutus he made a clumsy mark on the scroll and rolled it up.

"You won't see the harbour-master today," he said curtly, "there's nothing for you."

"Who told you that?"

"Captain Ephraim, who else!"

"Where is he? I was waiting to see him?" challenged Brutus.

"He won't return until late tomorrow."

"What has called the captain away?"

"Is it any business of yours?" The man looked as though he was spoiling for his five hundredth fight, but was disconcerted when Brutus smiled at him and said, "Only brotherly concern, that's all."

"Well his mother is very ill. He got word only a few hours ago and left to see her right away."

"That must be very sad for him," declared Brutus, but the irony was lost on the fellow as he shepherded Brutus through the door.

Brutus departed elated.

He now knew his adversary, and to his advantage this particular enemy thought himself undiscovered. But he felt in need of an ally, so he hurried down to the fort to see centurion Felix.

Felix had a message for him, which had been two days on the road. It was a simple square of parchment, folded so that each corner met at the centre where it was sealed with wax. It was addressed,

'Centurion Felix. Joppa Garrison. For the attention of centurion Brutus.'

Breaking the seal he read,

'General knowledge in Judaea you are at Joppa awaiting boat. Herod knows.' There was no signature just a square of green silk pierced in the centre.

Brutus laughed as he passed it over to Felix.

"Maas! What a staunch friend that Syrian is!"

Brutus proceeded to disclose what he had found out at the port office. Felix was silent for a minute then said,

"Men like Ephraim don't have mothers, their birth is a collaboration with the devil. He's obviously seeking a reward from Herod for betraying you. He won't want to share the reward so he can't send anyone to represent him. My guess is he's ridden to Caesarea and is arranging to hand over your head on a platter."

"Would the harbour-master own a horse?"

"No he would have to hire it from the livery stable and there's only one in

Joppa. Shall I go and enquire if he hired one there? I may be able to find out his destination."

Brutus agreed and they arranged to meet in an hour. He had decided to quit the inn and live rough in the area until they could sail. That way they wouldn't be easy prey should Ephraim bring back a squad of Herod's soldiers on his return, so while Felix was making his enquiries he explored the potential for concealment at the Phoenician fort.

When they met again Felix was pleased with his efforts.

"Ephraim hired two horses to ride to Caesarea and is returning tomorrow. I pretended I needed to get in touch with him urgently, to arrange some troop movements by sea, but no one was forthcoming as to his whereabouts."

"I guess he will be at Herod's palace. Pilate would be inaccessible to a lowly harbour official. Herod could send a company of soldiers to arrest us here, but is unlikely to do so if Ephraim is prepared to deliver us to the port of Caesarea by sea."

"It would be impossible to escape anywhere near Caesarea as there are half a dozen imperial naval vessels there, including a war galley," concluded Felix.

"So we know we are being misled and as like as not Herod is preparing a reception party right now, and intends to seize us aboard a boat we can shortly anticipate Ephraim finding us."

"Why go on such a boat? Why not delay a few days and make passage on another, or even go south towards Alexandria instead?" voiced Marc, anxious not to expose Mary to danger.

"We could delay but what will it avail us, a message can easily be sent to Caesarea concerning our movements, but if we change our plan completely they will deduce we know of Ephraim's intentions. No, we must not let them know we are suspicious. At the moment they think we are completely unsuspecting and that gives us a great advantage."

"Don't fear for me," said Mary. "I have seen you two in action and you must decide the best plan. I will place my trust in the Lord and you, and follow Peter's advice."

"Peter's advice!" echoed both men simultaneously, "what's that?"

"Pray, show no fear and be prepared to break any heads that get in the way!" she exulted seizing the hair of each of them in her widely extended hands. They capitulated, rather than risk her wrath and with their explosion of mirth, the seriousness of the discussion was dispelled.

Abraham appeared from the shop, looked disapprovingly at the two men and adoringly at Mary and withdrew.

"He's never going to forgive you for forcing me to accompany you. Nothing will convince him I am doing it voluntarily."

Mary was looking so much better, recovering surprisingly quickly from the battering she had taken. Her spirit had not been bowed at all.

"I have a plan in mind to foil Ephraim," said Brutus. "It will need resolve and courage from all of us, but it is our best hope."

Having gained their full attention the centurion elaborated on his plan. Both of the listeners were overwhelmed by its sheer audacity and debated it well into the night, agreeing finally that although hazardous it might well succeed.

149

On the evening of the second day following the return of the port captain, a large, shabby Arab dhow arrived in the port and tied up alongside the quay. On its bulwarks, well back from the high-raking stem, a carved dolphin was fixed to each side. The boat was riding high in the water as it had little cargo below, although on deck were secured some massive balks of timber. The word soon circulated around the dock that she was on her way to Tyre, where she was to be slipped and have some hull planks replaced. She was light on cargo because of ingress of seawater into the hull and would be sailing first thing in the morning.

Brutus only received the information that she leaked as he handed over eighty denarii to Ephraim for their passage, although he had known she was due for extensive repairs. He wondered whether to withdraw from sailing even now, but had no wish to delay implementing their carefully worked-out plan one day longer.

"Centurion Felix has given us supplies for the voyage to Tyre, so can we use a hand-cart and load them on board now?" requested Brutus.

"Take one from the quay. Here is a letter for the ship's master Joseph. Make your arrangements with him but remember she sails just before dawn."

He rejoined the others waiting on the quay and they quickly made their way to a warehouse and loaded the provisions onto the cart.

"Right, Mary, we'll take these to the *Dolphin* and stow them on board. When you see us approaching with the next load, you and Abraham must do your bit."

Mary hurried off to collect Abraham, as she had promised he could see her board on the eve of their departure.

Brutus and Marc trundled the cart to the quay and hailed one of the villainous looking crew.

"Ahoy. Is Joseph on board?"

The man called something indeterminate and disappeared, only to reappear two minutes later with a dishevelled, shifty looking man, who called, "I'm Joseph. What do you want with me?"

"The port captain has booked our passage to sail with you to Tyre. We want to stow our baggage and spend the night on board."

"I haven't heard from Ephraim," said the man doubtingly, "have you any authorization?"

Brutus applauded the man's acting, he really seemed indignant.

"Here's his letter," he said offering the paper.

Joseph took his time over the letter.

"It says three of you. Where's the third?"

"Mary is saying goodbye to a friend and will be along shortly."

"Mary! We don't have women on this boat!" he bluffed disapprovingly.

"Then you won't have any of us, and we will get our eighty denarii back from the port office. Come on Marc," and they turned as though to retrace their path.

"Will you keep her out of the way and be responsible for her when she's seasick?"

Brutus nodded agreement.

"Alright come aboard. Stow your stuff in the fore-hold and that can double up for your accommodation. Show them where, Levi," and Joseph disappeared.

Quickly they manhandled their belongings into the small space they had been allocated.

"We've another load to collect so we will be back shortly," called out Brutus as they hurried off with the cart.

Levi let out an oath and said something about it only being a two days passage, not two weeks.

"We must be quick," said Brutus, "Ephraim won't be around much longer."

As they approached the office, a flame guttering in the window was extinguished and the shutters drawn closed. They heard the office door close and Marc called out.

"Captain Ephraim. Joseph on the *Dolphin* is making trouble about Mary."

Ephraim had never spoken to Marc and he suddenly loomed out of the shadows to confront the boy.

"What's that about Jose ..." was as far as he got as Brutus, with the stealth of the hunter, felled him with one blow of his sword hilt to his head. Quickly they bound and gagged him and, enveloping him in a large square of sackcloth threw him in the cart.

Noisily they returned to the *Dolphin* and Mary hearing their approach quickened her step from the opposite direction, so that Abraham had to run to keep abreast of her. About ten paces from the bow of the boat she caught her foot, tripped, and with a shrill cry fell over the edge of the quay. The pandemonium that ensued was incredible

Abraham ran to the quayside shouting for help. Mary was thrashing about likewise shouting as first Levi and then Joseph appeared at the gunwale peering down. Grabbing a stout length of rope the two men descended the gangplank and ran towards the commotion ahead of the boat, followed belatedly by a third crew member just as the handcart was approaching from astern. Tipping their unconscious prisoner onto the quay they quickly manhandled his inert body up and into the hold.

"You watch him. I must see that Mary is safe," called Marc, and without waiting for a reply he ran to the quay. A lantern cast its baleful light on a distraught Mary who was clinging to the rope, but kept on falling back into the sea as the men sought to pull her up. When she saw Marc he was sure he detected a suggestion of a smile for a split second.

"Mary," he called, "look there's a loop at the end of the rope, put your foot in it, hold the rope higher up and let us haul you out."

After two or three attempts, all of which terminated in failure, Marc was sure she was inviting him to come to her rescue. Abraham was nearly prostrate with anxiety and pleaded that she was so weak from her injury she must surely die, unless she were quickly rescued.

Marc jumped in and nearly laughed aloud at the look he got as she thrashed away. He coaxed and cajoled, and was finally rewarded by the sight of her being lifted up. The last thing she did was to place her foot on his head and push him well under.

"What a woman," he thought, "oh what a woman!"

Finally they were standing side by side on the quay looking very sheepish under the searching scrutiny of Joseph and the crew of the *Dolphin*.

"By all the gods, is this the woman to travel with us to Tyre?" demanded the master, and when Mary gave a little curtsy in acknowledgement it was as much as Marc could do to keep a straight face.

151

Mary proceeded to placate everyone and to calm a distraught Abraham, by complimenting them sweetly on their resourcefulness in rescuing her. That she pointedly omitted to include Marc in her profuse thanks made him wonder if she thought him a little tardy to throw himself into the water. They were beginning to shiver in the cool air, so Mary took a last farewell of the silversmith and they ascended the gangplank before entering the gloomy hold of the boat, where an inadequate lamp spluttered fitfully throwing out more fumes than light.

Brutus didn't wait for Mary to shed her wet clothes but clutched her to him tenderly and reassuringly.

"Oh my love, you were truly marvellous. I watched from the bows and that was the most impressive acting I have ever seen."

Mary pushed him away.

"I can't swim," she said.

"What!" exclaimed both men, simultaneously.

"I can't swim a stroke," she repeated her face turned to hide her imminent tears.

"Then why did you agree to my plan to create a diversion? You might have drowned!"

"What option was there, a diversion was essential and it had to be convincing. Would you have had me push old Abraham in? That would have created a diversion! You probably would, you stupid insensitive warriors."

Both men were standing completely nonplussed by the unexpectedness of her attack. Suddenly awareness dawned on Marc. He moved close to Mary and took her hand. She tried to pull it away but he held on to it resolutely.

"Oh Mary you were scared to death by our plan weren't you?"

Mary gave an involuntary sob.

"You were scared to death all the time you were in the water weren't you?" Mary's sobs were now beginning to merge into an uninterrupted succession.

Marc moved in close and clutched her to him, so closely he could feel the convulsions of her breathing through their wet clothes.

"Oh brave heart. You must have wondered if I was ever coming in to aid you." A shudder passed from her body to his and he eased her hair away from where it was clinging lankly to her cheek, and kissed her so gently she knew he was asking for forgiveness.

She flung her arms around his neck and half laughing, half crying said, "It wasn't an accident when I put my foot on your head and pushed you under."

"Never mind dearest, I deserved it."

"But I didn't want to do it to you, Marc," and bursting into a fresh spate of tears she exploded, "I wanted to do it to him!" pointing at Brutus who looked totally bewildered.

The tears now flowing were all that was needed to release the tension and choking them back she was able to give Brutus a wan smile as she sought to reassure him.

"Oh poor boy. I am being unfair to you aren't I. You devise a brilliant plan to keep us all from being killed and it nearly goes wrong because I can't swim." She held out her arms to him and Marc backed away to let the centurion bury himself in her embrace.

As though to warn that the next twenty-four hours would test them in the

152

extreme there was a commotion from the dockside. A voice was calling out for Joseph insistently. Brutus had smelt wine about the master when he had presented the letter and it was a couple of minutes before he heard Joseph asking who wanted him.

"Tiasus."

Brutus recognized the voice of the pugnacious stevedore above those of the small crowd with him.

"Captain Ephraim has disappeared and nobody knows where to find him. His woman says he hasn't been home for his supper."

"Who saw him last? Hold on, the Roman brought me a letter from Ephraim two hours ago, maybe he knows something. They're on board so I'll find out."

Quickly checking that their prisoner was unconscious Brutus decided to meet the threat half way, and moved out of the hatch onto the deck just as Joseph was about to enter. Together they moved to the side of the dhow from where they looked down at the small group on the quay.

"I collected the letter for the master of the *Dolphin* nearly three hours ago and paid eighty denarii to the harbour-master. I haven't seen him since. Perhaps his mother is worse and he's been called to her again."

"I am his mother. What do you mean about my being worse?" called out an elderly woman.

"Tiasus told me a few days ago that your son was summoned to your bedside because you were very ill. I'm really glad to see you so well recovered."

This disconcerted the shore party and nobody was confident to make a reply. Brutus decided to keep the initiative.

"Has anyone been to the office?"

"Of course we have," snarled Tiasus. "It's locked."

"Well eighty denarii is a lot of money, people would kill for less than that. You should make sure he's not been robbed, he may be lying injured inside."

They conferred together anxiously and the women demanded that they look in the office. Joseph was unsteady and obviously affected by his drinking, for which Brutus silently gave thanks, as an alert and shrewd man might have connected the recent histrionics at the quayside with the disappearance.

Still arguing the shore party departed and Brutus nonchalantly moved towards their quarters requesting Joseph to keep him informed of the outcome of the search, as he was concerned for the helpful captain's well being. Wondering if he had overdone it a bit Brutus rejoined his uneasy companions.

"He's just starting to come round," said Marc, "and I was wondering whether to give him another blow with this." He held up a hefty belaying pin.

Holding the lamp close Brutus found himself confronting the hate filled visage of their prisoner.

Putting his dagger close to the man's throat the centurion said icily, "One sound and I'll cut your throat without a qualm. I know you have been to Caesarea and made a deal to deliver us to Herod somehow." He saw fear momentarily in Ephraim's eyes, and then malevolence dominated every feature of the man.

"My guess is that you are a coward who would prefer to save your worthless skin. Well, you do have one chance and one only."

The momentary flicker of hope he glimpsed assured Brutus that he had got Ephraim's measure as he continued, "and that is to get us to Tyre safely. The moment I know we cannot avoid capture you surely die, your throat cut," sliding the point of his dagger slowly across his neck from ear to ear.

Whatever hopes Ephrain entertained that his cunning might yet successfully accomplish his scheme were now dashed. Brutus moved his knife to the man's purse and cut the thong binding it to his belt. It was heavy in his hand and he held it close to Ephraim's face.

"You will never see the reward you agreed with Herod, but I agreed eighty denarii for our passage to Tyre and that still holds if you get us there. Otherwise ..." and he left the threat hanging in the air.

A few barely audible grunts through the heavy gag suggested their prisoner was anxious to say something.

Brutus said, "Listen carefully it would be easy to keep you bound, gagged and unconscious until we are nearing Caesarea tomorrow. Then you, the rest of the crew, and probably my son and I will die, but you first. If your gag is removed now and you call out it will be your last, and any of your men who get in our way will die before we take to the hills. Or you can tell us what you have conspired with Herod so that we can plan to avoid capture and sail us to Tyre." He signalled to Marc to undo the gag.

As the gag was about to be released there was a resurgence of calling from the quayside.

"Mary, go ashore and make your way to Abraham if we have to flee. We'll get in touch with you there. Marc, slit his throat should things go wrong and have your sword ready!"

He enjoyed the fear-filled look of their captive as he moved on deck.

For a minute he listened to the account of the shore's party's singular lack of success. They had broken down the door to the office but found it deserted.

"Did you find the denarii I paid him in the office?" challenged Brutus.

"No," said Tiasus, "but that means nothing."

"He might have unwisely told a trusted companion how much money he had on him. I think you must look for his body at first light, or maybe he will just walk in and you will realize your alarm was unwarranted. Well, whatever you decide my companions and I want some sleep before our early start tomorrow." Dismissively Brutus turned his back on them and made his way to the hold.

Gradually the voices outside petered away leaving the fugitives to discuss the options open to them.

CHAPTER THREE

The boat got underway while it was still dark. Emerging onto the deck Marc saw that there were four crew manning two sweeps on each side, preparatory to rowing out of the port. There wasn't any breeze yet, that predictably would follow close on the sunrise. Then the Melteni would start lightly ahead, later backing to strong on the beam from across the Great Sea. It was then that they would hoist their sail on the high raking spar.

For an hour they continued, breaking a vivid track of phosphorescence through the black water under a star filled sky. Marc, in his heart, sang a hymn to his creator as Miriam had taught him, and thinking longingly of her, wondered when and where they would meet next. He was glad she was not with them that day!

It was still too dark to reconnoitre the boat looking for concealed weapons or the most advantageous place from where to confront the unsuspecting crew. The stars were deserting the sky, and the fixed star towards which lay Tyre faded as the rose coloured dawn over the massive plateau to the east intensified by the minute. Wisps of cloud caught fire glowing larva red and burnished gold as though heating to iridescence on the hearth of a primeval forge. The unendurable energy suffusing the firmament radiated out reaching heavenwards, and across the sea beat a golden path to their boat. Marc watched entranced as the glowing ball of the sun struggled free of the clutching rock and earth. As it triumphed it illuminated the yellows and ochre of that sandstone mass where the deeply etched scars of ravines and passes lay darkly ominous.

Now he could clearly see the backs of the four rowers who were sitting astride the bulks of hardwood timber running the length of the deck. To a steady rhythm they propelled the boat across an unruffled blue sea and Joppa faded into the distance. He felt a slight rustle of air on the back of his neck and simultaneously heard the slap of wavelets on the bows. Their course was now parallel to the coast about one mile off shore, a course that would take them directly to Caesarea.

Returning to the cabin Marc related the situation to Brutus, who decided the time had come to confront Joseph. Unbinding Ephraim's legs he allowed him five minutes to re-establish the circulation to his cramped limbs before hauling him roughly to his feet.

"It's time to present you to the crew and put an end to their speculation concerning your disappearance."

Noisily they moved through the hatch onto the deck turning the heads of all four of the crew. The oars hung motionless as each face registered the full range of complementary emotions. Alarm, anger, fear were all to be seen, most markedly in the face of Joseph, the only one of the crew who was party to the treachery planned. The drawn swords of the Romans together with their advantage of surprise curtailed any spontaneous response.

"Stay exactly where you are, keep your heads to the stern and resume rowing," said Brutus stationing himself behind the forward rower on one side as Marc did likewise on the other.

Mary stood behind Ephraim with the belaying pin in her hand.

"Listen to captain Ephraim as you continue rowing but heed this, any threatening move will mean instant death as we can be ruthless executioners."

Ephraim started talking hesitantly, but gained in confidence as he continued.

"I was abducted by these Romans last night and bundled on board while you were distracted by the woman falling in the water."

As he hesitated Marc was disappointed that the faces of the listeners were turned from them, he would dearly have loved to see them.

"I deserved what I got, as together with Joseph I had devised a plan to hand our passengers over to King Herod at Caesarea. This may sound like treachery, but we had been led to believe these men are killers and that there was a duty to see them arrested. I am now convinced that I was wrong and that they have but angered Herod and Pilate in some way. The centurion is anxious that you know they are not loath to kill if necessary. They killed all four assassins that Herod sent after them two moons ago."

Two of the faces jerked around at this revelation but a threatening lift of both swords quickly returned them aft. Ephraim continued,

"They will be safe once we reach Tyre as neither Herod nor Pilate has any jurisdiction there. I have agreed to set our course to avoid closing Caesarea, where a Roman galley is probably on the lookout for us. I am not able to persuade the Romans that I no longer pose a threat, so they are keeping me bound throughout the passage. They are resolved to slit my throat at the first show of any challenge so I urge you not to threaten them."

There were some angry noises from a couple of the men, but no interruption to the steady sweep of the oars. Brutus marked the men who had expressed their anger for closer watching.

The wind was freshening but still from the north, and had not yet started to back around to the west as it would when the land heated under the remorseless sun.

It changed around mid morning and was suddenly strong from nearly astern on the port side. The oars were quickly shipped, and the crew hoisted the large sail as Joseph moved to the helm. Immediately the boat leapt forward with a comfortable heel, and the Romans moved their prisoner aft where they secured him to a bollard. They were staying in a close group to make a formidable front if the crew decided to rush them.

"Bear up wind so that we are at least ten miles off Caesarea," ordered Ephraim and Joseph put the helm over so that they were moving at an angle away from the coast.

"We will soon be so far out to sea they will not spot us from the land or from the galley. At this rate we will have cleared Caesarea in five hours, and can then gradually close the land to Tyre during the night and tomorrow," Ephraim explained to the passengers anxious to allay their suspicions.

The broad coastal plain could no longer be distinguished in the haze nor the high hills behind, fading by the hour. Brutus felt reassured but remained vigilant.

Aboard the bireme galley *Hermes*, centurion Hedylus was standing on the raised

156

bow deck looking intently seawards. He glanced back to the sailor who had been hoisted up the aft mast to the crow's nest, and when he received a negative gesture made his decision. He could see that Tribune Communis and King Herod under the stern awning were getting impatient. He didn't need a sixth sense to tell him he would incur considerable wrath if he waited for the prize to come to them, and lost it.

He signalled to the drum master who immediately gave a single beat of his drum. The seventy slaves naked to the waist and each chained to their station, seized the oars to respond in unison to the steady beat that followed. The rate was unhurried and the brightly painted vessel slid smoothly away from the port, punching its way through the waves as it headed west. It was now midday and the wind was strengthening so that white crests were forming and spray occasionally swept over the foredeck.

Looking along the open length of the hull the two tiers of oarsmen on each side were bending to their task with well drilled precision. They were muscular, well-fed and valuable slaves, who were the engine of a powerful war machine. Hedylus thrilled to the power that was the summation of their individual efforts, and knew they could keep this pace up for hour after hour. He had got rid of the barbaric practice of lashing to drive them to maximal effort, and had a better ship as a consequence.

They held their course for two hours, and he was thinking of the possibility of failure, when a new lookout called out "Sail ahoy", pointing ten degrees to starboard. The steermen heaved on the starboard paddle to bring the galley around, and the drum master increased the rate. The boat was now surging through the steep, short waves at an angle, and rolling quite considerably with a corkscrewing motion. The oarsmen were well able to adjust to this motion but for the legionaries in the centre of the hull it was no longer easy to keep their balance.

Hedylus was soaked with spray that was flying half way along the hull. He saw the tribune moving along the keel to climb up on the foredeck. Pointing ahead the buff coloured sail of the dhow was clearly visible about three miles away.

"So Centurion Brutus got wind of the harbour-master's treachery and is forcing a course to avoid capture. In view of the manhunt being stood down I can't see why we are pursuing them now," said Hedylus, with evident reluctance for his task.

"I'll forget you said that," rasped Tribune Communis. He had recently replaced Tibullus and was anxious to ingratiate himself favourably with the Judaean king. "Our duty is to serve our legitimate rulers to the best of our ability, not to be questioning their orders. How long before we overhaul them?"

"We can't increase our speed in these seas, so about one and a half hours."

Brutus watched the galley steadily gaining on them and Ephraim looked at him with fear. Tension was mounting amongst the crew, and the suddenness with which it erupted took their captors by surprise.

Joseph suddenly released the helm, turned, and threw a knife. It took barely a second, but the accompanying lurch of the boat, caused it to whistle harmlessly within an inch of Brutus' head. As his sword amputated Joseph's forearm and cut deeply into his chest, Brutus turned to see Marc parrying a blow from a cutlass and as the blade harmlessly passed, Marc swung his own sword up into the soft flesh at the junction of chest and limb, all but severing the man's sword arm. The remaining crew sat cowed, as though accepting their deaths at the hands of these executioners.

With no control at the helm, the dhow swung head to wind pitching and rolling violently. Mary was poised ready to strike Ephraim, who fully expected to die as Brutus approached with drawn dagger. Instead he cut through the ropes binding him and pulled him to his feet.

"Take the helm and steer the boat," ordered Brutus and as the dazed man took control he called the crew to help haul on the wildly flapping sail, and as they brought it under control the boat settled on a course reaching away from the closing galley.

From the foredeck of *Hermes* Hedylus saw the bodies thrown overboard, and as they passed them some minutes later somberly asked the tribune,

"Will we lose some of our men to seize a retired centurion and his son, just to appease Herod's anger?"

Communis turned away contemptuously and made his way aft to report to the eager king, resolved that Hedylus would be relieved of his command on their return.

Evening was near and to the west the lingering gold was dying in a sunset flare of resplendent light.

"We can't outrun the galley," urged Brutus, "but we have just the one chance. If you strive honorably and fail, then only we Romans will die and we will not be your executioners. If my plan succeeds, you will be rewarded and have an epic achievement worthy of recounting to your children." He outlined his course of action.

Leaving Ephraim at the helm, they moved along the deck unlashing two of the balks of timber. Each was over twenty feet long and needed the four men to move them as far aft as possible, where strong ropes were lashed to their rear-most ends. Brutus hammered in some heavy nails to ensure the ropes couldn't slip off.

The galley had closed the gap to a hundred paces, and Brutus decided the time had come for their desperate gamble.

"Run down wind now," he ordered, and as the *Dolphin* came around so did the *Hermes*. They could see the soldiers taking up station for boarding along both sides, and Hedylus and two other men on the fore deck were clearly visible as Brutus uttered his prearranged word of command,

"Now!"

They instantly manhandled one of the bulks until it was poised on the capping rail.

"Correct for the drag, Ephraim. Don't let her slew," the centurion called, and the baulk was pitched overboard and the rope to which it was attached became bowstring taut, and although the helm was put hard over the dhow slewed to port and slowed. They rushed to the other side and quickly threw the second over. With both beams dragging astern the *Dolphin* slowly gathered way as Marc and Brutus stood with swords raised, ready to sever the ropes.

The oars swinging in perfect unison had brought the galley within thirty paces of their boat, and it edged a fraction to one side positioning to overhaul and to board. Its unblinking oculus close to the surging bow wave regarded them malevolently.

On the stern deck Herod was straining his body against the rail to see every detail of the capture. His face was contorted by a grimace of pure malice and exaltation. He praised the gods that brought him this human sacrifice, the consummation of his relentless hunt.

The speed of *Hermes* as it hurtled through the *Dolphin*'s wake was electrifying. Its power was stunning in its ominous beauty.

"Now!" called Brutus yet again, and he and Marc severed their ropes simultaneously.

Their boat bounded ahead as would a hunting cheetah when freed from the leash and Ephraim instinctively attempted to throw their pursuers off course although the steersman of the galley responded instantly to negate any advantage.

Hedylus saw the two-pronged threat a split second before the *Hermes* surged onto it. The massive beam dead ahead rose up in the air as the protruding ram drove under it, and with a fearsome impact smashed into the stem. Its twin on the starboard side burst through the planking at water level, six feet of it protruding into the hull, crushing the forward oarsman against the mast step. Hedylus and a dozen soldiers were thrown into the sea. Herod, straining till the very moment of triumph, was catapulted from the heights into the bone crushing depths of the slave filled hull.

There pandemonium reigned. Strewn bodies lay under torrents of water forced in by the galley's momentum as the crippled Leviathan floundered, losing all way and the eager waves rolled her at their will.

From the *Dolphin* a triumphant cheer rang out as they bore away jubilant and elated. Enmity was buried as they celebrated achieving the impossible.

The four men were each at an oar sweeping them steadily northwards. A vortex of glowing light followed the oars as they stroked the water, and phosphorescent pearls dripped from each blade as it came clear at the end of its sweep. The gentle bow wave gleamed as if it held the essence of the moonlight, lazily rolling the length of the hull.

Under a star filled sky with a crescent moon to light their progress, Mary stood motionless at the bow, singing a silent psalm to God at the wonder of his creation and giving thanks for their deliverance. Then, out of nowhere, her eye was caught and then transfixed by a series of iridescent arcs carving a path across the smooth surface of the sea. They multiplied in number and grew in magnitude as they converged on the boat. Mary knew in her heart the creatures of the sea were celebrating in dance the victory of the *Dolphin,* as they took up position a hand's breadth distance in front of the stem. It was the first time she had ever seen these men sized creatures, and Brutus and Marc had relinquished their oars to join her.

"Dolphins," breathed Brutus reverently, "come to welcome their namesake."

"Dolphins," echoed Marc and Mary wonderingly.

They were cleaving six fluorescent lines abreast, their dorsal fins breaking the surface. The two outermost surged in a high arc nearly clear of the water before plunging back and peeling off to each side. Successively each pair did likewise and always, as though by magic, were replaced. The sea became a turmoil, as more and more joined the dance. Two leapt clear of the water, seeming to hang momentarily, dripping shining pearls, before falling back into the depths. These manoeuvres were repeated time and time again, in varying combinations, and were encouraged by Marc clapping and talking to them. Brutus put an arm around Mary drawing her to him.

"Have you called down a blessing on us, Mary?" he asked tenderly nuzzling his face into her luxuriant mass of hair.

"I'm sure you're right it is a blessing but I didn't call it. It is freely bestowed by our Lord to ease away the ache that violence and discord leaves in the human heart."

Marc was leaning as far over the side as he possibly could, talking to a wise old dolphin that was swimming alongside, turned to fix its inquisitive eye on his. That they communicated in a wordless way is beyond dispute, but whatever was said could not be spoken in human tongue.

The same stars looked down on a very different tumult on the bireme galley. As the crippled ship floundered impaled by the gigantic bolt, there was a very real risk of it sinking with the loss of all hands. The massive weight, protruding from the bows, was keeping the hole below the water line and the sea surged in through the splintered planks. The rocking of the boat, which had broached too and was receiving each wave along its length, made any effort to sort out the nightmare daunting. Communis assumed command, and realized they were lost unless they could get some way going and lift the bows out of the water. He ordered the first twenty oars on each side to be slipped and the slaves unshackled and moved aft. The forward mast was unstepped and thrown overboard, a fearful task in the violently rocking boat. Every available bucket, helmet and other miscellaneous receptacle was pressed into baling out. Cloaks and other items of clothing were stuffed into the raggedly splintered planks, and then tentatively the oars were brought into action. A little way was gained so that the steersmen could start to point the boat away from the waves and head home.

Daylight was long gone and the gloom in the hull was hard to penetrate. Still the bows were well down, pulled by the prodigious weight of the beam that extended some ten feet forward of the stem. Communis led a dozen slaves to the mortal wound in the hull.

"Our only chance of seeing the dawn is to move this beam back into the hull. Six of you on each side seize it in your arms and pull strongly at my command. Ready? Then heave, release, heave, release, heave, release, heave."

At the fourth pull, when the slaves had secured better footholds and were coordinating, there was the first perceptible movement, just enough to free most of the clothing rammed into the wound, so that the sea rushed in torrents over the struggling men.

"Keep it moving now, steady, steady, hold it there," he called as four to five foot of the timber now extended beyond the empty mast step. Calling another dozen men forward, the tribune put half of them on the beam and the others to finding the clothes in the flooded hull, stuffing them back urgently to reduce the ingress of water. Delegating one man to move to the foredeck to ensure they left a few feet of the baulk protruding, the massive timber was eased back into the hull. The radiating splits and tears were closed with anything that came to hand and the unceasing baling gradually reduced the water level. It was a precarious balance between the ingress and the baling out and Communis ordered all way to be taken off the boat.

The wind had now abated and the sea calmed, so it was comfortable to lie unmoving on the water. The crescent moon cast its baleful light helping the tribune to take stock. The galley was low in the water so that the holes for the lower tier of oars were only just above sea level, and with a start he realised how near to foundering they had been, literally a matter of a few inches. At least they were now on an even keel. As a precaution he had all the lower oars shipped and the holes closed.

Half of the soldiers thrown into the sea had managed to swim back and clamber on board. Hedylus was lost with five others and there was no chance of making a search, as the situation was still perilous. Herod was unconscious and a cause for concern, but there was nothing to do other than to cover him where he lay, and hope he didn't die from his injuries.

A further hours hard baling gained six inches of free board and Communis felt able to resume rowing. It was now possible by redistribution of weight to lift the bows so that the bolt that had pierced the galley was almost clear of the water.

Dawn saw the stricken vessel ease its side up to the crowded quay at Caesarea.

CHAPTER FOUR

The beams of the setting sun lit up the imposing water frontage of Tyre, as the *Dolphin* sailed into the channel between the mainland and the protective island of this ancient Phoenician port. The tall imposing sandstone buildings looming along the sea front hid the narrow entrance into the inner harbour.

Ephraim, confident at the helm and rejoicing at the remarkable turn to his fortune, put the helm over so that the boat glided into the crowded harbour before dropping the sail.

From the vast array of every type of ship, two rowing boats glided to take their ropes and move them to a vacant space on the quayside. As the Romans stepped ashore the look they exchanged revealed their lightening of mood. They knew nothing of Herod's injuries but they did know he had no power here as Tyre came under the jurisdiction of the Governor of Syria, Vitellius, and from his headquarters at Damascus he would certainly have no interest in a conflict between Pontius Pilate and an obscure centurion. They were finally free of pursuit.

Mary was delegated to find them rooms, but for tonight an inn close to the harbour would have to suffice. Striding through the crowded streets, they all rejoiced at the joyful cacophony of sound around them. These were a different people from the Jews, unconstrained spiritually, un-trampled by heavy-footed religious authority. They made their living by craft or commerce, with a quiet confidence from roots going back over one thousand years of a great trading tradition.

Drifting, relaxed, and eager to be delighted by simple pleasures, they came to a small square, where to the music of trumpet, tambourine and drum, a troupe of dark hued acrobats were cart-wheeling, somersaulting and forming human pyramids. Rush lights were already lit around the court of a small inn, and on enquiry their accommodation for that night was arranged.

As there was some time before eating, Marc lay relaxed on a low couch, dreamily recalling the wonderful evening at the inn in Joppa with Miriam and her family and the Syrians. Suddenly his reflections were cut short by the man crossing the room to ascend a staircase at the far end, and with a shock he recognised the pharisee from two previous encounters. The first when they had delivered the bruised body of Alexander to his parent's home in Jerusalem, the more recent when he had stood, sword drawn, over the battered, prostrate body of Mary. He was Saul of Tarsus.

Saul disappeared without any acknowledgement or flicker of recognition, but he had shattered Marc's feelings of security, and he was impatient to mention it to Brutus. This he did over dinner and the impact on Mary was frightening, the colour draining from her face as she clutched her hands over her heart, wringing them anxiously.

162

Putting a reassuring arm around her Brutus said, "Dearest that will never happen to you again. Marc will accompany you when you go to the Synagogue."

"I would hate not to go because of fear, so I will be glad to have Marc with me. It's in my nature to speak out against tyranny and injustice, but I think I've learnt my lesson as far as Saul is concerned, he's a very dangerous man."

Brutus wished she had spoken with more conviction, but let it pass as the room suddenly filled with the troupe of acrobats and their musicians. They were from Carthage, and a more vivacious, extroverted band could not be envisaged. Brutus unguardedly let slip he had served in Carthage and there followed a lot of searching for common ground.

Marc, challenged to test his ability as an acrobat surprised everyone, including himself, by achieving a respectable somersault.

Mary applauded heartily and Brutus declined to try, although he willingly accepted a challenge to arm wrestle with a broad squat man who was the lynchpin of their pyramid formation. Worsted on the best of three, Brutus conceded that he was getting soft in retirement.

"I doubt if any of the crew of the *Dolphin* would agree with that," said Marc in an aside to Mary, which made her chuckle delightedly.

That was the cue for Brutus and Mary to retire to their room, leaving Marc to bed down, "one Celt among a cartload of Carthaginians," as he expressed it to considerable amusement.

Most of the next day was concerned with sorting out the ownership of the *Dolphin*. The port authority had Joseph listed as sole owner and master, unmarried and without any dependants. As a consequence of his unfortunate death the boat would have to be sold by the authorities, and after deducting their commission, the balance would be shared among the crew, unless the crew wished to purchase it themselves. The port authority was prepared to consider a reasonable offer from any of the crew.

Ephraim wondered if he had much future as the harbour-master of Joppa, and he whispered to Brutus, "We both know how vengeful Herod is when he is denied. If you allow me to keep the eighty denarii I have enough to make an offer."

Brutus grinned and produced the purse from his baggage.

"Fancy forgetting to return it to you. I appear to be getting forgetful as well as soft in my retirement."

This casual quip sent Marc into such uncontrolled laughter he incurred a frown from the port captain.

Ephraim made an offer of three hundred denarii, which was accepted.

"I'll pay you eighty now and the balance on my first trip. Unfortunately I left Joppa in such a hurry I thought to bring little with me."

Marc again incurred the disapproval of the port captain as he tried to cover his uncontrollable laughter under the guise of a coughing fit, and had to leave the office.

Having collected their baggage they took their farewells with the crew of the *Dolphin*, and departed to meet Mary at the inn, where she had been making enquiries among the staff.

One of the maids hearing of this asked if she would be kind enough to look first at her mother's house.

"I was thinking of looking for a Jewish house and I think you are Phoenician or Greek?"

"That is true I am Lucia and a Greek, but in our house you will find no idols, we believe in the one true God as do you."

"We need two rooms, for me and my husband, and for our son Marc."

"Then I can sleep in my mother's bed and Marc can have mine," said Lucia eagerly.

"What will your father do?"

As Mary asked she saw the girl's face cloud and knew there was no man in the house.

"He died in a sea battle when I was a baby. I never knew him."

Mary's heart warmed to her. She knew how hard it was for a widow and child in Judaea, where the culture insisted on alms being given to widows and orphans. Here there would be no such provision and they would have known many a night without supper.

"Tell me where your house is and I will bring my men when they return."

"My work is finished in an hour. May I please take you?"

As Lucia replied she was thinking what a strange way to describe a husband and son, 'my men.'

When later she found them together awaiting her, there were a few further surprises. The father had a Roman name and his appearance was consistent with his nationality, but their son had a Greek name, looked unlike either of his parents or unlike anyone from these parts. That she also thought he looked like a God she hardly dared admit even to herself. Both men were also armed with Roman swords, something never seen within the city except for patrolling soldiers.

Bursting with curiosity, she led them to a quiet tree-lined street off a large square, where the houses, all identical, tall and narrow, presented a continuous façade to similar houses on the opposite side, and they approached a formidable oak door that opened on the gentlest pressure.

Entering into a large cool room, simply furnished with two couches on either side of a long low table, and a beautiful cedar dresser, Lucia opened the shutters and the light streamed in. She crossed to the stairs and called out.

"Mama, hello. I have some people to meet you!"

The disembodied voice that answered had a vibrant happiness about it.

"Ask them to sit down Kunaria, I'll be down in a minute."

Lucia blushed as she ushered them to sit down, especially when she caught Marc's eyes, which were twinkling mischievously. Fighting back an inexplicable nervousness, she offered them some cordial, and gladly retreated to the kitchen.

Marc had noticed how pretty she was, her dark eyes full of fire and the lifting corners of her generous full mouth promising a ready laugh.

At her entry Flora's resemblance to her daughter struck the visitors, only the laughter lines a little deeper, at the corners of her eyes and mouth. As she smiled her even teeth glistened as white pearls in a dusky shell, which puckered so that the dimples of both cheeks were emphasised beguilingly.

Mary instantly felt drawn to this woman and arose to embrace her.

"Lucia informs me you have two rooms that you would happily let for a month or two."

"Well, we have only one large room which I don't think would be suitable."

164

Her regret was tangible, but before she could continue Lucia entered with a tray of freshly pressed, cordial and said, "I said their son could have my room, mama."

She deliberately avoided using Marc's name, but to her surprise she found her duplicity made her blush even more.

"Thank you, Kunaria," said Flora as she relieved Lucia of the tray, "would you run and fetch the cakes on the kitchen table."

Lucia was only too glad to do so and hurried from the room.

"Kunaria is a very pretty name!" said Marc, feigning innocence.

"Please, it is a familiarity that only I use. Try to forget it as her name is Lucia!"

Marc bowed an acknowledgement, but something in his eye told her he was unlikely to, but she was too preoccupied discussing with Mary the practicality of Lucia's suggestion to give him any more thought.

Lucia returned eventually and handed around the cakes with averted eyes as the women got up to view the rooms.

Marc arose to go with them but Mary said quite firmly, "No Marc! It is totally inappropriate for you to see Lucia's room until she has vacated it!"

This time Marc reddened confusedly, and Lucia gave him a dazzling smile as she followed them up the stairs.

Marc asked Brutus, "Are women always so puzzling and contradictory?"

"Definitely they are, and I've observed it is proportionate to how pretty they are."

Marc looked uncertain for a few seconds and then his face cleared and smiling he retorted, "Then I might as well give up trying with both Miriam and Lucia!" and they both burst out laughing.

Later that day when they had settled into their rooms Mary wanted to go shopping, having agreed the women would share the kitchen, cooking independently, except on the eve of the Sabbath when they would all eat together.

"Do you want either of us to come with you?" asked Brutus.

"Certainly not. Neither of you can conceal how bored you are when I linger but a short while over any purchase! It's time you got some exercise and explored the area. Let's eat an hour after dusk."

They didn't need more urging and armed the men made their way to the foothills, which crowded close to the city. The more height they gained, the more impressive was the panorama before them. Brutus explored the terrain with a soldier's eye, and he was patient explaining the significance of things to Marc.

"That would be a good spot to conceal an ambush," he said pointing to where a narrow gully opened onto a wider, boulder-strewn riverbed, or "what a good position to defend from a pursuing force!" as they traversed a narrow goat path flanking a high cliff.

Many hours later when they returned, tired but exhilarated, Mary congratulated herself on her perceptivity. She resolved to encourage their rugged affinity for the wide-open spaces and adventure. It was part of what she loved about them, and as her future was now pledged to theirs, she knew her mettle was to be truly tested as she adapted to this new relationship.

In the centre of the square at the end of the street was a raised stone dais, around which there was always a crowd listening to an endless variety of speakers. Marc loved to mingle with the good-humoured crowd, who listened to the more outrageous tirades with unconcealed mirth, and the more seriously political or philosophical with varying degrees of attention. Disputes were not uncommon. Sometimes to the crowd's delight, when one orator was particularly long-winded, the normal courtesies might not be observed and his challenger might forcibly jump up to dispossess him.

By attendance at this place information could be gleaned on the affairs of the whole known world, and it was there that Marc heard, related in fairly accurate detail, the fate of the *Hermes*.

Marc rejoiced at the emphasis on the disparity between the *Dolphin* and the *Hermes*, and when the dramatic skewering of the hunter was described a big cheer went up, and a little Greek standing near him was hopping with excitement. Marc felt like saying it was he who had cut one of the ropes. He rejoiced that Herod was still confined to his bed by his injury, and learned that Tribune Communis had received a commendation to the Emperor. He listened eagerly to every detail of the *Hermes'* struggle home.

Returning elated he recounted all he had heard to Brutus and Mary.

Brutus expressed some reservation.

"I don't know, there may be repercussions because of the damage to the galley and the loss of life, and if the injury to Herod proves to be fatal the Provincial Governor may be forced to look into the affair, as Pilate would be directly accountable to him for such an irregular fatality aboard a Roman ship. Even the emperor may be concerned as Herod's kingship is appointed by Rome! I think we will be well advised to stay clear of the port authority and the *Dolphin*, and keep a very low profile."

The following day was the Sabbath, and Flora indicated she would like to go with them to the Synagogue. She sat with 'the God fearers' in the clearly prescribed area separate from the Jews, and Mary chose to associate herself with her gentile friends. Listening to the elder of the Synagogue announcing the guest speaker, Mary had an ominous premonition and seized Marc's arm anxiously.

"We are honoured to have a leading Pharisee who has been appointed chief prosecutor of the heretical sect of Jesus of Nazareth. The Sanhedrin have given Saul unlimited authority to purge this false doctrine from Israel. I commend we heed him well."

Even as her premonition was confirmed, Saul was striding to the lectern with the confidence of one who has no doubts and is resolved in his purpose. He raised his arms and held them aloft until a respectful silence fell on the assembly, disturbed only by Marc insisting on leaving accompanied by the three women. This required considerable force as every seat was occupied and many in the congregation were intolerant at being asked to make way for the youth. Saul regarded them with annoyance, and then for but a few seconds the rearmost turned and looked searchingly at him, before hurrying after her companions.

That one look was enough. Saul recognised the woman who had been mobbed by the assembly at Joppa, and all his composure was set at naught. He clutched the lectern fighting back a crushing feeling of defeat. He had last seen this woman near to death a few weeks ago following his incitement of the crowd at Joppa, and now here she was to taunt him. He dare not relinquish the lectern as he felt his head spinning. For some time he stood there incapable of any coherent action, and then the rabbi and the elders of the Synagogue led him away and summoned a physician.

The first of their shared meals started inauspiciously, everyone hesitant to start despite the enticing dishes on the long low table. The lamb and chicken, lentils and vegetables and bread, cheese and olives, all lay untouched while desultory conversation passed between them.

Finally Mary said, "This is ridiculous. We all believe in one God so however we think of God let us give thanks for this wonderful supper you have prepared and do it justice."

Flora smiled and said, "Amen," and the unease evaporated.

Brutus had purchased a skin of wine and under its influence inhibitions quickly broke down and friendliness and intimacy prevailed.

"You haven't yet told us of your reasons for visiting our city, or how you got here," said Flora casually as though it were a matter of small import, although she and Lucia had speculated on it many an hour in their shared nights.

Brutus began, "That is a story of such length it would take a week to tell it fully. For Marc it started some three or four years ago when in northern Gallia his brothers and father were slain and he was enslaved. He became my slave when I plucked him from the sea as his slave galley sank in a storm."

After a momentary pause Mary continued.

"Brutus was a centurion in the Roman legions until two months ago, and now Marc is no longer his slave but his adopted son." Again Mary paused, as she didn't wish to go faster than they could follow.

"I first came into their lives on the most dreadful day I will ever know, the day of the crucifixion of my Lord Jesus."

There was a cry from Lucia and she hurried around the table to sit beside her mother who clasped her tightly.

"There now, Kunaria. We can stop now if you wish."

"But I don't wish, Mama. I'm just so frightened to hear what happened to Jesus from people who were there."

"Oh we were there on that awful day, the three of us and the mother of Jesus and many more. Oh yes, let us not forget Marc's friend, Miriam, who held out the only kindness and compassion Jesus knew that day. You tell it, Marc, you saw it unfold."

Marc told it as it had happened, and he spoke of Miriam with such tenderness and adoration that there was not a dry eye among the three women. Some of the tears from Lucia were at the realisation that this young god had pledged his heart to another.

Marc moved onto their escape from Joppa.

"You may have heard the tale of how we came here at the agora today. The speaker recounted it as though it was the story of David and Goliath. We were David in a small Arab dhow, the *Dolphin*, and Goliath was a ninety oar Roman bireme galley, which we nearly sank through the brilliance of my father."

Lucia was shaking with excitement.

"Oh mama I've heard the story twice. It's unbelievably thrilling and heroic. And to think the heroes of it are in our house, in my bed all this time?"

The two heroes preened themselves simultaneously.

"Well actually it was only a seventy oar galley," said Marc casually, but Brutus quickly interrupted.

"Marc says it was my brilliance that saved us but it isn't that simple. I had no ideas at all as I cut the bonds of our prisoner, Ephraim, other than to regain some control as the boat wallowing in the sea and the sails flapping made it impossible to think, and it was only as he brought it around that my brain resumed functioning. I saw the massive timbers on the deck and simultaneously I recalled the vision that I had the night of the crucifixion. This vision climaxed with the Son of God as mankind's champion defeating a monster, a creature formed from countless Roman legions. His weapon was his sword that flashed across the sky time and time again until the scorpion lay slain at my feet, so I looked, wondering if a bolt of lightning was about to strike the pursuing galley. Then my eye fell on the long balks of timber and the conviction grew in my mind that they could be used somehow to strike and disable our enemy. You know what followed."

He studied his spellbound listeners searchingly then concluded,

"It was a revelation from Jesus, once again my saviour, and I can only thank God for it."

The heroine, smiling quietly, reflected on the panic that had gripped her when she had found herself in deeper water than she had bargained for at the side of the quay, but decided not to tell of that.

"Now you know our story, we want to hear yours. I know somehow it isn't pure chance we are here and that God's purpose has brought us together," insisted Mary.

"Please tell them, mama. I'm really happy you tell it to these friends."

Flora smiled.

"Only if you're sure, Kunaria," and it was at her daughter's insistence she continued.

"This same Jesus of whom you talk, visited Tyre just over a year ago - no nearly two years, as it was summer then. Since about her tenth birthday Lucia had been unable to leave the house for fear of injuring herself, for at that age she started having frequent and violent seizures, for many minutes throwing herself about in a frenzy and sometimes really injuring herself. It could take four men to restrain her, she was so strong when in its grip, and afterwards so weak and so wretched. The doctors were baffled and diagnosed that she was possessed by a demon."

Flora clutched Lucia to her tightly as the memories flooded back.

"I was at my wits end. I couldn't go out to work and had spent most of my savings searching for a cure. Lucia couldn't leave the house and life was one long agony of suspense. Then a wonderful friend told me that the miracle worker from Galilee had arrived at Tyre with his disciples. I was convinced that he was our only chance. I only knew his name, Jesus, and that he was with a dozen followers.

"My friend, bless her, said she would stay with Lucia and I was not to worry how long I took. I searched for two days and I knew he was the miracle worker as soon as I saw him, but he had such an air of abandonment about him, although surrounded by his followers. I had resolved to entreat his help, so I forced a way through the circle of men around him and cried out, 'Sir, Son of David, have pity on me! My daughter is grievously afflicted by a demon!' but it was as though he didn't hear me.

"His disciples tried to shoo me away, but I was determined they would not prevent me reaching him. They tired of resisting me eventually, and one who dwarfed all the others went up to Jesus and said, 'Send her away, we can't stand her shrieking!'"

"That's Simon Peter. Only Peter could be that blunt. Shame on him!" said Mary angrily.

"No bless him. For now Jesus looked at me and beckoned. I went and kneeled before him and he said, 'I was sent only to the lost sheep of Israel.'

"I didn't know what he meant so I simply said, 'Lord, help me!'

"Jesus looked at me searchingly and I felt my soul was bared to him as he said, 'It is not right to take the children's bread and to throw it to the pet dogs.'

"I knew so much depended on my answer, and I believe he was searching for God to reveal something that eluded him. I said, 'True, Lord, but even the dogs eat of the pieces which fall from their master's table.'

"His smile was radiant and I knew somehow I had answered a question that had been deeply troubling him. He said, 'Woman, great is your faith! Let it be done for you as you wish.' I hurried home and Lucia has not had a seizure since."

Above the general rejoicing at Flora's words, Brutus agitatedly insisted, "Do you mean that if you had given some other reply, less pleasing to him, he would have continued to disregard you, and Lucia would still be having these seizures?"

Mother and daughter looked at each other anxiously. They had never thought to question what might have been, and now were dismayed by the suggestion it could have ended differently. Flora looked imploringly at Mary who moved to put a reassuring arm around Brutus.

"You are still deeply troubled by the interaction of chance and destiny aren't you, Brutus. It is an unanswerable paradox for me too, but I do know there are moments when God to achieve his purpose uses the best of what is available, and so it was with Lucia and Flora. I don't believe God afflicted Lucia with her fits to use them to advantage later, but that God saw in Flora an indomitable spirit that would never cease to strive for a cure."

Mary felt they had come to a crisis and that the future happiness of their relationship hung precariously on her next words. She looked to Flora for help, but the entranced look of mother and daughter as they sat hand in hand was support enough.

"Jesus was nearing thirty years of age when God revealed his full purpose for him. God needed that maturity for what he asked of him, and for a few years he did everything that was humanly possible to show he was the Son of God. He preached a message of love and with parables explained the relationship of a loving God to his children and tried to reveal what he meant by 'the Kingdom of Heaven.' He healed the sick and the lame, comforted those that were oppressed. He raised the dead, drove out demons and explained how his coming was the fulfillment of scripture and of the prophets.

"Thousands from the tribes of Israel were converted to be his disciples and to believe he was the Messiah. Ordinary people for whom life could be hard with daily problems and setbacks, but still they believed in him and followed him. He must have had high expectations that his message was getting across.

"Then he came up against a brick wall, a barrier of mistrust, unyielding and opposed to everything he was saying. Resentment turned to hate as the Pharisees and the Sadducees realized all their privileges were threatened by his teaching. They closed ranks to get rid of him and Herod had John, he who had baptized Jesus, beheaded.

"Overwhelmed Jesus just had to get away and he came to Tyre. But here he was confronted with a new challenge; the whole pagan world was thirsting for the message of God's love. But his message for his own people was leading to a confrontation with the authorities that he knew would end with his death. How could he take on so much more at that time?"

Mary moved over to Flora and put her arms around her.

"When the agonizing of Jesus is at its most intense, along comes Flora on behalf of her afflicted daughter. She meets a brick wall, a barrier as unyielding and opposed to her erected by the disciples, as any that Jesus encountered from the priests. Is she going to allow anything to prevent her from asking for that she has set her heart on?

"No. Undeterred she resolves to strive harder. So she ceaselessly searches for a way through, until she achieves her goal and kneels at his feet. Jesus reveals his own dilemma to her, as though he wishes her to tell him the way he should go. And she does! Brilliantly, so appropriate and wittily that Jesus rejoices with her. So we see God using Flora's strength to his own purpose. It was the same with you at the time of the crucifixion. You were there, so I'm sure your strengths were needed and used by God. Who other of the centurions could have had your role?"

"Well Josias had a high fever so he couldn't. That left only Petrus, but I would have hated for him to have carried out the execution."

"Why is that?" exclaimed Marc, "I knew you would have to because there was such unrest and you had greater command of your legionaries than any other centurion. But why would you not want Petrus to have had command?"

"Petrus would have broken the legs of all the victims."

There was a simultaneous gasp of horror from the women, and Marc who was deeply affected, said, "Why on earth would he do such a brutal thing?"

"He is greatly feared of ghosts. The victims of crucifixion often curse those who drive in the nails, their executioners. By breaking the victim's legs, Petrus knew not only would they die quicker but they would not be able to walk from the grave and haunt him."

There was an involuntary shudder from Mary as she said, "Then I thank God that it was you and not Petrus. And I thank God for the good things that have followed and led to our being here."

She received a reassuring smile from Brutus and sitting at his feet she laid her head on his knee.

Marc, reacting to the somberness of all that he had heard, felt an urge to lighten the mood.

Turning to Flora he said, "I know I'm inquisitive but when you were talking to Jesus did he talk to you in Aramaic or Greek?"

"He knew I was Greek so we spoke in Greek. Why do you ask?"

"Well when Jesus said it was not right to take the children's bread and to throw it to the pet dogs ..."

He stopped and looked laughingly at Lucia who knew exactly what was coming and hurried to try and reach him before he could finish. She failed as he blurted out, "did he use the Greek word for puppy - Kunaria?"

Marc never got an answer as he was knocked from the couch and submerged under an outraged harridan, or so he thought as he was pummelled, sat on, shaken by the ears and generally abused.

"Help me somebody," pleaded Marc, but nobody moved a muscle as they all thought he was getting his just desserts.

"What must I do to get this fury off me?" cried Marc.

"Promise on your absolute honour, never to use that word again, never."

"I promise on my absolute honour never to call you Kunaria again Lucia."

Everyone joined in the laughter as his pummelling continued, if anything with greater enthusiasm.

That night Marc lay awake for a long time in Lucia's bed, but his longing was for Miriam. He liked Lucia well enough, and enjoyed the company of someone of his own age, but his heart ached to know if Miriam was well, and if she was missing him.

It was as well he didn't know she had cried herself to sleep that night, distressed by that which she had witnessed in the Temple that same day. Every detail was clearly etched in her mind and she kept awakening to the recurring nightmare.

CHAPTER FIVE

The storm clouds had been gathering for some weeks, with occasional acts of violence against the followers when they persisted in their slanderous attacks on the temple authorities. As the apostles responded to the threats by stepping up their criticism, calling on the Sanhedrin to publicly acknowledge guilt and plead for forgiveness, it was apparent to everyone they were on a collision course.

One morning in the meeting room Peter had beckoned Miriam to meet the stranger with whom he had been conversing.

"Simon the tanner brings news from Joppa, so I'll leave you together," and smiling conspiratorially the apostle moved away, leaving Miriam looking anxiously into a pair of brilliant blue eyes sparkling as sun on wind ruffled sea, from a face those same elements had tanned to the deepest brown of any hide.

"I bring news received by my silversmith friend, Abraham."

He waited until Miriam's eager look of entreaty forced him to continue.

"The fugitives are safely arrived in Tyre!"

Had he had more to communicate, the light in Miriam's eyes would have encouraged him to continue, but just then Steven, a young Greek speaking Jew from Corinth, burst agitatedly into the room, galvanizing every one by his news.

"Saul of Tarsus is in Jerusalem and right now he's at the temple, calling on the faithful to stone any heretic who persists in preaching the resurrection of our Lord!"

Mirian hurried home, anxious to bring to her family both items of news, but the agitation of her mother reinforced her misgivings.

"Daddy has been talking to Saul of Tarsus who has just left and ..." Naomi stopped as her daughter jerked at that name as though she had received a slap across the face.

"Saul here!" she shuddered violently. "Mama don't ever let me see him here after what he did to Mary!"

Just then Simon entered and shaken by the virulence of Miriam's words, clutched at a chair visibly shaken, and sat down.

"Saul came to warn me that you are in real danger if you associate with the followers of Jesus at the Temple. They plan to arrest the leaders, and there may be rioting among the followers, which will be stamped on by the Romans. Saul regrets what happened to Mary and supported the service of atonement at the synagogue. I wouldn't like what happened to Mary to happen to you, so don't go there until the situation is more settled."

Miriam was deeply dismayed, but respecting her father's concern, and not to distress him further, she yielded.

"I must be allowed to go to the communion room," she insisted, "and my promise not to go to the Temple must be reviewed in a few days when things are clearer."

Anxious the followers should know of Saul's intentions, Miriam hurried back to the meeting room, as they were assembling for midday prayers.

"Peter, my father has heard from Saul of Tarsus. They are going to arrest you all when next you go to the Temple!"

"Thank you, Miriam. Then that will be tomorrow," and he gave her one of his brilliant smiles as though he had not one care in the world.

Miriam did not go to the Temple the following days because of her promise, but on entering the assembly room, she found the greatest alarm and despondency among the followers. Steven told her that the Temple guards, reinforced by a century from the fort, had seized all the apostles and thrown them into prison overnight.

"They had only a few hours earlier seen Peter heal a lame man who has sat at the Beautiful Gate for years. But still they arrested them - it's unbelievable," he shook his head in disbelief, and Miriam noticed the bruise disfiguring his cheek.

Returning home dismayed at the news, Miriam beseeched her father to release her from her promise.

"Not until they have appeared before the Sanhedrin," insisted Simon.

The following evening Miriam returned home rejoicing.

"Daddy, they have released Peter and the other apostles and there has been no rioting. My promise to you I have kept faithfully, but I must be free to join them in worship at the Temple now!"

Simon knew the time had come to withdraw his objection.

The next three days were filled with incredible happenings as countless sick and lame people were brought to the Temple and many were cured. There was a further arrest of the apostles, then they were released again, and it was rumoured that through the advocacy of the Pharisee, Gamaliel, the apostles were no longer to be arrested. They were under an injunction not to preach in the name of Jesus in the Temple, but this they totally ignored.

One evening Miriam and Steven were talking in the assembly room when Peter came over to them and said, "I rejoice, Steven, that you are among the seven chosen. They have chosen well!"

"What was that about, Steven?" asked Miriam, and Steven explained that seven of them had been appointed to supervise the daily collection and distribution of alms within the community.

"It's quite an important job, as we should be able to help reconcile the Greek speaking and Aramaic speaking Jews who are not disposed to seeing each other's problems objectively."

Miriam wished him success, and was glad she was not living in one of the communities that were taking over some of the larger houses in the city.

Steven had the gift of healing and the sick and lame were brought to him all the time. Miriam had been with him often and had rejoiced with their loved ones at each miracle, but always Steven was more drawn to debate, at which he excelled.

His fame was recognized widely, and the leading theologians of the day from the synagogues and academies throughout the world, disputed with him as he declared Jesus to be the Messiah, quoting the authority found in the Prophets and the Torah.

"They murdered him, these self righteous priests and Pharisees, as they frequently did the prophets," was his typical conclusion to many a speech, as he was always intemperate in his scathing criticism of the Temple officials, urging them to repent and ask for forgiveness, and always he incurred their condemnation.

Late one afternoon, after a particularly bruising encounter as he sat drained and exhausted in the colonnade, an agitated Pharisee cried out insistently to all around.

"This man is always blaspheming against Moses and against God and should be arraigned before the court of the Sanhedrin. Seize him now while we still have witnesses here to testify to his blasphemy!"

As the temple guards arrested him Miriam protested, "This man lies. Steven has never said anything against Moses or God, only against the priests!"

One of the guards struck her across the mouth and she fell heavily, lying dazed until some of the crowd helped her to her feet. Frightened, blood streaming from a cut lip, she ran after Steven only to see him being dragged into the administrative complex of the Temple, and the two massive doors slammed closed behind him. A squad of guards dispersed any followers, and Miriam formed the ominous opinion it had been orchestrated to seize him while the apostles were occupied elsewhere.

Seeking out the apostles, to bring Steven's arrest to their attention, Miriam was confounded to stumble upon her brother Rufus, who she had thought still to be in Cyrene. Not having seen him in over a year she was both confused and distressed and ran to him sobbing, to throw herself into his arms.

He was truly alarmed at her dishevelled state and her bleeding mouth, and even more so when she urged him to help save Steven before they kill him.

"You look in real trouble yourself, little sister, what on earth has happened?"

"Oh one of the guards struck me, when they were dragging Steven off and I protested."

"Is violence acceptable in the Temple these days? Father said these were troubled times but I would have expected women to be safe here."

"Mary Magdalene was nearly killed in the synagogue at Joppa two weeks ago."

"Who is Mary Magdalene, do I know her?"

"No she is one of the bravest followers of Jesus. But mama and papa know her."

Rufus looked pensive, but as Miriam was still pulling at him he said, "Alright, take me to find your friend Steven now they've arrested him?"

They were stopped from getting near the guarded doors and Rufus tried to coax his sister to tell him what had been happening since he had last seen her, but she was too distraught to make any coherent reply. So they both waited apprehensively, as if anticipating the violence about to erupt around them.

From behind the closed doors was heard an increasing commotion before they suddenly burst open to the press of an angry mob, who were hauling the semi-conscious man by his arms, his feet bound and dragging uselessly. Priests were tearing at their beards and robes, and an insistent cry issued from every throat.

"Stone the blasphemer, kill the heretic!"

Pulling desperately at Rufus, Miriam tried to force a way through, but found a spear held barring her path. She went to push it aside, but the guard thrust her violently and she fell back against Rufus.

It was in a state bordering shock that they followed the bloodthirsty mob pouring out of the Temple, and from the high city wall overlooking the Kidron valley saw Steven thrown from the wall onto the boulder-strewn floor below.

Fearing a riot, Roman soldiers poured from the fort, but when they saw the larger part of the mob were priests and Pharisees they withdrew to let things run their course.

It was all Rufus could do to stop his distraught sister rushing to the gateway and down to where Steven lay. Some Jews had done just that and were massed along the lip of the valley facing them.

Suddenly a gasp went up from the onlookers. The crumpled figure rolled onto his side and slowly thrust himself to his knees. He raised his bloodied head to heaven and beseechingly clasped his hands before him, but the words he uttered failed to reach the ears of those on the wall.

Then stones fell in a violent fuselage from the valley slope, battering the body into stillness. Two men removed their robes and passing them to the erectly approving Saul, descended to the unmoving body, where the leader raising a large rock in both hands, brought it down to crush the cranium of the already dead disciple.

The roar of approval was lost to Miriam who overtaxed beyond endurance had slumped unconscious. Rufus stood shocked with disbelief, looking at the now rather subdued mob that was breaking up and skulking away. He felt a deep sense of shame, to have witnessed such barbarism from his own people. He surveyed for one last time the whole desolate scene, and found his eyes locked in an unbreakable hold with those of the zealous fanatic across the valley. He recognised Saul of Tarsus but never before had he known such enmity as now seized him.

They made a very sorry pair as they trod their weary, hesitant path across the city, and Miriam enervated by the stressful day needed to rest frequently. Entering the court the voice of Simon conversing with another man came to both their ears, and with questioning looks they moved to the side of the house. There, seated on the terrace, were their father and Saul.

Miriam shrieked, ran to the closed door at the front of the house and cowered behind the pillar to one side of the porch. Rufus followed behind her, and was relieved to see the door opened by their mother, concern etched on her face. Each took one of Miriam's arms and led her into the cool interior.

"Take care of her, mama," said Rufus as he relinquished her arm to a servant and turning on his heel, he emerged as Simon and Saul came around the corner of the house. Acknowledging his father with a bow, Rufus challenged Saul, all normal courtesy evaporated in the heat of his anger.

"One question, Saul of Tarsus!"

They eyed each other warily.

"You approved the murder of Steven that we have just witnessed?"

"I approved the stoning of the blasphemer, yes."

"Then leave our house. My enmity for you and your like makes it impossible for you ever again to be seen here."

"Rufus! Saul is our guest!" cried an anguished Simon.

"No father. He has the freshly shed blood of the innocent on his hands, as I witnessed to my shame this day."

Simon buried his face in his hands and sank down to his knees as Saul and Rufus confronted each other in a silent battle of wills.

Then Saul turned and left the house. The rage burning in his breast, hidden by his stony features, was to burst forth in an explosive violence that same night.

Providence urged Alexander to ride hard from Joppa that day. He just felt uneasy and kept pushing the eager young stallion, and both were grateful when he reigned back at the stable in the old city of David. That same instinct told him to take his sword for the ten minute walk to his home, although it was his habit to leave it at the stable, rather than bring such a symbol of violence into the peace that invested his family home.

Following the narrow cobbled streets he could feel the tension in the air. It was palpable, like the pulse of a fevered comrade at the approaching crisis. Dusk had fallen and he thought it an omen to find the outer gate locked, necessitating him pulling the bell two or three times before one of the nervous servants came to admit him.

Within the family there was a heightening of suspense as the bell sounded so insistently and their relief when Alexander entered was too much for Naomi, who burst into tears.

"Why such sombre looks to greet me?" he chided them, looking apprehensively from his clutching mother to his brother and father. His father appeared more aged than he had ever thought possible in the interval since last he had seen him.

"Welcome to our troubled house, Alex," said Rufus embracing him, and glancing at his belted sword, "I think that those seeking vengeance are about to be unleashed in Jerusalem today."

"That's colourful language brother, but then you always were the poet!" Alexander bantered, although the remark was only half in jest.

At his father's embrace Alexander made the traditional Jewish greeting of shalom, but his nervousness and flitting eyes made him realize Simon was far from at peace.

Seated around the low table over supper, Alexander was impatient with every one at their jumpiness. He still hadn't seen Miriam, who was sleeping fitfully, hinting of her inner turmoil in half choked, incoherent outcries.

Their meal progressed uneventfully until one of the servants entered and addressed Simon, but getting no further acknowledgement than a hesitant shake of his head she approached Alexander.

"There is a rabble assembled threateningly at the front gate," she said, noticeably nervous.

"Come brother, I think we need to show some louts there aren't just women in this house," called Alexander and the two of them went to the front door.

As they stepped out into the court the dozen men milling outside the gate fell silent, until one shouted, "Blasphemers, heretics, Jesus lovers!" and all the rest joined in the chant. The air was suddenly threatening. Not believing in meeting challenges half way, Alexander moved nonchalantly to the gate and studied the riff-raff contemptuously.

"Well, well," he said, "you must be surprised to find two men here. That you are so few, you were obviously expecting only a couple of women and the servants."

He seized the gates and shook them violently, and the men pressed up against them backed away nervously, then the brothers assisted the servants in securing all the shutters and moved back into the house. As though this was a signal, they felt the crunch of the first stone thrown at the door, which was the precursor to many more.

176

Reassuring Naomi there was no real threat if they kept their heads, they moved to their sister's room and found her sitting up in bed, wild eyed and distraught. Seeing Alexander, her face brightened, her bruised lip distorting the intended smile.

"What's the banging, Alex? she asked

"It's only some louts throwing stones to frighten us," Rufus said, instantly wishing he hadn't as Miriam's lip trembled so that she had to bite it.

"Well Steven didn't show any fear and nor shall we," said Miriam tremulously, and indicated she would be getting up, the better to face any threat.

From the hall landing a ladder gave access to the flat roof through a hinged skylight. From this vantage point, Alexander could see their own courtyard and a considerable part of the city. He saw a few fires burning in the old part and was glad it was a windless night, as any blaze amongst those houses huddled so closely together, was likely to get out of control and to burn down the city. He also saw a squad of legionaries, who passed the rabble at their gate with nothing other than a few laughing words and then moved on.

"So that's how the land lies, we can expect no help from the military," he thought, and then as though the soldiers had instigated it, he saw two of the men scaling the gate.

"Quickly," he called, "we must deter them from coming over the gate. Get your sword but try only to frighten them."

As they launched themselves at the men who were trying to force the lock from the inside they were met by a fusillade of stones. Most missed, although one caught Alexander a glancing blow on the jaw. Angered and dazed, as the two intruders desperately scrambled back over the gate he slashed at a kicking leg, severing the tendon of the heel. The man screamed and fell into the arms of his companions, while at the same time Rufus, jabbing his blade through the bars, impaled another's forearm.

They fled in complete disorder dragging their wounded, and then stood some way off taking stock of the situation. Deciding to seek easier prey elsewhere, there was a last half-hearted flurry of stones before they moved away.

Nobody quite realized the scale of the persecution that was being initiated that night. All of the communities were raided and their leaders seized and thrown into any available prison, both men and women alike. All monies and any valuables were stolen, and treasures that couldn't be taken away were smashed.

Those not imprisoned were urged to flee, their tormentors threatening they would be back tomorrow. Fires were started at the meeting rooms, but this the military regarded as overzealous, and the soldiers quickly put them out fearful they would spread out of control. It was a night of vengeance by the righteous Jews orchestrated by Saul of Tarsus, whose name was from that night on to become infamously linked with the persecution of the followers of Jesus.

The next day, those that were brave enough to ignore the taunts of the guards, assembled pitiably at Solomon's colonnade. Miriam and her brothers joined the apostles, just as Peter was declaring that the Lord had bestowed a beatific smile on Steven when his soul had soared to heaven on angel's wings.

Miriam was mindful of the soaring eagle she had seen on the way to Joppa, and she looked to see if Alexander registered any sign of remembering, but his attention was solely on Peter who was continuing.

"You all know that terrible things happened throughout Jerusalem last night, at the instigation of the priests and elders of this very Temple. Not content with murdering the Son of God, they are now attempting to eliminate us followers. No longer can we hope for our priests to ever welcome Jesus as the Messiah. But I say to you, Israel is more than the Temple and its authorities, more than the court of the Sanhedrin with its priests and Pharisees. Israel is all of you, who share in this new covenant revealed by the Son. This dynamic and living covenant which comes from the Father to fulfil and complete that given to the Patriarchs, and anticipated by the prophets. It is your inheritance now, you thousands of Jews who are the disciples and followers of Jesus. Take pride to be chosen to be a light to the gentiles. Shake the dust of this desecrated place from your sandals; go out into the world proclaiming the message of Jesus wherever you go.

"Go into Samaria and Lebanon, to Egypt and Syria, to Gaul, Rome and Africa even to the very ends of the world. Everywhere tell of the Lord's teaching and his parables. Tell of his miracles and of his death and his resurrection. Teach them to pray as he taught you. If the Holy Spirit gives you the power, lay hands on the sick and the lame. Jesus promised that where two or three are gathered in his name, there he would be also.

"We apostles will stay here in Jerusalem, at the centre of a church radiating to the furthest limits of the world. Jesus prayed for his church to be united in faith, so when you are troubled seek our guidance, and we will always listen to you. If you need help we will send help to you. Our prayers go with you wherever you go."

Peter looked towards Miriam and beckoned her to join him. Kneeling she said, "Our family will leave for Damascus tomorrow. Give us your blessing for the days ahead."

Peter took her hands and brought her to her feet.

"That is only the start, I foresee you going much further than that. As I was talking of taking the message to the furthest corners of the world, I clearly saw you. But look at these bruises you carry from yesterday. Wear them with pride, as did Mary at Joppa! Now who are these young men?" and Peter smiled warmly, with a very genuine interest that was more than curiosity.

"My elder brother Alexander, and my brother Rufus."

Both men bowed, aware of the close scrutiny of the imposing giant.

Looking piercingly into Rufus' eyes, his own shining with that clarity of purpose that knows no denial, Peter said, "So you are the young man who challenged Saul of Tarsus? The Lord needs you. Will you abide with us and be my acolyte?"

Rufus fell on his knees, overcome with such rejoicing his chest felt inadequate to confine his overflowing heart.

"Willingly, master."

Peter blessed him then raised him to his feet.

"Will you have no qualms at leaving the business?" asked Alexander petulantly.

Rufus looked at Peter and said with great joy, "No more than Peter had when Jesus called him to leave his boat beside the Sea of Galilee."

Peter rejoiced with them and praised the Lord. He blessed Miriam and Alexander as they departed brotherless, to take the news to their parents and prepare for the journey to Damascus.

Marc and Lucia had become good friends, and when not working at the inn or helping with domestic chores, Lucia liked to show Marc much of the ancient Phoenician city. The agora in the square became one of their favourite spots, where they could catch up on any news, or delight in some novel philosophy being expounded.

On this particular day it was immediately apparent there was an event of great moment being related because of the large, silent crowd gathered around the rostrum, and the dramatic posturing of the speaker. Moving quickly to the rear of the audience they heard only his final words.

"So the scale of the disturbance has led to hundreds of families fleeing. The roads out of Jerusalem are choked with carts and wagons, and people on foot, carrying whatever they can of their possessions, so that in places movement has come to a standstill, and the Romans are out in force trying to keep some order. The first refugees can be expected in Tyre tomorrow, and the city council is meeting now to decide what action may need to be taken."

Looking anxiously at each other, Marc asked a bystander what they had missed of the bulletin.

"I think there has been rioting in Jerusalem and the heavy hand of the legions has fallen on the Jews," he stated, as a merchant taking the rostrum called out, "I rode out of the city of David early yesterday after a night of considerable rioting. Many houses were burning and the mobs were targeting any house where followers of Jesus are known to live."

Another man leapt up onto the rostrum. He was wild haired with gaunt ascetic features, and a hunted look to his deep-set, darting eyes.

"I fled just before being arrested. I belong to the Essenes of the Qumran community, and was sent to Judaea to try to establish whether this Jesus was the Messiah, and if so to persuade him to talk to our assembly of the 'Sons of Light'.

"I stayed in Jerusalem at a very humble dwelling with a cripple and his widowed mother. Anthus has been lame from birth and both his legs are paralyzed, and I helped push him daily to the Beautiful Gate in the Temple Court where he has been begging for the past twenty years."

Responding to the gasps of incredulity, the speaker continued,

"You have heard nothing yet, wait until you hear the rest!" and absolute silence fell on the crowd.

"This only happened last week and I was there so I saw everything! Two disciples of Jesus came through the gate and heard Anthus calling for alms. One of them is a giant named Peter, who stopped and fixed his eye on Anthus thrusting out his bowl expectantly.

"Peter said clearly for all of us to hear, 'Silver and gold I do not possess but what I have I give you. In the name of Jesus, walk!'

"Anthus was stunned! This wasn't the hand-out he had expected! He just looked at his misshapen, atrophied legs, bent and contorted under him and shook his head in disbelief, as did all of us standing there. Then Peter put out his right hand, removed his alms bowl and lifted him up. There isn't much of Anthus, so such a man could easily pluck him up in one hand, but as we watched his legs straightened, and his feet and ankle bones strengthened, and he leapt about rejoicing and walked with them into the Temple praising God."

As the cries of joy and wonder seized the crowd, the Essene silenced them by raising both arms.

"You may be asking yourselves what has this miracle to do with what is happening in Jerusalem now? I will tell you. I was in the house of Anthus the night before last, when a Pharisee led a squad of Temple guards to arrest him and his mother, and imprison them."

A roar of anger erupted and it was some time before it simmered down for him to continue.

"The reason they gave was that Anthus had ignored the command of the High Priest to keep silent about how he had gained the use of his legs. Could anyone keep quiet about such a miracle? Of course not! I managed to flee the house as the guards were chasing Anthus, and a fine chase he gave them I can tell you. But when he saw they had seized his old mother and things might go badly for her, he gave himself up."

The howls of outrage that ensued at the conclusion were obviously going to continue for a long time so Marc and Lucia hurried home anxious to tell their shattering news.

"Marc we have to assume that Miriam's family will be amongst those fleeing Jerusalem, but we can't find out anything today," said Brutus, "so hire a horse first thing tomorrow and ride back along the Jerusalem road, following the coastal plain south to Acco. Somewhere along the way you will encounter the leading refugees and maybe Miriam and her family. I will go and see the local commander, who should know what's happening."

Marc was desperately worried about Miriam, so much so that to wait until the morning was almost unbearable.

"I'll go to the stable and arrange for a horse to be ready at dawn," he said unhappily, and as he departed Mary expressed her concern.

"He won't sleep at all tonight. His chance of stumbling on anyone who knows what has happened to Miriam and her family tomorrow is remote, so he is going to get more and more worried. I think I ought to go back somehow, to find out more and make contact with Peter, if he's not in prison."

"Only if I come with you!" insisted Brutus. "No, it makes better sense to find out what we can from the first refugees to arrive, the situation is so confused. Someone should keep an ear on the agora."

Lucia agreed to do that, and consequently it was she who brought unwelcome news an hour later, a few minutes after Marc had returned.

"The city council, has ruled that no one from Jerusalem will be allowed to stay here unless they have a place to stay with a house owner as sponsor. There is to be a road-block set up half a mile south and any refugees without sponsors will be turned away."

"Then we women of Tyre must busy ourselves organising for these poor people, so that they cannot be turned away! We can take a family here, and I know a lot of our friends will do likewise. At last we can do something to repay all that Jesus has done for us, Lucia," and Flora set purposefully about her self-imposed task.

An hour before dawn, after a sleepless night, Marc left the house with cloak and sword to be at the stable when they opened, and by the time he was cantering along the coast road a red streaked sunrise loomed over the high hills to his left. At least he was doing something instead of idly waiting, and his raw nerves responded to the anodyne of activity.

180

Had he not been so driven he would have taken a lot more notice of the spectacular terrain he was riding through, the road closely following the contour of the hills where they met the narrow coastal plain. But always his eyes were scanning the limited horizon ahead, willing the cart with the outriders to come over the next crest, as it had over the Judaean hills above Joppa but a few weeks before.

For three hours Marc rode unstopping, and then over the rise a mile distant, silhouetted against the azure sky, he saw the first horse drawn wagon breast the slope and move down the open valley, then another and another in unending sequence.

He urged his tired mount on, reigning back as he came abreast of the first cart. As he did so his exaltation froze, his questing eyes searching the empty, listless gaze, of someone who had lost everything. Hesitantly, as though intruding into an unfathomable sorrow, he moved up to the wagon. He coughed, and the down-cast eyes of the young woman suddenly became aware of him. She held the rein in clumsily bandaged hands and as he watched wordlessly, her husband moved to look over her shoulder from the interior of the wagon. The sight of his burnt and blackened face with frizzled hair and beard caused Marc to shudder, and conveyed more eloquently than any words uttered from the agora the full horror of the persecution. Marc was barely able to utter any words.

"Forgive me. I've ridden from Tyre to search for Miriam, do you know of her?" he stammered.

Something of the depths of his concern penetrated the despair engulfing the woman.

"I wish I could say she is with us," she said, "but we have only the bodies of our dead angels."

Baffled by this daunting reply, Marc leant over and drew the flap of the wagon aside. He saw the diminutive, charred bodies lying embracing each other, as they had in bed when the flames had surged with unbelievable vehemence through their modest house. The horror tugged at his heart, as nothing had since Miriam had held him to her breast on the way to Calvary.

He tied his horse to the tailboard and climbing to sit beside her took the reins and urged the horses forward saying, "Truly they are angels and you can be sure Jesus is there to welcome them to heaven."

The woman gave him a bewildered smile, as though afraid that doing so be-trayed her absolute desolation, and silently they rode at the head of that funeral procession to Tyre.

As they breasted the last rise and came to the road-block, Marc desperately beckoned the awaiting women over,

"Please take care of these devastated souls. Their dead children are all they have brought from Jerusalem."

He jumped down and passed the bridle to Mary, who was enjoining her anxious heart not to fail her now, fearful of what she would find within the wagon.

"I must find Brutus to help me search for Miriam," he said as he mounted and rode away.

It only took Brutus five minutes, and then both were ready to resume the search.

They passed the road-block and the long, despondent line of refugees, riding hard fearful to ease back for a moment. As dusk deepened and the glow to the west vanished quickly into night, they passed the place where Marc had first come across the refugees and turned back to Tyre.

There were very few stragglers on the road now, as they moved away from the coast along the ravine towards the high Plain of Esdraclon. The moon was not yet up, and they were forced to slow as the road fell away at places precipitously.

The sound of many horses made them hold back, and then they were in the midst of a troop of cavalry milling around them.

"Whoa," called a disembodied voice, "what the devil are you up to at this hour of the night?"

"Searching for a wagon that may have fled Jerusalem. There will be an elderly couple and their teenage daughter. Have you passed them?"

"How many were there at that overturned cart we passed sergeant?"

"Two women clambered up to the road, sir. One was young, the one who pleaded for our help." The sergeant fidgeted with embarrassment.

"Where was this, captain?" demanded Brutus urgently.

"About two miles back. They won't have moved as their wagon had plunged off the road."

"There are enough of you. Why didn't you right their wagon?"

Detecting the menace in the centurion's voice, the commander bristled defensively as he replied, "Our role is not wet nursing every Jew on the road who gets into trouble."

"What is your role then, captain?" snarled Brutus sarcastically, "ensuring you get your troop home in time for bed?"

"Who are you to challenge a troop of the imperial cavalry?" rejoined the officer, but with a querulous note, as though he was aware of the authority of his interrogator.

"Centurion Brutus, formerly attached to the Jerusalem garrison. Lead us to these unfortunate people commander."

The effect of declaring himself was electrifying, the troops shedding their slovenly disinterest, and assuming a new alertness.

"I can easily find the place, sir," said the sergeant, though it was uncertain whom he was addressing, as he turned the troop around and led at a swift gallop.

His night vision was excellent, and having but minutes previously covered the same road he led with justifiable confidence, and in fifteen minutes they reached the spot, but in the darkness nothing was visible.

"Ahoy there," called the sergeant, and a man's voice answered faintly from some way off, disembodied and forlorn.

"Is that you, Alexander?" called Marc.

There were a few seconds of silence, and then his ears resounded to his own name being called over and over again, in tones so tremulous and beseeching that he threw himself from the saddle, and nearly fell into the deep gully to the side of the road. Groping his way down, he heard the sobbing of someone moving towards him on hands and knees, and then they collided in a heart-stopping embrace, the stars cavorting in the heavens. Marc was so overwhelmed at finding them alive he was incapable of coherent thought or appropriate action.

The sergeant found some brushwood and soon had a feeble torch flickering hesitantly. This was quickly added to, until there was sufficient light for all to realize the serious consequences of the accident they had ignored, and the culpable indifference they had shown by riding away.

"Come on, dearest, we must see how bad things are!" Marc urged gently moving towards the wreckage of their wagon.

As they saw the horse with broken back lying between the shafts, and a man, with a broken arm sitting forlornly, beside an older man pinned under the over-turned cart, the appalling scale of the tragedy quickly became apparent. Naomi was not to be seen anywhere, but at Miriam's desperate tugging they followed her a short distance to the rear of the wagon, where a deep cleft opened in the rock. Naomi lifted her head as the searching torch was thrust into the cleft where she had fallen, and her eyes opened vacantly.

"And you led your troops away to seek the comfort of your bed," was Brutus' only scathing comment, before assuming command and organising the rescue.

They split in two separate groups, Marc, the sergeant and two soldiers to rescue Naomi from the cleft, the rest to assist Brutus to free the dead horse and take the crushing weight off Simon.

The darkness and the instability of the scree-covered incline made the work difficult and dangerous. Wooden staves had to be found to prop the heavy vehicle, and to lever it off the still body. Eventually Brutus was able to pull Simon clear of the precariously balanced cart, but even as he did so one of the levers snapped under the strain, and the wreckage of the cart began to pitch out of control down the slope.

Brutus grabbed the extended arm of a soldier, and heaved Simon clear a split second before it rolled away into the darkness. The flaying end of the broken shaft struck him heavily on the shoulder, knocking him over, and he couldn't hold Simon as he spun away. They were only arrested in their fall by scrub and boulders, while the cart continued its splintering course into the dark depths.

Meanwhile Marc had worked his way into the cleft to Naomi, where he assessed her twisted leg and foot wedged firmly into the narrowing embrasure.

"She's broken her leg and her foot is trapped," he called up to the sergeant, "pass me down a rope so that you can take her weight while I free her foot."

He tried to reassure Naomi as they waited for an eternity.

"Simon's dead," she said with dreadful finality and Marc realised she was not far from that end herself. Her eyes kept closing and he thought she was about to pass out as he placed a reassuring arm around her shoulders, as she had around his that Passover eve following the crucifixion.

Fighting back his tears he said, "Please don't give up Naomi. As soon as we can free your foot, we'll have you out of here shortly."

He looked up and saw Miriam's tearful, anxiety wracked face, peering down at them. Naomi looked up at Miriam hesitantly, as though focussing was difficult, then at Marc.

"You will look after her won't you?" she said, and closed her eyes.

The rope was passed down and he secured it around her body, hardly able to see what he was doing, blinded by tears that could not be contained.

"Take a little weight and see how it holds," he called and he felt a slight upward surge, "hold it there."

Rotating the smashed and broken lower leg he knew she wouldn't feel any pain from it now, but he felt it incumbent on him to be as gentle as possible as he worked it free and guided her dead weight as she was pulled up.

Following quickly he came to Miriam's side, kneeling beside her mother's body, and it tortured him as he tried to clasp her to him that she was inconsolable and wracked by an unending succession of convulsive sobs.

CHAPTER SIX

"Nobody will ever know the full horror Miriam endured that evening, but we can be sure it will never be forgotten. Had they not been stragglers they would have been helped by the other refugees, and why they were so far behind only Miriam knows. She will already be blaming herself because she and Rufus were followers and prepared to challenge Saul, and so a prime target for Saul's anger. But Miriam is strong, her grieving will ease in time, you must support her through the desolation that grips her now," said Brutus placing a reassuring arm around Marc's shoulders.

His reassurances did little to allay Marc's fears and his face showed the strain he was under as they sat on the high promontory, the whole city spread out before them as far as the glittering azure sea in the distance.

"I can't lose this feeling of guilt. Had I pressed on instead of turning back I could have prevented everything from happening."

"That might be so, but you did what seemed right when you came across those lost souls with their dead children. You saw a duty to help them and you did. I don't think you should punish yourself for that. The officer leading that troop of cavalry deserves to be condemned, not you." Brutus grew angry merely at the recollection of his indifference and continued, "Tomorrow I will make a formal complaint to the garrison commander, as this tragedy should have been avoided."

"I haven't the courage to tell Miriam I could have reached them before the accident and escorted them safely to Tyre."

"Nor should you. It would be turning a knife in an open wound. Talk to Mary about it, she took that desolated family from you, and she knows how desperately Jacob and Ruth needed you. Come on, we will be late getting back for supper."

Although they met and ate at Flora's house they no longer slept there, as the bedrooms had been reallocated to cope with the refugee crisis.

Mary now had a palliasse on the floor of Flora's bedroom. Miriam was in Lucia's bed, and the couple whose children had lain dead in the cart had the room Brutus and Mary had vacated.

The two Romans, together with the injured Alexander, shared a room at the inn where Alexander was still confined to his bed because of severe concussion. His broken arm was splinted and Lucia was always lavishing attention on him, which made his room mates feel such intruders they were glad to escape into the hills.

Only today had his concussion cleared and he had learned of the death of his parents.

Miriam's situation was quite the opposite. She could not erase the frightening images of their deaths, which interrupted her sleep and gnawed at her unceasingly throughout the day.

Alexander had been at the reins when the boulder had fallen, frightening the horse to shy away and plunge off the road, dragging cart and occupants into a tumbling nightmare, before coming to rest on its side with bone shattering impact. Miriam and Naomi had been thrown clear but not Simon who lay trapped, pinned under the cart. Alexander, unconscious, still clutched the reins where he had been thrown, close to the horse thrashing about in its death throes.

These nightmarish sequences of events were ineradicable in Miriam's mind and it was as though she would have to live with the distorted kaleidoscope for the rest of her life. The desperate but futile effort of the women to lift the crushing weight of the cart off papa, and the thrashing hooves as they dragged Alexander clear of the dying horse. Then the arrival of the troop of soldiers, raising hope of rescue as they frantically scrambled to the road, only to be ignored and abandoned as the soldiers rode away. Naomi, distraught and confused, had wandered away in the deepening gloom and fallen into the cleft, while Miriam, resigning herself that they would all die, could only sit beside Alexander who was looking around in the dark uncomprehendingly. She hadn't heard the horsemen return, and it was only when Alexander cried out beside her that she had heard Marc's call.

Instantly hope had revived yet again, but the despair that had engulfed her as her mother was pulled from the cleft and lain forlornly beside her husband's body, still had its icy grip around her heart.

Mary and Flora, anxious at Miriam's depression and despair, resolved that day to do something about it.

"Right, Miriam, we need you now at the hospital. We've too few volunteers and we need your help with some poor starving wretches who have arrived today," said Mary firmly.

"But I've never worked with sick people. I'd be useless."

"Not for long. Someone will show you what to do and you'll soon gain confidence."

"Tomorrow, Mary. I'll start tomorrow."

"No, we need you now. Flora has something urgent to attend to, and that leaves just me! I need your help so come along."

As Miriam reluctantly walked alongside, Mary was glad she hadn't been asked what so urgently required Flora's attention, and to prevent the possibility kept up a desultory conversation, until they entered the dingy hall that was doubling up as the woman's hospital.

A dozen straw palettes were occupied, while some children were listlessly sitting in a corner. A helper called to Mary asking if she had the ointment, and brandishing an earthenware jar, she replied, "A little. Use it sparingly as the city council are getting stingy about buying any more."

While one helper applied it to the raw, bleeding feet of an old woman, her daughter looked on, waiting her turn.

"They carried the children the last two days on bare feet, after their sandals fell to pieces," said the helper.

"Where were their men?" asked Miriam, her initial horror giving way to curiosity.

"My husband was too ill to make it, and he collapsed and died on the Judaean hills. We piled up stones to cover his body from the wild animals, and then walked a further three days here," said the grandmother.

Miriam felt the stirring of compassion, but before she could express it the younger woman said dejectedly, "My man was thrown into prison."

"Why?"

"Because he's a Temple guard, and he should never have got involved with the followers of this Jesus prophet."

A barefooted waif of about four or five came and stood beside Miriam, picking at a scab on her elbow. Miriam took hold of her hand and rebuked her gently.

"Stop picking at your scab, you will make it bleed. Leave it to drop off on its own." The little girl looked at her with large eyes, but left her hand in that of the stranger.

"I never thought of a temple guard becoming a follower," mused Miriam, "they always seemed to be the enemy, to mean trouble."

"Not all. My Joseph was one of a few that were baptized by the giant. Some of the priests and Pharisees were as well. I told him it would lead to trouble but he just laughed."

"Is that why they threw him in prison, for being a follower?"

"No, for being a fool," said the woman vehemently, and seeing the puzzled look of her listener she continued, "a brave fool but a fool nonetheless. Some of the guards had seized a young man at the orders of the priests. They brought him before the Sanhedrin who ordered him to be taken away and stoned."

"Steven!" gasped Miriam.

"That might be his name. Anyway my Joseph cried out loudly in the court that this man had worked many wondrous healings in the Temple which all had witnessed, it must be wrong to put him to death. 'Throw him in prison with the others!' he suggested.

"Well they threw him in prison all right, my Joseph, and doubtless he's still there. We fled when a mob threatened to burn us out of our home."

Miriam felt the pricking of tears at recalling the stoning of Steven and the thought of her Joseph's fearless plea, and suddenly they were flowing copiously, unstoppable and healing. These weren't the angry tears she had shed over her dead parents, full of reproach at everyone who had failed to help them in time. Nor the bitter tears of self reproach at her insistent, reckless following of Jesus, that had brought these troubles on their heads. She kneeled and embraced the startled woman as the waif stood silently watching.

The change in Miriam was apparent to everyone in Flora's large room. It was the first time Alexander had left the inn, and he was unprepared as she suddenly turned and said, "Flora will you help Alex and I to find a really imposing tomb, big enough to lay out twenty dead?"

There was a stunned silence for a while before Flora replied.

"One that size would have to be built. It would cost a lot, at least three thousand drachma."

"That can be arranged can't it, Alex?" queried Miriam, regarding her brother insistently.

"Yes, drachma, denarii, we can draw on a few letters of credit among the traders here. But why such an imposing tomb for our two parents, I don't want to be buried here."

"Nor me Alex. I want this tomb to be for the victims of the persecution. I really want all those followers who have died as a result of that holocaust, to lie together until the coming of the Day of the Lord."

Alexander looked perplexed but not Mary, who said enthusiastically, "What a lovely idea, Miriam. Far better than them lying in that lime pit, which makes me shudder. What made you think of it?"

"It is many threads coming together, but the final one was that old woman at the hospital, piling stones around her dead husband to keep away the jackals and the vultures. There are many like them and they died in a common cause, that of being true to Jesus. So I would wish to have mama and papa, the two children of Jacob and Ruth, this woman's dead husband and all the others in one memorial tomb together." Miriam's eyes were shining, and there was an urgency about her that would have been inconceivable earlier.

"We can go tomorrow to find a site and enquire of a mason I know well!" said Flora looking directly at Alexander, who nodded agreement if not enthusiasm.

"I won't come, can I leave it to you please. I want to be at the hospital with those really unfortunate people." The emphasis Miriam placed on those last words was not lost on some of her listeners, and as though on cue Jacob and Ruth entered the house to quietly seek their room.

"Please stay a while, we have a proposal that we hope you will agree to," said Miriam, shooing Marc off the couch to make room for them.

Seizing Ruth's hands, which she seemed always to be wringing in anguish, Miriam stilled them as she explained what she wished to do. Vast oceans of tears welled up in Ruth's eyes as she listened, and then a flood such as nobody had witnessed since Noah, engulfed the two women.

Brutus caught Marc's eye, and they suggested to Alexander it would be a good time to check that all was well in the neighbourhood. Two of the women noted with shared amusement, how eager Lucia was to accompany them as they made a discreet exit.

Lucia returned alone an hour later, conveying the respects of the men who were returning to the inn. She was a little breathless, her eyes were shining and she talked excitedly.

"How were Jacob and Ruth mama?"

"They went to their room leaving a little of their sadness behind, Kunaria. I think tonight will be a watershed in many lives around here," and for some inexplicable reason Lucia felt the blood suffusing her face, and she hastened to give her mother a cursory embrace, as she wished a hurried goodnight to all, and fled to her bed.

"What on earth has come over Lucia?" asked Miriam with amazement and was slightly put out when Mary and Flora seemed amused. Finally Mary said,

"Have you not noticed that your handsome brother is greatly admired?"

The dawning of comprehension on Miriam was accompanied by such a succession of facial expressions that the woman's amusement was amplified. First incredulity showed, then bewilderment and finally disapproval.

"Lucia," she blurted out, "but she's only a girl!"

"No younger than you, Miriam, and you know how it is to have your heart captive."

"But Marc is a boy, Alexander is a man!" she protested.

"Your parents' age difference was greater than theirs. Time makes a few years seem an irrelevance," said Mary pointedly.

Suddenly Miriam realized how totally self-absorbed she had been, and that she had paid no attention to the people who had supported her through the buffeting of this crisis. She brought her hand to her mouth in dismay.

"Have I been really awful to Marc and to all of you? Oh Mary, why didn't you slap me? Flora, how can you forgive me?" She moved over and knelt before the sympathetic woman, clasping her hands tightly.

"There now dearest. Don't trouble yourself. We were happy to be around as you wrestled to come to terms with all your suffering. We knew we only needed to be patient and loving," murmured Flora soothingly. "I know the torment of bereavement. It's always there but time does make it more bearable."

"Bless you, Flora. Faith in Jesus and in the resurrection does too. That's why I want this tomb so much, then on that glorious day our Lord won't have to look very far, for all these saints will be lying together." She smiled at Flora through swimming eyes, and abandoned herself to the loving sympathy that the older woman was so joyful to bestow.

The Garrison was quartered in part of the old Greek acropolis overlooking the city. This was the first contact of the two centurions, and Antony was pacing the large room in a state of agitation caused by Brutus's stinging criticism of one of his officers.

"Catullus is at Damascus right now, but Sergeant Tiasus is somewhere around." He moved to the door and ordered his clerk to fetch the sergeant. There was a letter on his desk, sealed and stamped with the imposing head of Tiberius, although it came from Damascus, from Vitellius the Governor of Syria.

"This is for you," said the centurion with a smile, "so you were expected. Please read it as an acknowledgement will be required."

Brutus broke the seal and read the contents, his face registering surprise. Then he read it a second time before looking up and addressing Antony.

"I'm summoned to Damascus a week today, to explain exactly how an Arab dhow came within a whisker of sinking a seventy oar bireme galley of the imperial fleet. All the commanders of Syria are to attend, to see what lessons can be learnt from the incident. Well, well, so we nearly sank it did we! We knew it was crippled, but nearly lost! I'm glad it wasn't, that would have been a disaster!"

"And one they want to avoid in the future, obviously. I will be there and look forward to hearing your account of the action."

A knock at the door admitted sergeant Tiasus who saluted and stood rigidly at attention.

"At ease, sergeant. You know centurion Brutus?"

Tiasus affirmed that he did.

"He has been highly critical of the delay in the rescue."

"I don't think any of us appreciated the seriousness of it sir. We could see the cart was written off, so we expected the occupants to get on the next wagon to come along that road."

"Did you stop to ascertain if anyone was injured?"

"No sir. We still had a three hour ride ahead of us and captain Catullus knew we would be back patrolling the road the next day."

"I think more could have been done, but whether you would have prevented the death of the man crushed under the cart is doubtful. I'm pleased you were able to lead the centurion to the accident and assist in the rescue. Thank you, sergeant, that will be all."

After Tiasus had left Antony said, "Well the sergeant tried to cover up for Catullus which is to his credit. He's a good man and should get promotion. Catullus was at fault and could have prevented the fatality to the woman. He will get no further as I will give him an adverse report. Please convey my regrets to the surviving children. Now, how do you propose to get to Damascus, and have you anywhere to stay when there?"

They spent the next half-hour discussing the various options, and Brutus left without any firm commitment other than to keep Antony informed of his intentions.

He arrived at a house in turmoil.

Marc and Miriam had just returned from visiting a site for the tomb accompanied by Flora and a mason, and they were studying some drawings he had left with them. Alexander was sorting out some letters of credit to obtain the funds needed for the construction, and Jacob and Ruth were moving their belongings into a handcart as they had found rooms to move into.

Lucia, bursting into the room with the latest news from the agora, became the focus of all their attention.

"Saul of Tarsus is here in Tyre. He has a commission from the Sanhedrin to work with the elders of the synagogue to root out the revolutionaries here!"

There was a flurry of protest at the terrible implications of further violence against them.

"How can we be revolutionaries?" demanded Mary. "We don't wish to destroy anything to do with the Temple or the Synagogue."

"Don't we, Mary? Doesn't the teaching of Jesus challenge the whole concept of building a vast Temple for God to dwell in? Hasn't he shown that God dwells in the hearts of those that love him, and now that we see God revealed in Jesus do we need the Temple any more?" Miriam fell silent leaving the challenging question to be answered.

Flora was the first.

"You have told us of the speech of Peter in the Temple, and he said to shake the dust of that desecrated place from your sandals and go to the far corners of the world preaching the message of Jesus to the gentiles. That is revolutionary!"

"But the Temple and the priests could be at the centre of this world shaking movement, if they were only willing to listen," sighed Mary.

"Your own words tell why they will never listen, because it is a world shaking movement and most of the priests want to continue as they have always done, isolated within the security of their privileged world."

Miriam looked at everyone in turn before continuing.

"Look at us here, five Jews and four gentiles all drawn together because of Jesus in a way that would have been unbelievable last year. We Jews would have to make a ritual cleaning offering at the Temple just because of being in the same house let alone sharing a meal! But the idea that we are unclean is unbelievable to us and we reject it. But it truly is revolutionary Mary, these new thoughts and ideas. To the priests it is more challenging and dangerous than any zealot uprising."

"I can see it clashing violently with Rome. Our whole edifice of empire is built on conquest, subjugation and slavery, and these can't be reconciled with the kingdom of Jesus," said Brutus emphatically.

"Didn't Jesus foresee an inevitable conflict and prophesy that his followers would have to endure great persecution before their ultimate triumph?"

This sobering thought caused all to remain quietly pensive, then Mary said urgently, "Ought we not to concentrate on the threat that Saul's mission here in Tyre poses. This man's implacable hatred has already brought about the deaths of four people very dear to us."

"I think we are vulnerable in three areas," said Brutus checking the points against the fingers of an upraised hand.

"Firstly, can anyone feel safe at the Synagogue? Mary has had two brushes with Saul there and still bears the scars.

"Next, could there be rioting outside of the Synagogue such as we saw in Jerusalem? I don't think the city council would allow it at large, but they might not concern themselves with what happens in the Jewish quarter close to the synagogue."

There was a frightened gasp from Ruth and Jacob took her hand soothingly.

"That's where we have found rooms," he said dejectedly, his hideously scarred face a picture of suffering, as his wife clutched nervously at her robe with her free hand, her eyes showing the terror threatening to overwhelm her.

"Then you must stay here," insisted Flora, "at least until that man leaves the city."

Brutus reasserted himself to continue his analysis.

"Thirdly, and this is the most imponderable, to what extent will the Roman authorities cooperate with the temple to put down what they might believe to be sedition?"

"Not here surely," interrupted Alexander, "this isn't Jerusalem and the elders of the Synagogue don't have the same power as the priests of the Temple."

"No, but Jesus does claim to be the King of the Jews, and now the whole world is being brought within his Kingdom. The Emperor of Rome will not sit idly by and watch that happen, while an ambitious Governor might decide there is a lot of credit to be gained from crushing such a seditious movement quickly. Saul is a fanatic but a very persuasive one, and so a very dangerous threat. I want you to move into a room at the inn with me, Mary, I will be able to sleep a lot more soundly with you under the same roof!"

"Of course, dearest," said Mary, with such acquiescence that Brutus was immediately suspicious, only to have his misgivings confirmed as she continued, "and we women would be grateful for the same protection from you when we worship at the Synagogue."

Hoist with his own petard, Brutus could only look around for help, his mouth half open and silenced. The merriment he saw in Marc's eyes momentarily made him regret ever giving him his freedom, and then he immediately launched into his counter-attack.

"Agreed. Marc or I will accompany you to the synagogue, and as we have just been summoned by Vitellius to Damascus to address all unit commanders in the Province, we would like you to accompany us, Mary, and I propose that you address the court of inquiry as well."

"Me address the inquiry!" exclaimed Mary her face draining of all colour at the thought. "Never, I would die if I had to stand up and talk to a room full of soldiers."

"This from the woman who stood up and challenged Saul of Tarsus in the Synagogue at Joppa! Why shame on you, Mary."

Something in his tone put Mary distinctly on her guard, and she studied his face to see if he was joking. It was set stern and inflexible, but for some inexplicable reason Marc was shaking disconcertingly just within her vision.

"What on earth could I have to talk about, Brutus? You're being absurd!"

"Not at all. I think you are the undisputed master of diversionary tactics, which are a vital part of any battle strategy."

As Mary was pondering this reply, Marc had visions of Mary standing on his head and forcefully submerging him, as she was pulled out of Joppa harbour. Not for one second longer could he constrain himself, and eyes watering and his whole body shaking with paroxysms of laughter, he subsided into a gibbering idiot. Brutus was the next to succumb to the contagion, then Mary, until the whole room throbbed to their laughter sweeping like gusts of wind in a gale.

The change of mood prevailed in the house that night, and even the departure of Mary with the accompanying shedding of tears from her and Flora could not dissipate it significantly.

Mary had tried to backtrack on her agreement and defer her move a night or two, but when the two Romans conferred, and declared themselves quite prepared to commandeer Jacob's handcart and repeat a recent kidnapping, she gave in.

CHAPTER SEVEN

Brutus and Miriam, seated on two matching bays, gave a cheerful wave as they set off on the journey to Damascus, which was not responded to by a subdued Alexander, his arm still splinted and supported in a sling. The women being left behind were more responsive and Marc at the reins of the wagon had to chide Flora to make her disengage from her embrace of Mary, as though they were parting for a year rather than a week.

Marc rejoiced inwardly at the excited manner in which Miriam was cantering ahead. Until yesterday it had been impossible to persuade her to come, and she had found reasons to keep her in Tyre with which Marc had disputed in vain.

Anxious to get to the underlying problem, Marc had urged Miriam to walk with him to a promontory giving a spectacular outlook over the whole city. There they had sat quietly, watching the sea in the distance turn into fire, which was only dampened as the red ball of the sun sank below the horizon and the glow of the embers vanished into dusk.

"Sweetheart, I think this is the moment to tell you why I can't leave you behind on this trip without breaking my solemn promise."

Miriam looked at him apprehensively, but left her hand resting in his. He saw the uncertainty in her dark eyes, and knew he had to seize this moment of crisis.

"When I was down that cleft in the rock with your mother, we didn't say many words as I was trying to organise the rescue efforts of the soldiers. There was a quiet time when I tried to reassure her we would soon have her out but she suddenly said, 'Simon's dead!' just that, and her eyes kept closing."

Miriam's sobs were now heart-rending to him and he wanted only to love and comfort her, but knew he had to continue or he might never have another opportunity to say what had to be said.

"I pleaded, 'stay awake please Naomi,' and put my arm around her shoulders as she had around mine that night I was first in your home. Then you were peering down at us and do you remember, your mother looked up and saw you?"

Miriam took a hand away to brush the tears that were blinding her and nodded mutely.

"Then she said, 'you will look after her won't you?' and closed her eyes not to open them again. That was your mother's last request, Miriam, and I made that promise I will always keep. So now you know why I can't go unless you go with me!"

He had said not one more word to urge her, but the reconciliation had been sweet, and as he sat on the wagon it was that memory that was with him.

The road quickly climbed up into the hills behind Tyre and then meandered its way eastwards following a dried up riverbed. That night they hoped to rest at Lake Huleh on the upper Jordan, before following the trade route skirting the hills that formed the eastern side of the great cleft running all the way to the Red Sea. It was high summer and the countryside lay desolate and arid.

Marc and Brutus changed places, and he and Miriam rode their horses towards a col a short way ahead, and as they breasted the slope they saw before them the gentle decline to the green region around the lake. Turning back to encourage the trailing wagon, they were surprised to see four horsemen closing rapidly. Urging their horses, they arrived but a moment behind the horsemen who had stopped around the stationary wagon.

Miriam seized at Marc's sleeve, "It's Saul of Tarsus! He's come to arrest us Jews!"

Marc found his hand going to the hilt of his sword, but he let it rest as they sidled up to listen to Saul urging them to turn back.

"Return to Tyre. You have nothing to fear there now, but woe to you if you continue to Damascus. I am on my way there to seize all Jews who follow this Jesus, and bring them before the Sanhedrin."

"Which will sentence them to be stoned as they did Steven!" exclaimed Miriam angrily.

"Steven had the chance to recant, and if he had taken it he would not have been stoned. But because he persisted with his accusation that the priests had murdered the Son of God he had to die! Why do you continue this calumny that they murdered the Messiah, and not accept that it was a regrettable but politically necessary execution of a minor prophet who was inciting the people?"

"Because it was I, centurion Brutus, who had to kill your Messiah at the instigation of those precious priests, knowing all the time that he was innocent of all their charges. I nailed him to the cross and drove my spear into his heart to ensure there was no doubting he was dead!"

"Could you but convince his disciples of that, this myth of his resurrection would be discredited and I would have no need to hunt them down?"

"His resurrection is no myth! Mary here was the first person to talk with him three days after I crucified him."

Saul had a desperate look in his eyes as they wavered between the Roman and the Jewess. He brought his hands to cover his ears crying out passionately.

"You lie! Annas and Caiphas have told me that the body was stolen from the tomb by his disciples. That same High Priest, who alone dared enter the inner sanctum to offer incense to the Most High on the Day of Atonement."

Mary cried scornfully.

"And as the bells around the hem of his robes tinkle, you believe he has the ear of God that resides there! Does not the midrash tell us that God does not wish to have a sanctuary to dwell in? When the priests pressed him to allow the Temple to be built did God not say, 'My children, earthly Kings need this, but I do not.'

"But no, you deceive yourself into believing the Lord God resides only there, as you deceive yourself into believing that the High Priest could not lie to you about Jesus being resurrected."

"Why do you torment me, woman? First at Joppa, then Tyre and now here."

Saul tore at his robe in vexation and hardly noticed that he was rending it.

"Did the High Priest tell you that the veil of the Temple was rent in two, when the spirit left the body of Jesus as he hung on the cross? Ask rather why do you deceive yourself, Saul of Tarsus; why pretend that you are righteous as you carry out the devil's work?"

Mary was punching him with her words and he was reeling, as she had from the blows his words had provoked in the synagogue at Joppa.

Bruised and confounded, as he now was, he could not disengage from this confrontation, which he believed fate had decreed was inevitable. These people were some of the instigators of that myth which he was resolved to discredit and destroy, that which threatened to tear the Jewish nation asunder, and so he watched her spellbound as she moved her lips wordlessly, as though entreating someone invisible to come to her aid.

When she opened her eyes they burnt with an intensity that matched those of Saul's.

"If I show you proof of his resurrection will you stop this persecution of the followers of Jesus?"

"Prove that and my mission is invalidated, and that can never be so as my work is for the Temple and for Israel's God. So yes, try what you will, but don't think I am easily swayed."

As he accepted the challenge Saul felt his spirit surge. Convinced that righteousness was his he was eager to confront and confound this mistaken woman.

"I must ask you all to leave us, this is only for the eyes of Saul, just give us five minutes alone, that is all I ask," pleaded Mary.

Reluctantly Brutus climbed from the cart and they moved some way down the road, where they stood a perplexed and silent group.

She insisted Saul climb up onto the bench, and briefly left him to move into the gloomy interior under the awning. After a short interval she summoned Saul to join her where he found her sitting confidently on a sack with a roll of cloth on her lap, and for the first time he had a premonition of danger.

"I must ask you to promise that you will tell no man of what I am about to reveal to you," she entreated.

"If that is necessary so be it, you have my word."

"I ventured into the tomb after the disciples had seen it was empty and had left to tell their news to the followers. I saw the two cloths that had bound the body and face of our Lord wound up and lying there, and I picked up the smaller of the two."

"Is that it?" asked Saul, his mind rejecting its significance even as his body felt the threat of some impending catastrophe.

"Wait until it is unrolled, only then will it become clear."

As the seared image of the face of Jesus was revealed Saul let out a scream.

"Stop it, no more!" he gasped, his left hand covering his eyes, but with his fingers separated sufficiently for the image to penetrate and burn itself into the deepest recesses of his consciousness. He felt his soul branded with a torturing, red-hot iron, and his heart as torn as was the veil of the Temple.

In his anxiety to escape he half fell onto the dusty road, before staggering towards the greatly agitated party of onlookers. He mounted with difficulty, requiring the assistance of one of his escorts, and then at a gallop led his alarmed men away.

Brutus and Miriam running to the wagon were apprehensive and fearful, but the nonchalance of Mary as she carefully tucked the package away, was really most vexing to them. Nor was it less so, that she would say not one word of what had passed between them in those few minutes.

The descent to the area of Lake Huleh was uneventful, but after that dramatic confrontation their serenity was shattered and all were left with a wary apprehension about the journey ahead.

Mary was deeply disturbed at Saul's reaction, as she had expected something more reassuring. She had responded to the inner voice that guides her through crises when she listens for it, although the consequences can sometimes be bewildering.

It was that same inner voice that set her walking into the wilderness, where she had found herself pressed to be wagon driver for the Romans. She laughingly nudged Brutus, and reminded him of that frightening descent to the Jordan, and he laughed with her. It was her response to that same clear inner voice that had unleashed the mob on her at Joppa, she reflected philosophically, and which she had chosen to totally ignore as she had thrown herself in the harbour a week or two later.

They started off early from the small oasis, at the first milky lightening to the east as the stars deserted the sky, to fade away in the approaching dawn. There was a full day's journey to Damascus, and they were all very edgy at the threat made by Saul, which had only been intensified by his dramatic withdrawal.

As they climbed the small foothills away from the lake, the chain of high hills bending away to the north, opened up to the far horizon, dominated by the cloud-capped summit of Mount Hermon. The road was leading towards a high col through which they would have to pass before they commenced the descent to the plain, where they would flank the range before moving east to the city.

The sun was overhead and in the far distance a handful of pearls danced in the heat ripples over the varied ochres of the sun-scorched earth.

"Damascus!" exalted Brutus, reining back the frisky horses, eager to descend after the long haul.

Mary was excited by the panorama, but drew the attention of the centurion to the purple black mass, that now obliterated much of the high mountain a few miles ahead.

"I think that build up of cloud is ominous," she said, and even as she spoke a flash of blue forked lightning threw the lower slope into sharp relief for a few seconds, and the rumble of the thunder lingered oppressively in the still air. The horses tossed their manes nervously, and demanded the full attention of the driver to restrain their skittishness.

"The sooner we're down on the plain the better," said Brutus, assessing the winding road with many steep inclines where the hill plunged precipitously. He was aware of Mary's nervousness, and they were quickly joined by the youths who suddenly wanted to stay close. Marc suggested it would be wise if he rode just in front, with a halter to one of the bridles.

"Good idea, Marc, the horses are uneasy, but between us we will be better able to control them."

The rapidity with which the slate gray, mass of cloud spread out and moved towards them was unbelievable, and as the sun was blotted out noon suddenly turned into twilight.

"Not since the day of the crucifixion have I seen such sombre gloom at this hour," Miriam whispered to Marc, her fear showing in the nervous glances she threw all around.

"You'd best get under cover as the heavens are going to open soon. Don't worry sweetheart, I know you're fearful after that dreadful day, but we're going to be ready so that nothing like that can happen again! Anyway, lightning never strikes twice ..."

Marc's words were never finished, as the gloom not one hundred paces ahead of them was riven by the blinding brilliance of a bolt of lightning, that tore up a large cedar of Lebanon adjacent to the road, holding it suspended, before it plummeted smoking and aflame down into the valley.

The frenzied stampede of their horses was only averted by the sinew-straining exertion of the two Romans, as they struggled to subdue the panicking animals. Miriam was thrown in an instant, her mount rearing before hurtling away as though resolved not to stop until Tyre.

Converging on it with devastating rapidity from behind was a Roman supply wagon, the ears of both mules laid back, the whites of their eyes glinting as they exploded in one inevitable collision, bodies, and timber impacting and spinning off the road to the accompanying crescendo of thunder.

Mary leaped down and rushed to Miriam where she lay crumpled on the hard rock, and fearfully she sought for any signs of life. At the same moment she felt the reverberations of the approaching column of horses pounding around the bend. Fearful for both their lives, she clutched Miriam to her as she threw herself off the side of the road.

The uproar as the legionaries fought their mounts to a standstill before crashing into the wagon was fiendish, many colliding with those in front, unseating riders and all milling around in pandemonium. Acrid smoke was drifting over them as the stricken tree ignited the dry undergrowth on the slope.

Marc now surged into them with reckless panic, searching despairingly for his love where he thought to find her trampled under hoof. A soldier threw himself from his horse knocking Marc to the ground, and then pinned both his arms to his sides in a rib cracking bear hold.

"Hold on lad, let's not make matters worse," he roared above the general mêlée, easily constraining all Marc's desperate efforts to break free.

"What's happening there, sergeant, who have you seized?" came an authoritative voice.

"I don't know who but I know why sir, this youngster would have got himself killed."

"There are two injured women down here, sir," came a call, and the sergeant realised the cause of the lad's desperation. Looking intently at Marc he said, "I'll release you now and we'll go and see what's happened to your friends. Bear up lad."

He relaxed his hold and together they hurried to the side of the road. Some soldiers had already climbed down to the wide, scrub covered ledge, where the two women were sitting receiving attention.

Mary looked up and saw Marc's haggard face peering down, fearful of the worst. She gave him a wan smile and a wave, as she called out, "Miriam's alright, Marc, but I fear her horse is in that carnage," pointing to the bodies of the horses and the mangled wreckage a short way down the slope. Marc was too stunned to reply, so convinced had he been that he had lost her, pounded into the road by the hooves of the horses.

Brutus now joined them hardly believing their incredible escape, and quickly appraised they were still at risk.

"By what miracle you two are still alive I'll never know, but you had better get up here quickly as that fire is leaping towards you. I'm coming down to help!"

Marc went to climb down with him, but soldiers were milling around everywhere, and the sergeant put a restraining hand on his shoulder urging him to leave it to the military, who were experts in this sort of situation. Feeling weak with reaction he concurred, and sat and watched the efficiency with which the well-drilled men coped.

A firebreak was created by uprooting or hacking away the tinder-dry scrub and bushes. The seriously injured driver of the wagon was brought up to the road on an improvised stretcher and anything salvageable from the wreckage retrieved. The women were helped to the road, where they stood around in shock as their men attended to them.

"Centurion Brutus, by all the gods!" cried out a voice that he instantly recognised.

"Firmus, by all that's wonderful!" echoed Brutus peering through the gloom at the familiar wrinkled face, screwed up joyfully at the unexpectedness of the reunion. "What on earth are you doing riding so recklessly towards Damascus?"

"Ha. Never expected to find you loitering at such a bad stretch of the road," rejoined Firmus, "and we were over-eager to hear how you nearly sank the *Hermes*."

Their laughter and banter were a welcome relief to the grim business of clearing up after the near catastrophe, but to demonstrate the disapproval of the heavens, there was a further rumble of thunder and the downpour began.

Nobody had the slightest awareness of the consternation among the small group of horsemen a few hundred paces ahead, three of whom were quieting the restless horses. The fourth, Saul of Tarsus, was writhing on the ground, as though it were he, not the cedar that had been struck by the awesome flame from heaven.

It had been every man for himself for a chaotic minute or two as they had fought to control their panicked mounts, and only now as they regrouped, did Saul pull himself to his knees, his eyes tightly closed and his dishevelled head lifted, straining to listen to the receding thunder.

Throwing his arms wide in entreaty he cried out, "Who are you, sir?"

And then in frozen immobility remained where he knelt, as the peal finally subsided. Nothing else moved in that tableau except the tears that flowed unchecked over his prominent cheeks, and fell on the dust of the road. As though to break the spell he said one word, filled with all the intensity of his supplication.

"Jesus."

He lurched to his feet his whole face suffused with inexpressible rejoicing, looked around blindly and then collided with one of the horses his companions held. He put out his hand, felt the horse's head and mane, then turned at the whinny of another horse and bumped into one of his escort.

"You can't see can you, sir. It must have been the lightning, it will wear off."

"Oh I can see. I can see with the eye of revelation. I can see more clearly than light of sun or moon can ever illuminate!"

Such was his exultation he counted his visual blindness as naught. For his escort it was a terrible affliction as he was quite unable to ride a horse, so they walked the last twenty miles, drenched to the skin and greatly perplexed. That their blinded leader, now totally reliant on being led, could remain so obdurately unperturbed throughout that nightmare of a journey was a constant amazement to his companions.

The convergence of these disparate and opposing factions on the great cosmopolitan city of Damascus was regarded as of no particular significance by any of them. By some unknown principal of alchemy, the mixing of them was to produce shock waves that would pulsate throughout the whole world until the end of time.

CHAPTER EIGHT

The gathering of Roman military leaders from the units throughout Syria and Judaea made an impressive assembly, numerically reflecting the great interest and speculation aroused by the near loss of the only Roman galley permanently assigned to patrol that coast.

Brutus was the guest of the Governor of Syria at a banquet on the eve of the formal enquiry, and among the press of officers milling around, he was delighted to see many familiar faces, but none more than the beaming, round, smooth face of Maas.

"Congratulations on your promotion," said the Governor and then turning to Brutus, "Maas has been recently promoted centurion and is the first Syrian to hold such rank."

"We know each other well, sir, as rivals in the spear throwing tournament. Congratulations, Maas, I can't think of a more worthy promotion!" Brutus exclaimed as the two men exchanged salutes.

"I should congratulate you on your remarkable victory over the *Hermes*," replied Mass with a laugh, "there are the wildest rumours concerning your encounter that need to be clarified tomorrow."

Before Brutus could reply the Governor introduced Tribune Communis, with the comment that only his resourcefulness had saved the *Hermes* from being lost with all on board.

"As that included the Tetrarch of Galilee we are indeed obliged to you, Tribune," concluded Vitellius.

Legate Venestus joined them bringing the apologies of Pontius Pilate.

"He greatly regrets, your Excellency, that he is too ill to undertake the journey from Caesarea to Damascus."

Vitellius conveyed his regrets and concern for the health of the Prefect, but Brutus felt only great relief that he wouldn't have to encounter the cause of all their troubles.

Accompanying Venestus was a centurion, who introduced himself as Cornelius.

"I should have been commanding the *Hermes*, not the unfortunate Hedylus, who was a good friend and a good officer," he said with evident sadness in his pale blue eyes.

"I greatly regret the loss of his and the other lives," rejoined Brutus, "but what kept you away from your command?"

"My century was engaged in a sweep against a group of zealots who were causing trouble near Caesarea Phillipi. The messenger bearing notification of my appointment to command the *Hermes* was seized and murdered by these rebels.

"But your sweep was successful?" asked Vitellius.

"A score of them are hanging from the gallows, your Excellency, two of them are boys."

Brutus gave an involuntary shudder at this, and again he saw sorrow clouding the eyes of the speaker.

"But old enough to bear a sword, centurion. If they choose to challenge their legitimate rulers, we have no alternative but to execute them!"

This with such finality that Cornelius bowed and withdrew as they were summoned to the table, groaning with a surfeit of all that the province could provide.

Peacocks were stuffed with duck and quail and songbirds. Spit roasted sucking pigs competed with young lambs and goats. Clay baked Tilapia fish from the Sea of Galilee surrounded poached sturgeon from the far Caspian. A whole legion could have subsisted many days on that which a few hundred officers demolished in two hours. If anyone questioned such abundance, in a region where meat is a rarity for the majority of the populous, it is doubtful if they voiced it. The accepted principle that might is right rested unchallenged for now, but Brutus was aware that he would be questioning that premise when he threw down the gauntlet on the morrow in this very same hall.

When that time came every seat in the huge auditorium was occupied. From their elevated position on the dias, the centurion and his son looked down on a sea of uplifted expectant faces. Each was eagerly anticipating a resolution to the conflicting rumours and stories that were still rife in every barrack room.

Vitellius called the meeting to order, and after a brief introduction and explanation of the protocol of the enquiry continued.

"I think the duel between the *Hermes* and the *Dolphin* is an epic, worthy of recounting alongside those of Ulysses, and the sea battles of Julius Caesar against the Veneti in northern Gaul. I hope we can learn any lesson that is to be learnt from listening to those who were on both the ships."

Giving the floor to Tribune Communis, the Governor took his seat, and every one listened in silence as the event unfolded.

The reason he gave for the pursuit of the dhow was that it was suspected to be smuggling arms to zealots north of Caesarea. Brutus and Marc were as fascinated as everyone, as the details of the hunt as seen from the *Hermes* sequentially unfolded.

"We had passed the two bodies of the crew an hour back and knew the *Dolphin* would not be captured without a battle, but we did not wish to ram and sink her, which was the easy option. As we rapidly gained on her and were closing from dead astern, we saw the crew of the dhow throw overboard two huge beams of timber, one each side of their boat. We guessed it was a desperate and futile effort to lighten their craft and never thought they were attached by ropes, and being towed like two massive prongs of a gladiator's fork."

He stopped for a moment to sip some water, looking at Brutus as though he still could not credit what happened next and shook his head in disbelief as he continued, "We were now so close behind we could see everything on board our quarry. This man and the boy were standing, their swords raised, one each side of the boat. Our soldiers led by centurion Hedylus were poised ready to board along our left side, and we were surging at tremendous speed, to overhaul them. We were about to ship our oars and engage, when both their swords flashed down simultaneously and their boat seemed to leap. Hedylus turned to shout a warning from the bows, even as we slammed into those massive timbers end on. One was lifted by the ram and smashed into our stem at the same instance as the second burst through the hull. Hedylus and a dozen soldiers were thrown into the sea."

There was a concerted gasp from the assembly, but any conjecture was cut short as the damage they had sustained was further revealed.

"We were badly holed at the waterline and one slave had been crushed against the mast by the inboard part of the timber. We were foundering, broached too, in the greatest danger of losing all our lives, and quite unable to attempt to rescue those lost overboard!"

Communis continued, telling of the subsequent actions necessitated by the crisis and their struggle home, having lost their captain and five soldiers. He sat down to absolute silence, the initial disbelief at the scale of the disaster taking a while to sink in, to be followed by a prolonged burst of applause from the excited listeners.

Vitellius was standing and applauding likewise until he raised a restraining hand.

"Thank you, Tribune. We are fortunate to have officers of your calibre to serve our mighty empire. The Tribune has received a commendation to Emperor Tiberius."

The jubilation with which this was received eventually subsided, then the Governor called on Brutus who arose to an apprehensive silence. It was as though everyone wondered how any speaker could follow the dramatic testimony of the first and not be an anticlimax, while at the same time knowing that the enquiry was now approaching its real purpose.

"The Provincial Governor has called this enquiry with a view to learning what lessons there are to be learned. Further he has compared our confrontation with that of Julius Caesar and the Veneti in Gaul. But I must emphasise the fundamental difference, for in Gaul there was a definable enemy and a definite objective, conquest, while here there was no enemy and no objective other than the quest for vengeance."

That the audience, hanging on every word were stunned by the implications of what they were hearing was apparent to Marc, who could see the powerful reaction of their faces.

"There were no weapons being carried to supply zealots and to pretend there were is deception. There was no enemy. We were Romans being pursued by Romans without any justification whatever. I have known many battles in my lifetime as a soldier and we could often not understand the politics or the purpose underlying the action, but relying on the integrity of our leaders we fought unquestioningly. But I am certain the battle between the *Hermes* and the *Dolphin* was the most futile and unnecessary engagement I have ever been involved in, and it cost the lives of six legionaries."

A rumble of protest was audible to those on the dais, and Vitellius was looking angry.

Brutus continued.

"I stated the objective of this hunt was vengeance. It is well known that King Herod Antipas was severely injured in this engagement. Since when, and under what circumstances, is such a ruler likely to be on board a Roman galley in an active engagement? The answer has to be never. It was because no resistance was expected that he was on board. King Herod and Pontius Pilate expected my son and myself to be delivered to them on a plate, merely to gratify their quest for revenge. Fortunately with the help of centurion Felix, I found out the master of the *Dolphin* had treacherously arranged to call at Caesarea where Herod was to seize us. The efforts of Herod and Pilate to hunt us down over the past few months are known to some of you. I don't wish to dwell on that other than to say they have nothing to do with military matters.

"I am, however, obliged to ask how Pilate is able to manipulate the military to serve nothing other than his personal desire for vengeance. He could only do this with the collusion at some high level of army authority, and it has sinister significance that such abuse of power goes unquestioned. I would suggest that Tribune Communis was only on the *Hermes* as representative of Pilate to liaise between King Herod and the unfortunate Hedylus and to give his authority to the king seizing us should the captain have demurred.

"I dwell on this at some length, because this is a serious enquiry into the near loss of a fighting ship and her entire crew. If we don't search for the undisclosed reasons behind the actions and our only interest is in the sequence of events, the abuse of the military in similar unwarranted circumstances will lead to further heavy losses of life. I believe the profession of soldiering to be honorable, but unless our leaders are vigilant as to the causes to which they commit troops, increasingly they will become the tools of injustice and tyranny."

Bowing to Vitellius and to the assembly Brutus sat down, aware that he had said things that would be very unwelcome and were certain to cause offence at the highest levels.

In the ensuing silence, Vitellius stood up to address the assembly, but before he could say anything, Firmus was on his feet, quickly followed by Cornelius, applauding the courageous speech they had just heard. Marc joined in enthusiastically and when Legate Venestus added his approval, the vast majority of the assembly did likewise.

As the applause quieted Vitellius held up an arm for silence.

"Centurion Brutus has made serious allegations concerning high officials who are not present to answer. I rule that such matters are beyond the jurisdiction of this enquiry and shall not be pursued here. As Governor of this province, it is my business to look into them. Now can we proceed to questions from the floor."

Everyone was seated except for Legate Venestus.

"Your excellency, I would like it put on record that I drafted the orders standing down the army throughout Judaea after the manhunt of Centurion Brutus was found to be unjustified, when we established that King Herod's so-called ambassadors had been killed while attempting to seize centurion Brutus and his son for questioning."

"If that is an established fact, I will allow it to be put on record Legate, but I want no more reference to King Herod or the Prefect of Judaea!" Vitellius sounded exasperated as he resumed his seat.

As the recently appointed commander of the galley that was still out of service for repairs, Centurion Cornelius was eager to put what he regarded as a very pertinent question.

"May I ask Tribune Communis what he was doing aboard the *Hermes*, and whether his presence was consequent to the king sailing on the galley?"

Communis looked ill at ease and glanced at the Governor uncertainly, who assented by inclining his stern, disapproving head.

"I was aboard *Hermes* at the insistence of Pontius Pilate. He was anxious that King Herod should have a liaison officer aboard, as he insisted on sailing in this action."

Vitellius was angrily on his feet.

"There will be no more questions gentlemen, I declare the inquiry closed. Thank you all for your attendance."

Without a further word he abruptly left, even as the assembly was belatedly rising to its feet.

Brutus and Marc left the dais and were immediately surrounded by a crowd eager for answers to questions that hadn't been touched on. Eventually their numbers dwindled, and it was a small group of friends that made their way out of the auditorium. Centurions Andreaus and Cornelius had attached themselves, and Cornelius pressed them all to refresh themselves at the large house he had rented not far from the forum.

As they sat relaxed and easy in each other's company the conversation flowed over the whole momentous events of the past few months. There was a lot of interest amongst the uninitiated at the part Maas and his company had played in these events, although the Syrian brushed aside his contribution as of little significance.

"Until your letter we had had no intimation that we were still vulnerable at Joppa, and it certainly made me more vigilant than I might have been." Brutus smiled.

Cornelius pressed Brutus further on his strategy to beat off the *Hermes*.

"How did you arrive at your final plan to hole the galley? I know the dhow was due for repairs, which explains the beams of timber being to hand, but the way you utilized them was inspired. I know it would never have crossed my mind to do anything other than throw them overboard."

Brutus was thoughtful for a while, and there was a heightening of anticipation among the listeners.

"I was inspired by remembrance of a vision I experienced after I had crucified Jesus the Nazarene when I lay tormented by guilt at his execution, verging on madness or suicide. That which brought me back from the brink was a vision of the Son of God at my side, girded as a mighty champion, his sword like lightning striking down the oppressive, bloodthirsty reptile that represented Rome and terrorized the world that I was surveying from a high mountain. He was my champion at that crisis, and faced with this new crisis I was aware that he was still my champion!"

Brutus paused as he found it difficult talking about the revelation and was unsure how to find the words to convey its relevance in the new situation.

"Well, as I stood on the deck of the *Dolphin* I hadn't any hope of escape, and Marc and I were resolved to die at the swords of our soldiers, rather than be captured by Herod. My eyes searched the sky hoping for another miracle, and then they fell on the timber beams and I just knew how they could be utilized to disable the *Hermes*. You know what followed."

His spell bound listeners were agitated by a variety of emotions. Elation and excitement predominated but Cornelius was very pensive.

"So you believe God spoke to you in a vision and told you or showed you what to do?"

"Yes," replied Brutus. "I now believe his Son, Jesus, spoke to me. Mary, my woman, was the first person to speak to Jesus after he had overcome death, and she has convinced me that he speaks to me and to you, we have only to know how to listen!"

"Is this Mary with you in Damascus?" asked Cornelius excitedly, and when Brutus assented, he urged him to bring her to his house, as he was most anxious to talk to her.

Andreaus added his pleas to those of Cornelius.

"Jesus healed my servant, so I count myself a follower or a believer rather, it's very difficult to be accepted as a follower by the tribes of Israel while remaining uncircumcised."

"I asked Simon Peter to baptize me in Joppa, along with a hundred Jews, but he said the time was not yet right for us gentiles," said Marc wistfully. "Wasn't it you at the temple, rebuking the crowd threatening to stone some of the disciples?"

Andreaus smiled modestly.

"How on earth did you hear of that?"

"We saw it from a distance and Mary Magdalene and my friend Miriam were there at the time, and said your courage and dignity cowed the mob, who were baying for blood."

"Then I am as anxious as Cornelius to meet these women of yours, if only to press them not to exaggerate my role in that minor disturbance."

Brutus agreed that they would bring the women the next day although neither of them was fully recovered from their near fatal encounter with a troop of cavalry on the Damascus road.

"Ah, I heard of that from Firmus! Then they must be carried here and I insist on arranging their transportation!" pressed Cornelius. "Say late afternoon they will be brought from your inn, the Phoenix I believe?" and when Brutus assented, Cornelius continued, "Would it be in order for a few sympathetically inclined friends of ours to meet your companions as well?"

The Phoenix inn was at the west end of the great street that bisected the city. As they hurried towards it, traders were dismantling their wares from the booths that lined both sides of the wide central thoroughfare, which still throbbed with the bustle of horse drawn wagons, caravans and hand drawn carts. The sandstone buildings rising on both sides served both residential and commercial needs, and a great assortment of people were entering or exiting, as it was approaching the evening meal.

Turning into the palm fringed courtyard of their inn and moving towards their rooms they simultaneously heard the masculine laughter from Miriam's room, and hurried to see who their visitor might be.

Miriam was sitting up in bed, her pale face animated with joy at some joke shared with the white robed stranger, and Mary was reclining on a couch, as eagerly partaking in the revelry.

"Ah Marc, Brutus, you haven't met my brother Rufus have you? These are the Romans who are our companions, Rufus. Mama placed me in Marc's care just as she was dying."

Although she shot him a heart-stopping smile of welcome, it was tinged with sadness.

"Then I must thank you for all you've done for my family. I've been six days walking here from Jerusalem, as we had received no news of their arrival at Damascus, and Peter urged me to put my mind at rest, even if it meant coming all this way to find out.

"Only on my arrival did I hear of their tragic deaths, and were it not for you I am convinced I would have lost my entire family, so I'm greatly indebted to you both. Mary was just telling me how only a thorn bush arrested her plunge off the Damascus road, and she was wondering if some of the thorns aren't still embedded in her, but has just declined my offer to give the matter my close attention, so perhaps you might have greater powers of persuasion than me!"

Marc instantly liked the easy friendliness of this brother, who he guessed to be about five years older than Miriam.

"I hope you can spend some time with us. Having you here may help Miriam to come to terms with so great a loss."

"Yes, a few days, but I must return to Jerusalem as the disciples need to be told of Saul being here. He is a real thorn in our flesh."

"Would it worry you to accompany us to the house of a Roman friend?" Brutus asked hesitantly.

"Do I worry about becoming unclean by joining you? I think that is something that has been swept away by the teaching of our Lord. I will be happy to join you and your friends."

"Which Roman friends are these?" queried Mary.

"Centurion Andreaus, the man you saw rebuking the mob in the court of the Gentiles."

Rufus looked elated at the invitation, and Brutus warmed to him, and realized why Peter had pressed him to become his acolyte, they were not that dissimilar in their nature.

Marc suggested hopefully, after her brother had departed, "I think he will be happy to bless our marriage when you are ready, Miriam."

"Be patient with me, Marc. I feel my childhood was but yesterday. I know I have grown up a lot these past few months, but I'm not yet ready for a woman's role."

The gently caressing way he nuzzled his downy cheek against hers was affirmation that he would not press her too urgently.

In the early afternoon a commotion arose in the court as two canopied and cushioned litters and a dozen bearers arrived to collect their passengers.

When Mary and Miriam were acquainted with their proposed means of transport, there was considerable excitement as neither had ever been carried in such opulence. Once ensconced inside they both felt conspicuous and preferred to drop the curtain drapes, allowing them to smile secretly at the two men trotting alongside to keep up with the bearers.

They were warmly greeted, the women being afforded the solicitous courtesies appropriate to their injuries, and after washing their feet in the traditional Jewish welcome they were ushered into the large reception room to meet the many strangers eagerly awaiting them.

Into that tranquil and harmonious setting burst Rufus like the clap of thunder on the Damascus road.

"Have you heard the rumours about Saul of Tarsus circulating at the Synagogue?" he blurted out looking around excitedly, as though oblivious that he knew only a few of its occupants. "Excuse me, I was carried away by what I've just heard concerning this menace of a Pharisee. I'm Rufus, brother of Miriam and acolyte to Simon Peter, the leader of the apostles of Jesus of Nazareth."

Judas, a large, black bearded man with piercing brown eyes scrutinized him intently and asked, "What are these rumours?"

"Some say he's been struck dead by lightning on the Damascus road, others that he has been struck blind and is in hiding."

Such dramatic pronouncements set everyone speculating wildly, and Andreaus had to assert his authority to calm his guests and to properly introduce the new arrivals. Then he claimed their attention.

"It is because we are all God fearers and concerned at this great schism that splits the fabric of our adopted faith, that we are gathered here today. I learned yesterday of four people that fate has united through their involvement in the crucifixion of Jesus, and I invited them here to talk to us. Rufus is not one of them, but as he knows the latest on Saul's persecution of the followers, perhaps we could ask him to speak to us first."

Speaking slowly, to get his thoughts in order because of the unexpectedness of this request, Rufus began.

"I am the newest and least important of the followers of the apostles of Jesus. Peter is their leader, and he invited me to become his acolyte the day after Miriam and I witnessed the brutal murder of Steven at the city wall. Steven is the first to be put to death for witnessing to the risen Messiah, but sadly there have been many others since. Nobody can have witnessed his stoning without wondering at the unshakeable faith he showed at his moment of trial." He paused closing his eyes as though seeing again that awesome and brutal death.

"Steven was the first to die, but Mary Magadalene was the first to suffer physical violence outside of Jerusalem that brought her close to death, and should have warned us of what was to come."

Mary gasped, and the colour drained from her face at this unwelcome reference to herself. Rufus bowed to acknowledge that he was taking liberties, beseeching her to bear with him.

"Peter often talks of Mary and says were she not a woman, she would be first among the apostles, because she was the first person to whom the risen Lord showed himself and to whom he spoke on the day of his resurrection."

He was interrupted by the eager cries of some of the listeners, two of the women having an irresistible urge to rush over and embrace Mary.

"Mary followed the Lord wherever his travels took him during his Ministry, and stood bravely at the foot of his cross when most of his disciples had fled. I'm also told, Mary, that you witnessed your own brother Lazarus being called back to life after lying three days in the tomb."

Mary nodded.

"My sister Martha and close on a hundred mourners witnessed it too; it was unbelievable."

"The point I'm trying to make is how greatly honoured you are, second only to the Lord's blessed mother. But Jesus never did anything by accident, so we need to look searchingly for the significance."

He paused as though hesitant to voice his conclusion, or rather his opinion at this early period of his discipleship. Then he took the plunge.

"I think he was honouring you as a woman, deliberately to challenge the most strongly entrenched prejudice in the whole world, which has to be the subjugation and humiliation of women!"

There were cries of wonder from some of his listeners and a petite and beautifully complexioned woman, who had never taken her sea blue eyes off Rufus exclaimed,

"Young man, you speak with God given wisdom and authority and your message is as fresh and invigorating as the first breeze of spring, at the end of a very long winter."

She would have continued but for an insistent knock at the door, to which Dicacus hurried as everyone waited expectantly. Returning quickly and in some agitation he said,

"It's elder Ananias, for you, Judas!"

As Judas arose, Andreaus said, "Bring Ananias to us here, we have no need to fear him."

Ananias was ushered in, but was greatly flustered to find himself in such a crowd until he saw Judas and calmed a little.

"I've been told to seek Saul of Tarsus, but your servants won't let me in your house, Judas."

No words could have had a greater impact on the gathering, all of them sharing in Judas' consternation.

"How did you know I was sheltering him in my house, Ananias? My household are sworn not to breathe a word of it."

"Nor have they. This morning I was awakened at cockcrow by a voice calling me. I could see no one, then my name was called again. Only then I knew it was a vision, and I realized it was the Lord calling me. I said, 'Here I am Lord.' Then the Lord's voice told me, 'Get up and go to the street called Straight; inquire in Judas's house for a man called Saul, a man from Tarsus. For, look you, he is praying; and he knows you will come and put your hands on him, so that he may get back his sight.'

"I answered, 'Lord I have heard from many about this man. They have told me all the hurt he has done to the saints in Jerusalem. They have told me too how he has authority from the chief Priests to bind all who call upon your name.'"

There was neither an eye nor an ear in the room that wasn't straining to catch every word, every nuance of what they were hearing as Ananias continued to reveal exactly what had been told him.

"Then the Lord said, 'Go, for he is a chosen instrument for my work. He is chosen to carry my name before peoples and kings and before the sons of Israel. I will tell him all he must suffer for my name's sake.'"

He fell silent as Judas further astounded his listeners.

"It is true, I have given Saul shelter in my house since he was brought to me by his escort, having been struck blind on the Damascus road. He can't tell night from day, nor has eaten in the three days he has been with me. But I am called away, come we must hurry Ananias, as you have to fulfil your assignment."

"Promise you will return before night, none of us will sleep until you tell us of the outcome of this meeting of Saul and Ananias," insisted Andreaus, and agreeing the two men departed, leaving a pensive yet excited party to ponder all that they had heard.

They fragmented into small groups, each with different priorities and viewpoint.

The petite Jewess, Corinna, said she had a large and empty house at her home town of Dura-Europas, which she would gladly place at his disposal if he wanted a mission house on the banks of the Euphrates.

"We are totally dependent on a few patronesses in Jerusalem or we would be living rough on the streets. Nor are our safe houses wherein we meet and worship any longer safe, so I will happily bring your generosity to the attention of Peter," said the acolyte.

"Oh that might mean waiting ages to receive the word from the apostles. I'll talk to Mary and persuade her and her friends to visit us in the meantime."

"You can hardly do better," said Rufus, but before he could elaborate further on Mary's credentials, Andreaus interrupted with a request.

"We would all like to hear how your worship differs from that of the Jews at the Synagogue."

"It is impossible to preach in the Temple, although they can't stop the apostles in the Court of the Gentiles, but many of the Synagogues allow us to recount the parables of Jesus and tell of his miracles, but there is always trouble if we refer to his resurrection."

Looking around he saw he had everyone's attention and continued, "Since the persecution we meet in safe houses known only to the followers, although our enemies are determined that nowhere can we find sanctuary. There we read from the scriptures, as well as recounting events that befell Jesus, and retelling his parables. But the high point of our worship is when the baptized are gathered to break the bread and pass around the chalice of wine."

"What is the special significance of the bread and the wine cup?" asked Cornelius with some despondency, as he and many present were Gentiles, and therefore not baptized.

"Well Jesus inaugurated it as a new covenant on the night he was betrayed. Knowing how close his death was, he arranged the Passover Supper with just his twelve disciples at table. He broke bread and offered it, saying it was his body, which would be given up for them. After the meal he blessed the chalice of wine and passed it to his disciples saying,

"'Take this and drink from it. This is the blood of the new covenant, which is being shed for many.'

"Then he led his disciples to the Garden of Gethsemane where he was betrayed and seized by the Temple guards."

"This new covenant is fundamental to any spiritual growth, so for how long are you going to deny it to us Gentiles?" entreated Cornelius.

"For myself, I would not withhold it one day longer. Peter is addressing this problem with the other apostles and they pray for guidance."

They were interrupted by the return of Judas who burst into the room.

"Oh you should have been there; I've never seen anything so incredible, truly amazing!"

To stop him pacing agitatedly around the room, Andreaus took his arm and insisted he sit in the vacated chair.

"When we entered my house, Saul immediately knew Ananias had arrived. He knelt stretching out his arms in silence. Ananias put his hands on his head and said, 'Brother Saul, the Lord Jesus, who appeared to you on the way as you journeyed here, has sent me that you may get your sight back and so that you may be filled with the Holy Spirit.'

"At that scales fell from his eyes and his sight was restored. The two men then embraced, and Ananias called for some water and baptized him. Saul was about to break his three day fast when I left to bring you news of all these wonders for you to marvel at!"

Seeing the anxiety etched on Mary's face, he recalled something Saul had requested and asked. "Are you that Mary whom Saul encountered on the Damascus road, shortly before he was blinded?"

"Yes, we had a dramatic confrontation, and he urged me to return to Tyre, or he would seize me and bind me if I continued to Damascus. I defied him and challenged him that he was working for the devil."

"Well he blesses you now, and begs forgiveness for the hurt he has caused you. His spirit is heavy with contrition at his persecution of so many followers of the Way, and he has said he will declare his error in the Synagogue tomorrow."

Mary was amazed by this conversion, of which she yet needed to be convinced. Magnanimously she said, "That will call for the greatest courage, the least I can do is witness his testimony."

The consensus among the listeners was that they too wished to witness such a momentous event. They broke into small groups debating the implications of the many marvels that had been revealed that day.

Among the many synagogues in Damascus, the principal one was an ornate building taking up the whole of one side of the Square of the Orphans, just off the street named Straight. Its cloistered court embraced the high pink stone assembly hall, colonnaded with a gallery around three sides. It was from this gallery those who had accompanied Mary and taken the front seats early, were now looking down on the sea of men earnestly filling the benches in the auditorium. The mosaic floor was a seething mass of black-attired elders and worshippers, and only the area in front of the arc was clear.

An elder approached the lectern, and gradually silence descended on the packed hall. In a high pitched falsetto he intoned a psalm, and then surrendered the lectern to a visiting priest who led the congregation in prayers and readings from the Torah.

The elder returned to the lectern, and with some complementary words introduced Saul of Tarsus.

Those who had seen him on the road to Damascus were shocked at the change in the man. His haughty arrogance was gone, as was his youthful vigour and the proud posture of the Pharisee. He looked unwell and hesitant, and even needed to hold the lectern to steady himself as his eyes searched the assembly. He raised them to the gallery, where they ceased their roving as they locked on to those of Mary, registering neither surprise nor vexation, and for the first time any of them had ever seen, he smiled.

Mary said afterwards, she had never seen as much rejoicing captured in the human face.

His voice was confident and clear, bordering on exaltation and he seemed to grow in stature as he began to speak.

"Brethren, elders, I believe I can say with confidence my reputation will have

210

gone before me. You will know how I persecuted the followers of Jesus beyond measure and tried to destroy them. How I went further in my zeal as a Jew than any of my age and race, so fierce a champion was I of the traditions handed down by our forefathers. No arguments, no pleading, no compassion could deter me, and I rejoiced as the stones fell on the head of the unrepentant Steven at Jerusalem. I instigated the terrible night of vengeance, when many thousands of the followers were driven out of Jerusalem for fear of their very lives. Many of them will have come here, and some will surely be in this congregation."

He paused, dramatically, and born orator that he was darted an inquiring look at various groups, all totally absorbed at his words. Such was the intensity of the interrogation in his eyes that wherever they alighted, people were disconcerted and fidgeted. Mary like everyone was spellbound by the vibrant magnetism of the man, and wondered if he was still an enemy.

"I have come with letters of credit from the Sanhedrin. I am to bind all those I find of the Way, both men and women, and bring them to Jerusalem to answer at the Temple court."

He produced a sealed roll of parchment, broke the seal and flourished it in the air.

A growl of approval arose from the floor of the hall, and for one awful moment Mary relived a similar experience in the synagogue at Joppa, and felt her heart pounding. She needed to grasp the firm hand of Brutus for that reassurance she so desperately needed.

The growl of the men was suddenly choked in disbelief, as Saul calmly tore the letter in two, and released the rendered parchment so that it fluttered pathetically to the floor. He resumed speaking.

"Let me tell you this, brethren, the gospel I now preach to you is not a thing of man's dictation, it comes to me by a revelation of that same Lord Jesus that I was determined to destroy. Four days ago on my journey here I was struck blind. I fell to the ground as my companions will testify, and then I heard the voice of the Son of God asking why did I persecute him. I wasn't sure whose voice I heard, so I asked who was speaking to me. He told me he was the same Jesus whom I had been persecuting. I was commanded to go into this city where I would be told what to do.

"My companions brought me blind to the house of Judas, and for three days I knew not day or night. Yesterday, elder Ananias laid hands on me and I recovered my sight.

"I now realize how spiritually blind I was, when I thought I could see so clearly good reasons for persecuting the followers of Jesus. I glorified in my ignorance until the glory of the risen Christ was revealed to me, and I repent of my past deeds. Henceforth I have been chosen to carry the name of the Lord Jesus before all peoples, and before kings, and before the sons of Israel. This is the first day of my life's mission."

As he bowed to the ark and to the presiding elder, there erupted unprecedented scenes on the floor below them. Many men were crying out in anger, and quite a few were raising lamentations to heaven and tearing at their beards and robes. The elders had to form a ring around Saul to keep him from being physically attacked.

Mary reflected she had had no such protection, and as she glanced thankfully at Marc, saw him giving her a smile as though he were reading her thoughts.

As Saul was ushered out he disdained to take any note of the abuse shouted at him, or the spittle that found its target. He was already putting on the spiritual armour that he would need throughout the remainder of his life.

They were a very reflective group that gathered in one of the open-air cafes that were plentiful in the squares of the city.

Rufus was elated and anxious to take the news of Saul's conversion to Jerusalem, so announced he had to leave that very afternoon.

Cornelius and Andreaus had to get back to their units, and were departing early the next morning.

Miriam was eager to see how the tomb was progressing.

Mary was conversing with Corinna, who was entreating them to come to Dura-Europas, and as Brutus joined them she was saying, "We are only a small community but eager to learn more. No one has received the gift of the Holy Spirit, and if you were to stay with us we would all benefit from your intercession. I have a lovely, big house, which I would happily give for your church and you would enjoy living there."

"Where do you live?" asked Brutus."

"Dura-Europas, which is a garrison town about ninety miles north east of here, on the western bank of the Euphrates. The valley is very wide there, where a tributary joins from the mountains far to the north. It is a verdant oasis and date palms and pomegranates create cool shade all along the banks of the river."

"I would like to go there, what do you think, Mary?"

"In time I really believe I might like it very much, especially as it would mean we would meet again. But there are many ties for Miriam and me in Tyre at the moment. Maybe later this year if the offer remains open."

"It would be a great joy if I can tell our church you will join us within the year, already we are past the longest day!"

"If we are coming we will send you a messenger some weeks before we can travel," said Brutus bowing as he went to take his leave of his comrades, all of whom were elated at the wonders they had witnessed in Damascus.

CHAPTER NINE

Their welcome on returning to Tyre was overwhelming, especially by a joyful Lucia, who had been bursting with curiosity to find out if the startling news of Saul she had heard at the agora that morning, had in any way been connected with the presence of her friends in Damascus. Seated in the agreeable familiarity of Flora's house they were surprised at news of Saul's conversion preceding them, and wanted to know how it had been received at the synagogue.

"It has caused a few ripples here," said Flora, "one of which is to have thrown the synagogue into confusion. The hot heads have been told by the elders in no uncertain terms to refrain from any harassment of the refugees. Jacob and Ruth have vacated their room, and you men are free to move back here if you so wish."

"For my part I have had enough of inns!" rejoiced Brutus who had not contemplated the return to their former sleeping arrangements with pleasure, and Marc gladly endorsed his sentiments.

Alexander was very subdued, and Lucia sitting at his side looked crestfallen. To Marc she said pleadingly, "I know you slept in my bed before the refugees arrived, but now would you sleep at the inn instead of Alex?"

Marc looked confused, as he had long ago ceased to have any claim on her bed, and Lucia continued, "Poor Alex needs more attention to his broken arm than he gets at the inn, so he can have my bed, and Miriam can sleep on the palliasse that Mary no longer needs."

Surprised to be consulted at all and his head spinning with who slept where, Marc looked at Miriam, gave a resigned smile and a shake of his head and said he wouldn't mind sleeping at the inn

Miriam, looking daggers, said she wanted to see how the tomb was progressing while there were a few hours of daylight remaining. Once outside she grasped Marc's arm tightly as she released her pent up feelings.

"The little vixen! The crafty fox! She had it all worked out so cleverly you didn't stand a chance! You fell for it completely, made it easy for her to wrap you round her little finger."

Miriam was obviously fuming and Marc, who had thought to milk a little sympathy from his sacrifice, instead found himself accused of being a simpleton, a pushover.

"How can I say what she is to do with her own bed, she can give it to her kunaria if she wishes!" he said trying to joke her out of her anger.

"That's just what she has done, only the pet poodle she has found for it is my brother. She is obviously out to catch him and he doesn't stand a chance. Oh men!" she ended scathingly.

Having given vent to her exasperation, she led Marc at the double to the plot where the tomb had sprung up during their absence.

The walls of sawn limestone rose well above head height and the wooden frame was in place to support the precisely dressed stone that would complete the domed roof. At the head of the columns forming the portal were palm-sculptured capitals supporting the lintel that was delicately carved in relief with Abraham's brooch, forming a continuous frieze along its span.

As they stood admiring the progress and the craftsmanship, tears welled up in Miriam's eyes and Marc put his arms around her and drew her tightly to him.

"Isn't life precarious, Marc? Liable to be snuffed out like a candle any moment. Were it not for Mary, I would be with mama and papa, waiting to be laid in there."

She felt Marc shudder at the recollection of his despair as he had searched for her trampled body among the milling horses.

"Only Mary could have put such trust in God and thrown both of you off the road's edge. Had you died, I would have wished myself dead. Instead I rejoice that my life is yours and one day you will be my wife."

Miriam's eyes held his and he looked into the dark pupils. For the first time he saw the yellow flecks that lightened the brown rings, floating exquisitely on a bluish white moistness as she blinked away her tears.

Smiling bravely she said hesitantly, "After we've laid mama and papa and the other victims in the tomb."

His heart pounding wildly at this promise, he placed his yearning lips tenderly on hers, and felt the thrill of her first womanly response.

Wordlessly they returned to their friends, where their shining eyes betrayed that metamorphosis from sweethearts to lovers.

One look exchanged between Mary and Flora confirmed the other's intuition, and their eyes lit up with the unspoken understanding they shared. Over the preparation of the meal the two women discussed the role that they had inherited consequent on the death of Naomi.

"This passion that is flowering is a bit heady for them," mused Flora, "with the normal constraints of family, things might evolve calmly, but as orphans in this turbulent world there is an imperative for us to do something."

"So we need to arrange a wedding!" exclaimed Mary as though concluding Flora's sentence.

They hugged each other with conspiratorial joy, just as Lucia burst in on them bubbling with happiness.

"Mummy, wouldn't Alex be an excellent son-in-law?"

As they both stared at her, struck speechless by the suddenness of it rather than its unexpectedness, Lucia continued, "He's just said he would like us to become betrothed!"

Again both women hugged each other, their joy no less heartfelt from lacking the zest of an element of conspiracy. Then hugging Lucia in turn, the women spilled out of the kitchen to scatter the troops, able bodied and injured, with a seemingly endless sequence of tears, hugs, smiles and more tears.

Miriam was far from overjoyed, as this confirmed all her fears, but she was overwhelmed by the speed of events.

Intuitively aware of her doubts, Flora embraced her saying, "I can see you're uncertain about all this, but I rejoice if I gain a daughter by our families being joined. Lucia is a bit scattered-brained but she will be a good wife, and Alexander is a husband to be proud of. I will not permit Lucia to displace you from your bed, and I'll tell Alexander he must stay at the inn for the present."

Miriam smiled at her wanly but gave her an appreciative kiss, and thereby many things were resolved. One of some significance was that Miriam converted to welcome the move to Dura-Europas, and of equal significance was her resolve to be Marc's wife before that happened.

Cornelius had returned to his battalion profoundly affected by all that had happened at Damascus. He fasted for two days, praying earnestly and reading the scriptures, and only his wife saw anything of him, as he even slept in the small sanctuary that he had built into the house. He knew the time was nigh to break his fast, as his military duties denied him the right to weaken himself unduly.

About mid-afternoon, he put his books away and lay on the couch emptying his mind of any worries and refusing to ponder the implication of what he had read. His eyes were heavy and it was a struggle to keep them from closing.

Then suddenly they were wide open and riveted on an ethereal light, as of some not distant star within the room. Without any conscious thought he knew he was being blessed with a vision from God, and he was awe-struck.

An angel called him by name saying, "Cornelius."

"What is it, sir?" he replied.

The angel said, "Your prayers and your works of mercy have not gone unnoticed by God. Now, send some men to Joppa to find a man named Simon Peter, who is lodging with Simon, the tanner, down by the sea-shore, and ask him to come and visit you."

Then the angel left him, just as his wife Delium, entered to see if there was anything he required.

Such a look of ecstasy about him she had never before seen. Sitting bolt upright, with dilated pupils and beatific smile on his face, Cornelius was oblivious to all around him. As he moved slowly to his knees in thankfulness, Delium, in awe knelt quietly beside him.

Rising abruptly, Cornelius hardly found time to tell her of his vision such was the urgency he felt to comply with this angelic command.

He called two of his servants and an orderly, and instructed them as best he was able, where to search out the house of Simon the tanner.

They were eager to start that moment, but Cornelius delayed them until first light the next day, when they set out an hour before sunrise; walking, as they had been told Peter would insist on accompanying them on foot.

Travelling light, they made good progress, and early the next day when they were close to the outskirts of Joppa, looking over the city, they sat down to share their morning meal.

The elderly Jew who approached saluted them and sat staring out to sea.

"Why do you sit so keenly searching the sea to the far horizon?" asked Silas, the senior of the two servants.

"Hoping to see the boat that took my heart's treasure from me bringing her back," sighed the old man.

"Is it your daughter who crossed the sea?"

"No, not a daughter, but Mary came like an angel into my life three months ago. She was companion of the Lord Jesus until he died, then she came to Joppa and revealed the wonder of God to me."

"She sounds a remarkable woman, why did you not keep her here?"

215

"Her companions were a Roman centurion and his freed slave who needed to flee King Herod, and she insisted on accompanying them."

The three travellers conferred earnestly, then Silas asked, "Is the centurion named Brutus?"

Abraham regarded them in amazement, shaking his head disbelievingly.

"Yes that's him. What can you tell me of him and his friends?

They explained what had passed in Damascus, and then moved on to tell of Cornelius' vision at Caesarea and that their present mission was to find the house of Simon the Tanner, where Simon Peter was lodging.

"Why, I can take you to the tanner's house and I know this Simon Peter, he visited my humble shop not long ago, and rebuked those who had attacked Mary in the synagogue!"

Now it was the turn of the travellers to show amazement, and Abraham had to explain what had befallen Mary in the synagogue, and how she had been nursed back to health in his humble room, and why nothing would persuade him that Saul had truly repented so that he felt obliged to warn them.

"Beware of Saul. He is deceiving you all to strike at the church from within! When nobody regards him as a threat, then will he strike like a cobra, to kill!"

The sun was high in the sky when Abraham led them to the beach, where those Jews lived whose work made them unclean by Pharisaic law. The door of Simon the Tanner's house opened at their knock, and his wife regarded them anxiously.

"Does Simon Peter lodge here?" asked Silas.

At the mention of his name Peter descended the steps from the housetop and stood dwarfing them.

"I am the man you are looking for. Why have you come?" he rumbled.

"Cornelius, the centurion, a good man and a God-fearer, one whose worth the whole nation of the Jews bears witness, was instructed by a holy angel to send for you to come to his house so that he can listen to the words you would give him," replied Silas.

Peter asked them in and the brethren that were with him made them welcome. Amongst them was Rufus, whose ears had pricked up at the mention of Cornelius.

Peter, looking very relaxed and confident said, "All accords with my own vision of this morning. Tomorrow I, and some of the brethren, will return with you to Caesarea. When we are in your master's house I will reveal to you all what God has revealed to me this day, that we may know better how to fulfil his will."

Abraham regretted that his age precluded him from accompanying them, as he was sure there would be many wonders to follow on from two such convergent visions. But he found consolation by contemplating how anyone as unworthy as himself, could be blessed by all that he had witnessed in the brief period since he had known Mary, to whom he attributed everything.

At the house in Caesarea, amongst those gathered at the invitation of Cornelius, there was a marked heightening of suspense with each day that passed, and every new arrival.

Andreaus, his wife and Corinna, accompanied by the faithful Dicacus, arrived on the third eve, just in time to rebut any misgivings amongst some of the more impatient as to what could be going wrong.

"Beware of misplaced optimism," he warned, "for we shouldn't impose a time scale on God working his purpose, which would be a sin as it evidences lack of faith."

Suitably rebuked, those who had expressed concern decided it might be in order just to send a small welcoming party, with a wagon and horses, to meet the weary travellers and assist their passage in any way they might need.

Cornelius, with an awareness of the inability of some people to wait patiently, put those friends who fretted over much, to preparing just such a welcoming party, which was to start out the morning of the second following day. This compromise satisfied nobody, as is the nature of compromises, but it restrained the impatient, and mollified the exasperated, and helped them to live together and wait.

As it happened that was not overlong, as Peter and his party arrived at noon on the next day. A lookout had been posted on the outskirts of the city, and the travellers found Cornelius and his guests awaiting them. As Peter approached the door Cornelius knelt before him, but Peter raised him to his feet saying, "Rise; I too am a man."

"So you may be but you have travelled two days to visit my humble abode, and me a gentile and unworthy! It is right that I should kneel before you, to give honour to your Lord and mine."

So they entered amongst all those who had assembled there, and Peter and his companions who were all Jewish mingled and talked with the gentiles. Then Peter raised his hands to make everyone aware he intended to speak, and a space was cleared as silence fell on the house.

"You know that it is against the Jewish laws for me to come into a gentile home like this. But God has shown me in a vision that I should never think of anyone as inferior, so I came without any objection when you sent for me. Now tell me what you want."

Cornelius had a look of rapture as he said, "Four days ago, I was praying in my house in the afternoon and an angel stood before me telling me I had found favour before God. He told me to send to Joppa for Simon who is also called Peter who is lodging in the house of Simon, a Tanner, on the seashore. Immediately I sent to you and I am most grateful that you have come. Now then, we are all present before God to hear all that God has enjoined you to tell."

Peter replied, "I must tell you of my vision as happened but minutes before your messengers arrived. I was at prayer on the housetop, when I became hungry and needed to eat. Then I saw descending from heaven a great sheet, let down by the four corners to earth. On it were all four-footed animals and all that creep on the earth and fly in the air. A voice came to me, 'Rise Peter, kill and eat any of them you wish.'

"'Never, Lord,' I replied, 'I have never in my life eaten such creatures, for they are forbidden by our Jewish laws.'

"I thought I was being tested but the voice rebuked me saying, 'Don't contradict God! What he says is clean, you are not to reckon unclean.'"

Peter paused and looked questioningly at his listeners, who were all familiar with the strict food laws of the Jews, even if they didn't see the need to apply them to themselves.

"Did not Daniel refuse the food of the Babylonians, the meat and wine of the king himself, and risk his wrath? How many thousands have been put to death for refusing the meat of the pig? So again I refused to break the Jewish food laws.

217

Three times this happened and then the sheet and all on it was drawn up to heaven.

"I was at a loss what to make of it all, and greatly worried, when the men of Cornelius stood at the door. Then the spirit spoke to me and said, 'Three men have come to see you. Rise and go with them without any hesitation, because it is I who sent them.'"

They were so enthralled at hearing Peter's words and had no wish to interrupt, but some just had to give thanks to God vocally for so honouring them, and he was forced to bide his time until their impassioned responses had quieted. Peter then went on to explain he had come to see the meaning of the vision, to understand that God had no favourites, but that all who fear him and act righteously were acceptable to him because of the sacrifice of his son who intercedes for all without distinction. To Jesus there is no significance of Jew or gentile, free man or slave, rich or poor. All are equal if they believe in him, and by following him receive forgiveness of sins through his name.

Such was the wonder this new message evoked in the hearts of his listeners that their faces glowed joyously and questions tripped off their tongues excitedly.

Peter and his attendants beheld the Holy Spirit descend upon all in the room, and when he heard them speaking with tongues and magnifying God, which accorded very much with what he had been anticipating, he said, "Can anyone stop water being brought and those who have received the Holy Spirit from being baptized?"

And he baptized them there and then, in the name of Jesus. Rufus rejoiced in his heart as he realized this removed any lurking doubts he had over the union of the Jewish women and the Romans.

Saul's escort showed great reluctance to return to the Sanhedrin at his urging, knowing that the Temple authorities would not be satisfied with anything less than the sect's leaders to make an example of. They would not be interested in any excuses for failure!

The actual circumstance of Saul being blinded on the Damascus road was difficult enough to believe, but his insistence that he could see with the eye of revelation more clearly than ever before was totally beyond them, and they dared not mention such words in the Temple. Only when he had pressed his purse bulging with temple funds upon them, and asked them to return it to the treasurer with the message that it was no longer needed, had they been persuaded to depart for Jerusalem. There they had encountered disbelief and hostility, until the news of Saul's testimony to the Synagogue at Damascus was brought independently to the Sanhedrin.

This betrayal of his mission fanned the priests' anger to white heat, and the bitter enmity they nursed to the followers erupted in a fresh burst of violence against those that remained. Only the apostles were immune, because of the innumerable miracles they had worked, those who would gladly have terrorized them being fearful of their supernatural powers.

The stream of refugees fleeing Jerusalem became a flood, escaping into Samaria and beyond, destitute and fearful, but always unbowed and holding firmly to their belief.

Panic was more in evidence among the priests and elders, as they realised the followers of Jesus rejoiced in sharing the suffering that had been inflicted on their leader, and that their numbers were increasing daily.

Accordingly, by the completion of Miriam's tomb, there were fifteen victims of the persecution to be laid to rest in it. How many hundreds there were scattered throughout the province nobody could guess but Miriam insisted on a carved stone being inserted to one side of the door, inscribed:

'To those victims of the persecution who may never be found.'

Those who knew her realised she was mindful of her mother, who in other circumstances might still have remained undiscovered in the rock cleft.

The evening before the burial of the victims a sombre gathering in Flora's house were resolved to fast until the following evening, so only a pitcher of water occupied the table which previously had served for their communal suppers.

Their desultory conversation was silenced by a persistent knocking at the door and everyone's eyes followed Flora as she investigated its cause, to erupt in excited greetings as she returned followed by an elated Rufus, who beamed with delight that at last he was to meet his sister's Phoenician friends of whom previously he had only heard.

"I've been three days on the road," he said, and Flora was suddenly anxious at the absence of any food to offer him, as she saw his eyes drawn to the pitcher.

"When did you last eat?" she asked hesitantly, and at his answer her worst fears were realized.

"Apart from some bread, olives and figs I carried with me, the morning I left Peter and the apostles at Jerusalem. Miriam's message about mama and father's burial arrived a few days ago, and Peter gave me unlimited leave, so here I am."

Miriam hastened to explain what was about to happen the next day, and the reason they were fasting, but Brutus, who had only reluctantly agreed as fasting was something he never did voluntarily, interrupted to suggest in the altered circumstance they might partake of a modest meal at the inn where Alexander and Marc still shared a room, a proposal welcomed by the famished traveller.

The innkeeper put a separate room at their disposal, and soon produced an enticing assortment of fare, which was eagerly partaken of by the men, although the women were resolved to adhere to their fast. Only at the end of the meal did Rufus feel called upon to tell them of all that had befallen the followers in Jerusalem, and the visions of Peter and Cornelius and the subsequent meeting of the two he had witnessed at Caesarea.

Miriam's eyes lost their sadness when he mentioned the silversmith Abraham, and Mary quickened to enquire of the lovely old man. Her eyes moistened at being told of the daily vigil that her worshipper kept at the outlook across the sea, where he had encountered Cornelius' servants.

"I would like to see the dear, sweet man again," she said, "our farewell was marred by my having to try and not drown in Joppa port!"

"Could we not send for him? A cart could be sent to bring him from Joppa." suggested Brutus.

"Rufus, can you stay a week and bless my marriage to Marc?" said Miriam to everyone's amazement, not the least Marc's.

"Thankfully I can, and gladly will I do so! Because of the visions of Peter and Cornelius, the old barriers between Jew and gentile have been swept away."

"Mama's last words were to Marc as he was freeing her leg, when she said, 'You will look after her won't you?'"

Miriam was sobbing quietly fighting back the tears, and Marc placed a comforting arm around her shoulders.

"So when our father and mama are laid to rest you wish to fulfil that last request?"

Marc almost swelled with pride as he replied, "With all my heart sir. That will be my greatest joy. I only wish it could all have been less tragic for you."

"In these tumultuous times tragedy is never very far away. As long as we meet it bravely and hold to our beliefs, we will triumph ultimately. And please don't call me sir, we have no rank in the army in which I am enlisted."

"I would happily serve under you in any Roman legion where I have commanded a century!" affirmed Brutus vigorously.

Rufus smiled as he rejoined, "Have no fear, our commander is a demanding master and uses the skills of his followers to their very limits. If you allow me to baptize you into his army, you will be undertaking the mighty task of conquering the whole world."

Mary was watching with bated breath. She knew that behind the banter, Rufus was throwing down a challenge that the centurion could accept or turn his back on, until now he had been absolved from making the choice.

Reaching his hand into a pocket of his tunic, he slowly withdrew it to reveal the rough cross from the hilt and shattered blade of his sword.

"I made my choice at the foot of the cross many months ago. I have only been awaiting the right time and circumstance to affirm it."

"And I too recognise this as the right time to confer on you baptism in the name of Jesus."

As Brutus knelt, Rufus took a pitcher of water from the table and poured it liberally over his hair, and laid his hand on his head saying, "Receive the Holy Spirit," then lifted him to his feet and embraced him.

It had all been so stunningly simple and brief, but the joy radiating from the new initiate was unmistakable, and the querulous, worried look he often wore was erased without trace.

Those who now crowded around the centurion were aware of some subtle change in their companion, although he had never lacked in authority. Now his authority rested on true credentials that were ageless and enduring.

An overjoyed Mary embraced him, and then reminded Brutus of his proposal that they send for Abraham.

"And he must be here for the wedding to share in our joy!"

"A messenger will be dispatched in the morning," Brutus assured her.

"I would like to tell you one of the favourite stories of Jesus as a young man before he had begun his mission. It has to do with a wedding at Cana, and how Jesus changed some jars of water into wine when they had run short at the wedding feast."

Rufus had everyone's attention, especially Mary's although she had heard it from Peter at Pentecost, and as he was already an accomplished storyteller, with a poet's ear for turn of phrase, he delighted his listeners, and they rejoiced at the appropriateness of this first of his miracles.

"I wish Jesus could have been around for our wedding," said Miriam sadly, "without mama and papa I fear it will hardly be joyful."

"Jesus will be present if you welcome him into your lives," insisted Rufus, "by the sacraments of baptism, and the sharing of his body and blood as bread and wine he has promised he will always be with us. I am aware of his presence even as I talk with you and he talks to me when I pray."

"I asked Peter to baptize me at Joppa, but he wouldn't because I am a gentile!" said Marc, who had witnessed the spontaneous baptism of Brutus with amazed bewilderment.

"He would gladly baptize you and welcome you now. It needed the visions of Cornelius and his own, to make that clear to him. If you wish to be baptized while I am with you, I will arrange that we celebrate together. Now let us pray for the dead victims of the persecution that will be laid to rest tomorrow."

As he knelt, and all present joined him easily and naturally, Miriam wondered at the stature of her brother, who seemed to have absorbed unwittingly the authority of his leader.

The burial day dawned clear, although it took a full hour for the sun to burn off the autumnal mist that lingered over the hills. The victims were taken from the lime pit and laid on biers, and after a relative had signified recognition, the body was covered with a white linen sheet and a carved plaque bearing each victim's name was placed at the foot.

Hundreds of mourners, many shaved of both hair and beard and wearing sackcloth, formed a simple procession, and as the flute players began their lament, raised the biers and began their funeral passage through the city's narrow streets.

Constantly the crowd grew as ordinary townsfolk, as well as representatives of the city council and a few elders of the Synagogue joined the procession. The military kept a very low profile, although in the side streets the occasional squad of soldiers was to be seen, resentful at this early morning readiness in case of disturbance.

By the time they exited the city gate for the winding country road, the last of the mist was gone, and the stark whiteness of the tomb gleamed in the morning sun, drawing all who wished to show respect to the victims. Few witnessing the tiny occupants of two of the biers could restrain the lumps rising in their throats, or the flow of tears that were induced by the wailing of the mourners and the flutes.

To one side of the entrance stood the huge millstone that would be rolled across the entrance to seal it, propped up by two staves of wood. Brutus and Marc exchanged significant glances, for they were their contribution and had been hewn from the baulk of timber that had speared the *Hermes*.

The bodies had lain too long in the lime pit for the traditional embalming, and Miriam had obtained a sarcophagus from Egypt for her parents. After the lid had been placed over them and the biers with the others placed around the tomb, the two Romans removed the staves and used them to lever the heavy stone into place.

Looking at each other they were then disconcerted as to what to do with them. Neither felt inclined to discard theirs, so of one accord they placed them over their shoulders, and rejoined their amused women for the reading of each testimony.

Alexander was the last to do so, and was greatly honoured by the leader of the city council who presented him with a gold medal commemorating his generosity.

221

Miriam was not pleased at the delight shown by Lucia, but when Rufus embraced her speaking quietly, she was contrite and buried her sobs in the folds of his cloak. Gradually her sobs eased and then ceased as she looked up at Rufus and smiled feebly. She slid away from his arms and moving quickly to Lucia put her arms around her and kissed her. Only one barely audible word was said, "Sorry," and then the two girls were like two inconsolable sisters, who had feared the other lost and just found them alive and well.

At the conclusion of the psalm and the prayers for the dead the crowd began to disperse. This was Rufus's awaited moment and moving quickly to stand at the entrance to the tomb he raised his arms and called, "Stay a while if you are eager to learn more of this same Jesus for whom these victims died, for he is assuredly the long awaited Messiah."

That last word was enough to arrest most of those who were dispersing, and the crowd quickly gathered around the young man who had called out so challengingly.

"My friends, we mourn these fifteen saints who died in the name of Jesus and many hundreds more killed in Jerusalem and throughout Judaea and Samaria. Jesus himself was laid in a tomb not dissimilar to this some four months ago, after his cruel crucifixion. Around the tomb were posted guards, vigilant to prevent his followers from stealing his body, so that they could not claim he had risen from the dead, as he had said he would.

"Because of the wonder at what happened there, we can rejoice that all these victims will be glorified on the day of the Lord, for he did indeed rise from the dead, and his disciples found the stone rolled back and the tomb empty when they went to it the morning after the Passover."

Among the cries of wonder that greeted these words were raised dissenting cries of blasphemy, and a section of the crowd showed considerable agitation.

Brutus looked at Marc, and with a wordless nod the youth began to push his way towards the dissenters.

"Indeed not only had the Son of God risen from the dead, but he appeared to his disciples many times over the next six weeks, his body still bearing the wounds of the nails and his side pierced by the centurion's spear. He spoke with them, ate with them and prayed with them, until the day of his ascension to his Father in heaven. They then awaited the Holy Spirit, that Jesus promised would follow his ascension, to guide and strengthens them to carry the message to the whole world.

"I was not one of them, I did not even know of them until a short while ago, when I became an acolyte to the apostle Peter. But it is the Holy Spirit you hear now speaking through me, as it does through his apostles and many other followers, who are commissioned to carry his message of redemption to both Jew and gentile throughout the world."

Marc had worked his way to the periphery of the crowd and saw three men scouring the area for large stones, which they were gathering into pouches formed by holding up the hems of their robes. He pushed his way more urgently to bring this intelligence to Brutus, but before he regained his group he felt the ripple of excitement around him, and heard the name of Mary Magdalene from the wondering lips of the listeners.

He arrived breathlessly at the side of the centurion just as Mary had moved to stand with Rufus and an awesome silence descended on the crowd, aware that they were about to hear something mysterious and momentous.

Mary's voice rang out clear and joyous as the two Romans pushed their way through the bodies to the area where the men had been gleaning the stones.

There was no sign of them now, as they had mingled back into the press of people, but Brutus had noted well the place where the agitation had been focused, and they moved around the rear of the crowd before pushing towards where they anticipated trouble It needed all their determination and resolve to penetrate the unyielding and protesting bodies, but eventually Marc recognised first one and then a second of the men, who were huddled in a group close to a corner of the tomb.

Mary's voice rang out.

"Then he said, 'Mary,' and I realised it wasn't the gardener I was addressing, but the risen Lord himself. I was blinded with tears as I knelt and breathed Rabbini, and went to kiss his feet but ...,"

A cry rent the air, piercing and shrill.

"Blasphemer, harlot! Stone this devil's spawn!"

As of one accord the huddle of men broke into its disparate members, each running with raised arms, stones clasped in hand, towards the stunned speaker. Although they found their path barred by two men with clenched staves, such was their frenzy they were undeterred, and surged to pass them to reach their intended victims. Their leaders were felled by simultaneous blows to their unprotected heads, then two more. None of them was a match for the battle-hardened warrior, or his enthusiastic son, and as the bodies piled up around them the frenzy evaporated, and the remnant of the mob jettisoned their stones and fled.

A few of the half dozen men they had felled were hesitantly attempting to regain their feet. Brutus gave one of them a contemptuous kick, as he and Marc raced towards Mary in case an attack came from any other quarter.

Mary was deathly pale and shaking, but she hastened to explain with vexation not fear.

"As soon as I begin to testify to the Lord all hell seems to break out around me. First Joppa, now here!"

"It's because you are a woman and fearless, and they feel threatened when you challenge their prejudices," said Rufus.

"I've never known a race so determined to humiliate and subjugate their women as you Jews," protested Brutus passionately.

"That is one of the things Jesus had no time for. While he was with her he loved and valued Mary because she was such a fearless woman, and he wanted to sweep away all the prejudices that mankind has built up over millennia," explained Rufus.

"Could anything be more formidable, to sweep away all the world's prejudices. No wonder I had to crucify him," mused Brutus, allowing himself to relax as the crowd dispersed without posing any further threat.

The rest of their party had joined them, and a litter was being improvised by some resentful Pharisees to carry away their unconscious leader.

"Don't expect his kingdom to be welcomed by Rome," asserted Brutus.

Rufus gave him a disarming smile as he said confidently, "As his kingdom has no borders or territorial ambitions, only to gain the hearts of mankind, I am sure the emperors of Rome will gladly become his most ardent subjects eventually."

All the way back to Flora's house he pursued his vision of what was to happen, and such was his faith that not even Brutus was prepared to gainsay him.

Rufus had requested that the elders of the Synagogue allow him to address the assembly on the Sabbath. They had agreed, but after the incident at the tomb sent a deputation to withdraw their approval.

"Jarius is still concussed, and he is a leading elder of our assembly. It could inflame the congregation if you were to address them after today's unnecessary violence," stated one of the elders critically.

"Then I will stand outside and address them as they are about to enter," said Rufus determinedly, "it would be a mistake to allow Jarius' claim that he is the victim of unprovoked violence to go unchallenged. He was leading a mob intent on stoning Mary Magdalene, as many other than us will testify."

"I advise against that as feelings are running high, and we elders cannot guarantee your safety if you continue to provoke violence," and with that warning he led his party away from the house.

Inside all had heard the disputation, and one look at Rufus' resolved face was enough to deter everyone from trying to dissuade him from his intention, except for Alexander.

"You made your point very convincingly at the tomb, brother, and there will be many who remember your words and ponder them. But if there is further violence, that is all that will be remembered, and the merit of your message will be obfuscated," he argued persuasively.

"Thank you, Alexander, you are right, so I will not be the orator that I was intent on being, and I will quietly attend the worship instead. I will take my place among the Jews in the synagogue alone, and it would be best if none of you accompany me this time!" he said, looking pointedly at the Romans and Mary.

There was considerable dissent to this, but such was his authority that he easily vanquished any opposition.

"Don't misunderstand me. I was really thankful you were vigilant this morning, and did what you had to do. But my own people worshipping in their synagogue, even if misled and errant, do not need their heads cracked by you two formidable warriors. I must learn better to search for ways to reach them. My whole life's work depends on learning to handle my own race sensitively. I was too blunt and challenging today as Alex has pointed out, and only your intervention saved Mary from paying dearly for my error."

Miriam was amazed at the change in her brother in the two months he had been with the apostles and a little daunted by him. She was now completely at ease with Lucia and they were often giggling girlishly at some shared joke, which had been unknown prior to Rufus' words with her at the tomb. Lying in her bed that night she heard his words again.

"Alex's hurt is greater than you know. Because he bottles it up inside him don't think he isn't suffering. He needs Lucia and all the love she will give him. Don't burden him with your resentment."

The fresh outpouring of tears carried her into sleep, and for once she neglected her prayers.

CHAPTER TEN

The next day, it was a very anxious group that awaited the return of Rufus from the Synagogue. As the hours passed their fears grew disproportionately and any conversation was desultory.

His whole body urging action Brutus finally said, "Anyone ready to join me for a walk?"

He was surprised at the immediate response, everyone jumping to their feet eager to accompany him. Scribbling a note should Rufus return while they were out, they grabbed their cloaks as rain was threatening and there was a feel of winter in the air. Instinctively they walked past the agora, through the city gate and along the road past the tomb. The wind was freshening and the sparse trees tossed agitatedly with each gust. It was all very exhilarating, and distracted their thoughts from what might be happening elsewhere.

Rounding a promontory the spume covered sea opened to their view, stretching to the far horizon glistening deep blue, flecked with white in the sunshine. Chaotic waves surged in to break against the cliff face, shooting spray high in the air to be blown far inland by the capricious wind.

Miriam seized Marc's arm and pointed excitedly to a small brown sail, that rose and fell regularly into the troughs between the waves. It seemed inconceivable that a small boat would put out in such weather, and they watched it being tossed around with a deepening awareness of impending disaster.

There were two men on board, one wrestling with the rope from the sail, the other throwing his weight on the steer oar, trying to hold a course parallel to the coast to seek shelter in the lee of the island. There was no chance of this, as the boat could not point up wind and each successive wave was moving it steadily shorewards.

Simultaneously all saw the rogue wave looming over the others, surging in from the west with its awesome crest arched and threatening. Some instinct made the helmsman look over his shoulder, perhaps a stupendous noise as the crest fell towards them, tumbling the boat in a succession of rolling cartwheels which stripped it bare of mast, spars, everything. As the torrent of foaming angry water moved past, it left the vessel wallowing, filled to the gunwales in the trough, before the smaller siblings of waves gradually pummelled it towards the cliffs. As they all recoiled in horror, Brutus was the first to react purposefully.

"Run back to the city and fetch help. Make sure some long ropes are included, as we will be hard pressed to recover their bodies from the foot of these cliffs. Come on Marc, this path leads down to the shore."

Alexander and Mary followed the Romans as they raced down the winding path, while the others hurried off to raise the alarm. The path ended in some steps carved into a narrow ledge of rock, which in calm times would have been a good landing place, but now was awash with spray shooting up the vertical wall behind it.

"We can't make our way around against these waves and the under tow. Can you two go back to the cliff top and keep a look out, the sea may wash them past and we will need to be quick if we are to stand any chance of reaching them," roared Brutus above the howling of the wind.

It took a while before the head of Alexander could be seen peering down, gesticulating wildly and pointing behind them. As they were trying to interpret the significance of the signals, both realised shouting was no longer necessary, the wind having dropped. Alexander withdrew from the cliff and in a few minutes rejoined them with Mary not far behind.

"The boat is drifting this way close inshore and one of the men is clinging to it. With this lull in the wind we could make a human chain that might be able to reach it as it drifts past."

"Oh if only we had a rope," said Brutus with the anguish of defeat, but Mary had removed her cloak and was offering it to him.

"Tie it to yours and the others, and improvise one," she said breathlessly.

"Bless you Mary, it's worth a try," and they tore the cloaks into strips as Brutus knotted them together, coincident with the slow drifting appearance of the wreckage of the hull, the inert man lying across it.

"I'm the strongest swimmer," insisted Marc, pulling off his tunic and securing one end around his waist. He plunged into the water, swimming resolutely towards the wreckage, but he was pulled up some way short and found himself drawn back by a more resolute centurion, who overruled his protests.

"You left you dagger behind with your tunic, you must have a knife!" sliding it into a knot of the improvised rope. "Quickly now!" and Marc plunged back in, aware there would not be another chance. Approaching the boat, he was constrained by the limits of the rope, and was about to untie it when its drag eased, and with a desperate lunging kick he was able to grasp the edge of the hull.

The effort of holding the drifting wreck was enormous, and Marc knew he could do nothing to help the man whose deathly face was so close. He felt himself being pulled in two directions and the strain on muscle and sinew was becoming unendurable, and he cried out to cut the rope, just as he felt the strain ease and he was able to heave himself over the splintered planking into the hull.

Seizing the line tying the unconscious youth to the stern post he went to sever it, but in the nick of time and amazed at his own stupidity he stayed his dagger, and severed the line at its fastening to the post, tying the free end around his waist. The wind had risen to a shriek again, and waves were breaking over as he threw himself and his companion into the sea, struggling to hold his head clear of the water, as they were steadily pulled shoreward.

Then hands were taking the body from him, searching for signs of life as they hauled both of them from the ledge, clear of the cheated sea still plucking angrily at limb and body and sending spray head high over them as they moved away.

"Keep a look out for the other. Although there's little hope, the wind and sea will be working on both alike," urged Brutus holding the drowned youth upside down, and Alexander moved tentatively along the ledge, while Marc lay exhausted by his efforts close by.

Water trickled from his blue lips as Mary pummelled him, forcing more of the sea from his lungs.

"Lay him here," she said indicating an inclined flat rock, and lying him face down, Brutus removed a gold torque from his slender neck.

"Some lady will be grieving for her high born son this night I fear. I'll conceal this for the moment, as princes are unlikely to wash ashore unless there are great troubles at the palace!"

Mary was applying her whole weight alternately to his shoulder blades and his lower rib cage, forcing brown stained water from his lungs. Her lips were forming unspoken words as she beseeched a miracle and Marc now looking on, felt deep anguish and despair. He hadn't considered that he might only have recovered a corpse, but now that with each minute this reality was increasingly apparent, his grief knew no bounds, and Brutus could not console the sobbing boy.

"There's the other one!" called Alexander, excitedly pointing to a spar drifting near, tied to which was a limp bundle of rags.

Marc, jerked out of his despair, went to knot the improvised rope around him again, but Brutus took it from him to attempt the rescue himself, knowing his son was all but exhausted.

Even as he tightened it, a crowd from the city spilled down the steps and quickly took over. Two fishermen stripped, secured lines around their waists and plunged in, forcing their way towards the vulnerable flotsam being blown out to sea by the capricious wind, now coming from the high hills behind them.

Mary was the only one not watching the drama of this second rescue, so only she heard the faint involuntary cough from the youth. Urged on by this, she reapplied herself with greater vigour, ignoring the protest of her exhausted body, and was rewarded by his feeble inhalation, followed by a sudden vomiting as the sea water stimulated its own rejection. With a silent prayer Mary ceased her exertion, and looked around for something to wrap around his cold body.

The stronger of the swimmers, at the full limits of his endurance, was now closing to grasp a rope trailing from the spar. It was enough to arrest the continued seaward movement of the boy, and as the second rescuer secured a hold, those paying out the ropes slowly started to draw the bodies back towards the shore.

Everyone's attention had been held by this drama, so Mary's plea for something warm to cover her charge excited their wonder, reviving hopes that the incredible rescue in which they were participating might end well after all. For the first time there was an easing to the grimness of their task, which had had all the makings of a double tragedy. Lucia and Miriam carried blankets from the house, and hastened to wrap them around the convulsing body, glancing at each other with disbelief.

Brutus cut the halyard binding the body to the mast and carrying him inverted, lay him beside his companion.

"Well done, Mary, you've achieved the impossible, can you do it again?" he asked, lying the second gently alongside his friend.

"I'll pray for another miracle while you do the work this time," she said, and he realised how desperately fatigued she was.

Ten minutes later, he too felt exhausted with a deep ache gripping his chest and arms. Marc took over as Mary urged everyone looking on to kneel down and pray. The two men who had swum to the body were the first to join her, and then most did likewise.

The miracle, when it happened, surprised all except Mary. Only a flickering of an eyelid for a few seconds preceded the violent vomiting followed by shallow paroxysms of breathing. Their joy was unrestrained, and the fishermen embraced Mary in turn, regarding her with a mysterious awe, as though aware that her contribution had been greater than theirs in some inexplicable way.

There came suddenly an influx of notables from Tyre. Centurion Antony, accompanied by Sergeant Tiasus and a squad of soldiers, insisted his physician be allowed to make an assessment. When he had checked all the vital signs with evident satisfaction, he supervised the placing of the unconscious youths on stretchers so that they could be transferred speedily and safely to the garrison.

The parting words of the commander to the exhausted rescuers were, "It would be best if we attend to them now in our sick bay. Your rescue of these lads has been truly remarkable centurion and I salute you. Please visit them at the acropolis whenever you wish," and he marched away proudly at the head of the column

Many of the city council and elders of the synagogue were present with Rufus, who detached himself to embrace his siblings, and a soaked and bedraggled Mary, who gave him a wan smile as he said, "Get this woman home quickly, Brutus, before she collapses, she is absolutely all in. I'll join you there shortly."

Brutus only realized how exhausted Mary was as she staggered against him, clutching to steady herself. Helping her up the narrow steps, they disgorged on the cliff top to find half of Tyre assembled there, drawn by word of the dramatic rescue that had swept through the city. They milled around the heroes excitedly, and a protective ring of soldiers was necessary around the stretcher parties, and of her companions around Mary, all the way to the city.

Mary took to her bed on arrival and, apart from Brutus and Flora who ministered attentively to her, nobody saw her until the following morning when she appeared and was surprised to see Marc astride a bay horse.

"I decided to ride myself and bring Abraham to the wedding," called out Marc cheerfully, and the joy that suffused Mary at the thought of a reunion with the silversmith brought a radiant smile to her tired face.

"Be back for Wednesday!" remonstrated Miriam, whose every instinct was to ignore the preparation of her wedding gown and ride with him, "or you will miss the baptism, and I don't intend to marry a heathen!" she added peevishly.

"We will be back for something as important as that!" laughed Marc, and Miriam stamped with vexation at his emphasis on the last word. Lucia took her by the arm, whispered something, and giggling together the girls feigned indifference as they disappeared into the house, cleverly reversing the situation by the casualness of their farewell. Marc had a bemused look as he swung his mount and rode away.

Mary and Flora were hard put to conceal their amusement at the masterly stroke of the youngsters, and embraced each other happily.

Arriving at the barracks Brutus was escorted briskly to the commander's office where an agitated Antony was pacing the floor.

"Ah I'm glad you're here, centurion, I think you may have rescued two very important personages. Read this!" passing him the communication he had just received by mounted messenger.

Brutus read,

'To unit commanders throughout Syria,

Maintain a vigilant lookout for two fourteen-year old youths
abducted from King Herod's Palace, Caesarea. One youth is a
nephew of Herod Agrippa, and his companion is related to Legate Quintilius Varus. Give assistance to such persons, and
hold while contacting Tribune Communis at Caesarea.

Pontius Pilate.'

"I haven't questioned them to be sure yet, but I think it time I did. You are welcome
to accompany me. Oh, the physician says they will be no worse for their experience
in a day or two!" said the elated commander, already anticipating the glory that
would follow his rapid restoration of the youths to the Proconsul.

Brutus smiled with satisfaction, but decided not to mention the torque he had
removed from the boy's neck. Not yet anyway!

Both youths were awake as they entered, and the darker of the two hopped
back into bed smartly on seeing the uniformed centurion.

Antony addressed them in Latin, but got a wary puzzled look, and the youths
exchanged a glance before replying in perfect Greek.

"I'm sorry sir, we have no knowledge of that language you speak. Is it Latin?"

Brutus smiled at the sheer audacity of the lads, as he realized they did not wish
their identity to be known. Antony was stern faced as he replied in hesitant Greek.

"I am centurion Antony, the commander of this fort, and this is Brutus, a former
centurion to whom you both owe your lives. Would you kindly identify yourselves?"

"I am Malchus, son of Boaz, a merchant in Alexandria. My friend Dan is from
the same academy in Alexandria, but his father is a government official in Antioch.
We were hoping to find a passage from Tyre to Antioch, when we ran into the
storm yesterday. The weather was settled when we hired our boat at Acco two
days ago, but I fear we underestimated how quickly it can change."

"They don't teach you Latin at your academy?" queried Antony incredulously.

"Oh they do, but to our shame Dan and I both opted to study Hebrew as a
preference."

Brutus could hardly suppress a smile, which the perceptive youngster recognised
and responded to.

"If we are to be detained a few days, is there anyone who might give us a few
hours instruction to help us correct this omission?" he asked, with the slightest
hint of irony which was not lost on Brutus.

"Might I have that pleasure?" he said, "it would afford me the opportunity to
find out a lot about Alexandria, a city I am interested to visit, but I'm afraid my
Latin is more colloquial than grammatical."

"Then if your assistance of us rendered a service to you, you would be a most
welcome tutor," replied the youth courteously, and Brutus felt himself drawn to
him by some indefinable charisma, and resolved to do whatever he could to help
in whatever crisis had driven them to such desperate measures.

Antony seemed disinclined to press his interrogation at this time and said curtly,
"Get yourselves well and we'll have a further talk tomorrow," and led Brutus back
to his office. His disappointment could not be hidden as he spoke to the centurion.

"They are evidently well educated young men, but they obviously haven't been abducted, so they aren't the Herodian prince and his Roman companion. However I would like to know more of their background, so can you spare a few hours and see what you can find out?"

Brutus looked pensive for but a moment, before he replied, "I'll start right now if you have no objection. I would hate to see my native tongue totally dominated by this pervasive Greek," and gaining approval, he returned eagerly to the sick bay. There he had to wait impatiently while two orderlies attended to dressing some minor wounds, before he was left alone with the casualties.

He put his hand into the pocket of his tunic and withdrew the gold torque and as his pupils saw it they exchanged questioning glances, before the one calling himself Malchus exhaled deeply, as though a great anxiety was being shed.

"So it was you removed it. I knew anybody who had risked their life to pluck us from that maelstrom could not have removed it with dishonorable intent, but I couldn't understand why I wasn't wearing it when we recovered and found ourselves here."

"I thought it best nobody knew you were of the royal household, as it would have caused unending speculation, and certainly have frustrated whatever you are attempting." He saw them exchanging hesitant glances. "Would it help you if I tell you I am no friend of Herod Antipas, and had to kill his assassins and flee to Tyre?"

"It would help greatly, for it was the discovery of a threat to assassinate me that precipitated our hurried departure from Caesarea. It's Antipas' cousin, Herod Agrippa, who wants me out of the way, especially now Emperor Tiberius is ailing, and nobody feels sure who his successor might be. Caligula seems the most likely and he is very volatile. It's best if I don't reveal my name, but I am a blood relation through the line of Herod Antipater the third, who was executed by King Herod the Great. My mother was only fourteen years old at the time but still remembers the anguish of it all. Assassination has always been a possibility and I have been brought up to be on the look-out for it."

"And so you took the desperate decision to sail for Tyre in an open boat. Do you have a place of safety for which you were headed?"

The fair-haired youth, who had previously remained silent, broke in.

"My father is highly ranked in the Imperial Roman army, and we thought to make our way by ship and overland, to join him in Gaul."

"Are you the son of Quintilius Varus?" asked Brutus, and got pleasure from the amazed look on both their faces.

"No, I'm his nephew, but how on earth did you know that?"

"Because all units throughout Syria have been alerted of your abduction and are looking out for you!"

"What are they requested to do if they find us?" asked Malchus, greatly concerned.

"Hold you, tend to you, and contact Tribune Communis in Caesarea!"

"That would be my death sentence. Communis is in the pay of both Herods, and plays one off against the other, and both of them between Tiberius and Caligula. I would get in the way of all their scheming if they left me free, with my royal blood and my Roman friend here."

"It might be possible for me to get you a passage to Antioch on a boat sailing soon, but nobody must know who you are. Can you keep up the pretence for a few days, while I make enquiries?"

230

Just then an orderly was heard approaching.

"Amare is the verb to love and it declines amo, amas, amat, amamus ..." He broke off as the orderly entered, and was amused to hear his pupils echoing his words in varying but convincing accents.

For two hours they elaborated their strategy, punctuated by ludicrously declining the occasional verb, and then Brutus made his report to centurion Antony.

"Well we can be certain those foolhardy lads have not been abducted as you deduced. I can't see Herod having any interest in them and as for tribune Communis, well they aren't likely to further his ambitions, so he won't be interested either."

"You don't seem to have any time for the tribune do you, why is that?" asked Antony.

"I hold him responsible for what happened to the *Hermes*, and the deaths of Centurion Hedylus and the legionaries. Herod should never have been aboard a Roman galley in action, and it was Communis who made it possible." The anger of Brutus surprised Antony, who had a more flexible attitude, never having been threatened by Herod.

"How's the teaching progressing?" he asked, wishing to change the subject.

"Tolerably well, they're bright lads. But I think their interest is more a courtesy than genuine and they are only likely to be here a few days."

"Have they told you of their intentions?"

"Only that they wish to find a boat for Antioch and wondered if you might be able to assist them."

Antony shook his head, as he had little knowledge of the commercial movements from the port.

"Would you like me to enquire of Ephraim? The master of the *Dolphin* that brought us here from Joppa?"

"Yes I am happy for you to do that. Please keep me informed," said Antony, indicating by his tone that he wished to end their discussion.

Brutus resolved to waste no time, but to get them away from Tyre as quickly as possible, and arriving at the port he was relieved to see the familiar lines of the ship tied up to the quay. Ephraim was signing a bill of loading for some cargo that was piled up on the deck, and smiled broadly when he saw the centurion approaching him.

"Our first cargo since the refit," he said gleefully, embracing the Roman as though he was a brother, "but why do you look so worried?"

Brutus was displeased that his concern showed, but made light of it.

"An old wound is causing me a little discomfort and I should never have let it show," he said dismissively, but he knew he lacked conviction and Ephraim was not fooled. "When and where are you sailing?"

"For Byblos, the day after tomorrow. Are you wanting a quiet passage?" A huge grin distorted his shrewd face.

"Two young friends of ours are wishing to sail to Antioch, and Byblos is half way there. Would you go the extra? You will be well rewarded."

"It wouldn't be the two you saved from the clutches of the sea the other day would it?"

Again Brutus was caught off guard, and he wondered how much Ephraim knew concerning the youths and whether to entrust their well being to him. His delay in replying prompted Ephraim to continue.

"It was my friend and partner Horatius swam out to the second victim as he was being swept out to sea. He never stops talking about your woman Mary. He says nobody else in the whole world could have got him on his knees praying to the God of the Jews, when he thought he had recovered a dead body. He didn't believe anyone would revive that drowned boy. He's not been the same man since, which is a great pity as I liked the reckless way he had, and the jokes he was always making." He shook his head in pretended dismay and not waiting for Brutus to reply, continued.

"After picking up some cargo we are unloading at Seleucia, which is not a day's walk from Antioch, so we will gladly take your young friends."

"I will confirm with you tomorrow if they are fit to travel," said Brutus, feeling that he had been completely outsmarted in this encounter, and suddenly realizing he had prevaricated with exactly those same words about Mary when Ephraim offered them a boat calling at Caesarea.

That evening he revealed to the women the events of the day, although he kept to himself his knowledge of their true identity until he was alone with Mary.

"I wondered when you would confide in me," she said, "I was with you when you removed the torque remember?" and Brutus embraced her, wondering at his great fortune to be the recipient of her trusting love.

Antony received the news of the *Dolphin's* suitability with little more than indifference. It was as though his disappointment that they were not the nobles he had hoped to bring him fame, had led to his disinterest and he wished to be shot of them. Their continued presence was a constant reminder of what might have been.

"You will find them up and about, so if they are inclined to leave there is no reason to detain them," he said peevishly.

Consequently two hours later, Brutus was escorting the youths as they descended through the city to the port. Antony had been mollified somewhat by the genuine warmth of their gratitude, and the promise of a gift of some wine from Dan's father when they reached Antioch.

"If the deception can be kept up I'll arrange the wine in a few days as though it has come from your father. I don't know how long it will take for news of your rescue to reach Caesarea, but there they won't be hoodwinked as easily as centurion Antony. Don't delay overlong at Antioch, it wouldn't take long for an assassin to track you down.

"Will you be in danger when they find out how you aided our escape?" queried Dan.

"From Antony, definitely not. My rank still protects me and I'm unknown to Herod Agrippa, although I've incurred the wrath of Herod Antipas. Anyway I'll pretend I was just as deceived by your plausible story, as was Antony."

When the boys went aboard, Ephraim showed them to the fore cabin.

"You will be very comfortable here," he said his eyes twinkling mischievously. "I shared this same cabin with centurion Brutus and his two friends all the way from Joppa, and I was never once worried at being a little cramped," and he gave a bellow of laughter in which the Roman had to join.

232

Brutus saluted his two charges and confidently left them, rejoicing in the part he had played in aiding their escape from the murderous Herods. As his hand strayed into his deep pocket, the absence of the torque alongside the hilt of his sword emphasized a sadness that was creeping over him.

That same evening there was not an inkling of sadness in the whole excited body of Abraham. The moment Marc had communicated that they were there to escort him to Tyre for his wedding to Miriam, he was impatient to be on his way. Such was his excitement each limb seemed to be competing with the rest of his body to show its awareness of its good fortune. So he would dance first on one leg then the other, or throw out an arm in a dramatic gesture as though to clutch at something elusive and tantalising. One thing he didn't do all night was to sleep, his imagination soaring at the thought of being with Mary again, after the daily vigil he had unfailingly fulfilled over the past months.

When his escort appeared at first light, with cart and driver he was as ready and eager as though it were but an hour's journey, although after his sleepless night he frequently dozed, and Tobit was anxious that he didn't fall off the bench seat beside him. He was the same Tobit who had driven Mary and Miriam to Joppa, having also had to flee the persecution. Marc had recognised him at the stable, and requested he drive the cart and join them for the wedding, as it would add one more face from a quieter period of Miriam's youthful life.

In conversation Abraham soon found out that he was seated beside the twin of one of the apostles, and the hours passed quickly as he pumped everything the youngster could tell him of Thomas.

"And all these quotations of Jesus that he is writing on these scrolls. What does he intend to do with them?"

"They are in a sealed jar which lies in a cave at Qumran. He doesn't need to read from them as he can repeat all of them word perfect, although there are thousands. But he says every time someone else memorizes them, they change the words a little and the emphasis, so eventually they may say something quite different. He regards it as vitally important to leave behind an authoritative source of reference."

Abraham was quiet for a while then he mused to his young listener.

"Many people think we are at the end time, and that any day soon the old order will be swept away. Your brother obviously doesn't or he wouldn't bother to write it all down."

"The disciples asked Jesus about how long it would be until the coming of the day of the Lord, and bear in mind that John the Baptizer called on people to repent saying the kingdom of heaven was at hand, but Jesus said nobody knows the time of the coming except the Father.

"Thomas thinks if they are to carry the message to all peoples, to the ends of the earth, it is going to take a very long time."

So the hours passed quickly, and as they neared Tyre Abraham became increasingly excited, straining to see around each bend, sometimes dismounting from the cart and walking impatiently ahead. Marc, riding alongside, pointed out the tomb on the promontory overlooking the sea. So excited was Abraham, he pressed them to make the small deviation to it, and saw the youthful figure in the distance at the same time as Marc. Recognizing Miriam, Marc broke his weary horse into a reluctant gallop, and was still happily embracing his betrothed when Tobit reined back his horses. Nearly stumbling with excitement, the silversmith leapt from the cart like a boy, and laughing and crying simultaneously embraced the maid, recognising instinctively how quickly she had grown up since last he had seen her.

She was fighting back her tears as she took his arm and led him to the impressive tomb, and when he saw the beautifully carved stonework, with the motif of the brooch he had made, he was overcome. He fell on his knees protesting at his unworthiness for such an honour.

As the three of them rode the last mile to the city, Tobit learnt of all that had befallen the family since he had driven with them to Joppa earlier that same year. Abraham had a comforting arm around Miriam as she recounted the details of their tragic end, and had no eyes on the streets through which they were passing. Then he became aware of someone calling his name, and he saw running down the tree lined avenue his Mary, her long black robe gathered in her hands to clear her feet of any impedance.

The reunion was sweet and heart warming, and but for missing the wedding, Abraham would happily have been taken up to heaven there and then, such was his transport of delight. While the men attended to the horses, the women bundled him indoors and lavished their attentiveness on him after his bone-shaking journey. Finally they persuaded him to rest on one of the divans, where he slept soundly for the next few hours, while everyone tiptoed about their business careful not to disturb him.

Marc meanwhile had been urged by Miriam to hurry and seek out Rufus, who was baptizing at the seashore. His more conciliatory approach in the Synagogue had won him many converts including some of the elders.

Standing up to his waist in the water, Rufus was immersing convert after convert when he saw Marc from afar off, and raising a beckoning hand in greeting, rejoiced in his heart because he knew how ardently the youth yearned for this, and it simultaneously washed away any impediment to the imminent wedding.

Emerging from the water Marc felt a strong arm around his shoulder, and recognized the rugged, craggy features of the man who had rescued the second of the drowning youths.

"I'm Horatius, I'm happy we can celebrate this second immersion together! Last time to save the lives of two strangers, and this time to save our own. Do you not feel we share a unique bond?"

Marc smiled at him and said, "Tomorrow I am to be wedded. I would like you to be in my party as we celebrate through the streets."

"Gladly I'll join you. I didn't sail with the *Dolphin* yesterday so I've a few days free, apart from a little fishing."

Making their leisurely way home, the strident sound of a trumpet caused Rufus and Marc to step off the path, as a column of mounted legionaries passed at the gallop, and swung away at the gate towards the high dominating acropolis. Something about the bearing of the scarlet robed leader stirred a faint recognition, and for a while Marc fell silent, although Rufus noticed his agitation.

"Communis!" said Marc suddenly, "Tribune Communis. Brutus will want to know of his arrival," quickening his pace at the importance of the news they carried.

Brutus was sitting dejectedly on the low balustrade around the agora. He was only half listening to the speaker and feeling thoroughly fed up. He had been happy to be banished from the house that was filling with seamstresses, cooks and provisioners, but his mind was at sea on the *Dolphin*, and he was concerned for the well-being of the two boys he had entrusted to Ephraim.

Marc had no sooner returned with the silversmith, over whom Mary doted as though he were a baby, than he had hurried off to be baptized, leaving him alone in a madhouse. The suggestion that he was hardly alone in the midst of so much frantic activity was on the tip of Mary's tongue, but she realized that he was concealing his concern for the boys rather unconvincingly and needed a man with whom to talk things over

Fretfully getting to his feet to take himself to the port, Brutus was thankful to see the young men hurrying towards him, until he caught their urgency.

"We've just seen Tribune Communis and a column of mounted soldiers galloping to the acropolis," Marc blurted out.

Immediately Brutus shed his languor and resumed his decisive normality.

"Then news of the rescue of the youths will have reached Pilate, thank goodness they're two days from here."

He saw Rufus and Marc looking at him uncomprehendingly and so he hastened to explain their true identities.

"Phew," whistled Marc, "a royal prince and the nephew of a Legate, and you arranged their escape from Herod. I'll wager centurion Antony is getting a roasting right now."

"We can expect visitors very shortly, but I don't want them to disrupt the house with all the wedding arrangements going on," said Brutus.

"Then let us await them here at the agora, they have to come past."

Having agreed on that, the three sat listening with one ear to the speaker informing them of an outbreak of fever in Venice, while the other was listening for the sound of hooves on cobbles. They hadn't long to wait before they heard the four horsemen approaching quickly, and they moved out into the street feigning casualness.

"Don't look as though we are in any way expecting them, and we know nothing of their purpose," stressed Brutus. "Remember we merely aided two youths from Alexandria on their way to Antioch, after we rescued them from drowning, nothing more."

It was only as the horsemen were nearly on them that Brutus looked around, and feigning surprise raised his hand in salute as they reined back.

"Why greetings, centurion, what brings you this way?"

He looked questioningly at Communis and continued before Antony could reply, "Tribune! What brings you all the way from Caesarea?"

"As though you don't know," snarled Communis, "where is this whelp of Herods?"

"Are you meaning those youths abducted from Caesarea, why don't you enquire at the agora over there. There's nothing they don't know that's worth knowing?"

"He's one of those you rescued from drowning! Where are they now?" interjected Antony.

Brutus looked puzzled.

"The boys from the academy at Alexandria?" he queried. "They're on their way to Antioch by boat. Dan's father is a government official there."

"Dan's mother is the sister of Legate Quintilius Varus and his name is not Dan," roared Communis angrily.

Brutus smiled broadly as he replied soothingly, "No, it's not these lads you are looking for! Not a nephew of Quintillius Varus! Why neither of the boys could speak Latin," and he looked for confirmation at centurion Antony, who seemed too discomfited to sit quietly on his horse.

"They fooled you both, or you would have us believe they did," snarled Communis.

"Would either of us have helped them on their way if we had had the slightest suspicion?" said Brutus holding out his arms deprecatingly as he turned to Marc. "Did you see anything to make you think either of the boys was high born?"

Marc frowned thoughtfully before replying, "After we had plucked them from that maelstrom their attire was in ribbons, but it was hardly the sort of boat a noble would ever be in. I don't remember seeing any jewellery. No, I would not have thought they were high-born. I think you must be mistaken, sir," he said politely to Communis.

"Why, you insolent puppy, who asked you what you thought. Let's get the name of the boat on which they sailed, and when they may be expected to reach Antioch," and with that command Communis wheeled his horse around and rode angrily away.

The moment the last of them had disappeared, Brutus showed his concern.

"Communis will not spare himself or his cavalry to win favour with Herod. They will have fresh horses and be riding for Antioch within the hour. I must ride to Byblos, the *Dolphin* may still be loading there. I didn't mention it was calling there to Antony, but I wouldn't put it beyond Communis to enquire at the port, and they will tell him for certain."

"I can't put off my wedding or I would gladly ride with you," said Marc, his voice conveying his regret. "Why don't you take Horatius, he must know this coast well? He would have sailed with the *Dolphin*, but for the baptism this afternoon."

"Do I know this Horatius?" asked Brutus.

"He swam out to the rescue of the other drowning boy."

"Then I would gladly have him ride with me! Where can he be found?"

"You hire two good horses. I'll go to the port and bring him back here within the hour."

Brutus was surprised at the assertiveness of his son, but it was a sign of his growing up, which he welcomed.

Arriving ten minutes late, both were out of breath as Marc blurted out, "I'm sorry, Horatius really took some tracking down, and then he needed to collect a few things for an enterprise like this."

Brutus looked hard to see what he was carrying, as apart from a large pouch strapped around his waist, and a rolled blanket across his shoulders, he was one of the most unburdened travellers he had ever seen.

"No sword?" he queried uneasily, but was answered by the lift of the man's tunic where the hilts of six throwing knives protruded from leather sheaths.

"I'm glad you weren't part of Joseph's crew when we requisitioned the *Dolphin.*"

"I would never have sailed with that old pirate. He would throw his mother overboard if he needed to lighten ship in an emergency," laughed the sailor showing a row of unblemished white teeth.

"I hope you can keep your mouth closed tight, the moon reflecting off your incisors would be like flashing a beacon."

"Are we to conceal ourselves then? Our young friend has been reticent to tell me much, except that you can be trusted, and the boys we rescued are in danger."

"I'll tell you more as we ride, and we may be riding all night."

With an embrace of Mary, and a wave to the small gathering, the men rode into the late afternoon sunshine, their long shadows leading them along the glowing facades of the houses. They left the city by the gate at the north-west corner, and rode along the narrow rocky cliff top to the far promontory jutting out into the fast reddening sea.

Brutus moved from the path to the rougher ground when the high hills reared up close on their right.

"I don't know whether the Tribune is already ahead or is following behind," he said, "but I don't want them to know anything about us."

"Not far ahead!" rejoined Horatius, his lips tightly concealing his teeth as he smiled. "Did you notice the horse droppings ahead of us were still steaming when we moved off the path?"

Brutus could not believe he had failed to see such fresh spore, and challenged his companion on what exactly he had seen.

"There was a small scattering about one hundred paces ahead, when we moved off the road. I thought you had seen it and left the road for that reason. There must have been a few riders because the droppings were scattered by following hooves."

Brutus was impressed by the acuity of his companion's vision and said generously, "My eyes can't match yours, you must tell me anything you notice immediately."

They were rounding the promontory now hugging the cliff face closely, and just discernible in the rapidly deepening twilight was a group of horsemen over a mile ahead. They were momentarily silhouetted against the fading, purple glow of the cloud low on the horizon, and then they were gone.

"Six of them," breathed Horatius, "and two spare horses."

"You really amaze me!" exulted Brutus, "I would have needed to get much closer to know that. So they are confident of bringing back those two unsuspecting lads. They must know the *Dolphin* is loading at Byblos."

"Do you think they will ride all night?"

"Quite possibly, there's a lot at stake for Tribune Communis if he hands over a potential rival for Herod's' kingdom. Knowing the Roman legionary they will make a brief stop for food soon, and then ride until day break."

"It will be nearly a full moon and the sky's likely to clear," stated Horatius, dismounting and scratching around at the stony earth.

Brutus watched him wondering until he stood up, securing a buckle on his waist pouch. From the blanket roll across his shoulder he produced and unrolled a small package, which had the distinctive look of a well-crafted sling.

"I'm from Cyprus originally and for ten years from a boy, was with a Roman legion as a sling-man. I've not lost the art."

"Let's bind our horses' hooves with strips of the blanket while we can still see, it will help us to follow close enough to seize any opportunity to best them," said Brutus tearing his blanket and holding out the strips to his constantly surprising companion.

Ten minutes later they regained the road, confident that the muted thud of their hooves would not carry far even in the still air.

It was a full hour before the glow of a campfire loomed in front of them on rounding a bend, close enough for the unguarded voices and laughter of the soldiers to carry clearly.

Dismounting Horatius said, "My night vision is good, would you like me to scout ahead to assess their disposition?"

"You are the only man for whom I would agree to that request. I'll wait here."

As the Cypriot disappeared silently into the darkness, Brutus wondered at his good fortune in having him along on such a fraught mission. He talked quietly to the horses, fondling their muzzles and they stayed calm and quiet, not even responding to the whinny of one of the mounts ahead, except to prick up their ears.

The suddenness with which Horatius materialized at his side, was uncanny, as the centurion had not relaxed his vigilance for an instance.

"Two officers and four men," he said. "The man with the horses at the side of the road is not very alert. He's probably waiting to be relieved by those eating at the fire, just off the road."

"Have you formed any plan to get past them?"

"Without stealing their horses that will be impossible. I'm sure I can get very close without being detected, and then take out the soldier guarding them."

"I don't want him killed."

"Is a severe headache acceptable?" queried Horatius, fingering a round stone, caressing it in his free hand. They discussed details for a few minutes and then Horatius stole away into the shadows, and Brutus waited impatiently, before slowly following with both horses on shortened bridles.

The moon was threatening to lift clear of the bank of low cloud, and approaching stealthily he heard the snorting of the horses not far ahead, and then he stopped awaiting the call.

Horatius was no more than twenty paces from their horses loosely tethered to a fig tree, and he clearly saw the sentry sitting looking enviously towards the fire a short way off, remove his helmet and run his hand through his close-cropped hair. At the whinnying of one of his charges he turned his head towards Horatius, who crouched immobile, hidden in the shade of a large cedar.

Sling in hand, he waited for the man to turn away before he could release his missile, but was stayed by a voice calling out from the fire. The reply of the sentry was short and he didn't change his position, so deciding this was as good a moment as he would get, Horatius threw the stone with one dexterous swing, and heard the thud of it impacting as the man keeled quietly over. He made one owl hoot, and then hugging the ground moved quickly to the tethered horses, talking quietly as he gathered their halters, knotting four of them together.

He wordlessly passed the knot to Brutus as he materialized out of the gloom and started on the remaining halters coincident with the moon breaking clear of the restraining cloud, bathing the hillside in white light. Ignoring the impulse to

238

hurry he completed his task and was starting to move them away as the challenge rang out from the startled party relaxing at the edge of the stream.

Horatius glided towards the centurion, sprang into the saddle of his horse and with a whoop of elation they leisurely galloped off. For ten minutes they sped until the angry cries of dismay had died away far behind them, and then they eased back to a comfortable trot, and exulted at the perfect execution of their manoeuvre.

"By Jupiter, I have never known a warrior as resourceful as you," laughed Brutus and was rewarded by an answering flash of whiteness, as Horatius grinned without restraint.

"I wondered if my sling arm might have lost some of its accuracy, casting a fishing net is a very different art. What shall we do with their horses?"

"Hide their saddles and sell them. We must make it appear as though the motive is robbery so they may not immediately suspect me and make life very uncomfortable for us all."

"Leave me to sell the horses, I am unknown to them if anyone should think to give my description later."

"Keep anything you get, you've earned it! You made the stealing of them look so easy it was masterly. I would merely have tried to get ahead to warn them at Byblos."

Approaching the town of Sidon, Brutus suggested it would be a good place to separate, as Horatius could strike inland with the horses and double back towards Caesarea Philippi, while he continued along the coast to the port.

His comrade was reluctant, as he had thought to rejoin the crew of the *Dolphin* at Byblos, but realizing the horses could be a source of trouble until they had been sold he concurred and they separated.

Dawn was well past when Brutus rounded a bend and saw glistening white in the blue distance, the buildings around the busy port. He was weary in every limb, and the wintry sun was not yet strong enough to warm his aching body, as he spotted the distinctive familiar features of the dhow. Stevedores were already working, running precariously balanced bundles up narrow gang-planks, where Ephraim was directing them to various holds.

One of the two young heads in earnest conversation suddenly jerked on seeing him, and raising an arm called loudly to the captain, pointing excitedly to the approaching centurion. All three of them tumbled down the gang-plank together, all but throwing a sure footed man and his cargo into the water.

It took but a few minutes for Brutus to explain what was happening, and both the youths were thrown into agitated indecision.

"You must get under way soon, as Tribune Communis will not let up in his pursuit while he thinks there is the faintest chance. His rage must be spurring his efforts and I would think you have five hours at the most."

"We will be loaded and can sail in three, if everyone gives a hand," said Ephraim looking pointedly at his young charges.

"But they will be awaiting you at Seleucia for sure!"

"Then we will sail for Cyprus. I know it well and there is always good trade to be found there. I will continue to Seleucia after seeing our young friends on a boat bound for Ostia or Massilia."

This accorded well with everyone, and the youths removed their cloaks and set to with the men, stowing cargo and readying the boat for a speedy departure. It took longer than Ephraim thought by a full hour, and Brutus was looking nervously around as he took his farewell and the crew prepared to man the sweeps to row them towards the open sea.

"We are forever in your debt," said Malchus. "I hope one day I will be able to repay you." Tears were brimming in his youthful eyes as he embraced the older man.

"Repay me by living honourably," replied Brutus, a catch in his voice as he turned away quickly.

He stepped ashore as the ropes were being thrown off the bollards, and the boat was being pushed away by two men with long poles.

Even as the plank was being hauled on board, Ephraim stayed the hand that was pulling it. Weaving between the boxes and bales on the quayside ran a figure he had recognised, Horatius! In pursuit, but slowed by their armour, were two legionaries. Horatius sprang onto the gang-plank as the sideways momentum of the *Dolphin* carried the extreme end of the plank to the edge of the quay. With the sure footedness of desperation he sprinted up it even as the free end started to fall towards the water. Two hands stretched out over the bulwarks grabbed his extended arms as he felt himself falling, and with a bruising impact, he crunched into the wooden topsides to be hauled on board by a grinning Ephraim calling out,

"One of these days you're going to miss the boat."

His words were lost to the ears of Brutus who had disappeared quietly amongst the piled up cargo. To the breathless soldiers, who watched impotent as the gap widened between boat and shore, it sounded like a taunt.

The elation at the imminent marriage feast was subdued, not only by the absence of Brutus, but by everyone's awareness of the dangers he could be facing. Mary tried to put a brave face on it, and threw herself into the preparations with vigour.

Abraham was constantly assuring her that she should have faith in the Lord who would protect her husband, and although part of her believed him, another part was raising nagging doubts.

All the other men had been banished to the inn, where there were assembling some children with cymbals, two flute players and a blind musician with a six stringed lyre. They were to accompany the procession through the streets when night had closed in, illuminated by the torches of the bridegroom's friends.

Marc was resplendent in a new, sky-blue tunic, edged with gold braid around neck, arms and hem. He sported a conical hat, the rim circled by a garland woven of ivy and olive shoots. Over his tunic, his well-worn robe had been embroidered with gold thread in the Celtic designs of his homeland, which he had carefully drawn for Flora and Lucia to work for him.

He was greeted with great enthusiasm by everyone, and flanked by his bride's two brothers they moved out of the inn to the exciting rhythmic beat of traditional Yiddish music. Mingling with the last of the shoppers, or the homeward bound workmen, their procession added joy to the streets they passed through, until they approached the house where within, all was excited anticipation. Suddenly in an instant, all the lamps were extinguished and the house lay dark and silent.

This caused the musicians to increase their clamour, and the torchbearers made a waving, flickering line to the front door.

Marc, chest thrown forward manfully, swaggered up to the door and knocked loudly. Three times he knocked and he could hear the giggling from within. Then the door was opened a little, and a querulous, disembodied voice asked what was the cause of the disturbance.

In well practised, mishraic Hebrew, Marc sang out, "I am the bridegroom Marc, come to claim my betrothed and to admire her beauty!"

To great merriment the door opened widely, and a stream of maidens in simple Greek style, white linen shifts, with brightly coloured mantles draped over their shoulders spilled down the step. Each had an unlit oil lamp in her hand, and approaching the bridegroom's attendants requested a light for their lamps.

"What do you give me in exchange?" each enquired of his maid, and as though well practised turned an expectant cheek, on which was planted a demure kiss.

As the lamps sprang into life to be swung gently by the bridesmaids, the music burst into renewed clamor and the bride appeared at the door. Her cream, elaborately embroidered gown was festooned with jewels, and it was just possible to see a suggestion of a smile through the veil, draped over a pretty, cream coloured skullcap. Her maids hurried to form a ring around her, and as Marc approached to claim her he was repulsed time and again.

"What must I do to claim my own?" he cried

"Sing of her virtue and her beauty," they chanted in unison.

At that the clamour ceased except for the gentle plucking of the blind lyre player, as his beautifully modulated tenor voice sang out a traditional hymn to the virtuous wife.

"A good wife who can find? She is more precious than jewels."

"than jewels," echoed Marc and one of the maids pirouetted off to stand beside an attendant.

"The heart of her husband trusts in her."

"trusts in her," echoed Marc and likewise another maid removed herself. So it continued.

"She does him good and not harm, all the days of her life."

"All the days of her life."

"She seeks wool and flax, and works with willing hands."

"works with willing hands."

"She is like the ships of the merchant, she brings her food from afar."

"food from afar," and Lucia hurried off to stand holding the hand of Alexander.

"She rises while it is yet night and provides food for her household."

"for her household."

"Her lamp does not go out at night."

"out at night."

"She puts her hands to the distaff, and her hands hold the spindle."

"hold the spindle."

Only one maid was now left between the groom and his bride.

"She looks well to the ways of her household, and does not eat the bread of idleness."

At Marc's chant, "of idleness," the last maid curtseyed and moved aside, and an expectant hush fell on everyone.

Marc approached Miriam and tentatively lifted her veil.

It was the sweet, shadowed light in her innocent eyes that made his heart bound, so that momentarily he was silent, forgetful of what was expected of him. He saw her eyes glint with amusement, and remembering, emitted a cry of wonder to convey his delight at his good fortune, before embracing his bride.

The hours sped away in a whirl of eating, drinking and dancing, which belied the anxiety gnawing away, maggot like, at many of those whose thoughts were elsewhere.

The door was closed against the cold night air and midnight was approaching. The mood had become mellow, and the final plaintive notes had died from the blind minstrel's last song, when suddenly the tranquillity was shattered, by an insistent banging on the door. Flora hurried off, followed by an apprehensive Mary, and then there was an explosive sound of exultant joy from Mary as she threw herself into the arms of Brutus. As he disentangled himself from her embrace he looked a parody of the man who had departed the previous dusk.

Blue streaks blending with purple covered his face, his tunic and bared limbs, and were mingling with tears coursing over Mary's cheeks. Powder dusted his hair and cloak, down to the sandals on his feet.

"That damned sea snail," he cried, "the only boat sailing from Byblos had just unloaded a cargo of the powdered shell of the murex sea snail. I was so tired I fell asleep on a pile of empty sacks and awoke to find myself covered from head to toe. I've had some funny looks from people I passed on my walk from the port I can tell you." A grin was creasing his face as he beheld his blue streaked woman, and such was their relief everyone was overjoyed to join in the laughter evoked by their comical appearance.

Even the bride and groom delayed their departure to the bridal chamber at the inn, to listen to the gripping disclosure of the exploits of the last two days. Certain climaxes excited comment only to be quickly suppressed to allow the narrative to continue. At the dramatic conclusion of the pursuit of Horatius, not one throat could restrain from joining in the cheering, and there was unending speculation as to what must have happened as he rode away with the eight horses.

"My guess, and it's only a guess, is that he ran straight into a second squad of cavalry making a more direct route from Tyre to Antioch. I should have thought of the possibility. Has anyone from the Acropolis enquired of my whereabouts?"

On being assured that nobody had, Brutus said, "I had better get rid of this dye before they come, as they most certainly will. Everyone keep up the story that I never left Tyre for an instant. They won't believe you, and a bitterly resentful tribune and centurion are going to make life very uncomfortable for me here. I think the time has come to leave for Dura-Europos!"

The innkeeper was greatly alarmed when an impatient centurion demanded to be escorted immediately to the room of centurion Brutus, very early on the morning of the Sabbath.

"Allow me to bring him to you here, your excellency. He has not risen yet." Antony was surprised that the centurion was to be found there at all, as he had expected him to be somewhere north between Antioch and Tyre.

"Be quick about it," he snarled, indicating to his escort to dismount in the court.

Very shortly the innkeeper reappeared with a distraught and tearful Mary, who approached the centurion averting her eyes and wringing her hands together as though greatly troubled.

"Please officer, centurion Brutus is too ill to rise from his bed. I have nursed him all night and greatly fear for his life, as I have never seen pestilence like it. Come back tomorrow, if he is still alive," she pleaded.

"Take me to him immediately!" demanded Antony, suspecting trickery, and pushing a supplicant Mary aside, he followed the innkeeper as he led him to his room and opened the door.

The room was dark, and he strode arrogantly to the shutters and threw them open. As the light of the early sunshine filled the room Antony turned towards the bed, and was stopped in his tracks by the piteous sight of Brutus lying all but naked, half covered by a thin sheet. That of his body revealed, was of the most ghastly colour, such as Antony had only seen on bodies after battle, when putrefaction was imminent.

Involuntarily he recoiled, and when the corpse-like body tried to rise from his bed, such was his fear of some virulent plague, he turned and hurried from the room slamming the door behind him as though afraid the pestilence was at his heels.

As Mary was about to enter the room he went to stop her, but withdrew his hand, fearful of contacting the contagion.

"How long has he been like this?"

"It started that night you came to him two days ago, but last night the fever was at its worst. He needed bathing every hour to stop him burning up. Do you think it is the rat-borne plague?"

At the mention of plague the centurion's eyes showed alarm as the soldiers instinctive fear of illness asserted itself, and without a reply he hurried away, and ordering the soldiers to mount led them out of the court as though pursued by a hundred demons.

"Sergeant Tiasus must have been mistaken when he thought he recognised the centurion as one of those who stole their horses," he said. "I greatly fear he may be dead before they return."

Had he seen the way the centurion leapt from his bed and embraced an exultant Mary as they rode away, he would have drawn his sword and slain them instantly; but the soldier's fear of dying of illness is the counterpoint to his fearlessness of death in battle, and Antony's regret was genuine.

Mary had scrubbed every inch of Brutus' body that night to remove the clinging powder of the murex snail shell, that is so highly valued for dying the imperial purple and noble blues worn extensively by the high born Roman. But so ingrained was it in every pore of the centurion's skin, it had denied her efforts to completely erase it, and so he retained his plague riven hue. Far from being the give away they had feared however, it had proved to be the suspect's salvation.

Only at Mary's insistence had Brutus sheathed his drawn sword and taken to his sick bed, prepared to give her ruse a chance, although neither had been confident of it succeeding.

"What did you do to frighten him so?" asked Mary between convulsive peals of laughter.

"I tried to rise to embrace a comrade as I do you, Mary," he said with a straight face, and as she backed away from his death like clutch, such was the vision she

243

saw, she collapsed on the bed, her body shaking with each successive peal of laughter.

When much later they were joined by a demure Miriam, and a modest, but proud and confident Marc, they recounted the story of the earlier confrontation.

Marc remonstrated with Brutus that he had thought to battle alone should they have seized him.

"No Marc, no longer are you to risk your life to defend mine. You are still my son, but you have taken Miriam as wife and it is to her that you should cleave not to me."

"But are we not all linked together by fortune and does not our strength depend on our support of each other?" queried Marc.

"Indeed it does la ...," Brutus had been about to say lad and suddenly realised how inappropriate it was now, "but men too often resort to the sword in answer to any threat. Has not Jesus died to show us there is a better way? Mary has learned that, and it worked miraculously. Had you been at my side, a few Romans would be dead and both our women would be widows."

As Miriam shuddered at this utterance and sought the reassurance of Marc's arm about her, she said, "Let us promise each other to always search for the peaceful way however difficult it may be, and to only resort to arms when no other way remains open."

"Well spoken, Miriam," rejoiced Mary, "that is also my prayer. Let us pledge ourselves so."

Solemnly they linked their hands forming a circle, complete and strong, as each affirmed such a pledge to the others.

No further action was taken by centurion Antony, with regard to the escape of the youths, and Tribune Communis returned to Caesarea resentful and angry at his futile quest.

A sublimely content Abraham finally wrenched himself away from these foreigners who had transformed his whole life. He had prevailed upon Mary, who he knew to be an incarnate angel, to once more reveal the wonder of the precious prize she had seized at the tomb on that monumental morning of glory.

Now his treasure chest of memories was full of priceless jewels, and as he waved beside the reliable Tobit, he knew he would never see them again, but his cup of happiness was filled to overflowing.

Mary and Miriam both shed tears at the poignancy of his parting. Somehow this modest little silversmith had influenced them both in a unique and wonderful way, and his departure signified the end of a phase of their lives.

Rufus before he had returned to Jerusalem had urged them to go to Dura-Europos.

"I know it is at the most easterly boundary of the Roman Empire," he had said, "but beyond the Euphrates lies all of Arabia, and beyond that India and China and undreamed of lands. We need a safe house there for our message to go out to the furthest corners of the world."

As he embraced each of them in turn, he rejoiced that it had fallen to him to confer baptism on them, Jew and Gentile alike, and recruit them to the service of his Lord.

The Journey

CHAPTER ONE

The restlessness troubling Brutus became too strong to ignore, and finally he was driven to cross the Euphrates once again and explore the vast Persian desert to the east. The centurion had occasionally felt the same urge previously, but never had he felt it as strongly as now. Mostly he went by himself, setting testing excursions that honed his mind and body to the pitch that he had known throughout his years of service, but this time he was accompanied by Marc, and as they sat under a canopy of brilliant stars, grilling a pair of quail he had trapped over a small fire, they pondered his unease, not coming to any conclusion but aware that his intuition had never previously let him down.

"I guess it's the pull of these vast spaces on us veterans," he confided, "but I'm also reminded that in Caesar's time, Marcus Crassus lost a whole army around here. Forty thousand men slaughtered by the Parthians! The army seldom dares to venture east of the Euphrates since and even now I'm aware of the ghosts of that disaster around me, and sometimes I think I hear their voices warning me to be on guard."

Marc shuddered, and thought he would be glad to be back with Miriam and Simon in the town, away from this overwhelming emptiness that cried out to the imagination, whilst defying man's futile efforts to subdue it, dwarfing them into insignificant tokens of conceit.

Life in Dura-Europos had its more predictable pattern for their companions, where Mary played a leading role in the developing church, while Miriam rejoiced in the joys of motherhood, and young Simon, approaching his fifth birthday, could always coax the taciturn Roman into periods of playfulness.

Isolated at the extremity of empire, news of events in the wider world arrived long after they were resolved. They heard of the disturbances in Jerusalem from Rufus, whose regular letters maintained a cheerful optimism. The affairs of the Levant they learnt of from Alexander and Lucia, now three years married but still in Tyre, living with Flora in the house where first they had met.

Brutus didn't feel drawn to either of these cities, but nor did he feel drawn to spending his life in Dura-Europos, and although nothing other than a temporary suppression of his restlessness was ever achieved by his desert excursions, on his return he happily slotted back into the routine and normality of town life until he felt the stirrings once more.

Mary was patient, and said to Miriam that all would be revealed in God's own time.

The sunset was filling the sky over the western wall with that primrose yellow that proceeds the final flaming at each day's end, when the cry went up that the expected caravan from the Great Sea was approaching. The news quickly filled the streets with all who had been eagerly awaiting its arrival, not only the merchants and craftsmen, but also those who were just curious, and every sort of vendor of every sort of delicacy the credulous might be persuaded to buy, all hurrying to the great square to the east of the city where the laden animals would be rested, and much commerce transacted.

As Brutus strode along, with Simon squealing excitedly from his shoulders, there was speculation on how it would vary from the caravan some two months earlier.

"I would like some amber beads to match that necklace you bought me, Marc, those deep honey coloured ones from the cold northern lands!" exclaimed Miriam hopefully.

"Doubtless Rome is ridding itself of more gold and silver than it mines, to satisfy its insatiable craving for pearls and spices and silks," mused Brutus half to himself, but his young passenger was eager for different fare.

"Will we see tigers and black and white bears and horses!" he cried out with excitement.

"Not when the caravan passes this way, Simon. They trade the money and the wine for lots of things at the head of the Persian Gulf and should come back with wild animals next month," explained Marc.

"Never mind, precious," consoled Miriam, taking one of his outstretched feet in her hand, "you will see acrobats and funny men with painted faces, and we can buy some wonderful sweetmeats," which caused his face to brighten considerably.

The press of people was restrained by a cordon of soldiers lining the square, keeping everyone at bay except for the tax collectors as the camels and mules were unloaded, and their wares stowed in two large transit warehouses. All around was a babble of strange tongues, of animal noises and the cursing of impatient soldiers, resentful of being dragged from their barracks.

From his elevated position the boy saw the soldiers part, allowing a young man in the homespun Nazarene broadcloth to move out from the caravan. In one hand he grasped a stout staff, which he raised in greeting as he approached the smiling centurion. The two men embraced, while the precariously perched boy searched his memory to put a name to this faintly familiar relative.

"Rufus!" cried Miriam, suddenly realising who had materialized from nowhere and throwing herself into her brother's arms.

"How lovely you look, motherhood must agree with you," said Rufus, and after embracing his sister he put up his arms to the silent boy who was studying him intently.

"Simon, what have you to say to someone who has been walking ten days to see you?"

The boy regarded him silently, too shy to utter the formal greeting he knew for grown ups, and then found himself being lifted off the centurion by the strong brown hands of his uncle who exclaimed, "How like papa he looks yet there is a gentleness in his eyes that is mama!"

Brutus seized the cloth bound package that Rufus had laid beside his staff, urging them away from the crowd, who were now pouring into the square as the soldiers dismantled their cordon.

"What brings you here? They're not sending you across the Arab sea to India are they?" queried Miriam anxiously.

Rufus smiled and shook his head.

"No, for some strange reason until now the apostles have thought me useful in

248

Jerusalem. But they were happy to send me on this important mission, possibly the most important I will ever be entrusted with, and it involves all of you!"The press of passers-by prevented him from saying more until they were seated in the house, but Brutus knew that his restlessness was about to be explained.

Simon, seated on Rufus' knee, never took his eyes off his uncle as he explained that his arrival with the caravan was coincidental and had no bearing on his mission, which caused the exchange of a few apprehensive looks between his listeners.

"This mission concerns the well-being of Mary, blessed mother of our Lord Jesus," Rufus had commenced portentously, and the gasps of surprise were only the precursor to a great many more as he continued, "She is no longer safe in Jerusalem or in Judaea, or anywhere where Jew or Roman can be incited to harm her. There have been many mysterious incidents in the past few months, all of which might have caused her death. A so-called, accidental fire burnt down a safe house in which she was sleeping, and only the alertness of three of the brethren who broke down the door saved Mary! Two others died trying to reach a maid trapped in an upstairs room, and the whole house was gutted."

He paused for a moment inviting comment, but his listeners were awed into silence by the enormity of what they were hearing.

"Again many of the sisters died of poisoning at another house Mary was visiting, where they care for the orphans. Had Mary not been fasting it is certain she would have been poisoned along with the sisters. The latest incident was very sinister, and happened a week before I was sent on this mission. A column of Roman cavalry galloped recklessly into the group of women on their way to the garden at Gethsemane, killing one and seriously injuring three more. Mary escaped unhurt, but our protest to the Roman governor fell on deaf ears. He said the obligation was on the citizen to get out of their way, not on the horsemen to avoid them. This led to a lot of protest, and some activity by the zealots, a few of whom are now hanging from the crosses as a warning."

Brutus was greatly disturbed by this,

"Then whoever is trying to harm Mary has the cooperation of the prefect, or some high Roman officer."

"We think so too, and you know what a dangerous combination that makes," and the women and their men exchanged knowing glances.

"We have received intelligence from sympathizers amongst the elders, that a party within the Sanhedrin are trying to cause the death of Mary precisely because she is the mother of our Lord. They hope that Jesus would be completely dis-credited if his mother was mutilated or killed in what appeared to be an accident. They cannot accept his resurrection, but realize every day hundreds more are converting to join us Christians, and that they are losing control."

"So they wish to break down his following by targeting his mother," said Brutus reflectively, "and somehow they have persuaded the Prefect it is in Rome's interest to make common cause."

"What is this word Christian you use?" asked Marc.

"It is the word the citizens of Antioch have coined for the followers of Christ. They always are subtle in their play on words, and they changed followers of Christ into Christians mockingly, but by welcoming it we have turned it into our distinctive name and given it great meaning."

"And are you here to ask us to protect Mary from those who would harm her?" asked Brutus perceptively.

"Much more than that. We need a reliable escort to take Mary across the Great Sea into Europe. I have suggested you and Marc as the only men capable of such a mission."

The silence that followed, as each pondered the implications of such a task, was suddenly broken by Mary, "When do we start?" she asked eagerly, but it catalyzed an animated period of dispute and discussion.

Mary flatly rejected Brutus's suggestion she was not included and remain behind in Dura-Europos with Miriam and Simon.

"What, and leave the mother of my lord at the mercy of you insensitive warriors, as you track across most of Gaul. She will need a companion and I intend to be there when she needs me!" This she said with such finality, Brutus smiled sheepishly at Rufus and shrugged his shoulders at its inevitability.

"Excellent," Rufus laughed, "I hardly dared suggest it, but it was in my thoughts that you wouldn't stay behind."

"And where are Simon and I in your thoughts, brother?" asked Miriam, with a steely edge to her voice that put him on guard.

"Wouldn't you be happy here, with Corinna and the other sisters?" he asked tentatively, but was surprised by the violence of her reaction.

Throwing herself from the couch, she seized Simon from his lap so brusquely, the little boy burst into tears as he caught the anger in his mother's voice.

"Let's put Simon in an orphanage, and me in widow's robes, and say goodbye to papa!" she cried irrationally, glaring angrily at her brother.

"These men can handle this task and come through unscathed, but you wouldn't want to expose Simon or yourself to danger. They could well be home within three months."

"Danger! Where can you avoid it? Isn't it dangerous just being a Christian! If Marc goes we will most certainly be going with him. Anyway, if we go as far as Gaul we are nearly in Britain, and you've talked many times of wishing to see the land of your birth again!" This last she threw at Marc with triumph, daring him to contradict her.

The eagerness in his eyes as he looked enquiringly at Brutus reassured Miriam that this was the best line of attack.

"Your mother doesn't even know you're alive, and it's over ten years since you were enslaved. Could you be as close as Gaul without having to see your family?"

Brutus held up his hands in surrender.

"I promised many years ago, when we were in Jerusalem, that one day we would visit your homeland. I think the time has come, so we had better make plans for us all to escort Mary."

Rufus was shaking his head in disbelief at the turn his original plan was taking.

"Now I know why we Jews keep our women in subjugation or try to. It's the only way we can make our decisions with total objectivity, unhampered by emotional considerations!"

He ducked just in time to avoid the cushion that Miriam threw at him, and laughingly conceded defeat.

"Is there a safe haven in Gaul or in Europe? We Jews are so widely scattered because of the Diaspora, a vengeful Sanhedrin would still be able to strike any-where," asked Mary Magdalene shrewdly.

"We believe there is such a place but are uncertain of its exact location. It's all buried in myth and legend and the memory of the mother of our Lord. When Jesus was an infant some wise men came to Mary bearing gifts. These gifts were gold, frankincense and myrrh. The bearer of the myrrh was named Casper, who said to Mary the myrrh was to anoint the body of Jesus after his suffering and death.

"She remembers clearly what he said next, and I quote her very words;

'Casper said to me, although I didn't understand its significance then, "To the far west in the foothills of the high mountains, my people will prepare for the day when you must flee your own. We are the Jentillak, descendants of the sons of God. Because of our forbearance of earthly pleasures, we were spared the flood and told to await the birth of the Saviour, as has come to pass. Read the stars, listen for the wind that will bring you to us. We will know when you are coming and welcome you to our hearth." Only now do I realize why I memorized his exact words to me.'

"That is what this whole undertaking is based upon, and that alone!"

As Rufus ceased speaking he surveyed his avid listeners and for a while no one spoke. Then Brutus said, "Go on. Tell us where these Jentillak are to be found?"

"I've told you all there is to tell. Nobody knows any more than that."

"And we are to embark on a voyage with Mary in our care and an ultimate destination that is unknown, that could be anywhere, that might not even exist! It's impossible. Worse, it's foolhardy!"

"From any viewpoint I have to agree with you, absolutely. It might be the most foolhardy voyage in the history of mankind!"

All waited expectantly as they knew that was not his final word.

"But the mother of our Lord wishes to embark on such a voyage. Melchior, a high priest of Zoroaster, and the most respected astrologer in the east, says that next month, the conjunction of all the five planets and a rare comet is the most significant in a hundred years. Further, Peter has been praying for guidance and the voice he hears always tells him to listen to Mary."

He spread his hands out deprecatingly and smiled at their consternation.

"When do we start?" asked Mary, looking challengingly from one to the other, seeing the unspoken doubts in each face. "Oh if only you knew how to pray and how to listen. Now I add my voice to that of Mary and Peter, we must be discussing when and how, not doubting the issue at all!"

Such was her advocacy she won the day, in no small measure due to the respect she had gained for the power of prayer many years previously at Tyre, when the bodies of the youths plucked from the sea had appeared lifeless and beyond resuscitating.

Brutus affirmed the *Dolphin* was the only boat for such a voyage. First however he would have to locate it and make the arrangements, so he would leave for Tyre in the morning. With a good horse he stated he should be back in three days, four at the outside, and wished them all to be prepared to leave within the week. One thing led to another and they sat up until the early hours of the morning discussing every aspect of the preparation.

It was still dark when Brutus passed by the sentry at the western gate, who reluctantly let him through the small, side door, before bolting it securely behind him.

"Watch out for some Parthian activity. They have got wind of the trading caravan and stragglers last night ran into a mounted war party."

Brutus was thankful for the warning, as these Persian raiders were a constant threat to the Roman grip on Mesopotamia, and skirmishes were frequent. Although they controlled much of the silk-road to China, and collected tax on every item passing through in both directions, the Persians resented their lack of control west of the Euphrates and on to the Great Sea.

Brutus and Marc had sometimes scouted and tracked Parthian war bands, usually supported by their redoubtable and innovative armoured cavalry. When in full battle order, the horses were protected with chain armour draped across the entire length of their powerful bodies, and together with each mailed rider with their unmistakable high pointed helmets, they made the most formidable and awe-inspiring cavalry in the region. When he had last spotted them at Ctesiphon, opposite Seleucia-on-the-Tigris three months ago, Brutus had estimated a force of five thousand cavalry and a thousand chariots. The Roman Garrison commander had responded to this information by requesting reinforcements from Damascus, which were still awaited.

Quietly Brutus rode his mount off the road following the sluggishly flowing Euphrates, and moved up to the crest of the lower hills. He dismounted as he neared the top, not wishing to be silhouetted by the blood red dawn behind him. Lying hidden he studied the Syrian Desert, normally an empty vastness to the far horizon, but not this day.

The fires flickering around the whole panorama confounded him, as in an instant he knew he was observing an army preparing to lay siege. They made no attempt at concealment, and shadowy figures could be seen moving around each fire, and laughter, or the occasional barked command, carried clearly to his ears. His trained mind quickly assessed their disposition, and he realized a ring of iron had been thrown around Dura-Europos, cutting it off from the Roman province that sustained it.

At each fire, about every two hundred paces, were milling fifty or sixty men as breakfast was being prepared. Two wagons, two chariots and an indeterminate number of horses, accompanied each company.

Looming between the nearest fires he could see the stark silhouette of one of the outposts of the garrison, square and silent, ominous for the lack of any movement around it. There were a dozen of these stone buildings, each with a wooden stockade and a deeply dug ditch, forming a first line of defence of the city, and that no warning had been sounded could only mean all their occupants were dead.

A rock-strewn gully led down to the plain, hardly deep enough to conceal him and his mount. He knew it flattened out into a lined culvert, taking flash flood water to the cistern built adjacent to the outpost. He could work down it unseen while the sun was still hidden behind the eastern hills, but time was rapidly running out, and what use would he be without his horse?

Momentarily he thought of returning to Dura-Europos and raising the alarm, but simultaneously he was aware only the mobilization of the whole legion in Syria could defeat this besieging army.

252

As he hovered undecided, his dilemma was resolved by the strident call of a Roman trumpet sounding out the alarm. It came from the front of a column of reinforcements from Damascus, rounding a bend of the road and stumbling on the Persian force.

The sound reverberated throughout the valley drawing all eyes towards it, galvanizing the Parthians into ill prepared and uncoordinated attacks. Brutus knew if he didn't seize this distraction there would be no second chance.

Mounting, he urged his horse towards the approaching column, now fanning out into a 'V' formation with shields and spears readied. Ahead of the column, scarlet robes flowing and plumed helmets held bravely, the lead officer and two companions faced the onslaught of the Persian cavalry, a score of whom had responded with greater speed than judgement to the trumpet's challenge.

Brutus rode at their heels, and almost felt the impact of the two colliding forces. The three officers stood no chance, positioned vulnerably at the forefront of the battle, and had been struck from their horses by the sheer number of their assailants.

Resolved to ride by, Brutus saw from the corner of his eye, the scarlet robed tribune striking at the four horsemen who surrounded him. Pulling his horse to the right, sword swinging mightily he joined the battle, and with one blow decapitated one unsuspecting man. At the same moment, he saw a partially parried blow impact on the cheek piece of the Roman's helmet, bloodying him as he fell dazed onto his knees. Before the assailant's arm could deliver the mortal blow, Brutus thrust his sword into his neck, even as he reined back his horse to face the remaining two. A well thrown spear from an advancing legionary hit one rider on the cheek, cleaving his face open, his instinctively raised hand holding his avulsed eyeball as he tumbled mortally wounded at the feet of the tribune. The assault petered away, and Brutus jumped from his horse to stand guard over the injured officer as they were both suddenly engulfed in the advancing Roman column, which parted and then closed protectively around them.

Bending to remove the helmet of the dazed officer Brutus saw the deep laceration to his cheek, but his eyes were drawn and then held by those of the wounded man, and he was puzzled by the amused gleam he glimpsed behind the pain.

"I'm Dan!" the tribune said simply, and instantly Brutus saw the face of the youth he had helped to pluck from the sea.

As they embraced the tribune said, "So once again I am indebted to you for saving my life, but this time sadly too late to save my comrade," looking regretfully at the fallen centurion beside him. "It was reckless of us to ride so far ahead of our soldiers, but we were eager to reach Dura-Europos, and unaware that you were under siege!"

The two cohorts making up the force, were steadily fighting their way through the Parthians, whose determined but uncoordinated attack was unable to overpower the disciplined troops. A wagon stopped and Brutus helped the tribune on to it.

"I must get to Tyre. I will raise the alarm at Damascus and return with the legion. I can't delay a minute, or we're all trapped," said Brutus, mounting his horse and urging it towards the rear of the column.

The soldiers parted to allow him to drive into those few Parthians pressing their rear, and such was the element of surprise, he drove through them without need to strike with his readied sword.

The road appeared clear ahead to the promontory from where the trumpet had sounded, and casting a glance backwards, he was relieved to see no cavalry in pursuit.

Rounding the bend he was unaware of the outcome of the delicately balanced battle behind him, but he was confident the greater part of the column would supplement the defence of the city, and felt reassured for his loved ones, provided he reached Damascus.

At the realisation that the lives of everyone in Dura-Europos depended on him, he became aware of the hair rising at the nape of his neck, and all his senses elevated to a level where they transcended into instinct.

So it was that after an hour's hard gallop along the meandering road, he started to feel uneasy there was no pursuit. The road closely followed the river for the next fifty miles until it branched, where he was to leave the river heading south towards Palmyra and Damascus.

He had planned to change horses at Palmyra the following morning.

To the left, the arid hills flanking the wide valley were uninviting, even threatening, but he felt an overpowering urge to climb up into them, to where the vast expanse of the Syrian desert would open up before him.

At a suitable goat path he deviated, riding up a shallow rock strewn gully. For fear of his horse being lamed, he led it for the rough part approaching the high pass and tethered it to a sparse acacia before ascending the last hundred paces to look over the crest, at the waterless plain spread out to the shimmering far horizon.

The column of twelve horses stood out with stark clarity about one mile away, and he saw that half of them were riderless, including two carrying fodder and water skins. Even as he watched the riders stopped to feed and water their horses, before pressing them hard across the desert at an angle diverging from the Euphrates.

"So I was spotted and they're trying to cut me off before Palmyra," mused Brutus, "and with spare horses they can continue without stopping and set an ambush for me anywhere."

For nearly an hour he watched them move until out of view, plenty of time to decide the only option that remained open to him. He had to head directly across the desert to Damascus, there was no other way to avoid capture. If he stuck to the road there were many places where he would be ambushed, but the direct route he contemplated was close on a hundred miles, without any change of horse and over a hostile, waterless terrain.

"I've no choice but to attempt the impossible," he thought, leading his brave stallion down the steep, scree-covered slope to the level plain, and mounting he rode unstopping that day and night, a clear moon lighting their southwesterly course.

Next morning the sun heated air distorted the whole country they crossed, causing mirages to make the occasional shriven tree appear to dance mockingly to the pulse beating in his temples, suspended against the azure blue sky, or a whole grove around a verdant oasis appeared inviting him to enjoy its coolness.

Can man or beast continue hour after hour in this heat, he wondered, the remorseless glare necessitating the use of his free hand to cover his aching eyes, trusting his horse to hold a good line. Once or twice it faltered, and glancing around he realized it was negotiating some obstruction that had broken its rhythm.

He rationed his meagre water between his mount and himself, and marvelled at its endurance and sure footedness. The time came when they had to rest and escape the noon sun, so finding a deep gully, they hugged the little shade that could be found, while Brutus soothed the horse, massaging its limbs to prevent cramp until they could resume their journey.

Some fixed point on the horizon was essential to hold a true course, and this often eluded the centurion, as there was a monotonous emptiness to the arid panorama, devoid of hill or tree or human habitation. So they continued without a break, the stout hearted beast treading its way across the never-ending desert. As dusk approached the setting sun hung malevolently over the western horizon, and the centurion recalled the vision that had tormented him the night following the crucifixion.

Then he had stood transfixed, looking down on the world, one vast arid plain turned to a field of blood by the tramp of endless legions. Now, the whole world turned red by the dying sun, he hallucinated that he alone was alive on it. The eagle that had soared overhead carrying sacrifices to the monstrous scorpion, now plunged lifeless from the scarlet streaked sky and lay crumpled on the rock, its extended wing pinions fluttering lifelessly in the hot wind, and he was irresistibly drawn towards it.

Slowly he crossed the intervening miles as night blotted out everything except for the gentle flapping of the barely discernible wings. He felt desolate and alone, and even the champion who had dismembered the scorpion with his flaming sword and stood beside him on the summit of the mountain had deserted him. So god-forsaken was he, that in despair he threw himself off the mountain, and felt himself falling into a vortex as the earth opened up beneath him.

He never felt the impact of the bare earth or heard the whinny of his horse, but Claudius Lysias cocked his head and signalled his comrades to silence. Hearing the horse again, he seized his sword and led the small group of officers from the tent. It took but a few seconds to reach the horse standing by the fallen man, a mere hundred paces away.

The coolness enveloping him was delicious, and in his delirium Brutus thought he was plunging into the cooling waters of the oasis that had beckoned to him in the desert. He struck out with arm and leg and resented the restraining hands, at the same time as he heard the man's voice.

"It's a bad case of sunstroke I fear. He's quite fevered and the next few hours are critical."

Responding to a fresh moistened cloth placed on his forehead he opened his eyes, and by the light of the fluttering oil lamp, distortedly viewed two appraising eyes anxiously searching his.

"Where am I?" asked Brutus, suddenly alarmed that he had been captured.

"In the officer's tent of the Italian cohort. Claudius Lysias is my name." A second, older face appeared alongside the youthful Lysias.

"You're lucky to be alive and don't try to sit up yet. Sunstroke can easily leave you permanently blind, if it doesn't kill you!"

"It's done neither," replied Brutus smiling feebly, and he rejoiced to see the answering smile of the younger man, although the older frowned as though disapproving of levity at such a time, but this was nothing to the change of all their countenances at his next utterance.

"I've ridden from Dura-Europos with the most urgent news for the Legate."

Their thunder-struck appearance and stunned silence encouraging him to continue,

"The city is under siege from a Parthian army!"

Disbelief immediately replaced any other expression as Claudius Lysius exclaimed, "We dispatched a cohort to reinforce them only four days ago!"

"I know. I left them fighting their way into the city at dawn yesterday. One centurion was killed in the battle and Tribune Dan injured."

Brutus found his shoulders seized by Claudius Lysias, his eyes anxiously searching his.

"Dan is my best friend, how badly is he injured?"

Brutus watched their consternation as he recounted what he had seen of the battle, and his assessment of the situation. Claudius Lysias strode to the entrance, and calling a company commander ordered that they ready themselves to ride to Damascus immediately. Brutus made to raise himself but the dizziness induced by this effort persuaded him to lay back.

"Be on the look out for some Parthians who thought to ambush me near Palmyra. I spotted five men and a dozen horses heading across the desert to cut me off."

"You did well to spot them. So that's why you appeared from out of that vast desert, there was no other way to avoid ambush! I'll send two companies of cavalry after them. You wait here and recover while I inform the Governor. It will take a few days to mobilize the full legion, which we will need to relieve this siege. Try to sleep."

"Have I reached Damascus, time and distance became a vague blur to me?"

"No, you would have another three hours ride on a fresh horse. Our cohort is on manoeuvres, luckily for all of us as I don't think you would have made it!"

Knowing he was spent, and the imperative need to recover physically sufficient to continue to Tyre, Brutus reluctantly agreed. It was mid morning before a slave brought him his breakfast and he raised himself tentatively from the bed, only breathing freely when he felt no dizziness.

It wasn't long before a column of soldiers flanking the legate and the Governor of Syria approached the camp, preparing to move off at short notice.

Festus was anxious to have a first-hand account of the seige of Dura-Europos not least because he had a big stake in the caravan that was trapped in the city. Brutus stressed it was a powerful army, which would prove overwhelming for the garrison even with the relieving cohort.

"How long do you estimate they can hold out?"

"A week, possibly two if their food stores are full. Certainly no longer."

As though to confirm this a squad of soldiers entered the tent with a Parthian captive. He had already been tortured, revealing that the invading army was in excess of eight thousand men and a thousand cavalry.

That was sufficient to decide Festus and he ordered the army to march to their relief with the greatest urgency.

Claudius Lysias thought they would need three or four days preparation, and as Brutus knew he needed all of that to reach Tyre and return to Damascus, he lost no time and departed on his trusty horse within the hour, only this time leading a spare mount loaned him by the tribune.

Dura-Europos was a city under siege. Martial law ruled and life was grim with food and water rationed, and a curfew imposed from dusk to dawn. Soldiers had commandeered all the houses close to the city walls, and every horse and wagon. Men between the age of fourteen and fifty were ordered for weapon training, where Marc's ability with the sword had been quickly noticed, and he was second-in-command of a company of townsmen, who alternated for twelve-hour periods reinforcing at the western gate.

Rufus had volunteered to be in the same unit, but Marc was anxious one of them would always be with the women, and had insisted he be attached to the alternating company.

Sergeant Longinus was their commander, a strict but fair cavalryman who had twice already ridden out with a column to harass the besiegers, disrupting their preparations of the heavy siege equipment they needed to make a determined assault and have any chance of breaching the city wall.

During one night's vigil, Longinus and Marc sat talking.

"Jerusalem is the place I like least. Even this hell hole is preferable to Jerusalem," said Longinus vehemently.

"I was there as a slave of centurion Brutus and we ..." Marc began, but Longinus interrupted,

"Not the same Brutus in charge of the execution of the Galilean Jesus?"

"Yes, the same. I was his spear carrier!"

"Then you saw him thrust it into the heart of this Jesus?"

Marc felt confused how to answer.

"Were you there?" he asked.

"I was the one who certified that Jesus was dead when they asked to take his body for burial. Centurion Brutus should have done it, but you would know about that funny business, how he called out he had killed the Son of God and collapsed."

"Then you must have heard he came back from the grave, back from the dead."

"I've heard it, and I believe there are thousands think that happened. But me I confirmed him dead, and dead is dead. Which is what we shall all be if they starve us much longer, and then attack when we are weak with hunger." He paused reflectively and then continued bitterly.

"Just my luck. One more month and I would be leaving this accursed, disease-ridden country, with the 10th legion for Gallia."

"Where in Gallia?"

"Right up north. They're building a vast fleet to cross the sea and conquer Brittania. If you want to get on in this army be with the legions that conquer, not with those that garrison the empire. The 10th Legion was Julius Caesar's own when he first invaded Brittania."

"When was that?" asked Marc, recalling stories he had heard as a boy.

"Long before I was born, but my grandfather was there."

"But Caesar didn't conquer Brittania did he! Why not?"

"He was too occupied conquering Gallia, but he had some mighty battles with

257

the tribes, some of which charged into battle naked, their bodies painted blue. They were urged on by Druid priests, wild, long-haired men, hundreds of them invoking their Gods, but the Roman Gods prevailed."

Marc could well imagine the overpowering might of the legions, remembering how ineffective his family had been confronted by the superior weapon skills and discipline of the legionaries.

"Do you anticipate a long campaign of conquest?"

"Probably. The terrain is difficult with oak forests and high mountain ranges, or else frightening marshes, which can swallow a wagon in a few minutes, and there are no roads only tracks. If the tribes combined they might be impossible to conquer, but always fighting amongst themselves they make it easier to pick them off one by one." They both fell silent for a moment then Longinus asked, "What is your country?"

"Brittania!" replied Marc simply, and the Roman's mouth fell open in surprise. Then a chuckle emitted that grew into great bellows of roaring laughter, which engulfed Marc too, succumbing to the funny side of all that had been said.

As the laughter subsided, the serious aspect of what he had heard dominated his thoughts, although he kept those to himself.

"You will still go with the legion, after Brutus has raised the alarm in Damascus! He left for Tyre before dawn the morning the siege began."

"How could he get through their encirclement? Why, the cohort lost many men fighting its way to the city gate!"

"I've spoken to tribune Dan. Brutus saved him from being overwhelmed after he had been wounded, and then raced away to the west, to warn Damascus. If they had captured him his head would be on one of their lances to taunt us."

Marc was referring to the line of heads that the Parthians had hewn from the fallen Romans, and stuck upon sticks on both sides of the road. One of the most furious cavalry forays that Longinus had been part of was to recover their comrade's heads, and now but a few remained in the far distance after that bloody encounter.

"I hope you're right, but I'm resolved to take many of them with me when I die!" The finality of Longinus' words silenced Marc, now feeling an overpowering desire to see his homeland again.

The debate in the large, richly adorned tent of Prince Ardashir, was heated and contentious. Hours before news had been received that Damascus was alerted to the siege and was mobilizing a relieving army, which could be on the march in a few days.

Polybius, an experienced general in many campaigns, had the floor. He was a heavily whiskered man, with huge side burns and moustaches hiding much of his weather browned features, and his deeply set eyes were shrewd and penetrating.

"Your highness, they will march thirty miles a day, day after day, and still arrive full of fight. They can outmatch any army, and will confront us with four to five thousand, war-seasoned soldiers. Half of our army have been conscripted from the fields and are far from battle hardened. I say we must bring this siege to a rapid conclusion and withdraw back across the Euphrates."

A lean, shaven, wolfish man, Agathobus, arose to address the assembly. As he spoke he continuously stroked his chin, and his hungry eyes were fixed on his Prince.

"Your highness, over the centuries we have fought great battles with the Israelites, the Phoenicians, the Hellenists and the Romans. Only by fierce resistance have we retained our homeland and prevented it from being overrun. I know our objective is booty and to sack this city, but we have an army that can defeat this Roman legion sent against us, as we slaughtered their army in the time of your illustrious forebear. We will gain all our objectives and the acclaim of a great victory. This will establish you as the undoubted successor to your honoured father."

As he sat down there was considerable enthusiasm among a section of the staff and it was obvious they had been polarized into two opposing factions.

Prince Ardashir raised himself from the silk adorned settee, his mind resolved.

"Thank you all for your considered opinions. This will be our overall strategy. We must force the city to yield within the week and seize the gold of the caravan and any treasures, before destroying it completely. Then we can face the legion on one front without any threat from our rear. Otherwise we abandon the siege and withdraw. We have no interest in the conquest of Syria, so such a battle simply for the acclaim of victory would not bring us honour."

He nodded dismissively and the war council dispersed.

The first attack was launched the following day. It was a determined storming of the whole perimeter wall, simultaneously. Using scaling ladders under a protective barrage of arrows from the ranks of archers at their rear, the Parthian infantry stretched the resistance of the smaller defending force to its limits.

Rufus killed for the first time that day thrusting his sword into the throat of the leading man ascending one of the ladders. As the mortally wounded man fell on his companions, Rufus felt an elation such as he had previously never known, so much so, that recklessly indifferent to the arrows flying past him, he threw himself against the top of the ladder to send it and its occupants crashing back onto the bloodied rock. Marc seized him and pulled him down under the protection of the battlements, and was amazed at the excitement of his companion.

To their right a pitched battle of swordsmen was storming along the ramparts where the attackers had managed to establish a foothold. A century held in reserve was thrown into the mêlée, quickly eliminating this threat as another materialized nearer them.

Four scaling ladders swarming with infantry appeared simultaneous with a lull in the fusillade of arrows. As the helmets of the lead men appeared over the wall they were thrusting their swords violently at those defenders confronting them.

Marc and Rufus surged into the fray, and seizing a long wooden pitch-fork Marc located it on one of the ladders, but the topmost man had a firm grasp of the stone embrasure and resisted his efforts to topple them. Others were clambering over their leader as Rufus plunged his sword into the man's mail protected neck. Somehow he found a chink through which to thrust, and as the blood spurted, the man's grasp loosened, and the ladder hung poised momentarily before pitching backwards with its half dozen occupants.

As suddenly as it had begun it was all over, and the Roman archers were sending their parting arrows after the Parthians. Bodies were scattered over a large area and heaped up at the base of the high walls.

Within the city there was euphoria at the sight of the beaten back invaders milling around the massed line of their cavalry, who hadn't been used in this unsuccessful attack. There were two score of dead and as many injured amongst the defenders.

Mary descended the stairs leading from the ramparts by the main gate. She was spotted with pitch, which a dozen of her companions kept permanently bubbling in vast cauldrons and ladled liberally over any unfortunates who were storming the main gateway. She sought out Miriam and Simon at a safe house on the square where the caravans unloaded, where they had been preparing clean dressings and horsehair sutures, as well as pounding herbs into ointments to dress wounds.

She arrived coincident with Marc and a very subdued Rufus.

"I'll fast for one day in atonement," he said, genuine remorse in his voice.

"What have you to atone for?" demanded Mary impatiently, "you all did quite splendidly, beating back such a determined attack!"

"But I killed two men and rejoiced at it. What is far worse I enjoyed it and found it exhilarating."

"Of course you did. Those men you killed would undoubtedly have slaughtered every one of us here if they had won the day. It's that exultation of your body and mind that overcame fear and made heroes of you. Any more talk of atonement and fasting will make me really angry!"

Rufus flinched at the chastisement he had to take, and relenting a little, Mary laughingly said, "Mind you, fasting might be preferable to eating. I hear they are now having to slaughter some of the camels!"

Leading the way she entered the spacious room at the same time as the walking wounded started to arrive.

Marc seized Simon thankfully, and took him up to the ramparts to look over the whole desolate scene.

The side gate was opened to allow two horsemen to ride towards the Parthian lines and halt halfway. Two of the Persian cavalry came to meet them, and they conferred briefly before wheeling their horses and returning each to their own line. Within a few minutes unarmed parties were scouring the field of battle and treating the injured, while a dozen wagons collected the dead before woefully returning to their lines. The Romans made a large fire outside the walls on which they cremated their fallen comrades. All was discharged in complete silence, a sombre legacy of the battle.

Brutus was too pressed to allow his imagination to dwell on what might be happening to his loved ones. Riding hard he arrived at Tyre on the second day, but found the *Dolphin* was nowhere to be seen, and enquiries at the port office established it would be some four or five days before it returned from Antioch.

Distrustful of leaving such an important message with the port officials the centurion made his way through the crowded streets towards Flora's house, where he hoped to find Alexander. In this he was more fortunate, and an overjoyed Flora assured him they would be home within a couple of hours. She could see how fatigued he was and pressed some refreshment on him before allowing him to sleep on the couch.

The voices of Alexander and Lucia awakened him, as they noisily burst into the room, and it was apparent they were greatly excited, too much even to enquire what had brought Brutus and of those left behind, they were so bursting to tell their news.

"Herod Agrippa has been struck down in front of us as we watched his enthronement, at the Acropolis!" blurted out Lucia.

Brutus was startled, not only by the event but by mention of an enthronement.

"Surely Herod's realm doesn't extend over Tyre?"

"Not exactly but this was a reconciliation between our city council and Herod after a long and bitter disagreement. It's to do with his granting favourable duty on trade through Caesarea and Joppa, and penalizing boats that call at Tyre. When our council retaliated by doubling the tax on cargoes loaded in Palestine, Herod threatened to cut off our supplies of food."

"Which would threaten your very lives."

"Exactly. Anyway Blastus, the king's chamberlain, acted as mediator, and his efforts brought about this ceremony, where Herod was to have had freedom of the city conferred on him. He entered the assembly hall in his royal robes of silver cloth, looking and acting like a benevolent god. As he lapped up the adulation of the crowd he suddenly clutched at his stomach and stumbled to lie writhing on the dais.

"The consternation amongst the nobility was incredible, and we all stood stunned into total silence. Finally we were all dispersed and told to go home and to offer up prayers for the recovery of King Herod!"

Alexander looked pleased with his summary.

"I'll not offer any prayers for such a bloodthirsty tyrant!" said Flora vehemently.

"He had the apostle James, brother of John, cut down with the sword and threw Peter into prison intending to do likewise."

"Is Peter in prison?" queried Brutus anxiously.

"No, the Lord broke open his shackles and set him free. Herod had his guards executed instead."

"These times are very dangerous for followers of the Way!" exclaimed Brutus. "Mary, the mother of Jesus is in danger for her life, and that is what has brought me to Tyre!"

He explained how Rufus had conferred this mission on them, and how he had to leave immediately to be with the legion when it marched to the relief of Dura-Europos.

His news alarmed them all, and Alexander could hardly concentrate to write a letter at Brutus' request, which he agreed to personally deliver to Ephraim, asking him to decline all trade and hold the *Dolphin* in a state of constant readiness, until such time as they joined them.

"We may have to sail in a hurry!" were the centurion's simple and prophetic words.

Prince Ardashir sat immobile on his white charger. Around him thronged the Parthian lords, their finest cloaks worn over their beautifully worked and be-jewelled bronze armour. Pennants flew from a hundred lances as the fully mailed cavalry anticipated their moment of triumph, when they would pour into the city, plundering its wealth and putting the despised conquerors to the sword.

261

To both sides of the cavalry the massed ranks of infantry formed a crescent of iron around the walls of Dura-Europos, scaling ladders and siege towers ready to be thrown onto its walls when the gates had been breached.

The four sections of the ponderous battering ram that was to achieve this had now been assembled into one formidable whole, at a distance just beyond the reach of arrows from the ramparts. A hundred slaves filed under the protective wooden canopy overhanging the massive tree trunk, suspended at eight points from the joined frames. Each slave had been offered his freedom if the gate was breached and the city sacked.

The trumpet sounded and the chocks were pulled from the wheels. The favourable slope of the road aided their efforts and slowly the most formidable ram the defenders had ever seen trundled towards the western gate. The ranks of the besiegers let out a concerted roar of triumph, rattling their weapons against shields, so that the valley reverberated to the menacing cacophony.

The Roman cavalry were outnumbered ten to one, and much the same discrepancy between the opposed forces applied generally. Dan knew how desperate their plight was but had never even thought of negotiating a surrender, rather he and his staff applied all their energies searching for some inspired strategy that might redress the imbalance.

As he saw the elaborate assembly of the ram, he mused aloud to himself and to those officers nearby.

"If we regard ourselves as a ship surrounded and beset by every sort of danger, all can be withstood as long as the integrity of the hull is maintained. One breach of that and nothing can hold back the flood and all is lost, and the intention of these Parthians is to breach the western gate!"

Turning he disclosed the plan that had come to him as he had been talking, of how to respond to the greatest threat.

"We must divide our cavalry into two squadrons, each to take up position by the northern and southern gates, and await the signal from the trumpeter. When they hear one long blast both must sally forth immediately and engage the ram with a pincer movement. Don't lose a second as surprise is essential to achieve our objective before they can respond and counter-attack, and our objective is nothing less than to seize their ram!"

Quickly the cavalry took up their position, amazed at the daring of their commander, while Dan briefed Longinus and two companies of infantry on their crucial role and assigned the troops to back them up.

Now Mars, the God of War needed to smile on them, they had done all they could to redress the overwhelming imbalance of the forces.

Turning to his officers Dan asked, "Are all in position?" and receiving an affirmative he signalled to the trumpeter.

As the shrill blast rang out from the tower, both the secondary gates of the city opened and the sorties galloped out, even as the battering ram began its shattering onslaught on the heavy doors.

As each column converged towards the ram the outer ranks of Parthian soldiers were forced to bring their shields down to face this immediate threat, and for the first time became vulnerable to the archers, and the salvos of arrows and spears that were loosed on them from the ramparts.

Prince Ardashir signalled to Agathobus, who had been impatiently sitting his charger since seeing the sally of the Roman cavalry. Smiling wolfishly he led his section in a thundering charge towards the action, eager for battle.

Each thudding impact of the ram was threatening to shatter the heavily planked and bronze sheathed doors, and the tribune knew the critical moment had come.

At his signal, Sergeant Longinus led his squad to lift the heavy securing beam, and at the next impact the doors flew open and the momentum of the ram carried the greater part of the machine through the gateway.

Prince Ardashir turned to General Polybius his eyes glinting excitedly.

"We've breached their gate, launch the attack!" and he signalled to the two horn bearers to make the call to battle.

"I fear a trick, your highness, delay a while," was uttering from Polybius' lips, as the strident call launched eight thousand troops into battle.

At the gate three murderous salvoes were fired into the mass of slaves now unprotected and thrown into confusion under the canopy. As the arrows ceased, two companies of swordsmen attacked the disordered Parthians at the gateway, as two pairs of legionaries struggled to engage heavy grappling irons on the vertical posts of the machine.

As soon as this had been accomplished a dozen soldiers threw their weight on each of the attached ropes, dragging the whole contraption through the opening, excelling even the tribune's expectations of his men.

The gateway was now clear of the ram as the Roman cavalry had been anticipating, and each horseman struck out to both sides, fighting their way through the confused mêlée of infantry around them, to re-enter the city, with Agathobus and his horsemen harassing them from behind.

They streamed through and between the testudo formed up just inside the gates, weaving between the waiting legionaries, their linked shields protecting them above, their sword arms free to stab at any enemy trying to pass between them.

Many Persian cavalry had fought their way through the gate, but were cut down by the testudo and the Roman cavalry regrouping inside.

Longinus, and his company were frantically clearing the piled up bodies obstructing their critical objective, that of stemming the tide of battle by shutting the doors on the massed Parthian cavalry.

With only seconds to spare the doors slammed closed, the securing beam was slotted home, and Prince Ardashir and his nobles found their progress blocked.

Now they were exposed to the unremitting bombardment from the ramparts and arrows and spears fell upon them relentlessly. Forced to turn and withdraw they had to ride down their own infantry, who were closing on the walls over the whole battlefront.

Such was the confusion and so great the carnage it was more than could be borne. The centre of the attack broke and fled, generating its own momentum that spread along both flanks, so that scaling ladders and siege turrets were abandoned without being used.

Bodies lay strew over the battlefield, heaped up in front of the western gate where men and horses lay together, the wounded suffering further injury from the thrashing hooves of their frenzied mounts. The white charger lay motionless, its crushing weight pinning the fallen prince, so that only his purple cloak fluttered pathetically around the piercing, broken shaft of the Roman spear.

A signal rang out, and the defenders sheathed their arrows and stood silent witness to the slaughter they had inflicted.

At the very base of the gate, Polybius came to his feet, helmet-less and shaken, his cloak stained with other men's blood. Looking disbelievingly around him his eyes fell on the fluttering purple and he picked his unsteady path to his dead prince.

Tears flowing unceasingly he turned and looked up at the battlements, where his eyes fastened on those of the tribune.

"I salute you on your great victory," rang out his proud yet broken voice, "we were but a few paces from our triumph when your heroes closed the gates on us. My prince lies dead and our nation has lost a great king. We will break off the siege and withdraw across the river, only allow us to collect our dead that we may honour them on our own soil."

Tribune Dan lifted his sword in acknowledgement before sheathing it.

"The Gods gave us the day. Only guarantee the safe passage of the caravan confined within our walls and agree to receive a delegation from our Governor at your imperial court, and we will place no other demands upon you."

Polybius bowed agreement, and made his unsteady path to his dejected troops, standing massed in disarray, where but minutes before they had stood in arrogant confidence of triumph.

Dan raised his arm in salute as he turned to face his troops.

"Let Rome rejoice at our accomplishment today. We will honour our own dead with a feast of victory two days from now; let the priests prepare. I proclaim the hero of this battle to be Longinus, the gate closer, and I will commend him to the Emperor."

A great cheer erupted from those crowded inside the gate.

Marc embraced the beaming sergeant.

"Now you will be promoted and posted to Gaul as a renowned hero of Dura-Europos."

Brutus was cantering, impatient at the steady pace of the army, stretched out over two miles like a segmented, sinuous serpent, meandering along the valley below. The Euphrates glittered in the clear daylight ruffled by the strong hot wind in their faces.

He knew no body of troops could march with greater urgency than this and arrive able to do battle, but his anxiety forced him to ride to the crest of the hill range flanking the valley, his eyes constantly scanning the far horizon.

Accordingly it was those eyes that first beheld the lone mounted figure appearing unexpectedly from the east. He was oblivious of the hot sun beating down on him, his head swathed with an untidy turban that his recent sunstroke had forced upon him, as the man rapidly approached and he could make out the red plume to his helmet.

Brutus galloped his stallion to rejoin the mounted vanguard grouped around the Governor. Festus had taken command of the one and half legions he had mustered, and the white plume of his helmet stood out among the coloured plumes of the centurions and tribunes.

Claudius Lysias spotted the urgent closing of the centurion, and drew the attention of the legate, who reined back and waited quietly.

"There's an ensign approaching two miles ahead," Brutus panted out as he pulled back his lathered horse, before pressing it ahead towards the far bend in the road, and the high bluff, limiting their outlook.

Claudius Lysias glanced imploringly at the Legate, and receiving a nod of approval, sent his mount galloping furiously after the receding centurion. His mind was afraid to contemplate the significance of this courier, as no word had been received from Dura-Europos since Brutus had raised the alarm.

Try as he might he could not close the gap, and as he rounded the far bluff he nearly ploughed into the two horsemen who were conversing excitedly where they had converged. One look at their beaming animated faces banished all anxiety, and he rejoiced as he listened to the words tumbling from the excited messenger.

"The Parthians have withdrawn; there was a great battle and Prince Ardashir was slain."

"The siege is really lifted?"

"Absolutely. There isn't a Parthian this side of the Euphrates."

"But they outnumbered the garrison ten to one?"

"True but they're not Romans, and Tribune Dan was an inspired leader!"

"Are all the civilians safe?"

"All. And I have a message for centurion Brutus," he raised a quizzical eyebrow, "from a Mary Magdalene."

"What is it? I'm he!" pressed Brutus, the smile erased from his face.

"Only this. We're all safe and ready. God speed you safely to us."

Brutus let out a great bellow of laughter, and wondered how long it had been since he had last emitted such a sound. He embraced his two companions exulting in the rediscovered feeling of being carefree, and realized how much anxiety he had suppressed in fulfilling his mission.

Rejoicing they remounted and cantered unhurriedly towards the eagerly awaiting army.

Riding hard, driven by an imperative that was impatient with the relaxed pace of the cohort now the crisis was resolved, Brutus arrived at the western gate at dusk on the day of the thanksgiving. The sentries recognised him and offered a quick summary of the celebratory options open to him.

"Go along to the temple of Ishtar because tonight the Queen of Heaven descends to mate with the Prince of the underworld. This only happens every seven years and the celebration will continue until dawn."

The soldier offering this advice was impatient to go off duty and participate.

Brutus knew of this cult, which met in secret in a cave temple in the hills and catered to the more esoteric sexual proclivity of some of his fellow officers, as the priestesses were prostitutes in all but name.

"Thank you, but no. Riding hard for two days does not leave a man in a state for such games."

The sergeant in charge interjected, "You are in time for the victory feast at the temple of Augustus and must be in need of sustenance after your journey."

"Indeed I am, I'll bear it in mind," said Brutus lightly, although he had never had much time for the Roman gods, and deified emperors he regarded as an absurdity.

He made his way through the thronged streets and after depositing his horses at the stables, made an impatient path to Corrina's house.

Only Simon and an elderly servant were there, and he looked down fondly at the sleeping boy, wishing to awaken him and hold him tightly even as the woman told him where Mary might be found.

Striding purposefully to the church, as they called the large, meeting-house that Corinna had bestowed on the followers, he was disappointed to find it all but deserted. The lamps were still burning, and he was amazed to see a life-sized and very life-like wall painting of Mary hurrying to the tomb, with a casket of ointment and lamp held in her hands. Her black hair had been skillfully highlighted with henna and glowed in the lamplight, and her eyes seemed to follow him as he moved along the unfinished mural.

His heart rejoiced as he studied her, how truly the essence of her brave, devoted nature had been captured. He smiled, appreciatively, and how typical of her to insist on the painting continuing even while they were under siege. He recognised her defiant refusal to contemplate the possibility of defeat, a conviction that came from her unshakable faith in God's purpose, rather than her confidence in man's striving.

He averted his eyes from the end wall dominated by the three crosses. He had refused to model for the painter, but knew he would be depicted with equal realism by the skilful artist.

The noise of someone entering caused him to turn towards the entrance.

From the gloomy interior the centurion could only see the intruder in silhouette in the open doorway, and then as he closed the door and moved towards him he recognized a familiarity of face without being able to place him.

"Centurion Brutus? I'm Sergeant Longinus. Well, actually Junior Calvary officer, as I had a field promotion to replace Facilis who was killed in the siege."

"Congratulations. I heard of your victory from the ensign."

He was scrutinizing the officer all the time, trying to make the connection.

Longinus laughed.

"You don't remember me do you? If I tell you I'm now immortalized over there you may remember," he pointed at the mural of the crucifixion and the soldiers throwing dice for the Galilean's robe at the foot of the cross.

Brutus saw one of the soldier's faces had been repainted, and Longinus had been written across a shield leaning against the cross.

"There!" breathed Brutus passionately, "you were there! I've tried to erase that terrible day from my memory but fate won't allow me to forget."

"I had to certify his death to the Prefect and to the temple court. A few days later I had to stand a grilling from that same court: 'Might he only have appeared dead? Could I have been mistaken? Could ten gold pieces persuade me that he feigned death to avoid having his legs broken? Did I know there were magicians who could arrest all signs of life for many minutes, breathing, heartbeat, pulse?'

"I replied, he was dead alright, and your lance had pierced his heart to ensure it was so. After that I was dismounted and given every unwelcome job in the legion and many of the most dangerous. I believe they wanted to get rid of me."

He stopped breathless, wondering if he had said too much to the retired centurion.

"Why is your face painted on that soldier?"

"I talked to Marc much as I have to you. He asked me to tell my story to Mary, the woman they have just painted there, and somehow she persuaded me to repeat all of this to the assembly in this hall."

"Oh I know how persuasive Mary of Magdelene can be alright," laughed Brutus, "she persuaded me that I needed her as my wife and she was most certainly right."

"Then why aren't you persuaded to seek her out first, instead of in your own sweet time," came her melodious husky interruption, and spinning on his heel Brutus felt his heart stop as he beheld her, hugging the shadows by an open side door.

In an instant they had met and were embracing, with all the fervour that danger and distance intensifies in the human breast.

Longinus knew the moment had come to retreat.

That night as they sat talking nearly until cockcrow, they each recounted their experiences of the past ten days. Simon, although often falling asleep where he sat on the lap of the centurion, from which he refused to budge, had the uncanny knack of waking up when anything exciting was being voiced. Perhaps it was the excitement aroused in the man that awoke the boy, and Brutus had to hear every last detail of the battle that ended the siege.

"Truly Dan has a great future in the imperial army. It's an interesting speculation but if you hadn't swum out to save him from the sea, Marc, or if I hadn't thwarted Communis, this city might be a smouldering ruin by now. I must make a point of calling on the tribune and hearing his view of the battle."

"Don't let him know that we are aware of the 10th Legion being posted to Gaul in readiness for the conquest of Britain," urged Marc, still agitated at those ominous words of Longinus.

Brutus nodded, but as he did so his eyes closed and he nearly fell from the couch. Miriam plucked the boy from his arms as Mary helped him to his feet and they made a somnolent departure.

It was mid afternoon before Brutus was led into the anteroom of the fort, where an eagerly awaiting tribune jumped up from his desk and hurried to greet him.

The spontaneity of their embrace belied the years separating them, and their affection for each other was as natural as it had been in the acropolis at Tyre.

"How's your Latin coming along?" queried Brutus and was delighted when Dan frowned and then with a beaming smile cried out.

"Amamus!" and their enjoined laughter echoed around the building.

"My purpose in visiting you is twofold. Firstly let me congratulate you on your leadership of the defence of this city. Your renown as an inspired commander will have spread throughout Syria by now and will soon reach Rome."

Dan was deprecating and modest in his telling of the decisive battle, and deflected all inspiration back on the centurion.

"When we fled Byblos on the *Dolphin*, Captain Ephrain told us of your escape from the *Hermes*, and of how you utilized the massive baulks of timber you were carrying so effectively.

"As I saw the tree being hung in preparation for breaching the gates, I thought of the city as a boat afloat in an angry, hostile sea. One breach of the hull and it would not have been possible to hold back the torrents striving to pour in, any more than they were able to on the galley. I knew I had to risk everything to nullify that ram before it stove in the main gate. Had the Parthians launched their attack on the whole front and the gate simultaneously, all would have been lost." He smiled self-effacingly.

"Had the *Hermes* altered her tactics of pursuit and not overhauled us from astern?" Brutus held up his hands deprecatingly and left the sentence unfinished, although their enjoined laughter completed the unspoken words.

"Now for your second purpose?" and Dan raised a quizzical eyebrow.

"I entreat your help for a mission I am about to undertake with Mary and my companions. I regard it as the most important mission of my life."

At some length Brutus expounded on their situation and the task Rufus had given them.

Dan was silent for some minutes reflecting quietly on all he had heard.

"I am not a religious man or I would find it impossible to make my career in the army. Conquest and control are often brutal and harsh, especially when there are millions who would like to pull the whole edifice of our mighty empire down into chaos. Shortly I, along with the 10th Legion, will be posted to Gallia, to prepare the invasion and conquest of Brittania. The best way I can help is by urging you and your charges to flee Palestine, and placing any resources you may need at your disposal."

"You can do a great deal more than that. You are now a famed hero throughout the province and a tribune. A letter of commendation from you to any commander who may be able to help us would be invaluable."

"Then you shall have one. I'll have it drafted now," he said beaming at the centurion.

Half an hour later Brutus read the parchment that was ready to be sealed. It was signed Danius Galerius, Tribune, 10th Imperial Legion.

"Danius?" he said, with a barely suppressed smile threatening to master his features.

"Dan to all my friends. Only my parents and my superiors ever call me Danius Galerius. I hope this will assist you in your mission and may your God go with you."

As they saluted and then embraced, Brutus momentarily regretted the necessity to terminate their reunion as their duties scattered them to different parts of the wide Roman world.

"Do you think Malchus will be safe at the Herodian court following the death of Herod Agrippa?" queried Brutus as an afterthought, and when he saw the puzzlement on the face of the listener, he realized no news had yet reached the garrison of events outside the besieged city.

He sat back in his chair and told of his visit to Tyre.

CHAPTER TWO

Even as Brutus was telling Dan of the dramatic death of Herod Agrippa, in an anteroom of the court of the Sanhedrin, Caiaphus was expounding to an intimate group of like thinkers the implications for themselves.

"This is a great blow as we had the ear of this king and saw eye to eye on a number of matters. Agrippa shared our concern at the diminishing income of the Temple and recognised its origins in the cult of these Christians; these renegades who have renounced the Temple. For this reason he readily executed James and would have done likewise with Peter had his followers not contrived his escape from prison. His arbitrary justice is the only sort that works in our current crisis and while there are liberal thinkers like Gamaliel and his sons in the Sanhedrin, prepared to give the benefit of the doubt, and to wait and see, our hands are tied, and to have lost a champion of our cause like Agrippa is a terrible set back.

"Shortly Rome will appoint a new ruler, who may be no more sympathetic than Pontius Pilate, so we have but a few weeks to crack down on this embryo church during its gestation, as once born the monster may be more than anyone can control."

There were rumblings of approval from the dozen or so ardent activists, drawn together by the fervour with which they would defend their traditional privileges.

Caiaphas held up his hands and as they quieted he continued.

"The first action of the new ruler is likely to be to remove me from office and appoint a High Priest who is more compliant."

At the growls of disapproval this elicited he smiled and bowed graciously,

"Thank you but that will be of small significance if by then we have succeeded in discrediting this spurious Messiah."

"How can anything be done now to discredit what happened eight years ago? We lost the opportunity then, and nobody believed the guards at the tomb when they claimed to have been drugged by his followers," said Zadoc, a young and intense Pharisee, who had angrily heard Saul's testimony in the synagogue at Damascus.

"None of the guards are alive now to contribute one way or the other," avowed Caiaphas significantly. "No, the only way of discrediting a resurrected Messiah remaining open to us is to eliminate those close to him. The apostles enjoy an immunity following Gamaliel's intervention, but this does not extend to the women upon whom they depend so much. I have a list of half a dozen to whom any injury would greatly shake the faith and resolution of the followers.

"So often it is the women who lead in embracing this cult and then the men follow sheepishly, and why does it appeal so strongly to certain rebellious women? They embrace this Christianity because it offers women an unmerited status foreign to our traditions, and likely to undermine our whole society. Let's switch our attack from the sheep, to the shepherd or rather the shepherdess."

This suggestion was greeted with an enthusiasm that surprised Caiaphas, and he realized he was on the right track with these arrogant and sternly disapproving men, jealous of every privilege they enjoyed.

"It will cost a lot of money and we may have to dip deeply into our personal coffers to pay these instruments of retribution, and then to ensure their compliance and silence afterwards. If each here will pledge five thousand shekels, we should be able to achieve our purpose!"

There was a gasp from many of the conspirators but the High Priest regarded them unrelentingly.

"You all supported me previously and we achieved a limited success even though we failed to injure the daughter of Anna. They are alerted to the danger around them now but we still have the support of the palace," he paused and looked towards Blastus, Herod's chamberlain, who inclined his large aristocratic head in agreement, "and there is a group of Roman officers prepared to commit troops to our cause. It is not a time for your resolve to weaken, any of you!"

The menace in his voice silenced all dissent.

It had been many years since they had set foot in Jerusalem, and for each of the travellers nostalgia was tempered by apprehension.

They all felt the tension that gripped the city, as though some malign influence was straining to tear its very buildings down around its cantankerous citizens. Squads of stern faced troops tramped its streets, while a sullen, resentful shiftiness caused passers by to avert their eyes for fear of betraying their feelings, or simply to avoid attracting unwelcome attention.

The occasional burnt out house testified to the intermittent episodes of orchestrated persecution.

Silently they made their way to the square bordered by tall elegant houses, one of which Mary, the widowed mother of John Mark, had bestowed to the emergent church.

They split into pairs and mingled separately with the few people in the square, their eyes alert for any danger.

Miriam drew Marc's attention to a minor dispute between a young girl with dishevelled long hair, and a burly, brutish fellow, gripping her tightly by her upper arms and shaking her at the same time as he remonstrated with her. As he became aware of the onlookers he released his grip, allowing the girl to run away sobbing inconsolably.

Grinning unconvincingly the man said, "Too bad children are so wilful and disobedient in these troubled days," as he shuffled away.

Marc hadn't heard a word although he nodded agreement. His memory was searching without success to place those coarse, unkempt features that had jolted his composure.

"I recognize that man but can't place him," he said to Miriam, swinging Simon around by his arms as though concerned only to play with his son.

"Well he won't recognise you, you've changed so much in the past eight years."

"Leave me sitting here alone for a while and I'll try and think back to those distant days," requested Marc, and he rejoiced watching his wife play chase with the boy.

It was warm in the late morning sun and he closed his eyes, and emptied his mind of all thoughts.

Suddenly he recalled the guard peering down on him and signalling recognition to his companion the day they had found Alexander beaten and robbed. Brutus had all but strangled and warned him off then, but it was definitely the same man!

Marc caught up with Miriam, and she could tell from his elation he was pleased with himself.

"Where is Brutus?"

"He and Mary have gone to look at the Temple and Fort Antonia. Brutus said he was anxious to know if Firmus is still adjutant."

"He must be told that ruffian will recognize him! Brutus all but throttled him when he followed us through the back streets before we fled Jerusalem. He's one of Herod's guards!"

They made their way to the Temple court and were surprised at the few worshippers. There seemed to be more priests than visitors, despite the closeness to Passover. But few pilgrims were yet in evidence and the vendors had very little to sell, either goods or sacrificial animals.

They quickly spotted their companions and hastened to join them.

Mary greeted them with lamentations.

"Did you know that the main rains and the spring rain have failed this year, and all Palestine is threatened with famine? This is the second successive year of drought, and explains why we didn't find any crops growing along our route. Most of the food has to be brought in from Egypt and Cyprus and is prohibitively expensive."

After expressing his concern, Marc took Brutus surreptitiously to one side and told him of his encounter with Herod's guard.

As he did so Miriam explained the same to Mary, and they both laughed at the conspiratorial pose the men were adopting.

Realizing they were being laughed at the men rejoined their women rather sheepishly.

"I suppose you know what we have been talking about then?" asked Brutus.

"Of course we do. What Herod's spy outside the meeting house means, and what to do about it," laughed Mary, and the men could not do other than join in.

"Well can you tell us likewise, what we have decided to do about it?"

"Probably always wear your swords, and make sure one of you is always with us to protect us," said Miriam with barely constrained delight at the crestfallen expression on both men's faces, and the women dissolved into giggles bordering on hysteria.

In mock exasperation both men by common accord, seized their respective wives and threatened to throttle them.

Such unseemly behaviour in the outer courts of the Temple elicited a rebuke from both a Sadducee and a priest, and the companions were forced to escape from the court, before someone summoned the guards to throw them out.

"Oh goodness," wheezed Mary, "I'm weak with laughter. Oh you men, if you could just see yourselves, how disapproving you look," and she and Miriam clung to each other as Simon and their husbands regarded them in wide-eyed disbelief.

It was late afternoon, an hour before dusk, when they were ushered into the house and up the stairs into the large assembly room, bustling with activity. Rufus took charge, introducing them to the various groups scattered about the room.

"I especially want you to meet our famine relief workers," said Rufus, "Paul and Barnabas have brought us much needed funds from the brethren in Antioch."

Mary was devastated at the meeting and the impact on Saul, now called Paul, was equally profound.

Seizing Mary's hand, he knelt at her feet and bringing her hand to his contrite face said, "A few hours after we last met I saw the truth you tried to reveal to me, the truth of the risen Lord, even as I lost my sight. I have often thought of the harm I brought upon you and regretted it always. Only the stoning of Steven has grieved me more. I can only entreat your forgiveness."

Mary withdrew her hand and urged him to his feet.

"As you can see I am not bearing any scars from our encounters, so you have my forgiveness as I think you have had to suffer more than I. This is my husband, centurion Brutus."

"Ah, a man of the sword I see. I bid you welcome."

They were interrupted by the arrival of a party of women, accompanied by the most imposing man Brutus had met since the day of the crucifixion, with the possible exception of Simon Peter.

His mother they instantly recognized, but James, the younger brother of Jesus, was unknown to them. He had the same Semitic features as Jesus, but his chestnut brown hair cascaded on both sides from a central parting, breaking in massed curls on his shoulders. His eyes, deep-set and pale blue, glittered with humour at the same time evidencing shrewd intelligence and a questioning mind. He held his head with that natural grace that confers the unmistakable air of the born leader.

"At last the long awaited Romans to escort our mother across the seas to a place of safety. You are welcome to our church, doubly so for we also welcome you as baptized brethren. Your timing is auspicious for I see you have met Paul. Talk to him of your plan, he too is planning a missionary journey to take the message of salvation across the seas to Cyprus and all of Asia Minor and with Barnabas and young John Mark, they sit up half the night talking of nothing else."

Paul smiled disparagingly.

"We talk of it yes, but it is not to be in the immediate future as we have much to sort out in Antioch, where we left the saints awaiting guidance from the mother church."

"Without the aid you have brought us from Antioch, it would have been necessary to fragment the community throughout the region to survive this famine. There would be no mother church in Jerusalem!"

The women were conferring with great fondness and affection, when a loud banging at the door shattered their serenity.

The servant who hurried to the top of the stairs looked frightened, and as she turned Marc recognised the dishevelled girl they had seen manhandled in the square earlier. Signalling to Brutus he quickly drew him aside, and in a few rushed words prepared him for trouble.

The loud noise of those ascending the stairs was ominous, and the squad of armed legionaries that spilled into the room confirmed their fears, forming two lines at the top of the stairs. Their commanding officer pushed the cringing servant forward.

"Point out the women," he ordered, and hesitantly she pointed at Mary mother of Jesus and two of her companions.

"There is a complaint against these women and others of this cult, that they are using the orphanages for the purpose of abducting children and selling them into slavery."

Jesus' mother stepped forward, although the draining of all colour from her face belied her brave appearance.

"Who makes such false accusation? I challenge anyone to accuse us so to our face."

"Esther here for one, was stolen from her house at the first burst of outrage against your heretical cult many years ago, and is now your slave," asserted the officer.

"Esther's parents were both killed in that violent persecution when she was seven years of age. She was cared for in our orphanage until she was old enough to become our valued servant, she is not a slave. Tell them it is so, Esther."

The girl was crying piteously, bordering on hysteria, and as Mary reached out a hand to get her attention, she jerked away with a shriek and ran to the stairs.

"What more evidence do we require? You have terrorized the poor girl and many more. Come with us to Fort Antonia, and tomorrow you can defend yourself at Herod's court."

Two of the soldiers moved to stand one each side of the outraged Mary, as others moved to secure the other women Esther had picked out.

"Hold! It is I you want!" rang out an unexpected voice and Paul stepped forward to face the startled officer.

"It was I who instigated the persecution of the followers of Jesus, and I who am responsible for the death of this girl's parents. Let me answer for their death at Herod's court."

The soldiers wavered, looking indecisively at their commander, who momentarily looked ruffled.

"Stand aside we have no interest in you," and putting out his hand he went to brush Paul aside as though he were a fly.

Paul stood immovable staring at his adversary, and as his anger welled up, the officer drew his sword and smashed the hilt of it into Paul's face. Even as Paul hit the floor a sterner, commanding voice rang out, "Hold still, Communis you cur, and you too, Sergeant Tiasus!" The power and menace in the challenge arrested every other movement in the room, as Brutus strode from the shadows to within a few feet of the paralyzed officer.

"So no longer a tribune, but merely the commander of some pestilential fort in Jerusalem. How you've come down in the world."

Communis' face was blazing with anger, but all response was suppressed by the dominance of his challenger.

"You chose to draw your sword against women and unarmed civilians. Don't sheath it for now you must use it against me. I challenge you to settle this between us."

Eyes locked, the two men warily circled each other as all in the room scattered, hauling tables and fallen chairs to clear an area for the dual.

Aware of the advantage he had of being armoured, Communis regained his wits and struck the first blow, which Brutus easily parried. All the hate that had been suppressed surged to the fore, as he attributed all his shattered hopes and ambitions to this centurion, and he exulted at this chance for revenge.

Now cold cunning rather than heated blood directed him, and as Brutus stumbled against an overturned chair, a thrust of Communis' sword caught him on the chest, opening up a wound across his ribs. The blood staining his adversary's tunic goaded Communis to prodigious swings of his sword, taxing all Brutus's strength and skill to parry and deflect them from his unprotected body.

His adversary with breast-plate, and arm and shoulder armour, presented but few points of vulnerability, so Brutus was forced on to the defensive, conserving his strength for when the younger man tired.

Silence gripped the room except for clash of metal, grunts of exertion and the sudden scrape of metal studded sandal, as only quick footwork averted disaster. No sound came from the tightly packed spectators, who had never before witnessed such violence, but were held spell bound by the life and death struggle.

Communis, breathing hard from his exertion, his feet losing their spring, made a despairing lunge, moving forward and off balance. Brutus ducked under the blade, pivoted on one knee as Communis tried to chop down with his extended sword, and then from his kneeling position thrust upwards. He felt his sword point impact on the pelvic bone as it penetrated his opponent's unprotected groin. Withdrawing, he parried one last weak and desperate blow thrown out by Communis as he fell, his right leg collapsing under him.

As he lay writhing on the floor, the blood spurting with each heart beat from the severed femoral artery, Brutus knew he had inflicted a mortal injury, yet he could feel no regret, such was his impassioned hated of this officer for abusing his position and power for self-advancement.

Two men moved forward to try and stem the bleeding, which could only be achieved by applying continual pressure on the wound.

Sergeant Tiasus looked uncertain how to behave towards the centurion. Battles to the death between comrades he had seen often enough and the authorities reluctantly accepted them, but this bloodied, panting centurion, had wounded his commanding officer in the execution of his duty, and ought to pay for it.

As though reading his thoughts Brutus said, "You're in command, sergeant, but before you decide to arrest me read this," proffering the sealed scroll that Tribune Danius had given him.

After breaking it open and reading it twice, Tiasus handed it back to him.

"This does put a different complexion on things. I was about to arrest you to bring you for trial before Governor Festus at Damascus."

"I was with Festus on the march to relieve Dura-Europos. I don't think he wishes to see me on trial, or hear of the death of the commander of Fort Antonia arresting Jewish women in such circumstances as these."

"What is your mission for which you carry this letter of commendation?"

"To escort these women, important to our church, to a place of safety where their lives are no longer at risk."

Turning, Tiasus ordered his men to make up a litter for the unconscious Communis.

As he departed he said, "I will cover this in some way. The wound appears to be inflicted by the tusk of a wild boar, or some such animal. Don't delay over your mission, they must have powerful enemies in Jerusalem and this will incense them."

Only as the door closed did the reaction set in. Two of the women swooned and Mary Magdalene and Miriam bathed Brutus' wound, bandaging it tightly to stem the bleeding.

Simon had seized a stick and was challenging everyone to a sword fight, while Marc tried to calm him down. Some women were mopping the spilt blood from the floor tiles, as others restored the room to a semblance of normality.

Paul sat on a chair, nursing a swelling the size of a hen's egg above his eyebrow.

Rufus called all those not active elsewhere to form a prayer circle, to give thanks for the safe deliverance of Mary and the other women.

Her eyes gleaming mistily Mary breathed into Brutus' ear, "You were magnificent my darling, like a raging lion."

Brutus squeezed her hand by way of reply. He didn't trust himself with words at this early stage of his reaction.

A subdued James came over.

"You present us with a paradox. We are both thrilled and repelled by what we have witnessed. Had I been asked an hour ago if swords were needed to protect our women I would have said no. Now I know nothing else would have sufficed. Rufus knew what he was doing when he pressed us to enlist you for this mission."

"I know nothing of your organization but I do know the Roman legionary. Communis is the worst sort of officer, and had he provoked a reaction from your community, would have happily used the blade not the hilt of his sword. I had little option but to challenge him, but it is not the first time we have been adversaries.

"There must be powerful people behind this attack, as Communis would not be bought cheaply, so it would be best if we move mother Mary to the boat as soon as possible."

"I have been ready many days now," said Mary, her eyes reflecting her gratitude and complete confidence in her escort, "won't your wound delay you?"

Brutus smiled.

"I will have my physician looking after me, so whenever it starts to feel comfortable she is bound to want to redress it, despite my protestations."

"Which will be loud and heart-rending, he is such a baby really," laughed Mary Magdalene, her mischievous eyes belying her concern at the pain his laughter provoked.

Recognising the time had come Mary said sadly to her son, "James, we will part tomorrow not to meet again in this world. At least you know you have entrusted me to reliable people. Can you spare yourself from your committees just for one night?"

"John Mark will deputize for me mother, we have so much to talk about."

"Marc and I will look to the wagon and the horses as there is much to prepare. Who other than yourself will be making this journey?" queried Brutus, anxious to finalize the arrangements.

"Only Mary, widow of Clopas. Only we three and Miriam, whom we are glad to have with us."

"Then only one wagon is required, and Marc and I will take turns driving."

"Include me as I will accompany you to Tyre!" said Rufus suddenly at their side, "I have matters to discuss with Alexander."

"Have you forgotten so quickly my prowess as a wagoner?" challenged Mary

Magdalene, and the very thought of their descent to the Jordan nearly sent Marc into a panic.

"Forgive me, Mary. There are now more drivers than passengers, and with Mary Magdalene we should prove unstoppable."

Mary never knew whether this was the compliment it sounded.

The journey was uneventful taking the three days that had been anticipated.

Twice they encountered mounted cavalry, but nothing other than a cursory interest was shown in them.

The dominant impression was of the arid parched landscape, and even the coastal plain and valley of Jezreel, normally rippling with green corn at this time of year, lay sun scorched and uncultivated. Judaea was in the grip of drought, famine stalked the countryside and many family groups were on the move, unable to feed themselves on their traditional land.

Approaching Tyre they passed close to the tomb of the victims of the persecution, and mother Mary, as the mother of Jesus henceforth was to known to the men, insisted on spending a few hours there, conferring sympathetically with Miriam and Rufus.

For their part Brutus and Marc gave their heavy wooden staves, still leaning where they had left them, against the millstone, a touch of oil, to rekindle their lustre, and reflected nostalgically on the last time they had been used in the vicinity.

Now they were approaching the *Dolphin* and even at a distance Brutus could see the time of waiting had been well used. She had new rigging and the halyards gleamed white, proclaiming their newness. A new sail was furled hanging from a newly adzed spar. Only captain Ephraim peering out over the raised bow looked familiar and old.

He raised a disbelieving hand in greeting then called Horatius, and they regarded the wagon expectantly as it drew up to the boat. The smile he flashed at Miriam as she stepped prettily down from the bench was frozen, as one Mary after another followed until the last, Mary Magdalene, stood smiling up at him.

"Oh no," he said pointing with a perplexed look, "how can you do this to me, centurion, after all these years? Just when I am beginning to forget, and not wake up at night with Mary standing behind me brandishing a huge belaying pin, you bring four women to complete my destruction."

Those Marys unknown to him were looking at each other with some consternation. This was definitely not the greeting they had expected.

"Why you old pirate," called out Mary Magdalene with evident glee, "hasn't your life changed greatly for the better since we last sailed together from Joppa?"

Ephraim rubbed his head as though expecting to detect the residual bump from Brutus' manhandling.

"Come on board if you must and I'll tell you the whole gruesome consequences of doing favours for centurion Brutus."

They hurried up the gangplank determined not to show any fear at its narrowness and absence of any handhold, but were grateful to Horatius extending them a helping hand at the top. As Brutus hurriedly introduced one Mary then the other, Ephraim's consternation knew no bounds.

"Don't tell me. I've only met one of triplets, and to complete my cup of happiness you thought it time I met the other two."

276

Horatius, noting the older woman's fatigue, took her arm and said, "Come over here and rest. Don't take any notice of his bark, he never bites," and settling Mary on some soft bales, he hurried off to fetch them a cordial.

Much later when all was stowed and the sleeping arrangements sorted, the men gathered on deck.

Simon had insisted that he be included with the men, and his mattress had been moved into the main hold that was free of cargo, other than provisions. He now stood listening as their proposed voyage was discussed, and although his comprehension of the subtleties was lacking, he quickly latched on to encountering pirates or risk of being wrecked by storms.

"If we don't set our course with such things in mind, and just await some conjunction of planets and a comet, and then run before the prevailing wind, heaven knows where we will end up!" protested Ephraim.

"That's it exactly, captain, Heaven does know. This is a journey of faith, much as Noah made in the ark. If there hadn't been a prophecy that this voyage was to happen, and if you weren't carrying the mother of our risen Lord, I would agree it's unbelievably stupid to attempt."

Rufus smiled ruefully at Ephraim, who looked confounded at the way his protest had been turned against him.

Horatius blurted out excitedly, "Can it be true? Are you saying mother Mary is the mother of Jesus the Nazarene, in whose name Marc and I were baptized eight years ago?"

"Exactly that," confirmed Marc.

"Why can't she stay with her own people? They must revere and adore her? Why must she undertake such a perilous journey and leave her land of birth?"

"Those of her own people who make up the church would love her to stay, but those who oppose the church and all it stands for are unscrupulous about how they are prepared to attack it. Mother Mary has had four attempts on her life, the last only a few days ago when Communis tried to seize her at one of the houses."

"Communis, that plague ridden thorn in my flesh! Is he still around in Jerusalem?" queried Ephraim with such vehemence everyone was taken aback.

"Roman soldier's dead," said Simon, "uncle Brutus killed him with sword in here," and he poked his finger in Ephraim's groin.

The incredulous look on both men's faces provoked a laughing centurion to state the simple facts of the fight. He tried to tell it as a simple summary, but Simon wasn't having it and insisted on a blow, by blow account, which had to accord with how it was engraved in his memory. When Brutus had concluded to Simon's satisfaction, he asked,

"How has he been such a thorn in your flesh?"

Ephraim explained after a brief pause.

"You will remember when Horatius and the two boys, Dan and Malchus, escaped the Roman soldiers by the skin of their teeth?" Brutus nodded. "Well Communis knew they had evaded him on board the *Dolphin*, that same boat that nearly sank the *Hermes* when they were after you. So he ordered our arrest if we should ever be seen in Palestine waters.

"We haven't been able to sail south of Tyre ever since, as you Romans have long memories when you have been worsted. We've had to decline some lucrative cargoes, even now the grain run from Egypt to Caesarea is denied us, while every other boat on the coast is enjoying rich pickings."

"I've always wondered what happened after you left me, with the stolen horses tied behind you," Brutus eagerly enquired of Horatius.

"I tried to sell them to a second party of Roman cavalry, didn't I? I didn't realize they were Romans when I saw them silhouetted against a dawn sky, heading north of Caesarea Phillippi. I thought they might be Arab traders and rode up to them eager to make a good sale. As I drew close I realized my mistake, at the same time as they saw I had their horses. I scattered the horses with a few stones from my sling, and then the chase was on. Luckily they only sent two of their party after me, while the rest rounded up the horses. You witnessed the end of the chase!"

His face broke into a broad grin as he recollected leaping onto the precariously balanced gangplank, and for the sake of those who had missed the climatic ending, Brutus filled in the culmination of the chase as he had seen it.

The concerted laughter brought the women up on deck, eager to escape the gloom of the hold and to hear what was so funny.

In fact the solicitous attention showered on the older woman by Horatius was the funniest thing of all, but everyone had sufficient delicacy and generosity not to refer to his slavish devotion. He was quite overawed with his undeserved honour of being able to serve her, as to him she was greater than any queen.

It was as yet unknown what a ready wit she had, that waited to be revealed as she recounted many stories in the weeks ahead.

Turning to her and rather at a loss, Ephraim said, "It appears we await your guidance on when and where we voyage."

Mary nodded regally as though the responsibility did not overawe her, and the disconcerted captain continued, "All I ask is that in matters maritime, relating to the safety of the boat and your lives, I must have command."

"That is as it should be, captain. I don't think you will find any conflict between what we ask of you and your concern for our safety."

The complete confidence in her tone reassured him that his nagging doubts were unworthy, and only testified to his lack of faith, of which he was well aware.

"Then when do you wish us to set sail? The boat is readied, the winds may be favourable for another month, but I'm unsure of the conjunction of the planets."

"Tomorrow we set sail, God willing. Today we all have other things to occupy us."

She didn't elaborate, but each had different priorities, only agreeing to be back on board by dusk.

Brutus insisted that he and Rufus accompany two of the Marys as they visited the church in Tyre.

Mary Magdalene was anxious to see Flora and would go with Marc, Miriam and Simon, who was excited at meeting his cousins for the first time.

"I'll let Alexander know you will be calling on him after we have sailed," Miriam assured Rufus as they went their various ways.

None of them was aware of the blind beggar who held out his alms bowl as they were dispersing. Had they seen him hurrying towards the office of the port captain, before departing urgently for the Acropolis overlooking the city, still the quarters of the Roman garrison, and still commanded by an embittered centurion Antony, they would have set sail immediately.

There Caiaphas' spy was frustrated by the absence of the commander and the obstinacy of the chief clerk, who was no Jew lover and shared in the average soldier's contempt for this pious, ungovernable race.

"When will your commanding officer return? My information is most urgent and it's for his ears alone."

"After his business is completed with the city council and the deputations from Antioch and Silicia. The necessity to ensure the supply of grain in this famine is a priority second to none."

"He would regard my information as of greater importance I can assure you!"

"If you care to put it in writing I will see it is delivered to him immediately."

For some minutes his informant considered his options, then accepting there was no way of bypassing this intransigent clerk, he requested quill and parchment and wrote,

'Centurion Brutus who murdered commander Communis in Jerusalem is about to sail aboard *Dolphin* with Jewish Christians. Imperative you apprehend same.'

Abihu (Agent of the Sanhedrin.)

Sealing it he handed it to the clerk who took it casually and indicated the interview was over.

"You will be in great trouble if centurion Antony doesn't receive it immediately," insisted Abihu as he was ushered out of the office.

"I'll see he gets it," growled the clerk.

He knew that Antony had a liaison after the meeting, with a lady of the town who he regularly visited, and woe betide any interruption of his arrangements. Still there was something about the insistence of this pathetic informant that worried him, and after a while he decided to take it personally to the city hall and hope to catch the centurion.

Abihu was returning to the harbour as fast as his legs would carry him, and it was his haste that caused him to trip over a raised cobblestone and strike his head so that he sprawled unconscious on the pavement.

At the harbour office there was consternation as dusk approached and no further instruction had been received. The insistent Jew had asked them to delay the *Dolphin* sailing, as there was a fugitive wanted by the Roman commander on board.

The *Dolphin* had been tied up more than a week and extensively refitted, but no indication had been given that it intended sailing that day.

Captain Ephraim was respected as a competent skipper who never made trouble and soon the staff would be going home leaving only one official in charge for the night.

The port captain decided that everyone could go and the only action necessary was to inform the night watch not to allow her to sail.

Ephraim paced the deck for some hours eager to see the last of his passengers on board.

A half moon lit the quay and only the family with the boy, were not yet returned.

Ephraim saw John, the deputy port captain, gesturing from the quayside and made his way down the gangplank and they conferred briefly.

Hurrying back on board Ephraim called to his crew to prepare to sail immediately.

Brutus, curious at all the activity, came on deck to the captain's brief explanation of the urgency of their sailing, that otherwise the ship was confined to port, and he would be arrested shortly unless they ignored the restriction and departed immediately.

"But Marc and his family are still ashore with Mary Magdelene!"

"Centurion Antony is after you not them, and possibly mother Mary! They can be contacted and picked up later. Stand by to let go forward."

"Ay ay, skipper," replied Levi.

"Stand by to let go aft."

"Standing by," said Joab, a youth on his first voyage.

"Here they come!" called Brutus and all eyes saw them running, a hundred paces from the boat.

They were breathlessly scrambling up the gangplank, when the clatter of hooves on cobbles was heard, and a column of cavalry burst on to the quay close by.

"Let go both, quickly now!"

As they tumbled on board Marc turned and hauled in the plank, while Horatius and Ephraim threw their weight on the poles to move them slowly away from the quayside. Levi and Joab added their weight, and the gap was opening steadily as the cavalry reigned back and tumbled from their horses.

"You're under arrest," called an apoplectic Antony, "surrender your fugitive!"

The boat had its own momentum now, and the gap was formidable as a brave soldier ran and leapt, his arms embracing the overhanging gangplank. He hung there a few seconds, and was about to fall in when Brutus reached over to grasp him, and with Marc's help hauled the man on board.

Immediately he was disarmed and brought to his feet, and holding him as a human shield Brutus moved to call to the soldiers lining the quayside,

"Your commander is misleading you. He and I are old enemies as gold buys his allegiance. He acts now for Caiaphas, the Jewish High Priest, not for the Roman Governor of Syria. I have a commendation here from Tribune Danius Galerius, gallant defender of Dura-Europos, asking all army commanders to assist our mission. Were Antony not in the pay of the Jerusalem Temple, you would be assisting me, not arresting me. Your comrade will be put ashore at the first port we come to."

The oars were now sweeping the boat away as Antony, failing in his exhortation to his men to throw their spears, seized one and threw it himself, only to see it plunge harmlessly well short.

As he stood stunned by his failure yet again, his Junior Cavalry Officer ordered the troop to mount up and return to barracks.

It was a long time before Antony remounted, and he knew he was a discredited commander and a laughing stock.

They found his body the next day. The sea had deposited it at the foot of the ledge where Dan and Malchus had been plucked from its grasp eight years earlier. Nobody appreciated the irony.

CHAPTER THREE

Ephraim had never encountered such consistent easterly winds, carrying them speedily to Cyprus, and on the fourth day they were running down the southern coast towards Paphos elated at their progress.

"Truly Horatius, there must be something remarkable that Mother Mary can summon up such favourable winds," but even as he said it, he knew his mate would refute the slightest disparagement of their remarkable passenger.

"God breathes over the oceans to speed his mother to safety, what would you expect?"

"The wind to swing on to our nose as it usually does. Each day I think it can't last, it must turn. But no it stays steady even during the night, and if you don't agree that's remarkable, I'll sail right by Paphos for Crete."

Horatius smiled, Paphos was his home. He knew they needed to take on some more provisions as the next leg could take weeks, and if they encountered strong westerlies, they would have to turn north for Lycia and work a long passage across the Aegean islands.

"Then you would miss out on some of the best wine in the world," he said, which he knew Ephraim would never contemplate. "What is remarkable is how the passengers are handling the voyage, as the women and Simon have never been at sea before. Not a hint of sea sickness, no boredom or irritableness, and you so convinced that women and boats don't mix."

"Well these aren't ordinary women, and young Simon is a sailor if ever I saw one." Ephraim made a small adjustment to the two steer boards, which he had ingeniously lashed so that they operated in unison by the movement of one tiller.

He became aware of the scrutiny of the blue eyes of the boy, who so resembled his father. Only his olive complexion attested to his Jewish mother.

"What's over there?" he asked, pointing at the hills in the far distance.

"That's Cyprus, and you'll be walking around a grand city instead of telling stories in your cabin tonight!" exulted Horatius, and both men grinned as the boy whooped excitedly and rushed off to tell everyone the news. This brought them all on deck, where they watched the progress along the coast clustered around the mast.

"No story tonight," said Simon, then with a plea in his voice, "tell Simon a story now."

"Come on, Horatius, we're arriving at your city. Tell us a story about Cyprus," urged Ephraim, and everyone moved aft to sit at the steersman's feet, as it was now Horatius' watch at the helm. Even Joab, after a long look around from the bow deserted his post and moved aft, such was the hold that story-telling now had over all on board.

"From when I was a boy of Simon's age I used to look after one of our flocks of goats in the foothills outside the town of Paphos, which lies just around that headland."

He went on to describe the day to day duties of finding them grazing and herding them into the stone walled pen at night, which his father always came to make secure before taking him home for supper.

"Did you have to fight lions, or wolves or bears, like King David?" asked Simon hopefully.

"No, but there were hyenas and wolves and wild cats and eagles. All of these could seize a young kid, especially if the mother was trying to look after twins. I would drive them off with stones from my sling."

"Just like King David," breathed Simon, his eyes gleaming excitedly.

"Then one morning we awoke to see a vast troop galley anchored off shore. We all took to the hills as the Romans rampaged through the region seizing everything they needed. I scattered the herd by shying small stones at them, but they kept regrouping just out of range, and then suddenly a troop of soldiers were seizing the fattest kids and hoisting them over their shoulders. I let loose a large stone and knocked the helmet off the leader, so they seized me and led me away with their booty.

"On board their troopship there was a centurion named Maximus. He gave me two choices, agree to serve ten years in his brigade with the other Cypriot slingers or be his slave. So I became conscripted as an auxiliary in the Roman army."

As he fell silent a few protesting voices expressed their dismay at his treatment but Marc interjected.

"I wasn't given such a choice - it was slavery for me. If I hadn't encountered my father I might be slaving away in one of your copper mines."

Horatius asserted quickly, "Instead of which we have fought in some notable battles, seen all sorts of wonderful things, and here we are embarked on a venture of great excitement and mystery under the guidance of God himself. I wouldn't change one thing in my life," and he gave all his listeners a beaming smile.

That night they spent a little while walking the streets of the town, but such was the hospitality thrust upon them when they came to Horatius' family home, they saw nothing further of Paphos that day. A feast was prepared and all the surrounding kinsfolk summoned to meet the illustrious visitors.

Inevitably there were some who had embraced this new religion that was sweeping across the eastern part of the Great Sea, and news of the significance of the three Marys brought a great crowd to the gates of the house. Just recounting the events that had stood out momentously in the brief ministry of Jesus occupied many hours, and all were enthralled when his mother talked of his boyhood and the unique way he had with all around him.

"Even the animals were at one with him. Birds would take crumbs from his hands and mice from the fields would burrow up the arms of his tunic and you could see them gliding across his shoulders before emerging on the other side. All the time he would chuckle merrily, gleefully watching his entranced friends."

Ephraim leaned over towards Simon.

"We've a few mice live down in the hold of the boat, Simon. You can try and coax them to run up your sleeve, or up mummy's!" he added, his eyes twinkling as he watched her involuntary shudder.

Mary continued, "He enjoyed playing with the other children, but also he loved studying the Torah with the scribes and the elders. He would learn great sections off by heart. The fables and legends of the Aggadah always held him, especially when a skilful rabbi would elaborate on the underlying meaning. It wasn't unknown for him to question and make his own suggestions. Many times I've heard teachers express their amazement at the wisdom that could come from one so young."

Tiredness eventually caused the crowd to disperse, and the travellers were persuaded to sleep with their hosts that night.

Although pressed to stay a few days further, Mary wished to continue while the winds were so favourable. Accordingly after a morning re-provisioning, the next dusk saw the island disappearing on the far horizon, only a mixture of joyful memories lingering, as they headed serenely over the waves, shimmering gold in the last plunge of the burnished sun.

That night was to be forever engraved in the memory of Brutus. He and Mary Magdalene were watching the fast fading purples and mauves streaking the soft banks of cloud beckoning them on. Mary tightened her grip on his upper arm and putting her lips close to his ear whispered, "Beloved, I'm carrying our child."

As the clouds cavorted in a cart-wheeling, maelstrom of colour, and his heart compacted into a kernel of inexpressible adoration, Brutus slipped to his knees so that his face could lie wonderingly against her belly. He clasped her to him, hardly trusting to allow himself to speak the unspeakable, aware of the inadequacy of any words. Eventually he looked up and saw her dark moist eyes lustrous with tears of joy. He rose and drawing her to him buried his face in the folds of her loosened hair, seeking by submerging himself in her to commune with that incarnate love in her womb.

That night was also to be engraved in the mind of Simon, for they struck a whale. It was in the early hours of the morning, when only a thin crescent of a moon was hanging suspended over a sea as blue black as the star filled sky surmounting it. The motion of the boat was arrested with a jolt, throwing the sleeping passengers against the forward bulkheads, and an inattentive Livy against the high-raking prow of the ship, which was all but dismasted.

As everyone rushed on deck a fountain of water shot into the air forward, and the boat was enveloped in a moist fog into which was distilled the olfactory essence of every sea creature that had ever existed. As the fog cleared, the boat lurched first to one side and then the other, and then settled evenly to be overhung by the curved flared tail fin, its span as great as that of the sail hanging from the spar. As it flipped forward it was drawn spectacularly into the seething sea, and everyone crowded to the gunwales peering anxiously for any sign of its reemergence. Ephraim put an arm around the excited boy.

"You've just seen your first whale!" he said, and watched his eyes grow proportionate to his amazement.

"A whale," breathed Simon, mouthing the word as though he could still taste it on the moist salty air.

"Leviathan," murmured Mary Magdalene, and mother Mary crossed herself, as though aware that this encounter with the malign omen was a threat to them all.

The boat surged through the waves responding to the freshening wind, leaping each wave as though anxious to put as much distance as possible from the encounter. The white spume from each crest blew forward as though reluctant to be left behind by the speeding boat.

"Shorten sail," roared Ephraim, suddenly aware of how loudly he had to shout to be heard over the wind.

Each man moved to one of the half dozen ropes secured to the gunwale on the starboard side. In unison they threw their weight and watched the loose foot of the sail to which each rope was sewn, ruckle up in folds. Horatius then lowered the long spar half way down the mast, and as though by magic the worse of the pitching and rolling abated. A creaming crest of a wave swept over the stern engulfing the helmsmen and soaking everyone on deck.

"All passengers into the hold and lie on the boards. Fasten all hatches and everything on deck!"

The last thing the fearful passengers saw as they tumbled below decks was Horatius lashing Ephraim to the stern post.

Inside the noise of the rushing water on the hull, but a few inches away, was magnified into a continuous roar over which normal conversation was impossible. The darkness was absolute, the lamp having been thrown from its fastening, and all they could do was clutch each other where they lay and pray.

Some hours later, although nobody was aware of time in the complete dark, the hatch cover was removed and the head of Ephraim could be seen silhouetted against the square of yellowish, sullen light. The howling of the wind through the open hatchway carried his words away unheard, as Brutus pulled himself upright and moved to the opening. He returned with a line he handed to Marc.

"Secure this around the boy and we can all go on deck for a while," and then he passed the same message on to each in turn.

Mary nodded her acknowledgement and stood beside her anxious husband, until he pulled himself through the opening onto the heaving deck. Two lines had already been secured the length of the boat, one each side of the hatchway. This gave him a hold from which he could reach down a free hand and help up Mary and then Marc, followed by the anxious mother and boy.

The spar of the sail was lashed to the deck and they were running on bare poles, Horatius trimming the ship so that each mountainous wave rising astern passed safely, lifting the boat and surfing it forward in a turmoil of white foam. One miscalculation so that the crest broke slightly on one side, and the ship would have skewed off, losing all way and foundering in the deep trough. He was grinning in exaltation, as though relishing the challenge, and once again Brutus rejoiced at having him at his side in danger.

They moved up to the mast, and huddled there under the lowering, cloud-filled, yellow sky. Water was no longer sweeping the deck, although the occasional storm driven crest of a wave would stream spume along its length, drenching them with its warm spray. Nobody had any desire for food and a skin of water met their only need until they were forced back into the hold by the storm worsening, and the waves again threatening to sweep them overboard.

How the crew endured the next three days, was a constant amazement to the passengers on the rare occasion they were allowed on deck.

That it was taking its toll was evidenced when a semi-conscious Joab was lowered through the hatch, and lay shivering and mumbling incoherently on the boards. At least there was a little light from the restored oil lamp, and his white clammy look suggested he was near death from exposure. Two of the Marys lay embracing him one each side, and cloaks and sacks were piled on his body and his limbs massaged constantly, while Mary Magdalene prayed with all the intensity that had saved the boys from drowning years before.

Marc volunteered to take Joab's place, and the eight hours he endured until the wind died convinced him he would never be a sailor.

The cessation of the wind was eerie, dying from a full storm to nothing in a matter of minutes, but the waves continued, slate grey and sullen, and as though resentful of being cheated, rolled the boat mercilessly now there was no way on her. Ephraim lashed the tiller and for the first time in his life was violently seasick, as was every living soul aboard that unmanageable bit of flotsam on that vast heaving ocean.

The gradual easing of the waves allowed some respite to the crew, who lay exhausted by both fatigue and sickness. Miriam and Mary Magdalene were the first to recover and busied themselves tending to their less fortunate companions. Eventually all motion of the water ceased and they lay unmoving, on a completely flat sea under a quarter moon and the star filled sky.

For the first time they became aware of their empty stomachs and a charcoal fire was lit in the galley and the provisions raided for anything edible. Joab had recovered and joined everyone on deck where mother Mary led a short but heartfelt prayer of thanksgiving.

As though to emphasise their good fortune they could see the waters around them littered over a vast area with the wreckage of a less fortunate vessel. A few motionless bodies lay scattered among the debris beyond any hope of resuscitation. Mary Magdalene insisted they sweep the *Dolphin* to the nearest, but it was clear the body had been immersed too long in those merciless waters.

Everyone's sadness was dispelled by the arrival of steaming plates of lentils and vegetables that were produced by the women, and soon the nourishment banished their exhaustion.

"We would be better rowing than just lying at the mercy of this swell," said Ephraim authoritatively, and the crew took their places at the long oars.

"Don't let that boy row," Mary insisted pointing at Joab who was still reeling, and Brutus took his place at the sweep, while the women led him below to recover.

Taking his bearing from the moon and stars, Ephraim set a steady pace they would be able to sustain for many hours. A brilliant sunrise saw them carving a rose red wake across the smooth sea, and a revived Joab and Marc relieved the most exhausted rowers, establishing the pattern of allowing two to rest in rotation that was to prevail there after.

So they continued mile after mile, hour after hour and as the sun rose higher they rigged the sail as a canopy, under which all could find shade without interrupting the rowing, which only ceased briefly at meal times.

Simon became a little fractious until Miriam involved him with a stylus and a waxed slate, and the two of them became totally absorbed for some hours.

At dusk when the meal was ready and the rowing suspended, Miriam said, "Simon has a poem he wishes to recite!"

Everyone fell silent as Marc lifted him to stand on a bale, and no longer needing the tablet as he had memorized his poem, he began.

"The Dolphin ran into a whale,
That dived with a flip of its tail.

The night wind turned into a gale
Captain Ephraim cried, down with the sail.
He headed us west without fail,
With him at the helm we'll prevail.

There was stunned silence as all looked at the little boy with amazement, and he looked at his mummy for encouragement. She silently mouthed something at him, and losing his puzzled look he called out gleefully, "Three cheers for Captain Ephraim!"

The cheers rang out mixed with applause, and it was immediately perceptible how much the mood had lightened and Simon basked at the centre of unfeigned admiration.

"What a remarkable little poet you are," affirmed Ephraim, and everyone laughed as Simon replied magnanimously, "Mummy helped me a bit."

"Just like his father," mused Miriam half to herself.

That night they sailed in the company of dolphins, and Simon insisted on hearing twice the full saga of how the *Dolphin* had escaped from the *Hermes*. The only difference between the two renditions was that the second time he knew what was coming next, and fairly burst with excitement as each climax approached. His excitement was contagious, and the albatross flying overhead momentarily hesitated in the steady majestic beat of its wings as the roar soared heavenwards.

For five breathless days they continued their journey, only the sweep of their oars causing the slightest disturbance of the glass smooth sea. Then as Ephraim stared for the last time that day westward into the sinking sun, he saw the ripples coming towards them along a path of burnished gold. His raised face felt the breeze on his cheek as the *Dolphin* responded to the caress with a gentle curtsy.

"A wind," he called, "a head wind from the west! Ship your oars. Ready the sail!" and turning he saw four disbelieving faces regarding him, all etched with fatigue and resignation, resigned to sweeping a sea of liquid glass for the rest of their lives.

The awning over their heads flapped as the breeze lifted its leading edge, and then like reprieved men they were galvanized into action. No longer faced with four hours rowing and two hours rest unceasingly, they stowed their sweeps and hoisted the sail and as it filled, tipping the boat to starboard and gaining way in a more northerly direction, let out a concerted cheer that brought everyone on deck.

"Where do you reckon us to be?" asked Brutus, concerned they had not seen land for nigh on ten days.

"I would put us two hundred miles from Crete at a very rough guess. Now we are on a more northerly course we must keep a sharp lookout for land fall, so we'll post two lookouts throughout the night."

"We will help with watches," volunteered Marc eagerly, with Brutus' full approval.

They didn't make landfall that night, and the sun was high overhead when the youthful eyes of Joab first glimpsed the white, snow-covered crest, only slightly more substantial than the white cloud wreathed around it.

"Land ho!" he called, excitedly pointing to the left of their heading.

Ephraim and Horatius conferred briefly, then the Captain ended all their speculation.

"We both think it's the Dictaean mountains on Crete. We'll bear off for three or four hours to clear the eastern end of the island if we're right."

"If you're right Ephraim that will be incredible navigation on your part, and we're all indebted to you," said the centurion, confidence exuding from his face.

"It will be more by luck than judgment!" responded Ephraim, only to be gently rebuked by Mary.

"Bear in mind that the wind over the waters is the breath of God, captain, and that it will carry us to our ultimate destination."

Looking contrite Ephraim bowed submissively.

"Wherever that might be? If it's western Gaul we are about one third of the way to Massilia."

He failed to add his unworthy thoughts of what the wind would have done to the boat, if Horatius and he hadn't wrestled at the helm to counter its destructive threat. He did express such thoughts to Horatius later as he stood down from his watch, but his mate rebuked him more strongly than Mary would have.

"God could only let loose such a wind to speed our distinguished passenger to her destination, in the knowledge that you and I were able to control the boat. It's probably your questioning and lack of faith, that made him arrest the wind to show us how far we would have got on our own."

They both looked at their calloused hands, and Ephraim realizing he was on a hiding to nothing and fearful of tempting providence further, declined to reply.

When in the late afternoon they were in the lee of the island and had to use their oars to sweep them to the ancient port of Mochlos, Ephraim was amused to see Horatius looking at him as though it was his fault.

The delight everyone felt at feeling solid rock under their feet contributed to their euphoria, and even this run-down, little quay and the cluster of stone built houses around it seemed inviting and full of promise. Not that it lived up to their expectations as now it boasted but a few small fishing boats and no real prospect of provisioning.

"We will follow the coast to the port of Amnisos which lies at the foot of the ruins of the palace of King Minos, who was once the mightiest king in all these seas!" said Ephraim, thereby exciting the imagination of Simon who demanded to know much more.

"It was more than a thousand years ago that Minos was king of the powerful Cretan states, which had palaces all over this island. Then the mightiest of earth-quakes shattered them all and brought a huge wave that engulfed everything, killing all the lords and nobles, all the farmers and soldiers and smashing their great fleet of galleys. Now they all lie in ruins, end of story."

Simon wasn't prepared to let it rest at that so Ephraim promised to take him to the ruins of the palace, as they would be spending a few days at Amnisos.

Accepting that nothing further was to be gained from Ephraim, Simon switched his efforts to Miriam and asked, nay pleaded, for the story of Jonah. Miriam felt more inclined to rest after such a passage and tried to dismiss him.

"Another day dearest, mummy's tired."

"Captain Ephraim hasn't heard it, mummy."

Turning to the sailors he said, "It's all about storms and being thrown overboard and swallowed by a whale. You would like to hear it wouldn't you?"

287

"Most certainly," they all affirmed, and Ephraim added,

"Why it sounds like what nearly happened on board the *Dolphin*."

"Who did you think to throw overboard?" asked Simon, his eyes wide open with wonder.

"Why the only one too small to man an oar of course!" and Simon ran to hide behind his mother.

"You win, you little rascal," relented Miriam and began.

"It's a story with a moral. Jonah was a prophet who was called by God to go to Nineva and tell the pagans living there, how much they had displeased God. Jonah would happily have gone if he had felt certain that God was going to punish them, but he rather thought God was too forgiving, and as soon as they repented he would leave them alone. So he decided to leave them to stew in their wickedness, but to escape the wrath of God himself he boarded a boat at Joppa sailing to Tarsus."

That Ephraim had been the port captain of Joppa caused much speculation and amusement among the audience before they allowed Miriam to continue. "Well the Lord sent a great storm, and so afraid were the mariners of sinking they threw everything they could over the side to lighten ship. Searching in the hold for anything to jettison the captain found Jonah fast asleep. 'Get up' he insisted, 'and pray to your God to save us.'

"But the crew thought someone must have displeased God, and decided they would draw lots to see who he was, and then throw him overboard to placate the Almighty. Of course the lot fell on Jonah, and he admitted it was he who God was displeased with and the storm would cease as soon as they had got rid of him.

"The mariners were reluctant to throw Jonah into the waves, and thought they would see what would happen if they just dangled him over the side up to his waist. Sure enough the storm stopped and they decided to leave him dangling until they reached port.

"But the Lord was vexed and got some sea creatures to help him. An octopus wrapped its tentacles around his legs and some crabs nibbled at his toes. He pleaded to be pulled back on board and the sailors did so from compassion, but immediately the storm resumed more violently than ever, so they had no alternative but to cast him completely into the sea.

"A great whale swallowed him whole and he lived in its cavernous belly for three days. Then the whale told him that Leviathan, the greatest monster of the deep, was going to swallow them both, but Jonah answered him, 'He is the devil and our Lord will vanquish him, take me to him.'

"So Jonah confronted Leviathan and told him that in days to come he, Jonah, would catch him and drag him from the sea, and feed his flesh to the righteous, in paradise.

"Leviathan took fright and swam away, and the whale in gratitude for Jonah's intervention, swam to shore and spewed him out onto the dry land, exactly where he would have landed for Nineva had he heeded God's original command."

With a sigh of contentment Simon fell fast asleep on Marc's lap, and he awoke when they were well on their way to Amnisos and the ruined palace of Knossos.

The sun was burning off the morning mist as the party of men ascended the limestone cliff. Steps had been hewn into the cliff face a thousand years before and the constant train of mules plying between the palace and the port had trodden a deep hollow in each step. Now, filled with debris, they were habitat to shrub or bush that greatly impeded their climb, so all were sweating and breathless when they tumbled on the plateau, and viewed the ruined palace beckoning in the distance, with the snowcapped mountain looming behind. Before them the rock-strewn slope was festooned with wild flowers, not yet scorched by the heat of the day.

Marc swung Simon on to his shoulders as Ephraim broke a trail through the slabs of stone, scattered as by some giant. Half way to the palace a gully cut at right angles across the path and two rough-hewn planks were their sole means of crossing.

Marc was relieved to step off on the far side and as he turned to watch Horatius and Levi bringing up the rear, a movement in the dense undergrowth caught his eye, and his companions joined in scrutinizing the area before they resumed their climb. The occasional flock of partridge or grouse took fright, beating into the air and calling their protest. Nothing else moved.

A cave off to the left drew them, and in an alcove near the entrance, freshly scattered petals adorned the head and bared breasts of some unknown goddess. Standing to Simon's height the statue held in each hand a writhing snake.

"Well someone has been here before us," remarked Ephraim, "probably some goat herd seeking pasture up on the plateau."

The sound of trickling water drew them into the gloomy interior where a natural spring welling from a cleft in the wall gave them needed refreshment.

Resuming their ascent of a wide staircase balustraded to right and left they suddenly spilled onto a wide terrace, fronting a stupendous pile of tumbled stone blocks where once had stood the royal apartments.

It was from these cavernous ruins that Marc first saw some movement and instinctively his hand fell on his sword hilt. The others had seen it too, and they stood stock still as the phalanx of ghastly figures moved slowly out to stand silently watching them. They were of both sexes, although it was difficult to tell man from women as all had long dishevelled hair and wore rent rags. Many staggered on their feet holding on to their neighbour and the faces staring at them were hideous distortions, many lacking eyebrows, some without noses or covered with ulcerating nodules and scabs.

"Lepers," breathed Marc with an involuntary shudder, and he saw the fear in the faces of his companions whose instinct was to turn and run.

"Don't panic!" he said urgently, "they aren't threatening us but may expect alms and luckily I have my purse. Let's go quickly but don't run."

A voice wheezing and hoarse called out.

"Do you bring us alms for the love of God?"

"No, we didn't know you were here!" called Marc, reaching into his purse and moving to place its contents on a stone. "Take all of this, you are welcome, it will buy you much food."

"Take it with you to the shop of Eliphaz in Amnisos, he will load up a mule with provisions for us. Go quickly!"

None of them needed the slightest urging, but Marc was intrigued as to why the man had urged them to make haste. As they approached the plank bridge he saw three armed men barring their path, all exhibiting the early manifestations of the disease without having progressed to the crippling deformity of those they had left behind.

"We will let you pass when you have given to us all you possess, purse, money, jewellery, swords, everything!"

The leader who made these demands was greedily assessing their worth, and Marc was drawing his sword, when he saw a fourth man on the far side who had removed one of the planks to his side of the deep gully, and was threatening to haul back the other.

Simon caught the menace in the situation and started to cry.

"Do as I say and we will not detain you, but resist and you will have no choice but to join our community."

"I offered all my money to those at the ruined palace, but they told me to buy provisions at the shop of Eliphaz in the port. If you let us pass to our ship, I promise on oath to buy twice as much and send it up to you."

Marc had little hope that this would succeed but he was not going to surrender his sword and be at their mercy.

The man's eyes gleamed greedily,

"You go to the ship and fetch all you possess and bring it here yourself," he said, and as the relief showed on Marc's face and he removed his hand from the hilt, the leper added, "and then you will be allowed to take the boy, who you will leave with us while you're gone!"

Enraged, Marc drew his sword as the man watching across the gully pulled the plank, trapping them on that disease-infested plateau. Ephraim put a restraining hand on Marc's arm, alarmed by the burning anger in his eyes, and fearing he would strike out without thinking of the consequences.

"Let me stay as your hostage," he called. "I'm the captain of the ship and there are two hundred denarii on board to ransom me. Let the boy stay with his father."

"You may not be worth ransoming, old man," sneered the leper, "I think we will hold on to the boy."

"Let them pass, Pekah, and you other men," came the hoarse voice of the leper who had urged them to go quickly, and turning the prisoners saw he had stolen up behind them.

"Go back and don't interfere. This is not your concern!" snarled Pekah angrily.

"It is the concern of all of us. Last time you brought great trouble on our community by your robbery. If you persist you will pay with your life."

Pekah smiled malevolently,

"With two hundred denarii we will not stay to account to you old fool."

Ephraim paced up and down indecisively.

"I've said I will stay instead of the boy, are you not going to agree?" he called, greatly distressed and emphasizing his words with dramatic gestures of both his arms.

"Never. Only the boy will do as our hostage!"

As Pekah's defiance rang out, Ephraim's skillfully thrown dagger impaled his throat, his last word choking on the blood gurgling from his mouth, the surprised look staying on his face as he struck the ground. Marc leapt with raised sword, parried the blow aimed at him and stabbed his assailant in the stomach, while the third man dropped his sword and jumped into the deep gully.

Bewildered and fearful, Marc scooped his crying son into his arms, not aware of any escape from this hellish hole into which he had precipitated them.

He looked up despairingly to Ephraim and could not understand the smile on his face, his eyes fixed through and behind him. Marc's heart momentarily stopped as he turned and his eyes fell on the stern face of Brutus, his sword poised over the quaking leper who was inching the first of the planks back across the gap. Only when both of them were in position did Brutus relax as he prodded the shaking man across.

"What shall I do with this scum?" he asked.

"Leave him with us, he won't be any further trouble now Pekah's dead. It's hard for you to understand, how resentful we who have leprosy feel towards you who are free of it. When it is compounded, by seeing your evident wealth compared with our abject poverty, it can push the weaker of us into doing stupid things. We crave your forgiveness," pleaded their anxious leader, moving to the edge of the gully from where they could peer down into its gloom, at the dazed man looking up from the ledge where his fall had been arrested.

"We can deal with him. My fear is for the reprisals that will befall us when they hear of what happened today in Amnisos."

"They will not hear a word of what passed from us," Brutus assured him, "we would not wish to add to your suffering, but I think you should put up a sign so that travellers do not unwittingly stumble into your refuge."

"How can we be sure you will receive the provisions from Eliphaz?" asked Marc dubiously.

"Because he is my brother, and he looks after my wife!" The poignancy of that simple utterance was not lost on his listeners, and it was a subdued group who returned that day to the boat.

"Thank God Brutus was with us at the Synagogue. I've never seen such alarm on anyone's face as those women, when he told them you were looking at the ruins of Minos' palace. And when they cried out, 'but that's a leper colony,' Miriam felt faint and I was nearly sick with fear."

Mother Mary was retelling them from her viewpoint, what Brutus had explained during their descent.

"I wished I had wings, or the winged horse Pegasus, and knowing speed was essential bade the women not to leave the synagogue until we returned. I've never run so fast in my life, and when I rounded a clump of bushes and saw your stand off with those robbers, and the plank bridge dismantled, I concealed myself and crept up stealthily on my man. Ephraim saw me and created quite a diversion until I was in position, and then he was able to get in such an effective first strike. You know the rest."

"So the ring-leader and one of the gang are dead, and the others won't be any further trouble so I guess it has ended better than it might have," said Miriam, who hadn't released Simon from her grasp since they had been reunited.

"I'm not sure it might not have been turned to better advantage. I really feel concern for that leader and all those hideously deformed people abandoned to eke out their wretched lives amongst those ruins. I feel we ought to have done more," said Brutus, a frown creasing his brow, "but there is nothing one can do, it's so incurable!"

"What's incurable mean, mummy?"

"It means it can't be made better darling," said Miriam with a shudder at the thought of how close they had been to the contagion.

"Didn't Jesus make lepers better?"

"Yes darling but he isn't here!"

The room had suddenly become charged and Mary Magdalene rushed over and embraced Simon.

"Out of the mouths of babes, oh bless you child! How can we be so blind? Jesus is here! I was the first to see him after his resurrection and it's unforgivable that I should be so blind."

She looked at Mother Mary with an ecstatic smile,

"Let us go to the palace and tell these poor people of Jesus and how he wasn't afraid to touch lepers and how he healed them. It would be wrong not to take his message of salvation to them for fear of their dreadful disease. That would truly be cowardly of us!"

"Go back there! Amongst them?" Brutus threw up his arms in mock dismay knowing that any protestation of his was as whistling at the wind.

"I don't think we will go if you don't mind," said Miriam emphatically.

"Simon want to go, mummy," said the little boy his face screwing up as he fought to keep back his tears.

"I think we should all go," said Marc, "even you, or rather especially you, Ephraim," although the captain was shaking his head in disbelief.

"Someone has to stay with the boat," he protested.

"I'll stay!" said Levi.

"You're marooned on the next lion infested island we pass, Levi, for insubordination."

"Simon wants room on lion vested island with Levi," and the little boy's plea broke the somber atmosphere as they all joined in the laughter.

Quite a procession breasted the cliff top and great was the variation in the mood of the climbers.

Although short of breath from the exertion, the three Marys were sustained by an exultation that was close to ecstasy.

Anna Eliphaz, leading a laden donkey, was fearful of how the ravages of the disease would have altered her husband in the two months since she had last seen him.

Miriam, leading a second donkey with Simon proudly astride it, felt like Daniel being thrust into the lion's den.

Brutus conferring with Horatius, let slip that inexplicably he felt something momentous lay ahead, although he had no idea what.

Ephraim plodding reluctantly at the rear, kept fingering the dagger in his belt as though it was a talisman against the evil eye.

Spotting the cave they made their way there and the women were intrigued by the goddess, and the fact that it was still a shrine to some locals.

Anna said, "Many women from the town still come up here and make an offering to her, if they are barren, or seeking the attention of an indifferent young man, or going on a journey. Probably she has heard the same petitions over a thousand years."

"It has sufficed all this time but the new way of my son will sweep it all into history!" exclaimed Mother Mary.

They moved on, and as they stepped onto the terrace found the assembled community of lepers anticipating them.

Eliphaz held up his hand, both in greeting and at the same time arresting them.

"Greetings, but come no further in case the contagion is in the very stone we walk. We knew you would keep your promise but why have you honoured us by all of you making so much effort?"

"Because the boy revealed a truth to us that we hid from ourselves under a cloak of fear," said Mary Magdalene, in her husky rich voice.

"And what is this truth that you wish to share with us?"

"That we are all children of the one God. And so whether leper or whole we are brothers and sisters in one family."

"You talk of the God of the Hebrews, but he is not a God to be shared; his countenance shines only on the circumcised."

"No longer. Listen to Mother Mary here. Her first born, Jesus, is the long awaited Messiah, and before he was crucified he went throughout Palestine talking of the kingdom of God, driving out devils and curing the sick. He laid his hands on the lepers, and they became clean."

There was a great agitation among the listeners, many of whom were openly weeping and Eliphaz said angrily.

"Why tell us of this. Your own words tell us he was crucified."

"He was. I was the centurion who crucified him and thrust my spear into his heart to be sure he was dead!"

"I carried the spear as servant of the centurion!"

"I ministered to him when he fell on the way to the cross. My tears fell on his face as he lay under the burden!"

"We all stood at the base of the cross as the sky darkened and the heavens were rent with God's lightning, and the Temple shaken to its foundations!"

The lepers had clustered together, reeling under each testimony as though to a succession of physical blows. Eliphaz held both hands over the holes where once his ears had been and sank on his knees.

He raised his eyes imploringly to Mary Magdalene and cried out,

"Torture us no more I beseech you. Tell us no more of this Roman wickedness, we cannot bear more suffering!"

"Let me end your suffering and offer you hope. I was the first to see him on the third day, when he had conquered death and broken free of the tomb. He spoke to me, called me by my name and told me to tell his disciples that they were to await his coming. He spent many weeks guiding them in their role of spreading his message throughout the world. Now he has gone to his father in Heaven, but he has sent the Holy Spirit to guide his church on earth. It is this Holy Spirit speaking through this boy that has led us to you. Now listen to Mother Mary."

The Magdalene's eyes were shining, moist with tears of joy that recollection of her unique privilege always provoked.

Interest and anticipation now gripped every listener, and even their ravished faces revealed that hope is indomitable no matter what the affliction. The hours sped by and some of the food was shared between them. There was wonder when Mary spoke of the miraculous cure of the ten lepers, and dismay that only one of those cured sought out Jesus afterwards to give him thanks.

"Have the healing miracles ceased with Jesus ascending to heaven?" asked a hesitant young woman, who was evidently carrying her unborn child.

"What is your name, daughter?" asked Mary.

"Ruth."

"No Ruth, many miracles of healing are happening through the Holy Spirit and the laying on of hands by the disciples."

"But not by you?"

"No Ruth, regrettably not one of us has this gift."

A long silence followed this somber answer, and Eliphaz had his eyes closed and his hands raised as though in supplication.

Suddenly he exclaimed, "Forgive me but I hear a voice telling me you may have this gift without knowing it."

This electrifying challenge seized everyone's attention, and Mary beseeched him to explain his meaning.

"Well, have you observed there are many children here?"

Mary nodded but remained silent.

"Even among us afflicted as we are, love sometimes blossoms between man and women and as you can see with Ruth, a new life springs from that love. When her baby is born it will be free of the affliction, perfect in every way. It is so for the first few years and only then does it steal in like a thief in the night, with an inevitability that is soul destroying."

Everyone hung on his next words, as they knew they were witnessing the working of the Holy Spirit.

"Would your church endow a house for these children, that at the edge of town they can grow up free of any contamination, cared for by a substitute mother, maybe a widow, while their parents watch them from afar and rejoice in their wholeness."

The stunned silence that followed this plea was followed first by Mary Magdalene and then the other women falling on their knees and giving praise to heaven. All followed without exception, Ephraim being the last, but no less sincere for all his dilatoriness.

Aware of the presence of the Holy Spirit, Mary Magdalene avowed that she would baptize all who sought it. She led them to the cave of the goddess and there cupping water from the spring, baptized twenty-eight souls. The last to receive it was Ephraim.

"Have you baptized before?" Mother Mary asked as they descended.

"No, but I felt it to be right, as your son honoured me uniquely for a purpose. Previously there have always been men so one would naturally leave it to them!"

"Yes, there's no point in upsetting them unnecessarily. I wonder what Peter would say."

"I ask what Jesus has to say, and I still can hear his warm kind voice so full of compassion. He would not have denied those unfortunates this blessing."

Anna pointed out a house on the outskirts of the town.

"That is for renting and very reasonable. It could house eight children easily. I would be happy to be their foster mother for just the room and my keep, and so free my brother-in-law from providing for me."

"Then I'll give you a letter of credit for one year's rent. It's drawn against the Tyre Merchants Trading Federation and they have an office in Massilia. I'll arrange for my brother to see that the next ten years rental are paid, and then we can review the arrangement."

Miriam's offer was received with a warm smile from Anna, appreciative of both her decisiveness and her generosity.

Likewise when they had returned to the ship, and were discussing the many wonders of the day, Mother Mary said, "It was lovely to see their faces when Simon gave them the donkey. Those children couldn't believe we were leaving it with them. We will all have some warm memories of Crete to carry with us on our travels. I'm glad we've been able to leave some behind."

It was some weeks before they were in port again. The wind held steady from the south-west and they reached ever westward until they passed through the Straights of Messina between Italy and Sicily. They were now on the corn supply route from Alexandria to Rome, and they passed or were passed by many of the vast grain galleys swept along by hundreds of slaves banked row above row.

Twice they were stopped and had to heave to while a party boarded them. Brutus' letter of commendation from Danius Gallerius always stood them in good stead and they were allowed to proceed. The second time they were able to buy some fresh provisions as the galley had but shortly left Rhegiem, at the very tip of the toe of Italy.

As though the vast leg that protruded into and split the great sea in two, had likewise divided the waters and the vault over them, the whole pattern of the winds changed dramatically.

Each day dawned windless, the sea a tranquil pond reflecting the blue of the heavens and the white tenuous cloud, or if they were close inshore the rugged browns and ochres of the sun-beaten cliffs.

They would then swim in the warm waters, the length of the boat separating the men from the women, only Simon being permitted to cross that imaginary line

Ephraim had initiated what had now become ritualized, when they had descended from the palace of Knossos. Suspecting contamination in every fibre of his clothing and pore of his skin, he had leapt into the sea to everyone's consternation and removing every garment he had splashed and cavorted, and finally reached up a hand to Brutus to help him up on to the quay. The women were modestly averting their eyes and about to hurry ahead as Brutus naively offered his hand, only to find to his disbelief that when clasped Ephraim thrust with his feet on the quay jerking the centurion in with him. Simon needed no second bidding to leap in too, and as he could barely swim Marc felt obliged to plunge in as well.

The three Marys wondering if this communal bathing was the final urging of the spirit that had earlier led to the baptism in the cave, and aware of their proximity and time with the lepers, leapt in likewise. Miriam was the last to succumb, after Ephraim had ordered the crew into the sea or face banishment from their boat.

It was a joyful cleansing, so refreshingly reviving and so simple. Later it needed but a plea from Simon or a look shared between two of them to precipitate a reenactment, although it never quite achieved the immodest spontaneity of the first time.

Then as the land heated the sea breeze would start strengthening to a good wind, blowing them along the Tyrrhenian coast for six or more hours, before dying to a flat calm around dusk. Sometimes to find a more protected bay they would row an hour or two, or drop anchor and watch the flaming sunset to the west light up with unbelievable intensity the yellows, browns and greens of the pine clad mountains behind the narrow coastal plain.

Ephraim often looked westward wondering whether to use the oars and head for the southern end of Sardinia, but he knew that was a week's hard rowing, and one strong Libeccio blowing from the south-west could set them right back. He knew also as they neared Rome they could expect to pick up the more northerly Tramontana, sweeping down from the high Apennines, but that too might weaken, leaving them to fight a hard passage through the narrow straight between Corsica and Sardinia. He concluded it would be better to follow the coast as they were.

On the third evening as they lay at anchor with the precipitous cliffs making any landfall dangerous, a small fishing boat approached them from the north. Responding to their calls the boat came close, and the four oarsmen slipped their oars and sat looking at them silently.

"Is there a harbour and town over there?" Brutus asked in Latin, but the colloquial dialect in which the leader replied left him none the wiser. By gestures and the occasional half recognized word they were persuaded to follow, but to be on the safe side Ephraim coaxed them to swap Levi with one of their crew before they upped anchor and rowed towards the cliffs.

Rocks jutted out of the water and there was no channel marked as a cleft loomed out of the gloom into which the leading boat disappeared. The *Dolphin* followed into the gap where there was barely room to use the oars so close were the rock sides, and then they were through with a natural basin lying before them, tumbled stones forming a rough beach in front of a dozen, low houses.

As this was their first landing in weeks it generated a lot of excitement aboard the *Dolphin* and as such a ship had not called all summer, all the occupants of the houses driven by curiosity congregated on the beach.

This was a most informative meeting from which the travellers learnt that Emperor Claudius had expelled the Jews from Rome, and had resumed direct rule of Palestine following the death of Herod Agrippa.

The man making these pronouncements was Petrus, a merchant hoping to enship from Reggio for Alexandria.

"Who rules Palestine now?" asked Brutus wondering how it might affect the apostles and the church there.

"The governor is Cuspius Fadus. A hard man who will crack down on any dissent and impose necessary tax reforms."

"Have you news of the famine in Palestine?"

"It continues. That is my purpose in journeying to Alexandria, as my normal grain suppliers are diverting their corn to Caesarea, it's so lucrative."

That night they discussed the welcome they might get if they entered the cities. Had Claudius expelled the Jews from Neapolis as well as Rome?

"If we avoid the bigger cities and keep well away from Capri and the Emperor's summer palace, we shouldn't encounter trouble," argued Brutus.

"In two days we will be at the old city of Poseidonia where we should get a good idea of how the wind blows," said Ephraim and when he got some funny looks from the listeners, hastened to clarify, "the wind from the mouth of Claudius, not the wind from the mountains or from the sea."

"I don't know of this city of Poseidonia yet I know this province well?" queried Brutus.

"Poseidonia is its original Greek name, the city of Poseidon, the god of the sea and hence of sailors. You call this god Neptune and renamed the city Paestum."

"Ah well I know it. It lies at the mouth of a river and is little more than a village in a swamp. I was stationed there years ago and we were plagued by mosquitoes! A lot of our soldiers caught swamp fever, so they moved us from the fort near the shore up into the high hills behind. That was much better!"

"Then we will make our visits as brief as possible, the last thing we need on board is swamp fever, it's not much better than leprosy," and everyone agreed with the captain.

Brutus received an enthusiastic greeting from centurion Felix.

"You are a survivor against all odds, aren't you! I thought you were still basking in the glory of the victory at Dura-Europos."

"Oh news of that has reached here has it?"

"It most certainly has. All units had a feast day a month ago in celebration!"

"Then you will know the hero of that siege was Tribune Danius Galerius."

"He came through here last week with a veritable fleet of troop galleys, at least ten."

"Ten galleys! Why that's enough to move the whole legion."

"That's exactly what it was doing. First for a great victory parade before Claudius in Rome, then after a couple of weeks re-equipping, shipping for northern Gallia."

"The last time I saw you was at Damascus, at the inquiry into the near loss of the *Hermes*. What happened to you after that?"

Felix looked uncertain what to say and then squaring his shoulders and looking Brutus in the eye, he said, "After your speech I was moved to every unpleasant job in Palestine! Hunting down zealots at Qumrun, garrison duty at the city of salt, escort duty for the caravans coming north from Arabia!"

"You poor chap. What did I say to bring so much wrath on your head?" pleaded Brutus with evident dismay.

"You told the inquiry that I brought your attention to the treachery that was to deliver you into Herod's hands at Caesarea!"

"So you had both Pilate and Herod seeking revenge!"

He fell silent for some minutes then said, "I am sorry. Is there anything I can do to make amends?"

"No, it's all in the distant past now. Pilate's dead. His body was found in the Tiber a few years ago, suicide I believe! Herod Antipas is banished to Gallia! This is my last posting and I have a villa and a small estate in the hills, just inland a few miles."

He clapped his hands and an orderly hurried in.

"We will take refreshment on the terrace," he said, leading Brutus from his office onto a splendid balustraded area looking down a colonnaded avenue to the magnificent temple of Claudius. To the right was the jagged outline of the mountains, pine clad to the occasional snow capped peak; to the left, through the columns, the sea glittered to the far horizon, the *Dolphin* bobbing with half a dozen other boats in the small harbour.

"Idyllic isn't it!" he said, but with an irony in his tone that wasn't lost on the visitor, "except for the swamp fever. Sometimes I lie burning hot for days on end, and my servants must fan me continuously and cover me with damp towels until it abates. In the barracks it takes its toll, three men have died this year. It's better in the winter. But enough of my woes, is there any way I can assist you?"

Brutus produced his letter of commendation, which Felix read before saying, "It would carry more weight if it was from the governor, but I'll help wherever I can."

"Mostly information. I am escorting some important Jewish women to Gallia, and we have heard of the Jews being expelled from Rome."

"They have been by Claudius' edict, from Rome, from Napoli and Pompeii and from here!"

"Do you know why?"

"The old, old reason. They refuse to venerate the Emperor's statue in the Temple, or to swear allegiance. Also there's been a small rebellion led by a man Chresstus, a Jew, which was easily put down. But probably the most damning of all, they refuse to advance more money for an additional palace to be built on Capri unless they are given title as security. They had the temerity to tell Claudius that they needed more than his oath, as that would not be binding on his successor!"

"Ha, that would have been hard for Claudius to swallow. Thank you, we will avoid these places. Also I am out of funds, the last pension I received was at Dura-Europos over two months ago."

"I'll get the adjutant to authorize it by this evening. Tell me, these Jewish women, you're not delivering them to Herod in Gallia are you?"

"Hardly. I've not a particularly wise head on my shoulders, but I still think I might lose it altogether if I encounter the banished king."

Holding Mary close to him on the stern deck Brutus said, "I'm glad you stayed on board dearest. There is a lot of fever in the garrison and probably throughout the city. Here, at least you're away from those blood-sucking mosquitoes and I'm sure they have a lot to do with passing it from one man to another."

"I wouldn't expose our baby to that risk," and as though in agreement the baby jumped, and taking his hand Mary placed it on the swelling of her belly.

"I thought I felt some movement earlier but this is really definite. There it is again!" and Brutus' eyes lit up at that first communication from their child.

"I never thought to know this joy," breathed Mary, blinking back her tears as Brutus kissed them gently from each eye.

"Nor I. I never thought to have a child of my flesh or such a wonderful woman to bear it."

The sail suddenly began to flap. Levi ran to tighten it, but Ephraim's knowing eye had seen the wavelets coming from the north-east.

"Let her go, the wind's changing quickly. We'll bear off westward." As he put the helm over the sail filled on the broad reach and they surged forward under the freshening breeze rushing down from the far Alps, across the intervening plain and the Ligurian Sea, as though eager to propel them speedily to their destination. Four days it continued uninterrupted, and each helmsman rejoiced in the clean wake he left behind him.

"If this holds but two more days we will be in Massilia," exulted Ephraim as they left a group of three islands on their starboard bow and the high hills of the mainland beyond them.

They were quite close enough to see the boat running out of the gap between the most westerly pair of islands. It was slightly smaller than the *Dolphin*, an open boat with two masts, each with an ochre coloured square sail and two fore and aft triangular sails, which flapped idly as it ran down wind towards them.

As Ephraim altered his course away from the coast the other boat did likewise. Suspicion aroused, Ephraim called Brutus and together they watched the approaching vessel.

"Does this mean trouble?" asked Ephraim. "They seem determined to intercept us and follow my change of course."

"They wouldn't need all those men if they were fishing. I think they're pirates. Can we outrun them?"

"No, they are a fast boat, and with those loosed sails hauled tight would sail well upwind."

"Then we must arm ourselves for battle and see if they have a stomach for a fight."

Calling everyone in the hold, Brutus checked them from showing themselves and told them of his fears. His manner was calm but Mary recognized the excitement and elation that came to him with the promise of battle.

"We need every man to arm himself and be ready for when they try to board. Mary, can you take the helm and relieve Ephraim, while we see what weapons we can muster. The rest of you stay concealed as you will be a much more effective force if they are not expecting you."

Ephraim showed Mary Magdalene the course he wanted her to follow, and then went down into the hold with Horatius.

"Mother Mary, will you keep Simon safely down in the fore cabin?" said Brutus, and Mary nodded, and took the hand of the reluctant boy who protested that he wanted to fight.

The two Roman swords, three cutlasses and assorted knives and daggers they collected looked formidable, even more so as Marc proceeded to hone them to razor sharpness on a wet stone.

Mary passed the tiller to Levi and taking one of the staves that had cracked a few heads at Tyre many years previously, lashed a murderous looking kitchen knife to one end.

"Now I'll feel happier at the helm," she said, the steely glint in her eye belying any humour in her smile.

A discussion followed on whether to brandish all their weaponry in the chance of scaring them off, or to keep the element of surprise.

"They will probably think us easy pickings, a few rough sailors and soft merchants, so when they board they will be expecting little resistance." Brutus was speaking his thoughts aloud as he analyzed the situation. "They think there are only three men so let's keep the three they don't know of hidden.

"Can you show yourselves and look fearful as they approach, Mary and Miriam? If you brandish these long quant poles from each end of the ship and try and stop their boat coming alongside it will look like a gesture of desperation and the futility will lull them into overconfidence.

"They'll be expecting to overcome us easily, but if the rest of you stay concealed until they board, surprise will be total. When I call you on deck crawl from the hold to hide against the bulwarks on the side from which they are attacking. You will then be positioned to inflict fearful injury from where they're not expecting it. Give no quarter, slash and thrust until you are sure they are finished. Show no pity, as none of us can expect any from them!"

"Won't they see us lying against the bulwarks?" asked a white faced Joab.

"Not if you hug the deck. Our boat rides higher than theirs, and they're bound to overhaul us to windward if Mary holds us on this reach. They will have to leap up on to our rail and will be momentarily off balance. That's the moment you strike!"

He looked at Ephraim for approval of his plan and grinning with admiration the captain said, "I'll stay at the stern with you, Mary, as you may need help at the helm. You take the bows, centurion, and Levi, you stay amidships. To action stations then!" and Ephraim moved aft swinging his cutlass in anticipation.

From the deck they watched as the vessel quickly gained on them and the faces of the motley band of pirates could clearly be seen. Scarred, unkempt, unscrupulous, each leered mercilessly, anticipating a quick slaughter of the men, some lustful pleasure from the women and a good prize. A convincing display by the women provoked cruel laughter, which carried clearly across the intervening water.

The leader at the helm was a broad ox-like man, his bald head shining above his villainous face with long drooping moustaches and two gold earrings. A cutlass hung from his belted, dirt-stained tunic, and he called out a few orders as he brought the bow within a boat's length of the *Dolphin*.

Ephraim called the hidden men on deck just as Miriam flourished her pole from the stern as though challenging them to come close, drawing all the crew's attention to her and evoking a few anticipatory expletives.

Both boats were sending up a fine bow wave as they cleaved the blue waters, keeping about ten paces apart, and as the pirate vessel angled their course to close, Ephraim murmured to Mary, "Just as they're coming alongside, turn hard into them, so that we smash against them."

Mary nodded.

Miriam's pole was now making contact but was ineffectual in holding their pursuers at bay, and laughing loudly, a man leant over the side to seize it.

This was Ephraim's chance, and seizing Mary's improvised lance he stabbed at him across the gap. As he saw the gleaming blade the pirate pulled back, but not in time to prevent it slashing across his forearm, cutting through to the bone. At his anguished cry and the sight of blood his comrades let out an incensed roar. The injured man put his hand to the hilt of his cutlass but found he was unable to clasp it, the severed nerve paralyzing his thumb and forefinger.

The Captain put his helm over to come alongside and for three seconds Ephraim held back, then he called, "Now, Mary," and threw his readied dagger an instant before Mary thrust the tiller away from her.

The collision of the boats was shattering, and there was a rending of wood as the hull of the *Dolphin* bore down on the bulwarks of the other.

Thrown off balance the pirates poised amidships, fell forward searching for handholds on the *Dolphin*, and instead of springing on board they scrambled in disorder across the locked boats. To the concealed swordsmen, they were vulnerable for but a few seconds, sufficient however for one to be eviscerated by a slash from Joab's cutlass, while Marc and Horatius were no less daunting, thrusting and cutting into the soft exposed parts of their adversaries' bodies.

Mary brought the tiller hard back, and the boats separated, the grappling hook and attached rope dangling ineffectually from the *Dolphin*, the pirate, who was to have made it fast clutching at Ephraim's dagger hilt protruding from his groin and slowly sinking onto his knees.

The helmsman was the only uninjured spectator to the slaughter of his crew, as all five that had boarded were struck down, to be picked up and thrown one at a time overboard, their bodies bobbing in a macabre line in the wake of the receding boat.

Ephraim took the tiller from the shocked hands of Mary, and in them placed the lanyard from a bucket and a brush handle.

"Clean the blood off the deck before Simon sees it," he commanded and Mary moved in a daze to do so.

Not however before Simon broke free, and burst on deck in time to see the last of the bodies thrown over the side.

Miriam ran to him and seized him in her arms, crying and shaking hysterically with reaction to so much death being meted out. Marc joined them talking reassuringly as he clutched his family to him, wondering if violence and death was always to be their lot. Those quiet years in Dura-Europos had been shattered forever by the arrival of Rufus and his mission.

It seemed impossible to exorcise the spectre of such an awesome slaughter, especially for the women to whom it was as alien to their nature as anything could be. Mother Mary looked searchingly into the eyes of the men as though she hoped to find some answer there.

Horatius was the closest to her of them all, and he tried to dispel her melancholy by assuring her nothing had been done that wasn't needful.

"I feel the responsibility is mine. It's because of me we are here on the *Dolphin* in the first place, and I said to ride the wind that brought us to these islands," lamented Mary, fighting back a further flow of tears.

Horatius countered, "No, you aren't responsible. Wickedness exists and had you seen the faces of that crew you would have seen the murder that was in their minds. Maybe they would have spared Simon's life, but only to be brutalized and brought up as one of them. We did what we had to do, no more. Why don't you lead us in prayer, asking God to have mercy on their souls and to purge our hearts of over-rejoicing at our triumph, and give thanks that the next boat to pass these islands will be safe from the threat that lay waiting for them because of our victory."

Mary chided herself on her self-pity, and thanking Horatius for helping her to see things as they were, did exactly what he suggested, thereby lightening the prevailing mood although not dispelling battle fatigue. It took Marc and his talent for mime to do that.

Borrowing Simon's slate and stylus he disappeared into the hold for half an hour. Suddenly to everyone's amazement he burst into their midst on the stern deck, attired in Ephraim's long sea boots, a cloak over his tunic, scarf tied around his head and a black eye patch. Brandishing a cutlass he paced the deck and began his epic poem.

"Behold me, captain of this pirate band,
Bolder at sea than ever on land.
To give no quarter is our valiant boast
And all men fear us along this coast."

He paused, snarling at his captive audience and waving his cutlass wildly. After a few seconds of disbelief, instead of the encouragement he had anticipated he received only derision and boos. Undeterred, indeed seemingly encouraged he continue,

"Look o'er our lee sails the Dolphin bold,
Up sail lads, for to steal their gold.
The women and boy could be sold for slaves
So chase them lads, cross the stormy waves."

Simon was screaming with excitement, and Miriam looked reproachfully at Marc but still he continued,

"Only three their crew, we'll soon o'er power
And leave the women for a later hour.
The boy might grow to a pirate wise
And the lovely ship will be our prize.

"Close to board her and to plunder all,
What's this? The women repel us with a pole
Our cries of laughter at their efforts vain
Echo o'er the water again and again."

As Marc's laughter rang out, excruciating tears coursed over Mary Magdalene's cheeks, and she cried imploringly to be spared any more, only to be overruled by an insatiable boy, demanding,
    "More, daddy, more!"
    Suddenly switching to a conspiratorial whisper, finger held up to his lips Marc continued,

"Biding their time and concealed aboard
Three valiant men lay, each with his sword.
No way could we see them, no way did I know
Three executioners hiding were waiting below.

"Their woman at the helm gave the tiller a push,
The boats came together with a fearful rush.
We pitched and we rolled and nigh fell in the sea,
As we clambered on board her to gain mastery.

"Then from under the bulwarks with total surprise
These swordsmen flew at us, right under our eyes.
My men were all butchered and cast into the sea
All my crew now are done for, all except me."

302

As he took his bow to prolonged and enthusiastic applause there was not a dry eye on the boat. Although it is certain the tears weren't only from unconstrained merriment, it proved the old adage that laughter is the best medicine.

CHAPTER FOUR

They all crowded the starboard rail as the *Dolphin* rounded the white rocky cape, and there was a feeling of both relief and excitement at the imminent end of the long passage, started in the spring and only now approaching its end in high summer. The frightening encounter with the pirates had made them press on with greater urgency to make their final landfall.

The sail suddenly came across and they were reaching along a rocky limestone shore, drawn towards the two stark white islands, and the buildings climbing the high hill over looking the harbour.

Marc had his arms around Miriam to reassure her as Brutus turned to them and said, "Did you know it took the Romans three years to drive out you Celts from Massilia?"

"Why couldn't you let them stay, I can't believe they were a threat to Rome?"

"Probably not, but there was no stopping the spread of empire at that time and Massilia was the most important harbour in this region. Julius Caesar sacked it a hundred years ago as it had sided with his rival Pompey."

Simon had been listening avidly, and pointed excitedly at some soldiers who were scrutinizing them from a fort clinging to a massive rock at the approach to the harbour. A modest galley lay against its small quay.

"Are they going to chase us, uncle Brutus?" he asked, eagerly anticipating another battle and was disappointed when the centurion shook his head and replied, "I doubt if they will, Simon, as we are a trading vessel and they don't know about the pirates. If we looked like pirates they would be after us for certain."

Simon wished he had one of the cutlasses so that he could brandish it like a pirate but Captain Ephraim had stowed them securely away.

"I wish your head wasn't so full of pirates, Simon," remonstrated Miriam, knowing her plea was falling on deaf ears as he had talked of little else the past two days.

"It will fade after a few days ashore, Miriam," soothed Marc, "but it's so vivid in all our minds at the moment."

"Let's agree not to talk about it then, as I can hardly close my eyes without seeing every gory detail of that encounter," pleaded Miriam.

The harbour they were entering was huge, massive stone blocks forming the four sides of the vast basin with only the narrowest entrance to the west. Boats of all sizes and all types lay moored against the high quays as hundreds of stevedores loaded or unloaded every type of cargo imaginable. Two rowing boats worked them into an appropriate gap and as the gangplank was positioned, port officials hurried aboard to enter into earnest dialogue with Captain Ephraim. Eventually, smiling and satisfied they left, and the impatient travellers were allowed ashore.

"They wanted to know where we've come from and where we're going, what cargo we carry or intend to load, and if there is any illness aboard. They're afraid of plague being brought in from North Africa where there has been an outbreak in Libya."

Brutus clasped Mary to him protectively, sharing the soldier's fear of disease, the great reaper against whom their swords are useless. As he recounted his encounter with the plague as a legionary in Carthage, so vivid was his description that all shuddered and hoped never to confront it themselves.

The women were anxious to visit the synagogue, and accompanied by their reluctant men hurried there to give thanks for their deliverance.

The Elder who welcomed them was one of the oldest men they had ever seen. His name, Abiathar, denoted his priestly lineage went back to the time of King David, and such was his antiquity one could be forgiven for wondering if he had been an acolyte in his court. Long, perfectly groomed whiskers of a brilliant whiteness hung down to his waist, and his twinkling eyes peered eagerly from a mass of wrinkles, surmounted by a sea of white waves cascading over his shoulders.

His rich, resonant voice enquired their origin and when he heard they had journeyed from Jerusalem, he too wished to join them in their thanksgiving, but not before they had told him something of their voyage.

It was their intention not to dwell much on their journey, but so quick was his intelligence and shrewd his questioning, that they were quickly ushered into a private chamber where they found themselves telling all. Simon was honoured to sit at his side, where he felt like a young Samuel sitting at the feet of Heli. Abiather eagerly encouraged him, and was filled with wonder as he recounted the adventures they had shared. He called for refreshment, and then urged Simon to tell him more of the whale, his evident joy at all he heard both delighting and spurring the boy on.

Finally he said, "My goodness, what an adventure, and how mysteriously God moves and works his purpose. I must run and officiate at the evening worship, but promise me you will return tomorrow as there is someone in town right now you must meet, before he moves on."

Despite all their entreaties he kept the identity of his visitor a secret, promising all would be revealed the next day.

As the harbour was conveniently located close to the centre of the city the crew of the *Dolphin* were spending this night together with their passengers, but Ephraim was already looking for cargo for the return journey now the epic voyage was at its end.

There was a quayside inn where they celebrated their safe arrival but their rejoicing together was tinged with sadness. Simon was clinging to Ephraim and Horatius, as though by sheer will power he could put off their leaving forever. There was no singing and absolutely no poetry that night, just friendly banter and discussion of all their many shared experiences. Then the conversation swung to the cause of the whole enterprise and to Mother Mary and what she was expecting now they were arrived in Gaul.

"I don't know what will happen. Maybe tomorrow's meeting will hold the key, but I know I am here because all of you responded to the voice of God, who entrusted my well being to valiant and resourceful men."

There was a general dismissing of her praise of them by the men, but Mary was undeterred.

"I can't thank you all enough. I do not believe the whole of Rome's might, could have guarded us more diligently and I thank you and will remember you always. May I reveal a little of my thoughts, to put all that has happened and what is to come into perspective?

"I have told you much of the boyhood and early years of the ministry of Jesus but I think it important you know something of what led to that ending on the cross at Jerusalem in which we all became so much involved. Indeed but for that we would probably never have come together, or be here now, even though to some of you it must have seemed a brutally premature end and cause you to wonder at the mysterious ways God works his purpose, using such contrary and rebellious creatures.

"Jesus used to confide his innermost thoughts to me, both his hopes and his doubts. He grew up aware of his royal lineage, and that it was expected of him, the first-born, to fulfil the prophecies and at the appropriate time reveal he was Israel's long awaited Messiah. After the death of Joseph, his earthly father who he always honoured, he listened more and more to God, his heavenly father. He knew great hopes hung on his claiming his inheritance but he was uncertain what it was. He looked at men's kingdoms and the tyrannies that flourish under kings and emperors, and yearned for something more meaningful.

"It was then that God revealed his Kingdom, his eternal way of relating the past, the present and the future within his purpose for mankind. Jesus tried to explain it through his parables, likening the Kingdom to everyday things that people would recognize. A mustard seed, growing into a mighty tree, the land-owner with his vineyard and the vine that bears everlasting fruit.

"But those who most urged him to declare himself Messiah already knew what they wanted, and they didn't find this sort of message met their expectations at all. They sought a warrior king like David, to challenge and overthrow the Romans, a great priest performing miracles and uniting the sectarian groups of Israel into one triumphant nation. The Pharisees, the Sadducees, the Essenes and the Zealots all expected to be vindicated and to unite behind one leader, the Messiah. But Jesus chose to ride into Jerusalem on a donkey, both to fulfil the prophecy of Zechariah and to announce he was his own man, and that he rejected David's sort of kingship although he was of David's line. He said to me, 'Why, even the priests were divided about which son was to succeed King David. Zadok was for Solomon, but Abiathar supported the younger Adonijah and was banished for it.'

"He knew among the princes of the Davidic dynasty there were those who wished for his brother James to assume the role of Messiah and lead an uprising against the Romans, and James was very tempted to usurp his brother's right, and was urging the Priests to give their support to an uprising even as Jesus was entering Jerusalem astride that donkey!"

"The same James we met at the house of the widow of John Mark?" asked Brutus and when Mary concurred, "he has the bearing of the born leader, no wonder he had so many backing him, I would follow him into battle with confidence."

"From you, that is indeed an accolade. Jesus could see he disappointed their expectations while James promised to fulfil them. Jesus used to say to me there is not a dynasty since the world began where brother hasn't striven against brother, not since Cain slew Abel."

306

Mary looked at each of her listeners and, reassured she had their attention continued hesitantly, her sadness weighing on her.

"For this reason he remained unmarried and without a bloodline heir."

Mary Magdalene's unconscious start betrayed what Mother Mary had always known. How much her son and this beautiful woman had been drawn to each other by a love never to be consummated.

"He chose to remain celibate, denying the demands of his powerful supporters to provide an heir. This way he knew he could serve both God and all mankind. As his sponsors fell away from him bitterly disappointed he knew it would lead inevitably to his death, and the only question was when and how? You probably know how Pontius Pilate so gravely miscalculated when he brutally overreacted to kill and humiliate those youths who attempted to ambush his coach. Far from cowing the populace and making an example of how he treated rebellion, he inflamed them to such a pitch a widespread riot was imminent, and it only needed one word of encouragement from the priests and everyone in the city would have risen.

"So the priests knew they finally had Pilate where they wanted him, and they were able to coerce him to crucify my son, thereby putting an end to his open and unrelenting criticism of them, which they found increasingly unbearable!

"They were also able to align themselves with the all the Jewish factions by calling on Pilate to release his prisoner Barabbas, even though he was anxious to torture him for information of the zealots. But I rejoice for the release of the boy, and if my son had to be sacrificed for it, well Jesus always said the greatest act of love is to lay down one's life for another. Probably it was as he had foreseen it would be, and accorded with God's will and the perverse nature of mankind!"

The inevitability of it left them quiet and subdued, yet in some inexplicable way each felt more reconciled to their involvement and the part they had played in his death.

The next day the travellers took their farewell of the *Dolphin* and her crew. A tearful parting that left not one eye dry, and as Ephraim remarked, "The only time I can remember four women crying to see the back of me, and the only time I've been reluctant to turn it and sail away."

Afterwards Miriam went to solicit the help of the Tyre Merchant's Association for the leper orphanage on Crete, and such was the standing of Alexander within the association everything was agreed satisfactorily.

Brutus felt it incumbent on him to call on the commanding officer of the garrison fort, and he was overjoyed to find it was Cornelius, who had been in post two years and was shortly to be moved on.

"There's a big build up in northern Gallia going on at the moment. We're moving vast quantities of goods up the river Rhone although nobody seems to know when the army will invade Britannia."

"Don't you have further trouble from the Helvetia, or the Allotroges?" queried Brutus, having known a few skirmishes with these tribes controlling the central mountainous region of Gallia.

"Quiet as lambs," laughed Cornelius, "we pay such a good price for their grain and wine and timber, they are more than happy."

"When we sailed from Tyre there was a severe famine in Palestine. What's the latest news from there?"

"It continues and of course it leads to local disturbances. Caspius Fadus the Governor has his hands full, but there is nothing abnormal about that. What brings you to Gallia?"

Brutus explained how they had the role of escorting Mother Mary, which caused Cornelius to ponder a while.

"The followers of the Way grow daily throughout Gallia although the authorities are trying to contain it, for the moment they're not sure whether to regard it as a sect of Judaism and tolerate it, or whether it's a new religion and to clamp down on it."

"Oh it's new alright! If it had a great deal in common with Judaism I would have shied away like a frightened horse! But I don't need to tell you that, do I?"

"Hardly, but it serves our purpose not to emphasise the distinction, not at the moment anyway. Tell me how I can be of assistance in your mission now, and what you are looking for here."

"We wait for the Spirit to show us, or rather Mary, what to do, or where to go. I'm not very attuned to receiving divine guidance!"

"Nor was I but I've always believed in prayer. Peter and the apostles were praying for guidance at the same time I too was praying for full communion in the new church. We both had visions and ever since we gentiles have been having an increasing say in the church."

"Oh there are plenty of good prayers in our party I can assure you, they hardly need my contribution," shrugged Brutus, "I'm just the man to get on with the job whatever it might be."

"Even if it's crucifying the Son of God on a tree?" mused Cornelius, his searching look not wishing to be unkind.

"Even to doing that if it is a necessary part of God's plan," said Brutus quickly.

"Then I rejoice for you and a prayer of mine has been answered," exclaimed the centurion, "I knew how troubled you were by your role of executioner."

"So I've your prayers to thank for reconciliation to my role, have I? Well I'm grateful but please no more prayers for me, save them for more deserving causes," and laughing the men parted.

Expectations were high when they were admitted to Abiathar's chamber, and his contrast with the man who rose to greet them couldn't have been greater.

The man to whom they were introduced was stocky and fair, with a short well-trimmed beard. He looked at them keenly, his dark brown eyes deeply set under prominent brows and a curving intelligent forehead. He was dressed in very fine clothes denoting his status, and his firm handclasp and deeply mellow voice declared his authority.

"Joseph of Arimathea has been impatient to meet you since I told him of your arrival," beamed Abiathear, his shrewd eyes assessing their different reactions.

Mother Mary and Mary Clopas knelt and held his proffered hand to their lips.

"You honour us, prince!" said Mother Mary, her surprise not negating the demands of protocol.

"Mine is the honour and I rejoice in your safe arrival. Your son James wrote saying you would cross the Great Sea this summer, but I was afraid I might be in Britain when you arrived as I leave shortly."

Brutus and Marc exchanged uncertain glances, neither expecting reference to their intended destination from this urbane, cultivated man. It was only during the spirited and enlightening conversation that followed, that they realized they were in the presence of a great prince and diplomat, known and welcomed at the court of Celt or Roman, and by the Germanic tribes across the Rhine.

"I had to flee Jerusalem within a few days of the resurrection of Jesus. When I pleaded with Pilate for his body to be placed in my tomb it was with the bitter taste of defeat in my mouth, and the realization that all we had worked for over the years had been brought to nothing.

"Then when Pilate and the priests were interrogating me as to where had I removed his body and at whose instigation, I knew that something stupendous had happened. Caiaphas was really angry that he hadn't been thrown in the pit with the other criminals, and blamed me for offering the tomb and Pilate for authorizing it. Pilate was scared of rioting and disorder if the news ever got out that the tomb had been found empty, and my life wouldn't have been worth a fig had I stayed.

"Then James indicated he had no interest in the dynastic succession or leading the uprising we had planned, so greatly troubled I fled to Antioch to take stock of the situation."

He stopped aware that his listeners might not be able to keep up with him.

"Where in Britain are you heading?" asked Marc his heart beating excitedly.

"For Camulodumum in the east, do you know it?"

"Of it. It's the stronghold of the Trinovantes. My tribe is the Catuvellauni to the west."

"Well they are united now under the leadership of King Cunobelin".

"I know him, he's the son of Tasciovanus, our king!"

"Tasciovanus died two years ago, but not before he had forged an alliance between the two tribes against the common enemy."

"The common enemy?" queried Brutus, although he already anticipated the reply.

Joseph looked questioningly at Abiathar for agreement to say more. The old man nodded compliance.

"Why the Romans of course. Remember they invaded Brittania once and are preparing to do so again."

Joseph noted their reaction before continuing,

"For ten years prior to the death of Jesus I travelled the courts of Europe as ambassador to the Davidic princes of Israel. I know every king of every tribe in Britain and the large island to the west that the Romans call Hiberia. Also the kings of the tribes throughout Gaul and Germany and the lands east of the Euphrates ruled by the Parthians. My task has been to persuade them to restrain from quarrelling among themselves and to prepare for a common war against Rome.

"This worldwide uprising was to have been initiated by the Messiah declaring his rule over Israel and the rallying of all the factions to his cause, then all the other nations were to rise up simultaneously."

"Rome could not prevail against a concerted uprising throughout the Empire and from the adjacent nations beyond its frontier. You would have won the day. What went wrong?" asked Brutus, perching eagerly on the edge of his seat, his white knuckles indicating how tightly he was gripping the arm-rest.

Joseph reflected for a few minutes then said poignantly, "None of our concepts of the Messiah accorded with those of Jesus, so much so that many tried to persuade James that Jesus had abdicated in his favour. Throughout Jesus' mission as we realized he would not comply with our expectations James encouraged us to believe he would succeed him when Jesus abdicated."

He paused looking pensive.

"Of course he never did! Jesus established a different Kingdom from what we expected by his death and resurrection, James became his ardent disciple and our whole strategy disintegrated around us. Instead we are left with a legacy of armies eager to fight Rome but lacking coordination, and now they fight each other or squabble among themselves."

"Not altogether, a Parthian army besieged us at Dura-Europos three months ago, and would have seized the city and sacked it but for the brilliance of our commander," countered Marc.

"Who was your commander and tell me more of the siege?" demanded Joseph anxiously.

After Marc had related the events of the siege, culminating in the death of Prince Ardashir, Joseph was very agitated and sorrowful, to the extent of fighting back tears.

"The flower of a great assembly of knights, all slain. I had not heard because I was travelling and I tremble at all these armies raised and now not needed, what will become of them. Israel cannot be held back for long, the zealots are straining at the leash and the famine will push many further into desperate actions."

He looked uncertainly at Abiathar, who looked troubled as he said, "You must continue with your efforts in Britain, prince! Although now there is no possibility of the tribes uniting and attacking Rome in Gaul, you may be able to keep them from fighting each other so that they are a more united country, especially as Rome is about to launch its invasion."

"I would like to support you and so would my father," implored Marc, "as soon as we have discharged our mission regarding Mother Mary! We all wondered if you would point us towards the next step of our journey which is as yet unclear."

"I'm afraid not. I depart on a boat for Britain in a few days. If you ever seek me there, enquire of King Arviragus of Siluria, brother of Caractacus the Pendragon. He will know of my whereabouts, as he has given me twelve hides of land to support the church I am to establish there."

Mother Mary said, "You don't need to stay with us, Marc. You have been courageous and loyal in our service, but now your courage and loyalty belong to your own people. Go with Joseph with my blessing and our heartfelt thanks."

Marc knelt at her feet and taking her hand said, "It is my honour to accompany you on this journey. When it is completed I will feel free to go with my family to my own people. Until then I wish nothing other than to serve you."

"Likewise, I wish only to fulfil this mission before we proceed for Brittania, but you greatly disturb me, Joseph of Arimathea." Brutus looked challengingly at the prince.

"Then I hope I can reassure you so please continue."

"Raising and equipping armies for war is very costly. Half the revenue Rome raises in taxes is used to support her legions. None of the barbarian kings can raise the money to maintain armies year after year without incurring huge debts?" He let the unspoken question hang in the air.

"We are funding them," Joseph said grudgingly.

"Who are the we, exactly?" parried Brutus.

"We, the Jews of the Diaspora. Our merchants have accumulated vast wealth from trade across the known world."

"So can I summarize the present situation as I see it. A vast amount of Jewish wealth has been channelled through your trading associations to the kings and rulers of a great many nations?"

Joseph nodded.

"To raise, equip and maintain standing armies in a state of readiness for war?" Again Joseph nodded.

"Awaiting only your invincible Messiah to raise his standard and launch that war, driving the Romans back over the Dolomitic Alps."

Looking very unhappy Joseph wordlessly nodded a third time.

"And now it will never happen!"

The accusatory thrust drew blood and Joseph, wounded, cried out.

"No it can never happen now! We turned deaf ears when Jesus told us we misunderstood the role of the Messiah. We preferred to believe what we wanted to believe."

He was holding his hands to his ears and rocking his head from side to side as though to emphasise his disbelief at his own words.

Brutus' face registered his shocked incredulity, but swordsman that he was he knew when to press his advantage.

"So you Jews of the trading associations have equipped a dozen armies, with hundreds of chariots, thousands of horses suitably accoutred for battle, many tens of thousands of swords and shields, of spears and arrows, full body armour for knights and attendants. All this enough to ransom a hundred kings but not one of them in a position to redeem their borrowing.

"These nations face impoverishment because they heeded your call to arms and allowed you to supply them in good faith, confident in victory. Now what are your trade federations doing to redress the situation?"

Joseph and Abiathar both looked confused by the change of emphasis of the question.

"Oh we are not pressing the loan repayments too strongly. Some are not repaying the borrowing at all, only a modest interest yearly. Britain's kings borrowed ten thousand shekels of gold and have repaid only half. But we are very patient and the interest charged is minimal," pleaded Joseph in mitigation.

"Where could you find armaments on the scale you needed them and how could you move them across the Roman Empire without them being seized?" asked Brutus as though satisfied with his answer.

"From the large land to the east of the tip of India. There thousands of furnaces redden the night sky so it can be seen from a hundred miles away. They are superb metal craftsmen in iron and bronze, and they forge swords that stay bright and sharp year after year. Our ships bring them to the head of the Persian Sea, and we have developed new and hazardous caravan routes to the Caspian Sea and then westward to where they are eagerly awaited." Joseph looked happy to be on firmer ground unaware of the trap that Brutus had prepared for him.

"It must be very distressing to have all these ships idle now there is no further demand for arms."

"Oh no, ships can be switched to other trading. Right now shipping grain to Palestine is a priority and there is a steady trade in silk and carpets from China, and in spices and perfumes and metal goods and luxuries from India."

"Then your federations would not face ruin if they were to write off the debts owed by all the countries to which they supplied arms?"

The innocent way in which Brutus slipped in the deadly question dismayed the two Jews who could only look at each other uncertainly.

"It would be the honorable thing to do and avert a great deal of strife across the known world. It was probably the burden of repayment that contributed to the siege of Dura-Europos by the Parthians, which so nearly succeeded. Had it done so I suppose the plunder seized would have repaid all their debts, but instead Prince Ardashir lies dead and half the noble families of Persia are grieving their lost sons!

"I place most of the responsibility on you, and the Jews of the Diaspora. You will incur the hatred of the impoverished nations amongst whom you live, unless you accept your responsibility and shoulder much of their burden!"

Brutus was shaking with rage that he found hard to control, and the faces of his listeners were drawn and white. Finally Abiathar said hesitantly,

"You speak with justifiable anger and present a viewpoint that if it ever occurred to us, we pushed from our minds. Because of our separateness, to which we cling as the chosen race, we expect to incur distrust and jealousy, but it will be a disaster for all Israel if we are hated and incur the wrath of our host nations. Would you be prepared to speak to our trading federations here in Massilia. You are truly a powerful orator?"

"If you can arrange such a meeting in the next few days I will say to them what I have said to you, but our journeying may be resumed at very short notice."

Brutus indicated that he had said all he wanted for the moment and together they departed for the inn.

"Thank you for pleading the cause of the British tribes," said Marc, "my blood was boiling at the injustice of my nation being held to ransom by the trading federations, but I couldn't trust myself to speak as you did."

"Likewise I'm glad too, as I feel a great burden of guilt," said Mother Mary, her evident distress showing in her ashen face and the nervous wringing of her hands.

"You have no cause to feel guilt. Jesus made it very evident he wanted no part in a warrior kingship or insurrection against Rome," urged Mary Magdalene passionately.

"No, but my son James went along with such ideas without regard to the full consequences. Only after the death and resurrection of Jesus did he realise how better to serve God's Kingdom!"

The implications silenced everyone, and they felt crushed after the eager expectations with which they had set out for the Synagogue

Two dilatory days passed before word reached the inn that an extraordinary meeting had been called of all the Jewish trading federations in Massilia, at the Grand Hall of the Tyre Federation that evening. Mary Clopas agreed to stay with Simon but all the others were anxious to support Brutus, who had spent many hours of enquiry and preparation.

Miriam was the only one not surprised by the splendour of the building. Rich tapestries hung covering the walls, where rolled scrolls were stacked in pigeon holes from floor to ceiling. The marble pillars glowed pink and rose in the flickering candlelight of a hundred candles in silver candelabra. The polished ivory and ebony inlaid table reflected the warmth of the pair of solid gold, seven-branched menorah and the ornately moulded candles burnt fragrantly.

Jarius, the president of the association called the meeting to order, and nearly a hundred men fastened their speculative eyes upon him. Briefly he introduced their guests at the president's table, and pleaded for the indulgence of the members at the presence of women for the first time at one of their meetings.

"All I can plead in mitigation for this break with tradition is that this is an extraordinary meeting, and this is an extraordinary band of travellers passing through our city. I call upon Brutus, a former centurion in the imperial army to address us."

An intense silence hung over the assembly, and Brutus from the slightly raised dais looked down on a sea of shrewd, questioning faces.

"Merchant Jews of the Diaspora, I wish to disclaim any suggestion that I am an orator. I am simply a retired centurion of the Imperial Roman army, whose viewpoint has been formed by a lifetime's service to the imperial cause.

"As a result of fate and fortunate association, I no longer have any sympathy with the concept of conquest and empire, which I regard as fundamentally brutal and oppressive. I don't need to tell you that, for you are successful and valued merchants and only too aware of the tyranny that demands tribute and taxes so remorselessly.

"What, however, is new to me, and possibly to many of you, is the vast build-up of armies you have financed throughout the countries around the borders of the Roman Empire, and the frightening legacy for all of these countries.

"Had your Messiah led a worldwide invasion of the Empire there can be little doubt the legions would have been driven back over the Dolomite Alps. But the whole idea was ill conceived and failed to materialize, so with the death of the prophet Jesus the idea of the invasion also died.

"But the armies haven't disbanded, nor has the indebtedness of the kings and knights who borrowed so greatly from your federations to finance their rearmament! There is nothing more destructive than a well armed and disaffected army, and you have contributed to more than a score such armies!"

Pausing to study the faces of his listeners in the front rows, he knew what he was about to say would be unwelcome to most, but that was not going to deter him, the stakes were too high.

"Only you wealthy merchants can remedy the situation, by writing off the greater part of their indebtedness!"

The reaction was immediate, a sharp intake of breath and exchanged angry glances, followed by howls of protest and angry gestures. Brutus held up his arms coaxing a gradual quieting of the outburst.

"I don't make this proposal lightly for I know it must be unpopular, but I am convinced it is in your own self interest to do so. The anger of the impoverished nobles, of the unpaid and under provisioned soldiers, of the peasant farmer taxed and pilfered to starvation, will erupt in unrestrained violence against those they see as to blame.

"Your goods, your houses, your ships, your very lives are likely to be taken in retribution. Close to your hearts, in Palestine where you might expect to find refuge, the zealots are armed and impatient to battle with Rome. They steal from and threaten the farmers who hold back from joining them, to pay for the weapons that you continue to supply. Armed as they are it will not be possible to restrain them for long, but when the battle begins the legions will stamp it out ruthlessly. The zealots will hang from crosses the length of your country, your temple will be razed and your cities laid waste.

"Similar catastrophes could befall Parthia, Arabia, Armenia, Germania, Brittania, Hiberia! The world is poised on a knife-edge of disastrous military actions, either against Rome, or against neighbour in the vain hope of seizing wealth, sufficient to pay off their debts. Write off these debts, encourage the rulers to pay off and disband their armies, and you will create a safer world in which your commerce will flourish and your associations grow in influence."

As he bowed and resumed his seat dissension broke out on the floor, with a great deal of shouting and pushing as the more dominant attempted to assert themselves and gain the podium.

Jarius stood resolute and authoritative, his hands held in the position of prayer, his eyes fastening on and subduing all challenge. Eventually he spoke.

"Please, I beseech you, let us remain calm, and study carefully and question critically this challenging hypothesis that we have heard. I personally found the scenario very frightening and have one question I wish to ask," turning to Brutus whose stern face inclined in agreement. "What is the source of your information on the contribution of us merchant Jews of the Diaspora, to this world wide rearmament?"

"One of your number here present. Let him declare himself," called out the centurion.

Joseph of Arimathea arose, "I revealed our involvement in arming the Persians, when our visitors told me of the siege of Dura-Europos in which they fought. I was greatly saddened by the death of Prince Ardashir and many of his knights. I also indicated that I doubted my ability to persuade this and similar federations to waive the debts of the kings of Britain even as Rome is preparing to invade."

"Honoured President, if Rome is preparing to invade Britain that is a reason for pressing for the earliest repayment from the various kings, as most certainly it will be impossible to retrieve our money from a conquered land."

"That's one point of view, Simon, but one I don't share as it would further Rome's cause."

"What's wrong with that! Our federations flourish under Rome's protection and I for one don't wish to bite the hand that feeds me."

Joseph of Arimathea interrupted.

"That is a deplorable attitude and one I hope few members share. For over a decade I promoted abroad the coming of the anointed Messiah to lead an uprising that would free Israel of the tyranny of Rome, and lead all subject or threatened nations to freedom. This was the message I carried on behalf of the Davidic dynasty and it places us under an obligation to bear much of the cost of its failure. We have done well from the trade it generated and we can continue to do so, if we announce a jubilee on these war debts."

An hour later a dispirited party returned to the inn, carrying their memories of the bitter and heated debate, convinced it would end inconclusively and be no help in holding back the hounds of war.

314

"At least you tried, dearest, so when the reckoning comes the responsibility will rest where it belongs," said Mary soothingly as they lay together.

"I owe it to our unborn child to do all I can to make this a less war driven, crazy world," were his words as sleep overcame him.

CHAPTER FIVE

Brutus was instantly awake to the urgency of the banging at the door, and although it was totally dark the panic in his voice brought Mary to respond equally quickly, so they both saw the fear in Marc's face accentuated by the fluttering candlelight.

"Simon is desperately ill and Miriam is fearful of losing him!" he blurted out. "Please help us."

"What is wrong with him?" asked Mary, wrapping her robe around her as they hurried along the corridor.

"He's in the grip of the most malignant fever I've ever seen!" said Marc, but one look at the restless boy, his eyes glazed and unresponsive while all the time he was throwing himself around with convulsive movements of his limbs, conveyed his desperate plight. Mary bent and listened to his rapid shallow breathing placing her hand on his forehead.

"He is burning with a fever and the light is troubling him," she said indicating to Miriam to take the flickering oil lamp well away. "Fetch some towels and cold water to cool him and lessen his fever. Quickly, wake the innkeeper, we must get a physician for him immediatly!"

"See to the towels, Marc, I'll go and ask the aid of Cornelius. A garrison this size must know the best physicians!"

Brutus was glad to have something to do as illness always emphasised his feeling of utter uselessness. He returned shortly, accompanied by Cornelius and his personal physician, a Greek named Luke. Together they examined the boy methodically feeling his feverish pulse, listening to his breathing with a metal cone placed on his chest, looking at his eyes. Luke was alarmed at both the exaggerated response of each reflex he tested while the pupils of his glazed eyes were unresponsive to anything. His own eyes betrayed the critical state of the young patient.

"I greatly fear for him," he said brusquely, his manner failing to hide his anguish. "He is at the crisis, which his young body may find beyond its resources. Keep his fever down with the damp towels and don't stop fanning him. Moisten his lips frequently and entreat the mercy of the Gods who give and take back at their will. I'll go and prepare some herbs into a tincture that may help bring the fever down."

As he left he threw a backwards glance and saw the women on their knees on either side of his bed. Outside the room he was sombre in his assessment.

"The rapidity and intensity of the fever is alarming. Has he been in contact with any noxious vapours or contagion?"

"Briefly, we were at Poseidonia but knowing its notoriety for swamp fever the child stayed on board," said Brutus.

"This isn't swamp fever, he's tinder dry and he would be sweating profusely. No it's something malign but I don't know what."

He looked quizzically at Cornelius.

"Do you think we could send for Pothus, he's the most renowned healer in this region?"

"Where would we find the old hermit if he's still alive?"

"Oh he's very much alive. A month ago he trepanned the skull of Catullus after his accident and he has fully recovered. My servant will lead you to him."

"Then do so right away, time seems to be running out for the boy," urged Cornelius.

"He will be with you in fifteen minutes. Go on foot as nothing will persuade Pothus to climb on a horse."

Brutus quickly informed the distraught parents of their plan and he and Cornelius girded themselves for their trek up into the high hills overlooking the city.

Breathless after an hour's intense exertion they approached a limestone high cliff as dawn was just casting its rosy tint on the weathered rock face.

A voice called out, "Come no further and state who is seeking Pothus and why!"

"It's I, Cornelius, the garrison commander."

"I know what you are and what you represent. What is your mission?"

Cornelius smiled at Brutus and whispered, "He's no Roman lover, this one," then he called back, "there is a sick child with a high fever that alarms all of us, and our physician Luke said to send for you."

This was received with a grunt then the disembodied voice demanded a few pertinent details before telling them to await him. Ten minutes later he appeared, and Brutus was amazed as the old man stood head and shoulders over him, towering on his spindly limbs in an awe-inspiring uprightness. His deep-set eyes, peering from a walnut brown face, scrutinised the visitors critically, the colour of his skin contrasting with the halo of white hair that now captured some of the dawn's hue.

Wordlessly he nodded and then led their brisk descent at a pace that belied his age. Brutus was convinced he took three paces for every two of the hermit's and they quickly regained the inn.

Untying his cloth bag Pothus demanded to be left alone with Simon. Marc led Miriam into an adjoining room, where the dread clutching at each heart was evident in the drawn faces and the ominous muteness constraining any speech. The waiting seemed interminable, only the muffled sobs of Miriam pulsing away the minutes. Finally the old hermit glided into their midst. His face was drawn and fatigued as he took Miriam's hands, and said in a voice barely louder than a whisper.

"He's going to be alright, dear lady," and as his brown capable hands were drawn to receive her kisses and covered with her tears, Pothus' eyes caught those of Mother Mary.

He stood transfixed, his face betraying considerable perplexity, prompted by some subconscious awareness of a previous encounter.

"My son, now gone, worked many healing miracles but never has one moved me to greater joy than yours today," said Mary.

Releasing Miriam's hands, Pothus knelt at Mary's feet. Even so his eyes were level with hers as he hardly dared breathe the question.

"Your son, my lady?"

"The Galilean, Jesus of Nazareth."

His awestruck face in other circumstances might have been thought comical, such intense surges of joy, of wonder, of adoration sweeping like ripples across the sands of the Arabian Desert, changing the configuration of his wrinkles haphazardly.

"Hail, Holy Queen!" were his portentous words, echoing and reverberating around the room.

Cornelius fell on his knees, aware that once again God had graced him with a glimpse of the divine, and every one joined him in a tableau of wonder.

"I am but the handmaid of the Lord," said Mary in confusion, "please don't praise or worship his honoured servant."

"As you wish, my lady, but I have lived here for forty years as eyes and ears for my master, the Magi Gaspar. I was with him watching when he knelt at the cradle in Bethlehem, and gave you his gift of myrrh with which to anoint Jesus' body after his suffering and death."

Mary's eyes were now wide with incredulity.

"Then you are to take us to the Jentillak to fulfil God's purpose?"

"Indeed, that is my mission, but oh happy day for me and my people that our long wait is approaching its promised fulfilment."

His face still radiant with the ecstasy of the revelation, Pothus took the anxious parents in to their sleeping son. Simon was bathed in perspiration and the fever still had its course to run, but it had lost its malign virulence, his breathing was easy and measured, and the eyes closed peacefully instead of fixed and staring.

Leaving them with a balm to rub over him and some drops to be taken regularly Pothus took his leave, promising to return the next morning.

The anticipation he had left behind him generated much speculation and discussion over breakfast. Who and what were the Jentillak, was on everyone's lips.

"I believe they will prove to be the lost tribes of Israel," said Miriam, "but whatever they are, Pothus will have my lifelong thanks for giving us back Simon when I feared to lose him."

"Tell us more of these lost tribes," urged Marc, and aware of everyone's interest Miriam continued.

"After the death of Solomon, a thousand years ago there was a deep split between the ten northern tribes and the southern ones, into Israel and Judah. Divided they were not strong enough to resist the warring Assyrians from Messopotania. The resistance of Israel centred on the city of Samaria, which fell after a three-year siege. The Assyrians carried off thirty thousand of its citizens into captivity who were never heard of again. They are the lost tribes of Israel."

Pondering that thought, nobody had a better explanation of these mysterious people they were soon to encounter, although Brutus was resolved to ask Pothus when next he saw him. That was later that day and although Simon was still febrile and greatly weakened, such was his improvement that Pothus was instantly aware of the lifting of mood as he entered. He was equally pleased with his patient's progress, and felt happy to discuss plans subsequent to his patient's full recovery.

"I have sent word to our homeland as they will require time to prepare for such a momentous event," he assured Mother Mary. "We all should be ready to journey in one week and I will accompany you as my waiting role here is finished now all that remains is to see the fulfilment of our purpose on earth."

"Have we far to journey?" asked Miriam concern showing in her slight frown.

"No, weeks by land, but by boat two days sailing and then another two walking."

"A pity the *Dolphin* has sailed," mused Brutus, "Ephraim has our full confidence. No doubt you will know of a suitable boat?"

"Yes indeed, there are many to choose from."

"Can you tell us more of the Jentillak, they are a tribe I never encountered during my service in Gallia?"

"You will have to ask our leaders. They do not encourage us to discuss our role with strangers."

Not so easily dissuaded Brutus persisted.

"Miriam thinks you may be the lost tribes of Israel?"

Pothus smiled tantalizingly.

"I would like to know why she thinks that?" he said, and listened as she repeated her conjecture.

Then he changed the subject, as he wanted to hear of their travels from Palestine. A feeble protest was heard from Simon's room and they were forced to relocate, surrounding his bed so he would not miss one word, or so they thought, but it soon became obvious he was determined they would not be allowed to miss out one word.

Marc did demur at Simon's demand for 'daddy's poem' and that was one disappointment the boy had to accept.

The week flew by. Abiathar and Joseph both called to enquire of Simon and to convey their sadness that they had made little impression on the trading federations in Massilia, which had no intention of waiving any debts.

"The best we've achieved is an agreement not to press for their repayment, which wasn't easy with regard to Britain under the threat of a Roman invasion."

"Well they will reap the whirlwind!" said Brutus,

"Let's hope it doesn't engulf us all!" sighed Joseph.

The three Marys accompanied by a vigilant escort visited a local Christian church comprising mostly of Gentiles and a smattering of Jews, who were eager to hear such direct witness from those intimately involved in the earliest days of the movement. There was pressure for them to stay longer but Abiathar warned of a Temple oriented section of the Synagogue, who was meeting with an envoy of the Sanhedrin from Jerusalem.

Accordingly it was with a certain relief that they boarded the small vessel to continue westwards, towards the high mountains that reared far beyond the horizon. The day was clear, the sky a translucent blue, with only the faintest wisp of white cloud over the hill tops.

Pothus was excited to be heading home and was already bonding with Simon.

Cornelius waved sadly, as with white sail hoisted they reached steadily seaward under the brisk, offshore wind. The land ahead stretched flat and featureless as far as the eye could see; behind the white limestone headland glistened and blinked its farewell.

The sudden elongated white streaks of cloud appearing off the low lying shore to their right meant nothing to the travellers, although the crew hurried to shorten sail in anticipation, but the suddenness with which the sea heaved into short steep waves as the wind hit them on the beam, laid the boat over on its port side so that the gunwale was awash. They had been hit by that most unpredictable of winds, the Mistral, roaring down from the high Alps, along the valley of the Rhone before heading unimpeded across the Gulf of Lion.

The precipitate strain on well-worn rigging initiated a succession of snapping and breaking, and in an instant they were dismasted, the sail wallowing in the waves as the splintered end of the mast gyrated wildly.

Brutus grabbed Simon and led the women to the clear area at the stern and securing a loose rope for an additional handhold, urged them to sit on the heaving deck, where Marc joined them and tried to reassure Miriam. Pothus sustained a nasty laceration across his temple from a flaying, wind-maddened spar, and instantly concussed lay on the deck not far from the group, who took it upon themselves to protect him from further injury.

Hastening to the aid of the crew Brutus drew his sword and severed the ropes entwined and holding the mast until it fell clear over the port side. Unconstrained the boat came on to an even keel, rocking violently to every wave.

The wind coming off the land had too small a fetch to build up fearful waves but the motion was distinctly uncomfortable and frightening enough. As their drifting ship came shuddering down on to the sand bank Brutus saw two of the crew heaving the long boat up to the leeside. Two pairs of oars were lashed across the thwarts and one man jumped in while the other held the boat.

"Bring the women and the boy," he called, "we have to abandon ship!"

Brutus hurried aft and ushered them forward, but his Mary refused to get in the waiting boat.

"Take Pothus, his need is much greater than mine!" she insisted, pointing to where the dazed man sat dolefully with Mother Mary nursing him, and no efforts of Brutus could persuade her otherwise.

Handing Simon and the women and the injured hermit into the long boat, Brutus restrained the second crew as he went to leap in.

"Let Marc go with them instead," he insisted, "he can row as well as any man and they may need his sword ashore."

They exchanged places and throwing in a leather bucket, Brutus pushed the boat off to head for the distant shore.

The frightened faces, peering at them over the spray-drenched transom as the boat rose to each wave, seemed hardly to move away. Then suddenly the gap widened as the boat moved more easily.

"They will make it for certain, dearest," said Brutus with relief, "and it should be easy to beach on that shore."

He looked at Mary quizzically, "That was brave of you to give Pothus your place."

Holding aloft the package she had retrieved from the hold, Mary laughed, her dark eyes gleaming, "I needed time to search for this, the greatest of my earthly possessions!" The ship was rising with each wave, and then shuddering with the impact as its keel hit the hard seabed. The crestfallen captain had now joined them and was inconsolable at the imminent breaking up of his ship.

"I know these cursed Mistrals, they blow for days, getting stronger with each hour. Nothing can save the boat, so collect your most valued possessions to take with you when we have to abandon her."

He fell silent looking forlornly at the long boat now closing the shore in the distance. Two hours later they too stepped ashore, where many friendly fishermen and their families offered them refuge at their humble dwellings. The first arrivals awaited them anxiously, wet through and bedraggled, and the locals looked on with disbelief as they all knelt on the sand and gave thanks for their safe deliverance.

"You'll never persuade me to step aboard another ship," vowed Mother Mary and was not the least surprised at the loud amen from her companions.

Pothus was slow to shake off his concussion, and was troubled by dizziness and double vision. The thought of him stumbling or falling from his lofty height deterred their travels for ten days, days that the local provincials utilized to create myths and legends that would be handed on in perpetuity.

Remote as they were from the cities of Arelate or Massilia, they had heard but whisperings of the new religion that was sweeping across Provence. Now, not only did they hear of the world shattering events that had reverberated from Jerusalem, they had some of the principal witnesses to these events, that for the time being they could claim their own. The beach where they had landed was thronged daily, with both the credulous and the curious, all spectators to the disintegration of the ship, that later legend was to claim had brought three Marys and a baby all the way from Palestine.

Simon never reconciled himself to his diminished status, but the captain even as he lost his ship reconciled himself to being the owner of the long boat, which daily gained in value to become a veritable treasure. Eventually he sold it to some enterprising man from Arelate, who thought it would adorn the church they were building in that city, where it was to become the altar.

The travellers deported themselves with quiet dignity, Mother Mary telling of the childhood and early years of Jesus' ministry, Mary Magdalene of the redeeming love that her saviour had shown her. Women, identifying with her total surrender as their own path to salvation venerated her very shadow, and attributed miraculous healing to gaining proximity to her. The moving stories she told, with the clear light of witness shining in her eyes, convinced them of the raising of the dead youth at Nain and her brother Lazarus from his tomb. Assured of this they found no difficulty in believing her witness to the resurrection of her Lord following his crucifixion, and always her testimony led to baptisms at the seashore.

Brutus was desperate to get away, more so as the daily increase of pedlars, entertainers and troublemakers changed the ambience from worship to carnival. Only once had he inadvertently testified to his role, when a dispute had arisen as to whether Jesus had really been dead when he was taken down from the cross. Mother Mary had been telling of Nicodemus and Joseph of Arimathaea standing aside, so that she could clutch the ruined body of her son to her breast before he was laid in the tomb.

"You lie!" rang out a shrill challenging cry from a prophetess of Mithras, who was greatly venerated at the temple at Arelate. "Only Mithras the sun god can bring back life, through the blood of a sacrificed bull. Your son can't have been dead. He can't have been!"

She had her hands to her ears, refusing to hear any reply. Mary said nothing, her composure shattered by this shrill challenge. The prophetess then brought her hands down to the neck of her robe, locks of her hair plucked in her closed fists, and then as the locks fell she rent her robe to bare her breasts.

"You lie, he wasn't dead! You lie, you lie!" rang out the chant of the supporters of the prophetess, many of the men having the cropped heads that Brutus recognized as those of Roman soldiers. Stepping between, to shield Mary from their chanting and to challenge their leader, Brutus hissed menacingly, "I, centurion Brutus of the tenth legion and the Jerusalem garrison, I killed him with a thrust of my spear to his sacred heart!"

Everyone's attention was held by him and the anger blazing in his narrowed eyes, from whose relentless look the legionary was forced to avert his own. The prophetess rolled her eyes so that only the whites showed, and then collapsed as though dead. Brutus turned and gently led the distraught Mary back to their lodgings.

When later, Mary Magdalene tried to coax him out of his black humour, as they were discussing their immediate plans, he only avowed that the sooner they got away the better.

The day they could leave finally came, but such was the build up of emotion in the area they would have found it impossible to escape during the day. Brutus knew from Pothus that their route lay westwards, but found the hermit so limited in his local knowledge of the terrain that he decided to rely on his own instincts.

He quickly established that the coastal delta where the Rhone split into many tributaries was impassable on foot, and the extensive lakes adjoining the shore were marshy and dangerous, so he decided it would be better to strike north following the bank of the small Rhone to the higher region where the river could be crossed near Nemausus. From there they would have to move west for many days through pine forests and scrub, but such terrain he had often negotiated in former days of soldiering and he was quietly confident this could be achieved, even though his party differed greatly in their stamina and endurance from a company of legionaries.

So for two days he took himself off to reconnoitre a route they would be able to follow at night, after they had managed to slip away unobserved.

Now that night had finally come.

Pothus was recovered, everyone was readied so that an hour before moonrise they stole out of their rooms and met on the seashore. It was too dark to see even where they were treading but Brutus knew every inch of the important first miles, and had a thin hand line for everyone to hold as they followed him blindly in single file. Simon found it incredibly exciting between his mother and father bringing up the rear of the column.

Progress was slow but once the moon broke through the cloud, bathing them in its pale light, they were able to stride more confidently through the sparsely wooded scrub. By dawn they had gained a hamlet at the crossing place, but as the ferryman was not yet eager to be roused they patiently rested and shared their breakfast until they were rowed across the sluggishly flowing Rhone, and began the hard day's walk to the first big town.

Dusk was falling as they approached Nemausus, the neat fields dominated by a high defensive tower that long predated the Roman conquest, that once had strengthened a Celtic oppidum against marauding bands. It was unoccupied, as the Romans had built new barracks within the city wall, along with an amphi-theatre, temples and baths, all of which are essential feature of any colonia built to accommodate a great number of veterans.

Brutus approached the guards at the southern gate to make enquiries.

"They'll be closing the gate shortly until dawn," he said on his return, "so we either rough it at the tower or find an inn."

"We don't need to provision and might well be recognized, so let's stay outside!" urged Mary Magdalene, and as no dissent was voiced, that was the first of many nights they camped in the countryside.

The weather held up, and although it was cool at night a deadwood fire could always be lit to warm them. Brutus exhibited his hard earned skills of living off the land, and many a rabbit or duck contributed to the aroma permeating the air around their camp, supplementing that which they could buy from the occasional farm or village.

On the fifth day they were climbing steadily through dense woodland, follow-ing a narrow valley down which tumbled an exuberant stream from the hills looming in the distance. Brutus began to fear for his companions, knowing the nights would get colder and they were without adequate clothing when the weather broke up, and resolved to ensure that they be better prepared at the next town they came to.

"Tolosa is an important city on the trade route between the ocean to the north and the Great Sea, and we will be able to find all we need there!" he reassured them confidently.

Mother Mary was unable to sustain a protracted march especially at these higher altitudes, and aware they were travelling slower than he intended, Brutus kept a look out for a couple of mules and a muleteer. He was lucky at the next village they passed through, where a few enquiries took him to the vineyard of Abihu, who readily agreed to accompany them.

"We're still two weeks away from harvesting so I can guide you to the western hills. Let me saddle one of my donkeys for the boy and the other will carry your provisions," he said eagerly, having negotiated generous payment from the relieved centurion.

Simon watched wide-eyed with anticipation as their saddles were secured and then he was lifted with uncontrollable excitement on to the larger beast as Abihu instructed him.

"There, Hannibal will be the most reliable but hold the bridle loosely."

Brutus laughed quite disproportionately, and they regarded him with surprise.

"Hannibal!" he gasped, "how can you name a donkey after the great Carthagi-nian general?"

"Generals can be more stupid than donkeys. I've got four and this one's name is Pompeii and the others are Caesar and Scipio."

When Brutus' laughter had subsided, he tried to briefly summarize the campaign that had brought Hannibal and one hundred thousand men from Carthage over those very hills they were about to cross, to invade Italy. Once he had mentioned the innovative use of elephants Simon no longer allowed any summary, but insisted on hearing every last detail of the campaign.

"I'll tell you the whole battle when we make camp tonight," Brutus promised and the impatient boy had to satisfy himself with looking for elephants through the trees as they progressed. After a few hours his sore backside made him more than happy to walk and the weariness of Mother Mary helped Brutus to persuade her to ride Hannibal in his place.

In this manner they made good progress and two days brought them to the bustling trading town of Tolosa.

Their descent into the broad valley of the Garonne River, with the walled city perched on its eastern bank was spectacular, and now through breaks in the dense woodland they could view the high mountains of the Pyrenees to one side, and the city beckoning at the centre of the endless rolling plain to the north.

Passing through the gateway was an urgent movement of people and pack animals in both directions. The double gate was wide open such was the volume of traffic, and a column of Roman cavalry approaching along the road scattered everyone as it rode through.

Brutus felt a surge of excitement, at the haughty spectacle of coloured plumes and flowing red cloaks, splendid horses and gleaming weapons and armour. Mary grasped his free hand, the other holding the bridle of the donkey.

"I always feel anxious for you when we encounter the army in action, you must miss the excitement so much!" she said.

"Mostly it's boring garrison duty punctuated by uneventful patrols. I can assure you each day since I retired has been more rewarding and there's been no lack of excitement!" and he gave her hand a reassuring squeeze.

The town lived up to expectation with all the appropriate monumental building to reflect imperial Rome's greatness. It also more importantly, lived up to expectations with regard to their necessary purchases and they elected to rest one night at an inn.

It had not been possible for any of the women to attend a synagogue for a long time, and they wondered if there was a Christian community in the vicinity, but their enquiries at the inn met with evasion. The porter denied any knowledge of the word Christian, but irritated Marc by drawing with his finger in the earth and then rubbing it out repeatedly. Mother Mary solved the mystery as she knelt down on the ground and drew an outline of a fish and then pointed at each of them. The eyes of the porter widened in disbelief, as he looked from one nodding head to another, each smiling inanely.

Finally he smiled at them and asking them to wait, disappeared smartly.

He returned with a goatee-bearded stranger who proceeded to ask many questions concerning Jesus. When and where was he born, the names of his parents, his disciples, the manner of his betrayal and execution? Each question they answered simply and eventually he declared himself satisfied.

"I am elder Caleb and we have an active community of Jewish and gentile followers. We meet most evenings at secret locations that are frequently changed, as we are frowned on and harassed by both Rome and the Synagogue. Where are you from?"

"Jerusalem!" said mother Mary, enjoying the electrifying effect of her word on her listeners.

"We meet tonight outside the town at the sacred pool of the Volques. I will have to guide you so be ready at sunset."

"What is the sacred pool of the Volques?" asked Mary, fearing some pagan temple and possibly some unsavory blending of new and old beliefs.

"Only a small lake in a grove of oak trees which once was sacred to the ruling Volque tribe of Celts, before the Romans desecrated it."

"What did they do to it?" asked Brutus resignedly.

"They drained it as soon as Tolosa accepted Roman rule, well over a hundred years ago."

"To eliminate a rival to their gods and their temples I suppose?"

"No, to seize the vast votive offerings of gold and jewellery that had been cast into it over many hundreds of years. The uprising this sparked took many years to suppress."

Marc felt his anger rising at this humiliation imposed on his Celtic cousins and resolved to treat the pool with appropriate reverence.

They eagerly followed Caleb through the darkened streets of the town, out of the western gate, across the arched stone bridge over the wide, slow-flowing Garonne, and into the countryside. Ten minutes along the road they overtook a smaller band, and together turned off the road to cross a few fields towards a darkly silhouetted copse. Lanterns were lit and they moved quietly approaching some lights flickering ahead. Suddenly they were in a clearing, where a large number of people were seated on the ground listening to the only standing speaker, who had their rapt attention and continued with his discourse uninterrupted.

"They have disappeared as quickly and as mysteriously as they appeared. Nobody has any explanation but all sorts of rumours are rife. The local followers feel deserted, after their euphoria at the very great honour they had been shown. Maybe the carnival was getting out of hand and so they left; but to receive the mother of Jesus and Mary the first witness to the resurrection, literally out of the blue, was bound to excite the whole region, and now there is a feeling of anti-climax that they find hard to bear."

The speaker paused, studying the newcomers, then continued,

"I ask you all to kneel and pray for our brethren at the edge of the sea. Pray that they are able to reconcile the loss they feel now, and that they grow in faith because of the great privilege they have received. Lord, help them to accept that all is in accordance with your will. Amen."

"Amen," echoed all in unison, as Brutus became aware of the scrutiny they were receiving from their escort.

Leaning across he whispered, "Trust us. All will be made clear in the fullness of time as your elder says, but we are on a mission of the greatest importance to the movement, and the less people to know of it the better."

The man nodded, although his reluctance to keep such a secret was transparent.

"We'll be gone in the morning but I promise we will send you word when our mission is fulfilled."

With that Caleb had to be satisfied, and late that night they re-entered the city, the side gate being opened to them by a sympathetic guard.

Shortly after dawn they were on their way, and Pothus was searching unsuccessfully for some conspicuous feature that would help him. Nothing looked familiar to him, so when Abihu suggested they follow the river to its source at the foot of the mountains he concurred.

This took two full days and as the high mountains reared up in the distance, some of the peaks glistening white with new snow, Pothus grew in confidence, for they were approaching his country where he knew his people would be preparing for them.

Lugdunum Convenarum came in view over the gently rolling fields, walled, turreted and threatening.

"We must cross the Garonne here and follow the hills westward," urged Pothus, "then I will find my people for certain."

Brutus warned, "This town is to be avoided as it is a settlement built to accommodate the retired riff-raff of many legions. Passers through are easy game for robbery, and if there is a magistrate here he is likely to want his cut. There are many such colonies in western Gallia to be avoided."

They had no need to enter and having crossed the bridge, deviated from the more northerly road to head into the sunset across open country.

The extensive forest covering the hills looked impenetrable and Abihu led them along the edge of the woods, which bordered the cultivated fields on their right. Mostly harvested and now awaiting the autumn rain, the earth was hard under foot. Simon was disappointed not to move through the forest, as he kept getting fleeting glimpses of Hannibal's escaped elephants, and couldn't understand the lack of interest of daddy and Brutus to hunt them.

"Just one," he pleaded, rejecting the excuse that there wouldn't be any around after a hundred years. His look of contempt sufficed where words failed him, although he was heard to mutter, "Elephants live to a hundred anyway!"

Widely skirting an unknown but typically Roman settlement, they moved through thick scrub at the forest edge, which seemed to lead imperceptibly towards the foothills.

Mary was seated on Hannibal when the quietness was shattered close by, as with a rending of saplings a black mass hurtled straight at the terrified Hannibal. Instinctively it reared throwing Mary with sickening impact to the ground, and as the boar passed under the belly of the donkey it swung its head viciously, its tusk opening and eviscerating the animal in a second, before it careered on down the escarpment, leaving its writhing victim and pandemonium behind.

Although Marc and Brutus were not slow in their reaction, it was all over before they had drawn their swords. The shocked muleteer knelt by his stricken beast as the women tended to its deathly pale and inert rider, while fearful of a second boar, a wary pair of swordsmen stood either side of the carnage, allowing Pothus to give Mary his full attention.

"There may be a mate and young lurking somewhere in the undergrowth!" called out Brutus, adding to the fear that still held everyone in its coils.

The pain filled shrieks of the donkey could only be silenced by the swift application of the centurion's sword, while Miriam soothed a distraught Simon who had grown to love Hannibal.

As the minutes passed their fears abated, and Marc sheathed his sword and helped calm the crying boy.

"We must find shelter for Mary. I haven't been able to assess her injury properly but it is essential she doesn't spend the night in the open!" insisted Pothus.

A river ran at the bottom of the escarpment and in the late afternoon light they studied the rock face on the opposite bank. The sun dropping behind the high peaks lit up the cliff, suffusing its whiteness with a rosy hue, and half a mile ahead a small stream joined the river where an area of deep shadow suggested the possibility of a cave.

Marc and Abihu descended the escarpment and had little difficulty in fording the river. They were watched anxiously as they rounded the prominence of the rock face and disappeared into the cleft from which issued the stream. The sun had now dipped behind the mountains but there was still an hour of daylight.

Some time passed and then Marc emerged, and giving a reassuring wave made quickly to rejoin them. Mary had now regained consciousness, and lay cradled protectively in the arms of Mary Magdalene.

"There's a small cave overlooking the stream that will give us good shelter!" blurted out Marc, his relief evident in his face, "I've left Abihu gathering wood for a fire."

Brutus had already improvised a litter, and carefully bearing Mary between them, they descended the bank and crossed the river for the sanctuary of the cave.

Brutus was aware of the proximity of someone, and shot out of his bed as Pothus laid a restraining hand on him. It was first light and through the entrance to the cave the stark outline of the high peaks appeared black against the palest of skies.

"I know where I am. My people await me but two days march from here so I must hurry to them and give them news of their eagerly awaited queen. Mother Mary has broken no bones and a week's rest in this cave will restore her. Don't move from here so that we know where to find you when we return to fulfil our destiny."

He departed, confidently walking towards the mountains unaware of the pensive look the centurion fixed on his receding figure.

"So the last part of our mission is near," said Mary Magdalene, "you and Marc have accomplished an incredible feat, bringing us this far, and I rejoice that for her it is ending. For the rest, this is but a new beginning which will take us to strange and uncharted places."

"Can you bear that with our unborn child so near? Would you rather we urge Marc and Miriam to go ahead to Britain and follow later?"

"Certainly not, we must go together as it has been since we stood at the foot of the cross. A child is more easily carried in the womb than any other way and ..." with a little laugh, "more easily guarded by my brave warrior."

"I hope it will be a little girl to grow up like you," said Brutus adoringly, slipping back between the furs that made their bed.

That cave was their refuge for many days. By the third day Mary had recovered sufficiently to walk a little way along the edge of the stream looking expectantly towards the high peaks dominating the far horizon. She had just nodded an acknowledgement when Brutus told her of Pothus' words, but he knew she was constantly on the look out for his return.

"This cave will always be most revered by me for I know I will be taken from here and from you all to fulfil my final destiny. I am concerned that someone is needed to stay and support the emerging church in this region of Gaul, which will always have my blessing. Could you make your home here, Mary?" she said, looking intently at Mary Clopas.

"Wherever you go I wish to go with you," pleaded her companion.

"You won't be able to, nobody will. All will be revealed when Pothus returns with his people, but I know I alone will leave with them. Please spend your allotted years here in southern Gaul where you will be able to tell the wonders you have witnessed."

A tearful Mary agreed without being able to find any words in her grief. Her sobs seemed to echo and be amplified in the cave, and then as the throb grew louder, rhythmic and melodious, they realized something momentous was approaching.

Rushing to the entrance their eyes beheld a hundred torches of the column moving joyously along the stream. Their chanting swelled momentarily to a crescendo, and then fell to a bare whisper as those watching moved out of the cave.

The men comprising the column amazed the viewers by their great height and their natural dignity. Each was bedecked in gold tunic and purple robe, befitting the escort of a queen. Arms and neck were bare, but surmounting their blonde wavy heads each wore a garland, as though they were a wedding party of woodland spirits. They carried two silk draped, and gem studded litters, the curtains of the first being thrown back to reveal a white bearded old man, peering eagerly and talking excitedly to Pothus, who walked at his side.

Still chanting, so quietly as to blend with the sighing night breeze, the column came to a halt forming a semi-circle around the cave, and Pothus offered his arm to aid the Magi to raise himself from the litter and slowly walk to the entrance.

Mary appeared from within. She had changed into a white robe; around her waist was tied a blue belt and her head was covered with a blue headdress, edged with gold. At the sight of her all fell silent and the Magi Gaspar knelt at her feet and said,

"Hail Mary, Queen of Heaven. We are come to escort you to your coronation."

All were kneeling before her, and her companions aware of the awesome significance of what they were witnessing, did likewise. Mary offered her hand to Gaspar who kissed it, and then led her silently to the second litter, which she entered and seated herself on the cushions. As the Magi assumed his seat the column of men resumed their chanting and prepared to move off.

Pothus went to join them but was arrested by Brutus' hand on his arm.

"Who are you?" he demanded.

"We are the Jentillak. Our patriarchs were the sons of God who thought the daughters of men so fair they coupled with them. Our forefathers were their sons. When our fathers beheld man's wickedness, long before the flood, they withdrew into the high mountains and so escaped the inundation. Ever since we have kept ourselves apart, occasionally making contact with and helping the Euskadi in a crisis, when ignorant of cultivation or how best to care for the animals around them. So we lived remote but in harmony with the Euskadi, teaching them of the healing in plants and of God's provision and care for this world.

"When we heard of the coming of the anointed one our Magi Gaspar ordered us to withdraw and await God's call. He and I journeyed to Bethlehem to bring gifts to the infant King. That was forty years ago. Since we have remained celibate and no children impede our fulfilment of God's purpose, which is to bring Mary to her coronation. She will be the Queen of Heaven and we are to share in her assumption."

He hurried to join the line of torches retracing their path along the dark valley. Gradually the glimmer faded and only the faintest of sounds vibrated around them. They stared fixedly into the enclosing dark, but each knew in his soul all was accomplished.

Her voice choking with emotion Mary Clopas whispered,

"She's wearing her wedding robes. Mary is going to join her Joseph!"

CHAPTER SIX

As though restrained unnaturally so that its anger had built up disproportionately, winter broke loose savagely the next morning. Storm lashed rain drove the inhabitants deep into the cave, where they huddled together to keep warm, unable to light a fire without choking on the fumes.

Venturing to its entrance they felt daunted at the torrent surging close to the cave, along the course of a stream that had but gurgled the previous day. Trees uprooted by the elements rushed past threateningly. Low on food and dispirited by the emptiness following the departure of Mary, there was a stultifying lethargy of body and mind, and every discussion of their unhappy predicament led to conjuncture on Mary's situation.

Finally an exasperated Mary Magdalene said, "We will never know, so don't let's try to guess. We have helped to bring about a mystery that will always remain so. We are faithless to worry over Mary now we have released her into God's keeping, and would do better to worry about ourselves if this continues, as I do believe we are trapped here while the rain persists."

"The water is within a few feet of the entrance and still rising. Our only option is to wait and hope," agreed a reluctant centurion.

"Oh Brutus. You must know by now we don't wait and hope, we pray," chided his wife mischievously.

"I know your prayers work for you and I don't doubt they will again, but I believe God helps those who strive to help themselves."

"So you strive while I pray and we'll make an invincible team," laughed Mary disarmingly, and her disconcerted man sat down with a rueful smile.

"Do you think Abihu will have harvested his grapes by now?" asked Miriam.

"He will have had four days and with his large family I would think so. He was wise to head home on Pompeii as soon as he knew we were stuck here."

Even as Miriam said this she regretted it for the mention of Pompeii reminded Simon of Hannibal and he started to cry. He remained inconsolable, and resisted all their efforts until Miriam agreed to tell a story.

"I have a story that will make a few days stuck in this cave seem like but an hour!" she said, and Simon's eyes gleamed at the thought of the cavernous belly of the whale.

"About Jonah and Leviathan, mummy?"

"Just you wait and see, my boy," and she suddenly realised everyone was listening.

"You will all know how Moses grew up as a prince in Egypt, until the day he realized how cruelly his brethren were being treated, and was provoked into slaying the Egyptian who beat the Hebrew slave. This was witnessed by Dathan and Abiram, who threatened to tell Pharaoh, forcing Moses to flee."

Their rapt faces assured her she had their attention.

"Well, Moses fled to Midian in Arabia, and there he saw Zipporah, who was so beautiful the flowers shed their petals so she would not have to walk on the bare earth. Moses wanted her for his wife, but Zipporah was the daughter of Jethro, a pagan Priest. Now in Jethro's garden was a marvellous tree. This tree was originally the rod that God had created on the eve of the first Sabbath and which he had given to Adam, who had it with him when he was thrown out of the Garden of Eden. Adam passed it on through his children until it came through the patriarchs into Jacob's family, and so into Egypt. There it came into the possession of Jethro, who was one of the advisors at Pharaoh's court. Jethro took it home and planted it in his garden, and it grew into a great tree in which nested a multitude of birds. A talking bird told Jethro in a dream, 'Beware the man who can uproot this tree, for through him will Egypt be humbled.'

"Now when Moses asked for Zipporah to become his wife, Jethro remembered this dream and he said, 'Show me you are worthy of my daughter, uproot this tree growing in my garden and she will be yours.'

"To Jethro's amazement Moses did as he was asked and the Priest realized that this was the man who would break the Egyptians' enslavement of the Hebrew people. He threw Moses into a pit and covered it so there was no way out, and then forgot all about him as he thought it would be his tomb. Zipporah cunningly managed to keep him alive by giving him food in secret and for seven years Zipporah fed him, and coaxed her father to refuse any suitor who asked for her hand."

Miriam stopped to give those trapped in the cave time to contemplate the thought of seven years in a pit, before continuing.

"At the end of that time she reminded her father of the man he had cast into the pit. 'Either take his corpse out because of the stench' she said, 'or if he is still alive you will know that he is perfectly righteous.'

"Jethro had forgotten his name even, but when reminded called out, 'Moses,' and when Moses responded he pulled him out, kissed him on the head and said, 'Blessed is God who has preserved you in this pit for seven years. I now believe that it is he that kills, and revives the dead, and that you are perfectly righteous.'

"He then gave Moses much wealth, and his daughter Zipporah to wed. They agreed that of any children born in his house half should be brought up to be Jew and half to be Egyptian."

A lot of comment was evoked by this story amongst the listeners, but unwisely it was Miriam's spouse who was most voluble.

"Seven years!" exclaimed Marc with disbelief. "Why in that time the beautiful Zipporah could have changed into an old hag."

Whether this was intended to elicit the outraged reaction of the women we will never know, but Marc was forced to seek sanctuary behind the burly centurion while Simon shrieked, whether to encourage or restrain Marc's assailants again remains a mystery.

Eventually the men concurred that seven days would not have been reprehensible on the part of Zipporah, but seven years just showed how slow women were on the uptake.

Even Mary Clopas partook in their chastisement, while Simon was thrown into a quandary whom to support. Finally he rejected any gender bias, and decided to align himself with numerical superiority.

Eventually a laughing Miriam asked if they wished to hear the sequel, and yielded to their entreaties.

"Moses was told by God to return to Egypt with all his family. On the way they came upon Satan in the guise of a serpent that immediately began to swallow Moses headfirst. He was however forced to stop when he came to the sign of the Abrahamic covenant, for he could not swallow that which carried God's sign. So he was stuck with Moses half swallowed, his legs flailing but unable to extricate himself. Then Zipporah realised the reason for the attack lay in their second son Eliezar, who being raised as an Egyptian was uncircumcised and God was showing his disapproval. So she seized a sharp stone and circumcised Eliezar with it there and then. She touched her husband's feet with the flesh of her son and said, 'Now we are betrothed in blood!'

"Immediately God consented to spare him, and the serpent had to regurgitate the frightened man, who lay prostrate on the ground while his wife tended to him."

Whether the sequel was told with the intention in mind, it had a very disturbing effect on both men, who were unusually subdued and looked distinctly queasy. Not so Mary Magdalene, who was holding her sides as tears of laughter rolled down each cheek. Miriam wore a self satisfied and superior look for many hours, and disconcertingly would suddenly bend and pick up a rough stone, looking at it pensively.

Retreating together to the entrance of the cave, and after a few minutes returning to dejectedly announce it was still lashing with rain, Brutus and Marc had the air of defeat about them. They all knew it would be hard to keep their spirits up for many days, but the grey clouds obscuring the whole world outside their shelter showed no respite.

"But we are dry and think of some of the places we have had to sleep in the open and how much worse off we would be there," said Mary Magdalene reprovingly when they were bemoaning their fate, "at least thirst won't be a problem and we can survive many days on what little food we have."

She was looking at the small pile of dried figs, a pair of loaves and the wedge of cheese, which she knew they had resolved was for Simon only.

With the passing of each day, Simon could hardly be coaxed to eat the stale bread, and the pain of empty stomachs grew harder to endure and what little laughter there was, was brittle and brief.

Brutus resolved that if the fourth morning dawned wet, not withstanding the danger, he would have to go hunting as food for their unborn child had become his overriding concern.

Thankfully the morning dawned clear and for the first time the mountains were visible in the distance. Quickly out and surveying the wide, fast-flowing river lapping the cave entrance, Brutus moved cautiously along the escarpment to his left until his way was blocked by a mass of impacted undergrowth. He moved back to try the other side but found everyone gathered, as eager as himself to get away.

"It's impassable that way," he said, "I'm going to work my way upstream to find a way out."

Marc proffered him the end of the landline they had used when setting out from the coast.

"Tie this around your waist and we'll explore it together," he said, as the older man chided himself for his lack of forethought, both now and for those wasted days while Mother Mary had lain recovering and he had not thought to explore up river.

A narrow ledge ran barely clear of the rushing water to a promontory which they carefully worked their way around and disappeared from the view of those watching.

A waterfall cascading out of a cleft from the cliff high above them, soaked Brutus as he passed along the narrow path, and he was frustrated only to find that the ledge petered out onto an impassable slope, lapped by the rushing water.

Looking up he realized that cleft in the cliff from which the water cascaded was their only escape route, but it was high and the rock lacked any real outcrops for foot or hand to grasp. However desperation was his spur and he started to scale the face, using what tentative holds he could find.

Marc, impatient and anxious, emerged through the waterfall to see Brutus spread-eagled half way up the cliff face above him, and inching his way up. He took a turn of his line around a stout root exposed by erosion of the rock, and made it fast as he willed Brutus upwards.

The clatter of a few stones preceded the breaking away of the rock under Brutus' foot. Momentarily he hung by his fingertips, his metal studded sandals scratching frantically, and then he slid down, crashing on the ledge and into the surging river like a libation to Poseidon that demanded the greatest urgency in its delivery to the god.

Mary, saw him hurtling towards her and was about to plunge to his rescue as his momentum was checked by the line, and the current thrust him angrily against the bank. Marc appeared simultaneously, and moved along the ledge to where he could reach down for the buffeted, half-drowned centurion. As he knelt to grab his tunic he found Mary was kneeling beside him.

Brutus grasped Marc's forearm but fearful of pulling his son into the spate he thrashed his legs ineffectually trying to get a purchase, only to find his ankle grasped by Mary as together they hauled him out horizontally, rolling him onto the ledge, where he lay gasping like a stranded fish. As his hair was brushed from his eyes he had a watery vision of a smiling Mary and heard her exult, "Now I know why Peter has given up catching fish to be a fisher of men!"

Such was Brutus' exhaustion her joke was completely lost on him, although Marc was more appreciative, and amazed that she could be resourceful and humorous at such a critical moment.

The fire had been rekindled in the cave and a shivering centurion sat as close as he could get to it.

"You were just unfortunate, your foothold collapsed under you," sympathized Marc.

"But I made no provision, that's what worries me. I nearly got us all killed!"

"Well you didn't and that won't happen again, and anyway it's given me an idea and I want you to listen to my plan which will get us out but it all hinges on Simon."

The others gathered around as Marc told what he had in mind.

"We're going to make a human pyramid, Simon, just like those tumblers from Carthage we've told you about and you will be at the apex, nearly at the cliff edge.

You will have this line to pull on and we want you to scramble up and onto the cliff. If you can do this we will be able to get away from here in a few hours instead of a few days!" encouraged Marc.

"You will be like King David, Simon. When he was a shepherd boy not much older than you, he would climb down into a ravine after a sheep that had fallen. Then he would climb back up with the sheep across his shoulders," said Miriam, aware that Simon was fighting back tears of fear.

An hour later they were all on the ledge, just beyond the waterfall. Marc secured a stout stick to the line and threw it up over the cliff edge and on the third throw it lodged securely, so not to tumble down when he pulled on it.

"Good, now for the pyramid," he said smiling reassuringly.

Brutus leant back, his legs braced to hold him against the rock face. Marc placed a foot in Brutus' clasped hands, and was quickly up on the centurion's shoulders. He tied a loop in the line and called out,

"Your turn, Simon!"

Mary and Miriam helped the boy scramble onto the centurion and Marc felt Simon clutching at his tunic.

"Put your foot into the loop and hold on to the line!" said Marc, grasping it in both hands to assist the shaking boy.

"Brutus will lift you now, hold the line tightly as you come up."

Brutus had hold of Simon's feet and extended his arms as Marc took up the slack in the line and then continued lifting as he felt his son scrambling up him until his feet came onto his shoulders.

Marc released the line into Brutus' keeping to grasp both ankles and felt the frightened boy shivering.

"Now up you go, Simon, just like King David! Pull on the line!" and he extended his arms until he had to let go of the kicking feet, and pebbles and earth fell around him. He hardly dared breathe, the future, indeed the very survival of them all, hanging on his young son.

He only relaxed when Miriam's proud voice called out with elation, "Oh well done, Simon. Now find the branch the line is tied to."

"I've got it, mummy," the boy's voice rang out.

"Take it round a tree and drop it back to daddy."

After a few minutes the branch hurtled down, narrowly missing Marc, followed by the smiling face peering at him over the cliff edge.

"Sorry, daddy," he called.

"You're a little hero," called Marc, "move back from the edge, I'm coming up now," and he put his weight on the double line and started climbing.

Within an hour all had gained the cliff top and they were cutting a trail through the dense wood. There was elation in their mood, which the hard going could not subdue, and when they burst out onto the cultivated fields, the heavy clay that clung to their sandals hardly checked their euphoria, although Brutus' next words dispelled it more effectively.

"I thought to avoid it, but the only place we can be sure of an inn is the Colonia at Tarbes," said Brutus hesitantly, "we could make it in about two hours."

"If there is a dry bed there, let's go to Tarbes," urged Mary. "With our three men to protect us we will not be threatened!"

She gave Simon a hug, and the boy's face beamed as he realized he was the third man, and he nearly burst with pride at his unexpected promotion. Miriam reflected ruefully on the contrast between his childhood and her own.

CHAPTER SEVEN

Tarbes in every way exceeded their worst expectation, and although long established and boasting the accoutrements of a Roman settlement, with baths, temples, theatre and arena, was still a frontier town. Drunken fights and disorder were daily occurrences and the only inn with a room for them was no exception and they were obliged to eat, drink and sleep in the one room, so that it seemed almost to be a cell.

There was no Christian community, nor a Synagogue, and the rains had resumed after a short break reinforcing their seclusion. Everyone was eager to be shot of the town but indecisive as to the next step.

Mary Clopas said, "Mother Mary's last request was that I stay in this part of Gaul. I have decided to return to Massilia, which is not that far away, where there is a Jewish community and a Christian church. Will you help me?"

Brutus looked enquiringly at Marc, wondering how this could be reconciled with their intention of travelling to Britain, but before either of them could speak, Mary Magdalene embraced her saying, "Of course we will. We'll escort you there as soon as the roads are passable. I can't wait to get away from here!"

Miriam was equally supportive.

The men accepted the inevitability of retracing their path and using the rivers to reach northern Gaul after they had seen Mary Clopas settled in.

As winter tightened its grip, the rain ceased and frost gripped the region. The river level fell, and Brutus was eager they recover their possessions from the cave. He recruited a donkey cart driver, named Ziba to go with him, nobody else being anxious ever to see the cave again.

"We will be back before nightfall," Brutus assured them as they set off.

The driver knew a path through the forest leading to the river. Easy to follow at first, it eventually became too narrow and they tethered the donkey in a clearing and proceeded on foot to the cave. It took but two trips before all was loaded in the cart and they began to retrace their route.

A shrill blast of a hunting horn shattered their tranquillity, and the very path they were treading shook to the thunder of hooves ahead.

The donkey pinned back its ears and reared as a pair of wild pigs crashed past, fleeing the dozen hounds at their heels. The lead huntsman was so close that even as he saw the obstruction all efforts to check his mount were futile and their collision was inevitable.

The frightened horse instinctively gathered its unstoppable momentum into a prodigious jump. For a second it looked able to achieve a miracle, but attempting to clear the donkey and cart was asking the impossible, and with a splintering of wood and snapping of bones its leap ended in a catastrophic impact, while the rider continued his trajectory, to be arrested by his sickening impact with a tree.

336

Two other horsemen drove into the mêlée, brushing Brutus carelessly into the dense undergrowth where he lay bruised and winded, as cursing the huntsmen dismounted to attend to their gravely injured leader and his mutilated mount.

Regaining his feet, Brutus surveyed the carnage all around. The broken horse lay spread-eagled across the upturned cart both forelegs shattered and convulsing violently. A shocked officer drew his sword and plunged it into the neck of the animal, and mercifully its spasms ceased as it exsanguinated from the severed artery, and the swordsman recoiled. Enraged, in the grip of an uncontrollable bloodlust, he raised his sword to strike Ziba who was struggling to disentangle his donkey from the shaft.

"Stop!" called Brutus, his voice strident with anger at the murderous intentions.

The centurion turned, sword raised, his wary eyes assessing who had dared to challenge him, and seeing the dishevelled civilian, smiled maliciously,

"You will pay dearly for your presumption, but first things first," and he turned back to finish the execution of the cowering driver.

"Fight me then," called Brutus, drawing his sword and lurching forward.

"Enough. Attend to Antipas," commanded the Tribune who had just dismounted, "put up your sword Gabinius and help!"

Reluctantly the centurion obeyed and while some of the lesser ranking huntsmen righted the cart, Ziba quieted the nervous donkey.

They laid Antipas in the cart, and the Tribune approached Brutus.

"I'm arresting you for causing grievous injury to King Herod Antipas!" he said, noting the incredulous expression on the face of his prisoner.

"But you know it was an accident, one of those things that happens in the thrill of the chase when caution is thrown to the wind. As a veteran and a centurion I deny any responsibility."

"Accidents don't just happen to royal personages, especially when they sustain grievous injury. Someone has to pay, and as you and the driver are responsible in my judgement, I am legitimate in arresting you. You will stand trial at Lugdunum Convenarum."

Any further protest being futile, Brutus went to pick up the scattered belongings and place them around Herod in the cart, but was told to leave them where they lay.

"I'll arrange for them to be collected later, but you won't be needing them where you're going!" threatened the tribune.

On arrival at the town the prisoners were roughly thrown into a cell adjacent to the guardroom at the gate. For two days their only contact with the outside world was their meagre food twice daily and the slopping out bucket, and all Brutus' efforts to get any message to Tarbes met with frustration.

The third day they were arraigned before a visiting magistrate. Their accuser was Tribune Varus, who as senior officer was responsible for the safety of the royal guest throughout the hunt.

"Your honour," he said in his opening speech, "we will show that King Herod was grievously injured as a result of an ambush, cunningly contrived to look like an accident, by a renegade Roman officer who nursed a long standing and deep hatred of the king from his service days in Jerusalem.

"Further we will present the testimony of centurion Gabinius that centurion Brutus drew his sword to complete the murder when he realised there was still life in the injured king. Only the action of Gabinius in standing between them dissuaded the prisoner.

"Finally in corroboration we will show that the accused caused serious injury to King Herod Antipas many years ago, when he was Tetrarch of Galilee.

"Our submission is that on two occasions the accused has made attempts on the life of King Herod Antipas and whether the king survives or succumbs, the court should sentence him to be executed."

This speech was followed by an excited clamour, among which many voices could be heard demanding his death without delay, as though no defence was possible. Varus bowed to the magistrate and sat with his officers.

Brutus looked to see the reaction of the magistrate, and was aware that he was being closely scrutinized by a youngish man, with distinctly semitic features, his deep-set eyes peering over an angular nose. His large lips seemed hard put to suppress a smile as they moved lazily,

"Let the court record that the prosecution brings two charges of attempted murder against veteran centurion Brutus. Not only that of three days ago, but another some years ago. Am I correct Tribune Varus?"

"Perfectly correct your honour."

"Thank you. Then the court needs to record the date of the previous attempt. Would you please oblige the court tribune?"

"Do you require the precise date your honour, it was many years ago?"

"The court does. It would like to know the year of which Consul tribune, so that our clerk can record it with confidence."

"May I briefly confer, your honour. This is really background to the latest attempt, and I did not pay close attention to the precise date it was so many years ago."

"Then you should have, tribune. The recent attack cannot be viewed in isolation, since you have chosen to cite a previous attack in support of your charge. Both need to be seen as substantive now you have brought them to our attention."

Varus had a thunderous look as he conferred with his advisors. Brutus felt the first surge of hope. This magistrate was obviously not in the pocket of the tribune and he started to believe he would get a fair hearing.

Varus rose and said quietly, "I regret we are unable to agree the precise year the first attempt occurred, your honour."

"Do you know the Emperor during whose reign it occurred tribune? Was it Tiberius or Caius?"

Such was the embarrassment of Varus as he had to admit even that was uncertain, but probably Tiberius.

"Then the court is adjourned and will reconvene in one week, hoping this period should suffice for the prosecution to clarify dates. Prisoners stand forward. Centurion Brutus you are to be detained until the trial. Custodians take note I wish this prisoner in no way to be harmed, and expect him to appear before us in exactly the health in which we see him today. Allow anything untoward to happen to the prisoner and I will call you to account. Driver Ziba, you are free to return to Tarbes but must appear to answer before this court in one week."

As he rose to leave chaos broke out in the courtroom and Brutus was certain the set of the magistrate's face expressed great satisfaction.

338

Mary Magdalene was in despair. She knew from their failure to return by nightfall that some catastrophe had befallen. For two days now they had enquired fruitlessly, and that the wife of the cart owner was likewise worried aggravated their wretchedness.

"We have only one fixed point from which to start searching," said Marc, "that is the cave, so I'll hire a horse and ride there tomorrow. If the packages are still there it will tell us something happened to them on their way, if they are gone it happened on the way back."

The ground was too frozen to leave a track but he had a good idea of the route having discussed it with Ziba's wife. He followed it faithfully, and as he penetrated into the forest caught a glimpse of a wolf, which surprised him, as they weren't usually so sluggish.

Rounding a bend in the path he nearly fell over the half-eaten horse, sending some carrion birds into the trees. Packages still lay strewn where they had fallen and Marc tried to piece together the clues to form a picture in his mind of what had happened. That he wasn't far out was confirmed as he led his heavily laden horse back past the town square where a large crowd was gathered around a wildly gesticulating man on a raised podium. Marc listened with incredulity.

"If King Herod dies of his injury then it's murder. The charge is attempted murder at the moment, but either will mean the centurion is executed. But what is really intriguing is the attitude of the magistrate who has adjourned the case for a week. He isn't satisfied with the prosecuting officer, who claims this is the second attempt to murder Herod by the same centurion. The idea of a Roman officer making two attempts on the life of a king beggars belief, and the magistrate is obdurate he wants corroboration. If any soldier served with centurion Brutus in Palestine, or knows anything likely to interest the court, take it to Tribune Varus at Lugdunum Convenarum."

"Brutus, did you say centurion Brutus?" called an unkempt man excitedly, and receiving confirmation he continued, "that's the man that threatened me when I stood up for the prophetess of Mithras last month, at the time of all that excitement at the seashore where the women and baby landed from Palestine." He paused and saw the crowd was hanging on his words.

"Well this man, his eyes blazing, seized me and said, 'I centurion Brutus of the tenth legion and Jerusalem garrison, I killed him with a thrust of my spear to his scared heart.'"

The reaction of the crowd was electrifying. The legionary was acclaimed as a hero, the champion of good over evil, and had Brutus been imprisoned in Tarbes a lynch mob would have pressed for him to be handed over there and then.

Marc hurried to the inn confused whether he felt elated or desolated, and uncertain how best to break his news to Mary.

He need not have worried for Ziba had but shortly left and they knew much the same, having heard the first hand testimony of the driver concerning the accident. Mary searched desperately through the packages.

"There must be the letter from Tribune Dan somewhere," she protested, and eventually it was found. "I must take it to Brutus. I'll go to Lugdunum tomorrow!"

"We'll all go, it's no good waiting here. Do you think Ziba would take us?" queried Marc.

"I doubt it," rejoined Miriam, "he's only just got back and has to appear in court in a few days."

They filled Marc in on the court proceedings and he felt some relief, but was eager to put Tarbes behind him and get to Lugdunum.

Travelling in two separate parties they entered the town together at dusk and enquiring at the inn, got the last available room.

"It's the trial of Herod's assassin!" rejoined the innkeeper rubbing his hands significantly, "the whole town is filling up with witnesses who know of this renegade."

"But Herod's not dead is he?" blurted out Mary turning pale.

The shrewd innkeeper noted her anxiety.

"It's touch and go, if he doesn't regain consciousness soon, well?" and he gave a meaningful shrug.

Their next days were frustrating as every effort they made to see Brutus was rebuffed. Nobody had been appointed to defend the centurion, and plea or petition to see him was redirected and disregarded. Sitting around forlornly with the realisation their efforts always fell on deaf ears, the door of the room burst open alarmingly, framing a man's figure in the doorway.

"I'm sorry, I thought the door was latched," he said.

"Maas!" cried Miriam, rushing to him to be seized in a crushing embrace.

"Princess, my memory plays me false you're more lovely than I remember," said Maas, releasing the breathless and blushing matriarch. Their spirits were lifted by his arrival, memories of his resourcefulness and courage in a previous crisis raising new hope.

"I'm going to press the court to accept me as prisoner's friend, so tell me all you can of the incident."

Maas had not lost his irrepressible sense of the ridiculous, and Simon was drawn to him, laughter having been non-existent amongst them for many days. He followed him like a shadow, and was the frequent recipient of a disbelieving shake of the Syrian's head as he looked from parents to son.

Following some hours of discussion, which had so absorbed them they forgot to send for food, Maas said, "Your testimony may be called for so be close to the court throughout the trial. They won't let you into the courtroom as its bound to be packed, the whole region is throbbing with excitement, but if I call for your testimony they will have to admit you as witnesses."

He left them confident that Brutus would be vigorously defended.

A cordon of soldiers restricted access of the aroused citizens to the vast square, of which the court occupied the northeastern corner. Only with the assistance of a resplendent Maas, were Marc and the women allowed onto the broad steps leading up to the colonnade that fronted the imposing building, to be available when called to testify.

Within, silence fell as the magistrate took his seat on the podium.

He was surprised at the emotion that had been generated by this case and his clerk had indicated many witnesses had come forward in the preceding week. He looked towards the table on his right, which was thronged with uniformed officers and black robed advisors. That on his left was sparse, only the one uniformed centurion and the two accused. The court was called to order and the indictment read out.

The magistrate allowed himself a brief smile, when centurion Brutus was indicted for the attempted murder of King Herod Antipas on two occasions, the first in the reign of Emperor Tiberius and the consulship of Severus, the second ten days ago, in the reign of Emperor Claudius.

Tribune Varus resumed his prosecution that had been so ignominiously interrupted a week previously.

"Your honour, in the week of the adjournment of this case such interest has been aroused throughout the province and beyond, that a lot of witnesses have come forward who will testify to the murderous activities of the accused centurion Brutus over a long period of years. Each witness thought only of their encounter in isolation, and failed to pursue the perpetrator, either because of intimidation or because he had fled beyond pursuit.

"Now because of Brutus' insatiable hatred of Herod Antipas, leading to the ambush last week, the whole saga of murder and vengeance can be revealed. May I call my first witness?"

The magistrate nodded agreement.

Herod's steward Caleb was called, an old man who had served the king for many years and had readily accompanied him into exile. He testified that he had identified the bodies of two servants of Herod's palace that had been murdered in the Judaean wilderness nine years previously. Their names were Phallu and Pua, and they had been trying to intercept Brutus and his slave, with a request that they attend an audience with the king. The two soldiers escorting them had also been murdered.

There was an outburst from the public area and Varus was unable to continue for some minutes.

"These were the first of many murders your honour, but I wish to emphasize that Phallu and Pua were servants of Herod's household and not soldiers."

Maas arose to question the witness.

"You state that King Herod requested centurion Brutus attend an audience with him?"

"That is correct."

"What was the relationship between them? Was there friendship?"

"Between a king and a retired centurion! I would very much doubt it. I would imagine it was to do with diplomacy."

"If I tell you there was enmity on the part of King Herod for an imagined affront by the centurion, and that he had illegally tried to seize the centurion's slave and throw him into jail, would you have any comment?"

"I know nothing of any affront, but yes there was an allegation the slave had stolen a valuable brooch and their had been an attempt to arrest him."

"I have no further question of the steward, your honour," bowed Maas, and sat down to a speculative murmur.

"My next witness is veteran legionary Horace, your honour."

Legionary Horace was a middle-aged, battle-scared veteran, still retaining the close-cropped head that characterized the serving soldier.

"Tell the court what befell the bireme galley *Hermes* eight years ago," urged Varus.

"We were carrying out a routine sweep off Caesarea looking for arms smuggling to brigands along the coast. King Herod Antipas was on board with Tribune Communis. Our commander, centurion Hedylus, gave chase to the *Dolphin* as there was suspicion it could be arms running. We were not expecting resistance and had ready a small boarding party when centurion Brutus tricked us, and holed the *Hermes* with a massive baulk of timber they were carrying."

"What happened to your ship and the men?"

"Centurion Hedylus and six legionaries were lost, two slaves were crushed at the oars, King Herod Antipas was very badly injured and the galley all but sunk."

There were gasps as he reeled off the casualties, and the outburst aimed at the centurion was angry and vehement.

Varus was elated as he looked at the judge.

"So far your honour, centurion Brutus has killed in peacetime, two of Herod's servants, two Herodian troops, a Roman centurion and six Roman soldiers and severely injured King Herod."

He resumed his questioning of the witness.

"What saved the *Hermes* from sinking?"

"Only the action of Tribune Communis."

"I would like a note made of that your honour. Tribune Communis saved the ship and thereby saved the life of King Herod, as well as everyone else on board."

Maas came to his feet as Varus withdrew.

"Legionary, how many times had you been involved in this sort of routine sweep aboard the *Hermes*?"

"Many times, maybe fifty or more!"

"And how often has King Herod Antipas sailed with you?"

"Only the once, not before or since."

"Thank you I have no further questions."

Varus resumed.

"My next witness is the key witness to show the devious and murderous nature of the accused. I call sergeant Tiasus."

Brutus could not help his involuntary gasp at this witness, and he looked anxiously at Maas, to whom the name held no significance.

"Sergeant Tiasus, how many occasions have you encountered the accused?"

"Three sir, maybe four."

"What was the first occasion?"

"Just after the rioting in Jerusalem seven or eight years ago. I was stationed at the Acropolis at Tyre, and my troop helped rescue two Jews, a brother and sister, from their cart that had fallen into a ravine."

"Were they badly injured?"

"The brother had a broken arm but sadly both their father and mother were dead. Both crushed."

"Was a complaint made by centurion Brutus?"

"Yes to Centurion Antony my commanding officer. When our troop had seen the upturned cart shortly before, cavalry officer Catullus had thought we had more urgent matters to attend to, and failed to stop to help."

"Do you recall the dramatic rescue of two youths from the sea?"

"Indeed I do. It was a very brave rescue by the freed slave of Brutus, and Horatius, a local fisherman. We attended to those youths at the garrison, they were some days in our sick bay."

"They recovered I presume. Then what happened?"

"They were released into the care of centurion Brutus, who had found them a ship to take them to Antioch."

"Your honour, I bring to your attention that they were found a passage on board the *Dolphin*, the very same boat that holed the *Hermes*." The ripples of excitement at this took some while to subside, and Varus exulted at his skilful disclosure.

"Was that the end of the episode sergeant?"

"No sir. No sooner had they sailed than Tribune Communis arrived from Jerusalem. One of the youths was related to King Herod, and the other to Legate Quintilius Varus. The youths had been abducted from the palace at Caesarea, and Tribune Communis was anxious to return them safely, but was obstructed in every way by centurion Brutus.

"Even our attempt to intercept the *Dolphin* at the port of Sidon failed, as Brutus somehow contrived to steal the horses from the pursuing company of cavalry. My own troop arrived just minutes after the boat sailed."

Brutus knew that damning, as this testimony had been, what was to follow would be more so. His face was grim in recognition of his predicament.

"Now tell us of your last encounter with centurion Brutus please, sergeant."

"It was earlier this year in Jerusalem. I, and a squad of soldiers under the command of Tribune Communis, arrested some Jewish Christian cult leaders who were abducting orphan children. At the moment of their arrest centurion Brutus appeared from hiding, and challenged Tribune Communis. They fought until the tribune lay mortally wounded. I was about to arrest Brutus when he showed me a letter of commendation from Tribune Danius Galerius, urging all commanders to assist him in his mission. Confused, and desperate to get my commander where he could be treated, I backed off and allowed him to go."

"So sergeant, centurion Brutus had mortally wounded Tribune Communis, who had saved the life of King Herod aboard the *Hermes*?"

"That is correct sir."

"And you let him get away with it because he showed you a piece of paper. A commendation from Tribune Danius Galerius, which might have been a forgery?"

Tiasus turned pale and looked distinctly nervous.

"Was it a forgery sir? It looked genuine."

"Nobody knows, sergeant, but you let the killer of your commanding officer go and he came here and may have murdered King Herod at last."

He took his seat, and for a few minutes Mass and Brutus urgently conferred. There was not a sound as Maas rose.

"Sergeant Tiasus, would you tell the court the names of the Jewish Christian cult leaders Communis was arresting.

"I'm not sure of names, they meant nothing."

"Well, was the giant Peter among them, or James the brother of Jesus, or Paul of Tarsus?"

Tiasus was perspiring, and wiped his forehead with the sleeve of his tunic. His nervousness could not be hidden.

"These men's names mean nothing to me."

"No they wouldn't, but they were there. But if I say Mary Clopas, Mary mother of Jesus what then?"

The startled look in his eyes betrayed his recognition, and he licked his lips many times. All confidence had gone as he murmured,

"I'm not sure. They could have been."

"No you're not sure, but you're quite sure they weren't Peter or Paul or James, because it was only women you were arresting."

"It wasn't for me to decide. I was only carrying out orders."

"The same excuse you plead for riding your troop past the overturned cart with two Jews crushed under it. Cavalry officer Catullus thought we had more urgent matters to attend to, your own words used to excuse complete indifference when you should have helped."

Tiasus stood silent and shattered, incapable of speech and evidently distressed. As the mutters started from the audience, Varus came quickly to his feet.

"I object your honour. Sergeant Tiasus is not on trial, and woe betide the Imperial Roman army when a soldier is berated for carrying out orders!"

"Woe betide the army when it acts as an instrument of the Jewish high priest to arrest women, because of collusion between Jewish Temple and a corrupt officer," retorted Maas indignantly.

Pandemonium broke out in the hall as howls of protest were thrown and rebutted by factions among the listeners. The magistrate declared an adjournment of fifteen minutes, and stated the court would be cleared if there were disorder on his return.

Maas made his way to Brutus' companions, who were dismayed by the anger welling out of the courtroom. He reassured them to be ready as their turn would come and returned to see a distraught and confused witness being led away. An angry Tribune was waiting, impatient to promote his prosecution with a more credible witness.

Centurion Gabinius gave the reassurance that Varus desperately needed. Tall, immaculately uniformed, handsome and composed, his youthful features belying his many years of active service, he restored the tribune's confidence.

"Centurion, tell the court what you witnessed as the first to see the carnage that terminated the hunt."

"Carnage it was indeed. Cirrus, King Herod's stallion, was thrashing about in its death throws where it lay on the donkey cart. I was distressed at its suffering, and ended it by piercing the horses neck with my sword, but as it was covered in blood I kept my sword in hand, as I searched the immediate area for the rider. The undergrowth was very dense where King Herod had been thrown by the brave but ill-fated jump of Cirrus, and only his moans led me to where the crumpled king lay at the foot of a tree. As I went to his aid I glimpsed centurion Brutus converging on King Herod with sword drawn. This didn't alarm me, I thought he had probably had to hack his way clear of some undergrowth, until I saw his eyes. They were murderous, blazing with anger and focussed on Herod. I don't think he saw me until I moved between him and his intended victim, then cowed by my confrontation he sheathed his sword. Tribune Varus saw his murderous intent as well, but wasn't positioned to intervene as I was."

"You are convinced centurion that your intervention saved King Herod from being slain by Brutus' sword?"

"I am sir. Even though King Herod was unable to defend himself because of his injury, he would have killed him."

Varus sat down with a grim smile, as growls of anger rippled from the listeners only to subside as Maas rose, and stood waiting patiently to conduct his cross examination

"Centurion Gabinius, what do you say to the allegation of centurion Brutus that you were so enraged by the accident, that after you had put Herod's horse out of its misery you were about to turn you sword on the donkey cart driver, whom you held to be responsible."

"Why sir, that would have been murder."

"Indeed it would, centurion. That however was your intention, until centurion Brutus threw out his challenge and drew his sword."

"No sir, it wasn't like that. Brutus has made up this calumny against me to try and save his own neck. I threw out the challenge not he, as I moved between him and King Herod!"

"Ziba the cart driver, states you had your sword raised to strike him."

"I had plunged my sword into Cirrus' neck. I was covered in the blood of the horse and Ziba was lying at my feet. From where he lay everything must have appeared distorted and threatening."

"You use the word cowed to describe the reaction of the accused when you confronted him. Did he cower before you?"

"He did to his shame."

"So, you accuse centurion Brutus of cowardice; this same centurion who raised the alarm in Syria six months ago, when Dura-Europos was under siege. The same centurion who went to the aid of Tribune Danius Galerius and another officer when they were overwhelmed, and then fought his way through the Parthians to raise the alarm in Damascus. You dare to accuse this man of cowardice. I leave the court to consider what value they can place on such discredited testimony."

Sitting down, Maas briefly conferred with Brutus, and receiving his agreement the Syrian came back to confront the confounded Gabinius. He brandished a piece of parchment as he called out,

"I wish to present to the court the letter of commendation from Tribune Danius Galerius, requesting all commanders to assist centurion Brutus in any way possible in fulfilling his mission."

"May I have that please, officer?" requested the magistrate.

The seal was broken but he recognised its validity as he opened it and read.

"When was the seal broken?"

Maas looked uncertainly at Brutus, who stood up and said,

"Your honour it was opened by Sergeant Tiasus, after I had vanquished Communis, his commanding officer."

"Why did you show it to him, centurion?"

"I knew he was about to arrest me, and that would have meant the end of my mission."

"What is this mission that is so vital?"

"I'm not prepared to disclose it in open court, but I will tell you in confidence if you assure me it will not be made public."

Howls of protest were hurled at him as the magistrate said,

345

"I recognise you will never reveal your mission unless I concur, even to save your life. Sergeant Tiasus, does he know?"

"Only as little as I had to tell him."

"Then I place an injunction on him to say nothing of this to any person in this court or outside of it. Come, let us go to my office. The court is adjourned for thirty minutes."

Ignoring the turmoil that spilled out from the court into the adjoining square, the two men left the room.

Varus was furious with Gabinius,

"You idiot, how could you fall into such an obvious trap? To impute cowardice of a veteran centurion is tantamount to insulting the whole chain of command. You are finished."

"If I go down, you go down with me," hissed the centurion and the two men stared at each other with undisguised enmity.

Although the assembly awaited their return with barely constrained impatience it was a full hour before the court reconvened. The face of the magistrate was stern and uncompromising as he addressed the assembly.

"I declare that no case has been presented to this court that justifies the arraignment of either of the defendants. However the time of the court has been wasted needlessly to serve the ambitions of certain officers who sought to evade their responsibilities. I refer particularly to Tribune Varus and centurion Gabinius, who both had responsibility for the well being of King Herod Antipas in the eventful hunt.

"You know that it is reckless in the extreme to abandon all restraint to the thrill of the chase, but that is human and forgivable. When the vicissitudes of life bring calamity it is the duty of officers to face up to the situation and deal with it manfully. To try and evade responsibility by shifting the blame onto innocent bystanders who become embroiled is shameful, and to press for the death penalty is a heinous crime deserving the full censure of the court. A report of these proceedings will be sent to the governor of the province and made available to the Senate in Rome. Let all beware of using the courts, the enthronement of justice, for their own purposes."

A stunned silence hung over the listeners as they dispersed and they spoke only in whispers, if at all. It was as though they all felt the lash of the magistrate's tongue applied to themselves, because of their prejudgment and prejudices.

The officers, knowing their careers to be finished, were ashen with shocked disbelief.

One party rejoiced with undisguised relief, unable to quite believe the suddenness with which the trial had collapsed.

Brutus emerged with Maas and informed them they would be accompanying the magistrate to Massilia the next day, but in the meantime to stay in the inn, as there were quite a few aggrieved persons who would welcome the opportunity to settle scores.

Their reunion with Maas, although brief for he was in transit to northern Gaul, was as memorable as on the previous celebratory night when Brutus and Marc with his help had escaped the manhunt around Jerusalem.

Brutus' ten days incarceration had made him edgy and dented his confidence and he knew it would take him a while to really believe he was free.

"With my reputation of both murderer, and mighty slayer of Parthians, which-ever people choose to believe, I don't think anyone will cause us trouble if we celebrate in the large dining room tonight and sleep there too," he said.

Mary realized the small room was too reminiscent of his cell.

The innkeeper was obsequious and they quickly sent him packing, with the request that one of his pretty maids would serve them better.

In contrast to the insolent casualness they had received, they were now provided with the best the inn had to offer. Maas felt irrepressible, and as yeast adds zest to the juice of the grape, he fermented considerable merriment amongst them. When they had imbibed enough wine Marc was easily persuaded to render his poem, and whenever he forgot a line or mixed up his words Simon could be relied upon to assist him.

Encouraged by his father's glory, Simon recited his poem of their encounter with the whale, and they all thrilled to the retelling of their odyssey, which Maas insisted was the most extraordinary voyage ever to have been undertaken, and not a few of those who had embarked on it were amazed how extraordinary it sounded in the retelling.

Dispersing the next day was not without the shedding of some tears, but embers still smouldered in the breast of each, to lie dormant awaiting only the reunion of comrades for it to be fanned into flame again.

The Roman magistrate enjoys many privileges, and is entitled to demand of the authorities, civil and military, any assistance he requires.

Accordingly in addition to a mounted escort, a cart was provided for the two Marys and Simon, and horses for the remainder of the party, when they set off on a crisp, frosty morning with a full days journey ahead to Tolosa.

Dionysius was the name of the magistrate, and relieved of the sombre robes of his office he likewise shed his serious, intense manner, and was witty and carefree.

"Well now Lugdunum Convenarum is behind me, and now I no longer have to regard you as a possible villain I can tell you where I met you many years ago, centurion," he laughed joyously, leaving Brutus in suspense, watching his face frowning with concentration as he searched desperately to recall any encounter, until he gave up.

"Forgive me, it's unfair. I was one of a hundred you met that night. At the banquet thrown by Vitellius the Governor of Syria, and afterwards I heard you address the enquiry into the near sinking of the *Hermes*. I was very impressed at the time as a junior advocate in Damascus, and when Varus referred in his opening remarks, to a previous attempt you had made on the life of the Tetrarch of Galilee I half remembered, and then veteran Horace confirmed it."

"I thank God for your good memory then sir, I was beginning to think they were concocting a water tight case against me."

"You should have had more confidence in your friend; Maas was brilliant! His shrewd questioning is an example in economy of words that I wish all lawyers could study, and he probes for the vulnerability of a witness with the scalpel of the surgeon. How did you gain him to your cause?"

"That is a very long story sir, and deserves better than I should try to tell it from the saddle of a horse. I ask your indulgence."

347

Brutus was gratified to receive a smiling acknowledgement. He knew he was going to enjoy the journey to Massilia.

Dionysius was a man of great curiosity and fine intellect, and he was anxious to probe deeper into the background and experiences that had welded his fellow travellers from their disparate backgrounds into such a unity of purpose. He envied their conviction that each person's destiny originated from his or her unique encounter with Jesus, and he wondered at the power of this eastern prophet whose death added to the momentum of his movement. Skillfully befriending everyone, and coaxing them to confide their innermost feelings and experiences, piece by piece he built up a picture of the crucifixion at Jerusalem and the momentous events following.

Mary realised he needed but a small nudge and he could become one of their most influential converts. They were talking one evening as he sat beside her in the wagon.

"Your Jesus didn't have much time for lawyers did he? But for me the law and the courts through which it is administered are of paramount importance!"

"They are in a world that has lost sight of God's law, where men are seeking dominance of neighbour and striving for power and wealth and title. Only imperial laws and courts can supervise the enslavement of half the world to Rome, and the distribution of all the wealth that is demanded as tribute. Our lawyers, the Scribes and Pharisees, are masters of those sorts of law, and have elaborated such a complexity of regulations they could fill the library of Alexandria.

"Jesus summarized God's law in two simple commandments, to love God with all one's heart and soul, and to love one's neighbour as oneself."

Dionysius was silent for a while, then, he said wistfully,

"No wonder they had to eliminate him, he challenged the whole edifice of their power and authority."

"Brutus tried to challenge the Jewish trade federations at Massilia a few months ago. Most of the kings at the periphery of the Roman empire owe great debts to these federations, through which they acquired armaments for a common war on Rome, initiated by an uprising in Palestine led by the Jew's Messiah."

"What exactly did Brutus try to persuade them to do?" asked the intrigued magistrate.

"To cancel the outstanding debts so that the kings could pay off and disband their armies peaceably. Brutus attributed the recent Parthian attack on Dura-Europos to the crippling debts they had incurred!"

"He's probably right, though you might as well ask a leopard to change its spots, as ask a merchant to surrender a claim for payment."

"Brutus argued they would not lose out, as they would find increased demand for luxuries that they would trade to the grateful rulers and their courts."

"Which are essentials for any ruler if he is to hold the allegiance of his nobles." mused Dionyius.

They were interrupted by the insistence of Simon who had a question of great urgency that wouldn't wait.

"Mummy says at the top of a mountain God wrote the laws for the Jews on tablets of stone using lightning as his stylus. Did he do the same for you Romans?"

"No, but we do know of the commandments God gave to Moses on Sinai, and our laws are based on them."

"Then do all your slaves rest on the Sabbath as God commanded?"

"I regret not. We choose to ignore those that don't suit us."

"Could we write to the Emperor and remind him?" and when Dionysius concurred, he rushed off and reappeared with a waxed board and stylus, and began writing in Hebrew.

When the magistrate suggested that perhaps the Emperor couldn't read Hebrew, Simon shot him a scornful glance, and delighted them by writing in Latin as together they worked on an appropriate letter.

"I'll see he gets it," promised Dionysius, carefully wrapping it away amongst his belongings, and Simon beamed at him with happiness.

At Arelate the court session was spread over two days so they had time to explore. Though of lesser importance than Nemauses it was full of monumental buildings with a magnificent circus, its tall Egyptian obelisk standing proudly in the centre of the arena.

"If we were staying you would be able to watch the horse racing and the charioteers in a few days," said Dionysius, and described the whole spectacle to an entranced boy.

They moved on past a complex of water cisterns and baths and stood watching the water cascading from pipes and fountains in a small square near the city centre.

"This water comes from the hills on the other side, and is syphoned through miles of lead pipes even crossing the bed of the Rhone. We Romans build our cities only where we can guarantee fresh flowing water, throughout the year," said Dionysius proudly.

On a colonnaded forum, fronting an imposing temple a noisily excited crowd drew the travellers.

As they approached Mary Magdalene pulled reluctantly on the sleeve of Brutus, but just then the crowd parted and a decapitated cockerel, wings beating, ran towards them pursued by a dishevelled, wild haired priestess, brandishing a curved sacrificial knife. As though guided by some malign force, the cock sped directly at them, the blood spurting from its neck making a clear trail, and the half naked priestess seized it at their feet.

Her eyes lustful and crazed encountered those of Mary, wide and horror filled. For but a brief instant they communed, then screaming the harpy threw herself at Mary, knife raised to strike in one hand and cockerel in the other. Mary was rooted to the spot and none of her party responded quickly enough to parry the blade as it flashed towards her slightly rounded belly. Her arm, naked except for a wide copper bracelet, absorbed the frenzied blow, and then, saliva frothing from her mouth, the priestess collapsed, her limbs twitching convulsively.

The ensuing silence hung over the forum like a shroud as Mary sank to her knees before the prostrate woman, raising her bloodied arm and calling out,

"In the name of Jesus Christ I command you Satan to depart this woman."

The shriek that emitted from her foaming lips echoed malevolently through the arches of the cryptoporticus and the colonnades, before fading away. The silent crowd saw Mary enfold the quiescent body, holding her protectively to her lap and covering her nakedness with a cloak. She had recognized the prophetess of Mithras from their encounter at the seashore, and she resolved to confront this manifestation of paganism and conquer.

349

She rocked the woman and smoothed away the tumbling hair from her brow until the priestess opened her eyes and gazed quietly into hers. Realizing there was a bond linking them, the woman smiled, and surrendered to the love that emanated from her intended victim.

As the baby kicked the priestess grasped the encircling arm and looked with wonder at the small laceration, just above the wrist, where the bleeding was already congealing. Rotating the bracelet she saw the dent and the two-inch gash in the metal and again felt the baby kick, and the enormity of what she had come so close to doing overwhelmed her. As the tears flowed at the unspoken words each read in the others eyes, Mary helped her to her feet and said simply,

"Come with me," and the traumatized party moved to their accommodation at the inn.

That night the decision was made not to continue to Massilia.

The prophetess was Helena and she remained cloistered with Mary for some hours while Brutus fretted about getting her arm seen to.

Dionysius was bewildered by both the casting out of a demon that he had witnessed, and by the speed of their subsequent decision to head north at the earliest opportunity, curtailing his chance of fully satisfying his greatly aroused interest in all their affairs. He knew this brought forward his decision making, which he resented as it was not in his nature to commit himself until he had made exhaustive enquiry into anything that interested him.

The innkeeper announced three Elders of the town wished to see them. They were ushered in and after exchanging greetings came directly to the point.

"Judas here," they said indicating the black bearded younger man of the three, "heard the woman cast out the demon in the name of Jesus Christ. We would be fearful of declaring ourselves Christians otherwise, as the followers of that priestess are zealous in their persecution of our church. We have come to enquire if these are those women that were blown ashore in the little boat earlier?"

"Yes, we are that same party," admitted Brutus reluctantly.

"We give you greetings from the brethren here in Arelate, and our sincere prayers for your sister Mary who was attacked. We pray for her well being."

"Then your prayers have been answered," called a cheerful voice, and Mary smiled at the visitors who bowed deferentially. Behind Mary a tremulous Helena followed in her footsteps.

"I want you to welcome a new sister in Christ into our church. Helena wishes to be baptised as soon as is possible."

There was a beatific smile on Helena's tear streaked face, in stark contrast to the dumbstruck look on that of all the men.

"But she is renowned as the most ardent prophetess of Mithras throughout Gaul!" stammered one of the delegation plucking nervously at his beard.

"No longer. Sister Mary has revealed the risen son of the one true God to me and I can no longer worship idols!"

She saw the confusion and fear in their faces,

"You need not fear me, I swear on the cross on which they hung my Lord that I am now his follower!"

"The whole town is seething with the news of your attack on Mary from the sea. Step outside of the door and you will be mobbed by your followers or attacked by ours!"

"Then I must plead for forgiveness and face their wrath," said Helena the colour draining from her face.

"Forgive me for interfering, but you will gain nothing by confronting a mob of any persuasion, they won't listen to what you say. I council that you lie low for a few days and then follow the advice of these elders," said Dionysius, and then turning to Mary he entreated, "and can you in your turn baptize this woman and myself, as we are both anxious to receive the Holy Spirit?"

Mary's eyes lit up with amusement,

"God does move in mysterious ways, but I really wish to be less involved in any future conversions," she said, bringing her cut arm up to her mouth.

Before they departed the elders went into earnest conclave with Marc and Brutus then left them both in a state of great agitation.

Brutus revealed that they had been informed of Joseph of Arimathaea passing through Arelate but a few days before, and informing the Elders that the invasion of Britain would almost certainly be launched in the summer of the approaching year. This resolved both men to move as quickly as possible to northern Gaul from where they could sail for Britain.

Mary Magdalene officiated at the baptism of the two converts in the Rhone just north of the city. The word had spread and there were upwards of sixty souls that she immersed that day. When some of the Elders questioned her fulfilling this role, she had offered to stand down for any man who had followed Jesus as faithfully as she had throughout his ministry.

"Beware," she said, "if you devalue the role of women in the offices of your church, you are not following the example of our Lord, who greeted me the first of his apostles, on the glorious morn of his resurrection. Mary Clopas has elected to stay with you and guide your church at the last request of Mary, mother of our Lord. Value her, she has been consecrated for she too was at the tomb!"

There was great sadness both ashore and amongst the small party of travellers as they waved farewell from the stern of the flat-bottomed troop transporter, taking them and part of a cohort to the city of Lugdunum, far up the river Rhone. The river flowed sluggishly because of the snow and ice in the mountains to the north, but come the spring and the thaw, when it was no longer held back at its source it would be impassable for many weeks.

Armed with a fresh letter of commendation from Dionysius, Brutus was confident their journey would be unimpeded, but he had not appreciated the high standing of the magistrate throughout Gaul or the help that would follow as a consequence.

The tribune commanding the cohort greeted them cordially.

"Congratulations on your acquittal at Lugdunum Convenarum, and I can tell you the trial has been of tremendous interest throughout Gallia. You are welcome to travel with us to Alesia where I am to assume command."

"Isn't that where Caesar gained the final victory over Vercingetorix in the conquest of Gaul?" asked Brutus.

"It is and I'm proud to say that alongside Caesar was my great grandfather,

Legate Licinius Crassus, commanding four legions that he had force marched from Aquitania across the snow covered passes."

"Did he have any of Hannibal's elephants?" asked an eager boy, and Crassus smiled at him with wonder.

"No he didn't. Roman legions prefer horses to elephants, and I doubt if there are any elephants still around."

"But we nearly saw some, that were hiding in the forest," insisted Simon.

"But they're too good at staying hidden, that's why we never use them. When we reach Alesia I'll show you where the final battles took place," promised the tribune.

They were quickly underway, their shallow draught troopship propelled by the oars of the soldiers.

"We never use slaves as we would carry fewer soldiers. They will shortly find their rhythm, and it's good for them to work, as they get up to all sorts of mischief when idle."

Brutus concurred with Crassus' sentiments, and they were soon making progress against the current, a man either side at the bows keeping an eye open for underwater hazards, alternately swinging a lead line for shallows.

Pink flamingoes and white egrets waded at the edge of sandbanks, and at their approach took to the air in a flash of premature sunset.

The forest on both banks of the wide river rolled away to the far low hills, hiding the hamlets and villages with their cleared fields waiting the spring planting. The short hours of daylight limited the boat's progress, and at dusk each evening they dropped anchor and prayed for a good catch, as two Palestinian soldiers cast their circular nets. With luck they could net a dozen good size fish each, a welcome augmentation of their bread and boiled vegetables.

Each day saw the hills moving nearer to flank them on both sides, and looming far ahead, the high white crests warning of the savagery of winter.

Then suddenly on the fifth day, from a crystal clear, pale blue sky, the mistral hurtled down the valley from the north. The river became a maelstrom of short, steep wavelets that broke on the boat hull, soaking the leading men with freezing spray. The temperature plunged, and even the oarsmen had frozen hands and bodies little warmer, in spite of their exertion. For those with enforced idleness it was unbearably cold, hunched behind the woven branch hurdles that had been improvised to give some protection.

When Crassus edged the boat into a shelving beach on a bend in the river, everyone was thankful to jump ashore in the lee of a low cliff.

Brutus watched critically the precautions that were taken to protect their camp and was impressed how they set to work with well drilled precision, clearing peripheral trees and building a ditch and earthen wall surmounted with wooden staves. Sentries were posted both inside and outside the stockade, and surprise attack would have been impossible.

He happily volunteered to go on a foraging party, armed with a borrowed pair of spears. An hour later they proudly returned bearing a sow and eight sucking pigs. The odours emanating from their campfires were enough to draw every Allobrogue within twenty miles stated Crassus, ordering the sentries to be especially vigilant.

It blew for three days and from the shore they looked across a river of white foam, until the fourth morn dawned windless.

Within the hour they had broken camp and were under way, but now that the river was narrowing they were making less gain against the stronger current. Twenty soldiers pulling on a long towrope were able to compensate and keep them moving, even where the path narrowed and had been hewn into the rock face. On one such stretch a boulder crashed down from the cliff edge above, narrowly missing the rearmost of the towing party.

Crassus responded by detailing a company of legionaries to scout ahead for any Gauls who might be lying in ambush, but such was their knowledge of the terrain they quietly disappeared into the forest rather than face a confrontation.

A smaller, flat-bottomed barge had joined them, and seemed glad to stay in convoy for the protection afforded by the soldiers. Apart from its eight crew, it carried two black bulls, their fodder and an elderly priest.

Crassus was greatly excited when he rejoined his ship after conferring with the priest.

"They're transporting two sacrificial bulls to Lugdunum and Vienna, which we will reach tonight, where there are temples to Cybele and Mithras with a splendid fossa-sanguinis".

"What is a fossa-sanguinis?" asked Marc.

"It's the pit at the foot of the altar stone where the priest performs the sacrificial cutting of the bull's throat. He wears a newly sewn white tunic, and catches as much blood as he can in a bronze dish. Then he ascends the steps to where the priestesses are waiting to strip him of his bloodstained vestment, and to smear the bull's blood on their foreheads, before anointing the congregation with the blood. For those who are sick they tear his tunic into strips and sell them to be applied to the afflicted part of the body."

Mary gave a shudder but her curiosity made her ask, "When will this ritual slaying take place?"

"At the winter solstice in three weeks. This time it will take place simultaneously at Arelate, Vienna and Lugdunum, to appease the Gods for the defection of the priestess Helena of Arelate who has become a Christian."

"Are you certain of that, or is it just a rumour?" asked Mary with trepidation.

"No, it's a fact. She has been baptized in the Rhone, and because the river has been defiled, they will be sacrificing three bulls along its course simultaneously to placate the Gods."

Crassus' involvement with the cults of Cybele and Mithras was not lost on the listeners, and even Simon intuitively refrained from any reaction at the name of Helena. That evening they saw the unloading of one of the garlanded bulls as it was led away to the high looming temple.

A discussion followed as to whether they should declare themselves and challenge this paganism, but the consensus was that nothing would be gained, and a lot might be lost if they alienated themselves from their travelling companions.

The following two days that brought them to Lugdunum were uneventful, and because Crassus wished to transact some important business there, they sought out an inn for the night.

Crassus had a great liking for Simon and wished to take him on his visit to the barbaricarius, Constantius Aequalis, the following day.

"What on earth is a barbaricarius?" queried both men simultaneously.

"Constantius Aequalis is the finest craftsman of ceremonial and parade armour

353

and maker of cloth of gold. His silver and gold gilt work is renowned throughout the empire."

"A little beyond the pocket of an infantry centurion for sure," mused Brutus, "he will show you some wonders, you lucky boy," and picking Simon up he whirled him shrieking above his head, before placing him in the arms of Miriam.

Mary felt her eyes misting at the thought he would soon be doing the same with their own child, and prayed fervently for their safe passage.

Returning from their encounter with the barbaricarius, it would be a mistake to say that they returned empty handed. True, Crassus' purse, which had held three hundred denari was empty, having been put down as deposit on breast plate, helmet and cuirasses, but clutched in the loving hands of Simon, was a fiery bundle that would have been lost in one of his mother's pockets.

"It's six weeks old mama, and Constantius Aequalis has given it to me!" Simon looked gleefully from one parent to the other as his charge attempted to lick or devour all the excrescencies on his face.

"It's true. Simon soon got bored with gold and silver, but when he saw the litter of their bitch guard dog, he was totally absorbed. The pup comes from hunting stock, and this little monster hunted the boy wherever he hid," laughed the tribune.

"Then he found his future master didn't he, Marc?" said Miriam, looking at her bemused husband.

"I guess so," was all Marc said, and the matter was settled except for a suitable name.

That was going to tax them most of the journey up the Saone before Simon was happy with Jup.

"That's no sort of name for a dog, Simon," remonstrated Marc, despite the instant recognition of its appropriateness by the recipient, who wagged his tail approvingly every time Simon barked it at him.

"It's short for Jupiter daddy, and as Jup grows he will move like lightning in the chase, and launch himself like a thunderbolt on the prey."

So that too was settled.

The impact of the new passenger was disproportionate to his size and he affected every one with his insatiable quest for fun, making the four days to Cabillonum pass more agreeably than any of the previous. There they disembarked hoping never to be confined to a troop transporter again, and contemplating the two days by road north to Alesia with a certain relief.

Simon's eagerness to get there grew daily, as Crassus told in detail of Caesar's long campaign to subdue the uprising of most of the Gallic tribes.

"The complex moves and counter moves of the vast armies spanned the length and breadth of Gaul until Vercingetorix was finally pinned down at the strongly defended oppidum at Alesia," he said. "It stood on an isolated hill at the confluence of two streams and was ideal to defend. Caesar settled down for a long siege and his legions dug in. They threw up an earth bank twenty-five miles long surrounding the oppidum. Part of the ditch they excavated to form the bank filled with water from the streams, and behind it they laid down barbed iron spikes called stimuli and set sharpened wooden stakes in the ground. They half buried foot traps, called lilia with vicious spikes that played havoc with the poorly shod Celtic infantry. All these prevented Vercingetorix and his force from breaking out."

Crassus was unaware of the anxiety this elicited from the boy but Brutus put a comforting arm around him as the tribune continued.

"But the Gauls had assembled a vast relieving army of eight thousand cavalry and a quarter of a million infantry. Caesar dug more ditches and built a rampart with towers, with redoubts for detachments of troops behind them, that was all of fifteen miles long. The Gauls attacked the besieging Romans on both fronts, but couldn't break through their siege works. There were enormous casualties and finally the relieving force lost heart and withdrew to their tribal lands. Vercingetorix surrendered and most of his men became slaves."

"What happened to Vercingetorix?" asked Simon fearfully, and when Crassus told him he was executed in Rome, the boy burst into tears.

"The Romans knew there was always the threat of his raising another army while he was alive so they had no choice!" explained the disconcerted officer.

"They could have kept him prisoner," insisted the boy tearfully, until his father explained how that would have been worse than death.

Simon never became reconciled to his execution, and his affinity with the Celtic cause and his aversion to Rome could be traced to that day. That evening he was heard calling 'Caesar' as he threw sticks for Jup to chase and retrieve, until the name of the Roman emperor became synonymous with stick in the canine brain.

When Crassus accompanied them, searching out traces of the siege, Simon was more interested in the oppidum than the siege works.

Brutus challenged Crassus on his ceremonial armour.

"When do you expect to wear it?" he asked.

"I will be in the second wave of the invasion of Brittania next year. As an aide to emperor Claudius, I will wear it on our triumphal procession into Camulodunum, and later at our victory celebration in Rome!"

The assurance with which he spoke convinced Brutus there was no time to be lost, as he was resolved to offer his military knowledge to the kings of Britain.

They were glad to be travelling unaccompanied at last and hired a waggoner to take them north, to the river that would bear them to the channel. Known by the Romans as the Sequana because of its snake-like course, it flowed for over three hundred miles to the sea.

The boats plying the upper reaches were called water shells, and were little more than large baskets covered in skins. Their smallness necessitated they hired two, each with a boatman to navigate their passage along the fast flowing river. Brutus and Mary were in the leading shell, so that if they met with any accident, the following one with Simon and his parents would be able to avoid it. At places the river ran between tumbled rocks, where the skill of the boatmen was all that averted disaster. At others the water was too confused to navigate, and they had to porter the boats considerable distances along the bank.

"They're so fragile they should be named eggshells," avowed Mary, as they shot between two rocks with but inches to spare.

At an unavoidable collision with a submerged rock one of the slender frames was staved in. Within the hour the boatman had cut a green willow branch, trimmed it, and lashed it to double up for the damaged one, and they were under way again.

Some way short of Paris a tributary joined from the east, and the river became wider and more sedate. They paid off the boatmen, and watched as they negotiated a ride on a cart, and then threw their 'eggshells' onto it for the return journey. Then they embarked in their own wooden boat which was not dissimilar to the troopship which had brought them up the Rhone except that it was piled head high with bales of straw being transported to the city down river.

A week later they were at the vast estuary looking out at the channel towards Britain.

The small harbour of Honfleur had three sea going vessels which were loading or unloading, but on enquiry none was bound for Britain.

"One of the fishing boats will take you across if you can pay," advised the captain of a large boat. "We're all too busy supplying the Roman fleet in its preparations. In six months you will have hundreds crossing the channel."

"Where are they assembling?" probed Brutus, anxious to get as much intelligence as possible.

"At Portus Itius, but the whole coast north of here, every river and inlet for a hundred miles, is a hive of ship building."

"Portus Itius is where Julius Caesar launched his invasion and you can see the cliffs of Britain from there, so my guess is they will cross at the same place," Brutus confided to Marc while they were enquiring in the quayside inns for a passage.

A very rotund, bewhiskered man, who spoke only a local dialect none of them could really understand, finally agreed to take them across the following day if the weather was good. Marc was able to make out the occasional word as he used a Celtic tongue similar to that of his boyhood, but such was the man's accent most of their communication was in sign language.

The boat that the man proudly showed them was quite beamy and solid looking, with two masts from each of which hung a spar with a furled red sail. It was only half the length of the *Dolphin* and completely open to the elements.

Accordingly all were clothed in everything that they could put on when they rowed out of the harbour an hour before first light. As the sails were raised the boat settled comfortably to the cold easterly wind, and they danced eagerly to the slap of each wave on the hull. The flood tide still had two hours to make, but they more than held their own as the boat slowly gained on the north running coast of the estuary.

The passengers were less able to hold their own, indeed such was the rolling motion of the boat, first Simon, closely followed by Miriam and then Marc, heaved all they had eaten that night over the side. Jup was unhappy too, with his ears laid back and tail limp, but he had been starved in anticipation. Brutus clutched him protectively while Mary ministered to the afflicted. As the sun rose in the clear sky they moved out of the protection of the low coast, and the sea rolled them even further, although more predictably, and the waves sent spray flying across to add to their misery. Mary draped a storm sail across them and lashed it to the gunwale.

"Our captain is saying it will get better in an hour as the tide will be running the same way as the wind," Brutus called out encouragingly, and then added, "as far as I can understand anything he's trying to tell me!" the two of them nodding reassuringly at each other, smiling all the time.

Mary thought it more of a grimace than a smile on the part of Brutus, but was too concerned with her companions' miseries to be analytical.

As the tide set increasingly westward, the movement of the boat quieted and the shore on their right faded quickly into the distance. For many hours they held this course with no sight of land, but the spirits of all were lifted by the knowledge that the first sight they had would be the coast of Britain. Journey's end for one as well as a homecoming, but for the rest a big mystery, with which their imaginations could not attempt to grapple.

"Land-ho!" sang out Brutus, a surge of relief adding stridency to his call as he saw the low cliffs, infused red by the sinking sun, dead ahead.

The helmsman took a look and then muttering unintelligibly, bore away slightly.

As darkness descended they prayed for a clear moon, as otherwise they would be unable to make landfall until the next day. It arose out of the eastern sea, clear and full and as they rounded the white chalk teeth rising from the sea like the spines of some sleeping monster, the captain raised two fingers and nodded his head with satisfaction at his navigation.

So they proceeded eastwards between the island to their right and the low wooded mainland on the left. The last of the incoming tide carried them up the river for a mile or so, to tie up alongside a quay where a spluttering lantern hung at the entrance to a mean inn.

Their arrival brought out the landlord and his wife, disbelieving of the likelihood of paying guests at that time of year. To be asked to accommodate four adults and a child made the man lose his wits, but his wife set to, bringing in some straw for their bedding, chivvying a slovenly barmaid to stick some mutton in the pot over the fire, and generally settling them in. The captain had no sooner helped them unload than, five denarii the richer, he turned his boat around and was gone.

Marc was grinning with irrepressible elation as he said,

"He thought it best to get away quickly. Everyone is so nervous at the imminent invasion he was afraid of being seized, and they might have kept him here days for questioning."

That night, while his companions slept the sleep of the exhausted, Marc lay awake his mind seething with tantalizing memories of home, and fears of what he might find with daybreak.

357

The Conquest

CHAPTER ONE

He must have dozed, for Marc was awakened by the sound of horses' hooves receding from the inn. It was still dark but with that lightening of night that precedes dawn. Rising and wrapping his cloak tightly around him, Marc stole to the door and slipped out onto the frost-covered quay. Two small fishing boats that hadn't been there were now tied to the iron rings, lying on the shiny grey mud awaiting the flood tide. A few shadowy figures moved near the inn and he recognised the wife of the innkeeper.

She looked surprised when he greeted her and nervously she asked,

"You're not from around these parts, are you?"

"Not far away. We could see the dragon's spine rising out of the sea from our village. It can't be more than fifteen miles."

"Who is your chief then?" and Marc noted the edge to her voice.

"The son of Tasciovanus of course, King Cunobelin."

The quizzical look evoked by Marc's pronouncement alerted him to some hidden significance to her questions, and he realised how suspicious they were. Jup had followed him and was investigating the riverbed, so Marc had to go and retrieve him before he became one small ball of mud. He washed his legs and the underside of his body off in a rill and carried him back to the inn, to find everyone awake and eager to explore their surroundings.

"Don't reveal you are a Roman," advised Marc, as he proceeded to tell them of the woman's suspicious questioning of him.

"You couldn't blame them for seizing me if they knew. There will be Roman spies sounding out who might be an ally to their cause in return for favours following the conquest. It's what they did in Gaul to prevent concerted resistance."

"The tribes are too busy raiding each other to fight as a unified army, but Tasciovanus was powerful enough to unite the tribes of the Catuvellauni and the Trinovantes, and the invasion will have to be through their territory. I wonder if Cunobelin is as strong as his father?" mused Marc half to himself.

After they had breakfasted they were eager to be on their way, as Marc was confident he could soon lead them to the oppidum he remembered as a boy, certainly by tomorrow if not today. But two hours along the west-leading path, following the coast through the bare forest, a body of mounted warriors overtook and surrounded them. Brutus restrained Marc's hand from flying to his sword.

"They're not robbers, Marc, they're a reception party alerted by the innkeeper."

The leader, a long haired man who looked too large for his stallion studied them warily, his shrewd dark eyes moving from face to face. When he finally spoke it was like an explosion that fanned his heavy moustache.

"Who claims fealty to King Cunobelin?" he demanded.

"I do," called out Marc.

"Then when did you last serve him?"

"Never. He was but a prince, the son of Tasciovanus when I knew him."

"How long ago was that?"

"Fifteen or so years ago – I'm not sure, slaves have little regard to one year or the next."

"How were you enslaved? Who sold you?"

"I was taken prisoner at Castillon in Gaul. My father and brothers were killed by the Romans, I was enslaved."

"Have you not been back to Britain since?"

"Not until today, no."

"So you had no awareness that Cunobelin was killed, and know nothing of that weakling Adminius who fled to Rome?"

"Is Adminius one of Cunobelin's sons?" queried Marc surprised that he could follow the man's tongue after all the years.

"Yes, the malcontent. May he die a thousand deaths. What is your name?"

"Calgacus is my father's name but I am called Marc." As the man jerked his head in surprise the whole party of warriors focussed their renewed attention.

"You must all come with us. Our leader is sure to want to question you."

They split into two, one group riding ahead, the other escorting their prisoners as they retraced their path a short way, before heading north through the dense wood towards the uplands of which they caught the occasional glimpse. The pace was demanding for the walkers and Marc had been carrying a tired Jup for some time when Simon, struggling to keep up, tripped and lay sprawled on the leaf-strewn path. As his mother helped him up he was fighting back tears.

One of the rear-guard dismounted. He was dressed in a coarser wool tunic than the warriors, and his felted brown cloak reminded Miriam of the Galilean broad-cloth in its appearance. Smiling kindly, he lifted the boy up onto his horse and remounted, wrapping the folds of his cloak so that only the boy's face could be seen above, and his lower legs bare and muddied below.

They were three hours gaining the high hill fort, and entered through a massive pair of gates between two large standing stones, overshadowed by a timber plat-form from which a few curious guards surveyed them. From both sides of the gate, raised earthworks surmounted by a palisade of rough staves encircled a vast area containing a number of round thatched huts and a big covered assembly hall. This was open to the elements, posts each side supporting the thatched roof, under which a crowd of warriors and servants milled around, and smoke meandered lazily into the still air from an inviting, flickering fire. Two old hags stirred a cauldron suspended over it, watched by a reclining, white-robed man, whose long white hair fell loosely from a circle of twisted gold on his forehead. He got up as they approached and stood watching silently as they were pushed to a corner where rough hides were draped forming an enclosure.

Ushered inside, the gloom at first hid the darkly visaged man seated on a chair hewn from the trunk of some massive tree. His eyes studied them, as following their escort they bowed before him, and stood silently as their leader respectfully addressed his liege lord.

"My Lord, we have a party landed from Gaul but last night. They stole in like thieves in the dark and their boat turned around and was gone. This one claims to be the son of Calgacus."

The noble beckoned Marc to approach him and appraised him critically.

362

"He has something of the look of Calgacus as I remember him. Where was your home?"

"Where the headland juts out into the sea at Hengist, to the west of the white spines."

"What was your mother's name?"

"Cartinua," said Marc simply, but the effect was electrifying on the noble, who jumped from the throne his face expressing incredulity.

"Then if you tell the truth we are cousins. We can take you to her tomorrow, as she has never left the oppidum since her man and her sons died in Gaul. She will know if you really are her son."

He instructed the warrior band to provide well for their captives and to assemble mounted at first light.

"We will save the celebrating until you have been accepted by Cartinua," he laughed, "don't try and leave the stockade, the guards have their orders."

The roundhouse they were allocated was already home to a few family groups and Kenan, he who had put Simon on his horse, led the boy and the frisky puppy to meet his two sons who were only a year older. Donal and Chadran were identical twins with the same reddish hair as their father, and their green flecked, hazel eyes gleamed mischievously in anticipation of a new playmate with a puppy.

From a wicker cage they rolled a ball onto the hard earth by the log fire. Jup looked at it quivering with excitement, nose twitching and tail wagging. As it warmed it slowly unrolled, and Jup pricked up his ears and his tail extended rigidly as the young hedgehog took a few uncertain steps after such a rude awakening from its hibernation. The hair on his back bristling black and erect, and responding too quick to be stopped, Jup launched himself to impale his soft nose on the prickly animal that immediately curled itself into a ball. The yelp of excitement turned to a whimper of bewilderment and pain, and laughing Simon placated the puppy. Hedgehog was the first word Simon learnt in Britain and hedgehog was the first animal Jup learnt to respect.

Marc was excited beyond belief that his mother was still alive, and he was to see her on the morrow.

"After my mother has seen me and knows you are my family we will have nothing to fear from these Britons," he rejoiced.

A shuffling sound drew their eyes to the entrance, which framed the tall figure of the white robed druid. As his eyes adjusted to the gloom they fastened on those of Mary and he moved to stand enquiringly a few paces from her.

"What is this emanation, this aura you carry about you?" he demanded his gaze scrutinizing the bewildered woman, who didn't understand one word although she understood their urgency. Marc had to interpret for them both as he replied for Mary.

"I am but a Jewish woman, wife to this retired Roman centurion."

"You are that and much more, for I feel a power that very few possess. Are you a shaman?"

"No. I can neither prophesy, nor have the gift of healing."

"Then what is your remarkable power, such that I know it without recognising it?"

"Any power I have stems only from my Lord whom I loved and followed for three years in Palestine."

"His name?"

"Jesus."

The priest's eyes narrowed at the name but never wavered in their scrutiny. Almost in a whisper he said,

"That same prophet of whom the Jew has told the Pendragon."

He inhaled through pursed lips and then exploded violently, "And now he renounces the old Gods and has given land for a church on the hill among the western swamps."

"The same, the one true Son of God. You speak of Joseph of Arimathaea. Is he here?"

"Look for him with Arviragus of Siluria!" and greatly agitated he turned and abruptly left them.

They assembled at dawn, most of the warriors mounted on horses, but there were two chariots of wood and wicker for the women and Simon, and one splendidly worked and burnished bronze chariot, on which the Druid stood holding the rein, accompanied by a young novice in a white tunic, who was seated because he was blind. He was about the same age as Marc and something about him stirred a germ of recognition.

They set off along the path following the ridge to the west. The forest was dense and only the occasional clearing allowed a glimpse towards the far sea. After three hours they descended a steep slope towards a river winding its way from the plain to the sea. When they remounted in the floor of the valley, they turned south following the river and Marc remarked to Brutus on features that he recalled from his boyhood memories, growing ever more excited at the imminent reunion with his mother.

The guards, alarmed by the approaching column of horsemen but recognizing the standard, hurried to open the gates, and the party swung into the large cleared space fronting the communal wooden house. Smoke was hanging lazily above the two holes in its roof and those of the dozen assorted round houses, and the smell of burnt wood hung over the whole settlement. Men from the outlying farms had abandoned hoe and plough to hurry with spear and sword as though called to battle, and the two blacksmiths suspended their insistent beating to join the throng around the arrivals.

"We seek Cartinua," called their leader as all dismounted, the foreigners clustered in a small group surrounded by the warriors.

"Cartinua, Cartinua," called one voice after another, and then a silence descended that even extended to the livestock and the birds on the thatch.

Three women moving very slowly, the old woman in the middle relying on the others to support her, appeared around the corner of the long house. Marc felt his heart pounding and his eyes misting as he was seized by an irresistible urge to run to his weakened mother. He released Miriam's hand, which he had unconsciously squeezed to numbness, and rushed through the crowd to her. She jerked back with fear as he fell on his knees before her, his hands raised imploringly as he studied her wrinkled, frightened face. For a moment he was afraid her eyes had lost their clarity and she would not recognize him but then such joy suffused her features, twenty years were erased as by the brush strokes of a magician painter, and her released hands clutched disbelievingly at his.

"Sucellus," was her only greeting as great sobs racked her frail body, and she misted to his tear filled vision. He rose and enveloping her in his arms crushed her to him, luxuriating in that delicious smell of her that stirred in his subconscious, remembered from the first time he suckled at her breast. As he felt her weight increase he knelt on one knee, and placed his right arm under her legs to catch her as she fell insensible, and guided by his sisters he carried her to her hut. Miriam completed the tearful gathering that disappeared within, while the crowd now regained its voice to demand what was happening. The leading noble explained what had transpired, and quickly the word spread of the son returned from the dead.

The blind minstrel shed unseen tears as he remembered the battle at Castillan, for he had been there alongside those slain. The Romans had gouged out his eyes, and sent him back on a trading vessel with the warning that they would do likewise to any other Britains who aided their Gallic cousins. For good measure they also decided to castrate him. Had they known that this was to contribute to his wonderful counter tenor voice, which captivated audiences wherever he sang his ballads the length of the south coast, they would undoubtedly have torn out his tongue.

That night there was to be a feast at the oppidum the like of which had not been held in anyone's memory. The conjunction of a noble's lost son returned from captivity, minstrel, Druid, Roman centurion and Jewish women, was unparalleled on this island since it had been separated by the inrush of waters ten thousand years before.

The Priest wanted to sacrifice a calf to the Celtic God, Sucellus, as this was the given name of the returned son of Calgacus, but he and many were dismayed when Marc declared his Roman name was that by which he wished to be known, as he had been baptized thus as a believer in the one true God, and follower of his son Jesus Christ.

The Druid, the minstrel and the whole assembly, were enthralled at the recounting of all that had befallen Marc since he had been seized. For most, the sequence of events was all that mattered and sufficient to marvel at in themselves, but for the Druid and the minstrel the conflict of ideas, the challenging message of how people were to think and worship was paramount, especially as this Jewish God offered hope of resurrection equally to noble and servant, freeman and slave, and both were disturbed by what they heard.

Talking to the nobles, who now felt easier about their visitors, Brutus spoke of the Roman strategy to weaken military resistance by subverting tribal chiefs, or playing on the rivalry and feuding that was second nature to neighbouring tribes.

"You can be sure they are active throughout Britain right now," he said, "under the guise of diplomats or ambassadors."

"What role has this Joseph the Jew, with the Pendragon?" asked the Druid.

"His is a two fold mission. To help the tribes to prepare for the invasion by supplying armaments, and to promote the kingdom of God through the teachings of the Son of God."

It was amazing the way different groups reacted, and feelings were running very high against Joseph.

"Tell them of Joseph's petition in Massilia," urged Marc, and Brutus told of the meeting they had all attended, when Joseph of Arimathaea had pleaded with the trading federations. When he had to concede the plea had fallen on deaf ears, there was an outpouring of vituperation against the Jews.

"Aren't your women Jews?" asked a burly warrior aggressively.

"By birth yes, but married to Roman citizens and converted to be Christians, they would not be acceptable within their Synagogues. I am Roman, but what of that, when we ally ourselves with you to help you defeat the imminent invasion?" said Brutus, glad that the women were not admitted to such a heated meeting.

Later they were to participate in the celebratory feast, unlike the tribeswomen who were merely servants to the men as their tradition demanded.

Two other exceptions were made to the women attending the feast. Cartinua, and Branwen the wife of the local warrior chief, joined the men when their business was concluded.

The long house was crowded, but when the minstrel plucked his lyre instant silence fell and all present rejoiced at the privilege that was theirs to hear again his singing of some epic legend.

Initially his voice was hesitant and shy, which was unusual as his repertoire had been sung in many a court the length of the land.

As the cadences rose and fell, like waves from some far distant source, seized by rapacious winds to tower threateningly before thundering on to their island shore, they knew they were hearing something never before sung. The familiar names skillfully worked into the fabric of song, evoked images of heroes surging across the waters to do battle with an evil of greater magnitude than the world had ever known. Shivers delighted the spines of all as they realized he was recounting the epic excursion to the aid of Castillon, and Marc felt the hair rising at the nape of his neck as he heard the long unspoken names of his father and brothers. Exquisitely anguished beyond bearing, his hand sought that of his mother at his side, and he felt the tears falling as counterpoint to the rhythm of the chant. As the bloody sequel rose to a crescendo the bard sang of his own loss so evocatively, that the sobbing of every listener, was as the chorus to a lament at the end of the world. The last note died, hanging tentatively in the ennobled consciousness of each listener, to be followed by an outpouring of such a catharsis as to recruit the hearts of all to battle against the legions of Rome.

Such a song could not be followed and only the minstrel knew he would never sing it again. It was both an anthem to celebrate the invincibility of life, and a requiem to the loss of a way of life he knew was looming with the threat across the narrow sea, no longer the barrier to invasion that it had been.

The following day it was hard to recapture the magic of the night but the awareness of having participated in something unique and ennobling could never quite be erased.

Cartinua was insistent in her questioning of Mary about Jesus, for she had quickly seen that the recovery of her lost son with his wife and new grandson, all stemmed from his impact on their lives.

Likewise, the Druid was demanding answers to searching questions, which he pondered.

Marc, as sole interpreter, felt quite exhausted as he was struggling to familiarize himself with the nuances of the Celtic tongue of his past. He was quite glad when Brutus said he and Mary were to accompany the warriors to a council of war, to be convened at the oppidum of the Maidens the following day.

"Lord Cassidun commands me to attend as my knowledge of Roman strategy might be useful. We may be gone a week before we return, but I want Mary to have our child here when her time comes. Your mother although frail, and your two sisters will be a great help at that time, when I will be of no help at all!"

It took but a day to reach the uplands where the iron-age fort dominated the surrounding fields, gleaming white with speckles of chalk turned up by recent ploughing. The setting sun suffused the terraced earthworks with a ruddy glow, which belied the frost that would quickly seize it in its chilling grip when it vanished.

Brutus was amazed at the vastness of it, and as they entered the northern gate noted the deep ditch surrounding the earth ramparts and the wooden staves surmounting it, and speculated on whether Claudius could throw a siege ring around this with his invading legions as Caesar had at Alesia in Gaul? He concluded he could do the same and dig in until the defenders were starved into submission.

Once they had penetrated the entrance maze with its twists and turns and blind ending deceptions, night had fallen and only the glow of fires illuminated the improvised dwellings thrown up to house the ever-swelling garrison.

Cassidun led his party to the greatest concentration of fires and burning torches and knelt at the feet of a youthful man, beardless but hiding much of his face under a pair of blonde moustaches, that fanned out to merge with his bushy sideburns. His pale blue eyes revealed his pleasure at their meeting.

"So Cassidun, you honour us with your presence. I knew only something of great importance would delay you, so now we are impatient to know what you have been doing," gesturing to include the throng of nobles who were attending all that was said.

"Sire, we have had cause to visit the oppidum at Hengist on the sea. The circumstances are really most extraordinary and intimately associated with the Roman centurion Brutus, whom I have the honour of presenting to my king."

The king shot out of his chair as though summoned by a call to arms, and the nobles expressed both incredulity and outrage.

Seating himself, Caratacus turned to Togodumnus his brother, who resembled him facially although wearing a well-trimmed beard.

"So brother, our informant was right, their spies are penetrating our courts! Where did you catch this one, Cassidun, and what have you extracted from him so far?"

"Sire you misunderstand me. I am not presenting him as a captive. Allow me but five minutes to explain and you will welcome him, as they did in the oppidum at Hengist."

Although trusted implicitly by the king, Cassidun found the few seconds they were scrutinized by the brothers interminable.

"Sire, he has his woman with him who is with child. What spy would do that?"

Mary was standing at the very periphery of the throng, but so imposing was her demeanor Caratacus knew who she was instantly, and as she became aware of his eyes upon her, she modestly averted hers and gave him a decorous curtsy.

Acknowledging with an inclination of his head the king smiled as he said,

"Indeed what spy would? You have your five minutes to convince us, proceed."

The five minutes stretched deep into the night, and was only interrupted for seats to be arranged so that food could be taken as the long saga unfolded. Language was a problem, for few among the nobles could follow Latin without interpreters, and so explanations seemed to drag on interminably.

The effect of the mead and ale with which they were plied and with which they were unfamiliar, on top of the long journey they had endured, caused Mary to fall asleep on her stool. Noticing this, as he had noted everything about the exceptional woman, Caratacus terminated further discussion, ordering that a place be found for their guests in one of the roundhouses, and departed unsteadily for his tent.

Late the following morning Brutus was summoned to attend the War Council that had been debating for some hours.

Caratacus presided and inviting Brutus to take a vacated chair, asked him to summarize how he saw their situation.

"There will undoubtedly be a Roman invasion, Claudius needs a conquest to consolidate his claim as Emperor, much as Julius Caesar did one hundred years ago. The preparation of the fleet is well on and the vessels have been designed to be easily beached on your shores, unlike Caesar's which went aground too far out and gave the legionaries great problems of gaining a foothold, a beach head.

"I know that at least four legions are moved to northern Gallia and approaching the state of readiness for a full campaign. They are the 2nd, 6th, 9th and 20th and a cohort of the 10th. They will be supported by auxiliaries and cavalry and together must number thirty thousand men."

This caused quite a stir among the assembly, although one boasted of being able to raise that number from just his own tribe,

"And we number more than twenty tribes," he affirmed.

Brutus continued, unprepared to deviate from his presentation of the facts as he knew them.

"They will cross at the shortest crossing possible, as the sea is one thing a legionary fears. So expect them to invade to the east much as Caesar did. That is where you need to assemble your army, and to successfully repulse them your warriors need to be united under one commander, as the Romans will be."

"But we can't leave the whole coast undefended apart from the eastern corner. Nor these oppida which are our tribal refuge when threatened," protested a veteran warrior who felt his age merited voicing his opinion.

"You will need two hundred thousand tribesmen to repel this invasion. Remember each legionary is skilled in weapons, as are your warriors, but most of your tribesmen will be putting down their hoes to pick up the sword or spear."

As he threw out this assertion he saw the anger of the man who had previously protested could not be contained.

"My Lord, why are we forced to listen to this? Are we warrior knights but the match of each Roman legionary? Must we throw eight or ten of our countrymen against each Roman soldier? I am incensed at having to listen to my tribesmen being so insulted."

There were murmurs of agreement from among the nobles and Caratacus raised his arm to quiet them.

"Well, Roman, what have you to say to all this?"

"Sire, the courage of no man of Britain is being questioned, their reputation as tenacious fighters is known throughout Gallia. But are your men able to march twenty miles day after day carrying arms, tent, ditching equipment and staves? Every legionary has to be able to do that. Let history speak for me. Julius Caesar forced a beachhead with fifty thousand troops although outnumbered five to one by Britons. From that beach head he marched his legions to overcome the tribes one at a time, until much of your island was conquered."

"But we drove him out within two years. Forced him to flee to the safety of Gaul!" challenged his adversary.

"No, don't delude yourselves. Gallia was getting hard to hold with the constant threat of raiding armies from across the Rhine. Caesar needed those legions to defend Gallia, that's why he withdrew. He had already achieved his objective, a new conquest to strengthen his claim to the throne."

"Then why not sue for peace if we stand no chance of success? The Romans are eager for client-kings, to rule their tribes peaceably and pay them tribute."

"They are, and if that is the option that you prefer so be it. Their ambassadors will be seeking agreement to non resistance from many of your tribal kings, you can be sure."

"Our younger brother Adminius to his shame has fled to Rome to promote his claim," growled Caratacus. "I fear we are not as united as we were under our father Cunobelin, and Tasciovanus before him."

The faces of the warriors looked gloomy at this pronouncement, which they all knew to be true.

"Then can we establish what tribes can be relied on to fight?" asked Brutus.

"The Catuvellauni and the Trinovantes for certain, and the Durotriges who rule these parts. The Belgian tribes are not so reliable to join with us, although they hate the Romans and will fight them. The Cantii to the east are the most immediately threatened by invasion, but their resistance will be overpowered unless they are supported by all of us. The Western tribes and those of the north will all fight, but will not send their warriors to the other side of the island. Nor can we rely on the Iceni who are always feuding with us."

Caratacus looked gloomily around the assembly before concluding, "I doubt if we can find as many to fight with the Cantii to the east as resisted the invasion of Julius Caesar."

He shook his head in disbelief, then said, "Thank you centurion you have spoken as an honest and knowledgeable man, please leave us to our deliberations."

To Mary, Brutus confided that there was little hope of the tribes combining to resist any invasion.

"I may be of some use as an advisor, but the tribes are too distrustful of each other to unite effectively. Do you want to have our baby here, there is not a lot to hold us now?"

"Oh yes, we need to stay together, all of us who have overcome so much to be here. Let us at least stay united, and see what happens when we are more settled."

The plea in Mary's eye to be settled for the birth of their child was not lost on Brutus, who suddenly realized they had been travelling for eight months with hardly a break.

They should have known from the excited yapping of Jup and the eager way

Simon ran to greet them, when the settlement first came in sight that something had happened in their absence.

"Come and see, come on," cried the boy, eagerly pulling at Brutus' sleeve.

The crowd gathered attentively around the communal hut parted to allow the visitors to enter, and before their eyes had adjusted to the gloom, Mary recognised the melodic urgency of the young man's voice.

"Rufus!" she said, turning in amazement to regard her astonished man, "can he really be here?"

"I certainly can be," laughed the man who had risen and was lunging towards them. He seized Mary so hard the breath was squeezed from her, and fairly spun her around in his arms before standing back and regarding her wonderingly.

"So sister Mary, the Roman and the Jewess are to be blessed with a little Christian. I rejoice for you," and he seized the bemused centurion as he ushered them through and proudly addressed the assembly, which seemed to comprise everyone from the oppidum with the children seated in an arc at the front and the women close by, with the men milling around the periphery.

"Sister Mary is the first among the apostles to witness the risen Lord, on that glorious morning. She thought he was the gardener, and asked where they had taken the body that she might anoint him with the ointments she carried."

"So that is her secret. Now I recognise the source of her power, she has been chosen by God!"

The old Druid whispered the words reverently, as though he was seeing every-thing for the first time with a clarity that had evaded him before, despite his lifelong searching.

"Indeed she has. Mary Magdalene will radiate like a beacon for women until the end of time. All those who listen to God's call as Mary did are chosen, and he uses the least of us to advance his kingdom. Myself from being a trader on the Great Sea, he called me to be his disciple, and his gift to me is the gift of tongues."

As he said it, they realized in an instant that he was comprehensible to all of them, the children with the limited and rough Celtic tongue of their parents, the Jewess and the Roman.

The Druid chanted the primal incantation to the unknowable God that he had learnt as a novice fifty years before.

> "Mine was the first breath over the waters that prescribed
> their limits,
> Causing the waves that fall upon the shore.
> I am the champion of the seven combats,
> Vanquishing the power of sin holding man in thrall.
> I am the hawk upon the crag
> And the glance of sun off eagle's wing.
> I drive the salmon to leap the fall
> And gain the lake on the high plain.
> I am in the fair plants that garnish the bare earth
> And the essences that heal the creatures that dwell thereon.
> I am the craft of the artificer
> And the questing mind of science,

It is my trumpet that sounds the call to battle,
And my spear that strikes down the oppressor.

I am the god that creates in man the fire of thought."

As he ceased a brilliant smile lit up Rufus' face as he responded,

"Who if not I, enlightens the assembly from the mountain top
and commands all creation to obedience?
Who tells the ages of the moon?
Who shows the place where the sun goes to rest?"

Astonished the Druid asked, "Where did you learn that?" but he already knew the answer as Rufus replied,
"That was an utterance of the Holy Spirit, it was never learnt by me."
The Priest sank on his knees and said, "Now all has been fulfilled. The old ways are no more; their days are numbered and we stand at a new beginning."
Rufus arose and embracing the old man as he left, retreated with the travellers and Cartinua to the roundhouse.

There it was that on a spring day three months later a son was born to Mary.
"I want him named Peter," said the blissful mother, "and Rufus is to Christ name him so that he grows up a member of the church."
There it was that a month later Cartinua was buried, the first cross placed over the slight mound to the west of the oppidum; the first of millions that would follow throughout the island of Britain for thousands of years, until time ceased to have any meaning.
The Romans came as they must, sweeping a destined bloody path from Dubris north to the estuary of the Tamesis. Claudius followed and with fresh legions and elephants, sought to emulate Hannibal, and triumphantly entered Camulodunum.
He was watched by a silent, hostile crowd, the widows and orphans of those killed in the brutal encounter a few days earlier.
The Trinovantes had underestimated the resourcefulness of their enemy, and feeling secure behind the rivers that separated the two armies had relaxed their vigilance. But for Claudius, Camulodunum was the jewel in the crown and by fording, and where necessary swimming his cavalry across, he had completely surprised and routed Caractacus and Togodumnus, forcing them to flee west with the remnants of their army.
Among those watching the ceremonial parade were Marc and Simon, Brutus and Rufus. They had been persuaded by Joseph of Arimathaea to try to persuade King Prasutagus of the great Iceni tribe to forget old enmities and join a belated alliance, in the forlorn hope of containing the Roman legions to the eastern corner.
They had travelled down the Tamesis and then moved north-east from Londinos, following the well-used path through a great forest, until they came to the extensive system of dykes between the two rivers. The guards at the crossing point had imparted the news they had so feared, that Caractacus and his Trinovantes had already been vanquished.

371

"The Romans have made a fortified encampment east of here and tomorrow they enter the town to accept its surrender. King Prasutagus of the Iceni is already there to swear allegiance to Claudius and Rome. We are a conquered Britain."

"What of Caractacus? Is he captured or slain?" asked Brutus, but the man shook his head to indicate he didn't know.

The procession was meant to impress, and all had to agree in that it was successful. They easily spotted Craccus wearing his ceremonial armour, and in the sun the bronze and silver of breastplate and helmet glittered magnificently. He was one of a dozen equally splendidly attired officers, knotted scarlet capes flying as they cantered ahead of the three elephants.

Claudius certainly looked the Emperor, his head circled by the corona aura of beaten laurel leaves, the gold crown of the victor. From the high castle on the lead elephant he surveyed the subjected crowd with disdain, as did Aulus Plautius who had commanded the legions in the initial landing and early conquest. He had reason to show disdain for had not sixteen of the tribes capitulated without a fight.

Vespasian was riding the third elephant, and he would much rather have been on his horse, leading his legion west after the fleeing tribesmen, and he turned and looked at the long column of legionaries snaking up the hill from the quay. As soon as Claudius has departed for Rome, he thought to himself, he would be free to pursue his campaign.

Brutus turned to his companions and noted the resolute defiance in the face of Simon, who was fighting back tears that wanted to wash away the humiliation he felt so strongly.

"He looks stupid up there!" cried the boy angrily.

"He looks precarious and that's not good for an Emperor," said Brutus putting a comforting arm around the boy's shoulders.

When the parade was over the legionaries were stood down, and with new denarii in their pockets quickly turned the town into one big market. It was amazing to see the expediency with which every tradesman opened his premises, every inn threw open its portals and opened a fresh cask of ale, and the town thronged with street vendors, musicians and pretty girls, scrubbed and wearing their finery.

Reconciling themselves to the inevitable, the travellers resolved to find a quiet inn outside the town for the night, before retracing their journey. Suddenly a voice cried out.

"Centurion Brutus, by the thunder of Jupiter!"

As they all turned Brutus instantly recognised the tribune with the vivid scar disfiguring his smiling face.

"Tribune Danius Galerius!" he exulted, delighted to embrace the beaming hero of Dura-Europos, "no need to enquire what brings you here."

"What other than conquest. But what else is there for us soldiers to do, other than boring garrison duty?"

He spread his arms deprecatingly and the centurion loved him as of old.

Marc reminded Simon of the siege at Dura-Europos and how they owed their lives to this young officer, every one of them, for Rufus had been there too, and the boy found his resentment evaporating. Gathering that they were about to depart, Danius pressed them to spend at least one night in his tent on the edge of the town.

"There's no way I'm going to let you go without hearing every detail of your mission, and if you need more persuasion Agricola here will just have to arrest you."

"On what charge?" laughed Brutus.

"Why of causing a disturbance of the peace of course. Is there any part of the empire where you haven't caused mayhem?"

Brutus had to concede that he had had his fair share of trouble, and as Simon was eagerly looking forward to telling of sailing into a whale, they accompanied the officers back to their lines.

News of Brutus' presence in the camp quickly spread, and as some of his exploits were legendary, a great number of officers called to pay their respects.

"Uncle Brutus is really famous, isn't he daddy?" said Simon proudly, and Marc affirmed it was so, and deservedly.

When an equerry of Claudius requested the attendance of the centurion on the emperor, Simon was heard to suggest they might send an elephant for him to ride just like Hannibal.

"Would you like me to arrange for you to ride an elephant?" asked Danius, instantly gaining a young friend for life, and as the centurion accompanied the equerry, the boy proudly accompanied the tribune.

Marc was surprised to be greeted by Longinus.

"Tribune Danius Galerius had me transferred to his staff when we reached Gallia, and we were the first cohort to establish a beach head at Dubris. Do you remember your words to me after we had routed the Parthians?"

Marc shook his head.

"You said, now you will be promoted and posted to Gallia as a renowned hero of Dura-Europos."

They both reflected on that remote time, although it was less than two years ago, then Marc said,

"I remember you thought the Parthians would keep up the siege until we were weakened and easily overcome. You were bemoaning your misfortune at missing the conquest of Brittania, and said that the British tribes were too preoccupied with fighting each other to offer effective resistance."

"And then I asked you which was your country."

"And I answered Britannia, and then you nearly died laughing."

At the memory they both laughed as though it was as funny in the retelling as in the original.

"There are great plans for this town. I heard Danius and Vespasian saying it will be a provincial capital with its own procurator one day. Emperor Claudius plans to make a new capital of Brittania on the Tamesis where Londinos is now, but is talking of Camulodunum becoming a colonia. If it does I might well decide to settle here in my retirement; the girls are pretty enough, if I could only get my tongue around their unspeakable Celtic language."

"But haven't you family in Sardia, your birthplace?"

"No longer. My father Matycus was in the Thracian cavalry and was killed on the borders of Dacia when I was a boy. My mother died three years ago."

"So, the army is your family like it is for centurion Brutus, or would have been if Brutus hadn't encountered Jesus of Nazareth, which changed his life."

"Yes, well I'll be surprised if that encounter will change mine. I was in the squad at the crucifixion you know?"

Marc's surprised look showed he had forgotten.

"It was I who collected his shattered sword hilt and placed it on his bed."

"You!" said Marc, and in an instance the years receded and he was the frightened slave back in Fort Antonia, in Jerusalem.

"He always carries it in his pocket as a reminder of that event that also shattered his life. I'm sure even as he talks to your emperor he is aware of his talisman, the bridge between the old life and the new."

"But he still carries a sword doesn't he?"

"Yes always, and has often had to use it to defend himself and his loved ones. But he will never draw it to advance Rome's cause after that day in Jerusalem."

They were interrupted by the triumphal call of an excited boy sitting astride the neck of an elephant, while Dan and the Moroccan elephant handler led the ponderous animal around the tent and back to its compound. He waved excitedly to Brutus and the equerry as they returned, and ten minutes later burst in to shatter their reminiscences with his delirious account of his adventure.

"Dan says," for so he insisted on being called, "Claudius has no further use for Sheba and we can take her home with us," implored the boy passionately.

"If you saw the trouble we had in shipping them you would know why. If the crossing had been rough they could have sunk the vessel, Sheba and her two companions," Longinus had a twinkle in his eye that belied the frown on his face and Marc gratefully seized the opportunity.

"We would have to take all three of them, Simon, they are inseparable companions and it would be cruel to take one from the others."

Simon's face fell and then lit up as he said,

"Brutus and you could ride one each, daddy. It's not that difficult."

"But we could never feed them, they need special things like ..." Marc stopped searching for inspiration,

"Like bananas and pomegranates?" suggested Dan.

"That's right, wagon loads of bananas and pomegranates every week," sighed Marc sadly.

Even Simon was daunted at this, although for months he thought they should have been able to think of alternatives.

"Why do grown ups always find difficulties?" he was heard muttering to himself, and it was with the greatest hardship they kept straight faces.

They eventually returned to the oppidum after a prolonged and frustrating journey up the Tamesis, retracing in part its course that had brought them to Londinus, only this time they were impeded by the current, not assisted as formerly. They had decided on this route, after refusing Vespasian's offer that they could accompany his legion as they moved westward to subdue the Atribates who were rallying around Caractacus.

"We're bound to get caught up in their battles somewhere along any route over land, but if we use the river we might avoid it," Marc had urged as they debated the alternatives.

He was right as far as battles were concerned, but finding boatmen who were prepared to go more than a short distance up river, away from their homes and families in those troubled times was almost impossible. Fortunately Brutus had exchanged some of the newly minted denarii he had drawn, for some gold coins struck at Camulodunum in the previous reign of Cunobelin.

Looking at the rearing horse image on one side of the coins and the wheat-ear on the reverse he wondered if he was being cheated by the trader, a bewhiskered old Judaean who still clung to his Jewish robes and demanded five silver for each gold.

"Who knows if anybody will want these Roman coins? Soon they might be worthless, they seem to be minting them as fast as they can," said the Jew, trying to bend one between his teeth without success, "soon they will be debasing them with tin and copper, you mark my word." But he seemed happy enough to lighten Brutus' purse by fifty of them.

Now as he negotiated the hire of a four-oared boat he was glad of his provenence, as the boatman spat on being offered denarii. For two gold coins, however he and his fourteen-year-old son agreed to row them for one day's journey.

"Then you must row yourselves, and when you can go no further ask for Kenan the coracle builder. Tell him you got it from Segovax at the tidal limits, and he will see the boat is returned to me."

So it had been agreed. At the end of the first day they had made a good way up river, mostly through thickly wooded terrain, with the occasional village built on the bank at crossing points or clearings.

"When the river branches for you tomorrow take the south branch. You should make Kenan after three more days rowing."

With that they were on their own as the man and his son swung their few possessions over their shoulders and started walking back along the bank.

Rowing steadily they made acceptable progress. Occasionally they were challenged but the mention of Caratacus always gained them passage. As it was high summer each night was slept on the riverbank, choosing a place with tree cover and plenty of bracken.

Near the head of the river they easily found Kenan, inspecting a net he had stretched across the river, into which he had driven a few fish by beating on the side of his coracle.

"Travel due south from here and you will see the huge henge. Keep going south and you should pick up the river that leads to Hengist on the sea. Maybe three days walk with the boy," said the fisherman, guiding them to the beginning of a south leading path, opposite a fording point on the river.

They stumbled on the concentric rings of broken weathered posts as they emerged from the woods and stood in astonishment looking across the fields of waving grain to the henge on the other side of the vale, and were compelled by some primitive, atavistic compulsion, to deviate to the west and stand at the centre of the massive ancient temple.

Rufus was disturbingly affected as he felt the hair rising at the nape of his neck and an urge to run from its over-powering and primitive aura. Simon, leaping from one fallen stone to another, was the least. Quickly Rufus pulled the boy outside of the circle of stones, into the waist-high standing corn that awaited the harvesting that would never happen now the men had been called to oppose the advancing might of the invader. With a shudder he exclaimed,

"I heard the chanting as human sacrifices were made here, and they weren't just from the distant past. I thought that was all over and would never happen again, but standing within that circle I heard a baying for blood and it wasn't from the past but from the future!" he said with a shudder.

"Do you think you're edgy because of all the conflict?" suggested Marc, but Rufus shook his head.

"No, this wasn't the brutality of war, not that sort of mindless, indiscriminate slaughter. This was deliberate, legally sanctioned killing, in the name of righteousness and hundreds were burning at the stakes."

He looked back across the valley they had crossed, "More than the number of all those posts over there, each with a victim fastened and all ablaze with the crowd howling insatiably. It wasn't here exactly, it was in a vast arena, in Rome, and the people burning at the stakes were followers of the way!"

"Just as Judaic law sanctions the burning alive of the daughter of a priest for laying with a man out of wedlock?" asked Brutus, "the very same that Mary Magdalene challenged Saul of Tarsus to justify in the Synagogue at Joppa, when he declared how far he was prepared to go to stamp out the followers of Jesus?"

"I remember hearing of that incident, and what did Saul reply?"

"Before he could think of anything the crowd mobbed Mary and would certainly have killed her, had not Marc and Miriam and some passing soldiers heeded the entreaties of the old silversmith Abraham."

Brutus could not even talk of it without anger seizing him so that he stood rigid, the blood pounding at his temples, his eyes blazing for expiation. Marc put a reassuring hand on his arm and said,

"Come father, we've been too long at this place."

They arrived back at the oppidum to find it overflowing with refugees, and a proliferation of simple woven wattle shelters filled the whole interior, within which milled the aged, the wounded, women and children. The stench and the noise were unbearable and when the travellers found their wives confined in one tiny part of the bursting round house, both women wept openly with relief.

As the tears flowed they remonstrated with their men for being so tardy about returning.

Although they did not know how they could have got back earlier, the men were distressed by the deterioration of the conditions within the oppidum, and the misery their women had suffered while they were away. It took them two minutes to decide to leave and twenty minutes to execute.

An elderly guard challenged them as they passed through the gate.

"All fit men and unencumbered women are ordered to arms. Why aren't you with the warriors?" His challenge was shrill and caught the attention of two men unloading provision from a wagon at the gate. They were armed and moved threateningly beside the guard.

"We are for the cause of Caractacus," said Marc, "I am the lost son of Cartinua of whom the bard sang back in the winter. We are instructed to make our way to the Durotriges where the decisive battle will be fought. We have our orders to join with the alliance of the western tribes and rally all warriors there. The oppida east of here are defended only to slow down the Roman advance, and nothing will be gained by us staying here, or you either!" he shot at the men, who suddenly seemed uncertain.

376

He had assumed such an air of authority, the men withdrew sheepishly to their unloading and with relief they left the oppidum behind them. Only after some distance had been put between them, did they stop to confer on where they intended to go.

Brutus thought Marc should first speak his mind.

"After that brilliant piece of improvisation back at the gate you had me believing we should go west," he laughed, "so I am eager to hear what you really think."

"I think we should retrace our route to Camulodunum!"

Marc's positive assertion surprised Brutus, who had not dared to hope he would choose to move east.

"If we make our way to where we left the boat Kenan may not have taken it back down river."

The women had no idea what the men were talking about, but Simon was already getting excited at the mere mention of Camulodunum.

Mary said, "The lie of this country baffles me, north, south, east, west, it's immaterial where we go. We know we can rely on you to choose the best option and put our faith in God who has cared for us throughout."

"Thank you for saying that. Now I am happy to tell you of an offer that was made to me by Plautius which I kept quiet about, as I didn't wish to compromise Marc in making his decision."

Keeping all in suspense, Brutus then astounded everyone as he continued,

"They want a coordinator of native affairs to liaise between the Governor and the tribes of the eastern province. Plautius offered me the job and the office is at Camulodunum!"

"Why that's fantastic news," cried Marc, "how could you have kept it from me?"

"I haven't accepted it yet. I wanted to be able to attend to the well being of the women and children if you had thrown in your lot with Caractacus and added your sword to his warriors. I decided I could not myself bear arms against my own, but I wanted you to be free to make up your own mind."

Marc was greatly moved by the loyalty of his father, and too overcome to reply immediately, but he knew he needed to explain his decision.

"Had the tribes united I would have pledged my sword to drive out the Romans. When I found out that sixteen of the tribes had sworn allegiance to Claudius and had no intention of fighting I was really angry. And then the early defeat of the Trinovantes convinced me our cause was lost; and remember I was captured and enslaved fighting for a lost cause once before. I knew had I been slain I could rely on you to care for my family as you would for your own, but I can't justify following that course in the circumstances."

As he fell silent the anguish of the decision showed in his tortured face.

Wordlessly Brutus placed a comforting arm around him holding him close. The memory of the last time he had done so following the crucifixion flooded back. He knew he was not a demonstrative man, and words often could not be found to say how proud he was of his son, but he also knew instinctively this assurance needed to be given now, more than ever before.

Both women rejoiced more openly as they embraced each other and allowed the tears to flow.

Simon, holding Peter nonchalantly, decided elephants were the least complicated of all animals and as the baby started to howl decided to apply for the role of assistant elephant keeper as soon as they reached Camulodunum.

Imagine his disappointment when they arrived there ten days later to find Claudius had returned to Rome, the elephants to Gaul and there was but a single cohort remaining in the town, under the command of Tribune Crassus.

The first time he encountered the tribune was when Jup broke away from his hold and raced towards the uniformed figure in the distance and jumped up in greeting only to be rebuffed by the uniformed officer, until he recognised the boy chasing up behind.

"Simon, by Jupiter," he laughed, "then this must be Jup!" and he fondled the handsome dog, laughing even louder at his inadvertent diminution of the God he had sworn by, "what a splendid animal he has grown into!"

No other words could have re-cemented the friendship between the Roman and the boy half as well, and the three of them walked together as though life long friends, down the easterly hill to the wooden quay that had been built at the river-bank. Bales and wooden crates were being carefully unloaded and moved into a nearby warehouse.

As the terracotta amphora followed, Craccus said, "This is the first of many such ships that will unload here if we are to make Camulodunum into a fine Roman town, Simon."

Simon had a stick that he was throwing as Jup barked excitedly at his feet.

"Caes ..." began the boy as his arm arched and the stick flew.

"Seize the stick Jup!" he said, and was abashed when the confused dog failed to give chase.

The Tribune smiled quietly to himself and recognised that Simon had the making of a good diplomat. To cover the boy's discomfiture he said,

"Come and see these fine hunters that will be sailing tomorrow."

Brutus quickly found a house in the old part of Camulodunum, where the river curved around the promontory that commanded the broad valley to the north and east. The wooden house had two storeys, divided into five rooms, giving privacy for sleeping. A spring nearby at the base of the hill ensured fresh water and an open drain vented into the river.

Each tide brought boats to the harbour quay, half a mile down river, provisioning the rapid expansion of the Roman town with those accoutrements that Romans insist on. Pottery, wine, olive oil, mosaics, glassware, lead pipes and luxuries streamed in endlessly. Barracks and temporary forum and administrative offices sprang up on the hill, spilling over the gently sloping west incline towards the ancient dykes.

One of Brutus' first problems was to allocate the proportion of each farmer's produce for the support of the garrison, and the wider ranging requirements of the army subduing the tribes to the west. As his remit extended from the Tamesis north including the tribal lands of both the Trinovantes and the Iceni, he was aware of the necessity of being even handed about this and decided to disregard the assistance that many Trinovantes were giving to the Atrebates in their hit and run tactics against the legions of Plautius to the west, and Brutus imposed equal taxes on both tribes.

This incensed King Prasutagus of the Iceni who protested at his farmers paying the same taxes as the war-mongering Trinovantes.

378

"If we were at war with Rome as is Caractacus, you would be entitled to punish us with such heavy taxes. But we are allies of Rome yet we pay the same as its enemies. This cannot be tolerated."

Although secretly Brutus would have taxed them double for being allies of Rome he knew that would never be allowed to happen.

"Why your men are free to sow and reap and your farms are very productive. Many of your neighbours' farms are managed by widows and children, while the men are away fighting. They cannot pay more than they do, although you could bear a greater share than is demanded!"

The veiled threat in the argument silenced the king and Brutus pressed home his advantage.

"Have you thought how much more grain you could grow if you cut back a quarter of your forest? You would gain twofold as I can guarantee we will buy all the timber you produce, and your corn will always fetch a good price."

The king thought about this and then shook his head.

"No my nobles need the forest for the hunt. Take that away and they will be dispirited and troublesome. Before you Romans came there was plenty of raiding against neighbouring tribes, and half a dozen slaves would buy a superb horse from Persia."

Brutus left him with the thought sown, and within months was requested to get a good price for a felled oak wood.

To the west it was a different story. Vespasian was marching ever westwards overcoming oppida, seizing towns and treating savagely any warriors captured, in retaliation for the scorched earth policy of Caractacus and Togoduminus, who were burning everything they couldn't carry in their vast convoy of wagons. Many a warrior hung from the cross as the Romans suppressed the tribes.

Togoduminus, trapped by a fast encirclement of Roman cavalry, called on his men to die rather than be crucified, and Longinus testified he had never known a bloodier encounter, as no quarter was given or asked.

The Romans relied on supplementing their rations by living off the country but there was nothing to be gathered from the devastated region, and the peasants were gathering leaves and roots to cook, in a desperate attempt to hold out until the conflict had moved on.

Longinus' squadron commandeered the stew a family was cooking at a burnt out farmstead. That night all had fearsome hallucinations and only those who vomited the stolen food quickly were alive in the morning. Eight were dead of the twenty.

In Rome, Claudius enjoyed a conqueror's parade, and was given the title of Britannicus in celebration of his triumph. Plautius was replaced by a new commander of the army, Ostorius, whose tactics and ruthlessness were effective in overcoming all resistance as far as the western mountains. The Durotriges were humbled, and all but those living in the wild, untamable mountains, subjugated.

Amazingly as tribe after tribe fell, the standing of Caractacus became legendary, and dismayed bards sang sagas to his prowess throughout the land. While he lived, and loved, and fought, some forlorn hope burned in the hearts of a conquered nation that all was not lost.

At Camulodunum a sombre centurion, with fixed eyes restraining pressing tears, brought from afar the news of the end of their dreams.

"Caractacus has been taken!" he said like a prophet of doom.

The fourteen year old boy at his side wept like a girl, and his six year old cousin clasped him disbelievingly, aware of an overwhelming sadness that he was too young to articulate. With every moist eye riveted on him, Brutus continued,

"Betrayed, as he tried to forge an alliance with the Brigantes to the north. Queen Cecilia tried to bed him, while her king assembled the priests and warriors to battle. Caractacus spurned her, and Cecilia rode on her white stallion to the camp of Ostorius to revenge herself by betraying him. The world knows no anger like a woman spurned, and Britain knows no infamy to match that of Cecilia, the queen of the Brigantes."

The pain of the betrayal was etched on every face and then Simon said,

"Will they execute him as they did Vercingetorex in Gaul?"

"Nobody knows. He, and his household, are to be taken in chains to Rome. Perhaps Claudius will extend clemency to him, I don't know?"

With the betrayal of Caractacus all resistance collapsed, and as the Romans rampaged along the north-west coast looting and violating, there remained one unfulfilled abomination to be accomplished.

On the Holy Island of Mona, at the western extremity of the world were gathered those druid priests and the bards so irrationally hated by the victors. As though they encapsulated the very spirit of this island people, the Romans regarded their annihilation as the final act of its subjugation.

But there was more to it than the last drama of a struggle for power.

The ancient truths and knowledge of the Druids challenged Roman materialism, which even Roman gods had been fashioned to serve. Unless crushed they would always be feared, as their challenge was unanswerable. Caesar had been the first to recognize that the druids embodied myth and ritual, poetry and law, and could not coexist with a Roman Empire. Tiberius had continued their persecution and now Claudius officiated at its consummation.

Mary Magdalene had taken to her bed that evening troubled by an undefined feeling of impending disaster. On an impulse, she had meditated over the linen cloth that had covered the face of her crucified Lord. Earlier she had responded to the urging of the spirit and bequeathed part of it to Donal, the old druid, that day he pleaded with her to baptize him before the end.

"Wait until Rufus returns," she had replied.

"I can't. The end is near!" he had insisted.

"The end?"

"Our end, that of we itinerant priests who have carried the traditions of belief from when the land emerged from the receding waters. The Romans say we are the custodians of all vehement instincts and bestial passions, and make false charge we condone human sacrifice. They will kill every last one of us!"

She could see the sublime joy now with which he had embraced the precious relic as she lay trying to control the turmoil in her mind.

She cried out at the flash of lightning that seared her mind and wondered if she would be blinded on opening her eyes, as had been Saul on the Damascus road. She was still sighted when she did, for what she had seen, but would not be revealed in its full barbarity for some days, was the plunging torch flame reflected momentarily from the blade of the sword that severed the head of the old druid, his eyes closed to exclude the brutality of the ending of his life and the passing of an era.

Tribune Danius Galerius exulted in this last rite his troop was executing on the high hill, overlooking the flame and smoke engulfed plain where the massed druids had been put to the sword. Then he saw the torches high up above, and had rallied his troop to follow, many of whom were reacting with revulsion to the unopposed slaughter in which they were participating. His horse reared, threatening to throw him as they approached the kneeling, white robed druids, upraised torches forming a burning cross.

Only with a supreme effort could he force his normally compliant stallion down and then forward, as he led the fearful charge.

Still one knelt, pathetic and insignificant among the scattered bodies all around, a soiled square of cream coloured cloth fluttering from the short staff held in one hand, a guttering torch in the other. The tribune's sword flashed in the torch light and as Donal's head fell, the staff toppled and the flag was engulfed in the flames.

Mary's cry called Brutus and he had never witnessed such paroxysms of sobs as racked her now. Holding her to him he rocked her gently and gradually the sobs subsided and she told him of Donal. He didn't question it, as he knew she knew things beyond his understanding.

The next day they assembled with a dozen followers in the small wattle church they had built to the south side of the colonia, which boasted the grandiloquent name of Colonia Claudia Victricensis. The natives still called it Camulodunum and made it a point of honour to deny any knowledge of the colonia to any enquirer using its Roman name.

Rufus called for the prayers of the community for their brother Donal, killed by the legions the previous evening, on Mona, the isle of the druids to the west.

"How can you know this?" queried the son of the Roman landowner, whose imposing villa set among the fields of golden corn was the envy of the town.

"Mary Magdalene was distressed by a vision of a great slaughter on the holy island of the Druids," said Rufus simply, and such was her standing, no-one doubted its authenticity, although it was four days before an official bulletin was posted on the notice board of the forum. Alongside this bulletin, as though to rub salt in the wounded pride of the Britons was the drawings and plan for a Temple to be built just to the east of the colonia which was to be dedicated to Emperor Claudius.

Brutus was given the responsibility of funding this huge enterprise.

"Are no funds to be forthcoming from Rome?" he asked with dismay.

"None!" said Crassus. "I've tried to get the treasury to pay some of it, but they resent the cost of this protracted war. They say it will give the natives a chance to show their appreciation of the benefits of Roman rule."

Brutus laughed derisively.

"What benefits? To post both bulletins on the same day is provocative, but when people realize the revenue consequences there will be trouble."

"It's your job to see there is no trouble. You have to convince them that their sacrifice is for a worthy cause."

The legions returned and the colonia was bursting with arrogant and bored soldiers, swaggering aggressively around the old town looking for diversion.

Fights broke out frequently sometimes ending in serious injury. A decree was issued banning the bearing of arms within the town, other than by soldiers on duty, and a curfew was imposed two hours after dark.

As the architects, surveyors, masons and carpenters assembled for the building of the temple the quartering and provisioning of the workers became a burden on the local community.

The tradesmen and merchants called a meeting to protest at the heavy duty imposed on all their trades and businesses, and on the town market. The large hall built by Cunobelin was the venue, and Crassus listened to the complaints for an hour. Then he grew impatient, announced that complaints could only be submitted in writing and cleared the hall.

That night the hall was burnt to the ground.

That night also a plea came for Mary Magdalene to urgently attend the garrison, as the physicians were worried for the life of Tribune Danius Gallerius.

"Why on earth would they send for me?" asked Mary, greatly agitated as she secured her cloak.

"It isn't the physicians who send for you, Mary, it's Dan, and I believe it's because you saved his life."

They hurried to the garrison where Longinus was waiting anxiously at the guardhouse.

"Come quickly, I've been at my wits end for a week," and as he walked them to the sick bay he quickly summarized the situation.

"It's since the final slaughter on the isle of the Druids, he's been like a man haunted. At first he wouldn't speak. As commander of cavalry he was expected to make a report, but he just sat mute in front of Ostorius, staring wildly around him, and then as though he heard something none of us could hear, he would become still, his head to one side as though listening intently. That was a week ago but he's rapidly deteriorated since as you'll see."

They entered the sick bay, the end of which was screened off to isolate Dan from his fellow officers, and they heard his shuffling walk even as they approached, and as they parted the screen and entered the gloomy interior, were struck by the travesty of the young officer they had seen off to war.

Thin and gaunt, he was pacing the room with shuffling steps. Then he would stop, reach out with hand eagerly as though to grasp something, and as though what he reached for eluded him, bring his hand hesitantly to cover his eyes, brush a lock of snow white hair from his forehead, turn and shuffle back.

Fascinated and appalled they watched him repeat the whole procedure over and over again, endlessly. The boards he trod were marked by the unvarying routine. Mary sank on her knees and prayed as she had over his prostrate youthful body at Tyre a life-time ago. He took no notice.

"How long has he been like this?" whispered Brutus.

"Three or four days."

"Does he never sleep?"

382

"Never. Occasionally he collapses from weakness, and then the orderlies lift him on the bed where he lies with his eyes staring at the ceiling. Then after a few hours he becomes agitated, drinks a little water and begins all over again."

"Eat?"

"Not a thing. He did at first but everything he ate he vomited up. Then he just stopped eating."

"Was it terrible there?"

Longinus stared uncomprehending.

"At the Druid's island. Was it terrible?"

Fleetingly panic disturbed Longinus' face, and his left eye twitched. Then he controlled himself and forced his face into a stony composure.

"I've never known a blood-bath like it. A thousand white robed priests and as many black robed women, all waving torches and chanting, or screaming blood curdling curses. Not one escaped our swords, not one."

"Did they not defend themselves?"

"They had no weapons. Afterwards we found a few dozen corn scythes and some staves, that was all."

Mary had joined them now and appeared to be listening although her lips were moving as she counted his steps.

"... Ten, eleven, twelve." Dan had reached the end and went through exactly the same procedure of reaching for something elusive, brushing back a lock of hair, turning and beginning again.

"Always twelve," she said, "does twelve have any significance?"

Longinus shook his head.

"Then think. Think about everything and see if twelve comes into anything."

She moved to stand opposite Dan as he approached to make another turn. As he stopped and reached out his sword hand, Mary grasped it in hers and looked beseechingly into his eyes. They were uncomprehending, staring and yet vacant, then he withdrew his hand to cover his eyes, brushed his lock of hair and turned to begin another twelve paces.

"What do the physicians say?" asked Brutus

"They say many things I don't understand, but I think it comes down to them being baffled, and they wonder if he has been cursed into madness by the Druids."

"Would that be possible?" Brutus queried of Mary.

"I don't believe so. I'm afraid something so awful happened he can't bear to think of it. Think back to the foot of the cross and you will know what I mean. What did you want to do then?"

"Kill myself!"

"And why didn't you?"

"I don't know. Maybe I lacked the courage!"

Mary's eyes blazed angrily.

"That's stupid and not true, don't ever say that again!" and as her eyes softened and filled with tears he drew her to him, pleading for pardon.

"The very last killing, the most bizarre of all, there were twelve of them," said Longinus tentatively. "I remember because I had a head count afterwards."

"What do you mean by bizarre?" entreated Mary, her mind spinning at the reply she feared and anticipated.

"Well all the priests and priestesses down on the shore ran around yelling oaths and curses, and trying to avoid our swords. When they had all been struck down, tribune Danius drew our attention to a cross, formed by lit torches up the hill above us. He led his squadren up to it and was nearly thrown by his horse rearing violently."

"Then what happened?" whispered Mary, fighting the icy hand clutching her heart.

"We all waited as Danius regained control of his horse, which surprised us as he prided himself on the unfailing obedience of his mount. There was no hurry the twelve white robed druids were kneeling, torches held in both hands in front of them, except for the white haired fellow at the centre, he held a torch in one hand and in the other a flag of surrender. It looked weird in the flickering light, dirty and creamy white, fluttering pathetically from a staff."

"And then?" Mary squeezed out the words as she welcomed the oblivion that was closing in on her.

"Tribune Danius led the charge and we cut every one of them down. It was eerie, not one tried to flee or pleaded to be spared. Dan beheaded the last one, the one with the flag and it was all over."

Mary had slumped to the floor and as the outraged centurion bent to lift her he saw from the corner of his eye the tribune standing rigid, before he too collapsed. Brutus carried Mary past the prostrate Danius, and as he did so gave him the most violent of kicks.

He cradled his woman past the startled guard and down the hill, his mind in such a turmoil he didn't notice the spasm that siezed his upper body, so that he had to call Marc and Miriam to come to his aid to lay her down.

Crassus accepted Brutus' resignation the next morning, but gave scant assurance that he would consider Marc for his replacement.

"I know it's a big job and you have often delegated the Briton to act for you, but I feel it is a job for a Roman."

"He is a Roman as much as I am. He has Roman citizenship as my adopted son, and has a letter of manumission to back his full rights," Brutus protested angrily.

"That may be so but I am referring to where his sympathies lie, which I feel are more with the conquered than the conqueror."

"Since when has conquering Rome looked for sympathy from those it forces into subjugation?" demanded Brutus contemptuously. "The job needs a fair minded and even-handed man and you won't find a better man than Marc in the province."

As he stormed out of the commander's office he remembered his angry kick of Dan the previous night, and wondered if he was becoming short tempered.

Mary was sitting up in bed when he returned, and when he referred to his losing his temper and kicking the unconscious Dan, she smiled sadly.

"Dan wouldn't feel anything you did to his body, his mind has shut out his body completely. There is a sensibility about him, as there is about you, that is the cause of an inner conflict because of the brutal reality of soldiering. I fear it may lead to his destruction. Now a kick might just make some impression on Crassus. Is it too late to go back and give him one?"

He had to smile at her bravery and rejoiced yet again at being the recipient of her love.

Sitting on a bench in the noon sunshine Brutus was glad to see the two boys returning from a walk in the high woods on the far side of the valley. Jup, now too old to chase 'Caesars' with much enthusiasm, walked proudly, tail held aloft, as though he wanted to assert his contribution to the hare they had caught.

"They're fine lads," he thought, "attentive both to their studies and to their weapon skills," not that he wished either of them to be a soldier, "and respectful of their parents," he added belatedly, as he reflected on the disruption to all of their lives that he proposed, and of which as yet they were unaware.

Mary emerged from the house with a small parcel under her robe.

"I want to see Dan," she said, anxiety etched on her normally tranquil features. "Will you accompany me to the sick quarters? You won't need to wait with me as I will be quite able to walk home today," she added confidently.

Reluctantly Brutus agreed as he was not convinced of the wisdom of Mary's mission, and he thought she was more vulnerable than she acknowledged.

As they entered the gloomy room she realised everything had changed. The screens had been removed and the whole length of the sick bay was revealed, but Dan's bed lay unoccupied and orderly as though for inspection.

"Where is Tribune Danius?" she asked an orderly, her heart pounding.

"Taken to the guard-room, I fear. He became so violent first thing this morning he frightened everyone. It's impossible to keep him here."

Mary ran to the door and called to Brutus as he was about to disappear. Quickly she told him what had happened and urged him to take her there.

"They may not let you see him, and if he's violent is it wise?"

She dismissed his worries.

"He needs me more than ever," she cried, her compassion driving any fear from her thoughts.

"If they let you I'll have to stay as well!" he emphasized, and she agreed.

The guard-room was built into the triumphal gate to the west side of the colonia. The earthworks surmounted by a wooden palisade spread out from it on both sides to encircle the garrison, with a smaller gate on the east side.

The guard commander, a young centurion, was loath to let anyone in with the mad tribune. He knew Brutus and his importance to the Governor and eventually was prevailed upon, although he insisted on locking the heavy door behind and slid the grid through which he could keep an eye on them. The only light was from a barred high opening on the south wall and the afternoon sun was barely able to penetrate within.

Surprisingly it evoked in Brutus' mind a clear recollection of standing watching the humiliation of Jesus in the guard-room of Fort Antonia all those years ago, but as though it were but yesterday.

Dan lay on a pile of straw in a corner, knees drawn up to his face and encircled by his arms. Only his white hair revealed his head hidden from scrutiny.

"Leave everything to me unless I lose control," whispered Mary.

As she approached she saw an eye watching her over the clasped arms. His hair half covered his eye and she reached out her hand and brushed it aside.

"It's me, Mary. Remember? We've just pulled you from the sea at Tyre, you and your friend Malchus. You nearly drowned both of you. Your little boat was smashed by the waves."

His one eye was watching her warily and she moved her hand to his. Gently she tried to unlock his fingers but withdrew her hand as she saw the fear register momentarily in the one eye. She resolved to hold that eye whatever she did. She knew hypnotists were able to dominate by maintaining eye contact, and she was prepared to try anything to penetrate the shell within which he had retreated.

After ten minutes ineffectually recalling the distant past, she decided to be more brutal and challenge him with the recent event.

"What are they holding on the hill there? Those lighted torches burning above the beach what do they make? Is it a cross, let's ride up and see. Lead the way tribune, ride your horse hard, let's get this slaughter over with."

Suddenly as the fear again flared in his eye he brought both his arms from around his knees and in one convulsive movement clasped his hands above his head, his upper arms covering his ears. Both eyes were now on her, but full of malign hate, not fear.

Never wavering in her eye contact, she voiced a silent prayer to her Lord, before resuming her attack.

"Ride it hard, fast as the wind. Exult in the power of your stallion and in your invincibility. Conquerors of the earth, can these pathetic priests defy you? Why, what are they, only youths and old men? Youths as you were, you and Malchus, when Marc and Horatius swam out and saved you from the sea!"

A moan that seemed to have its origins beyond conscious remorse and awareness, before even when sin first shattered man's innocence, emitted from his parted lips.

"How many are they, one, two, three, four, five, six, seven, eight, nine, ten, eleven, twelve. How many are you milling around on your horses, more than you can count? But why does your horse refuse your urging, isn't it always reliable and obedient? Now it rears, is it to resist the evil you propose by throwing you? Can this insensate beast know wrong while you are completely oblivious of it? Hold the bridle, hold it!"

Dan's arms reached out in front of him, his fingers seeking the reassuring feel of leather. Desperately he sought for something to hold on to and his eyes flitted wildly from side to side. Mary put her hands over his but he shook them off and grabbed the folds of her robe.

"That's right. Dominate everything; make your horse submit; force it down, down, now forward. Only twelve to kill and it will be finished."

Dan had pulled Mary down so that he towered over her. Brutus was poised to hurl himself at the tribune, but Mary's insistent voice restrained him.

"Now for the very last one, tribune Danius, he's all yours, the ultimate sublime act of this slaughter. He's old and his hands cannot defend himself. Go for him, Danius. His name is Donal, a teller of stories from the beginning of time. He's dangerous, Danius, threatening, with torch in one hand and flag in the other. The flag he holds Danius, look at it. Can you see whose image it carries, tribune? Look, look hard!"

Eyes wide and staring, fixed on a point above Mary's head, Dan's breath came in deep, rasping sobs, and then a scream arose from somewhere buried behind his torn heart. As it pulsated within the enclosing room, it grew in power and pitch so that every movement on the parade ground was arrested and every eye focussed on the narrow embrasure high up on the wall.

Mary's heart was ravished. Torn and bleeding, penetrated by the urgent need for love of this rapacious boy-man, deprived by the patrician aloofness of his growing up, and warped into permanent adolescence. She arose and clutched the sobbing boy to her bosom, caressing his head and murmuring those soothing words and sounds that a mother always treasures, but the boy grown big always forgets

"You can leave us now," she said to the centurion, "all is well. I just have something secret to show Dan."

The tightly closed eyes and total surrender of the tribune reassured Brutus it was safe to leave them alone.

The military authorities were loath to credit Mary Magdalene with any part in the recovery of the tribune. Indeed when he requested to be found a non-combatant role in the administration of the island, the governor decided he hadn't recovered at all.

"Is he bewitched? What do we know of the woman who was with him that day? Isn't she a priestess of the Judaean cult that practises cannibalism and incest? The best thing for tribune Danius Gallerius would be to get him away, back to Rome as soon as possible!" were Crassus' final words.

In the fortnight that took to arrange, Dan was frequently to be seen walking with Rufus along the bank to the fishing village, where the river widened opposite the low island and joined the sea. Nobody witnessed his immersion in that river and by the time they had regained the colonia the autumn sun had dried them both.

His friends' joy on hearing of his initiation into the church was tempered that same day by receiving news of his imminent departure.

"The Christians in Rome are having a bad time and have been driven to meeting in secret. You won't find any places of worship but there is a community. Find the Jewish area and look for the sign of the fish and you will have found them," said Rufus, drawing the outline with his moistened finger on the tabletop before wiping it dry.

Brutus decided this was an appropriate moment to broach something that was on his mind.

"I want Mary and Peter to return with me to Italia next spring - maybe to Rome!"

Mary's face registered amazement as this hadn't been mentioned in any of their intimate moments but she held her peace and Brutus continued,

"I haven't any role here now I've resigned as coordinator. Nor am I in agreement with the governor and Craccus. Their punitive attitude to the local tribes is bound to lead to trouble. I would find idly sitting by and watching it happen with no possibility of influencing the outcome too disturbing, and I don't envy you if you get my job, Marc. Anyway any appointment will be on hold until Ostorius is replaced by Suetonius."

A knocking at the door led to the entry of Longinus, bursting to give them his news.

"We have just received a message that Caractacus has been freed, he and all his retinue."

Watching their elation he rejoiced to be the bearer of such good news.

"Apparently when paraded through Rome he deported himself with such dignity, refusing to plead for clemency, and made such an impressive defence of his right to resist conquest that Claudius ordered all their chains to be removed."

"Can we expect to see him restored to his kingdom?" asked Marc, thinking excitedly of the new possibilities that could follow such an imaginative action.

"No. He can't leave Italia! They will probably give him one of Tiberius's former palaces on Capri."

Their disappointment was palpable, but Longinus was secretly relieved there was no possibility of this fiery chief leading another army in Brittania. Little did he know it would be of no consequence to him, for within the week he was thrown in a hunt and sustained head injuries from which he never recovered.

He was buried with full military honours in the cemetery to the west of the town, the day before Dan was to sail.

"Buy him a tombstone worthy of a hero!" insisted Danius, "we who were with him at Dura-Europos and throughout the campaign in Brittania have lost a staunch comrade."

Crassus promised to see to it, putting the hundred denarii carefully aside, but he failed to consult anybody as to its suitability, as Crassus wished it to reflect his view of Longinus' role and importance. Consequently although many admired the superbly sculptured cavalry officer astride his ceremonially accoutred horse, others were incensed at the submissive naked Briton he trampled under foot. The winged goddess and lions rampant surmounting the edifice, would undoubtedly have won the approval of the officer it commemorated.

"You can read more of Crassus than of Longinus from this stone," was Brutus' cryptic comment to Mary.

It encapsulated the attitude of conqueror to conquered, which was to prevail for a decade and would cause the inevitable and ferocious expiation to follow.

CHAPTER TWO

The west wind filled the sail and the small trading vessel drawing away from the quay moved quickly down river. The spring sunshine belied the temperature and the party on the stern deck needed the warmth of the cloaks they held close. The trees crowding the bank of the river were showing the first hint of green after the long winter and as the boat rounded a bend the passengers waved farewell to the forlorn group on the quayside.

From view maybe, but from the thoughts of those left on the quayside, not for a long while, as the reality of their breaking up after all they had confronted together had seemed more of a nightmare than an actuality.

Miriam refused to acknowledge that they had really gone, which turning away would have underlined. Marc put a comforting arm around her sob-racked shoulders and Rufus held her tight by her free arm. Neither had sufficient imagination to know all she was suffering at letting go of her only son, although they too felt saddened at this parting.

Miriam had taken a lot of convincing that if there were reasons their son should accompany their friends overseas, there were any reasons for them to stay behind themselves. Apart from the small Christian community, over which Rufus presided like a cock over the barnyard hens, an analogy that was particularly appropriate as the women greatly outnumbered their men, Miriam missed the great Jewish traditions and the Synagogue.

"If this job doesn't measure up I'll throw it in next year and we can join them," said Marc placatingly.

He had just heard that he was being offered Brutus' job for two years initially.

"We do need to earn a living you know, we can't expect Alexander to keep us, and it will cost quite a lot to put Simon through law school!"

This was the real bone of contention as Simon had his heart set on becoming a lawyer and there was nowhere in Britain to study law. He was seventeen, already a year late for enrolling in an academy, and so Marc had suggested that Brutus enrol him at an appropriate institution in Rome. There had followed a winter of discontent in the household.

Marc filling the native tribe coordinator job on a temporary basis, hoped to become permanent when he had proved to Crassus that he was up to the job.

The Jewesses, with their inborn respect for learning had ensured the boys had a good grounding in the torah and the prophets, and knew of Jesus' eventful life and his teaching and parables. They had also studied Latin and Greek and could read Hebrew, and there was no doubting that they had inherited their intellectual flair from their Jewish parents, and Simon his love of the outdoor world and his sense of adventure from his Celtic father.

Marc responded to the sad howl emitted by Jup with a pat and a fondle of his ear.

"You don't understand it any more than we do, do you old boy?" he said commiserating, blissfully unaware of how near he came to being pushed in the river.

Aboard ship, excitement at what lay ahead tempered the sadness of the parting.

"Dubris by morning," said Brutus reassuringly, "and there we shall find a stout vessel to carry us to Rome."

By common agreement two weeks on a boat was preferable to as many months crossing Gallia by land and river, and they were anxious to get Simon started as soon as possible into his studies.

They arrived before dawn, following the moonlit white cliffs close inshore, avoiding the hazardous sandbanks further out. The burning beacon atop of the lighthouse tower guided them into the harbour, and they disembarked coincident with the bustle of port activity initiated by first light.

They found an inn adjacent to the small fort overlooking the harbour that was itself dwarfed by the tall tower, the beacon of which was lit every night to guide in the many Roman vessels crossing from Gaul, and their first enquiries were fortunate in finding a suitable vessel sailing in two days, after it had loaded its cargo.

"The captain predicts the winds will change easterly with the spring equinox and is happy to carry us as far as Massilia. So, have a good look around Dubris while we can, as it will be a few weeks before we are on dry land again!"

Mary was disappointed at the close of her day, finding no trace of Synagogue or Christian community despite all her enquiries. Twice, after circuitous routes she had found herself back at the fish market, and gave up making that sign when inquiring thereafter.

The men returned elated after their exploration of the high chalk cliffs with their wonderful views across to Gaul.

"I'm sure we could see where you sailed from before I was born mama, Simon says he recognises the coastline as well!" called out Peter excitedly.

"Then he must be right, but as we sailed over so long ago, I've forgotten what it looked like, and everyone was so sea-sick I didn't take much notice."

"What's sea-sick like, mama?" asked Peter.

"You can't describe it. You have to feel it to know and then you would rather be dead than it continue a minute longer."

Both boys looked at each other apprehensively.

Not that they found out for a week, with the predicted easterly hurrying them down the channel they had turned south around the western tip of Gaul before any discomfort in the motion was felt.

"We must gain some seaway, the winds are bound to come around from the west soon and when they do we don't want to be near this shore," said the captain pointing at the low-lying rocky island on the left.

For two days they pushed south-westerly and then in the short space of a few hours the wind moved southerly, and a dark bank of cloud grew threateningly on the western horizon.

"Belay there, shorten sail," called the captain, and the topmost of the square sails on both masts were gathered on the spars and lashed.

With the rain the wind gusted strong moving ever more westerly. The waves built up, surging in to lay the boat well over as it rose, only to fall away sickeningly as the crest passed under and the next one loomed up. All the square sails were now lashed, and only two triangular sails set forward of each mast steadied the boat.

To three of the four passengers it seemed like an eternity of wretchedness although it lasted but a day and a night.

"I remember now, Brutus, that which I should have remembered two weeks ago!"

Brutus regarded her suspiciously as Mary continued.

"After we were rowed ashore west of Massilia, our boat breaking up on a sand bank, Mother Mary said, and these are her exact words. 'You'll never persuade me to step aboard another ship.' We all said Amen to that, now here we are again!"

The accusatory tone with which she said the last caused Brutus to grin.

"I never heard Mother Mary say that. I'm sure I wasn't present or I would never have brought you!"

He ducked but not in time to avoid the wet, knotted, coir fender that caught him on the crown of his head.

That was the only time she demonstrated her disapproval so violently, and another ten days saw them edging into the harbour. They paid off the captain, complimenting him on his splendid time, and with their few possessions made for the inn they knew from many years before.

Massilia looked exactly the same, disconcertingly so, and Brutus found himself looking for Ephraim and Horatius as though they could suddenly appear. After they had all bathed and changed Mary was impatient to attend the synagogue.

There all was far from the same, and the Rabbi who received them told them curtly that Abiathar had been dead five years.

"What of the Christian community?" asked Mary unguardedly, "and does Joseph of Arimathaea ever call?"

The Rabbi grew apoplectic, his red suffused face contorted and eyes bulging. With an effort he restrained his outburst and hissed,

"Get out. You're not welcome here. None of your cult has set foot here for five years, not since Abiather who was a traitor to Judaism. He just escaped being stoned, such was the anger when he brought that man Paul here.

"Paul of Tarsus was here?" exclaimed Mary, but the Rabbi would say no more as he herded them towards the door and slammed it behind them.

"So feeling is really running high between the different factions. It's probably so in all the synagogues," mused Brutus, not wishing to experience a similar confrontation.

"There always has been a large part of Jewry that rejects the Messiahship of Jesus, hasn't there?" said Simon.

"Yes, all the apostles and many of the early followers are Jews, so originally it is a Jewish movement. Saul, or rather Paul of Tarsus has been preaching largely to the Gentiles and many Jewish leaders distrust and reject him totally. Even some of the apostles won't recognise him as one of them," explained Mary.

"Do they recognise you as one of them, mama?" asked Peter, revealing a surprising perceptiveness.

"I think not. History might but it's too early in the church's development to challenge the pre-eminent role of men as priests and teachers."

"Jesus was challenging it when he invited you to join his band of followers and showed himself to you first on his resurrection!" said Simon, supportive of his friend.

"Maybe, who knows why I was so privileged. We can be sure he will reveal all in due time."

Before more was said a voice rang out incredulously.

"By all the wonders, is it centurion Brutus?"

The face of the clean-shaven man silhouetted in the arched entrance of the court was hidden, but as he moved towards them he was quickly recognised.

"Dionysius!" exclaimed Mary and Brutus together, greeting the stranger joyfully, as Simon searched his memory to identify his vaguely familiar face.

"The magistrate," he said quietly to Peter giving him a nudge, although the younger boy was none the wiser.

"I see you've unmasked me," smiled Dionysius, "I recognise you are Simon, although you were the age of your companion when last I saw you."

In recognition of the boy's altered status he offered his arm in greeting before asking, "Well what brings you all here?"

"Right this moment being forcibly ejected from the synagogue where we were making inappropriate enquiries," laughed Brutus.

To which Dionysius retorted there was nothing out of character there, although the centurion was uncertain to whose character he alluded.

As he wasn't pressed for time they dined together, and so they were all brought up to date on the events of the last years and the purpose of their visit. Before they separated Dionysius pressed them to dine at his house the following evening.

"I'll send a servant to escort you as I live on the outskirts of the city. He will call at your inn an hour before dusk, all right? I've something I particularly want to give Simon!"

He left them intrigued, and they had all that day and most of the next to ponder his intentions.

The following day they tried repeatedly to trace a Christian church but to no avail, and wondered why all their efforts and enquiries drew a blank.

"There must certainly be more than one in Massilia so they must have gone underground because of the threat of persecution," suggested Brutus losing interest in pursuing the matter further, "we should rather be inquiring for a ship for Rome."

That evening they followed their guide towards the limestone cliffs south east of the port, where Cornelius had taken Brutus to search out Pothus, when they feared for the life of Simon.

Telling them of this brought back anxious memories for Mary and caused endless speculation by the boys until they approached Dionysius' house that commanded a fine view over the bay, with its small islands scattered on the fire-suffused sea, ignited by the sun as it plunged behind the low headland far to the west.

"Until our other guests arrive tell me what you have done today," Dionysius enquired politely.

As he listened to their frustrating day trying to trace any Christians, Brutus observed the satisfaction in the eyes of the magistrate and wondered. He remembered his baptism together with Helena, the priestess who had attacked Mary with a knife at Arelate, and could think of no reason why he had withheld his help in their search.

Changing the subject Dionysius held out a rolled parchment to Simon.

"I thought this too precious to send by messenger and knew one day I would be able to give it to you."

It was tied with a crimson ribbon and the wax seal carried the deep indentation of a man's head. It was addressed,

'To Simon, son of Marc, and grandson of centurion Brutus.'

Looking closely Simon whispered,

"It's the head of the emperor!"

"That's right, Caesar Gaius Caligula. The emperor before Claudius."

Simon looked puzzled not knowing what to do with it.

"It's the reply of Gaius to the letter you asked me to give him. It was to remind him of God's command to Moses that slaves should have a rest day on the Sabbath."

As the faintest memory of the incident was recalled, it caused Simon some confusion and he blurted out,

"I hardly dare open it!"

"One should always read the reply to a petition," said Dionysius gravely.

Trembling Simon broke the seal and unrolled it. Every eye was on him as first he read it to himself and then, his face creasing up with a delighted smile, he read it to his elated audience.

"We thank you for your petition on behalf of all slaves. Your concern is most creditable. We have neglected to provide them with a day of rest in the past. It can't be the same day for all but we will rectify the omission, and every slave of our palace will enjoy a weekly day of rest. Instead of a Sabbath day it will be a Simon day hence forward. Caesar Gaius - Emperor."

The stunned silence was followed by the spontaneous applause of all present, which covered the entry of the servant leading a short rotund man and a woman into the room.

"Mary," exploded each woman simultaneously as Mary Magdalene and Mary Clopas tearfully embraced.

Dionysius introduced the unknown man to them as brother Crescens, a student of Paul carrying the message to the people of Gallia.

"I'm afraid we have been driven underground by the violence of the Jewish priests and the Roman Governor to our movement," said Dionysius, "which is why I said nothing when you told me of your difficulties. If you had found it easy to locate our churches so would our enemies!"

When it came to their departure some hours later, Brutus was angry with himself for not liking this messenger of Paul's, about whom he had misgivings. Was it because he exhibited the same unswerving confidence as his master, that inability to consider any doubt about his convictions, or restraint to his actions that had so nearly killed Mary Magdalene.

Brutus tried to be generous and open minded, but every uncompromising utterance of the man shut him up, aware that his opinion was not being invited, nor would it be welcomed. He wondered if this sort of man would always come to the fore in the church, just as a certain type of man always came to the fore in the army, neither of them prepared to listen to the dissenting voice.

When Brutus expressed his disapproval to Mary, she said Jesus could be relied upon to call those best able to serve him in the particular circumstance, and not to be put off by personality conflicts. He refrained from reminding her that Jesus had called Judas Iscariot to be a disciple, and wondered if his was just a simple personality conflict.

"I'll have Rufus any day!" he said petulantly, and as Mary couldn't dissent with that, they were reconciled.

Brutus wasn't aware of it, but his evaluation of the merits of the two acolytes was a microcosm of the fundamental differences that would deeply divide the Eastern Church with its mystical spirituality, from that gestating within the Roman womb, which following parturition would be suckled on wolf's milk and weaned on the riches that Rome's avaricious elite appropriated from the conquered world.

Paul was a citizen of Rome, but Rufus came from Cyrene where Grecian values still prevailed and mysticism flourished.

CHAPTER THREE

Back in Britain, as though to heap further misery on an intensely lonely Miriam, Rufus decided he should be more of an itinerant priest and try in some small way to fill the void following the slaughter of the Druids. For the nation his decision was salutary, and people flocked to hear him reconciling the tradition of the druids with the revelation of the cross, and thousands were baptized the breadth of the island. For Miriam it was a disaster and her homesickness became a source of desolation.

Marc adored her, remembering still the brave girl driven by compassion to comfort the fallen Jesus whenever he looked at her. He remembered also how Mary had first taught him to pray, by the salt sea after descending from the Judaean wilderness, and he found himself praying with that intensity that he had forgotten. He tried to listen as much as he petitioned and recollected the transformation in Miriam after the trauma of losing her parents. Then her desolation had only been assuaged when her compassion was drawn to the plight of the refugees from Jerusalem.

So anxious had he become that he confided his anxiety with Martina, the wife of their shoemaker neighbour, and asked her to look in on Miriam when his duties took him away.

The Temple of Claudius was rising impressively and the costs commensurately.

Marc had to collect the additional tax revenue from King Prasutagus, a devious ruler not averse to borrowing from the Jew to pay the Roman, and pledging his kingdom as security, and he was not surprised when assembling his dues in an assortment of carts, that an additional cart with five children was tagged on to the convoy. Each child was chained by one foot to his neighbour.

"Get the best price you can for them and send back five amphora of wine for the betrothal of the princess. Give the residue of the money they fetch to Crassus for the temple," were his instructions from the avaricious king.

The journey home was long and the weather hot. There was no cover for the children and inadequate provision for their feeding and watering. Marc was concerned for their well being as they made their slow progress, and had lots of time to consider his options.

At the outskirts of Camulodunum he sent the convoy to the warehouses adjoining the port but insisted that the wagon with the children accompany him to his house.

There he left them waiting in the afternoon sun, calling Miriam to fetch him some refreshment. Sitting complacently in the cool of the house, he waited some time before he told Miriam to take a jug of water outside to the children, aware of the crowd gathering in the street and their angry grumbling. Miriam returned greatly agitated.

"Those children are nearly fainting in this heat!" she said, "how could you leave them so callously?"

The reproach in her voice almost weakened his resolve but the thoughts of the high stakes for which he was gambling strengthened him.

"They're all chained together. It would be a lot of trouble to unload them and anyway there's nowhere for them to wait. I'll take them to the quay shortly."

A roar from the street drew both of them to the doorway, and Marc saw it had also drawn a patrol of four soldiers.

Martina berated him angrily,

"Those children will die if they aren't cared for!" she exclaimed.

"We can't let that happen, they are too valuable, and are to be sold into slavery. Give them some more water."

"Water! They are all skin and bones and need proper meals!" remonstrated Martina, "where are they from?"

"Durolipons. From King Prasutagus!"

"Shame on him. Are the Iceni selling their children to pay their taxes?" cried Martina, to a roar from the crowd that was swelling by the minute.

"Oh these are orphans."

"Orphans! Where would you find orphans amongst the Iceni? Not one of their men was killed resisting the Romans!"

"I didn't say they were Iceni. These are Trinovante, a band of vagrants caught stealing by the Iceni!"

The anger erupted in a moment and the squad of soldiers outnumbered ten to one hastily retreated to summon reinforcements. By the time they returned the street was deserted, only a few lengths of chain and splinters of wood marking the spot where feelings had run so high shortly before. Bewildered the soldiers looked around and told the exasaperated centurion that there had been a riot breaking out.

"Where are these rioters then and what was it all about?" demanded the officer.

"Who can understand their devilish tongue?" protested a soldier dejectedly, aware of the scorn they had incurred.

Within Marc's house anxious faces watched them withdraw towards the barracks, and then the boys resumed their places at the table and the first hot meal they had eaten for many a month.

"I'll go and make the arrangements with the trader," said Marc securing his sandals.

"What trader?" demanded the women with one voice.

"Why the slave trader of course. Who else, we can't keep them here."

"We can't just hand them over to be sold as slaves to these perfidious Romans, not orphans of our own tribe!" exploded Martina.

"Well who's got room to bed them or money to feed them? Not you Martina!" Marc knew that Martina's four children more than filled their rooms over the workshop.

"We have! We've more than enough room since everyone left," said Miriam, bitterness at what she regarded as a betrayal giving a steely edge to her voice.

"What here! Why that's impossible!" cried Marc, inwardly rejoicing.

"Of course here. Did we not look after our orphans at Tyre, and set up the house for the children of the lepers at Knossos. If these children leave so do I!"

"Well on your head be it," capitulated Marc begrudgingly.

Martina noted how vigorously he patted and fondled old Jup, who went into an ecstasy of tail wagging.

"If you had one you would be wagging it too," she thought shrewdly.

The seasons and the years passed. Jup died of old age, and Claudius died of poison. Nero came to the throne and an increasingly improvident king of the Iceni bequeathed half his kingdom to the Emperor to defer the day of settlement.

Claudius' temple was inaugurated with great solemnity, and the new Governor, Suetonius, commanded all the Legates and their officers to the ceremony and all the tribal chiefs and their courts. As the tables groaned under the stress of the feasting the impoverished Britons groaned under the burden of crippling taxes.

Marc wrote of it to Simon who was about to finish his final year at Law school. Dionysius had strongly urged them to allow him to study in Massilia and so they had never moved beyond Gaul. Simon passed the letters to Dionysius, who passed them on to Nero, urging him to install a civil magistracy in Britain as the military regime had been in place too long.

"I leave you to assess their requirements," said Nero. "We are too preoccupied with the rebellion in Palestine and the raids across the Rhine. Make an official visit to Britain and give us your advice."

Alexander on a trading enterprise from Tyre visited Massilia and told them of the scale of the rebellion throughout Judaea.

"It gets worse year by year and there is going to be a fearful reckoning soon as Rome has lost all patience with the rebels."

Simon reminded his uncle of the orphanage for the children of the leper colony on Crete, and its lease was paid for and renewed through the federation.

"Next time I come through I'll bring James so that you cousins can meet. It's time he undertook some enterprise on his own, he's twenty now," said Alexander.

"We will be sailing for Britannia when Simon has gained his doctorate," said Dionysius, "as I am commissioned by the Emperor to install a civic magistracy before the military lay waste the country, and I need his keen brain with all the problems of restoring law and order."

"They have pretty well done that already. Most of their traditional produce has dried up and as we won't trade slaves, there is little to tempt us to their shore. Be careful, it's becoming a very dangerous place."

"I wish to accompany you on that visit and see Marc and Miriam," said Brutus. "How about you, Mary, and you, Peter?"

"No more ships for me!" avowed Mary passionately, "but Peter is bound to want to go wherever Simon goes."

The young men smiled at each other, glad to have that agreed so easily, they had spent hours deliberating how to broach the subject.

Had news of the death of Prasutagus, king of the Iceni reached Massilia it might have influenced their plans, but news of the death of such a minor king in a remote country was carried first to Rome, to an avaricious emperor Nero.

"Good!" he said, gleefully rubbing his hands as though the anticipated riches were in his grasp, "so finally I come into my inheritance. Half his kingdom I have been promised, and as he has no son it is mine to collect. Have an inventory made of the estate and requisition anything that would grace our new palace."

"What of Queen Boudicca and her daughters?" enquired his chancellor.

"Is that her name? Well let her have the half of the kingdom that is of least value to us. How many daughters, two did you say? They should have adequate dowries from their mother's half!"

Two months later Marc was summoned to the office of Crassus. Governor Suetonius was present, obsequiously trying to ingratiate himself into favour with Plautianus, Nero's chancellor.

"We have a very big job for you, Marc. As you must know, King Prasutagus, in recognition of his indebtedness to the emperor for favours received, bequeathed half his kingdom to Nero. Chancellor Plautianus wishes to have an inventory of the assets of the kingdom to assist the apportioning of the estate. You are to accompany him and a cohort of the ninth legion on this delicate mission."

Marc was devastated.

"You mean Queen Boudicca is to be disinherited of half her kingdom in her lifetime, within months of the death of her Lord? This is the most dishonourable business I have ever heard of."

He looked pleadingly at the Chancellor, but the set, angry, patrician face gave no hope of comfort.

"Tell me I have misunderstood. Don't ask me to have any part in such ignominy!"

"Silence fellow. How dare you use such insulting words to the chancellor of your emperor? Do we have to put up with the insolence of this Briton?" roared Suetonius.

"Marc is the son of centurion Brutus and so enjoys the privilege of being a citizen of Rome. He knows more of tribal affairs than anyone in eastern Britain," said Crassus with dismay.

"Then kindly behave like a Roman and serve your emperor faithfully," snarled Suetonius, his whiskers bristling warningly.

"And if I refuse?"

"Then we might request an additional cohort, and make a very arbitrary and forceful apportionment," said Plautianus coldly.

"Then I will do it under protest, but I warn it will cause great unrest!"

That night Marc wrote a letter to Brutus and dispatched one of the orphans, now grown into a strapping youth, to take it to Dubris.

"You will need two changes of horse," he said giving him sufficient denarii, "but insist it goes by road across Gaul, if possible by the military couriers, but not by sea."

Although Marc accompanied the cohort under the command of Legate Vespasian, he deliberately kept himself to himself, knowing the rage he nursed could erupt at the slightest provocation. As they approached the rambling palace he had managed to regain his composure and realized if he was to act for the interests of the queen, he must remain as cool as the chancellor.

A hunting party was just unsaddling their horses and kennelling the hounds as the palace came in view, and the queen and her daughters remounted and galloped towards them. Marc rode ahead and they conferred agitatedly as Vespasian and the chancellor rode up. Introductions were brief and Boudicca said,

"At other times you would have received our welcome, but these are sad times for my family and my subjects and I wish you had not come. It is discourteous of you to impose yourself, with all the force you bring, at a time of grief."

"Discourtesy was not intended, ma'am," said the chancellor, the half suppressed sneer lingering at the corners of his mouth, "but it is not always possible with distances greater than two thousand miles between my emperor and your kingdom, to choose the most advantageous time."

The emphasis he placed on his emperor and the dismissive way he spoke of her kingdom made Marc aware the chancellor was resolved to humiliate the queen.

"We need to quarter the soldiers some distance from the palace," Marc said, indicating a large mown field close to the wood they had hunted that morning.

"The officers deserve better than tents in a field," asserted Vespasian, "the palace looks big enough to accommodate us!"

"Have I any choice?" Boudicca asked Marc, who shook his head sadly.

"Very well. On the assumption that your officers are honourable, you will be shown your rooms if you will allow me to make the arrangements, Legate."

He bowed stiffly as they rode away.

Marc urged the queen,

"Your majesty, I think these arrogant Romans need to see some show of strength, if you are not to be completely humiliated by them. I would suggest you send messengers to all your chiefs and headmen to assemble here, with every warrior they can find, and with the greatest urgency."

"It will be done. Can I rely on your loyalty?"

"Completely, even to laying down my life," said Marc, with tears misting his eyes.

"I fear we may all be doing that if our only recourse is to take up arms," said Boudicca prophetically.

That night Marc was summoned by one of the daughters.

"Mother needs your help," she said simply, and led the way to the queen's bed-chamber. An iron bound chest was being closed and Boudicca indicated a heavy hammer.

"Can you turn the end of this iron bolt with the hammer? All our royal jewellery is in here and we need to bury it before that man seizes it."

"Do you have somewhere to bury it? Somewhere you can be sure to find it next year or even later?"

"Yes, by the king's grave, but we must hurry, these Romans are rampaging through the house seizing anything of value!"

Marc gave half a dozen glancing blows to the thick pin and saw it was well spread and immovable. He lifted the chest to follow the queen when the door burst open and Vespasian was framed in the doorway.

Wordlessly he moved towards Marc, then lashed out with his fist smashing his jaw and knocking him unconscious. Seizing the hammer he demolished the lock with a few blows and stood looking at the contents that spilled out onto the floor.

"Stealing the crown jewels!" he said, "that's always a capital offence. But for you my fine lady, as you might claim half of them, I'll commute the sentence to a flogging and be satisfied with his head," throwing a contemptuous look at the unconscious Briton.

The queen glared at him with contempt as he brought his face close to hers, close enough for her to smell his wine-laden breath. She spat into his face and enraged he seized her robe in his hands, and with one violent wrench he bared her to her waist. Her cream finely veined breasts rose and fell with each measured breath and she held his eyes until he was forced to look away.

"Hold her," he ordered two of the officers, as he unclasped his bronze studded leather belt.

He slid his sword scabbard off, and legs braced wide apart swung the belt viciously, and with fascination saw the red wheal disfigure the unblemished whiteness of her back. Again and again he struck, straining to make her cry out with pain.

"Cry bitch, cry!" he growled with each blow, his venom rising as she denied him that satisfaction.

The wheals coalesced but still she held back the scream that tortured her lungs, tearing at her to break free of her scourged body, just one scream to declare her violation to heaven. The blackness came before that scream and she slumped to the floor.

Her eldest daughter broke free of a centurion's grip and threw herself at the legate, fingers reaching to tear at his rage-suffused face. His backhanded blow knocked her to the floor and turning he strode to the door. He felt aroused, and catching the eye of his most junior officer allowed a softness to replace his anger.

"Do as you wish with them," he called as they left the room.

Consciousness returned to Marc with the instantaneous surprise that he was still alive. Unmoving he squinted through one eye and saw the scabbard with loosened sword lying near him.

The thrusting naked buttocks rising and falling but a few paces away galvanized his reflexes, and he rolled, drew and thrust the sword in one violent eruption. He felt a coldness that bordered on exultation as he saw the spitted body convulse just once.

As he withdrew, he turned and saw the wine-bemused centurion's jaw, hanging slack with amazement. He had removed his sword awaiting his turn and in a trice found his consummation, Marc's sword entering and eviscerating him in one sublime movement. He felt like an avenging angel as he pulled the body off the sobbing girl but she clutched at him and said,

"My sister!" her eyes flitting to a chink of light from an adjoining door.

Marc eased it a fraction and as the smiling man turned saying,

"Your turn will ..." He received the executioner's thrust and uncomplaining rolled onto the floor.

His companion never had a chance to extricate himself before he was slaughtered on the altar of unrequited lust.

Only as he tried to speak was Marc aware of the pain in his jaw. All three women were clinging to each other seeking some solace for the hurt, some expiation of the violation they had suffered.

Pulling the torn robe to cover her nakedness Marc urged them all to flee.

Boudicca threw down her robe to reveal her lacerated torso.

"No, let these breasts that gladly suckled my two daughters proclaim our conjoined femininity. That in a man's world you have need to violate our womanliness must be to your shame, not to ours. Yes, flee and to arms. The stripes on my back will call every man to war. By violating their queen they violated every woman of this island and the expiation of this crime can only be Roman blood, until the last is driven back across the sea!"

400

The orgy of revenge began when Vespasian found his four dead officers. The palace was plundered and burnt to the ground. Then in every town and hamlet the cohort passed through, anyone who hadn't fled was killed and every dwelling torched.

This course of retribution was bought at a very high price, for it slowed down the cohort as the region rushed to war. Ancient chariots rolled across the fields and along the roads and paths, gathering a defiant following of every outraged Briton.

Marc riding ahead lost much of his advantage when his horse went lame. The cavalry of the cohort followed hard on his heels, as the Legate had declared,

"A thousand denarii to whoever brings me his head!"

Marc was frequently forced into hiding, but Vespasian was constantly harassed by the swelling ranks of the Iceni and Trinovantes.

Camulodunum was paralyzed at receiving word of the uprising.

Crassus organized the veterans and garrison soldiers he had at his disposal, but could not defend the whole perimeter of the colonia. He fortified the recently built Temple of Claudius for their last defensive stand, and moved in food and water in readiness for a siege. Two riders were dispatched to Lindum but word had spread there like wild fire, and they had already mobilized the ninth legion for a forced march to relieve Camulodunum before the riders were received.

Miriam and Martina were distraught over how to respond to the threat.

"If only Marc were here he would know what to do!"

"He would urge you to flee. There's no point in being caught between the uprising tribes and the Romans."

"You go. Take the boys and just go. I have to wait for Marc. I know he will look for me here."

Calling the youths she told them to go with Martina. It took but five minutes to gather their few possessions before they filed out among the crowds milling undecidedly along the narrow street.

As dusk fell, a red glow to the north indicated the inevitable progress of the cohort and the pursuing tribes.

The clatter of horses along the cobbled street stopped outside the house, alerting Miriam to the imminent intruders. As the door was kicked open, Vespasian and Crassus and two troopers stormed in.

"Where's you husband?" demanded the Legate as the troopers rapidly searched the vacant rooms.

"You tell me. I haven't seen him since last week when he accompanied you to the Iceni!"

The troopers confirmed he wasn't in the house.

"Then hide yourselves and wait here. He's bound to come soon with this mob at our heels. Kill him on sight, he's the cause of this uprising."

All colour drained from Miriam's face at the danger to Marc, who she was sure would walk in unsuspecting any minute. Bravely she challenged Vespasian.

"Marc is a Roman citizen, you can't just execute him without giving him a chance to prove his innocence!"

"We've enough proof alright. Four of my officers lie in a cart, murdered by him!"

He glared at her wondering whether to strike her down and vent the anger and frustration gripping him, but he wasn't sure of Crassus holding his tongue.

"I'm amazed that Marc single handed can have struck down four Roman officers!" protested Miriam scornfully, but more troops bursting into the house terminated any altercation.

"They've broken through the rearguard and will trap us outside the colonia if we don't hurry, they're everywhere!" called a cavalryman hysterically.

Through the open doorway could faintly be heard a surging clamour of sound, rising and falling as though waves were breaking on a shingle beach.

"To the colonia at the double, it's our only defensible position!" ordered Crassus, and Vespasian, torn between his twin desires of revenge and survival, mounted his horse and galloped away with a lightly laden wagon following.

The driver and his escort had been offered a handsome reward if the chest of Boudicca's jewels were spirited away from the approaching battle zone. Nero's chancellor had inexplicably been killed in an early skirmish with the rebels, and Vespasian felt no obligation to further the interests of the emperor. He already had aspirations on that elevated office himself, and knew it was essential to be backed by a personal fortune.

Only Miriam and the two troopers remained one standing either side of the doorway.

"I need to go upstairs for a moment," said Miriam, moving towards the stairs.

"You stay down here where we can see you," growled the soldier.

"I won't be two minutes but I must go. You men don't have these monthly problems."

"Thank the Gods," said the soldier with feeling. "Two minutes only or we'll be dragging you back down."

Miriam smiled sweetly at them and hurried to Brutus' former bedroom overlooking the front street. From a chest containing his centurion attire she seized his scarlet cape, opened the shutter and threw the greater part of it out and pulled the shutters closed securing it. She hurried down alarmed by the sounds like an angry swam of bees that had briefly carried to her.

One of the soldiers opened the door and as the angry sound swelled, moved into the street. Less than a quarter of a mile away some dwellings were blazing fiercely. Silhouetted against the flickering flames, enveloped in vaporous shrouds of smoke, he saw the leaping, naked, blue tribesmen, and then like a splendid apparition of vengeance the bronzed chariot burst to the fore. Two bared women were in it, likewise blue from the dye, leading their brave men in a sublime defiance of their arrogant conquerors. Their long, loosed hair streamed behind as the pair of white horses cavorted to complete the awesome spectacle.

The Romans' discretion prevailed and they abandoned their post and ran, capes flapping wildly, towards the colonia. A roar emitted from the tribesmen and nobody noticed the figure in the shadows that flitted through the open door, except Miriam who threw open her arms to her husband.

But the fleeing Romans had been observed and the scarlet cape flapping at the window, and in that paroxysm of revenge where they sought to obliterate every trace of the hated foe, the tribesmen torched the building as they raced past and in an instant the lower story was enveloped in flame.

Miriam's dead weight alerted him to her faint, and carrying her in his arms Marc made a dash through the flame-engulfed opening.

The pain of the spear as it entered his side and ripped its way into his heart was

402

momentary, and as he staggered back he was dead. In the pulse of that one last heartbeat, he knew he would remain clutched to the breast of the loving compassionate girl for eternity, because his Roman father had plunged his spear into the heart of the crucified Galilean.

On board the ship, hovering at the mouth of the river awaiting the flood tide to take them to Camulodunum, Brutus looked anxiously at the smouldering stumps of the forest that had clothed the east bank.

As the pain seared his chest wall, one cry emitted from his contorted lips,

"It is finished!" then he died.

On a high hill to the west, Rufus stood listening to the wind and watching the star filled sky.

Some embers set flying by the collapse of the upper part of the house were seized by the wind and carried heavenwards.

Rufus saw them, a trail of bright sparks across the sky. In that instant he was back in the stone henge and saw the hundreds burning at the stake. As that image faded he saw Jerusalem and Rome engulfed in the same conflagration, and then amazed he saw an incredible fireball that swelled to embrace the whole horizon and grew in intensity so that no eye could behold it. The prophecy of Isaiah echoed in his ears.

"Part the veil of Heaven asunder, so that the hills melt away as if burnt with fire, the waters, too, boiling with that fire."

The vision passed and girding his robe, staff in hand, he stepped out.

"So much to do," he said, "and so little time."

THE END

POSTSCRIPT

Boudicca continued her rampage. The ninth legion, already marching to the relief of Camulodunum, paid a heavy price for their zeal. The victorious Britons, elated by their sack of the colonia and gathering thousands of men daily, advanced to meet them and overran and slaughtered every legionary. The Commander Petilius Cerialis and the cavalry fled.

Boudicca likewise sacked and massacred south to Londinium and then Verulanium, her forces now swelled to more than a quarter million with a vast number of carts and families. Suetonius hit back and rallied the legions to seek vengeance, which was achieved with the massacre of every last rebel and the suicide of Boudicca.

Grieving bitterly, Dionysius and the sons of the Romans searched the smouldering shell of the house they'd known from childhood. The charred bodies embraced in death, were only identifiable by the silver brooch that had withstood the flames.

Brutus, Marc and Miriam were laid in a common grave with a simple wooden cross to mark it. So in death they remained united, as they had been since the crucifixion.

Mary, following the loss of her husband, stayed in Provence and served the only other man she had ever loved. Her good works throughout the region were legendary and the church flourished. Shortly before she died she gave Dionysius her fragment of that most precious possession snatched from the tomb at Jerusalem, half of which most appropriately he saw buried with her. It was wrapped around the hilt of a shattered sword.

Dionysius ended his life serving the law he loved, and the Lord he loved even more, in Turin. He bequeathed his scrap of the shroud to the embryo church there.

It took nigh on nineteen hundred years before a peasant girl of exceptional purity and spirituality, in the foothills of the Pyrenees, traversed the barrier of time to a timeless mystery and her first wondrous encounter with a queenly lady in a simple blue robe . But that has to be another story!